重庆市莎士比亚研究会　主办

西南大学外国语学院
西南大学莎士比亚研究中心　承办

莎士比亚评论

Shakespeare Review

第 2 辑
Volume 2

西南大学出版社

图书在版编目(CIP)数据

莎士比亚评论. 第2辑 / 罗益民主编. -- 重庆：西南大学出版社, 2024.4
　　ISBN 978-7-5697-2349-6

Ⅰ. ①莎… Ⅱ. ①罗… Ⅲ. ①莎士比亚(Shakespeare, William 1564-1616) - 戏剧文学 - 文学评论 - 文集 Ⅳ. ①I561.063-53

中国国家版本馆CIP数据核字(2024)第071488号

莎士比亚评论（第2辑）
SHASHIBIYA PINGLUN(DI-ER JI)

主编　/　罗益民

责任编辑：畅　洁
责任校对：张昊越
封面设计：钰　坤
排　　版：张　艳
出版发行：西南大学出版社（原西南师范大学出版社）
　　　　　地　　址：重庆市北碚区天生路2号
　　　　　邮　　编：400715
　　　　　电　　话：（023）68860895
印　　刷：重庆亘鑫印务有限公司
成品尺寸：175 mm×250 mm
印　　张：24.5
插　　页：2
字　　数：550千字
版　　次：2024年4月　第1版
印　　次：2024年4月　第1次印刷
书　　号：ISBN 978-7-5697-2349-6
定　　价：56.41元

莎士比亚评论
Shakespeare Review
编委会

顾问委员会
Michael Dobson(University of Birmingham, UK)
Jonathan Locke Hart(Harvard University, USA)
William Baker(Northern Illinois University, USA)
Richard Burt(University of Florida, USA)
苏福忠(人民文学出版社)
辜正坤(北京大学)
聂珍钊(广东外语外贸大学)
彭镜禧(台湾大学)
朱尚刚(浙江大学)
李伟民(四川外国语大学)
李伟昉(河南大学)

编辑委员会
Charles Alexander(North Arizona University, USA)
Youngmin Kim(Dongguk University, Korea)
Leonard Neidorf(南京大学)
Sandro Jung(复旦大学)
Reto Winckler(华南师范大学)
杨林贵(东华大学)
黄必康(北京大学)
从丛(南京大学)
郝田虎(浙江大学)
李正栓(河北师范大学)
朱小琳(中央民族大学)
肖谊(四川外国语大学)
冯伟(东北师范大学)
戴丹妮(武汉大学)

主编
罗益民(西南大学)

副主编
刘佯(西南大学)
史敬轩(重庆邮电大学)

主编的话

《莎士比亚评论》(以下简称《评论》)第2辑终于和大家见面了。这一辑在栏目设置、稿件组成等方面,较之于创刊号,有了明显的传承和不同。就传承来说,辑刊继续保持了贴近前沿、以问题为本、尽力言必有据等特色,努力做到有一说一、不故弄玄虚等。务实,是我们唯一的目的。

《评论》的作者群既有小荷尖尖初上路的人,也有莎学研究的名流。前者有攻读博士学位的年轻学生和学者。《评论》本着对文不对人的原则,不论门第,只论文章是否真有收获与发现。

在"名家论坛"栏目里,《评论》汇集了研究莎士比亚的台柱子学者,把最新的研究成果刊载于此,以利于与年轻学者进行思想交流与碰撞。这个栏目同时具有国际性、前沿性和相当的开拓性。

《评论》是一个真正期望为作者提供尽兴汇报学术成果的平台,因而给予作者足够的表达空间,不规定和限制篇幅。因为,这是学科性质所需的。我们强调对问题的透彻论证与探索,希望能真正地通过格物而达到致知的目的,不给读者留下言已尽且意也有穷之感。

在选材、组稿方面,《评论》秉承务实、求新的目标。除各个方向如文本、理论、历史与文化等的交汇,翻译、演出、专题讨论等方面的论文以外,还专门设置了短小的、与话题相配的,言简意赅、要言不烦的小文。在"人物专访"里,我们设计了两种莎学历史人物的素描,有林纾这种开先河者,其他如朱生豪的家人朱达先生,译莎士比亚十四行诗的屠岸先生,中国的约翰逊、编莎士比亚大词典的刘炳善先生等;同时,我们还设计了推出新成果信息的"前沿快递"栏目,一叶知秋式地介绍新近出版的著作、文集、教材等。这些文章虽然看起来不是那么系统、深入、全面,但它们有自己的作用,为学术提供了信息，展现了风采，设置了窗口，也成为回顾历史的有效渠道。

《评论》尽量保持固定的栏目，以形成特色，并对相关问题保持足够时长的追踪，比如文本、理论、前沿问题等。此外，一些栏目对课题目标等进行专题讨论，比如"马克思主义与莎士比亚"这个栏目，是从同名的重庆市社科规划项目展开的。这样，就可以把研究的奋斗目标，与研究领域内的实际工作结合起来，以项目促研究，使研究在项目中成长起来。

作为国内仅有的两家专业莎士比亚研究辑刊之一，《评论》希望为作者提供平台，也希望为研究交流提供阵地，为学者成长提供场地，为学术表达提供场所。这是《评论》的己任和奋斗方向。

莎士比亚在他的收笔之作《暴风雨》中，借剧中人之口说："要演一场戏，过往的历史都是一个序曲，未来这部正文，还得你我好好地奋斗一番"（To perform an act/Whereof what's past is prologue, what to come/In yours and my discharge）。这话好像正是说给创业中的《莎士比亚评论》及其作者、读者听的。

就让我们好好奋斗，写好"正文"！那一定是一道可人的风景！

2024年3月21日

目　录

主编的话/1

名家论坛

Shakespeare's Great Forgotten Poem
　　——*The Phoenix and Turtle*("Let the bird of loudest lay")　William Baker/3
Shakespeare's *Merchant of Venice* and the History of the Jews　Leonard Neidorf/23
Ethical Care Principles for Training Young People in Shakespearean Acting　Elspeth Tilley/46
Why the First Folio Matters to China's Shakespearean Studies　Huang Bikang　/69
朱生豪的中国化莎剧翻译与中国莎学　杨林贵/79

文本、理论、跨学科研究

小冰期术语与莎士比亚生态批评　张军/93
入魔之人与出笼之兽
　　——莎士比亚家国悲剧《李尔王》中的国王、女儿和动物　陈贵才/105
忧惧、绝望和死亡
　　——《理查三世》中的存在性选择问题　刘慧敏/121
莎士比亚十四行诗的迷雾与猜想　罗朗/137
莎士比亚戏剧中的复仇与司法危机　黄艳丽/153

饥饿、寓言与天气
　　——《科利奥兰纳》中吃的意图　胡鹏/168
《鲁克丽丝受辱记》中的"艺格符换"与性别政治　许庆红　李玉婷/184

跨国语境中的莎士比亚
17至18世纪德国对莎士比亚的接受　唐雪/199
莎士比亚与萧伯纳作家人格的形成　陈鑫/210
莎士比亚东瀛"行脚"论
　　——"美"的传播与接受历程　卢昱安/229

马克思主义与莎士比亚
《雅典的泰门》与莎士比亚时期炼金术情感生产及交易制度　史敬轩/243
唯物主义与莎士比亚：女权主义及以后　陈小凤/256

莎士比亚在中国
莎士比亚戏剧在中国戏曲中的重生
　　——以越剧改编为中心　刘昉/279
莎士比亚戏剧汉译批评百年回顾与展望　孙媛/292

译坛论莎
《无事生非》双关语的语内和语际翻译　袁帅亚/309
莎律朱韵　高山流水
　　——基于语料库的莎士比亚四大悲剧朱生豪译本音乐性研究　刘伴/322
近二十年国内莎士比亚汉译研究博士学位论文调查述评　杨斐然/337

人物专访

林纾：莎士比亚戏剧汉译的先声　柳杨/355

我的父亲朱达与朱氏一族的译莎、研莎之旅　朱小琳/358

屠岸与莎士比亚　章燕/360

刘炳善雕龙莎士比亚
　　——写在《刘炳善文集》出版之际　彭弱水/362

苏福忠及其对莎士比亚研究的贡献　洛州牧/365

前沿快递

《莎士比亚作品选读》的教学文化启示　今至/369

时代共鸣：与莎士比亚的永恒对话，写在《芳华》之后　朱鑫宇/372

画中有戏：从文字到绘画的舞台
　　——"莎士比亚漫画版"的特色和魅力　木子李/374

英文摘要/376

名家论坛

Shakespeare's Great Forgotten Poem
——*The Phoenix and Turtle* ("Let the bird of loudest lay")

William Baker

Abstract: The early *Venus and Adonis*, *The Rape of Lucrece* and the *Sonnets*, profound meditations on mutability, are not Shakespeare's only poems dealing with the mutability theme. This paper will focus on the very powerful and enigmatic lyrical poem of sixty-seven lines, *The Phoenix and Turtle* or "Let the Bird of Loudest Lay". It has three sections and is written in trochaic tetrameter metre[①] and to explore (1) Its dating and consideration of the question of why it is considered to be Shakespeare's given that it is so very different in formal terms from anything else attributed to him; (2) The form and style of the poem; (3) An analysis of the poem taking into consideration scholarly and critical reactions to it.

Key words: Shakespeare; poem; *The Phoenix and Turtle*

Author: William Baker is a distinguished Chair and Qiantang River Professor of Hangzhou Normal University. His interests include Shakespearean studies and Renaissance literature.

The early *Venus and Adonis*, *The Rape of Lucrece* and the *Sonnets*, profound

---

① Trochaic is a metrical foot composed of two syllables; stressed followed by a unstressed syllable, and tetrameter is equal to four feet.

meditations on mutability, are not Shakespeare's only poems dealing with the mutability theme. This paper will focus on the very powerful and enigmatic lyrical poem of sixty-seven lines, *The Phoenix and Turtle,* or "Let the bird of loudest lay". It has three sections and is written in trochaic tetrameter metre.

So firstly, the dating and a consideration of the question of why it is considered to be Shakespeare's given that it is so very different in formal terms from anything else attributed to him.

Attribution:

The poem, under the name "William Shakespeare"—only a very few instances of his name appearing with his work during his life time—originally appeared in *Love's Martyr, or Rosalin's Complaint* (1601), compiled by one Robert Chester (fl. 1601), who probably worked for Sir John Salusbury (c. 1566–1612) of Denbighshire in Wales, a poet and land owner. He was knighted in 1601, the year the poem was printed, for his loyalty to Elizabeth I during the rebellion of the Earl of Essex, a former favourite of the Queen: his own cousin, a supporter of Essex, was killed in this rebellion. Included is a lengthy poem by Chester announced on the title page of the volume as "Allegorically Shadowing the truth of Loue, in the constant Fate of the Phoenix and Turtle."

In addition to Shakespeare there are poems by poets including John Marston (1576–1634), George Chapman (1559–1634), and Ben Jonson (1572–1637).

The printer was Richard Field (1561–1624) who had printed *Venus and Adonis* and *Lucrece*. The text has no substantial errors, which suggests a clean copy handled by an experienced compositor.

Historically, the poem has appeared in most editions of Shakespeare.

The most pressing textual issue is the title. Until 1807 when the poem was given the title "The Phoenix and the Turtle" in two American editions published in Boston, it was known by its opening line, "Let the bird of loudest lay". The subsequent title seems to have been retained as a tradition although it seems not to have any textual authority.

Shakespeare's connections with Chester are unclear. Some critics (for instance Burrow) have found a few allusions to Shakespeare's narrative poems in his work. Other critics (such as James P. Bednarz) have speculated that Shakespeare may have written the poem as a favour to Salisbury in order to maintain his reputation as a poet while publicly competing with his fellow playwrights.

There is no evidence that the poem circulated in manuscript and "considering that Shakespeare uses Chester's motifs of the phoenix and turtle, a pairing that does not occur elsewhere in Shakespeare's work, he may have been invited or commissioned to contribute a pairing on this theme for the book"[①].

Others, for instance Duncan-Jones and Woudhuysen think that only the "Threnos" section in the poem can be confidently attributed to Shakespeare; however they do not press the case.

Dating:

It has been argued that his poem was written as early as 1586 to celebrate Salusbury's marriage to Ursula Stanley, sister of Lord Strange, the Earl of Derby (d. 1594), whose company (the Strange's Men) were led by Edward Alleyn and with whom Shakespeare as dramatist and actor was connected.

Whether Shakespeare's beautiful and complex allegorical poem was written as early as 1586 is speculation. The poem praises ideal human union through using a tale of the two birds, the legendary Phoenix and the turtle dove. Both may be found in the Biblical *Song of Songs* (2.12) and the "voice of the turtle" as the harbinger of the return of spring reverberates through the Hebrew liturgy. The turtle dove is associated with fertility, with procreation, and the mythical Phoenix with resurrection, rebirth. In the poem, the Phoenix, is female and the turtle dove, male. Probably com-

---

① Francis X. Connor, "Let the Bird of Loudest Lay", in *The New Oxford Shakespeare: The Complete Works Critical Reference Edition, Volume 1*, Oxford: Oxford University Press, 2017, pp. 1075–1077.

posed specifically for the 1601 volume, the poem responds to Chester's poem.

The form and style of the poem:

The form and the style of the poem are most interesting. The lines are short being in catalectic trochaic tetrameter

<u>Catalectic Trochaic Tetrameter</u>

Definition: Catalectic Trochaic Tetrameter consists of a stressed syllable followed by an unstressed syllable,

| DUM da | DUM da | DUM da | DUM |

As Shrank and Lyne observe "the poem draws together different types of style, syntax and vocabulary, from the artfully Latinate to the mono-syllabic Anglo-Saxon" [1].

Lines 1 to 52, i.e stanza 1 to 13, to before the "Threnos" are in quatrains.

They rhyme abba.

The final five stanza's, the "Threnos", i.e. the final 15 lines, are in rhyming triplets.

The poem has a three-fold division.

The first 20 lines, the first to the fifth stanza are ceremonial expressing simple ideas in a complex way through the use of *periphrasis*.[2]

Lines 21–52, stanzas six to thirteen (the *anthem*, the term from the Greek, antiphona, something sung or performed on ceremonial occasions, today the national

---

[1] William Shakespeare, *The Complete Poems of Shakespeare*, Cathy Shrank and Raphael Lyne, eds., Abingdon, Oxon and New York: Routledge, 2018, p. 257.

[2] A roundabout or elaborate way of saying something in deference to the high dignity and decorum as in Latin poetry. Used in 18th century poetry, for instance "the finny tribe" for "fish" and "the bleating kind" for sheep.

song, or a "passage of scripture set to music"[①] express complex, contradictory, paradoxical ideas in deceptively simple terms.

Lines 53–67, stanzas fourteen to eighteen consist of the *threnos*, a verse expression of lament, of grief when a specific person has died. Furthermore, in the initial printed text of the text there is a page break creating: "the appearance of two separate poems" reinforcing "the paradox of two entities in a single nature described in l.40": "Neither two nor one was called"[②].

So there is a "Proem": a "proem" is a poem or lines of poetry introducing a longer poetic work or sections of a longer work. In this opening section there is a meeting of the birds, "the death-divining swan" (l.15) is the priest, and they celebrate the funeral rites of the Phoenix and the turtle dove. They have "fled| In a mutual flame from hence" (23–24) In the seventh stanza, an anthem is sung by the birds:

So they loved as love in twain
Had the essence but in one,
Two distincts, division none:
Number there in love was slain (25–28).

They loved so completely: "Either was the other's mine" (36)

The final section of the poem is a threnos, or a mourning song, not in lines of four but of three in five stanzas. They are ironically

Leaving no posterity
'Twas not their infirmity,

---

① William Shakespeare, *The Oxford Shakespeare: The Complete Sonnets and Poems*, Colin Burrow, ed., Oxford: Oxford University Press, 2002, p. 374.
② Ibid, p. 376.

It was married chastity (59-61)

The Phoenix of myth, known for its regenerative qualities, reproduces no more; it rests eternally. The final stanza is noteworthy for its cumulative, moving and extremely effective monosyllables with the exception of the last word!

To this urn let those repair [go]
That are either true or fair;
For these dead birds sigh a prayer (65-67)

Shakespeare once again plays on meanings of "fair", with its legal and physical implications and the legal and literal meanings of "true": not only is the weight or measure of something correct/ accurate but there, too, is fidelity, loyalty.

To repeat, stylistically the poem is different from anything else of Shakespeare. It doesn't belong to the theatre and draws upon utilizes the tones and ways of thinking associated with the Inns of Court.

There are specific affinities with some of John Donne's poems especially "The Canonization" in which "passion transforms the lovers who die in flames (albeit the temporary death of orgasm), and whose love is similarly described as 'mysterious', or beyond reason." The most pertinent section of Donne's poem (ll. 19-27) has too an eagle, a dove (a turtle dove) and a phoenix. Both poems approach their subject similarly. "Shakespeare addresses abstract principles, drawing on a range of semantic fields from the alchemical" for instance "essence" (l. 26) and "compounded" (l. 44) "to the mathematical and logical" in for instance ll. 26, 27, 28, 37, and 42. However Donne's poem is much more worldly and sexual, synthesizing "metaphysics and basic desires with dazzling wit" whereas Shakespeare's poem "remains unworldly and symbolic"[①].

Analysis:

I will now draw your attention to some specific lines l.1: "lay": song. Paradox-irony here: if of all the potential birds the phoenix probably the least likely, since it is dead and in the poem has no heir however notice the alliterative quality of this first line. This opening line with its "heavily stressed imperative and alliterating superlative give the poem a great push forward into a rhythmical buoyancy which it never loses"[②].

l.2: "sole Arabian tree": probably a palm tree regarded as the traditional perch of the phoenix. The tree is "sole" as without the phoenix and hence alone or isolated.

l.3: "herald": as in state events, announcing

"sad": serious; "trumpet": a marshal and musical instrument and declaim or announce

l.4: "sound": punning on musical sense also has the meaning of a firm, sold: a solid foundation;

"to": the verb "obey" regularly used with the preposition "to" in Elizabethan English although only one other instance in Shakespeare noted in Troilus and Cressida 3.1.150-52["His stubborn buckles [...]|Shall more obey than to the edge of steel"];

"wings": example of synecdoche (Greek for taking together, as in for example where a part of something is used to signify the whole as in "wings" for the birds);

"chaste": the summoned birds like the Phoenix and the Turtle they mourn are said to be "chaste."

[①] William Shakespeare, *The Complete Poems of Shakespeare*, Cathy Shrank and Raphael Lyne, eds., Abingdon, Oxon and New York: Routledge, 2018, pp. 257-258.

[②] A. A. Alvarez, "Shakespeare's 'The Phoenix and The Turtle'", in John Wain, ed., *Interpretations: Essays on Twelve English Poems*, London: Routledge and Kegan Paul, 1955, p. 6.

l.5: "shrieking harbinger": the ominous owl, the forerunner, the harbinger of dire events to come.

l.6: "foul": possible pun on "fowl".

"precurrer": precursor, forerunner; possible misprint for "precurrent" or "precurse"; "precurrer"-"harbinger"!

"the fiend" = the Devil?

l.7: "augur": in the Roman period the augur would divine the future by observing the flights and actions of birds and other portents. An echo in *Hamlet*, 5.ii.219-20: "We defy augury. There is a special providence in the fall of a sparrow."

"fever's end": "prophet of the end of illness (in death or cure)."

l.8: "troop": company.

l.9: "session": the sitting of a court or parliament. Note Shakespeare's play on the legal and mutability implications of the word in his Sonnet 30 with its opening line: "When to the sessions of sweet silent thought | I summon up remembrance of things past".

This begins a series in the poem of the use of political vocabulary seen for instance in the words "interdict", "tyrant", and "king".

"interdict": prohibit-only one other instance of the word in Shakespeare but in a different form as "interdiction" in the Scottish play [4.iii.106-07].

l.10: "fowl of tyrant wing": bird of prey: pun on "foul", "fowl" bird general usage and something incorrect or bad.

l.11: The eagle traditionally exempt from the other birds of prey, regarded as the princely eagle.

l.12: "obsequy": funeral rites, at the graveside.

"strict": limited in number also implication of following tradition: also used in Hamlet regarding Ophelia's burial (5.i.226-7).

l.13: "surplice white": loose linen over garment worn by the clergy: the swan is to act the part of the priest as it has white plumage. Could also be a reference to

Elizabethan controversy concerning what was worn at funeral services by those officiating.

l.14: "defunctive": related to dying, first instance of use in *OED*.

"can" is skilled in (the music of death); able to.

l.15: "death-divining": swan believed to sing only once, that is before its own death.

l.16: "requiem": opening word of the Latin Mass for the Dead. Be sung in English "Give them eternal rest, O Lord." One other instance in Shakespeare, in *Hamlet* 5.i.236-8 where the Doctor prevents Ophelia's being given the full funeral rites.

"lack his right": punning on "rite", not to be properly observed. The swan-priest's presence is necessary to ensure the full performance of the ceremony; consequently, it is "his"-the swan's-right/rite.

l.17: "trebly-dated crow": refers to the reputedly long life of the crow, some held that it lives nine times longer than humans, also like the swan, and the cock, the crow is perceived as a prophetic bird.

l.18: "sable gender mak'st": black, crows offspring, believed to be engendered by touching beaks and exchanging breath.

"gender" refers to offspring.

l.19: "the breath thou giv'st and tak'st": chaste method of reproduction prefigures the union of the Phoenix and the Turtle. Also echoes lines from the burial service in the Elizabethan *Book of Common Prayer* "The Lord giveth, and the Lord taketh away."

l.21: "anthem": song of praise, particularly a passage of scripture set to music.

l.22: "is" use of the singular verb for what seems to be a plural subject—"Love and Constancy"—not unusual in Elizabethan English[①] as the singular use of the

---

① See Jonathan Hope, *Shakespeare's Grammar*, London: Arden, 2003.

verb suggests that Love and Constancy have become one indivisible unit.

l.23: "Phoenix and the Turtle": a mythical bird; turtle-dove celebrated for its constancy to its mate.

l.24: "mutual": together but could be ironic as one presumably outlives the other as in Donne's "The Dissolution"!

l.25: "as": with the result that; as if.

"twain" as together, one and the same.

l.26: "essence": being, existence-the Phoenix and the Turtle form a mysterious two-in-one.

There now starts a section of the poem that begins to attempt to come to terms with the process of categorizing"[1] or explaining something that resists categorization.

l.27: "distincts": individual entities; sense of distinct in person, yet in unity. The only citation in the *OED* for "distinct" as a noun, and no other Elizabethan instances are revealed by a full text-text search of the *Early English Books on Line*.

l.27: "division none": The Phoenix and the Turtle can no more be separated into their different parts than can the Trinity-God exists as a unity of three distinct persons: Father, Son and Holy Spirit. Each distinct from the other yet the same in essence in which three become one, essential in Christian theological belief. They are indivisible.

l.28: "Number there ... slain": as two-in-one, the Phoenix and Turtle disrupt the principle that everything has an individual entity and can be counted. The two birds have also become one, which-according to mathematical principles-is no number.

l.29: "remote": separate

"asunder": in two parts. Echo of the Anglican marriage service, *Book of Common Prayer* "Those whom God hath joined together, let no man put asunder." In

---

[1] William Shakespeare, *The Complete Poems of Shakespeare*, Cathy Shrank and Raphael Lyne, eds., Abingdon, Oxon and New York: Routledge, 2018, p. 262.

this poem the "celebration of the union of the Phoenix and Turtle coincides with celebration of their deaths; the two birds thus embody the marriage vow to remain together 'till death us depart'"[①].

l.30: "Distance and no space": quibble on the meaning of "distance": there is a difference between them but no measurable space.

l.31: "queen": Usually the faithful turtle-dove is depicted as female; here, however and throughout Chester's Collection in the poem the Turtle is male (to a female Phoenix).

l.32: "But" except.

l.34: "his right": that which the Turtle owns; or is due to him; or that which is appropriate for him to do or perform.

l.35: "Flaming": glowing; in flames.

l.36: "mine": see Burrow note: "(a) each bird belonged to the other, such was the mutuality of their love; (b) each of them was a source of riches for the other"[②].

l.37: "Property": right to possession. Burrow "(a) the abstract principle of ownership; (b) the principle that particular qualities inhere in one entity alone." The "natural manner of doing, which agreeth to one kind and the same only and that evermore." Burrow writes that "The pair of birds consequently threaten the logical principle that entities are distinct"[③].

"appalled": weakened, shaken.

l.38: "That the self...same": the phoenix as a paradox, as offspring to herself/himself, and as achieving love in death.

l.39: "Single...name": the punctuation reminds the reader that this is a poem in which the distinction between single and plural is being eroded. The verb that follows is the singular "was"!

[①] William Shakespeare, *The Complete Poems of Shakespeare*, Cathy Shrank and Raphael Lyne, eds., Abingdon, Oxon and New York: Routledge, 2018, p. 263.
[②] William Shakespeare, *The Oxford Shakespeares: The Complete Sonnets and Poems*, Colin Burrow, ed., Oxford: Oxford University Press, 2002, p. 375.
[③] Ibid.

l. 40: "Neither...called": numbers should be explicit as they are the least adorned of words however the line shows that there are some conditions for which the very concept of number is useless.

l.41: "reason...confounded": confused and possibly a synonym for what happens to metals in a foundry; in other words, logical tools, habitually used by the personified Reason for defining experience, or ineffectual when it comes to describing the Phoenix and Turtle in their two-in-oneness.

l.42: "division grow together": paradox, just as Reason is confused, single nature has a double name, and simplicity is compounded, so here the action of dividing becomes a means of coming together.

l.43: "To...neither": "each was its own being ('To themselves'), but neither of them was simply itself nor the other"[1].

l.44: "Simple...compounded": again, be read as a paradox or as a description of the alchemical process, in which "simples" are pure ingredients or elements that can be combined to make "compounds".

l.45: "it": Reason; the next three-and-a-half lines are spoken by Reason.

l.45: "twain": couple.

l.46: "concordant one". Notice that "A single sound or entity cannot of course be said to be in concord with itself. This is Reason's problem"[2].

l.47: "Love...none": Reason is habitually pitched against love, or passion, in Renaissance thought. However, within neo-Platonic thought, love and reason are not necessarily in conflict.

l.48: "what...remain": what separates also remains together.

l.49: "threne": a song of lamentation, uncommon as a word during Shakespeare's time and not found elsewhere in Shakespeare.

---

[1] William Shakespeare, *The Oxford Shakespeare: The Complete Sonnets and Poems*, Colin Burrow, ed., Oxford: Oxford University Press, 2002, p. 376.
[2] Ibid.

l.51: "Co-supremes": another paradox, since "supreme" is a superlative, here meaning the highest or greatest yet made equal with another. This is according to the *OED* the earliest use of the term "co-supreme."

l.52: "chorus...scene": in classical tragedy, the chorus commented on the action of the play.

ll.53−67: "Threnos": the song of lamentation is spoken by Reason. Remember that in the initial printed text there is a page break creating: "the appearance of two separate poems which this offers reinforces the paradox of two entities in a single nature described in l.40"①.

ll. 53−54: "Beauty...Grace": These can be read as personifications of these qualities, which are embodied in the Phoenix and Turtle (beauty and rarity in the former, truth and grace in the latter); beauty is certainly referred to as "she" in l.63. The pairing of Beauty and Truth is very important in the sonnets as in much of the love poetry of the period.

l.55: "enclosed": in the urn.

ll.59−61: "Leaving no...chastity": according to Burrow "the fact that they left no children was not the result of any physical weakness or incapacity, but was the expression of the chastity of their marriage.

l.62: "Truth...be": "Truth may appear to be true, but since truth died with the two birds, it cannot be truth itself. Reason imagines the world as a lesser place without the Phoenix and the Turtle"②.

l.63: "Beauty brag": "Beauty may boast of being beautiful, but she does not represent the reality of beauty"③.

---

① William Shakespeare, *The Oxford Shakespeare: The Complete Sonnets and Poems*, Colin Burrow, ed., Oxford: Oxford University Press, 2002, p. 376.
② William Shakespeare, *The Complete Poems of Shakespeare*, Cathy Shrank and Raphael Lyne, eds., Abingdon, Oxon and New York: Routledge, 2018, p. 266.
③ William Shakespeare, *The Oxford Shakespeare. The Complete Sonnets and Poems*, Colin Burrow, ed., Oxford: Oxford University Press, 2002, p. 377.

l.67: "For...prayer": the last "line hints at the pre-Reformation practice of intercession for the souls of the dead, a ritual at odds with Protestantism." It has been argued that "the threnos, - which proclaims the birds to be 'dead', cannot be taken as authoritative, because it is spoken by Reason, whose methods have been shown to be ineffectual"[1].

This poem has perplexed commentators and been read in various ways. One of the most helpful commentaries is found in an essay by the British poet and critic A. A. Alvarez (1929-2019) called "William Shakespeare, 'The Phoenix and the Turtle'" (1955). Alvarez indicates that if the poem "is not a direct love poem to a mistress, it is at least a description, a definition of perfect love." He points out that "the Phoenix was a medieval symbol for Christ, and the Dove might well be an unmarried lady devoted to piety and good works." The poem "can be read as a copybook example of technique; of how to take the abiding themes of love poetry-Love, Death, and the Absolutes-and give them a perfect aesthetic order"[2].

Alvarez attempts to unlock the meaning of the poem by examining its "technical complexity," its use of logic and paradox, and choice of words such as *Property* in line 37 "Property was thus appalled." The word "refers back to the line before ['Either was the other's mine']: it is the power of ownership personified (it becomes 'appalled')"[3]. Specifically "Property" refers to what is by the self, however "There is no with holding in Love; it is beyond greed and ownership." The word has other meanings as well, relating for instance to "the proper use of language, what we now call 'propriety'"[4]. So, the words of the poem reverberate and resonate. Alvarez concludes "The Phoenix and the Turtle are more than lovers; they are

---

[1] William Shakespeare, *The Complete Poems of Shakespeare*, Cathy Shrank and Raphael Lyne, eds., Abingdon, Oxon and New York: Routledge, 2018, p. 266.
[2] A. A. Alvarez, "Shakespeare's 'The Phoenix and Turtle'", in John Wain, ed., *Interpretations: Essays on Twelve English Poems*, London: Routledge and Kegan Paul, 1955, p. 11.
[3] Ibid, pp. 3-4.
[4] Ibid, pp. 12-13.

all the values of Love as well. Their vitality, like their purity and their sacrifice, continues beyond them"[①]. However, this poem is read, there is no doubt of its haunting, moving, powerful, beautiful, and enigmatic qualities.

Other perspectives include allegorical interpretations. For example, the British Shakespearian critic G. Wilson Knight (1897-1955), in his *The Mutual Flame: On Shakespeare's Sonnets and "The Phoenix and the Turtle"* (1955) views the Turtle as Shakespeare or "as his personified love for the young man to whom he addressed many of his sonnets"[②].

Other scholars and critics look to the dedicatee of the poem Sir John Salusbury or to Elizabeth I.

In their edition of Shakespeare's *Poems*, Katherine Duncan-Jones (1941-2019) and H.R.Woudhuysen (1954-)combine the two by placing the poem and the collection in which it appears, Robert Chester's *Love's Martyr*-"in the political context of summer and autumn 1601, when Salusbury was waiting for Elizabeth to summon parliament, and then attempting to be elected as MP for Denbighshire, and election which was abandoned" following violent churchyard fights between the supporters of rival factions. Consequently, when Parliament opened on 27 October, it was not represented by an MP from Denbighshire.

The readings relating to Salusbury, identify the Turtle as Sir John, and the Phoenix his wife Ursula. Such an interpretation seems flawed as the poem emphasizes married chastity. By 1601 the marriage of Sir John and his wife had produced 11 children!

More common readings are those arguing that Shakespeare's Phoenix is a representation of Queen Elizabeth I who evidence suggests "used the iconography

---

① A. A. Alvarez, "Shakespeare's 'The Phoenix and Turtle'", in John Wain, ed., *Interpretations: Essays on Twelve English Poems*, London: Routledge and Kegan Paul, 1955, p. 16.

② William Shakespeare, *The Complete Poems of Shakespeare*, Cathy Shrank and Raphael Lyne, eds., Abingdon, Oxon and New York: Routledge, 2018, p. 256.

[representations of biblical and non-biblical persons and events intended to have allegorical or symbolic significance-in painting and sculpture] of the phoenix...coupling her phoenix emblem with the motto *Semper eadem* (always the same), or occasionally with the motto *Sola phoenix omnis mundi* (the only phoenix in the world)." For those critics who identify Elizabeth with Shakespeare's Phoenix, the Turtle "can stand for the love and fidelity of her subjects"[①].

In spite of these and other readings, especially theological echoes relating to the mystery of the Trinity and the evocations of religious rituals and ceremonies during a time that was reacting to Catholicism, "none...offers the allegorical key to unlock Shakespeare's poem"[②]. This is perhaps fortunate as much of the fascination of the poem resides in its haunting allusive enigmatic qualities. To quote Barbara Everett "the reader halts, never quite sure what it is, to read this poem. We seem, even while finding it exquisite, to lack some expertise, some password." For Burrow "the poem slips between theological and logical registers, and blends voice on voice in a polyphony that has the resonance of ritual worship. This is partly an effect of its dominantly seven-syllable trochaic lines which end with a single stressed syllable. This metrical form begins and ends with a weighty syllable, allowing the poem to lift off the ground in the centre of the line: so 'Two distincts, division none' (27) welds abstractions within the solid buttresses of 'Two' and 'none.' The poem's mingling of gravity and airy lightness enables the physical and the spiritual to interblend." Furthermore this "is to describe the poem, rather than to explain it. But explanations will always fall short of this poem" (87–88).

The Phoenix and Turtle
William Shakespeare

---

① William Shakespeare, *The Complete Poems of Shakespeare*, Cathy Shrank and Raphael Lyne, eds., Abingdon, Oxon and New York: Routledge, 2018, p. 256.
② Ibid, p. 257.

Let the bird of loudest lay
On the sole Arabian tree
Herald sad and trumpet be,
To whose sound chaste wings obey.

But thou shrieking harbinger,   5
Foul precurrer of the fiend,
Augur of the fever's end,
To this troop come thou not near.

From this session interdict
Every fowl of tyrant wing,   10
Save the eagle, feather'd king;
Keep the obsequy so strict.

Let the priest in surplice white,
That defunctive music can,
Be the death-divining swan,   15
Lest the requiem lack his right.

And thou treble-dated crow,
That thy sable gender mak'st
With the breath thou giv'st and tak'st,
'Mongst our mourners shalt thou go.   20

Here the anthem doth commence:
Love and constancy is dead;

Phoenix and the Turtle fled
In a mutual flame from hence.

So they lov'd, as love in twain   25
Had the essence but in one;
Two distincts, division none:
Number there in love was slain.

Hearts remote, yet not asunder;
Distance and no space was seen   30
'Twixt this Turtle and his queen:
But in them it were a wonder.

So between them love did shine
That the Turtle saw his right
Flaming in the Phoenix' sight: 35
Either was the other's mine.

Property was thus appalled
That the self was not the same;
Single nature's double name
Neither two nor one was called.   40

Reason, in itself confounded,
Saw division grow together,
To themselves yet either neither,
Simple were so well compounded;

That it cried, "How true a twain   45
Seemeth this concordant one!
Love has reason, reason none,
If what parts can so remain."

Whereupon it made this threne
To the Phoenix and the Dove,   50
Co-supremes and stars of love,
As chorus to their tragic scene:

        threnos

Beauty, truth, and rarity,
Grace in all simplicity,
Here enclos'd, in cinders lie.   55

Death is now the Phoenix' nest,
And the Turtle's loyal breast
To eternity doth rest,

Leaving no posterity:
'Twas not their infirmity,   60
It was married chastity.

Truth may seem but cannot be;
Beauty brag but 'tis not she;
Truth and beauty buried be.

To this urn let those repair   65

That are either true or fair;

For these dead birds sigh a prayer.

Bibliography

Alvarez, A.A. "Shakespeare's 'The Phoenix and The Turtle'", in *Interpretations: Essays on Twelve English Poems*. Ed. John Wain. London: Routledge and Kegan Paul, 1955: 1−16.

Bednarz, James P. *Shakespeare and the Truth of Love: The Mystery of "The Phoenix and the Turtle"*. New York: Palgrave Macmillan, 2013.

Bradbrook, M. C. *Shakespeare and Elizabethan Poetry: A Study of his Earlier Work in Relation to the Poetry of the Time*. London: Chatto & Windus, 1951.

Connor, Francis X. "Let the Bird of Loudest Lay", in *The New Oxford Shakespeare: The Complete Works Critical Reference Edition, Volume 1*. Oxford: Oxford University Press, 2017, pp.1075−1077.

Everett, Barbara. "Set Upon a Golden Bough to Sing: Shakespeare's Debt to Sidney in *The Phoenix and Turtle*". *TLS*. 5.107 (2001):13−15.

Hope, Jonathan. *Shakespeare's Grammar*. London: Arden, 2003.

Knight, G. Wilson. *The Mutual Flame: On Shakespeare's Sonnets and "The Phoenix and the Turtle."* London: Methuen, 1955.

Shakespeare, William. *The Oxford Shakespeare. The Complete Sonnets and Poems*. Ed. Colin Burrow. Oxford: Oxford University Press, 2002.

Shakespeare, William. *The Complete Poems of Shakespeare*. Eds. Cathy Shrank and Raphael Lyne. Abingdon, Oxon and New York: Routledge, 2018.

Shakespeare, William. *Shakespeare's Poems*. Eds. Katherine Duncan-Jones and H. R. Woudhuysen. Arden 3. London: Cengage Learning, 2007.

Shakespeare's *Merchant of Venice* and the History of the Jews

Leonard Neidorf

Abstract: The present paper considers the value of Shakespeare's *Merchant of Venice* as a source for the history of the Jews in Europe. It examines the portrayal of Shylock in detail and argues that Shakespeare offers a more positive and humane conception of the Jew than many of his contemporaries. When compared with the figure of Barabas in Christopher Marlowe's *Jew of Malta*, Shylock can be recognized as a far more sympathetic and credible figure. Though far from admirable, Shylock is not a ridiculous caricature—he is a plausible and ambivalent character grounded in contemporary knowledge of European Jewry. The complexity of Shylock thus sheds considerable light on Shakespeare's use of sources, his engagement with his predecessors, and his ideas about Jews and Judaism.

Key words: Shakespeare; *Merchant of Venice*; Jewish history

Author: Leonard Neidorf is Professor of English at Nanjing University. He received his Ph.D. from Harvard University and his B.A. from New York University. He is the author of two monographs—*The Art and Thought of the Beowulf Poet* (Cornell University Press, 2022) and *The Transmission of Beowulf: Language, Culture, and Scribal Behavior* (Cornell University Press, 2017)—as well as the editor of three books. In 2020, Neidorf was awarded the Beatrice White Prize by the English Association for his research on medieval literature. Neidorf has published more than 90 papers in A&HCI journals. His work has appeared in a wide range of journals including *ELH, Folklore, Neophilologus, Review of English Studies, Tolkien Studies, Journal of Germanic Linguistics*, and *Nature Human Behaviour*. Neidorf is an Associate Editor of *English Studies* (Taylor & Francis) and the Editor-in-Chief of *The Explicator* (Taylor & Francis).

This essay was composed on account of my longstanding friendship with Professor Luo Yimin of Southwest University. Professor Luo has been a great champion of Shakespeare studies in China, and he has done much to ensure that future generations continue to understand and appreciate Shakespeare's works. Professor Luo knows that I am an expert in Old English, that is, in literature composed several centuries before Shakespeare's lifetime, yet he has always encouraged me to work on Shakespeare, in the evident conviction that Shakespeare's literature transcends its time and speaks to scholars of all periods. I therefore aim in this essay to put forward my own peculiar understanding of Shakespeare, informed as it is by my intellectual and personal background.

Part of that background, for me, is that I am a person of Jewish descent. My ancestors were Jews from Eastern Europe, who migrated to the United States at the beginning of the twentieth century. I knew personally very few of my relatives, and I have been told very little about them. Oral tradition in my family has preserved few details aside from names and occupations. Such amnesia reflects a common belief among Jews that it is the story of the Jewish collective rather than the Jewish individual that really matters. Indeed, for much of the past millennium, every Jew in Europe was affected by the same restrictions and prejudices, so their lives are assumed to be largely the same.①

It is therefore to literature depicting Jewish characters, such as Shakespeare's *The Merchant of Venice* (ed. Mahood 2018), that a Jewish person curious about the

---

① Irving Howe, *World of Our Fathers*, New York: Harcourt Brace Jovanovich, 1976.

individual experiences of their ancestors must turn. The status of *The Merchant of Venice* as a source for Jewish history is, of course, hotly contested. Some allege that the play is antisemitic, while others allege that it is philosemitic. Some argue that it displays minimal knowledge of Jews and Judaism, while others argue that it is well-informed about the contemporary Jewish predicament. Whatever the case might be, there is no doubt that *The Merchant of Venice* has become one of Shakespeare's most popular and enduring works, generating numerous adaptions on stage, page, and screen.[①] It is in *The Merchant of Venice* that we encounter Shylock, the most famous Jewish character in all of world literature and one of the greatest characters that Shakespeare created. The role of Shylock has been played by some of the most eminent actors of the past century, including Laurence Olivier, Patrick Stewart, and Al Pacino. As we will see later on in this lecture, Shylock is an extraordinarily complex and multifaceted character, a subject of endless fascination. But before we analyze the character of Shylock in depth, I'd like to briefly consider the treatment of Jews in English literature prior to Shakespeare.

Probably the earliest reference to the Jews in the English language is to be found in the Old English poem known as *Widsith*, which is believed to have been composed around the year 700.[②] In this catalogue poem, a far-travelling poet claims to have visited many of the world's peoples. He says: "With the Israelites I was and the Assyrians, with the Hebrews and with the Indians and with the Egyptians" (Bjork 2014:51). The poem does not tell us much about what contemporary English people thought of Jews. The presence of the Jews in a part of the catalogue dealing with oriental peoples, rather than in the part dealing with the Germanic peoples more familiar to the Anglo-Saxons, suggests merely that the Jews were re-

---

[①] For a sense of the play's reception, see Gross (1992); and Baker & Vickers (2005). On the play's value as a source for the history of the Jews in the early modern period, see Adelman (2008); Holmberg (2011); Shapiro (1996).

[②] Old English poetry is cited from the editions of Krapp & Dobbie (1931-53). On the dating of *Widsith*, see Neidorf (2013).

garded as a distant and alien people, likelier to be encountered in books or stories than in the daily life of Northern European peoples.

The Old English *Exodus*, one of several epic retellings of biblical stories to survive in Old English, is notable for its favorable depiction of the Jewish people as they struggle against their Egyptian enemies. In this poem, the terms of Germanic heroic verse are adapted to the biblical narrative, and Moses occasionally appears indistinguishable from a Germanic hero such as Beowulf. In one passage, Moses is described as *manna mildost*, "the mildest of men." The same phrase is also applied to Beowulf, who is eulogized by his retainers as the "the mildest of men and the kindest, most generous to his people and most honor-bound" (Fulk 2010: 295). For the Anglo-Saxons, Moses the Jew was apparently no less admirable than Beowulf the Scandinavian.[①]

This is not to say, however, that Old English literature is devoid of disparaging references to the Jewish people. In the poem *Elene* by Cynewulf, we find expressed the idea that the devil induced the Jews to crucify Jesus Christ, and that the Jews are perpetually cursed for it. Cynewulf writes: "the old enemy through wiles seduced them, misled the people, the Jewish race, so that they hanged God himself, the creator of armies. For that they have to endure banishment forever in humiliations" (Bjork 2013:157). It is notable, though, that Cynewulf blames the Jews for a crime they purportedly committed about eight centuries ago. There is no sense in his poem that the Jews of ninth-century Europe are engaged in nefarious activities.

And so we may concur with Samantha Zacher, who writes: "Anglo-Saxon conceptions of Jews had little in common with the derisive and far more damaging

---

[①] Gernot Wieland, "*Manna Mildost*: Moses and Beowulf", *Pacific Coast Philology*, 23 (1988): 86–93.

stereotypes that emerged in the centuries after Jewish settlement in England"[1]. Old English literature appears more or less devoid of references to "the contemporary Jew," to borrow a phrase from the title of Jacob Cardozo's (1925) book. For authors in the Old English period, the Jews are a literary people, not a significant population in the parts of the European world that were known to them. Many of the negative stereotypes about the Jews did not develop until later, when unassimilated Jewish communities became a prominent feature of major European cities. The difference is evident by the time we come to Middle English literature. Before we consider the most illuminating Middle English source, it is worthwhile to briefly review the history of the Jews.

Following the destruction of the ancient Jewish kingdom, the first millennium witnesses the migration or forcible relocation of populations of Jews to various parts of Europe, with notable communities emerging in France, Italy, and Germany. European rulers, aware that Jewish merchants could benefit trade, periodically invite Jewish communities to settle in exchange for heavy taxation. In the second half of the eleventh century, William the Conqueror becomes the first English monarch to invite Jews to settle in England. In 1290, Edward I expels all of the Jews from England, but in 1655, Oliver Cromwell invites Jews to return to England. Between 1290 and 1655, there were no substantial Jewish communities in England: there were only small numbers of Jewish travelers, secret Jews, and the socalled conversos or "New Christians," that is, people of Jewish descent forcibly converted to Christianity in Europe. One of these converts was Roderigo Lopez, the descendant of Portuguese Jews, who served as a doctor to Queen Elizabeth before he was accused of plotting to poison the queen and subsequently executed.

The Jews in Europe had no land and no nation of their own. They were toler-

---

[1] Samantha Zacher, ed., *Imagining the Jew in Anglo-Saxon Literature and Culture*, Toronto: University of Toronto Press, 2016, p. 5. See also Andrew Scheil, *The Footsteps of Israel: Understanding Jews in Anglo-Saxon England*, Ann Arbor: University of Michigan Press, 2004.

ated only because of the patronage they received from the lords and kings to whom they provided financial or professional services. The Jews were, moreover, barred from owning land, and thus prohibited from obtaining the landed stability fundamental to the European conception of nobility. Prevented from forming ties to the land, the Jews were required to rely on portable wealth, and to develop portable professional skills. Barred from agrarian pursuits, Jews applied themselves predominantly to professions such as finance, trade, and medicine. They were particularly notorious for the practice of usury, that is, the lending of money on interest. Since Christians were forbidden from engaging in this practice, Jews naturally filled that void, and they were both valued and despised for doing so. For much of the Middle Ages and the early Modern period, the Jews constituted segregated and non-assimilated communities in various European countries, and they were viewed with suspicion and hostility by the Christian majority populations. It is in this context that most of the antisemitic stereotypes and slanders against the Jews appear to emerge.

By the time we come to the writings of Geoffrey Chaucer, known to many of us as the father of English literature, we find that the intellectual tradition of antisemitism was fully developed. In his *Canterbury Tales*, written at the end of the fourteenth century, Chaucer (ed. Benson 1987) tells a story of a Jewish community that murdered an innocent Christian child for singing a Christian prayer while walking through the Jewish neighborhood. The story ends with a miracle: the child's mother discovers her murdered son, who continues to sing his prayers despite being dead; the Jews are then executed for their crime. The tale is told by one of Chaucer's characters, the Prioress, but it gives us no reason to doubt that Chaucer himself viewed Jews contemptuously.

The Prioress opens her tale by describing the standard predicament of the Jews in Europe. She says: "Ther was in Asie, in a greet citee, / Amonges Cristen folk, a Jewerye / Sustened by a lord of that contree, / For foule usure and lucre of vileinye,

/ Hateful to Crist and to his compaignye. /And thurgh this strete men mighte ride or wende, / For it was free and open at either ende" (Benson 1987). So, we are told that there was a Jewry, that is, a Jewish community, patronized by a lord of a country with a Christian majority so that they can provide financial services to their lordly patron. The Jews, according to this image, are not engaged in honest business. They are engaged in foul usury and profitable villainy. Here is Chaucer's description of the tale's climactic moment, when the Jews decide to murder the young Christian child. He writes: "Fro thennesforth the Jewes han conspired / This innocent out of this world to chace. / An homicide therto han they yhired, / That in an aleye hadde a privee place, / And as the child gan forby for to pace, / This cursed Jew him hente, and heeld him faste, / And kitte his throte, and in a pit him caste" (Benson 1987). And so Chaucer gives us a standard European conception of the segregated and non-assimilated Jewish community: it is a place, he thinks, that is rabidly hostile to all things Christian, so much so that its denizens would contrive the murder of a child who offended them by singing Christian prayers on their premises. He imagines a "cursed Jew," a murder-for-hire, who cuts the child's throat and casts him into a latrine.

A similar image of unbridled Jewish criminality is preserved in a play composed by Shakespeare's great contemporary, Christopher Marlowe, whose plays dominated the Elizabethan stage at the beginning of Shakespeare's career. One of Marlowe's most popular plays was *The Jew of Malta* (ed. Siemon 2009). It begins with a prologue from Machiavelli, who describes the play as "the tragedy of a Jew, / Who smiles to see how full his bags are crammed." The play was a huge commercial success and was frequently performed between 1592 and 1596. Shakespeare is believed to have composed *The Merchant of Venice* in 1596 or 1597. There can be little doubt that the success of Marlowe's Jewish play inspired Shakespeare to write one of his own. Marlowe's play tells of the rise and fall of Barabas, a comically evil Jew who is wronged by the state and then avenges these wrongs in elaborate ways. A notable feature of Barabas is his absolute disdain for the society around him. When he hears that the Turks will invade Malta, he says: "Why let'em come, so they come not to war; / Or let'em war, so we be conquerors. / (Nay, let'em combat, conquer, and kill all, / So they spare me, my daughter, and my wealth.)" (Siemon 2009: 17). Barabas, we learn here, has no attachment to Malta: he is a transient Jew, an international merchant, and he doesn't mind if the city is destroyed; he cares only about himself, his daughter, and his wealth.

At one point in the play, Barabas visits a slave market and purchases a Turkish slave to help him execute his villainous plans. After asking the slave if he is qualified to commit crimes against Christians, Barabas delivers an extraordinary speech reviewing his career and demonstrating his own aptitude for villainy. He says: "As for myself, I walk abroad a-nights / And kill sick people groaning under walls: / Sometimes I go about and poison wells… / Being young I studied physic, and began / To practise first upon the Italian; / There I enriched the priests with burials, / And always kept the sexton's arms in ure / With digging graves and ringing dead men's knells: / And after that was I an engineer, / And in the wars'twixt France and Germany, / Under pretence of helping Charles the Fifth, / Slew friend and enemy with my stratagems. Then after that was I an usurer, / And with extorting, cozening, forfeiting, / And tricks belonging unto brokery, / I filled the jails with bankrouts in a year, / And with young orphans planted hospitals, / And every moon made some or other mad, / And now and then one hang himself for grief, / Pinning upon his breast a long great scroll / How I with interest tormented him. / But mark how I am blest for plaguing them, / I have as much coin as will buy the town. / But tell me now, how hast thou spent thy time?" (Siemon 2009: 52–53). The speech is a remarkable monument to the literary tradition of European antisemitism. Barabas begins his speech by bragging about poisoning wells-one of the standard slanders against the Jewish minority believed to loathe the Christian majority. He then works as an itinerant professional, using his talents to deceive employers and create mischief. He is first a corrupt doctor, then a corrupt engineer, then a corrupt usurer, in each case using his profession to enrich himself and harm the society around him. Barabas entertained Elizabethan audiences not merely by embodying a wide range of antisemitic stereotypes, but by being an outrageous, larger-than-life figure.

Critics often find in the depiction of Barabas something farcical and even endearing. Stephen Greenblatt, for instance, writes: "Marlowe celebrates his Jew for being clearer, smarter, and more self-destructive than the Christians whose underlying values Barabas travesties and transcends"[1]. It would be wrong, then, to construe Barabas as a product of virulent, thoughtless antisemitism. There is sophistication behind Marlowe's Jew. Yet it is nevertheless clear that the comical and unrealistic figure of Barabas is fundamentally different from Shakespeare's Shylock. Shakespeare, as noted before, was Marlowe's exact contemporary, though Marlowe was the first of the two men to achieve eminence on the Elizabethan stage. Shakespeare's Shylock can thus be understood as an attempt to respond to Marlowe and demonstrate what he was capable of doing as a dramatist.

The plot of *The Merchant of Venice* seems rather simple and unpromising. Bassanio, a young and improvident Venetian nobleman, needs money in order to court Portia, a rich and beautiful noblewoman. Bassanio therefore asks Shylock, the Jewish moneylender, for a loan of 3000 ducats. As a security for the loan, Bassanio's friend, Antonio, agrees to give Shylock a pound of his flesh if the loan is not repaid in time. In a subplot of the play, Shylock's daughter, Jessica, elopes with Lorenzo, a Christian nobleman and friend of Bassanio. After their elopement, we learn Antonio's ships did not return to Venice in time, and he cannot repay the loan in time. Shylock thus intends to extract the pound of flesh to get revenge, but his plans are foiled by Portia, disguised as a male lawyer. Shylock is defeated in court and forced, in the end, to lose half his wealth and convert to Christianity. Let's take a

---

[1] Stephen J. Greenblatt, "Marlowe, Marx, and Antisemitism", *Critical Inquiry,* 5(1978): p. 307.

closer look now at the figure of Shylock.

Here is the scene in which Bassanio asks Shylock for the loan of three thousand ducats. Their interaction proceeds as follows: "BASSANIO Your answer to that? / SHYLOCK Antonio is a good man. / BASSANIO Have you heard any imputation to the contrary? / SHYLOCK Ho, no, no, no, no! My meaning in saying he is a good man is to have you understand me that he is sufficient...Three thousand ducats. I think I may take his bond." (Mahood 2018: 83) In the scene, Shylock emerges as a serious businessman and moneylender, one assessing the financial risk of Bassanio's proposition. In saying that Antonio is a *good* man, Shylock refers not to his supposed Christian virtue, but to his credit, and to the probability that his wealth will be sufficient to repay the 3000 ducats. Shylock goes on in the scene to ask to speak with Antonio, and so Bassanio asks him to dine with them. Shylock then offers a memorable reply. He says: "Yes, to smell pork! To eat of the habitation which your prophet the Nazarite conjured the devil into! I will buy with you, sell with you, talk with you, walk with you, and so following; but I will not eat with you, drink with you, nor pray with you." (Mahood 2018: 84) We could interpret Shylock's answer as the typical response of a Jew contemptuous of Christians, like Barabas, but there is more to it than that. The passage characterizes Shylock as a confident, self-assured, and observant Jew. He does not leap at the chance to ingratiate himself with Christian noblemen. There is a proud dignity to the man.

When Antonio, the Christian merchant, enters the play, Shylock delivers a lengthy aside expressing his contempt for Antonio. Shylock says: "How like a fawning publican he looks! / I hate him for he is a Christian, / But more for that in low simplicity / He lends out money gratis and brings down / The rate of usance here with us in Venice. / If I can catch him once upon the hip, / I will feed fat the ancient grudge I bear him. / He hates our sacred nation, and he rails, / Even there where merchants most do congregate, / On me, my bargains, and my well‐won thrift, / Which he calls 'interest.' Cursèd be my tribe / If I forgive him!" (Mahood

2018: 84−85). This is a problematic speech, for it makes Shylock sound positively similar to Barabas. He seems here to be the Jew who hates Christians simply for being Christians. Many directors of the *Merchant of Venice,* who wish to portray Shylock in a sympathetic manner, delete this speech from their productions. Yet there is no doubt that Shakespeare wrote it and that it is an authentic part of the play. I do not regard it as a speech that should be ignored. It makes us appreciate that Shylock is a realistic product of his circumstances, bearing the prejudices that one might expect him to bear. Notice, moreover, that theology is not really what Shylock hates about Antonio. The men have a professional rivalry. Shylock hates Antonio because, as a Christian merchant, he offers interest-free loans to his petitioners, which drives down the interest rates in Venice and thereby sabotages Shylock's business. Shylock's hatred, additionally, is framed as a response to Antonio's hatred. Shylock says of Antonio: "He hates our sacred nation." Indeed, the play leaves us in little doubt that this is correct, that Antonio genuinely hates Shylock not because he is a usurer but because he is a Jew. Shylock is therefore enticed by the prospect of having Antonio bound to him as the security for Bassanio's loan.

Furthermore, Shylock takes pleasure in the irony of the situation that has arisen. Bassanio and Antonio, two Christians who scorned and derided Shylock for lending money on interest, have now come to Shylock because they wish to borrow money on interest. To make his Christian interlocutors aware of this irony, Shylock delivers his first great speech in the poem, which reads: "Signior Antonio, many a time and oft / In the Rialto you have rated me / About my moneys and my usances. / Still have I borne it with a patient shrug / (For suff'rance is the badge of all our tribe). / You call me misbeliever, cutthroat dog, / And spet upon my Jewish gaberdine, / And all for use of that which is mine own. / Well then, it now appears you need my help. / Go to, then. You come to me and you say / 'Shylock, we would have moneys'—you say so, / You, that did void your rheum upon my beard, / And foot me as you spurn a stranger cur / Over your threshold. Moneys is your suit. /

What should I say to you? Should I not say / 'Hath a dog money? Is it possible / A cur can lend three thousand ducats?' Or / Shall I bend low, and in a bondman's key, / With bated breath and whisp'ring humbleness, / Say this: 'Fair sir, you spet on me on Wednesday last; / You spurned me such a day; another time / You called me 'dog'; and for these courtesies / I'll lend you thus much moneys.'" (Mahood 2018: 88)

The speech is a shocking one. Prior to this point, there has been nothing in the play or in the history of English literature to expect such a clever and multifaceted response to come out of the mouth of a Jewish moneylender. There is, first of all, the registering of resentment for the wrongs that Venetian Christians have committed against him. Antonio is accustomed to spit on Shylock, kick him, and call him a dog. Shylock remembers all of this persecution. And he bitterly makes Antonio aware of how ignorant and thoughtless such persecution had been. If I am a dog, Shylock asks, how can I lend you 3000 ducats? "Hath a dog money?" (Mahood 2018: 88) he pointedly asks. The speech can be interpreted as a sign that Shylock is uncharitable, bitter, resentful. But who would not feel that way if they were in Shylock's shoes? The speech also makes us question the character of Antonio, and others like him, who despise Jews for performing a useful service—a service that they need when their wealth is locked up in overseas ventures and no liquid capital is available.

Indeed, it is interesting to note that Antonio responds to Shylock's speech not by apologizing, but by insisting that he will continue to disdain Shylock. He says: "I am as like to call thee so again, / To spit on thee again, to spurn thee, too. / If thou wilt lend this money, lend it not / As to thy friends, for when did friendship take / A breed for barren metal of his friend? / But lend it rather to thine enemy, / Who, if he break, thou mayst with better face / Exact the penalty." (Mahood 2018: 88-89). The speech cannot help but make audiences question the expected character dichotomy between the good Christian Antonio and the evil Jew Shylock. Shylock's powerful words have no effect on him; they fail entirely to alter Antonio's habitual antisemitism. Since Antonio thinks it is wrong to lend money on interest, Shylock proposes an alternative bond for his loan: a pound of Antonio's flesh, to be extracted if the loan of 3000 ducats is not repaid in three months. The proposition can itself be regarded as an attempt to ridicule the Christian disdain for usury. If money is not be loaned out on interest, he seems to be saying, what would you have it loaned out for? A pound of flesh? Shylock calls his proposal a "merry sport," a friendly jest not to be taken seriously. Of course, once he feels sufficiently wronged by Antonio and Venetian society, he will insist on having his bond.

The next scene that sheds light on Shylock's character is one in which he is at his home, preparing to leave in order to dine with Bassanio and Antonio. It appears that, after rejecting the invitation, he decided to accept it after all. Before leaving his house, Shylock instructs his daughter Jessica to lock up the windows. He says to her: "What, are there masques? Hear you me, Jessica, / Lock up my doors, and when you hear the drum / And the vile squealing of the wry-necked fife, / Clamber not you up to the casements then, / Nor thrust your head into the public street / To gaze on Christian fools with varnished faces, / But stop my house's ears (I mean my casements). / Let not the sound of shallow fopp'ry enter / My sober house. By Jacob's staff I swear / I have no mind of feasting forth tonight. / But I will go." (Mahood 2018: 106) Here again we get another insight into Shylock's attitude: as a Jew, he is excluded from Christian society, but it is a society that he wants no part of. He even wants to keep his "sober house" free from the noise generated by the Christian revelers. We can read the passage negatively, as a sign that Shylock is a distempered puritan, but we can also read it as a sign that he is a morally serious and observant Jew, who is not tempted in the least by the licentiousness of Venetian society. Of course, Shylock's instructions to Jessica are disobeyed: Jessica opens her window and climbs out of it in order to elope with Lorenzo, a Christian, whom she will marry. To add insult to injury, Jessica steals bags of money and jewels from her father before running off.

Shylock's immediate reaction to Jessica's departure is not included in the play. His reaction is instead observed and recorded by Solanio, a minor character and friend of Antonio. Solanio says: "I never heard a passion so confused, / So strange, outrageous, and so variable / As the dog Jew did utter in the streets. / 'My daughter, O my ducats, O my daughter! / Fled with a Christian! O my Christian ducats! / Justice, the law, my ducats, and my daughter, / A sealèd bag, two sealèd bags of ducats, / Of double ducats, stol'n from me by my daughter, / And jewels— two stones, two rich and precious stones— / Stol'n by my daughter! Justice! Find the girl! / She hath the stones upon her, and the ducats.'" (Mahood 2018: 114) In a conventional play about a good Christian merchant and an evil Jewish moneylender, this should obviously be a scene that we are supposed to laugh at. Solanio certainly laughs at Shylock and regards him disdainfully as a "dog Jew." Here we have that apparently ridiculous sight, the Jewish moneylender obsessed with his money, who is no less concerned about the loss of his money than he is about the loss of his daughter. And yet: Shylock has done nothing to deserve his misfortune. Jessica had no right to run off with her father's wealth. Furthermore, when you are alienated from the majority society and can expect no charity from it, like Shylock, the accumulation of private wealth is important. If we laugh at Shylock here, we must also wonder: would we not react the same way?

The same question is raised by Shylock's greatest speech, which he delivers after learning that the ships containing Antonio's wealth have all been shipwrecked, and that Antonio will now be unable to repay the loan of 3000 ducats to Shylock. Shylock is pleased with the news: he will get revenge on Antonio and on the world by extracting the pound of flesh from Antonio and presumably killing him in the process. Salarino, hearing that Shylock intends to have his bond, doubts that he would really want a pound of flesh. Salarino asks him, "what's that good for?" and Shylock responds by delivering the most memorable speech in the play. He answers: "To bait fish withal; if it will feed nothing else, it will feed my revenge. He hath disgrac'd me and hind'red me half a million; laugh'd at my losses, mock'd at my gains, scorned my nation, thwarted my bargains, cooled my friends, heated mine enemies. And what's his reason? I am a Jew. Hath not a Jew eyes? Hath not a Jew hands? Organs, dimensions, senses, affections, passions? Fed with the same food, hurt with the same weapons, subject to the same diseases, healed by the same means, warmed and cooled by the same winter and summer, as a Christian is? If you prick us, do we not bleed? If you tickle us, do we not laugh? If you poison us, do we not die? And if you wrong us, shall we not revenge? If we are like you in the rest, we will resemble you in that. If a Jew wrong a Christian, what is his humility? Revenge. If a Christian wrong a Jew, what should his sufferance be by Christian example? Why, revenge. The villainy you teach me I will execute; and it shall go hard but I will better the instruction." (Mahood 2018: 121−122)

The speech is extraordinary, and it seems to confirm some of the interpretations put forward in relation to previous passages. Shylock is not inexplicably or essentially evil in the manner of Marlowe's Barabas. He is a normal person with a strong sense of personal dignity. When he is wronged, when he is kicked or spat upon, he remembers the injustice. Shylock does not accept the premise of Christian Venetian society that simply because he is a Jew, he deserves to be mistreated and abused, and he should just accept it. Antonio's default on the loan has finally given Shylock his opportunity to take revenge, and he intends to seize the opportunity and extract the pound of Antonio's flesh. What exactly does Shylock wish to avenge, we might ask? It appears that Shylock wishes to avenge no specific wrong but all of the wrongs he has suffered for his entire lifetime. He alludes to a lifetime of mistreatment in the speech when he says of Antonio that "He hath disgrac'd me and hind'red me half a million." Shylock must be referring here not to a single incident, but to a lifetime of lost income due to Antonio's intervention. A series of separate incidents seems to be imagined, moreover, when Shylock says that Antonio "laugh'd at my losses, mock'd at my gains, scorned my nation, thwarted my bargains, cooled my friends, heated mine enemies." Shylock, we can see, does not forgive and forget. And why should he, he asks? He is a human being, no different in his fundamental corporeality from a Christian. Shylock previously wished to separate himself from Christian society. He is now prepared to emulate it in one respect: revenge. Christians take revenge on Jews who wrong them, so Shylock will now emulate the Christian majority and follow its practice. He says: "The villainy you teach me I will execute." An argument is lodged in this line: Shylock is not innately villainous; he has no natural inclination to extract a pound of flesh from a Christian merchant. He has been driven to this point by a lifetime of abuse, culminating in the loss of his daughter and his ducats. We see a character here who is, perhaps, imbalanced, incoherent, frightening, and distempered, but at the same time, one that is undeniably sympathetic and convincing.

Shakespeare's nuanced and ambivalent depiction of Shylock is further developed in the scene in which Shylock learns from his friend Tubal about how Jessica has squandered her father's wealth. Shylock exclaims: "Why, there, there, there, there! A diamond gone cost me two thousand ducats in Frankfurt! The curse never fell upon our nation till now, I never felt it till now. Two thousand ducats in that, and other precious, precious jewels! I would my daughter were dead at my foot and the jewels in her ear; would she were hearsed at my foot and the ducats in her coffin. No news of them? Why so? And I know not what's spent in the search! Why, thou loss upon loss!" (Mahood 2018: 123) Again, in the conventional comedy about a Jewish moneylender, in the play that Shakespeare did NOT write, this seems like a scene we are intended to laugh at. It seems to say: look at the Jew's excessive love of money, which he values more than the life of his own daughter. Audiences might laugh at Shylock's histrionics, his apparently imbalanced and inhumane words. Yet any laughter must be tempered by the recognition that Shylock has done nothing to merit his misfortune. He has suffered one wrong after another, and he recoils at the loss of additional money in pursuit of his lost money. The scene develops his character further, continuing: TUBAL Yes, other men have ill luck, too. Antonio, as I heard in Genoa— / SHYLOCK What, what, what? Ill luck, ill luck? / TUBAL —hath an argosy cast away coming from Tripolis. / SHYLOCK I thank God, I thank God! Is it true, is it true? / TUBAL I spoke with some of the sailors that escaped the wrack. / SHYLOCK I thank thee, good Tubal. Good news, good news! Ha, ha, heard in Genoa— / TUBAL Your daughter spent in Genoa, as I heard, one night fourscore ducats. / SHYLOCK Thou stick'st a dagger in me. I shall never see my gold again. Fourscore ducats at a sitting, fourscore ducats! / Their interaction continues: "TUBAL There came divers of Antonio's creditors in my company to Venice that swear he cannot choose but break. / SHYLOCK I am very glad of it. I'll plague him, I'll torture him. I am glad of it. / TUBAL One of them showed me a ring that he had of your daughter for a monkey. / SHYLOCK Out upon her! Thou torturest me, Tubal. It was my turquoise! I had it of Leah when I was a bachelor. I would not have given it for a wilderness of monkeys. / TUBAL But Antonio is certainly undone. / SHYLOCK Nay, that's true, that's very true. Go, Tubal, fee me an officer." (Mahood 2018: 123−124)

  This is one of those scenes that must make us appreciate Shakespeare's artistry. Again, we enter the scene thinking that we are getting the comic figure we expect: the greedy Jew agonizing over the loss of his money. Yet that reaction is mingled with Shylock's ominous delight at the news that he will get to have his revenge. This revenge will not return the money to him, but it will give him a sense of vindication against a world that has wronged him. The mingled reaction reveals that Shylock's concerns are not exclusively financial. This is further suggested by the surprising revelation that Shylock attached particular value to the turquoise ring that Jessica exchanged for a monkey. Shylock had received this ring from his wife, Leah, when he was a bachelor. Leah, who is not mentioned at any other point in the play, presumably died before its action takes place. This revelation strongly alters our perception of Shylock and Jessica. Shylock is not the inhumane and unfeeling character we might expect him to be; the lost wealth had more than a monetary value to him. Conversely, we might think Jessica, the Jew who becomes a Christian, would be a positively depicted character in the play. Yet she seems here to be a callous, ignorant, and improvident girl, who heartlessly stole a precious heirloom from her father and went on to pawn it for a monkey. Certainly, the scene complicates any simplistic interpretation of Shylock. In one scene, he can seem farcical, greedy, vengeful, yet also sentimental and sympathetic. In other words, he emerges from the scene as a real human being, not a caricature.

A process of radicalization is evident in the play's depiction of Shylock. The calm and rational moneylender in the first scene transforms into a frighteningly intransigent figure in later scenes. Here he refuses to listen to Antonio's pleas for mercy and says to him insistently: "I'll have my bond. Speak not against my bond. I have sworn an oath that I will have my bond. Thou call'dst me dog before thou hadst a cause, But since I am a dog, beware my fangs..." (Mahood 2018: 138) And this is the attitude that Shylock brings into the courtroom scene. He wants revenge. He is no longer the comically greedy Jew. He is the radicalized everyman intent on getting revenge on the society around him, and he would rather have that revenge than have 6000 ducats or 60,000 ducats.

In the courtroom, the Duke attempts to reason with Shylock and persuade him to take the money rather than the pound of flesh from Antonio. Shylock is asked why he insists on his bond. To answer the question, he gives the following speech: "I have possessed your Grace of what I purpose, / And by our holy Sabbath have I sworn / To have the due and forfeit of my bond. / If you deny it, let the danger light / Upon your charter and your city's freedom! / You'll ask me why I rather choose to have / A weight of carrion flesh than to receive / Three thousand ducats. I'll not answer that, / But say it is my humor. Is it answered? / What if my house be troubled with a rat, / And I be pleased to give ten thousand ducats / To have it baned? What, are you answered yet? / Some men there are love not a gaping pig, / Some that are mad if they behold a cat, / And others, when the bagpipe sings i' th' nose, / Cannot contain their urine; for affection / Masters oft passion, sways it to the mood / Of what it likes or loathes. Now for your answer: / As there is no firm reason to be rendered / Why he cannot abide a gaping pig, / Why he a harmless necessary cat, / Why he a woolen bagpipe, but of force / Must yield to such inevitable shame / As to offend, himself being offended, / So can I give no reason, nor I will not, / More than a lodged hate and a certain loathing / I bear Antonio, that I follow thus / A losing suit against him. Are you answered?" (Mahood 2018: 148-149)

We see here the same triumphant, sardonic Shylock that we saw in Act 1, when he asked Antonio "hath a dog money?" Shylock again feels that he has the upper hand, that there is nothing in the law requiring him to explain himself. People are free to make economically irrational decisions and to spend their money however they see fit. A man can spend 10,000 ducats to have a rat exterminated. We also see here the same proud Shylock who disdains the prospect of dining with Christian. Shylock, speaking to the Venetian Duke, feels justified and protected by the law; he feels no need to placate those around him.

Shylock's defiance is again on display in this exchange with Bassanio, who says: "This is no answer, thou unfeeling man, / To excuse the current of thy cruelty. / SHYLOCK I am not bound to please thee with my answers. / BASSANIO Do all men kill the things they do not love? SHYLOCK Hates any man the thing he would not kill? / BASSANIO Every offence is not a hate at first. / SHYLOCK What, wouldst thou have a serpent sting thee twice?" (Mahood 2018: 149) In this exchange and others, Shylock emerges as wittier and more logical than the Christians around him. Although he will be defeated in the end, Shylock enjoys a series of brief triumphs over the Christians of Venice in the courtroom scene.

At no point in the scene is Shylock more triumphant than when he delivers the following speech: "What judgment shall I dread, doing no wrong? / You have among you many a purchased slave, / Which, like your asses and your dogs and mules, / You use in abject and in slavish parts / Because you bought them. Shall I say to you / 'Let them be free! Marry them to your heirs! / Why sweat they under burdens? Let their beds / Be made as soft as yours, and let their palates / Be seasoned with such viands'? You will answer / 'The slaves are ours!' So do I answer you: / The pound of flesh which I demand of him / Is dearly bought; 'tis mine and I will have it. / If you deny me, fie upon your law: / There is no force in the decrees of Venice. / I stand for judgment. Answer: shall I have it?" (Mahood 2018: 150-151) Shylock's speech receives no satisfactory answer because there is no answer than can be given. He exposes the hypocrisy of the Christian society around him. They cannot object to Shylock's ownership of a pound of Antonio's flesh when they themselves own the complete bodies of their slaves. No one asks the Christians to be merciful to their slaves, to marry them to their heirs and make their lives comfortable. So what right do they have to ask Shylock to be merciful to Antonio? For Shylock, this is a glorious moment. He has temporarily brought Venice to its knees, using the legal system to kill Antonio and thereby take revenge on the whole unjust world around him.

Of course, Shylock does not get to have his way. Portia, appearing in disguise as a young male lawyer, uses the law against Shylock. She points out that the bond entitles Shylock to the pound of flesh but not to a single drop of blood. If he spills any blood, then he will be guilty of attempted murder. Shylock relents at this point and gives up his claim to the bond. But Portia also finds him guilty of a law prohibiting aliens from plotting to take the lives of Venetian citizens. As a punishment, Shylock's wealth is to be confiscated by the state. He says in response to this verdict: "Nay, take my life and all. Pardon not that. / You take my house when you do take the prop / That doth sustain my house; you take my life / When you do take the means whereby I live." (Mahood 2018: 161) As in previous passages dealing with the loss of wealth, we could regard this as yet another indication of an excessive attachment to wealth. But are not Shylock's words reasonable?

Antonio takes mercy on Shylock by proposing that he be allowed to keep half of his wealth if he converts immediately to Christianity. The Duke agrees to this proposal. And so Portia says to Shylock: "Art thou contented, Jew? What dost thou say? / SHYLOCK I am content. / PORTIA Clerk, draw a deed of gift. / SHYLOCK I pray you give me leave to go from hence. / I am not well. Send the deed after me / And I will sign it." (Mahood 2018: 162) The ending of the plays confirms, I think, that we are to feel some sympathy for Shylock. His plans are not merely foiled. He is completely undone. In addition to losing half his wealth, he loses the Jewish identity that had previously defined him. Shakespeare returns, moreover, to the theme of shared corporeality in this scene. Shylock says: "I am not well." Perhaps we are to imagine that Shylock is about to vomit or cry or have a nervous breakdown.

Shylock is one of Shakespeare's most spectacular creations. He becomes a villain, but he is not inherently villainous. He is a multidimensional character, whose negative qualities are humanized and explained by the surrounding context. He is a credible character, at times sympathetic, at other times repugnant, just as real people are. Shylock's credibility is, I would argue, a sign that Shakespeare thought seriously about the predicament of European Jews and was probably more familiar with Jews and Judaism than scholars tend to assume. I see in Shylock many traits that I recognize in myself. I consider him an ancestor that I never knew, and I thank Shakespeare for providing me with this extraordinary record of human experience, however imaginary it might be.

I would like to conclude this lecture with a quote from Harold Bloom's book on Shakespeare and the Invention of the Human. I regard this quote as one of the most insightful statements I've seen about The Merchant of Venice. Bloom writes: "The phenomenon of a 'real' person entrapped in a play, surrounded by speaking shadows, is strongest in Hamlet, evidently by design. Yet this aesthetic experiment...is first ventured in The Merchant of Venice, where the ontological weight of

Shylock, from his first appearance through his last, places him as a representation of reality far distaining every other character in the play"[①]. I agree with Bloom, and I think it is such a testament to Shakespeare's genius that he would compose a play like this. Shakespeare's contemporaries would have assumed that in a play about an evil Jewish moneylender, the Christian characters would be attractive, witty, and humane, not the Jewish one. Shakespeare did the opposite. He gives us a play full of dubious, dimly depicted Christians alongside a highly nuanced, richly illuminated Jewish character, who dominates every scene in which he appears. Recognizing this, I believe we can better appreciate Shakespeare and understand why he should continue forever to be read, studied, and performed.

Bibliography:

Adelman, Janet. *Blood Relations: Christian and Jew in The Merchant of Venice*. Chicago: University of Chicago Press, 2008.

Benson, Larry D., ed. *The Riverside Chaucer*. Boston: Houghton Mifflin, 1987.

Baker, William and Brian Vickers, eds. *The Merchant of Venice: The Critical Tradition*. London: Thoemmes Continuum, 2005.

Bjork, Robert E., ed. *The Old English Poems of Cynewulf*. Cambridge: Harvard University Press, 2013.

Bjork, Robert E., ed. *Old English Shorter Poems: Volume II, Wisdom and Lyric*. Cambridge: Harvard University Press.

Bloom, Harold. *Shakespeare: The Invention of the Human*. New York: Riverhead Books, 1998.

Cardozo, Jacob Lopes. *The Contemporary Jew in the Elizabethan Drama*. Netherlands: H. J. Paris, 1925.

Fulk, R. D., ed. *The Beowulf Manuscript: Complete Texts, and the Fight at Finnsburg*. Cambridge: Harvard University Press, 2010.

---

① Harold Bloom, *Shakespeare: The Invention of the Human*, New York: Riverhead Books, 1998, p. 182.

Greenblatt, Stephen J. "Marlowe, Marx, and Antisemitism". *Critical Inquiry,* 5 (1978): 291–307.

Gross, John. *Shylock: A Legend and its Legacy.* New York: Simon & Schuster, 1992.

Holmberg, Eva Johanna. *Jews in the Early Modern English Imagination.* Burlington: Ashgate, 2011.

Howe, Irving. *World of Our Fathers.* New York: Harcourt Brace Jovanovich, 1976.

Krapp, George P. and Elliot van Kirk Dobbie, eds. *The Anglo-Saxon Poetic Records.* 6 vols. New York: Columbia University Press, 1931–53.

Mahood, M. M., ed. *William Shakespeare: The Merchant of Venice.* 3rd edition. Cambridge: Cambridge University Press, 2018.

Neidorf, Leonard. "The Dating of Widsið and the Study of Germanic Antiquity". *Neophilologus,* 97 (2013): 165–83.

Scheil, Andrew. *The Footsteps of Israel: Understanding Jews in Anglo-Saxon England.* Ann Arbor: University of Michigan Press, 2004.

Siemon, James R., ed. *Christopher Marlow: The Jew of Malta.* London: Methuen Drama, 2009.

Shapiro, James. *Shakespeare and the Jews.* New York: Columbia University Press, 1996.

Zacher, Samantha, ed. *Imagining the Jew in Anglo-Saxon Literature and Culture.* Toronto: University of Toronto Press, 2016.

Wieland, Gernot. "*Manna Mildost*: Moses and Beowulf". *Pacific Coast Philology,* 23.1–2 (1988): 86–93.

Ethical Care Principles for Training Young People in Shakespearean Acting[1]

Elspeth Tilley

Abstract: Ethical actor training is crucial in safeguarding students from harm, especially amidst challenges like Covid-19 and climate change. Balancing skill development and safeguarding against (re)traumatisation poses a significant challenge. Drawing from feminist ethics scholarship and personal actor-training experiences, my rehearsal approach combines Brechtian-inspired techniques and feminist ethics principles, fostering a context of care in drama classrooms. This approach to Shakespearean theatre training cultivates critical awareness of acting techniques, emotional observation, and self-regulation practices. It empowers young actors to consciously choose approaches aligned with ethics of care while delivering impactful performances, ultimately promoting their well-being and ethical engagement with dramatic texts.

Key words: ethical care; young people; Shakespearean acting

Author: Dr. Elspeth Tilley is Professor of Creative Communication at Massey University in New Zealand. Recognised internationally as an expert in the power of art to trans-

---

[1] An earlier version of this paper was presented in the panel 'Caretaking and Healing', Theatre and Social Change Stream, Association for Theatre in Higher Education Conference, Austin, Texas, 2022. My gratitude to panel chair Tara Brooke Watkins and the audience members for their valuable feedback.

form the world, her many research publications examine the ethics and effectiveness of art and creativity as communication forms.

As a feminist scholar, I want to start by acknowledging some of the women whose thinking has influenced the kinds of ideas I have used in developing my actor training technique. They're not the only humans whose ideas have influenced my approach to training and rehearsals, but I noticed when giving my students the genealogy of ideas that we use in actor training, many of the names were men - Lecoq, Laban, Copeau, Chekhov, Stanislavsky, Strasberg, Brecht, Meisner - with Adler, Hagen, and Bogart some of the few women who featured regularly. I wanted to add more women's names into the ways we talk about our theatre pedagogy, alongside the names most of us are already familiar with.

One of the women is Niki Harré, a New Zealand psychologist who thinks about the psychology of games and how games relate to the psychology of society. Another is Helene Weigel or Helli, as she was known, who, with other notable women such as Elisabeth Hauptmann, was a key part of the Berliner Ensemble alongside Helli's husband Bertolt Brecht. A third is Virginia Held, an American feminist who developed an "ethics of care" based on the idea of caring as a practice, not just an abstract value. Scholars including Elin Diamond[1] and Sue-Ellen Case[2] have observed the compatibility of Brechtian acting techniques with feminism, but it wasn't until I encountered sources indicating much of Brecht's approach was co-developed with Weigel and other women in his ensemble[3] that I felt able to articulate clear connections between the techniques I was using and a femi-

---

[1] Elin Diamond, "Brechtian Theory/Feminist Theory: Towards a Gestic Feminist Criticism", *TDR,* 32.1 (1988): 82-94.
[2] Sue-Ellen Case, *Feminism and Theatre*, 2nd edition, London: Palgrave, 2008.
[3] David Barnett, *A History of the Berliner Ensemble*, Cambridge: Cambridge University Press, 2015.; James K. Lyon, *Bertolt Brecht in America*, Princeton, NJ: Princeton University Press, 1980.

nist approach.

My thinking about this topic began, however, with an awakening to the importance of games. Drama games are routinely used in Australia, New Zealand, and elsewhere as core skill-building, strengthening, and role preparation for actors. Indeed, one of the things I love most about directing and teaching theatre is the opportunity to take actors through an increasingly somatic recognition of the importance of play, throughout the warmup process. Of course, drama games all have an immediate purpose, whether it is developing voice capacity, building memory, enhancing focus and concentration, listening, collaboration, or more. I always explain to my students the purpose of the game I am teaching them to achieve their goals as actors, but a few years ago I started to think far more deeply about the bigger purpose of drama games.

In 2015 I attended a conference presentation by Harré. She asked the whole audience, a couple of hundred of us, to make paper planes and throw them at each other. There were three phases, each with rules. In the first phase, we had to make eye contact with someone else and swap planes with them. In the second, the instructions were to throw our plane high in the air, and then the winner would be the person who grabbed as many planes as they could as they came down. In the third phase, the object was to try as a group to keep as many planes in the air simultaneously as possible.[1]

I use that game now with my students so that they, too, can recognise how the games we play, even as children, encode values and norms (Tilley, 2016). Which of the phases, I ask my students, represents how we organise our society and distribute resources in New Zealand? The second one, of course, is the model that best matches our capitalist economic system. The one in which planes are grabbed and

---

[1] Niki Harré, "Keeping the Infinite Game in Play in Life, the University, and Everything", *Social Movements, Resistance and Social Change* II: *Possibilities, Ideas, Demands,* Second Annual Conference and Social Change Forum: Auckland University of Technology, 2-4, September 2015.

ripped and damaged, in which people push past each other to grasp and then to hold to their chest as many planes as they can. The one in which some people end up with a lot of planes, and some with none. The one in which nobody feels good about themselves at the end of the round, even if they "won". The one in which we are separated from not joined to others and winning is acquisition, not sharing or connecting. After the game, we have a discussion, and it is clear that for the first time, many of the students have begun to see that there are other ways to organise the world than the competition of capitalism they have grown up in and that the games we play matter. The activities we use in the theatre classroom don't just reflect reality; when we are working with young people, the games we play also contribute to building the future world they (and we) will inhabit. This made me reflect deeply on the exercises I use in actor training.

To give an example: while I have never used musical chairs specifically in my classroom, I've seen them played often at children's parties in New Zealand, where I live, and it's an exaggerated, so useful, example to illustrate how games create meaning. A game like musical chairs is ableist. Several chairs are lined up, music is played, and when the music stops everyone must occupy a seat. There are fewer seats each round. People must compete to occupy a space. Those with physical differences will be out early, just as, in some of the games routinely played in the theatre classroom that require linguistic ability (such as Big Booty, in which participants must ad-lib a rhyme in synch with a precise rhythm) or intense concentration (such as the alphabet game, in which the group must speak in turn without pre-planning or overlap), people who are linguistically different or neurodivergent are "out" first, rejected from the group, and made to sit on the side and observe.

In real games of "musical chairs" that I have seen at children's parties in New Zealand, sharing is even punished—a child offers to sit on half their chair and give another child the other half, and both are deemed "out". They are sanctioned for their communitarian impulse with social rejection, one of the worst kinds of punishment for a child.

Many games that drama teachers play likewise encode values typically associated with patriarchy: might equals right, competition, a chain of command, and the privileging of, for example, rational, literate, and individualistic ways of seeing. Many drama games punish non-conformity, whereby those who might benefit most from being in the game longest, and thereby having more opportunity to develop the skills being used such as listening or focus, are those who are ejected early. So, the gap between the skills in the theatre class becomes wider, not closer together.

Values of capitalism, patriarchy, colonialism	Values of care, collaboration, empathy
○Competition, winning	○Working together to build something
○Elimination for "mistakes", elevation for being "right"	○Increasing interactive skill as a team
○Ranking, hierarchy, ambition	○Nobody is ever 'out'-making mistakes is celebrated as the root of creativity
○Ableism	○ There is no "wrong" or "loser", only different
○Battle for resources	○ Valuing different ways of knowing - oral, pluralist, Indigenous, contextual, autochthonous (grounded), embodied
○Neoliberal individualism	○Holistic understanding of personhood

After experiencing Harré's "infinite game" I started to think about modifying common actor training games to encode values that resist hierarchical ideas and instead reward practices of care and empathy; games where the goal is to encourage collaboration using different skills. Now, nobody is ever "out" in my drama classroom or rehearsal room. When we make mistakes during acting exercises and warmups, we laugh and keep going and problem-solve together. I see students supporting and peer-teaching each other the game to make sure that everyone can learn to succeed. Everyone builds the skills of fast reactions, memory, and vocal articulation, not just the "talented" actors. We will even change the rules of a game as we go to make it more caring. We talk about the value of making mistakes in terms of creativity. Everybody gets to stay in the game as we build the skills together. We rehearse "yes, and" improvisation techniques[1] and practice accepting others' offers and finding something in the offer to respond positively to and build upon. We build awareness of how our default responses to offers (such as offers of feedback on our acting performance) are often defensive, competitive, and self-elevation-oriented. We work on being better at caring, together, about the production as a whole rather than about individual "stars". I have seen firsthand that this translates into better theatre productions where the standard of acting is more even across the whole cast, rather than having some actors excel in their portrayals and others "weaker". Building collaboration right from the warmup phase translates into a cast that truly collaborates to lift everyone's performance.

We can call these values feminist as that is the field of ethical scholarship where most of them have been theorised, but we need to be clear that that must mean intersectional, inclusive feminism, if feminism is to enact the very values of care and diversity that it espouses. Held[2] is useful when thinking about creating care. Her theory has five main principles, which are interlinked and overlapping but to separate them out for the purposes of this article, they are: other focus, valuing emotions, concrete and subjective activation of caring, public and private are linked, and a relational understanding of personhood.[3] There is debate about whether Held's theory is or is not "better" overall than Kantian ethics, utilitarianism, virtue ethics, etc. but I'm not interested in which is the "best" ethics theory which ironically is a masculine value of competition. I am interested in what is most *useful* from Held's ideas of feminist ethics, in creating a context of care for actor train-

---

[1] Keith Johnstone, *Impro: Improvisation and the Theatre*, London: Routledge, 1979.
[2] Virginia Held, *The Ethics of Care: Personal, Political, and Global*, 2nd edition, Oxford: Oxford University Press, 2006.
[3] Marilyn Friedman, "Care Ethics and Moral Theory: Review Essay of Virginia Held, The Ethics of Care", *Philosophy and Phenomenological Research*, 77.2 (2008): 539−555.

ing. In Held's view, care is both a value and a practice; to me, this is what is most useful to learn from her; the specific need to think about how we *activate ethical values*, not just espouse them.

How can we create a drama classroom that is actively an environment of caring? We can start by understanding that students bring their personal lifeworld to the classroom; they don't leave it at the door even if we do try to use thresholding activities to clear their heads as they enter the space. They come with deeply ingrained trauma from immersion in experiences of pandemic and climate crisis, along with social values of elitism and competition and, increasingly often, mental health challenges. They may come to us already wedded to the neoliberal form of subjectivity, as I will unpack below. Before we can even begin to ask them to embody other characters from different times and places who faced different challenges, we have to actively train them to be aware of their own baseline subjectivity and associated cultural values and assumptions. Making that training seem like fun and games is a good place to start.

I had the honour recently to edit an important book chapter by an emerging Canadian scholar, Michael Ruderman[1], on the infiltration of the neoliberal form of subjectivity into acting schools in North America. Ruderman, inspired by high school encounters with the work of Augusto Boal[2], had been drawn to theatre to (he anticipated) make a difference in the world. He attended several different theatre programmes, and was finally accepted into a prestigious acting school, the elite school of his dreams in fact. But once there, he became more and more unhappy. He realised that he was being "broken down" to be built up again, and it was only when he began to ask questions about what exactly he was being "built up" to be-

---

[1] Michael Ruderman, "Training for What? An Autoethnographic Study of Neoliberal Subjectivity in Professional Theatre Training", in Elspeth Tilley, ed., *Creative Activism: Research, Pedagogy and Practice*, Newcastle Upon Tyne: Cambridge Scholars Press, 2022, pp. 243–262.

[2] A. Boal, *Theater of the Oppressed*, New York: Theatre Communications Group, 1979.; A. Boal, *The Aesthetics of the Oppressed*, Adrian Jackson, trans., New York: Routledge, 2006.

come that he realised that his own goals, and those of the acting school's actor training processes, were not compatible.

Ruderman became aware that the physical exercises he was trained in were not only meant to further his physical and vocal self-awareness, but also to create a specific and more desirable physical form and vocal timbre. His posture, walk, pitch, weight, muscularity, and even the way he held his head, were "corrected", as he worked towards an "ideal". He became aware that he was being trained to emulate ableist norms and to compete with his classmates to see who could reach those norms faster so that they wouldn't be "cut" after the first year of the program.

His chapter in my book also describes how he and his classmates were trained in using relationships as instrumental tools-"you never know where your next job will come from"-in ways that emphasised a neoliberal framework of utility, rather than a communal ethic of genuine connection and care. In general, Ruderman convincingly argues that the acting schools he attended were without exception focussed on producing a neoliberal form of subjectivity; one emphasising networking as hustle, the "business" of acting, a "Break you down to build you up" approach to actor training, disciplining the body to be "fit, able, and attractive", fitting graduates into (de Certeau's concept of) the grid of control[①], and encouraging trainee actors to aim to be a "star", even at the cost of friendships and collegiality. Ruderman writes that the neoliberal form of subjectivity.

conceives of the self as a competitive entrepreneur, or a business in and of itself in which one can "invest". As a result, one must constantly hustle to maximize the growth of the self-business, with the understanding that any "failure" is one's own responsibility. Recent work in psychology has shown that exposure to neolib-

---

[①] Michel de Certeau, "On the Oppositional Practices of Everyday Life", *Social Text*, 3 (1980): 3-43.

eral ideology is associated with increased loneliness and social isolation.[①]

Ruderman then quotes Kurt Vonnegut—"We are what we pretend to be, so we must be careful about what we pretend to be." And so, we must be conscious of how we ask our acting students to pretend and to play, in the classroom and on the stage, because theatre games and exercises emulate and prepare them for the big game of life. Those teachers who don't use competition in the classroom to motivate their students are probably exceptional, rather than the rule, at least in teaching institutions in the West. A 2016 United Kingdom survey found that most people in the UK believe that institutions of higher education and the arts encourage selfish values over compassionate ones.[②]

In another chapter I edited for my 2022 book, award-winning Michigan-based actor, director, and educator Rob Roznowski reported that, when working with his class on a production of Romeo and Juliet, "Some actors were unable to leave behind their character's sinister behaviours ... Personal safety could sometimes be compromised ... Numerous readings and techniques related to cooling down or de-rolling were shared with the actors, but this was still not enough for all"[③]. Roznowski describes one actor who, despite using de-roling techniques, was particularly impacted by the confronting themes that the production explored through the lens of Shakespeare's work:

[T]he actor complained of fear of coming into the performance space (also his theatrical classroom during the day) because of the trauma he endured the night before. This inability to distance or separate between artist, role, and activist was dis-

---

① Michael Ruderman, "Training for What? An Autoethnographic Study of Neoliberal Subjectivity in Professional Theatre Training", in Elspeth Tilley, ed., *Creative Activism: Research, Pedagogy and Practice*, Newcastle Upon Tyne: Cambridge Scholars Press, 2022, p. 245.
② Common Cause Foundation, *Perceptions Matter: The Common Cause UK Values Survey*, London: Common Cause Foundation, 2016.
③ Rob Roznowski, "Creative Activism: Creating Activists?", in Elspeth Tilley, ed., *Creative Activism: Research, Pedagogy and Practice*, Newcastle Upon Tyne: Cambridge Scholars Press, 2022, p. 190.

tressing and caused harm to the actor, as the role appeared to trigger past traumatic events that coincided with the show's messaging. The student sought assistance with untangling this artistic knot from trained professionals during and after the run of the show. ①

In her postgraduate research on New Zealand university students' memories of their experiences of high school drama classes, my student Jessica Ramage found that many of her interviewees recalled being deeply harmed by their experiences of high school drama training when they were asked to prioritize a good performance over psychological safety. She reported that young drama students were required to call upon their most traumatic experiences of grief and loss to inform characterizations, and that the majority of her respondents experienced "discomfort or distress with unrelatable characters or harrowing adult situations they were asked to portray"②.

Similarly, it is both my own industry experience as a former actor, and documented in scholarly research[3] and grey literature [4] that some forms of actor training can create deep-seated psychological challenges for some participants. In a comprehensive review of the literature, Arias concludes that "professional actors and per-

---

① Rob Roznowski, "Creative Activism: Creating Activists?", in Elspeth Tilley, ed., *Creative Activism: Research, Pedagogy and Practice*, Newcastle Upon Tyne: Cambridge Scholars Press, 2022, pp. 191–192.
② Jessica Ramage, *Actor-Kind: A Feminist-Theory Informed, Critical and Creative Approach to Developing Empowering Theatre for Aotearoa Young People*, MCW thesis: TeKunenga ki Pūrehuroa / Massey University, 2023, p. 3.
③ Mark C. Seton, "The Ethics of Embodiment: Actor Training and Habitual Vulnerability", *Performing Ethos: International Journal of Ethics in Theatre & Performance*, 1.1 (2010): 5–20.; Alison E. Robb and Clemence Due, "Exploring Psychological Wellbeing in Acting Training: An Australian Interview Study", *Theatre, Dance and Performance Training*, 8.3 (2017): 297–316.; Ian Maxwell, Mark Seton and M. Szabó, "The Australian Actors' Wellbeing Study: A Preliminary Report", *About Performance*, 13 (2015): 69–113.; Ross Prior, Ian Maxwell, Mariana Szabó, et al., "Responsible Care in Actor Training: Effective Support for Occupational Health Training in Drama Schools", *Theatre, Dance and Performance Training*, 6.1 (2015): 59–71.
④ Christine Brubaker and Jennifer Wigmore, "Actor Training in Canada: An Appeal for Change", *Intermission*, 19 June, 2018.

formers are more likely than their civilian counterparts to suffer from depression, anxiety, and various other mental health struggles"[1].

In my classroom I must comply with stringent codes of pastoral care to protect my students from harm. So, given the risks, how can I ensure that my approach to actor training for confronting roles such as those in Shakespeare's tragedies will do no harm? Especially when working with vulnerable young people and asking them to explore themes of suicide, mental health, and violence, I have a very high level of duty of care. Arguably at least 13 of Shakespeare's characters commit suicide—Romeo, Juliet, Ophelia, Lady Macbeth, Othello, Cleopatra, Mark Antony, Charmian, Timon, Goneril, Brutus, Brutus' wife Portia, and Cassius[2]-and almost all of the young women in my university theatre classes report that they have played either Juliet, Ophelia, or Desdemona, who is violently murdered, previously during high school drama training; Shakespeare "remains a dominant force in the curriculum"[3]. This would have seen them portraying either a suicide or a victim of intimate partner violence during their most vulnerable teenage years.

Of course, there are many benefits noted from engaging young people with Shakespeare. See, for example, Kelman and Rafe's[4] analysis of staging King Lear with 10-to 12-year-olds as one such success story, in which the cast found "courage and confidence" while engaging with one of Shakespeare's most heightened tragedies. Yet, "while Shakespearean drama provides rich characters, plots and ideas evidently suitable for adaptation into a range of more contemporary modes of per-

---

[1] Gabrielle Arias, "In the Wings: Actors and Mental Health—A Critical Review of the Literature", in *Expressive Therapies Capstone Theses*, MA thesis, Lesley University, 2019, p. 2.
[2] David K. Anderson, "Two Shakespearean Suicides", *Essays in Criticism*, 72.2 (2022): 125-147.
[3] Chris Hay and Robin Dixon, "'Until I Know This Sure Uncertainty': Actor Training and Original Practices", *Theatre, Dance and Performance Training*, 12.1 (2021): p. 46.
[4] Dave Kelman and Jane Rafe, "Playing on the Great Stage of Fools: Shakespeare and Dramaturgic Pedagogy", *Research in Drama Education: The Journal of Applied Theatre and Performance*, 18.3 (2013): 282-295.

formance, acting students do not always find it easy to work with these texts"[1]. Kelman and Rafe admit that, based on concern for their cast and audience that arose during "reflection-in-action" on feedback within the rehearsal process, they rewrote the ending of *King Lear* to provide an additional alternate "happy" ending, and "soften" the work "in ways that could be seen as patronising to the children and their community"[2] yet were essential to ensure actor safety. If we want to remain true to the text of a powerful tragedy, yet still protect young actors from harm, what other options are open to us?

Here's where I turn to a second inspirational woman, Helene Weigel. Long before she met Brecht, Weigel was exposed to an influential form of feminism during her education. As a teenager, she attended a progressive girls-only Lyzeum founded by Viennese social reformer Dr. Eugenie Schwarzwald. Schwarzwald had been inspired by Maria Montessori to deem that girls could excel in technical and scientific subjects, that both creativity and physical activity—to build strength and be able to defend oneself, not to move gracefully or elegantly—should be integral to women's education, and that women's learning should be driven by personal interest and choice. The school aimed to ensure women could enter university and that, once there, they could study whatever they wanted, right across the arts and sciences. Empowered by these ideas, at 17 Weigel began taking acting classes against her parents' wishes and gained professional acting work with the Frankfurt New Theatre at age 19.[3] From the beginning, she was known for her distinctive acting approach using stylized vocal delivery and bold, assertive movement, likely a

---

[1] Chris Hay and Robin Dixon, "'Until I Know this Sure Uncertainty': Actor Training and Original Practices", *Theatre, Dance and Performance Training*, 12.1 (2021): p. 46.

[2] Dave Kelman and Jane Rafe, "Playing on the Great Stage of Fools: Shakespeare and Dramaturgic Pedagogy", *Research in Drama Education: The Journal of Applied Theatre and Performance*, 18.3 (2013): p. 293.

[3] Sabine Kebir (2000, n. p.) notes that while Weigel's mother attended the theatre often, she refused to indulge her daughter's interest, and that Weigel "never forgave her mother for not taking her to see the last appearance of the great Josef Kainz as Marc Antony".

legacy of her schooling in which she was trained to both move and speak in uncompromising ways.

I have read multiple sources about Weigel, and they differ or even conflict in the detail, but in the general gist, they align. In the spirit of highlighting women's work, I want to draw attention to a play, *The Collective*, by New Zealand playwright Jean Betts, which I found particularly illuminating in terms of that "gist". Betts read John Fuegi's work, *Brecht and Company*[1], which has attracted some controversy, but not content with taking it at face value Betts also interviewed Fuegi about his work and checked many of the original sources before writing her play, which covers Weigel's time as director of the Berliner Ensemble. The play paints a picture of the Berliner Ensemble as largely run by women, with Brecht, who is referred to only as "Bert" (according to a cryptic note from the playwright it appears she was unable to use his full name due to copyright protections on his actual name, and she remarks how ironic this is for someone who called themselves a socialist), as happy to enthusiastically "absorb" women's work, both administrative and creative, into his better known "brand" and then conveniently "forget" who did the actual writing.

Of course, we cannot know exactly what happened, despite the work of archivists and historians[2], because history will always be partial and contested, but it seems clear from multiple sources that the women of the Berliner Ensemble were involved to a far greater degree in what happened there than my own mentions of "Brecht's Alienation Effect" or "Brechtian acting style" when I first began coaching actors did justice to. This is not to detract from Brecht's achievements, but to suggest that we may want to be broader in our terminology if we are trying to create a

---

[1] John Fuegi, *Brecht and Company: Sex, Politics, and the Making of the Modern Drama*, New York: Grove Press, 2002.

[2] Käthe Rülicke-Weiler, "Brecht and Weigel at the Berliner Ensemble", *New Theatre Quarterly*, 7.25 (1991): 3–19.

world in the classroom that reflects the inclusive operations of the world we want to see beyond the classroom.

Marston Jennifer William writes that:

Weigel's distinctive acting style consisted of a subtle combination of realistic and stylized dialogue and gestures, resulting in her own interpretation of the "alienation effect" promoted by Brecht. Her famous "mute scream" in Mother Courage, a move inspired by a photograph of a mother mourning her child's death after a Japanese attack on Singapore, exemplified this style. Influenced in part by Chinese theater, Weigel's movements on stage were employed deliberately and economically, as the actress believed that too many details would lead to an extreme naturalism that could ruin a character.

So, there were many sources for Weigel's acting techniques, including Chinese acting, and not all of them were Brecht. However, how, specifically, does this help us with a feminist ethics of care in actor training in the classroom? The alienation effect—which seems likely to have derived much if not all of its inspiration from Weigel's uniquely demonstrative acting style—can readily be adapted into a practical way to care for students, particularly in Shakespearian productions that demand difficult roles. Alienation-style methods can help students develop better emotional literacy and expand their self-care skills in dealing with emotions on stage.

Brecht's writings contain many theories and they are "moving, changing discourses, open to multiple readings"[1]. However, to give one reading of alienation, we can see it as requiring a separation between real feelings an actor has on the inside and the pretence of feelings an actor trains their body to show on the outside. Brecht wanted people to leave a theatre performance provoked to think about how the characters showed up the emotional problems that result from inequalities and problems in society as manufactured emotions created by unjust social structures,

---

[1] Elin Diamond, "Brechtian Theory/Feminist Theory: Towards a Gestic Feminist Criticism", *TDR*, 32.1 (1988): p. 82.

and therefore open to change, rather than as individual feelings created by the character's personality. He didn't want the audience given catharsis, or emotional relief leading to complacency, by seeing characters who seemed real, work through authentic-seeming emotions and find solutions within themselves.

Renowned theatre theorist Elin Diamond describes alienation as an acting theory this way:

In performance the actor "alien-ates" rather than impersonates her character; she "quotes" or demonstrates the character's behavior instead of identifying with it. Brecht theorizes that if the performer remains outside the character's feelings, the audience may also, thereby remaining free to analyze and form opinions about the play's "fable" or message. [1]

This requirement of distancing by the actor from how the character feels is the exact opposite of the technique that is normally called "method acting". The method has its roots in the acting system developed by the Russian theatre practitioner known by the stage name of Konstantin Stanislavski in the late 19th and early 20th centuries. Stanislavski argued that acting was about the "art of experiencing" rather than the "art of representation".[2] He wanted his actors to imagine themselves into the situation fully and react as they themselves might react if the circumstances of the drama were actually happening to them. In later adaptations of the method system, particularly in the United States of America, this came to involve actors using their own memories and experiences to try to create authentic emotional states on stage, living as their character, or staying in character throughout the run of a play or shoot of a movie, even when not performing the role.

There is a large body of literature suggesting that method acting is gruelling and even that it can cause psychological problems. This begins with Stanislavski's

---

[1] Elin Diamond, "Brechtian Theory/Feminist Theory: Towards a Gestic Feminist Criticism", *TDR*, 32.1 (1988): p. 84.

[2] Jean Benedetti, *Stanislavski and the Actor*, London: Methuen, 1999.

own observations that many of his actors using these kinds of techniques began to experience what he called "mental problems" and had difficulty "shaking off" the character.[①] In the present day, there are often media reports of cinema actors who feel damaged from being asked to use method techniques, and report "method" being interpreted as a license for them to relive their personal trauma for the sake of a role.

For example, one of the better-known proponents of the method technique, until his shocking 2017 announcement of his permanent retirement from acting, was Daniel Day Lewis. When filming the acclaimed movie *My Left Foot*, where Day Lewis played Irish writer and painter Christy Brown who was confined to a wheelchair, Day Lewis himself reportedly remained in a wheelchair throughout the production, including visiting a restaurants in character, where he would require the film's crew to spoon-feed him, and asking technicians to carry him to and from the set.[②]

It is my personal theory that this deep immersion in method acting may have been at least part of the reason why Day Lewis retired early and permanently from acting, and why Brecht favoured a very different technique of acting. Given the principal actor in many of Brecht's plays was Weigel, his wife and the mother of his children, and he was writing some incredibly brutal roles for her to play, her wellbeing as an actor would have impacted directly on him. Mother Courage, for example, is a woman who is so brutalised by war that she will even contemplate selling one of her own children to feed herself. By the end of the play, all three of her children have been killed, likely because of her profiteering, and she is bereft. Weigel had to play Mother Courage and then go home to her own children. She had

---

[①] Gabrielle Arias, "In the Wings: Actors and Mental Health A Critical Review of the Literature", in *Expressive Therapies Capstone Theses*, MA thesis, Lesley University, 2019.

[②] Calum Russell, "Daniel Day-Lewis' Extraordinary Method Acting in 'My Left Foot'", *Far Out Magazine*, 21 November, 2021.

to switch from being brutal and brutalised, to being caring, and the approach that she used was to implement an acting style that separates, rather than integrates, the physical and the emotional. She arguably brought with her from her early schooling in Vienna the assertive physical approach that Brecht called "gestus", meaning a series of movements, postures, facial expressions and gesticulations which the actor would learn and then replicate emphatically and precisely in performance, and she could put the gestus on and off in the same way one would put on and off a costume, to provide a symbolic external demonstration of a particular emotion, rather than trying to feel the emotion. This can be just as successful as more naturalistic or interiorised styles of acting, as multi-award-winning actor Meryl Streep has proven with her acclaimed stylized portrayal of Mother Courage.

In my own courses, then, I teach students the underpinning philosophical differences between method and alienated acting and train them to become aware, through such techniques as mirror work, of how their body looks to others. I train them to slip representations of emotion on and off without needing to feel them and support them to develop self-awareness about what works best in terms of physicality to communicate each state they want to portray. I ask them to make faces at each other, and to name and describe the emotions they see and compare them with what the actor thinks they are representing with their body. I require them to move emphatically with signature postures to convey an emotional state, but always, always to monitor their thinking versus their feeling to ensure that there is a separation between their external gestus and their internal emotional state. I ask them to try out different tones, timbres, intonations, and inflections for a line, to hear the different "sounds of emotion" (but without feeling the emotion). I ask them to riff between twenty different possible emotions for a line and to audio record this vocal activity using their phone and play it back to check whether the emotions conveyed vary between the different vocal attempts. I ask them to be conscious of the effect of their characterisation on them as an actor, not just on the audience. After several weeks of mirror and audio recording work they are in a much better position to take control of the physical and vocal aspects of their storytelling and work these into an overall acting performance in ways that can impact an audience, without damaging the actor. We visualise leaving the role on the floor of the rehearsal room, picking it up, putting it on, removing it again and leaving it on the floor, until they can confidently say that when they are acting trauma, they are not feeling trauma; while they are acting tragedy, they do not in the least feel tragic.

The results are impressive. I have worked with my students not only on deeply dramatic Shakespearean and other scripted roles, but also in applied theatre projects on incarceration, homelessness, and climate change. They have played victims of crime, people experiencing severe distress, people choosing never to have children, and while they are already stressed themselves, in the context of climate change, pandemic fatigue, and rising costs of living, learning to take on and off their emotional "costuming" in the role helps them also manage their emotions in real life.

When they create the mind/body separation characteristic of Weigel's style, through activities that encourage them to represent an emotional state on the outside, but to monitor to ensure they are not feeling it on the inside, they are able to develop emotional literacy and self‐protective capacity through these performances. I also find it helps them to tell them about Weigel and the roles she played and how she played them, and the reasons she may have had for deliberately cultivating a separation between representation and sensation, and about Held and her ideas of what makes a caring environment. The combined approach of thinking about self-care and thinking about other-care helps young actors become critically aware of the implications and origins of rehearsal techniques they have encountered previously and to develop emotional observation, self-regulation, and other-aware practices that can build wellbeing skills.

Not only the method but most other acting systems focus on integrating the physical and the emotional: and in class, we also review these, so that the students are familiar with their key tenets. Rasaboxes, for example, "trains participants to work holistically: the body/mind/emotions are treated as a single system...Rasaboxes integrates rather than separates acting, movement, and voice. Rasaboxes engages the whole performer in a single, powerful, and learnable approach." (Rasaboxes, n.d.) Even Viewpoints[1], which has a significantly greater focus on care than other approaches, does not fully separate body from effect, and so risks students taking difficult roles into their body—if the body "keeps the score" of trauma[2], I don't want my students to risk the possibility that embodying trauma for performance also "scores" the body in some way.

It always shocks me once we start talking about method acting in the classroom, how many of the young people were asked, in high school or even primary school while acting for school shows, to dig into their own emotions to fuel a character. Of course, this says more about the ways in which method is deployed than method in and of itself but, in my experience, drama teachers must recognise that method is not suitable for classrooms. Method acting can be a deeply harmful activity, particularly when working with texts such as Shakespeare that require representation of traumatic events and heightened emotion. When our students are already traumatised by a pandemic and by climate change, this is not something we can afford to risk.

Developing the ability to self-observe and actively recognize and moderate the connections and disconnections between physical and emotional expression develops skills in emotional self-regulation that are useful far beyond the acting classroom. It is my aim in drama classes to help students develop an "affective solidarity and mutual regard that, in turn, could be powerful counterweights to the exclu-

---

[1] Anne Bogart and Tina Landau, *The Viewpoints Book: A Practical Guide to Viewpoints and Composition*, New York: Theatre Communications Group, 2004.

[2] Bessel van der Kolk, *The Body Keeps the Score: Brain, Mind, and Body in the Healing of Trauma*, New York: Viking Press, 2014.

sions and disregard in a careless society"[1]. The responses I receive from students indicate that what they learn about emotional literacy and feminist care ethics expands and endures beyond the classroom; they report that they are learning to be different not just as actors but in their other "roles" as employees, flatmates, siblings, friends, etc. Feedback includes, for example, "She made a group of about 20 become very close friends, it was great to see everyone express themselves through her encouragement and teachings," and "We're encouraged to challenge ourselves, make mistakes and grow together as a group and individually. I've learned techniques that will help further a potential career as an actor, as well as feeling like I can open up and show vulnerability and be accepted." I know there are other teachers doing this kind of work slipping broader wellbeing-building into the drama curriculum by modelling a classroom in which ethical care is the modus operandi. I also know there are those who do not, and who will use any means to push an actor to a heightened dramatic performance.

Biesta[2], argues that teaching is world-building: "the responsibility of the educator, is not only a responsibility for 'newcomers' [the coming into the world of unique, singular beings]—it is at the very same time a responsibility for the world. It is a responsibility to create and keep in existence a 'worldly space' through which new beginnings can come into presence." So, what kind of world do we model in our theatre classrooms? In keeping in mind three women who thought about care, kindness, and harm reduction, in turning these values into practices that students enact towards each other every day in the rehearsal room and in their actor training, I hope to make a class world that is a little more along the spectrum towards the kind of outer world that I want to inhabit.

---

[1] James Thompson, "Towards an Aesthetics of Care", *RiDE: The Journal of Applied Theatre and Performance*, 20.4 (2015): p. 430.
[2] Gert J. J. Biesta, *Beyond Learning: Democratic Education for a Human Future*, London: Taylor & Francis, 2015.

The fun stuff—playing games in which nobody is out, making faces in the mirror—is of itself a just process, such that the games and turn-taking we engage in makes the classroom become not just a place of respite from the outside world, not just a safe space for learning to be emotionally literate actors, but something far more radical—an enactment, a practice, a rehearsal of practices, of recognition, redistribution, representation, and self-regulation that model the world as it could be.

Bibliography

Anderson, David K. "Two Shakespearean Suicides". *Essays in Criticism*, 72.2 (2022): 125–147.

Arias, Gabrielle. "In the Wings: Actors and Mental Health A Critical Review of the Literature". *Expressive Therapies Capstone Theses*. MA thesis. Lesley University, 2019.

Barnett, David. *A History of the Berliner Ensemble*. Cambridge: Cambridge University Press, 2015.

Benedetti, Jean. *Stanislavski and the Actor*. London: Methuen, 1999.

Betts, Jean. *The Collective*. Wellington: The Play Press, 2005.

Biesta, Gert J. J. *Beyond Learning: Democratic Education for a Human Future*. London: Taylor & Francis, 2015.

Boal, A. *Theater of the Oppressed*. New York: Theatre Communications Group, 1979.

Boal, A. *The Aesthetics of the Oppressed*. Trans. Adrian Jackson. New York: Routledge, 2006.

Bogart, Anne, and Tina Landau. *The Viewpoints Book: A Practical Guide to Viewpoints and Composition*. New York: Theatre Communications Group, 2004.

Brubaker, Christine, and Jennifer Wigmore. "Actor Training in Canada: An Appeal for Change". *Intermission*, 19 June, 2018.

Case, Sue-Ellen. *Feminism and Theatre*. 2nd edition. London: Palgrave, 2008.

Common Cause Foundation. *Perceptions Matter: The Common Cause UK Values Survey*. London: Common Cause Foundation, 2016.

de Certeau, Michel. "On the Oppositional Practices of Everyday Life". Social Text, 3 (1980): 3–43.

Diamond, Elin. "Brechtian Theory/Feminist Theory: Towards a Gestic Feminist Criticism". TDR, 32.1 (1988): 82–94.

Friedman, Marilyn. "Care Ethics and Moral Theory: Review Essay of Virginia Held, The Ethics of Care". Philosophy and Phenomenological Research, 77.2 (2008): 539–555.

Fuegi, John. Brecht and Company: Sex, Politics, and the Making of the Modern Drama. New York: Grove Press, 2002.

Harré, Niki. "Keeping the Infinite Game in Play in Life, the University, and Everything". Social Movements, Resistance and Social Change Ⅱ: Possibilities, Ideas, Demands. Second Annual Conference and Social Change Forum: Auckland University of Technology, September 2–4, 2015.

Harré, Niki. The Infinite Game: How to Live Well Together. Auckland, New Zealand: Auckland UP, 2018.

Hay, Chris, and Robin Dixon. "'Until I Know this Sure Uncertainty': Actor Training and OriginalPractices". Theatre, Dance and Performance Training, 12.1 (2021): 45–61.

Held, Virginia. The Ethics of Care: Personal, Political, and Global. 2nd edition. Oxford: Oxford University Press, 2006.

Johnstone, Keith. Impro: Improvisation and the Theatre. London: Routledge, 1979.

Kebir, Sabine. "'Shockingly Explosive': The Young Weigel". The Brecht Yearbook / Das Brecht-Jahrbuch, Vol. 25. Eds. Maarten van Dijk, et al. Waterloo, Canada: The International Brecht Society, 2000.

Kelman, Dave, and Jane Rafe. "Playing on the Great Stage of Fools: Shakespeare and Dramaturgic Pedagogy". Research in Drama Education: The Journal of Applied Theatre and Performance, 18.3 (2013): 282–295.

Lyon, James K. Bertolt Brecht in America. Princeton, NJ: Princeton University Press, 1980.

Maxwell, Ian, Seton, Mark and M. Szabó. "The Australian Actors' Wellbeing Study: A Preliminary Report". About Performance, 13 (2015): 69–113.

Prior, Ross, Maxwell, Ian, Szabó, Mariana, et al. "ResponsibleCare in Actor Training:

Effective Support for Occupational Health Training in Drama Schools". *Theatre, Dance and Performance Training*, 6.1 (2015): 59−71.

Ramage, Jessica. *Actor-Kind: A Feminist-Theory Informed, Critical and Creative Approach to Developing Empowering Theatre for Aotearoa Young People*. MCW thesis: TeKunenga ki Pūrehuroa / Massey University, 2023.

Robb, Alison E., and Clemence Due. "Exploring Psychological Wellbeing in Acting Training: An Australian Interview Study". *Theatre, Dance and Performance Training*, 8.3 (2017): 297−316.

Roznowski, Rob. "Creative Activism: Creating Activists?". *Creative Activism: Research, Pedagogy and Practice*. Ed. Elspeth Tilley. Newcastle Upon Tyne: Cambridge Scholars Press, 2022, pp.183−198.

Ruderman, Michael. "Training for What? An Autoethnographic Study of Neoliberal Subjectivity in Professional Theatre Training". *Creative Activism: Research, Pedagogy and Practice*. Ed. Elspeth Tilley. Newcastle Upon Tyne: Cambridge Scholars Press, 2022, pp.183−198.

Rülicke-Weiler, Käthe. "Brecht and Weigel at the Berliner Ensemble". *New Theatre Quarterly*, 7.25 (1991): 3−19.

Russell, Calum. "Daniel Day-Lewis' Extraordinary Method Acting in 'My Left Foot'". *Far Out Magazine*, 21 November, 2021.

Seton, Mark C. "The Ethics of Embodiment: Actor Training and Habitual Vulnerability". *Performing Ethos: International Journal of Ethics in Theatre & Performance*, 1.1 (2010): 5−20.

Thompson, James. "Towards an Aesthetics of Care". *RiDE: The Journal of Applied Theatre and Performance*, 20.4 (2015): 430−441.

Tilley, Elspeth. "Ethics and Gender at the Point of Decision-Making: An Exploration of Intervention and Kinship". *Prism*, 7.4 (2010): 1−19.

van der Kolk, Bessel. *The Body Keeps the Score: Brain, Mind, and Body in the Healing of Trauma*. New York: Viking Press, 2014.

Why the First Folio Matters to China's Shakespearean Studies[1]

Huang Bikang

Abstract: The speaker of this celebratory address claims that Shakespeare's First Folio is the rhizometic origin of centuries of Shakespearean studies worldwide, but fetishism of it does not avail anything in our study of his works. The speaker proposes that a granular engagement with the First Folio with editorial interests may empower us Shakespearean scholars with socio-historical context, cultural messages, materialistic references and even biological information of the Bard necessary for our understanding of his works for meaningful interpretation.

Key words: The First Folio; fetishism; history; materiality; biography

Author: Huang Bikang is professor of English, Peking University. He is currently the Chair of Shakespeare Society of China. His research interests include Shakespeare's history plays and American political history.

Respected Professor Cong Cong, Professor Michael Dobson, Dr. Jessica Chiba, Professor Li Weimin, Professor Li Weifang, my colleagues, and the stu-

---

[1] This is the author's speech delivered at the seminar celebrating the 400th anniversary of the publication of Shakespeare's First Folio at Nanjing University on November 4th, 2023.

dents who are here today with intensive interest in Shakespeare's First Folio and his plays, I am very much honoured to be invited to participate in this seminar celebrating the 400th anniversary of the publication of Shakespeare's First Folio.

We gather here today at the Shakespeare Institute jointly established by Nanjing University, Birmingham University and Phoenix Media and Publishing Group, to celebrate the 400th anniversary of Shakespeare's First Folio. Nanjing is a city of historical and cultural legacy. It was the capital city of six great empires in ancient China. It is also a city of theatrical inspiration. About four hundred and fifty years ago, the great dramatist Tang Xianzu, now known as "China's Shakespeare", came to Nanjing and studied at the Imperial Academy of the Ming Empire. Fostered by the rich theatrical culture of the city, he wrote his first play, *The Purple Flute*, and together with his fellow theatre enthusiasts, put it on stage, thus starting his career as the greatest dramatist of this country, thanks to his unsuccessful pursuit of his political ambition in a period when the great Ming Dynasty was in decline. That was in 1579, Shakespeare was then in his teens attending the local grammar school in his hometown Stratford-upon-Avon. Some thirteen years later, he emerged in London theatres as an actor, and shortly after began writing his first play, and when he died in 1616, he left us thirty-eight plays, thirty-six of which were collected in a single volume and published seven years after his death. This monumental book, known today as Shakespeare's First Folio, is the focal theme of our seminar today.

This year, 2023, marks the 400th anniversary of the publication of the First Folio, the first collection of Shakespeare's thirty-six plays on nearly one thousand big folio pages. This extraordinary book collects almost all of Shakespeare's known dramatic works in a single volume, thus elevating Shakespeare the actor, plotter, and stage scriptwriter to the status of an author who was empowered with the intellectual authority comparable to that of historians and philosophers in his time. The book provides the primary and reliable sources for multitudinous editions of Shakespeare's plays that flourished in the centuries after his death. It has been one of the world's most studied books giving consistent research momentum to generations of Shakespearean scholars, paleographers, and critics worldwide. For centuries, Shakespearean textual scholars and critics have persistently studied the plays originally printed in the First Folio with an archaeological zeal and the conviction that they are working on the greatest dramatic genius the world has ever produced. In a sense, we Shakespeareans, or "Bard's buffs" as we may call ourselves, all live on the First Folio, and more historically, we are indebted to Henry Condell and John Heminge, the initiator and promoter behind the publication of the First Folio, for their endeavour to convince the London printers to undertake this expensive but monumental project. But except for a qualified few Shakespeare textual scholars in China, such as the ones present today, what does the First Folio mean to most of our Chinese lovers of Shakespeare after centuries of exploration and excavation of its editorial and exegetic meanings mostly by Western Shakespearean editors and scholars? As a matter of fact, due to a lack of cultural intimacy and professional textual training, most Chinese students are not in a vantage point to explore this fetish book and the great variety of editions for important textual discoveries and gratification. Practically we are not expected, for example, to explore the Bodleian Library at Oxford University like Stanley Wells and Gary Taylor, find a manuscript buried in piles of classics, and after painstaking editorial examination, eventually prove that it is one of Shakespeare's lost poems that has survived the cruel hand of time. But the First Folio must not be worshipped as a rare book only. Fetishism does not avail anything in our pursuit of Shakespeare's literary greatness and the academic and cultural value of his plays. This great book does tell us about its past, the changing meaning of words over time, the process of its making and marketing, the theatrical transformation, the social and economic life of Shakespeare's time, and perhaps, Shakespeare the man himself. In addition, reading the First Folio and various Shakespeare editions may reveal to us the verbal changes or transformations that reflect various editorial decisions, annotations, emendations, and conflations that inevitably influence our understanding of how Shakespeare's mind worked and the changing tastes and beliefs of modern readers/audiences. In a word, the First Folio can inspire us in many ways. Let me briefly, for the occasion, illustrate how the reading of this monumental book can inspire us in our study of Shakespeare today.

First, editorial and paleographical interest in Shakespeare's First Folio will empower us with a sense of history necessary for contextualizing Shakespeare for social and cultural understanding. I am ever of the opinion that history, though itself may be a textual existence as post-structuralists tell us, is always a haunting presence for literary scholars. Literary text as a symbolic system is ever embedded in its social, cultural, and economic conditions when it is produced for human attention, reflective intelligibility, and aesthetic consciousness. Even ardent formalists like New Critics, in their impersonal analysis of the text, may leave room for the human concern of the past, as evidenced by its connection with modernist poetry which reflects the social turmoil in the beginning decades of the twentieth century. Deconstructionist famous "*Il n'y a pas de hors-texte*" or "there is nothing outside the text" sounds like an absolute denial of the existence of social-historical context, but we are aware that Derrida, in his later works seeks not to rule out historical presence at all. He turns explicitly to the problem of the relationship between testimony, historical memory, and cultural evidence. He used the terms "historical configuration" or "historical milieu" to denote these connections. In his lecture at Peking University in 1997, he talked of the signified elusiveness of "Pardon" as a historical category functioning in a historical context[1]. Most evidently, after the post-structuralists surge across the landscape of literary theory, historicist critics, both old and new, hold the belief that history is either a necessary background or co-text to unveil the hidden power relations and the circulation of social forces. They find

---

[1] This lecture was delivered in Peking University's largest lecture theatre in the autumn of 1997.

Shakespeare's plays particularly illuminating to the workings of Foucaultian "discursive practices" and the circulation of the social forces in the sixteenth and seventeenth centuries. It is in this theoretical framework, that our close textual examination of Shakespeare's First Folio and granular engagement with the printed words on its pages may unfold to us the messages of the social-economic condition of his time that will enhance our understanding of his plays for meaningful interpretation.

Second, as a corollary of the concern for the historicity of text, Shakespeare's First Folio can draw our attention to the materiality of the cultural, economic, and intellectual relations of the Elizabethan Age. This monumental work should not be hung up in monumental mockery to our intellect in this digital and cybernetic world. Instead, we need to situate the Bard and his First Folio to the lived experience and materialist process of his time for intelligible examination. We understand that ever since William Caxton started his printing business in London in 1476 and printed Geoffrey Chaucer's *The Canterbury Tales*, book printing and binding flourished in the city, thanks to the overwhelming sensation of the so-called "Triumph of English" of the time and the humanists' promotion of classical wisdom and rhetoric. Up to Shakespeare's time, printing as a trade grew to be a lucrative business. But to print a book was not purely an economic act for money. It involved social collaboration regulated by a guild made up of publishers who secured manuscripts and supplied the paper needed, printers who managed the type and press, booksellers who promoted the books in the main market situated around St. Paul's Cathedral, and bookbinders who lived on those readers with delicate taste or bibliomaniac indulgence. These cultural, social, and economic activities were understandably governed by economic/material rules and were overseen by the government authority. Our encounter with Shakespeare's First Folio may call our attention to the material and economic activities involved in its production and promotion. We are told by textual scholars that the folio format was not rife in Shakespeare's time, for it is used only for books of "superior merit or some permanent values"[①] such as the *Holy Bible* or the documents of regal and legal severity. Economically, folio printing is much more expensive than quarto. Take the First Folio for example, the printing cost a little less than one thousand pounds. That was a huge investment for any publisher and the printer. We can imagine how hard John Heminge and Henry Condell persuaded William and Isaac Jaggard the printers to make an affirmative decision for the project of publishing Shakespeare's plays in folio format. And small wonder that in their epistle "To the Variety of Reader" contributed to the First Folio, the two actors earnestly urge the reader to "read, and censure. Do so, but buy it first," and "Whatever you do, Buy!" That was a loud advertisement quite worth the money Shakespeare bequeathed them in his will for their mourning rings. These, and many other lived cultural messages encapsulated in the First Folio comprise what we believe to be the "material culture" that constructs the social history, and meaningfully informs our interpretation and appreciation of Shakespeare's plays.

Furthermore, the First Folio may help us know more about Shakespeare the man. Careful readers of the First Folio may notice on one of its prefactory pages that Shakespeare's name appears on the top of the twenty-six "principal actors" who acted in the thirty-six plays collected in the First Folio. Considering our understanding of Shakespeare as a distinguished playwright having appeared on stage only for some minor roles such as the ghost in *Hamlet* and Adam the elderly servant to Orlando in *As You Like It*, we may take this as a complimentary gesture by John Heminge and Henry Condell. Nevertheless, further research into Shakespeare's life in London may demonstrate that he was not only a playwright, and a shareholder, but a regular acting member of his company. He earned more money from acting than from writing plays. For, in Shakespeare's time, a playwright earned but a flat price of less than ten pounds for his manuscript of one play. While the payment

---

① Fredson Bowers, *Bibliographical and Textual Criticism*, Oxford: Clarendon Press, 1964, p. 76.

was made, he lost all the rights to his work. This may also explain why Shakespeare's original manuscripts did not survive. They were simply thrown away when the play was well rehearsed and ready to put on stage. Fortunately, unlike his acting partners Condell and Heminge who had large families with nine to fourteen children to support, Shakespeare stayed alone in London with a private family paying a small rent, he was able to devote all his time and creative energy to acting and writing. One prefactory page of the First Folio also informs us that Heminge and Condell's three apprentices also appear in the list of actors. In contrast, because Shakespeare had no family in London as his fellow actors had, he was not entitled to take apprentice to nurture and so he enjoyed easy mobility in the city. He ended up comparatively wealthy with some handsome estates and cash when he retired in 1613. In this sense, can we say that Shakespeare has provided a ready footnote, perhaps, for Francis Bacon's famous proverbial statement that "he that hath wife and children hath given hostages to fortune, for they are impediments to great enterprises?" One more point about the actors listed in the First Folio. The fact that Shakespeare is honoured as the top actor in the First Folio can prove to be a strong bulwark against the most recent Anti-Stratfordian attack on Shakespeare as the genuine author of the canon. In their book *The Truth Will Out: Unmasking the Real Shakespeare* published in 2009, Brenda James and William D. Rubinstein propose that Sir Henry Neville, a well-educated statesman and diplomat was the true author of all the plays attributed to William Shakespeare. They claim that Sir Neville "might have gone frequently to London, and it is highly probable that he would have visited the local theatres, doubtless sitting in the expensive seats reserved for affluent playgoers"[①]. This is the only biographical information offered in their book to connect Sir Neville with plays or the theatres in London. To my judgment, this hesitant speculation immediately ruins the foundation of the authors' arguments painstak-

---

① Brenda James and William D. Rubinstein, *The Truth Will Out: Unmasking the Real Shakespear*, New York: HarperCollins Publishers, 2009, p. 87.

ingly built by their scrutiny of historical documents and personal biographies, for it is unimaginable that a prolific playwright springs into existence with very little life experience in acting on a stage when Shakespeare's London provided ample opportunities of such experience.

Finally, comparative textual reading and research of Shakespeare's First Folio against various editions of Shakespeare's works will help Chinese Shakespearean scholars consolidate the foundation of China's Shakespearean studies, cultivate their linguistic and poetic sensibility, and maximize their research capability. This will in turn reinforce their competence in the adaptation of Shakespeare's plays for stage performance or film presentation, which I believe is crucial for Shakespeare's afterlife to thrive in a cross-cultural environment informed increasingly by AI technology. As Professor Cong has pointed out in her recent article on Shakespeare's First Folio in China, "The textual study of Shakespear's editions is identified as systematically insufficient in the past one hundred years for our research into the Chinese translation of Shakespeare's works. This is an issue that must be dealt with urgently"[①]. There are some Chinese researchers and adapters of Shakespeare who tend to take the multiple editions of Shakespeare's work for granted. They tend to work on their favoured editions of Shakespeare's work, not being fully aware that different editorial decisions may result in different interpretations for different purposes (or theories), and different adaptation strategies. They need to realize that, like the exuberant branches, sprigs, leaves and flowers of a tree, all the multiple interpretations and adaptations of Shakespeare are the natural growth of a rhizomatic origin. More specifically, they need to be exposed to the textual issues in their research of Shakespeare by asking the questions that will lead to the close examination of the linguistic, poetic, dramatic expressions and theatrical effects. For instance, we may ask why in the First Folio edition of *Hamlet*, more than two hun-

---

① Cong Cong, "Shakespeare in China: Editorial Problems of Translation and Adaptation", *China Reading Weekly*, 2023-11-08(14).

dred lines are absent which are originally present in its 1604 quarto, and why the editors of the New Oxford Edition of Shakespeare chose to "conflate" the 1608 quarto of King Lear with 1623 Folio edition of the same play, making this great tragedy the largest (also the most powerful) tragedy of the Shakespearean canon. Also, for the same play, why does the new edition by Royal Shakespeare Company edited by Jonathan Bates take a sort of "condense" strategy, striking out blocks of lines that sound redundant to the natural flow of dramatic action? And most strikingly, editors, lexicographers, scholars, critics and directors joined hands to bring *King Lear* to an enormous size of books. In 2020, MLA launched its *King Lear: New Variorum Shakespeare* which presents complete textual and critical histories of each line of the play, along with extensive essays on criticism, sources, stage history, and more. A single Shakespearean play in two volumes with a total of 1.6 million words on more than two thousand large octavo pages! A colossus of *King Lear* indeed! No matter what, one thing is certain for a serious Shakespearean scholar. That is, close textual examination of the words, phrases, and allusions across different editions and textual criticism may unexpectedly lead to new revelations of Shakespeare's cultural and dramatic values for various tastes and evaluations. For, as Professor Brian Vickers, the book reviewer of the New Variorum edition of *King Lear* puts it, reaching a "correct or least, a defensible comprehension of Shakespeare's meaning has been a collective process, accumulating both insight and confusion over time"[①]. So are our intellect and zeal with Shakespeare. That is, I think, what Shakespeare's First Folio means to a sworn Shakespearean scholar in China.

  Let me close my address with a wish inspired by a certain editor of the First Folio. I wish Shakespeare, in his grave undisturbed as he had wished himself, could have commented on his First Folio with his own lines included in his lyrics *The Phoenix and Turtle*:

[①] Brian Vickers, "Review of '*King Lear*': A New Variorum Edition of Shakespeare", *Shakespeare Quarterly*, 72.1-2 (2022), p. 154.

Beauty, truth, and rarity,
Grace in all simplicity,
Here enclosed in cinders lie.

Thank you for your patience and attention.

名家论坛

朱生豪的中国化莎剧翻译与中国莎学

杨林贵

摘要：对莎士比亚的引介和研究贯穿于中国现代文化的塑形过程当中，因此，莎士比亚作品中国化，不仅仅涉及翻译的策略和方法问题，更具有深广的文化政治内涵。朱生豪对莎剧的中国化翻译，渗透了中国美学精髓，可以讲是朱莎合璧的结晶，可谓经典神韵，雅俗共赏，影响了一代代中文读者、改编者和研究者。朱生豪译笔下的莎翁作品不仅以惊人的词汇量丰富了中文词库，为现代汉语的发展做出了贡献，而且他对中国古文典故的灵活使用，为变革中的中国白话文保留了中国文化的气韵和精华。因此，他对世界莎学的贡献不仅在于莎士比亚经典在中文语境中的传播，更重要的是，他探索的中国化处理为我们今天提倡的中国文化对外传播提供了很好的启示和参考；同时，也为我们翻译理论和实践中关于如何处理形式和内容的关系提供了可以借鉴的经验，即借船出海与改编移植并行不悖，或者说中国作品的西化处理与外国作品的中国化翻译和改编都可以是传播中国文化和智慧的有效途径。

关键词：朱生豪；中国化；莎剧翻译；中国莎学

作者简介：杨林贵，东华大学外国语学院教授，主要研究方向为英美文学文化、莎士比亚研究、翻译研究、女性文学研究。

一、引言

本文题目所言莎士比亚作品的中国化，不是泛泛的莎士比亚的中文翻译，不是讨论莎士比亚在中国的翻译史这个大题目。而且，中国化翻译这个提法也需要有所限定，不是所有的中文翻译都是中国化的翻译，也不是说中国化的翻译就是把外国作品彻底归化,让原作隐形。本文所讨论的中国化,是指以归化外国作品为旨归的翻译处理,不拘泥于逐字逐句翻译原文,甚至在形式处理上可能有所不忠,但在精神上与原作高度契合。所以,这里要谈的莎剧中国化,最重要的一点是,在总体上最大程度转化外来内容精髓的同时,找到两种语言文字之间的契合点,译者甚至可以大胆激活目的语文化的某些元素并将其有机地融入译作当中。这样听起来又好像是要探讨翻译策略问题,但笔者要谈的是翻译处理中所涉及的文化政治问题。这是因为,任何翻译策略的选择以及译文的接受,都不可避免地带有译者所处时代以及译作在传播过程中的文化政治烙印。本文以朱生豪翻译莎剧为例,讨论什么意味上的莎剧中国化才是我们需要的。他的中国化莎剧翻译,是对中国莎学乃至世界莎学的独特贡献,同时我们需要思考,朱生豪翻译莎剧能给当今中国文化、中国智慧对外传播实践带来什么样的启示。

二、呼应时代、影响久远:朱译莎剧的不朽魅力

朱生豪翻译莎士比亚呼应了那个时代的强烈需求。1936年夏,他在给女友宋清如的信中写道:"你崇拜不崇拜民族英雄? 舍弟说我将成为一个民族英雄,如果把Shakespeare译成功以后。因为某国人曾经说中国是无文化的国家,连老莎的译本都没有。"[1]其实,当时的有识之士都在呼唤莎士比亚全集中文译本的问世。鲁迅先生也表达过这种迫切心情:在日本,《吉诃德先生》《一千零一夜》是有全译的,莎士比亚、歌德等都有全集。[2]

朱生豪在艰难困苦、贫病交加和战火动乱中,用不到10年时间独自完成了31部半莎剧翻译,后经过其他译者补译,于1978年出版的《莎士比亚全集》[3]是再版次数最多的中文全集译本。天才翻译家朱生豪的译本,是很多中国人开始认识莎士比亚戏剧并与

---

[1] 杨林贵、李伟民:《云中锦笺:中国莎学书信》,商务印书馆,2023年,第8页。
[2] 鲁迅:《鲁迅全集·第5卷》,人民文学出版社,1981年,第471页。
[3] 1947年上海世界书局出版了朱生豪译的《莎士比亚戏剧全集》。1954年作家出版社出版了朱生豪译的《莎士比亚戏剧集》。1957年,以朱生豪译本为主,台湾世界书局出版了《莎士比亚全集》(虞尔昌补译);后来以此为基础,在台湾出版了多个不同版本。1957年,人民文学出版社收到了朱生豪莎剧翻译手稿,并由其他译者补译了朱生豪生前未能完成的莎士比亚历史剧和诗歌翻译;1964年打好清样准备出版,但没能付印;1978年,人民文学出版社正式出版11卷本的《莎士比亚全集》;1988年出版第二版;1991年出版6卷本校订本;2009年出版8卷本校订本。1998年,译林出版社出版了《莎士比亚全集》校订本。2015年,浙江工商大学出版社出版了由陈才宇修订和补译的《莎士比亚全集》。现今各种网络莎剧版本,大多为朱生豪译本或其修订本。

莎士比亚结缘的媒介,更是中国学者研究莎剧的基础。他的翻译并非十全十美,从某些批评角度看亦有瑕疵,但其译文所传递的神韵无可替代,是莎士比亚作品的经典译文。正如德国有多个德文版莎士比亚全集,但都无法取代施莱格尔的译本;又如日文翻译中不朽的仍然是坪内逍遥的译本。因为我们知道,翻译中体现出的神韵是任何语言形式的对等都无法企及的境界,因为其体现了译者和作者之间共通的文学灵性和创造性。如果莎士比亚的作品是广大莎士比亚爱好者的世界语,那么朱生豪翻译的莎士比亚就给这个语库增加了一种亿万中文读者能够读懂的文本。他对莎作的领悟和他本人的文学天赋,令他的译文成为值得欣赏的中文读本。中文莎剧演出参考的大多是朱生豪译本,或者以朱译为底本进行改编,莎剧翻译研究也是中国翻译研究的一个重要方面。

改革开放后读大学的一代人,差不多都有通过朱生豪译本研读莎士比亚的经历。广大中文读者能够欣赏莎士比亚,大多得益于朱生豪的翻译。笔者也是通过朱生豪,才开始认识莎士比亚艺术殿堂的辉煌。在从原文作品中汲取莎作提供的精神营养之前,笔者以为朱生豪的译本就是莎士比亚。不消说,英文原著对于一个英语非母语的读者来说有多困难,即使是对于英语是母语的英美大学生来说,莎士比亚的 Early Modern English 也是个挑战。笔者在给自己的美国学生讲授莎氏作品时,常常要用现代英语来翻译某些地方,或者解释某些已经在现代英语中消失的英语语义以及语言结构。笔者对他们讲:我最初接触莎士比亚要比他们容易得多,因为我开始读的是朱生豪为中国读者提供的通俗读本。朱生豪用现代汉语翻译莎士比亚作品,使我们感到和莎翁更加亲近。的确,笔者当年一下就被精妙得几乎可以和莎氏原作相媲美的个性化语言所吸引。正是朱译本中的这种灵性,引导着笔者一步步接近莎士比亚的文学圣地。大学时代,笔者找来莎剧原文阅读,开始时感觉非常吃力。幸好有了读朱译全集的基础,不至于望而却步。后来,开始比较译文与原文,自以为发现了译文与原文上的出入,但是无论如何也找不出比朱生豪的译文更好的处理办法。再后来,在美国大学学习莎士比亚作品、教授莎士比亚作品,虽然用的都是英文版本的莎士比亚全集,但是总有回头读朱生豪译文的冲动。因为朱生豪的散文译文中透着诗意,他不仅没有背弃莎作亦庄亦谐、亦雅亦俗的特色,语言符号内外还渗透着翻译家的个人气质,以及语言能指之外的中国文化内涵。比较了中英文两种文本之后,我们更加理解了朱译与莎剧之间的气韵神通。再比较了其他译文后,就有了"除却巫山不是云"的感叹。笔者不否认其他译本的价值,可以说各有各的好,在样貌或者形式上,以及个别细节的处理上,其他翻译可能比朱译更贴近原文。然而,从对莎剧意蕴的总体把握上来说,都无法与朱译相提并论。所以,人民文学出版社资深编辑苏福忠先生说:"朱译既出,译莎可止。"①我们倒不必因为朱译的高超无法企及,就放弃新的尝试,或者就认为朱译完美无缺;我们也不应故意抬高朱生豪的译本,而贬抑其他译本的价值。但是,任何重译的尝试或者对朱生豪译本的修修补补,都需要学习朱生豪译莎的精神气质,以无愧于莎翁经典,无愧于译界先贤。

三、博古通今、典用化境:朱生豪译文的遣词造句

首先,朱生豪的中国文学功底和惊人的汉语词汇量,是任何其他全集译者都无法比肩的。同时,我们可以这样讲,朱生豪译文甚至对变革中的中国文字做出了贡献。他为汉语贡献了很多词汇,这些词汇不仅包括他从莎士比亚戏剧中直接移植的词汇,还包括他根据莎士比亚的意思,结合中国古文经典,为现代汉语贡献的新词。朱译经常使用古文典故,为变革中的中国白话文保留了中国文化的气韵和精华。据苏福忠先生的不完全统计,仅仅是朱译的这种中国化处理,就为汉语增加了不下千种词汇。②这也是朱生豪能够把莎剧的神韵传达出来的一个重要原因。他在用莎剧丰富了中国文化和中国词汇的同时,让中国文化与莎士比亚实现了互通和互补。

正如莎士比亚的创作丰富了英语的词汇量,朱译本充实了现代汉语的词库。据统计,莎士比亚的词汇量是25000到30000个(一般作家6000个左右)。莎士比亚为英语创造了近2000个新鲜词汇,他的很多表达法成了英语俗语,如"all that glisters is not gold(闪光的未必都是金子)"③、"break the ice(破冰)"④、"fair play(公平游戏)"⑤等等,不胜枚举。朱生豪译文的用词量与莎剧高度吻合,在这方面现有的其他译本无一能够望其项背。

朱生豪的译文用词、用典的重要特征就是恰当。无论是新词的创造,还是旧字的沿用,其价值都不在于新旧,而在于使用是否熨帖得当。要看用词在何种程度上对应了原作的情节、人物和场景,以及译文激活的中国典故是否符合原文要表达的意蕴。笔者在

---

① 苏福忠:《朱莎合璧》,新星出版社,2022年,第7页。
② 同上书,第5页。苏著还列举了一些朱生豪译文中两字词汇和四字词汇,见第7—8页。
③ 出自 The Merchant of Venice 2.7.65。所有莎剧英文皆引自 David Bevington, ed., The Complete Works of Shakespeare, 5th edition, New York: Pearson Education, 2004。
④ The Taming of the Shrew 1.2.265.
⑤ The Tempest 5.1.176, Troilus and Cressida 5.3.43, King John 5.2.118。"Fair play"是指游戏、比赛或者竞争双方照规则行事,引申为公平竞争、公平待遇、条件均等等义。鲁迅在其杂文中使用了这个英文词的译音"费厄泼赖",见《论"费厄泼赖"应该缓行》,刊于1926年1月10日《莽原》第1期。

这里举几个朱生豪译文遣词造句的例子。

《无事生非》第五幕第三场，Claudio 误以为情人 Hero 因己而死，来到墓前凭吊，还事先写好了墓志铭：

Done to death by slanderous tongues
Was the Hero that here lies.
Death, in guerdon of her wrongs,
Gives her fame which never dies.
So the life that died with shame
Lives in death with glorious fame.
青蝇玷玉，谗口铄金，
嗟吾希罗，月落星沉！
生蒙不虞之毁，死播百世之馨；
惟令德之昭昭，斯虽死而犹生。①

朱生豪对这则墓志铭的翻译，在准确把握原文的前提下，激活了中国古典成语。其中"青蝇玷玉"出自宋代邓林的词；"谗口铄金"最早出自春秋时期左丘明《国语》。两个成语点出了"死者"的不白之冤，极为贴合原意。同时，整段译文既庄重又大气，匹配原文中主人公的懊悔和深沉悼念。

再比如《维洛那二绅士》第三幕第一场，公爵无意中看到了 Valentine 写给恋人 Silvia 的情书：

My thoughts do harbor with my Silvia nightly,
And slaves they are to me, that send them flying.
Oh, could their master come and go as lightly,
Himself would lodge where, senseless they are lying!
My herald thoughts in thy pure bosom rest them,
相思夜夜飞，飞绕情人侧；

---

① 莎士比亚：《莎士比亚全集（一）》，朱生豪等译，人民文学出版社，1997年，第548页。

身无彩凤翼,无由见颜色。
灵犀虽可通,室迩人常遐,
空有梦魂驰,漫漫怨长夜!①

我们看到,朱生豪对原文的比喻以及所借用的中文典故都做了变通处理。这里的"身无彩凤翼""灵犀虽可通"以及"无由见颜色",分别来自李商隐的两首诗;而"室迩人常遐"借用了《诗经》的典故。译者没有拘泥于形式的对应,而是抓住了原文缠绵悱恻的情思灵动,借用中国古诗将其准确充分地表达了出来。就是说,在不失原作意蕴的前提下,译文自然地融合了中国古诗的优美。

朱生豪的灵活变通不局限于字词的处理,他对整句台词的中国化处理更加灵活自如,比如:

Then, afterwards, to order well the state,
That like events may ne'er it ruinate.
从今起惩前毖后,把政事重新整顿,
不让女色谗言,动摇了邦基国本。②

这是《泰特斯》结尾路歇斯的台词,反思腐败祸国的悲剧。译文的变通处理,不仅在于用"惩前毖后"和"女色谗言"具体化了 like events 所指代的剧中的主要情节,而且用中国化的遣词造句提高了译文的语感,其节奏感也不输原文。另外,这样的台词是不是听着耳熟? 其实,当今流行的宫斗剧中经常出现这样的桥段。

朱生豪译文的用词不仅对应作品的时代,还回应译者生活的年代。因此,朱生豪译文用词的另外一个重要特征是语汇的适时性。正是这种适时性造就了永恒性。他在中国人民奋起反抗日本侵略者的年代翻译莎士比亚,在处理 To be or not to be 这样的经典独白时,考虑的肯定不是个人的生死,而是中华民族面临的困境。因此,"生存"与"毁灭"这样大气的词汇里面蕴含着困境中崛起的抗争精神,以及中国文学文以载道的经世致用精神,从而在汉语中得以广泛传播。

---

① 莎士比亚:《莎士比亚全集(一)》,第133页。
② 莎士比亚:《莎士比亚全集(四)》,朱生豪等译,人民文学出版社,1997年,第600页。

四、朱莎合璧、经典神韵：朱生豪翻译原则与中国诗学和译学

把莎士比亚恢宏的经典翻译成中文，不仅需要有中英两种语言的修养，而且还需要有深厚的中国文化功底，才能实现朱莎合璧，传递经典神韵。朱生豪译本之所以受欢迎，主要在于朱生豪以精彩的中文传达了莎翁经典的神韵，这是把外国经典文学作品本土化的一种尝试。

朱生豪提到的嘲笑中国的某国就是日本。鲁迅在1934年说的日本已经有了莎士比亚全集的翻译，就是指1928年出版的坪内逍遥的翻译，这也是把莎翁的作品本土化的一个成功范例。虽然坪内逍遥翻译的初衷是为了以莎剧为样板来改造日本歌舞伎，却并不忠实于莎剧的语言风格，而是将日语文学风格融入莎剧。坪内逍遥起初借用日本传统歌舞伎的语言风格来翻译莎士比亚，后来进行口语化的尝试，修订后的译文亦文亦白，是文白的巧妙融合。虽然这种翻译没有在形式上与原作对等，但契合了日本读者的审美，因而广受目的语读者欢迎。因此，坪内逍遥100年前的翻译令当今的日本读者都不觉得过时。

卞之琳曾经提到，坪内逍遥的译本据说日本有人认为比莎士比亚原著还好[1]。虽然卞先生认为它不忠实于原作的形式，或者不把莎剧用素体诗（blank verse）来翻译，就是对莎士比亚原作的不忠实。"比原著还好"的译文确实是一种翻译现象，本文无意对此类现象做出综合评价。这里只想讨论朱生豪"不忠"的莎剧译文如何成就了莎士比亚在中文语境的传播和接受，不仅为现代中文的发展做出了贡献，而且拉近了莎士比亚与中国文化的距离。反之，莎翁崇拜心态下对莎剧诗行在形式上的亦步亦趋，反倒可能疏远了广大目的语读者。梁实秋的莎士比亚全集译本看似忠实于作品原貌，虽不是貌合神离，却让很多中文读者望而却步[2]。卞之琳的《莎士比亚悲剧四种》可以讲是忠实于原作形式的翻译精品，在效果上与朱译不相上下，只可惜他的莎剧翻译仅限于四部悲剧。[3]其他译者如孙大雨[4]、方平[5]等前辈也曾经尝试以音组形式对应莎士比亚以五音步抑扬格（iambic pentameter）为主的诗行，虽有个别上品，但总体上译文的可读性不尽如人意，只

---

[1] 《外国语》、《译林》编辑部：《漫谈翻译》，江苏人民出版社，1984年，第189页。
[2] 1930年，梁实秋应胡适之邀开始翻译莎士比亚，1967年独自完成了全集翻译，在台湾出版。
[3] 莎士比亚：《莎士比亚悲剧四种》，卞之琳译，人民文学出版社，1988年。
[4] 孙大雨翻译的《黎琊王》《哈姆莱特》最早于20世纪30年代在《诗刊》（徐志摩主编）发表，2010年上海译文出版社出版了孙译《莎士比亚四大悲剧》。
[5] 莎士比亚：《新莎士比亚全集》（全十二卷），方平等译，河北教育出版社，2000年。

有少数研究者才肯细读。

我们认为,朱生豪成功的关键是以其深厚的中国古典文学的功底实现了中外经典的巧妙结合,在于他的翻译中自觉贯彻了中国美学的神韵理念[①]。他在译者前言中透露了他的翻译原则,这个原则就是以神韵说为基础。朱生豪的译者自序如是说:"余译此书之宗旨,第一在求于最大可能之范围内,保持原作之神韵;必不得已而求其次,亦必以明白晓畅之字句,忠实传达原文之意趣;而于逐字逐句对照式之硬译,则未敢赞同。"这实际上是朱生豪的翻译思想的概况。他认为,译文与原文在精神上的契合应该是译者追求的目标,要尽最大可能保存原作的"意趣"和"神韵"。他的思想根基是中国古代美学中的"神韵"说。中国美学从画论到诗论,都强调创作者的悟性对于事物本质的把握,而不计较外在形式的相似性[②]。状物抒怀,恣意舒展;师法自然,注重写意。文字之美、文学之美,在韵味、在意境;重神态毕现,不重外形逼真。应用到文学翻译上,神韵说是中国传统译论的核心,也应该是翻译的一种美学标准。中国传统译论,如"文质说""信达雅说""神似说""化境说"(钱锺书),无不遵循中国古典哲学和美学对艺术的认识,因此认为翻译的最高境界就是神似,也就是神韵,只有传神的翻译才能引起中国读者的审美共鸣。

对于译者来说,实现传神的文学翻译,需要将悟性转化为创造性,才能实现翻译创造与原作在神态上的异曲同工,从而调动读者审美的经验与感受。这种美感经验中的"悟性",是所谓科学的翻译取代不了的,也是机器无法取代的,是真正属于人的特质。有人会说这种靠悟性的翻译和审美不科学,这种"不科学"的翻译恰恰让几百年前的英国莎士比亚在中文语境下成功"转世"了。成功的根本原因在于,文学翻译是艺术,不是科学,文学翻译需要有深厚的人文底蕴。因此,朱生豪不单单是译者,也是翻译艺术家、翻译美学家。

文学艺术需要用心去感受。或许今天讲这话有些不合时宜,但我们需要警醒,需要更加关注人类的内心世界,才不至于在所谓科学理性的误导下越走越偏。即使是在后人类时代,人类仍然需要阅读人的文学,需要人的翻译,因为人类需要心灵相通。阅读朱生豪翻译的莎士比亚总能让我们感受到人性的光芒和希望,因为他在古与今、中与外

---

① 笔者颇为认同关于朱生豪翻译原则中渗透着中国古代美学的观点,参见朱安博:《朱生豪翻译的"神韵说"与中国古代诗学》,《江南大学学报》(人文社会科学版)2013年第4期。

② 参考朱安博关于朱生豪神韵说与中国古典诗学和中国传统译学的讨论,参见朱安博:《朱生豪翻译的"神韵说"与中国古代诗学》,《江南大学学报》(人文社会科学版)2013年第4期。

的碰撞中,把握了人类心灵相通的奥秘,将原作的人文气质转化为目的语读者的审美体验。

朱生豪处在20世纪的大变革时代。他在新旧转变的大潮中仍能秉承中国美学,实属可贵。他既有深厚的国学功底,又生活在新文化塑形的时代,受到的是新学的教育。那是个西学猛进的时代,当时的知识精英希图通过大量翻译来建设新文学。但朱生豪没有盲目跟随否定国学的大潮,而是把中国美学原则贯穿于他的莎剧翻译中。因此他的翻译中既有白话口语的通俗,也有经典神韵的古雅。中国化的莎士比亚翻译成就了一位民族英雄。或者说,朱生豪的英雄梦想,是通过翻译莎士比亚得以实现的。他在民族生死存亡的困境中,用莎士比亚的人文主义光芒给中文读者带来了希望。他的译文自发表以来,之所以一直广受全球华人读者欢迎,就在于他关注中国人的审美习惯和审美感受。①

五、散文体还是诗体,这不是问题

朱生豪以散文为主的翻译中的诗意、诗性,与莎士比亚要表达的意蕴异曲同工。其实,押不押韵、分不分行,只是诗的外在形式。莎士比亚的诗剧主体是无韵诗,每行以五音步抑扬格为主,不必押韵,押韵则是有意为之,这样的地方在朱译文中大都以韵文翻译。关于译文的分行问题,分或者不分行,不是诗的唯一标准。或者说,译文不一定要分行才是忠实于原文,才是诗。你分了行,念起来却疙疙瘩瘩,反而毁了莎剧的诗意。

当然,要以忠实原文为首要条件。但忠实什么? 什么才是忠实? 值得讨论。形式对等、字句对等就是忠实吗? 或者说,在形式上的对等与精神上的契合不能兼得的情况下,你是要比原文还好的神似的译文,还是要亦步亦趋的蹩脚的形似的译文? 这些问题的答案,对于我们今天的外译工作具有重要意义。朱生豪的中国化翻译实践为我们提供了很好的参考。

朱生豪抓住莎剧诗行的灵魂所做的灵活处理,可以说是朱莎之间的灵犀相通。虽然朱生豪在翻译莎剧中的素体诗台词时使用的是不分行的散文体,但他在翻译莎剧中

---

① 这里笔者非常同意李伟民的看法。他认为,朱生豪以散文译莎剧,诗意的审美上超越了以诗体形式翻译的莎剧,虽然是散文形式,但读起来更有诗意感。即便是莎剧原文中基本不押韵的独白,在朱生豪的译文中也押了韵,而且换韵不多,适合汉语读者的审美习惯。参见李伟民:《论朱生豪的诗词创作与翻译莎士比亚戏剧之关系》,《华南农业大学学报》(社会科学版)2009年第1期。

的诗和歌时则完全使用的是诗体。他不仅能够理解和把握莎士比亚戏剧的文学精髓,而且具备深厚的中国古典文学修养和诗词创作的实践基础,可以驾轻就熟地使用古今诗体的不同风格、不同句式,四言诗、五言诗、七言诗,以及长短句,无一不通,谙熟诗道以及各种诗体。因此,他的译笔文采飞扬,把莎剧的文学灵气充分转化、融入莎剧翻译中。朱译本完全是中文文学精品。

我们前面讨论的例子中 Claudio 为 Hero 写的哀悼诗文,是提前在纸上写好的。Claudio 将墓志铭挂在墓碑上之后,让乐师弹唱了另外一首挽歌。朱生豪给墓志铭对应了原文的韵脚,用了两句四言、两句六言的绝句形式。而后面紧接着的这首挽歌,却是另外一种中国化的处理方法。他翻译的这首歌中融入了骚体。

惟兰蕙之幽姿兮,	Pardon, goddess of the night,
遽一朝而摧焚;	Those that slew thy virgin knight,
风云怫郁其变色兮,	For the which, with songs of woe,
月姊掩脸而似嗔:	Round about her tomb they go.
语月姊兮毋嗔,	Midnight, assist our moan;
听长歌兮当哭;	Help us to sigh and groan,
绕墓门而逡巡兮,	Heavily, heavily.
岂百身之可赎!	Graves, yawn and yield your dead,
风瑟瑟兮云漫漫,	Till death be utterèd,
纷助予之悲叹;	Heavily, heavily.
安得起重泉之白骨兮,	Now, unto thy bones good night!
及长夜之未旦!①	Yearly will I do this rite.

从典故的使用,到歌赋的形式,再到主导意象,整首歌都完全中国化了。

原文 Goddess of the night 典故,是指罗马神话的月亮女神 Diana。朱生豪把莎翁笔下的月亮女神变成了中国神话传说中的月姊,也就是月宫嫦娥。莎翁动员月亮女神出来为白璧无瑕的女主鸣冤叹息,而朱生豪笔下的月姊眼见如此悲情不禁掩面而泣。

形式上,译文化用了楚辞的旋律和遣词造句,用骚调的句腰"兮"字对应原文出现四

---

① 莎士比亚:《莎士比亚全集(一)》,第548页。

次的heavily。整个译文亦诗亦歌,亦咏亦唱,完全符合原文的情境和功能;但在目的语的表达效果上,可与原文相媲美,甚至更美。这或许就是卞先生所说的"比原著还好"的译文吧。

如果说形式和典故的转换对应还不足够中国化,那么意象的汉化处理则更加彻底了。原作中衬托哀伤情愫的意象——深夜、坟墓、叹息之声等——在译文中不是简单对应,而是根据中文的语势变化层叠呈现。而且饶有意味的是,译者巧妙移植了楚辞的兰蕙意象,并将其放在了歌的开头,引领其他意象的叠进。因此,兰蕙幽姿的比拟,强化了悲剧效果。死者的身姿越是婀娜,德操越是高洁,其摧焚越是催人泪下。译文充分表达了懊悔、惆怅和悲伤的心境,可谓长歌当哭,悲痛欲绝。

可见,译者对莎剧的深层领悟和深厚的中国古典文学修养,使其能够化用中文诗歌和古典文化元素,最大化地转化了原文的神韵。这种处理不是形式和内容的简单复制,而是进入一种化境,一种传神的境界,有效地将原文的意趣传递给中文读者。我们知道,朱生豪生前没有来得及翻译莎士比亚诗歌集,这是一大遗憾。但从他对莎剧中诗歌翻译的传神处理,我们已可以窥见他的译诗之精彩了。除了上面举例的诗和歌,莎士比亚还在一些剧作中镶嵌了十四行诗,比如《罗密欧与朱丽叶》[①]。对应这些剧中的十四行诗,朱生豪的译文同样赋予神来之笔,篇幅所限,讨论从略。

六、结语:神韵翻译的影响及启示

朱译的中国化处理是让莎士比亚在中国更有路人缘的一个有效途径。朱生豪译本不仅是一代代华人了解莎士比亚经典的入口,也为中国莎学研究提供了必不可少的资源,更对中国莎学产生了深远影响。不仅如此,朱译全集推动了20世纪80年代的莎士比亚热。1984年成立了以曹禺先生为首任会长的中国莎士比亚研究会。该研究会于1986年筹备举办了盛况空前的首届中国莎士比亚戏剧节,让世界看到了改革开放的中国拥抱莎士比亚的气魄。莎剧节以及其后的很多莎剧演出,不论是话剧的还是戏曲的,大多都以朱生豪译本为底本。

朱生豪对莎剧的中国化翻译,渗透了中国美学精髓,可以讲是朱莎合璧的结晶,可谓经典神韵,雅俗共赏,影响了一代代中文读者、改编者和研究者。朱生豪译笔下的莎

---

① 参见莎士比亚:《莎士比亚全集(四)》,第629-630页。

翁作品不仅以惊人的词汇量丰富了中文词库,为现代汉语的发展做出了贡献,而且他对中国古文典故的灵活使用,为变革中的中国白话文保留了中国文化的气韵和精华。因此,他为我们的翻译理论和实践中关于如何处理形式和内容关系提供了可以借鉴的经验。同时,他对世界莎学的贡献不仅在于莎士比亚经典在中文语境中的传播,更重要的是,他探索的中国化处理为我们今天提倡的中国文化对外传播提供了很好的启示和参考。借船出海与改编移植,或者说,中国作品的西化处理与外国作品的中国化翻译,都是传播中国文化和智慧的有效途径,二者可以并行不悖。

参考文献

David Bevington, ed., *The Complete Works of Shakespeare*, 5th edition, New York: Pearson Education, 2004.

卞之琳:《文学翻译与语言感觉》,《漫谈翻译》,《外国语》、《译林》编辑部编,江苏人民出版社,1984年。

莎士比亚:《莎士比亚悲剧四种》,卞之琳译,人民文学出版社,1988年。

莎士比亚:《新莎士比亚全集》,方平等译,河北教育出版社,2000年。

李伟民:《论朱生豪的诗词创作与翻译莎士比亚戏剧之关系》,《华南农业大学学报》(社会科学版)2009年第1期。

鲁迅:《读几本书》,《鲁迅全集(第五卷)》,人民文学出版社,1981年。

鲁迅:《论"费厄泼赖"应该缓行》,《莽原》1926年1月10日。

苏福忠:《朱莎合璧》,新星出版社,2022年。

杨林贵、李伟民:《云中锦笺——中国莎学书信》,商务印书馆,2023年。

朱安博:《朱生豪翻译的"神韵说"与中国古代诗学》,《江南大学学报》(人文社会科学版)2013年第4期。

莎士比亚:《莎士比亚戏剧全集》,朱生豪译,世界书局,1947年。

莎士比亚:《莎士比亚戏剧集》,朱生豪译,作家出版社,1954年。

莎士比亚:《莎士比亚全集》,朱生豪译,虞尔昌补译,世界书局,1957年。

莎士比亚:《莎士比亚全集》,11卷本,朱生豪等译,人民文学出版社,1978年;第二版,1988年;6卷本校订本,1991年;8卷本校订本,2009年。

莎士比亚:《莎士比亚全集》(增订本),朱生豪等译,译林出版社,1998年。

莎士比亚:《莎士比亚全集》,朱生豪、陈才宇译,浙江工商大学出版社,2015年。

文本、理论、跨学科研究

文本、理论、跨学科研究

小冰期术语与莎士比亚生态批评

张军

摘要：文学，如同人类社会中的一切事物，都是特定时空环境的产物。对文本形成生态空间属性的考察，有助于更全面地理解文学表达的本质。本文首先强调了小冰期在文学经典与现代科学之间扮演的重要桥梁角色，接着从历史的角度梳理中西方文学批评中的气候议题，最后探讨了小冰期在莎士比亚生态批评中的运用现状及未来前景。

关键词：小冰期；生态批评；莎士比亚

基金项目：本文系教育部人文社科项目"莎士比亚戏剧中的瘟疫书写研究"（项目编号：22YJA752025）的阶段性研究成果。

作者简介：张军，重庆师范大学外国语学院教授，主要研究方向为莎士比亚戏剧及美国20世纪二三十年代小说。

小冰期（The Little Ice Age）原本是一个历史气候学术语，指地球曾经历长达五百年（公元14—19世纪）的持续寒冷袭击。[1] 1939年，美国地质及气候学家马瑟斯率先提出这一名词，引起了学界关注。瑞士历史学家克里斯蒂安·普菲斯特随后提出小冰期巅峰

---

[1] 目前科学界对于小冰期起止日期及其引发的确切天气现象尚存争议。有学者把时间限定在17世纪晚期至19世纪中期，也有建议1430年前后至1770年左右，但绝大多数专家认为小冰期发生在1300年前后到1850年之间（See Brian Fagan, *The Little Ice Age: How Climate Made History 1300-1850*, New York: Basic Books, 2000, pp. 48-50.; Wolfgang Behringer, "Climatic Change and Witch-hunting: The Impact of the Little Ice Age on Mentalities", *Climatic Change*, 43.1 (1999): 335-351, p. 336.）。

期(1570—1630)说,即所谓的"格林德瓦波动"(Grindelwald Fluctuation)。[1]另有学者认为,在1590至1610年的20年间,包括欧亚大陆在内的全球广袤地区,同期出现了极寒气象。[2] 15世纪至18世纪英格兰平均气温比今天约低2华氏度,这个温差貌似不大,却足以令作物生长期缩短三四周。有学者甚至推测,17世纪40年代欧洲谷物产量下降三到五成。[3]粮食减产带来全球谷价上升,饥荒与瘟疫频仍,故小冰期亦是暴乱、死亡及王朝更替的高发期。[4]

莎士比亚(1564—1616)的生卒年代与格林德瓦波动期大致吻合,其创作年代与小冰期巅峰期高度重叠:首部喜剧《驯悍记》成型于1589—1592年间,谢幕之作《暴风雨》完成于1611年。[5]埃文河畔的这只甜蜜天鹅,离不开斯特拉福镇上的那条蜿蜒小河。被誉为"时代的灵魂"的莎士比亚,其人其作与小冰期的关联究竟如何,存在无限阐释空间。

一

《尚书》有云:"唯天地万物父母。"这句经典文言文强调了自然界对于人类和其他生物生存的重要性。根据现代生态学基本理论,气候环境是决定生物生存的核心因素。在年际或更短的时间尺度上,变化频繁且迅捷的气象因子是生态系统最直接最根本的驱动力之一。[6]即便是哈姆雷特口中所称的"万物灵长"之人类,也时刻受到气候环境的制约。倘若没有风雨、雷电、阳光等气象因素的相态转变,人类纵有十八般武艺,也无法在虚无中创作出来。正如李尔王对其幼女考狄利亚的警告所示,其他生物的生存状况更是如此,没有适宜的气候条件,地球上任何生命都将无法生存。

在《生态气候学:概念与应用》(*Ecological Climatology: Concepts and Applications*)

---

[1] Wolfgang Behringer, "Climatic Change and Witch-hunting: The Impact of the Little Ice Age on Mentalities", *Climatic Change*, 43.1 (1999):335-351, p. 336.
[2] Ibid, pp. 335-351.
[3] 彭纳:《人类的足迹:一部地球环境的历史》,张新、王兆润译,电子工业出版社,2013年,第94-95页。
[4] Brian Fagan, *The Little Ice Age: How Climate Made History 1300-1850*, New York: Basic Books, 2000, p. 50.
[5] 尽管写于1613—1614年间的《两个高贵的亲戚》和《亨利八世》在创作时间上明显晚于《暴风雨》,但它们并非莎士比亚个人独立完成的作品,而是有其他剧作家的共同参与(See *William Shakespeare, Complete Works*, J. Bate and E. Rasmussen, eds., New York: Modern Library, 2007, pp. 2471-2475.)。
[6] 王连喜、毛留喜、李琪等:《生态气象学导论》,气象出版社,2010年,第20页。

中,伯南将小冰期主要阶段限定在1550年至1700年之间,并阐释了其对生态系统的重大影响:在此期间,冬季漫长而寒冷,夏季则转瞬即逝。阿尔卑斯冰川扩展到低海拔地区,而非洲北部气候则比现在湿润得多。[1]小冰期的成因复杂,其中太阳辐射与天文地质事件起着主要作用。太阳活动强度的周期性变化决定了地球的气候变化。早在1893年,英国天文学家就通过整理格林尼治天文台的档案发现,1645年至1715年间,太阳黑子数量极其稀少,与这一时期的寒冷气候相吻合。此外,火山喷发也直接影响全球气候,大量火山灰进入平流层会阻碍地球接受太阳辐射,导致全球气温下降。[2]

1815年4月5日,印尼的坦博拉火山喷发,造成周边近十万人死亡。这一地质事件对全球气候的影响到次年方才突显出来。1816年农历八月,"天气忽然寒如冬",万里之遥的欧洲则全年无夏,并出现八月霜冻的奇观。"嘉庆、吸血鬼、拿破仑、自行车,通通都因为一座火山联系在了一起。"坦博拉火山引起的蝴蝶效应也波及文学领域:英国浪漫主义作家如雪莱、拜伦、济慈等人一面感慨横扫欧陆的寒冷饥饿,一面登上个人创作生涯的巅峰;此次低温事件还诞生出世界首部科幻小说《科学怪人》及首部吸血鬼小说《吸血鬼》。总之,源自坦博拉火山喷发的气候丕变,对19世纪欧洲文坛的影响是不容忽视的。

反过来,通过观察分析艺术作品中的生态描写,自然科学家们往往又能获取本学科的理论洞见。在极地冰芯勘探尚未流行的时代,气象学家们时常利用古代艺术作品寻找地球气候变迁的蛛丝马迹。我国著名气象学家竺可桢通过唐诗宋词,揭示了物候学的重要规律。英国气象学家兰姆在《气候、历史与现代世界》(*Climate, History, and the Modern World*)一书中,则以荷兰画家勃鲁盖尔(Pieter Bruegel de Oude)创作于1565年的作品《雪地围猎》为例,阐明16世纪北欧天气的总体特征。纵观荷兰艺术史,对冬季风物的兴趣肇始于这一时期,气候变迁显然是这种兴趣产生的主要推力之一。[3]可以说,呈现北欧冬日寻常之景的《雪地围猎》,既是早期现代时期欧洲艺术主题转变的具象,又是现代气象学家理论的一个有力佐证。

科学家们借助人文艺术经典阐释气象学的基本原理,这种现象一方面说明了文化与气候的紧密关联,另一方面则暗示了运用自然科学知识去观照人文学科具有逻辑上

---

[1] Gordon B. Bonan, *Ecological Climatology: Concepts and Applications,* Cambridge: Cambridge University Press, 2016, p. 120, p. 436.

[2] Ibid, p. 128.

[3] Ibid, p. 2.

的可行性,甚至会洞开一片天地。而这一点,恰是生态批评者们的孜孜追求。2013年3月20日,英国《每日邮报》网站刊登了一则关于莎士比亚生平事迹的文章。该文援引贝特的一句话,即"小冰期时代的饥馑与粮食短缺问题可以为理解莎士比亚作品提供新的思路",以提醒读者在品味莎剧之时,莫忘剧作家所处时代的基本生态特征。乔纳森·贝特曾执教于毗邻斯特拉福镇的沃里克大学,其学术涉猎广泛,成就非凡,既是国际莎士比亚研究权威,又是英国生态批评的理论先驱。贝特对经典名剧《暴风雨》的生态解读显示,在剖析文化的过程中,生态批评理论只有与其他学科进行交叉或整合,方能全面且深入地探讨生态问题的实质,并探寻出更加有效持久的生态文化策略。诚如洛夫所言:"就其本质而言,生态批评应该体现在与其他相关学科特别是生命科学的某种新型关系之中。"①

二

韦勒克在《近代文学批评史》首卷中提到,17世纪的英国文人威廉·坦普尔认为,多变的英国气候与该国人古怪的幽默气质有关,其相关学说是用气候条件来解释文学的最早例证之一。②

19世纪初,斯达尔夫人在《论文学》中指出:"北方天气阴沉,居民十分忧郁,基督教的教义和它最早那批信徒的热忱加重了他们的忧郁情绪,并给它提出了方向……南方人民禀性偏于激奋,现在则易于接受与其气候及趣味相适应的沉思默想的生活。"③在谈论文学的地域差异时,斯达尔夫人又很明确地认为:北方人喜爱的形象和南方人乐于追忆的形象之间存在着差别,气候当然是产生这些差别的主要原因之一。④斯达尔夫人虽提出气候命题,但并未展开深入论证。⑤她的观点,出自孟德斯鸠的地理环境决定论。后者在《论法的精神》里用了整整一章的篇幅来讨论气候对法律的影响,指出人的精神气质和内心情感因不同的气候而有很大的差别,处于不同气候带的国家的法律因此也

---

① Glen A. Love, *Practical Ecocriticism: Literature, Biology, and the Environment*, Virginia: University of Virginia Press, 2003, p. 37.
② 胡燕春:《雷纳·韦勒克的文学史观述评》,《社会科学》2007年第12期。
③ 斯达尔夫人:《论文学》,徐继曾译,人民文学出版社,1986年,第110-111页。
④ 同上书,第146-147页。
⑤ 同上。

有很大的差别。①

19世纪中叶,泰纳不仅惯于谈论英国气候的阴晴无常,多雨、浓雾、寒冷、泥泞与海上风暴及其所产生的压抑性的影响,而且还时常将之与风和日丽的南欧加以对照。②然而令人遗憾的是,泰纳从未对自己的气候影响论的准确程度与适用范围产生过质疑,也未曾思考过人类在何种程度上可以从气候影响中解脱出来。③总之,在20世纪前,除去斯达尔夫人和泰纳,从气候角度深入分析具体文本内涵的论述相对较少。④

进入20世纪70年代,"生态批评"在欧美勃兴。但我们从艾布拉姆斯给"生态批判"所下的定义中可知,生态批评家们更多强调的是"人类活动给环境所造成的损害"。⑤对影响动植物栖息之地与生命形式的气候变量,尚未给予足够关注。

气候在出版于2000年的英国批评家库普的《绿色研究读本:从浪漫主义到生态批评》(*The Green Studies Reader: From Romanticism to Ecocriticism*)中,充其量只是影响文本的六大要素之一,地位甚至不如性别那么重要。⑥美国学者布伊尔虽屡屡宣称要让季节、地方与气候等自然存在成为艺术再现中心,但文化民族主义及比较文学,才是他真正的兴趣指向。⑦与其他生态批评者们一样,布伊尔时常带着一丝功利的道德说教色彩,即胡志红所指出的:生态批评学者研究自然现象(季节、气候)、海洋、地方以及人口在文学作品中的作用,旨在通过揭示自然或自然存在物与人类文化之间及人类存在之间密不可分的关系,或昭示自然对人之生存的影响或决定作用,从而激发人的环境意识或环境敏感性。以培养人的生态情感,提高人的生态意识,唤醒人的生态良知。⑧

以上是气候与文学之关系的国外相关研究综述。在国内研究方面:南朝文学理论家刘勰最早阐述了气候对文学的影响。在其经典文论《文心雕龙》中,刘勰说了两句至理名言:一是"春秋代序,阴阳惨舒,物色之动,心亦摇焉";二是"岁有其物,物有其容;情以物迁,辞以情发"。第一句中的"动"字强调气候变迁,"物色"指因应四季轮回而发生

---

① 曾大兴:《中外学者谈气候与文学之关系》,《广州大学学报》(社会科学版)2010年第12期。
② 胡燕春:《雷纳·韦勒克的文学史观述评》,《社会科学》2007年第12期。
③ 同上。
④ 参见曾大兴:《中外学者谈气候与文学之关系》,《广州大学学报》(社会科学版)2010年第12期。
⑤ M. H. Abrams and G. Harpham, *A Glossary of Literary Terms*, Beijing: Peking University Press, 2014, p. 96.
⑥ 参见胡志红:《西方生态批评史》,人民出版社,2015年,第146页。
⑦ 同上书,第229页。
⑧ 同上书,第232页。

变化的自然之景。[1]借用现代物候学的表达,"物色"就是"物候"。[2]而所谓"物候",其主要研究对象便是每年天气气候条件的反映。[3]第二句是对第一句的补充,两句共同揭示出文学的气候学生成机制,即节气变化引起物候变迁,触发心灵悸动,文思因此泉涌。虽然刘勰本意并非探究气候究竟如何影响了文学,但无论如何,他提到的气候变迁对文学的影响,体现的是一种朴素的气候生态学意识。对于气候,紧随刘勰其后的南梁人钟嵘有着比前者更为清晰的论述。在《诗品》中,钟嵘开宗明义说道:"气之动物,物之感人,故摇荡性情,形诸舞咏。"又说:"若乃春风春鸟,秋月秋蝉,夏云暑雨,冬月祁寒,斯四候之感诸诗者也。"这两处引文的大意是节气使景物发生变化,从而动摇了人的性情,诗人触景生情,又把节气变化写进诗中。

自刘勰、钟嵘以来,在中国文学批评界,气候命题几乎默默无闻,长期处于失语状态,这种状态一直持续到20世纪。近代以来,最先激发国人对气候产生兴趣的人物之一即是前文提及的气象学家竺可桢。作为中国现代物候学的奠基者,竺氏在与他人合作的《物候学》一书中,大量引用古典诗词以论证中国古代的物候问题。[4]古典诗词在王梨村的《中国古今物候学》中得到了更为充分的运用。尽管这两位科学家醉翁之意不在酒,而是以文本为数据,论证物候学上的定律,但这种研究本身足以证明这样一个事实:气候对文学的影响,或文学对气候的反映,二者之间的关系是密不可分的。

三

美国学者门兹曾用一个颇具生态意味的诗意表达,将莎士比亚戏称为"英语文学海洋中那条体型最为壮观的巨鱼",指其"漫长而鲜活的戏剧实践为彼时的生态困境提供诸多确凿证据"。[5]在当下全球环境危机日益加剧的背景下,生态批评理论取得了长足

---

[1] "物色"一词最早出现在《礼记·月令》中,指祭祀时所用牲畜的体毛颜色。刘向著《列仙传》有"候物色而迹之",此处"物色"指预兆不凡人物或事件发生的天气异象。在《史记·龟策列传》中,"占龟与物色同"的"物色"则指依据星相进行的推断过程(参见:兰宇冬:《物色观形成之历史过程及其文学实践》,复旦大学,2006年,第6—7页)。

[2] 竺可桢、宛敏渭:《物候学》,科学普及出版社,1963年,第1页。

[3] 曾大兴:《中外学者谈气候与文学之关系》,《广州大学学报》(社会科学版)2010年第12期。

[4] 参见曾大兴:《中外学者谈气候与文学之关系》,《广州大学学报》(社会科学版)2010年第12期。

[5] Steve Mentz, "Shakespeare's Beach House, or the Green and the Blue in Macbeth", *Shakespeare Studies*, 39 (2011), p. 84.

的进展,并且自然地延伸至莎士比亚研究领域。从时间上看,莎士比亚生态批评的起源可以追溯到20世纪90年代末期。

1999年,在《美国现代语言学协会会刊》编辑部举办的一场研讨会上,斯托克呼吁早期现代文学研究与生态批评理论进行"直接对话"。[1]斯托克一呼百应,欧美莎士比亚生态批评的队伍从此不断壮大。2006年,第八届世界莎士比亚大会在澳大利亚布里斯班举行,会议特设了一组研讨专场——生态批评与莎士比亚的世界(Ecocritism and the World of Shakespeare),由斯托克担任主持。[2]时至今日,与生态相关的研究成果正在以几何倍增的速度大量产生,莎士比亚生态批评进入烈火烹油、鲜花着锦的鼎盛时期。接下来,笔者将按照时间先后顺序,简单介绍21世纪以来出版的几部莎士比亚生态批评的论著。

2006年,英国青年学者伊根的《绿色莎士比亚:从生态政治到生态批评》(*Green Shakespeare: From Ecopolitics to Ecocriticism*)问世,由世界知名出版社罗德里奇(Routledge)出版发行,堪称全球首部莎士比亚生态批评专著。伊根以生态批评理论为主线,结合21世纪科学新知和全球化背景,对莎士比亚戏剧中的三对生态主题(自然与社会、食物与生物界、超自然与天气)逐一进行分析,涵盖不同题材的戏剧文本共计10个。[3]

2009年是一个标新立异的年份。是年,美国学者泰斯出版了《森林牧歌之邦:早期现代英格兰的森林书写》(*Writing the Forest in Early Modern England: A Sylvan Pastoral Nation*)一书。该书使用的"森林牧歌"(Sylvan Pastoral)术语系作者别出心裁的创造,被视为一种独特的文学体裁。在该书第一部分,泰斯以《仲夏夜之梦》《温莎的风流娘儿们》及《皆大欢喜》这三部莎翁早期喜剧中的森林描写、舞台地位及象征隐喻为聚焦对象,揭示自然和文化二者之间的复杂关系。泰斯认为,对木材匮乏的恐惧长期存在于早期现代时期的英格兰民众心中,森林对个体与国家认同的形成具有不可或缺的工具性

---

[1] Todd A. Borlik, "Simon C. Estok. Ecocriticism and Shakespeare: Reading Ecophobia", *Early Modern Literary Studies*, 16.1 (2012), p. 86.

[2] Simon Estok, "An Introduction to Shakespeare and Ecocriticism: The Special Cluster", *Interdisciplinary Studies in Literature and Environment*, 12.2 (2005), p. 110.

[3] See Gabriel Egan, *Green Shakespeare: From Ecopolitics to Ecocriticism*, London and New York: Routledge, 2006.

意义。①是年,门兹在专著《莎士比亚的海洋深处》(*At the Bottom of Shakespeare's Ocean*)中建构了莎学"蓝色文化研究"的批评范式。以回归海洋在西方文化传统中之中心地位为目标,取生态学与比较文学二者之长,门兹阐释了莎士比亚戏剧中各项以海洋为中心的人类活动。②

出版于2011年,由美国学者布鲁克纳和布雷顿担任主编的《莎士比亚生态批评》(*Ecocritical Shakespeare*)汇集了英美莎学界的最新生态研究成果。全书共计13篇论文,涉及植物、动物、气候和水体等4项主题。③布雷顿在其2012年出版的个人专著《莎士比亚海洋的生态探索》(*Shakespeare's Ocean: An Ecological Exploration*)中分析了海洋在早期现代英国人心中的现象与偏见。鉴于"莎士比亚持续性思考了人类与海洋环境之间的深层关系"④,布雷顿呼吁要建立一种"水陆两栖"(Terraqueous)式的批评模式⑤。

同样是在2011年,美国学者博利克出版了个人专著《绿色牧场:生态批评与早期现代英国文学》(*Ecocriticism and Early Modern English Literature: Green Pastures*)。此书出自作者完成于2004年的博士毕业论文,文本对象涵盖16—17世纪英国文坛大家,如莎士比亚、锡特尼、斯宾塞、马娄、邓恩及弥尔顿等人的主要作品。博利克认为,尽管早期现代作家们不是现代意义上的环保主义者,但森林砍伐、能源利用、空气质量及气候变化等议题在他们的作品中也初现端倪。⑥尤其值得注意的是,在该书第三章"宗教改革与自然的祛魅"(The Reformation and the Disenchantment of Nature)中,博利克论证了小冰期对莎士比亚时代所产生的深刻影响,时人对恶劣气候的宗教解读与心理顺应。这一小节名曰:"《仲夏夜之梦》、祈祷与1590年代的'小冰期'"(*A Midsummer Night's*

---

① See Jeffrey S. Theis, *Writing the Forest in Early Modern England: A Sylvan Pastoral Nation,* Pittsburgh and PA: Duquesne University Press, 2009.

② See Steve Mentz, *At the Bottom of Shakespeare's Ocean*, London and New York: Continuum International Publishing Group, 2009.

③ See Lynne Bruckner and Dan Brayton, eds., *Ecocritical Shakespeare*, Farnham: Ashgate Publishing Limited, 2011.

④ Dan Brayton, *Shakespeare's Ocean: An Ecocritical Exploration*, Charlottesville and London: University of Virginia Press, 2012, p. 6.

⑤ See Dan Brayton, *Shakespeare's Ocean: An Ecocritical Exploration*, Charlottesville and London: University of Virginia Press, 2012, p. 199.

⑥ See Todd A. Borlik, *Ecocriticism and Early Modern English Literature: Green Pastures*, London and New York: Routledge, 2011.

Dream, Rogation, and the "Little Ice Age" of the 1590s）。[1]

2014年，伦敦大学学者斯科特出版了名为《从农耕到文化：莎士比亚笔下的大自然》（*Shakespeare's Nature: From Cultivation to Culture*）的个人专著。通过分析《亨利五世》《麦克白》《冬天的童话》及《暴风雨》等不同戏种剧本中的农业活动，斯科特阐释了农耕语言与生产实践究竟是如何影响莎士比亚的创作的。来自英国农村，自幼便对母亲辛苦劳作的那片土地充满敬意的斯科特认为，早期现代农耕术语重新定义了人类与栖息地之间的相互关系。[2]同样是在2014年，麦克米伦出版公司出版了由杰恩·阿彻、霍华德·托马斯和理查德·特利等三位学者共同撰写的《食物与文学想象》（*Food and the Literary Imagination*）一书。该书论述了粮食危机对莎士比亚创作及其职业生涯的影响，还专门将小冰期和当时颇为盛行的饥荒叙事联系起来。[3]

不过，除去博利克和阿彻等人，以上莎士比亚生态批评文献对气候议题的总体关注度是远远不够的。尤其是对于小冰期话题，仅有只言片语。例如伊根的《绿色莎士比亚：从生态政治到生态批评》，仅有一句话提到莎士比亚年代属于小冰期时期，并未就此展开任何讨论。[4]伊根考察的主要是16—17世纪英国新、旧两种宇宙观的纠葛。[5]比伊根略进一步的是泰斯。他在专著《森林牧歌之邦：早期现代英格兰的森林书写》里提了一次小冰期这个概念，并难能可贵地将之与彼时的能源供应联系在一起："16世纪90年代的'小冰期'使得冬天寒冷异常，薪柴需求量因此急剧增长。"[6]不过，泰斯在提出这一结论之时并未援引其他文献，或列出推理过程，多少显得有些仓促。除此之外，泰斯没有在该书其他地方提及小冰期这个概念。门兹在《莎士比亚的海洋深处》里运用生态气候学的原理，解释海洋影响全球气候变化的内部机制。他说："（海洋）这个巨大的流体贮体吸纳了地球的热量和能量，促使洋流、热带风暴及厄尔尼诺现象的循环，为处于动

---

[1] See Todd A. Borlik, *Ecocriticism and Early Modern English Literature: Green Pastures*, London and New York: Routledge, 2011, pp. 118-129.

[2] See Charlotte Scott, *Shakespeare's Nature: From Cultivation to Culture*, Oxford: Oxford University Press, 2014, pp. 1-21.

[3] See Jayne Elisabeth Archer, Richard Marggraf Turley, and Howard Thomas, *Food and the Literary Imagination*, New York: Palgrave Macmillan, 2014, p. 82.

[4] See Gabriel Egan, *Green Shakespeare: From Ecopolitics to Ecocriticism*, London and New York: Routledge, 2006, p. 134.

[5] Ibid., p. 174.

[6] Jeffrey S. Theis, *Writing the Forest in Early Modern England: A Sylvan Pastoral Nation*, Pittsburgh and PA: Duquesne University Press, 2009, p. 17.

态系统之中的天气提供能量,对于这个系统,我们至今依旧无法准确模拟。"[1]与此同时,门兹在书中还把早期的美洲殖民与北大西洋环流(North Atlantic Gyre)紧密联系在一起。他的这种提法也是颇有新意的。[2]令人惋惜的是,虽然门兹已经认识到生态气候学理论对解读莎士比亚戏剧的应用价值,但他却在全书中完全忽视了小冰期这一极为重要的气候变量。

综上所述,当前莎士比亚生态批评多侧重于人与自然的关系,旨在提高人们的生态和环保意识,具有某种道德训诫的目的。正如"文学与环境研究学会"首任会长斯科特·斯洛维克(Scott Slovic)所言:"在最近几十年间,有关气候变化的科学与政治讨论大多集中在如下问题,即人类活动是否引起地球大气的变化,从而导致气候反常。"[3]在全球生态日益恶化的21世纪初,这种学术观点无疑是正确的思路,但其中的危害在于:人类的作用往往被无限夸大,批评也更容易陷入西方中心主义者们事先预设的话语圈套中。气候变化是2015年达沃斯论坛的关键议题,而文学作品早已成为气象学家们调查研究的重要参考资料。鉴于此,从小冰期的视角解读莎士比亚的作品,显然是一个具有潜力的研究方向。

参考文献

Brian Fagan, *The Little Ice Age: How Climate Made History 1300-1850*, New York: Basic Books, 2000.

Charlotte Scott, *Shakespeare's Nature: From Cultivation to Culture*, Oxford: Oxford University Press, 2014.

Dan Brayton, *Shakespeare's Ocean: An Ecocritical Exploration*, Charlottesville and London: University of Virginia Press, 2012.

Gabriel Egan, *Green Shakespeare: From Ecopolitics to Ecocriticism*, London and New York: Routledge, 2006.

Glen A. Love, *Practical Ecocriticism: Literature, Biology, and the Environment*, Virginia:

---

[1] Steve Mentz, *At the Bottom of Shakespeare's Ocean*, London and New York: Continuum International Publishing Group, 2009, p. 97.
[2] See Steve Mentz, *At the Bottom of Shakespeare's Ocean*, London and New York: Continuum International Publishing Group, 2009, p. 97.
[3] Scott Slovic, *Going Away to Think: Engagement, Retreat, and Ecocritical Responsibility*, Reno and Las Vegas: University of Nevada Press, 2008, p. 12.

University of Virginia Press, 2003.

M. H. Abrams and G. Harpham, *A Glossary of Literary Terms,* Beijing: Peking University Press, 2014.

Gordon B. Bonan, *Ecological Climatology: Concepts and Applications*, Cambridge: Cambridge University Press, 2015.

Jayne Elisabeth Archer, Richard Marggraf Turley, and Howard Thomas, *Food and the Literary Imagination*, New York: Palgrave Macmillan, 2014.

Jeffrey S. Theis, *Writing the Forest in Early Modern England: A Sylvan Pastoral Nation*, Pittsburgh and PA: Duquesne University Press, 2009.

Lynne Bruckner and Dan Brayton, eds., *Ecocritical Shakespeare*, Farnham: Ashgate Publishing Limited, 2011.

Scott Slovic, *Going Away to Think: Engagement, Retreat, and Ecocritical Responsibility*, Reno and Las Vegas: University of Nevada Press, 2008.

Simon Estok, "An Introduction to Shakespeare and Ecocriticism: The Special Cluster", *Interdisciplinary Studies in Literature and Environment*, 12.2 (2005): 109−117.

Steve Mentz, "Shakespeare's Beach House, or the Green and the Blue in Macbeth", *Shakespeare Studies*, 39 (2011): 84.

Steve Mentz, *At the Bottom of Shakespeare's Ocean*, London and New York: Continuum International Publishing Group, 2009.

Todd A. Borlik, "Review of Ecocriticism and Shakespeare: Reading Ecophobia", *Early Modern Literary Studies*, 16.1 (2012).

Todd A. Borlik, *Ecocriticism and Early Modern English Literature: Green Pastures*, London and New York: Routledge, 2011.

William Shakespeare, *Complete Works*, J. Bate and E. Rasmussen, eds., New York: Modern Library, 2007.

Wolfgang Behringer, "Climatic Change and Witch-hunting: The Impact of the Little Ice Age on Mentalities", *Climatic Change*, 43.1 (1999): 335−351.

彭纳:《人类的足迹:一部地球环境的历史》,张新、王兆润译,电子工业出版社,2013年。

王连喜、毛留喜、李琪等:《生态气象学导论》,气象出版社,2010年。

胡燕春:《雷纳·韦勒克的文学史观述评》,《社会科学》2007年第12期。

斯达尔夫人:《论文学》,徐继曾译,人民文学出版社,1986年。

曾大兴:《中外学者谈气候与文学之关系》,《广州大学学报》(社会科学版)2010年第12期。

胡志红:《西方生态批评史》,人民出版社,2015年。

兰宇冬:《物色观形成之历史过程及其文学实践》,复旦大学,2006年。

竺可桢、宛敏渭:《物候学》,科学普及出版社,1963年。

入魔之人与出笼之兽
——莎士比亚家国悲剧《李尔王》中的国王、女儿和动物

陈贵才

摘要:人物形象的动物化形变是莎士比亚家国悲剧《李尔王》的一大显著特征。通过自我形塑和他者形塑的动物化策略,莎士比亚将剧中对父权和君权入魔的古不列颠国王李尔化为一系列与其身份变化相适应的动物,将暂时摆脱父权和君权束缚而不择手段争权夺利的女儿高纳里尔和里根化为各种各样的凶禽猛兽,甚至是邪恶的毒蛇,从而将争权夺利的家庭小世界和家国大世界演化为一个危机四伏的动物世界,最终在国王、女儿和动物的巧妙链接中织就出了家破人亡、国将不国的家国悲剧。莎士比亚《李尔王》的家国悲剧是王位合法继承人的缺失、不辨是非不计后果的分治策略、权力的无序角逐、父权和君权中心的疯狂解构、行为主体身份的动物化之变以及内忧外患的国内国际环境等诸多因素共同作用的结果。

关键词:莎士比亚;家国悲剧;《李尔王》;国王;女儿;动物

作者简介:陈贵才,西南大学外国语学院博士研究生,滇西科技师范学院外国语学院副教授,主要研究方向为以莎士比亚为中心的文学动物批评。

一、引言

人物形象的动物化形变是莎士比亚家国悲剧《李尔王》的一大显著特征。为了衬托剧中人物的悲剧命运和渲染剧本的悲剧色彩,莎士比亚将龙、狗、杜鹃、鹈鹕、野猪、老虎

和毒蛇等54种或实或虚的动物巧妙植入文本网络[1]，适时将动物(animal)、野兽(beast)、怪物(monster)和恶魔(devil)等嵌入悲剧文本，精心营造了"笼中之鸟"(birds in the cage)、"洞中之狐"(foxes in the cave)、"金色的苍蝇"(gilded fly)、"金色的蝴蝶"(gilded butterflies)和"金色的毒蛇"(gilded serpent)等蕴意丰富的动物意象。在此过程中，莎士比亚娴熟地采用自我形塑和他者形塑的动物化策略，将剧中人物特别是对父权和君权入魔的国王李尔，以及因一时得势而暂时逃出父权和君权囚笼的女儿高纳里尔和里根，化作一系列与他们身份、地位和角色变化相适应的动物，他们的父女关系也随之演化成了弱肉强食的动物关系。这些人物形象的动物化形变和人际关系的动物化演变强化了戏剧人物的悲剧命运，增添了剧本的悲剧色彩，增强了文本的阐释力，同时也为方兴未艾的文学动物批评提供了重要的文本支撑。在已有相关研究中，约翰·C.麦克洛斯基(John C.McCloskey)在解析剧中动物意象的情感功用时指出，这些意象表达或强化了李尔的生气、反对、谴责和愤怒等情感[2]；娜奥米·科恩·利勃勒(Naomi Conn Liebler)依托法国戏剧理论家安托南·阿尔托(Antonin Artaud)有关"残酷戏剧"的论述，结合亚里士多德悲剧理论中的"亲戚相残"(kin-killing)和蒙田有关"残忍"的论述，紧扣文本细节但又突破文本局限，深入阐释了剧中"老虎—鹈鹕"般的暴力女性形象、破坏家庭关系的暴力行为和贪婪子女鹈鹕般的残忍手段[3]；麦瑞迪斯·斯库拉(Meredith Skura)系统解析了剧中怒龙般的父亲与鹈鹕般的子女之间争斗不止、互相蚕食的非自然关系[4]；迈克尔·C.克洛迪(Michael C. Clody)以剧中的动物声音为切入点分析指出，这些影射和再现人物悲剧命运的动物声音不仅表达了悲剧人物的痛苦和悲伤，而且传达出整个悲剧的中心议题是无以言表的虚无[5]；罗益民在深入考察剧中动物意象的基础上，详细阐释了其

---

[1] 这些动物分别为龙、羊(山羊、绵羊)、鱼、狗(母狗、恶狗、獒犬、灰狗、杂种狗、猎犬、哈巴狗、brach、寻血犬、懒狗)、毛驴、麻雀、杜鹃、马、鸢(kite)、蛇(毒蛇、小蛇)、狼、狐狸、牡蛎、蜗牛、鹡鸰(wagtail)、鼠(老鼠和田鼠)、翠鸟、鹅、猴子、野鹅、蚂蚁、鳗鱼、秃鹰、猫头鹰、熊、狮子、虱子、鹈鹕、pellicock、猪、野猪、蚕、麝猫、臭猫、蝌蚪、青蛙、蛤蟆、壁虎、水蜥、母牛、害虫、虫子、蛀虫、夜莺、鲱鱼、老虎、乌鸦、红嘴山鸦、甲虫、云雀、鸟、鹪鹩、苍蝇及蝴蝶。

[2] John C. McCloskey, "The Emotive use of Animal Imagery in *King Lear*", *Shakespeare Quarterly*, 13.3 (1962): 321–325.

[3] Naomi Conn Liebler, "Pelican Daughters: The Violence of Filial Ingratitude in *King Lear*", *Shakespeare Jahrbuch*, 143 (2007): 36–51.

[4] Meredith Skura, "Dragon Fathers and Unnatural Children: Warring Generations in *King Lear* and Its Sources", *Comparative Drama*, 42.2 (2008): 121–148.

[5] Michael C. Clody, "The Mirror and the Feather: Tragedy and Animal Voice in *King Lear*", *ELH*, 80.3 (2013): 661–680.

中所体现的虚无主义思想①。这些以动物为切入点的研究,增进了对莎士比亚悲剧文本内涵的理解,深化了对剧中人物悲剧命运的认识,为后续相关研究奠定了一定的基础。然而,就莎士比亚《李尔王》这个家国悲剧的研究而言,在从人物形象动物化形变的表现形式和内在机理系统考察人物悲剧命运的基础上,多维度深入探索家国悲剧的动因,仍有较大拓展深入的空间和较好的学术价值。

二、入魔之人：自我形塑与他者形塑中李尔形象的动物化形变

作为古不列颠国的国王和三个女儿高纳里尔、里根和考狄利娅的父亲,80岁高龄的李尔深知自己治国理政已力不从心,于是便在自以为是的政治正确的思想主导下,形成了不辨是非、不负责任和不计后果的财产分配原则和国家分治方略。这些原则和方略的施行满足了李尔大女儿高纳里尔和二女儿里根长期被压抑的国土、财产和权力欲望,为她们成为权力的操盘手奠定了坚实的基础,同时也断绝了小女儿考狄利娅的生存之需和发展之要,直接将她逼上绝路。对李尔本人而言,虽然他年事已高,财产已分配,权力已下放,但他非但没有功成身退,而是依然入魔于君权和父权,依然迷恋于权力所带来的快感体验,依然以君王和父王的口吻发号施令,依然想当然地认为周围的人和事还得由他支配,完全受控于强烈的权力欲望和强大的内心野兽而不能自拔,最终彻底丧失了自我,沦为动物般的存在物。而这种动物性存在又在自我形塑和他者形塑中,以龙、驴、篱雀、马、牡蛎、蜗牛、狼、猫头鹰、驮马、熊、笼中之鸟、洞中之狐等动物众生相展现出来。

当肯特伯爵试图劝告李尔要善待他的小女儿考狄利娅时,独断专横的他不仅置若罔闻,而且发出了警告:"闭嘴,肯特! 不要来批怒龙的逆鳞。"②在此,李尔将自己视为一条怒不可遏的蛟龙,一条誓要吞噬万物的狂暴之龙,一条具有强烈报复心的邪恶之龙。这样的警告还表明:作为国王,他像巨龙一样强大和危险。③在西方文化传统和文学传统中,"龙"一直是怪物般的存在物:《圣经·启示录》中头上戴着冠冕的大龙自以为是世

---

① 罗益民:《天鹅最美一支歌:莎士比亚其人其剧其诗》,科学出版社,2016年,第52页。
② 莎士比亚:《李尔王》,收入《莎士比亚全集·Ⅶ》,朱生豪等译,人民文学出版社,2014年,第133页。后文中该剧的中文引文均出自该译本,将随文标出《李尔王》的首字和页码,不再另注。
③ Karen Raber and Karen L. Edwards, *Shakespeare and Animals: A Dictionary*, London and New York: The Ardent Shakespeare, 2022, p. 149.

界之王,但它却被视为魔鬼和撒旦的化身;《金色传奇》中的巨龙狂妄自大、残暴无比、嗜血成性,每天都要城里居民用羊或人供奉着,否则它就怒不可遏地越到城墙喷出毒气将人毒死,但它终归还是被圣乔治所屠杀;[1]英国史诗《贝奥武夫》中的火龙发现有人盗窃了它所看守的财宝,十分愤怒,于是喷火烧毁附近的村庄,给老百姓造成极大的灾难。[2]但这样的怒龙恶龙最终还是被80岁高龄的贝奥武夫给斩除了。这些看似强大无比、怒不可遏的恶龙形象终归均未逃脱它们的宿命,它们最终都落得了命丧黄泉的下场。因此,李尔之怒也只不过是大难临头前的虚张声势,他的行为也只不过是盘踞在心中内隐之蛇的外显罢了,他的形象也成了内隐之蛇和外显之龙的集合体。

当李尔在大女儿高纳里尔那儿尝尽各种欺辱和折磨后,他便将希望寄托在二女儿里根身上,希望能到她那儿安享晚年,能在那儿有个归宿。但令他绝望的是,口口声声说好要照顾他的二女儿里根却根本不想收留他,只想劝他返回大女儿高纳里尔那儿去。本就在大女儿那儿吃了闭门羹的李尔现在已成了丧家之犬。在安全、归属、尊重和被爱等的需要都得不到满足的情况下,李尔的需要层次之塔随之断裂崩塌,情感世界之堤也悄然崩溃,情感洪水旋即一泻而出,于是他发出了无奈又无助的声音:

> 回到她那儿去?裁撤五十名侍从!不,我宁愿什么屋子也不要住,过着风餐露宿的生活,和无情的大自然抗争,和豺狼鸱鸮做伴侣,忍受一切饥寒的痛苦!回去跟她住在一起?嘿,我宁愿到那娶了我的没有嫁奁的小女儿去的热情的法兰西国王的座前匍匐膝行,像一个臣仆一样向他讨一份微薄的恩俸,苟延残喘下去。回去跟她住在一起!你还是劝我在这可恶的仆人手下当奴才、当牛马吧。(指奥斯华德)(《李》:178)

这些"宁愿"其实正是李尔心不甘、情不愿的心理反应,是他不得已而为之的现实选择,同时也是他生存境况突变后狼狈不堪的现实。他已意识到自己王威的不在和权威的丧失,内心已放下了国王的架子和面子,寻思着去被他抛弃的小女儿考狄利娅那儿,但他并不奢望得到应有的温暖和尊敬,只求能在那儿有个安身之所,哪怕做仆人也愿意。他还做好了最坏的准备,去给可恶的仆人奥斯华德当牛做马,任他驱使和欺辱。他内心已从人类世界走向动物世界,已做好了与凶禽猛兽为敌的心理准备,已预料到自己

---

[1] 褚潇白、成功:《金色传奇:中世纪圣徒文学精选》,浙江大学出版社,2016年,第59-64页。
[2] 李赋宁:《古英语史诗〈贝奥武夫〉》,《外国文学》1998年第6期。

会沦为猎物。

在经历如此巨大的落差和遭遇，以及如此强烈的心理震击之后，"何处是家""何以立命"成了他心中最迫切、最痛苦的追问，而这所有的追问无不尽显于他的叹息声中："啊！不要跟我说什么需要不需要；最卑贱的乞丐，也有他的不值钱的身外之物；人生除了天然的需要以外，要是没有其他的享受，那和畜类的生活有什么分别。"(《李》:180)从李尔叹息声的认知体验来看，人之所以为人而不是动物，是因为除了本能的需要外，人还有诸多其他方面的欲求，要是这些需要和欲望无法得到满足，人和动物就没有什么本质区别，也不可避免地成了畜类。当李尔的生存之需和安全之要被无情地剥夺之后，他沦为了卑贱的乞丐和低贱的兽类，过着乞丐般居无定所和动物般低贱无度的生活。

当被埃德蒙抓捕后，李尔的小女儿考狄利娅向其父亲李尔提议要不要去向大女儿和二女儿求助时，李尔坚决地回答道："不，不，不，不！"(《李》:234)这种决绝的态度表明，李尔已认清他的大女儿高纳里尔、二女儿里根和埃德蒙是一丘之貉，已认识到自己敌不过她们这群凶禽猛兽，于是便化身为鸟，化狱为笼，躲入其中，苦中作乐："来，让我们到监牢里去。我们两人将要像笼中之鸟一般唱歌。"(《李》:234)"笼中之鸟"这个奇妙意象直接道尽了李尔的生存现实：他的肉身已被囚禁和束缚，但心灵仍在自由飞翔：

我们就这样生活着，祈祷，唱歌，说些古老的故事，嘲笑那班像金翅蝴蝶般的廷臣，听听那些可怜的人们讲些宫廷里的消息；我们也要跟他们在一起谈话，谁失败，谁胜利，谁在朝，谁在野，用我们的意见解释各种事情的秘奥，就像我们是上帝的耳目一样；在囚牢的四壁之内，我们将要冷眼看那些朋比为奸的党徒随着月亮的圆缺而升沉。(《李》:234)

凄苦的牢狱生活使李尔身心备受煎熬和摧残，但也为他提供了一个冷眼看世界的窗口和一个笑看人生百态、世事难料的机会。虽然处在埃德蒙等人的严密监视下，李尔依然获得了从狱内往外看的窗口，他从中看到了人生别样的风景，看清了朝政，看破了红尘，同时也在静观时光长河中谁主沉浮。

当埃德蒙叫人把李尔和他的小女儿考狄利娅带走时，他还将自己称为"狐狸"："对于这样的祭物，我的考狄利娅，天神也要焚香致敬的。我果然把你捉住了吗？谁要是想分开我们，必须从天上取下一把火炬来像驱逐狐狸一样把我们赶散。"(《李》:234)为了应对穷凶极恶、凶禽猛兽般的埃德蒙，为了守护女儿考狄利娅，李尔必须像狡猾的狐狸一样躲在洞中，任凭他们采用何种办法，他都不会轻易出来，他只得以此来规避险恶的客观现实。

无论是"笼中之鸟",还是"洞中之狐",李尔的身份和处境已发生了根本性改变。肉体上受到严密监视和严加囚禁的他,在精神上仍保持相对独立,仍然能像笼中的鸟儿一样自由歌唱,仍然能像洞中待捕的狐狸一样誓死不出。这并不是表明李尔已躲进小楼成一统和已彻底退隐江湖,而是表明他已做出了不得已而为之的现实选择,已回归了生活本真。

考狄利娅之死给李尔留下了无限的惋惜、深深的忏悔和无尽的叹息:"我的可怜的傻瓜给他们缢死了!不,不,没有命了!为什么一条狗、一匹马、一只耗子,都有它们的生命,你却没有一丝呼吸?你是永不回来的了,永不,永不,永不,永不,永不!"(《李》:245)这何尝不是李尔对自己人生无常、生不如死的生命叹息,叹息自己连一条狗、一匹马和一只耗子都不如。

李尔的"一怒三叹"不仅体现了他对父权中心和君权中心业已遭受解构的心理认知,而且体现了他无可奈何权势去的客观现实,更体现了他人生轨迹的递变和人的动物化形变。李尔的动物化形变不仅体现在他的自我形塑之中,还体现在弄人和侍臣等的他者形塑之中。

当李尔将权力分成两份,全部分给大女儿高纳里尔和二女儿里根时,在弄人看来,这种行为无异于"背了驴子过泥潭"(《李》:152),自己不仅将深陷其中而不能自拔,而且成了驴一样的蠢人。当目睹了李尔将其国土和财产全部分给大女儿和二女儿之后,弄人觉得李尔连牡蛎和蜗牛都不如,牡蛎和蜗牛尚能用自己的硬壳保护自己,而李尔却不知为自己留下足够的财产和安身立命之所。而且,当李尔将权力、财产和国土的掌控权全部交出时,他就不再拥有既有的话语权,相反,他只能默默忍受频频沦为两个女儿发号施令的对象。弄人对此看在眼里,认为这是本末倒置:"马儿颠倒过来给车子拖着走,就是一头蠢驴不也看得清楚吗?"(《李》:154)从弄人对李尔的动物化形塑来看,李尔已成了蠢驴般的存在,蠢得连弱小的牡蛎和蜗牛都不如。

弄人还将李尔与大女儿和二女儿的关系视为篱雀与杜鹃的关系:"那篱雀养大了杜鹃鸟,自己的头也给它吃掉。"(《李》:154)弄人意在用这种关系去暗示"高纳里尔对待李尔的行为相当于杀父"。[①]李尔含辛茹苦把她们姐妹俩养大成人,倾其所有为其奉上权

[①] Karen Raber and Karen L. Edwards. *Shakespeare and Animals: A Dictionary*, London and New York: The Ardent Shakespeare, 2022, p. 392.

力、国土和财产,到头来不仅没有得到她们应有的关爱,反而遭受她们变本加厉的虐待和随心所欲的处置,甚至连寄人篱下的希望都成了彻底的绝望,而他的两个女儿却鸠占鹊巢,摇身一变成了掌控他生死大权的杜鹃鸟。

当李尔被迫流落荒野,遭遇大自然的狂暴时,他的侍臣感叹道:"这样的晚上,被小熊吸干了乳汁的母熊,也躲着不敢出来,狮子和饿狼都不愿沾湿它们的毛皮。他却光秃着头在风雨中狂奔,把一切托付给不可知的力量。"(《李》:182)在这种凄风苦雨的极端环境下,被小熊吸干乳汁的母熊、作为百兽之王的狮子和狡猾的饿狼等都已躲进藏身之处而不肯外出,而被榨干生命汁液、年老体衰、衣单食薄的李尔却被置于荒郊野岭,任凭寒风暴雨肆虐,任由神秘莫测、摧枯拉朽的大自然摆布。在母熊、狮子和饿狼的衬托下,李尔的处境和遭遇就显得格外凄苦和悲惨。在天灾和人祸的双重击打下,李尔已彻底丧失了抵御生存风险的能力,他已不再是自己的主宰,已沦为行尸走肉。

从李尔的动物化身份形变可发现,在争权夺利的家庭小世界和宫廷大世界中,他从大权在握、不可一世、君临天下、众星捧月的君王变成了唯命是从的懦夫和无人搭理的孤家寡人,从稳坐江山的君王沦为居无定所的流浪汉,他的居所从富丽堂皇的皇宫变为荒郊野岭的茅舍,他的形象也由叱咤风云的蛟龙变为寄人篱下的麻雀、束手就擒的困兽和忍辱负重的驮马。从空间结构看,李尔命运轨迹的戏剧性突变经历了从权力之巅到权力之谷的跌落。在如此急剧的跌落中,李尔心灵之弦被折断了,需要层次之塔坍塌了,欲望之兽被撞死了。曾经对父权和君权入魔的国王李尔,最终竟成了逃出父权和君权牢笼的凶禽猛兽毒蛇般的高纳里尔和里根的束手就擒的猎物。

三、出笼之兽:他者形塑中女儿形象的动物化形变

在通过口是心非的承诺,从年迈父亲李尔那儿获取权力、国土和财产后,高纳里尔和里根成功获取了掌握自己命运和掌控他人命运的筹码,暂时逃出了束缚已久的父权和君权牢笼,摇身变成了他人命运的主宰和恶魔般的存在:"魔鬼,看看你自己!千变万化的妖魔鬼怪都没你这样的女人恐怖。……你这变了形还自我掩饰的不要脸的东西,别把你丑恶的嘴脸露出来。"[1]虽然这是奥本尼对其妻子高纳里尔的警告,但同时也是对

---

[1] William Shakespeare, *King Lear*, George Ian Duthie and John Dover Wilson, eds., NewYork: Cambridge University Press, 2009, p. 84.

里根的警醒。因为在他看来,她们既不是柔情的女儿,也不是善良的天使,而是邪恶的魔鬼。不仅如此,她们还成了李尔、弄人、葛罗斯特、肯特和埃德蒙等人的言说对象,在他们心中成了鹈鹕、鸢、秃鹰、毒蛇、豺狼、狐狸、鹌鹑、金苍蝇、臭猫、骚马、母狗、猛虎、野猪和小蛇等凶禽猛兽毒蛇般的存在。

在王威不在却仍想保持国王形象和行使国王权力的李尔眼里,他的大女儿高纳里尔和二女儿里根是"鹈鹕般的女儿"(pelican daughters)。鹈鹕长大变强后攻击养父母的本性直接影射出李尔两个女儿残忍不孝的本色。而且,高纳里尔还被他看作"可恶的鸢"(detested kite)。作为食腐动物,鸢不仅是肮脏的代名词,而且还成了约定俗成的文化符号而被写入16、17世纪英国谚语之中:"食腐之鸢永远都成不了雄鹰。"[1]而且,"由于鸢不仅捕食人类饲养的弱小动物,而且为资源而争斗不休,因而被冠以盗贼、谋杀犯和叛徒之名"[2]。这一隐喻不仅折射出高纳里尔的丑恶嘴脸和肮脏手段,而且暴露了她争权夺利和不忠不孝的本性。不仅如此,李尔心中的高纳里尔还成了秃鹰一样的存在:"她就像一只秃鹰,用利喙般的恶行,猛啄我的心。"[3]"秃鹰与战场、暴力和死亡的关联性"[4]影射出高纳里尔的残暴手段,凸显了李尔的凄惨遭遇和痛苦感受,同时也暗示了李尔的最终下场。这些凶禽类动物隐喻不仅强化了李尔大女儿高纳里尔和二女儿里根的恶女形象,而且影射出她们肮脏可恶的嘴脸和贪婪残暴的本色。

为了进一步凸显她们的兽性本色,李尔还将他那不知养育之恩、只知争权夺利的大女儿高纳里尔视为毒蛇一样的存在:"她裁撤了我一半的侍从;不给我好脸看;用她的毒蛇一样的舌头打击我的心。"(《李》:176)在满怀期待他的二女儿里根会为他报仇雪恨时,李尔又将他的大女儿视为披着羊皮的狼:"我还有一个女儿,我相信她是孝顺我的;她听见你这样对待我,一定会用指爪抓破你的豺狼一样的脸。"(《李》:157)在想象中对大女儿高纳里尔和二女儿里根的审判中,李尔还将她们视为雌狐(she foxes)。这些动物隐喻不仅强化了她们外在的蛇性化、狼性化和狐狸化的动物化特征,而且影射出她们

---

[1] Morris Palmer Tilley, *A Dictionary of the Proverbs in England in the Sixteenth and Seventeenth Centuries*, Ann Arbor: University of Michigan Press, 1950, p. 359.

[2] Karen Raber and Karen L. Edwards, *Shakespeare and Animals: A Dictionary*, London and New York: The Ardent Shakespeare, 2022, p. 262.

[3] William Shakespeare, *The Tragedy of King Lear*, Jay L. Hali, ed., Cambridge: Cambridge University Press, 2005, p. 166.

[4] Karen Raber and Karen L. Edwards, *Shakespeare and Animals: A Dictionary*, London and New York: The Ardent Shakespeare, 2022, p. 423.

赤口毒舌、心狠手辣、阴险狡诈、人面兽心的兽性本色。另外,李尔还将他的大女儿高纳里尔和二女儿里根视为鹪鹩(wren)、金苍蝇(gilded fly)、臭猫(fitchew)和骚马(soiled horse)。这些动物化隐喻进一步影射出她们争权夺利、争风吃醋、不守妇道的本性和金玉其外败絮其中的丑恶嘴脸。

这些以动物隐喻为介质的咒骂语言表明,虽然高纳里尔和里根已暂时摆脱父权和君权牢笼的束缚,但她们仍然难以逃脱被言说的命运,她们依然是被言说的他者,她们的身份仍然是女性他者和动物他者的统一,而且这种统一还进一步体现在弄人、奥本尼、葛罗斯特和肯特的男权话语言说之中。

在弄人眼里,常说假话、阿谀奉承、口蜜腹剑、口是心非的高纳里尔和里根就是摇尾乞怜的母狗:"真理是一条贱狗,它只好躲在狗洞里;当猎狗太太站在火边撒尿的时候,它必须一顿鞭子被人赶出去。"(《李》:151)弄人极具讽刺意味的言说表明,以肯特为代表的讲真话的人是一条贱狗,必须乖乖地躲起来,而常说假话、阳奉阴违、母狗般留在主人身边坐享其成但又为非作歹的高纳里尔和里根,必须受到严厉的惩罚。然而,黑白颠倒的李尔不仅未防患于未然而采取相应的惩罚措施,而且依然养"犬"为患,让她们肆意妄为,最终成为猎犬般的她们露出了锋利的獠牙,李尔也不可避免地成了她们的猎物。不仅如此,弄人还将高纳里尔视为阴险狡诈的狐狸,并把她和狐狸被宰杀的命运联系起来:"捉狐狸,杀狐狸,谁家女儿是狐狸?"(《李》:157)弄人的言说表明,无论是母狗般的高纳里尔和里根,还是狐狸般的高纳里尔,她们不仅避免不了应有的惩罚,而且还逃不脱被宰杀的下场。

当目睹李尔惨遭大女儿和二女儿的伤害后,奥本尼对她们发出了悲愤之问:"你们干下了些什么事情?你们是猛虎,不是女儿,你们干下了些什么事啦?这样一位父亲,这样一位仁慈的老人家,一头野熊见了他也会俯首贴耳,你们这些蛮横下贱的女儿,却把他激成了疯狂!"(《李》:209)作为"嗜血成性之人"[①]的隐喻,猛虎意象不仅彻底将高纳里尔和里根的恶女形象及其残忍手段,以及为非作歹的行为暴露无遗,而且凸显了她们已成为政治丛林之王的客观事实。不仅如此,奥本尼还将高纳里尔视作一条金灿灿的毒蛇(gilded serpent)。这个意象将高纳里尔外表华丽、心如蛇蝎的形象栩栩如生地刻画出来:身为国王的女儿,高纳里尔穿着富丽堂皇,披金戴银,但在此伪装下却是一条邪恶

---

① Robert Allen Palmatier, *Speaking of Animals: A Dictionary of Animal Metaphors*, Westport and CT: Greenwood Press, 1995, p. 387.

的毒蛇,一条随时准备向其父亲发起攻击并可将他置于死地的毒蛇。

当狠毒的里根和她的丈夫康华尔怒斥葛罗斯特为何把李尔送到多佛时,葛罗斯特勇敢地答道:"因为我不愿意看见你的凶恶的指爪挖出他的可怜的老眼;因为我不愿意看见你的残暴的姊姊用她野猪般的利齿咬进他的神圣的肉体。"(《李》:203)葛罗斯特的强硬回答彻底揭开了高纳里尔和里根姊妹俩穷凶极恶的嘴脸,彻底将她们凶禽猛兽般的本性暴露了出来。从葛罗斯特的认知体验来看,里根已成了凶禽般的存在,她利爪一样的双手随时准备挖出李尔可怜的老眼。高纳里尔则成了一头凶残的野猪,她野猪般的利齿随时准备向李尔神圣的肉身发起进攻。性情"暴躁、易激怒、难驾驭"[1]的野猪意象直接将高纳里尔的残忍本性披露无遗。"野猪般的利齿概括了高纳里尔凶恶狠毒的行为;柔嫩的、近乎神圣的肉身与利刃般獠牙间的鲜明对比,勾画出了人类与动物他者的极端冲突。"[2]在与凶禽化的里根和猛兽化的高纳里尔的惨烈冲突中,无论遭遇谁的袭击或攻击,年迈体弱的李尔都在劫难逃,等待他的也只有白骨露于野的下场。

肯特还将李尔的大女儿高纳里尔和二女儿里根视为"犬狼之心的女儿"(《李》:213)。狗有摇头摆尾取悦奉承主人的一面,同时也会欺骗、背叛甚至违抗主人。这种两面性正好与高纳里尔和里根姐妹俩的双重人格一致:为了得到自己想要的事物和满足自己的欲望,她们会像狗一样取悦奉承主人,但一旦获取她们的所需所欲,她们就翻脸不认主,变得像疯狗一样违抗并报复主人。

埃德蒙则将相互嫉妒的高纳里尔和里根视为象征"谎言、欺骗、背叛和虚伪"[3]的小蛇(adder)。身为有夫之妇,高纳里尔和里根并未尽职尽责地担起相夫教子的本职,也未安分守己地树立贤妻良母的形象,相反,她们心怀鬼胎,不仅与臭味相投的埃德蒙朋比为奸,而且还在一系列的胡作非为中与他发展成了剪不断理还乱的男女关系。虽然她们都不相信他的忠诚,都害怕有危险,但她们最终依然被诡计多端的埃德蒙玩弄于指掌之间,彻底沦为他的玩物和言说的对象。

作为国王李尔的女儿,高纳里尔和里根因一时得势而得以暂时冲出父权和君权的牢笼,她们内心的野兽也随之释放出来。在强大的内心野兽的驱使下,她们忘乎所以地开启了系列清算父权和掠夺君权的疯狂表演,俨然成了自己命运的主宰和权力的操盘

---

[1] Aristotle, *History of Animals*, Richard Cresswell, trans., London: George Bell & Sons, 1878, p. 6.
[2] Karen Raber and Karen L. Edwards, *Shakespeare and Animals: A Dictionary*, London and New York: The Ardent Shakespeare, 2022, p. 70.
[3] Ibid, p. 15.

手。然而,在君权至上、男权占支配地位的社会主流文化语境下,她们的身份地位并未取得实质性的突破,她们被言说的命运仍未得到根本性改变,她们的女性他者身份也未得以跨越。不仅如此,她们还被披上了凶禽猛兽毒蛇般的外衣和背负上了动物他者的身份。在双重他者身份的裹挟下,冲出父权和君权囚笼的她们最终还是难以逃出男性中心主义文化的牢笼,她们也不可避免地成了男性中心主义文化的牺牲品。

四、莎士比亚《李尔王》家国悲剧的动因

在《李尔王》这部悲剧中,李尔一家所处的家庭小世界和家国大世界已在惨烈的权力争夺战中演化成了一个危机四伏的动物世界。在这个世界中,作为权力掌控者的李尔因一时失误而被从权力中心推向了权力边缘,不仅丧失了对权力的操控,而且成了动物他者般的存在物和权力角逐的牺牲品。作为权力争夺者的高纳里尔和里根,虽因一时得势而得以暂时成为权力的操盘手,但她们不仅未能改变自己女性他者的身份,而且还在他者的言说中成了凶禽猛兽毒蛇般的存在物和男性中心主义文化的牺牲品。这场惨烈的权力争夺战不仅直接导致李尔一家的骨肉分离和家破人亡,而且使整个古不列颠国都陷入了无序而衰、国将不国的局面。这样的家国悲剧是王位合法继承人的缺失、不辨是非不计后果的分治策略、权力的无序角逐、权力中心的疯狂解构、行为主体身份的动物化之变以及内忧外患的国内国际环境等诸多因素共同作用的结果。

王位合法继承人的缺失是家国悲剧的主要动因。根据君主制王位继承的传统,长子是王位继承的首选,然后是次子。如果国王没有男嗣,长女则是首选继承人,然后是次女。在《李尔王》这部悲剧中,虽然王位继承是李尔最基本的问题,但剧中从未直接提及可能的继承人。[1]而且,年事已高、治国理政已力不从心的国王李尔并未从国家长治久安、人民安居乐业和民族兴旺发达的大局和全局出发,去选定和培养合法的王位继承人。相反,他只遵循快乐原则,设定了爱的考验,并根据三个女儿爱的承诺去分配国土、财产和权力。于是说尽漂亮话的大女儿和二女儿就得到了她们想要的一切,而不愿吐露心声的小女儿则一无所获。这样的分配选择看似符合王位继承的传统和原则,实则违背了国家长治久安、人民安居乐业和民族兴旺发达的根本利益,同时也违背了李尔既定的意旨,因为他本想选小女儿考狄利娅作为王位继承人,但她出人意料的抵触行为不

---

[1] 布鲁姆、雅法:《莎士比亚的政治》,潘望译,江苏人民出版社,2012年,第110页。

仅打乱了他的政治计划[1],而且"使他的苦行付之一炬"[2],同时也使王位合法继承人处于缺失状态。这也是莎士比亚在剧末将奥本尼那样的忠义之士设定为治国理政的理想人选的原因。他希望奥本尼将埃德加和肯特等人团结起来,去担起"主持国家大政、将国家从疮痍满目的境况中拯救过来"的使命。[3]

不辨是非的分治策略是家国悲剧的诱因之所在。由于年事已高,李尔心想把国土、财产和权力一分为三,交由三个女儿掌管,由她们代他治国理政,以期实现三分天下、分而治之的目标。李尔对国土、财产和权力的分配本身无可厚非,但他行事的原则却成了问题的关键。他把国土、财产和权力全分给了说尽漂亮话却丧尽天良、作恶多端的大女儿高纳里尔和二女儿里根,而只愿吐露真情实感且一向诚心待他的小女儿考狄利娅却一无所获。这种不分是非、不计后果的分配方式满足了李尔的一时之快,成全了他蛇蝎之心和虎狼之行的大女儿高纳里尔和二女儿里根,满足了她们压抑已久的物质欲望和权力欲望,同时也截断了他小女儿考狄利娅的生存之需和发展之要,直接将她逼到了绝境。他的小女儿因爱神的眷顾和法国王子的垂青而暂时得以绝处逢生,但终归因他分而治之的祸根而断送了宝贵的生命。他的大女儿和二女儿获得了权力带来的快感,但她们最终还是成了权力关系的牺牲品。李尔一分为快的行为促成了他的终生之痛。他养虎为患的行径也使他成了落入虎口的羔羊。他不分是非、不计后果的分治策略不仅未能使国家达到分而治之的目标,而且还在很大程度上削弱了整个古不列颠国的政权根基,甚至将整个国泰民安的美好前程都葬送在了人类历史的长河之中。

权力的无序角逐成了家国悲剧的直接动因。在君权神授的主流政治文化语境下,国王至高无上的身份和神圣不可侵犯的权力是铁的定律,谁都不可撼动也撼动不了。然而,当君权神授的权力机制遭遇日趋没落的封建君主文化和日渐兴起的资本主义文化时,这种权力机制势必会在两种政治文化的交流碰撞中和两股势力的相互撕扯中丧失既有的能量并遭受重创,其运行效力也会在此消彼长中大大受阻、大打折扣,其生命力也会随着强势文化的不断增强而逐渐衰弱。在莎士比亚悲剧《李尔王》中,君权神授主导下的古不列颠国的国威已江河日下,以李尔王为代表的古不列颠封建势力已日趋衰弱,而以高纳里尔和里根为代表的新兴资本主义势力却在逐渐增强。在这样的背景

---

[1] 布鲁姆、雅法:《莎士比亚的政治》,第114页。
[2] 同上书,第116页。
[3] William Shakespeare, *The Tragedy of King Lear*, Jay L. Halio, ed., Cambridge: Cambridge University Press, 2005, p. 263.

下,李尔分配了国土、财产和权力,但他仍想维护自己的国王形象和神圣不可侵犯的王权。然而,在势不可挡的王权争夺战中,李尔却无能为力,无所适从,只能眼睁睁地看着自己至高无上、神圣不可侵犯的权力被疯狂蚕食。而且,在欲望交织的宫廷世界中和无序而衰的政治局面下,争权夺利已成了常态并愈演愈烈,制约与平衡早已在国土、财产和权力分配时被打破,一旦各种关系之间的平衡被打破,人就不可避免地沦为动物[①]。在权力争夺战中,成为凶禽猛兽毒蛇般的高纳里尔和里根也并未因一时得势而逃脱女性他者和动物他者的宿命,最终成了权力角逐的牺牲品。

父权中心和君权中心的疯狂解构是家国悲剧的一个主导原因。在巧取财产支配权后,高纳里尔和里根疯狂地进行了拆解父权和君权的系列恶行,完全不顾父亲的身份和国王的尊严,只顾如何将其权力夺到自己手中,然后忘乎所以地行使心之所向的权力。她们解构父权和君权的疯狂行动给她们的父亲留下了深深的创伤和无尽的痛楚,而这种伤痛又随着她们进一步的施暴被不断加深。随着施暴力度和强度的不断增强,本就年老体衰的李尔的需要层次之塔坍塌了,情感的洪水溃堤而出,发出凄惨的哀鸣:"我的可怜的傻瓜给他们缢死了!不,不,没有命了!为什么一条狗,一匹马,一只耗子,都有它们的生命,你却没有一丝呼吸?你是永不回来的了,永不,永不,永不,永不,永不!"(《李》:245)李尔的哀鸣看似是对权力关系的牺牲品考狄利娅的不舍,实则暗含着他对业已消解的权力中心的不甘。在不舍与不甘的激烈撕扯中,李尔痛不欲生,最终撒手人寰,回归了尘土。作为权力中心的疯狂解构者,高纳里尔和里根虽然成功拆解了以李尔为代表的父权中心和君权中心,但在居于主导地位的男性中心主义文化语境下,她们拆解中心的疯狂表演注定是昙花一现,她们的努力不仅不会对根深蒂固的男性中心主义文化产生重大影响,而且她们还难以改写自己女性他者的命运,也无法逃避动物他者的下场,成了男性中心主义文化和君权制文化的牺牲品。

行为主体身份的动物化之变是家国悲剧的又一主导原因。在《李尔王》这部悲剧中,无论是作为国王和父亲的李尔,还是作为公主和女儿的高纳里尔和里根,他们都是家国悲剧的行为主体,都经历了动物化的身份形变,都从人类自我变成了动物他者般的存在物,都成了名副其实的"政治动物"[②]。他们的动物化行为直接将争权夺利的家庭小世界和家国大世界演化成了一个危机四伏、凶残无度的动物世界。在这个世界中,特别

---

① 李毅:《二十世纪西方〈李尔王〉研究述评》,《四川外语学院学报》1996年第4期。
② Aristotle, *Politics*, Ernest Barker, trans., New York: Oxford University Press, 1995, p. 343.

是在高纳里尔和里根的世界中,人性几乎荡然无存,兽性反而大行其道。在人性与兽性的此消彼长间,李尔经历了从叱咤风云的蛟龙到任人驱使的驽马的动物化形变,但他身上的兽性元素却随着他动物化形变的增强而逐渐内隐和减弱;高纳里尔和里根则经历了凶禽猛兽毒蛇化的动物之变,但她们身上的兽性元素却随着她们动物化形变的增强而不断外显和增强。在弱肉强食的政治丛林中和无序而衰的政治局面下,弱势的李尔最终成了强势的她们的猎物。然而,在处于支配地位的男性中心主义话语体系下,无论她们如何肆意横行,她们的女性他者身份和动物他者身份依然未能得以根本性改变,她们依然逃不了被猎杀的宿命和下场。

内忧外患的国内国际环境是家国悲剧的现实语境。作为假丑恶的代名词,李尔的大女儿高纳里尔和二女儿里根为权力而争斗,为利益而争斗,为爱情而争斗。而且,在埃德蒙的离间下,相依为命的她们最终骨肉相残。这些构成了家国悲剧的内忧之基。然而,当面临以考狄利娅及其夫君法国王子为首的外敌入侵时,高纳里尔等人并未坐以待毙,而是率兵奋勇抵抗,去守护自己来之不易的权力、心之所向的财产和国土,以及保卫自己的国家和人民,但这样的行为选择并不能抵消她们破坏国家政权大厦根基的系列恶行。李尔的小女儿考狄利娅看似是真善美的化身,实则成了家国悲剧的外患之源。她和丈夫率兵对故国发动的战争看似是要推翻以高纳里尔为首的政权,为受尽苦难和惨遭虐待的父亲讨回公道和正义,实则是为自己报仇雪恨,去夺回自己的国土和财产。而且,由于她已不再只是国王李尔的女儿,她还是法国的王后,她所发动的对两位姐姐的讨伐战争就可能包藏难以言说的政治目的,本质上就是一场侵略战争[①]。这场使家庭矛盾上升为民族矛盾的侵略战争不仅殃及李尔一家四口,而且使整个古不列颠国都遭受了深重的灾难和创伤。

五、结语

在《李尔王》这部家国悲剧中,莎士比亚通过自我形塑和他者形塑的动物化策略,将人物形象的动物性淋漓尽致地展现出来。作为家庭矛盾的制造者和家国悲剧的行为主体,大权在握的古不列颠国的国王李尔老而不智,以想当然的政治正确为原则,以分而治之的臆想为目标,将国土、财产和权力视为私有财产,全部分给了德不配位的大女儿

---

① 李正栓、叶红婷:《莎士比亚〈李尔王〉中的伦理》,《外国语文》2023年第6期。

高纳里尔和二女儿里根,而他德才兼备的小女儿考狄利娅却成了名副其实的无产者和无权者。李尔不计后果的分治方略和不患寡而患不均的分配策略满足了大女儿和二女儿为之疯狂的物质欲望和权力欲望,截断了小女儿考狄利娅的生存之需和发展之要,同时也将自己、家庭和国家拖入了痛苦的深渊和悲惨的境地。

在激烈的权力争夺战中,李尔经历了从愤怒的蛟龙到任人驱使的驮马的动物化之变,高纳里尔和里根则经历了凶禽猛兽毒蛇化的动物之变,他们之间血肉相连的父女关系也演化成了弱肉强食的动物关系,他们所处的家庭小世界和国家大世界也随之演化成了一个危机四伏的动物世界。在这个人人自危的世界中,王威不在但仍想保持国王形象和行使国王权力的李尔,成了大女儿和二女儿父权中心和君权中心的解构对象,并最终成了她们权力角逐的牺牲品。一时得势而肆意妄为地举起反父权、夺君权大旗的高纳里尔和里根,不仅未能从根本上改变被言说的命运,以及女性他者和动物他者的双重身份,而且最终还沦为了男性中心主义文化的牺牲品。

如果说李尔及其大女儿和二女儿是家国悲剧的内忧之基,那么作为看似真善美代名词的远嫁法国的小女儿考狄利娅和她的丈夫就是家国悲剧的外患之源。他们对故国发动的侵略战争不仅激化了民族矛盾,而且使国家和人民都遭受了战火的摧残。残酷的战争不仅使李尔一家家破人亡,而且使整个国家都陷入了国将不国的局面。莎士比亚《李尔王》中家国悲剧是王位合法继承人的缺失、不辨是非不计后果的分治策略、权力的无序角逐、父权中心和君权中的疯狂解构、行为主体身份的动物化之变以及内忧外患的国内国际环境等诸多因素共同作用的结果。

参考文献

Aristotle, *History of Animals*, Richard Cresswell, trans., London: George Bell & Sons, 1878.

Aristotle, *Politics*, Ernest Barker, trans., New York: Oxford University Press, 1995.

John C. McCloskey, "The Emotive use of Animal Imagery in King Lear", *Shakespeare Quarterly*, 13.3 (1962): 321–325.

Karen Raber and Karen L. Edwards, *Shakespeare and Animals: A Dictionary*, London and New York: The Ardent Shakespeare, 2022.

Meredith Skura, "Dragon Fathers and Unnatural Children: Warring Generations in King Lear and Its Sources", *Comparative Drama*, 42.2 (2008): 121–148.

Michael C. Clody, "The Mirror and the Feather: Tragedy and Animal Voice in King Lear", *ELH*,

80.3 (2013): 661−680.

Morris Palmer Tilley, *A Dictionary of the Proverbs in England in the Sixteenth and Seventeenth Centuries*, Ann Arbor: University of Michigan Press, 1950.

Naomi Conn Liebler, "Pelican Daughters: The Violence of Filial Ingratitude in King Lear", *Shakespeare Jahrbuch*, 143 (2007): 36−51.

Robert Allen Palmatier, *Speaking of Animals: A Dictionary of Animal Metaphors*, Westport and CT: Greenwood Press, 1995.

William Shakespeare, *King Lear*, George Ian Duthie and John Dover Wilson, eds., New York: Cambridge University Press, 2009.

William Shakespeare, *The Tragedy of King Lear*, Jay L. Hali, ed., Cambridge: Cambridge University Press, 2005.

罗益民:《天鹅最美一支歌:莎士比亚其人其剧其诗》,科学出版社,2016年。

莎士比亚:《莎士比亚全集·Ⅶ》,朱生豪等译,人民文学出版社,2014年。

褚潇白、成功:《金色传奇:中世纪圣徒文学精选》,浙江大学出版社,2016年。

李赋宁:《古英语史诗〈贝奥武夫〉》,《外国文学》1998年第6期。

布鲁姆、雅法:《莎士比亚的政治》,潘望译,江苏人民出版社,2012年。

李毅:《二十世纪西方〈李尔王〉研究述评》,《四川外语学院学报》1996年第4期。

李正栓、叶红婷:《莎士比亚〈李尔王〉中的伦理》,《外国语文》2023年第6期。

忧惧、绝望和死亡
——《理查三世》中的存在性选择问题

刘慧敏

摘要：莎士比亚历史剧《理查三世》是早期现代人寻找自我存在与形塑意义的经典剧目。剧中理查三世作为道德教化的反面人物，被塑造成为遭受世人唾弃的失败者。然而，通过考察其人物出场戏份及台词占比，结合克尔凯郭尔哲学思想的有关维度，本文认为剧中理查三世的忧惧、绝望情绪与死亡终局思考，实则为读者展示了相对应的存在性选择焦虑，并体现了莎士比亚对早期现代个体主义精神的探索。

关键词：《理查三世》；存在；忧惧；绝望；死亡

基金项目：本文系国家社会科学基金重大项目"十六世纪英国文学研究"（项目编号：22&ZD287）的阶段性研究成果。

作者简介：刘慧敏，河南大学外语学院博士研究生，主要研究方向为文艺复兴时期英国文学和现代主义文学。

一、引言

1485年，"金雀花王朝"最后一位国王理查三世死于和亨利·都铎交战的博斯沃思原野，随后被潦草地埋在一个荒废已久的修道院中。2013年，莱斯特大学考古队通过现代技术，在一片废弃的停车场下找到了理查三世的遗骸。逝世530年后，理查三世终于迎来了符合其国王规格的葬礼。这也算是最终回应了理查三世生前"一匹马！一匹马！

我愿用我的整个王国去换一匹马！"的绝望。

对于这个费尽心机坐上王位,却只有短短787天统治时间的理查三世,托马斯·莫尔爵士在《理查三世史》(*The History of King Richard the Third*, 1513)里是这样描述的:理查德国王本人死在了战场上,诸位看官在后面就会看到,被他的仇敌砍死,死尸在马背上让人拉着,头发让人狠狠地揪拽得像一条杂种狗。[1]除了被称为"杂种狗",理查三世因为身体畸形在后世莎剧中还被辱骂为"野猪"、"驼背的蟾蜍"和"毒胀的蜘蛛"。有不少学者论证过理查三世的畸形身体是一种写作上的隐喻,象征着病态、失序、羸弱的英格兰国体。这种手法不是文艺复兴人的独创,实际上早在古希腊时期,柏拉图在《理想国》中把懈怠战事、痴迷物质享乐的城邦称为"猪的城邦"和"膨胀的、发烧的城邦"。由此可见,无论是在莫尔笔下,还是在莎士比亚的剧本中,理查三世无一例外被凸显成残暴、嗜血的形象,是冷酷无情、渴望权力的恶棍,畸形的怪物,被贬损为动物他者,是邪恶和非道德的表征[2]。500多年来的历史学家和文学评论者普遍同意莫尔和莎士比亚的结论。然而,胜利者所书写的历史,往往因其主观意志而扭曲了真相:失败者通常被描绘成对历史进程无足轻重的小人物。这种扭曲可能发生在最有影响力的人身上,国王也不例外,理查三世也许只是其中之一。笔者通过分析现当代资料,追溯对理查三世的极端负面评价的起源,试图说明理查国王作为一个怪物的形象,在很大程度上是一种文学建构,并结合克尔凯郭尔的哲学思想,揭示出理查三世在不同阶段的内省,将早期现代舞台上的理查三世如何艰难却义无反顾地做出生存性选择作为核心议题。

二、早期现代时期人的个体存在

关于现代性,学者们意见不一,众说纷纭。耶鲁大学的迪普雷教授将现代性的源头追溯到了14世纪后期。在他看来,中世纪后期神学的各种思潮以及早期意大利人文主义,摧毁了将宇宙、人和超验因素结合起来的传统。人变成了意义的唯一来源,而自然则降为客体。[3]这里所说的现代性与人的主体性觉醒有关。另外,哈贝马斯认为,现代性的真正内涵是西方文化由宗教性走向世俗性。刘小枫把现代性阐释为:个体——群

---

[1] 培根:《英王亨利七世本纪》,北京时代华文书局,2016年,第73-74页。
[2] 王晶:《论理查三世畸形身体中的动物他性和国体隐喻》,《外国文学研究》2022年第1期。
[3] See Louis Dupré, *Passage to Modernity: An Essay in the Hermeneutics of Nature and Culture*, New Haven: Yale University Press, 1993, p. 3.

体心性结构和文化制度之质态和形态变化。①可见,尽管大家对现代性的解释不尽相同,现代性的核心主题却是相对稳定的,即精神取向的主体性。

索伦·克尔凯郭尔(Søren Kierkegaard, 1813—1855)关注的是作为一个存在的、有限的人意味着什么。他将这种关注与"内在性"联系在一起。存在主义的许多核心主题和概念——自由、选择、焦虑、绝望和荒诞——都起源于克尔凯郭尔的著作。在克尔凯郭尔的思想中,人自身的内部对立就是他作品里经常提到的内在性,也称主观性。所谓内在性,更多指涉的是个体人面向自己的一种情感体验,严格地说,是个体人面对生存着的自己的一种严肃的关切态度,个人对自身的关切程度不同,表现出来的内在情感也不相同。

对于克尔凯郭尔来说,所有世代以及所有世代中的全部个体,都肩负着同样的任务,他们——每一代人和所有个体——构成了现在的时代。因此,当前的时代是一个被历史所理解的范畴。在这个范畴中,单个个体必须学会对那些区分他们特定时代的问题和辩论作出反应,通过接受他们最基本的任务,成为克尔凯郭尔在《恐惧与颤栗》(*Fear and Trembling*) 中所说的本质上的人。克尔凯郭尔所强调的转型,即是以孤独的、非理性的个人存在取代脱离人的客观物质或理性意识的存在来当作哲学研究的主要内容,以个人的非理性的情感活动,特别是厌烦、忧郁、绝望等悲观情绪代替感性或理性认知,特别是代替黑格尔主义的纯思维、理性和逻辑来作为揭示人与世界及上帝的真谛的出发点,而这也正是他的全部哲学和宗教研究的出发点。②

克尔凯郭尔认为,黑格尔哲学的根本错误在于把"纯逻辑,即纯思维或者说客观精神当做一个具有普遍性和必然性的统一整体和封闭的系统……世界无非是这种客观精神的必然显露……个人的存在也是被决定的……人的道德和宗教情感是普遍理性的附属品"③。这样一来,人实际上丧失了独立性和自主性,失去了做选择和决定的可能性,失去了个性与自由,进而丧失了激情和活力,使人的生活变得越来越平淡无奇,无聊乏味。所以,克尔凯郭尔设置了"个人",即单个的人。换言之,克尔凯郭尔哲学的出发点是在被总体解释的世界中那部分被消除的个人存在感。黑格尔的哲学关注的是宏大而抽象的历史进程,而不是微观而具体的人类。与之相反,克尔凯郭尔并不认为人类自我

---

① 刘小枫:《现代学的问题意识》,《读书》1994年第5期。
② 加迪纳:《克尔凯郭尔》,刘玉红译,译林出版社,2013年,第iii页。
③ 同上书,第iv页。

主要是一种形而上的实体,而更像是一种成就或目标。诚然,人类是某种物质;它们和实物一样存在于世界上。然而,人类自我的独特之处在于,自我必须成为它应该成为的样子,人类自我在定义自己的过程中扮演着积极的角色。克尔凯郭尔发展了一种个体哲学,个人并不需要把自己作为历史长河的一部分,而是作为一个自由的、焦虑的、终有一死的人,努力发现自己荒诞而悲剧性的存在的意义。

在某种意义上,莎剧中的理查三世就是克尔凯郭尔笔下的那个孤独、忧惧并且绝望的个体。

三、理查三世的自我选择

戏剧开篇是理查三世一段有名的独白:"说实话,我在这软绵绵的歌舞升平的时代,却找不到半点赏心乐事以消磨岁月,无非背着阳光窥看自己的阴影,口中念念有词,埋怨我这废体残形。因此,我既无法由我的春心奔放,趁着韶光洋溢卖弄风情,就只好打定主意以歹徒自许,专事仇视眼前的闲情逸致了。"[①](第一幕第一场)莎士比亚总是用许多独白来呈现那些无法与人交流的角色,他们要么邪恶,要么被人疏离,如伊阿古、理查三世及哈姆雷特等人;他们不能与人交谈,只得自言自语。这是莎士比亚借用独白对人物的存在性进行处理。

在这里不妨将科利奥兰纳斯与理查三世做一番比较。莎士比亚通过理查和科利奥兰纳斯两人,展现了他对人类心理最深刻的洞察:要么忠于自我,要么失去自我。理查选择忠于自我,科利奥兰纳斯则选择放弃自我。备受母亲宠爱的科利奥兰纳斯能够放弃自我是因为他尚有余地可退,他悔悟后还能回到亲人的怀抱。理查的母亲公爵夫人却说:"呵,一股阴风播散着苦难!呵!我这可诅咒的肚腹,死亡的苗床,是你产出了一个残害世人的恶怪,他生就一副毒眼,谁也躲避不了他那致命的目光!"(第四幕第一场)被母亲憎恶弃绝的理查无路可退,他的狂妄至极是一种极端个人主义的选择。

其实在《亨利六世》(下篇)中,理查还是葛罗斯特公爵的时候,他内心就被无尽的忧郁侵蚀了,他要找到一条属于自我的出路,即使要虚情假意的欺骗,痛苦的伪装,流下虚伪的泪水,也要不惜一切代价,把所有的幸福寄托在他所梦想的皇冠上面:"在我一生

---

① 笔者注:本文中莎士比亚《理查三世》的译文出自方重译本(《莎士比亚全集》(第6卷),人民文学出版社,2014年;《亨利六世》(下篇)译文出自《莎士比亚全集》(第5卷),人民文学出版社,2014年。

中,直到我把灿烂的王冠戴到我这丑陋的躯体上端的头颅上去以前,我把这个世界看得如同地狱一般。……我在争夺王位的时候饱尝了许多困苦,好比一个迷失在荆棘丛中的人,一面披荆斩棘,一面被荆棘刺伤;一面寻找出路,一面又迷失路途;没法走到空旷的地方,却拼命要把这地方找到。我一定要摆脱这些困苦,不惜用一柄血斧劈开出路。"(第三幕第一场)"我也多次听到我母亲说,我出世的时候是两条腿先下地的:那也难怪,有人夺去了我的权利,我怎能不快走一步把他们打垮?当时接生婆大吃一惊,女人们都叫喊:'呵呀,耶稣保佑我们呀,这孩子生下来就满嘴长了牙齿啦!'我确实是嘴里长牙,这显然表示,我生下来就应该像一条狗那样乱吠乱咬。老天爷既然把我的身体造得这样丑陋,就请阎王爷索性把我的心思也变成邪恶,那才内外一致。"(第五幕第一场)理查自我选择成为一个恶人。为了迎合他的形貌,他决定使自己的内心变得同样丑陋。他就像一个不让观众失望的优秀演员,要在舞台上当众彻底剖开内心的无限恶念与诸般不堪。

理查心里明白,亨利六世之子爱德华的遗孀安夫人在理查巧舌如簧的劝说下,勉强戴上了象征婚姻契约的戒指,但那又怎样呢,安夫人的夫君爱德华年轻、无畏、聪明、高贵无比。"我的所有禀赋怎抵得上半个爱德华呢?我这样一拐一瘸,这样残缺其形?……我只有花费一笔钱,置一面衣镜……让他们推究一下时装,为我打扮起来……照耀着吧,太阳,等我买到了镜子,好让我在镜前端详我的影儿。"(第一幕第二场)为什么理查在这里要买镜子端详自己呢?当他的眼睛盯着镜子中的自己,他的内心活动会有什么变化吗?德尔斐神谕"认识你自己"(Know thyself)的本质就是认识灵魂中最神圣最高贵的部分——理性。苏格拉底在此基础之上,将理性比作眼睛中最重要的部分——瞳孔。他认为,瞳孔是眼睛看到自己的工具,同时瞳孔就像一面镜子,使得眼睛在别人的瞳孔里看到自己的一切。对苏格拉底来说,认识你自己不是指认识你的外表和身体,而是认识你的灵魂,认识灵魂的理性部分。作为一个孤独的、独立的个体,理查的目的无外乎认识他自己。

古罗马哲学家普罗提诺在《九章集》(Enneads)中指出,有生命的东西并不完美,是一种非常贫乏、勉强和粗糙的东西,是在一种更高秩序的堕落沉积物中形成的,这是灵魂对万物的贡献。宇宙中的邪恶是必要的,也许更确切地说,没有邪恶,万物将是不完整的。因为大多数甚至所有形式的邪恶都为宇宙服务——就像毒蛇有它的用途一样——尽管在大多数情况下它们的功能是未知的。罪恶本身有许多有益的方面:它带来许多美好的东西,例如在艺术创作中,它激发我们深思熟虑的生活,不让我们在安全中沉睡。恶是一种绝对匮乏的状态,恶的本源是缺失。逐渐增强的缺失感会导致人向罪恶堕落,而完全匮乏就是绝对的恶了。[1]这种极端的匮乏导致理查嗜血、阴险个性的形成。理查曾诘问众人:"只是为了我不会谄媚或假作殷勤,不会在人前装笑脸,或花言巧语骗人,或者学着法国人那样点头点脑,像猴儿般假装讲礼,于是把我当敌人看待,怀疑我心狠。丑人就该死吗?就一定存心害人吗?"(第一幕第三场)理查三世造物主让理查生就这副皮囊,但他心有不甘,也曾经向上天发问。然而天助者自助,他要为自己的尊严而战,直到鱼死网破。"我真正需要明确的是我要做什么,而不是我必须知道什么……这是理解我自身命运的问题,理解神祇到底想让我做什么,寻找一个对我而言千真万确的真理,找到我愿为之生为之死的念想,我的灵魂就像非洲的沙漠渴望水一样渴望它。"[2]与哲学家克尔凯郭尔一样,理查三世解除了与俗世人的婚约,把自己作为献祭者,像犀牛一样孤独地流浪一生,决定做一个彻底的自我找寻的个体。

四、理查三世的忧惧、绝望和死亡

克尔凯郭尔的观点是,人的选择在于超越寻常生活的有限性,并以内在忧惧、绝望和罪等情感体验为动力。这种选择最终旨在追求与上帝直接面对并成为真正本我,即孤独个体(solitary individual)。内在分裂的程度不同导致自我的情感表达方式各异,克尔凯郭尔将这些扭曲形式称为忧惧、绝望甚至罪,而这些情感反过来又加强了人们的内在性。

托马斯·莫尔爵士的《理查三世史》为1483年王位继承危机的焦点提供了精确的环境细节。但在宫廷内外的官方和半官方资料中,对王子命运的提及仍然是暗指性的,除了表明他们已经死亡,理查对此也负有责任。1485年11月,理查和他的追随者在国会被指控"叛国,杀人,流婴儿血"时,对儿童的杀戮有一个独特的描述。[3]宫廷诗人彼得罗·卡米利亚诺和乔瓦尼·吉利斯评论说:"他残忍地杀害了这些男孩,他们被错误地托

---

[1] 阿尔特:《恶的美学》,宁瑛等译,中央编译出版社,2015年,第27页。
[2] Søren Kierkegaard, *Kierkegaard's Journals and Notebooks*, vol.1, Princeton: Princeton University Press, 2007, p. 22.
[3] R. Horrox, *The Parliament Rolls of Medieval England, 1275-1504, XV: Richard III, 1484-1485 & Henry VII, 1485-1487*, New York: Woodbridge, 2012, p. 107.

付给了他,而他们是'被交给了可怕的冥界之神的受害者'。"[1]相较之下,莫尔戏剧性地、完整地描述了这起谋杀案涉及的人员和下达的命令。莫尔运用人物塑造、对话、演讲和动作,将叙事带入戏剧性焦点。就像一个道德剧中的演员一样,他有时直接与他们讲话,通过强调道德要点和使用一种讽刺的语气来引导他们的反应,首先是俏皮的,然后随着理查的行为变得邪恶而愈加痛苦:

  理查德国王表面上一直生活在痛苦和烦恼之中,内心里则是恐惧、悲痛和忧伤。我曾从他寝宫里他身边的人那里得到可靠消息,说他干过这件坏事以后思想上从来都没有平静过,一直以为自己不安全。

  他外出时,两只眼睛左顾右盼,暗中护着身子,一只手一直握住匕首,其神情和架势就像一个随时准备出手还击的人。他夜里睡不安稳,长时间地醒着想心事,因忧虑重重而疲惫不堪,是打瞌睡而不是沉睡,受到噩梦的折磨,有时突然惊醒,从床上一跃而起,在卧室里跑来跑去。[2]

  在常人眼中,理查三世犹如麦克白夫妇,手刃他人后的战战兢兢、夜不能寐以及被梦魇死死纠缠,这些情感体验皆属于消极范畴;然而对于具有主观意识的个体而言,却具备积极价值。克尔凯郭尔将忧惧和绝望等内在心理经历视为实现个人内在性开启的关键要素,而内在性开启则象征着个体精神的觉醒。这种觉醒所蕴含的重要意义之一是:个人已察觉到自我面对之必要。这种内在恐惧正是克尔凯郭尔所说的"正确恐惧",它引导个体成为精神性的自我。

  理查三世主动选择成为孤独的魔鬼。在《亨利六世》(下篇)中,他说:"我本是个无情无义、无所忌惮的人……老天爷既然把我的身体造得这样丑陋,就请阎王爷索性把我的心思也变成邪恶,那才内外一致。"(第五幕第六场)理查三世不止一次强调他作恶的原因是"内外一致"。既然身体先天不足,相貌丑陋,缺乏母子之爱,也得不到手足之情,没有人能够接受他,因此他无法凭借自身融入社会和家庭,那么何必把自己禁锢在一个

---

[1] H. A. Kelly, *Divine Providence in the England of Shakespeare's Histories*, MA thesis, Cambridge University, 1970, pp. 319. "He, steeped in the blood of his own family, having been dispatched to the waters of the Styx (i.e. killed), appeased the spirits of his small nephews-victims given up to the hideous God of the Underworld, the avenger of crimes".

[2] 培根:《英王亨利七世本纪》,第74页。

有限的、令人窒息的环境里呢？这样只会让人变得消沉、具有奴性和依赖他人。理查的兴趣在于活成怎样的一个人。他的存在既是被动地承受，也是个人内在性焦虑，做出生存性选择的结果。Walk without meeting one single traveler（在成为自我的路上，我们孤身一人）。①在《忧惧的概念》(*The Concept of Anxiety*)②一书中，克尔凯郭尔认为，恐惧是一个人对外界威胁他的事物的担忧，对他的生命、肢体、生计和幸福的无数威胁是他无法控制的。而忧惧是一个人对来自内部、他自己的意识威胁到他的东西的担心。忧惧的人关心的是，如果他有选择的自由，他可能会选择做什么。他被自己的自由和自发性所困扰，意识到没有任何东西可以阻止他在任何时候做出愚蠢、破坏性或不名誉的行为，除非他选择不去做。因此，克尔凯郭尔说，忧惧是自由的眩晕(dizziness)。个体在被孤立的这条路上，面对存在和自由，眩晕、迷失、无措，我们站起来面对可能性的深渊的时候，这种眩晕不仅在深渊，更在内心。克尔凯郭尔没有把忧惧看作病理状态，而把它看作自我道路上必要的因素。

对照另一部莎剧《李尔王》，即便李尔勉强被称得上一个好国王[阿兰·布鲁姆(Allan Bloom)在《莎士比亚的政治》(*Shakespeare's Politics*)中提到，李尔曾是个让国家欣欣向荣的好国王]，但他仍是个僭主，因为他容忍不了自由，容忍不了肆意的善。后来他所付出的惨痛代价便是必须直面肆意的恶。李尔失去事实权力后，质问自己的身份和同一性："这儿有谁认识我吗？……谁能够告诉我我是什么人？"（第一幕第四场）李尔警觉并害怕失去自我。直到在暴风雨之夜离家出走，别人都以为他疯癫了之后，殊不知这才是他真正清醒的时刻。③理查三世无疑罪孽深重、邪恶可恨，他杀光了身边所有的亲信，要弄所有人，这些都是他个人的生存性选择，但他从来没有迷失自我的同一性，他将自我的生存性选择一直坚持到最后。

在克尔凯郭尔的写作以及其日记中详细描述了生存的多种可能性，特别是三个主

---

① Søren Kierkegaard, *Fear and Trembling and The Sickness Unto Death*, Walter Lowrie, trans., Princeton: Princeton University Press, 2013, p. 143.
② 《克尔凯郭尔文集》的译者京不特将此翻译成《恐惧的概念》。他认为应用"恐惧"一词来译Angst/Angest，而不是用诸如"不安""焦虑"等词。这是因为"不安"一词在汉语中的口语特性在这里不适合作为反复出现，而在心理学诊断中被频繁地用到的"焦虑"一词，是心理学上的症状描述词，它是不同于"恐惧"这个概念的。京不特说，在丹麦的高中哲学教学中，为避免对这个概念造成外行想当然的误读，人们常常会特地强调：绝不可混淆心理学临床讨论的Angst（焦虑）和哲学中所讨论的Angst（恐惧），这是两种完全不同的东西。社科院王齐女士称建议使用"忧惧"，京不特给予认可。在此，笔者采用了王齐的翻译。
③ 赫勒：《脱节的时代——作为历史哲人的莎士比亚》，吴亚蓉译，华夏出版社，2020年，第75—76页。

要阶段,他将其称为"生存的境界",即审美、伦理和宗教境界。他的基本观点在于强调:每个人首先必须或者说应该——因为并非每个人都能做到这一点——使自身从被给定的环境当中、从其父母和家庭当中、从其所出生和成长的社会环境当中分离出来。然后,他必须开始历经生存的各个阶段,在此进程之中他将获得其永恒的有效性,成为一个独立的个体。这个个体将成为其自身行动的主体,进而将成长为一个独特的、负有伦理责任的人。[1]莎士比亚通过理查三世这一角色,刻画了一个伦理层面恶人的生存性选择。我们现在必须跟随理查到战场上去,看看他何时才会发现这一终极的生存性失败所带来的致命威胁。如果一个人的生存性选择遭遇失败,那么,他的人格是否也将随之分崩离析?

第五幕第三场,博斯沃思原野,战前深夜,理查三世由噩梦中惊醒,口里嚷着:

再给我一匹马!把我的伤口包扎好!饶恕我,耶稣!且慢!莫非是场梦。呵,良心是个懦夫,你惊扰得我好苦!蓝色的微光。这正是死沉沉的午夜。寒冷的汗珠挂在我皮肉上发抖,怎么!我难道会怕我自己吗?旁边并无别人哪:理查爱理查;那就是说,我就是我。这儿有凶手在吗?没有。有,我就是;那就逃命吧……怎么!自己报复自己吗?呀!我爱我自己……呀!我其实恨我自己……我是个罪犯……犯的是伪誓罪,伪誓罪,罪大恶极;谋杀罪,残酷的谋杀罪,罪无可恕;种种罪行,大大小小,拥上公堂来,齐声嚷道,"有罪!有罪!"

在理查三世的睡梦中,爱德华亲王的幽灵、亨利六世的幽灵、克莱伦斯的幽灵、利弗所、葛雷、伏根、海斯丁斯、两王子、勃金汉的幽灵依次登场,每人都对理查三世扔下了恶狠狠的诅咒:"我要你绝望而死!"同时这些幽灵对里士满说:"你将是个战胜者!""拿起刀枪,为了美好的英吉利""功成名遂!"

"绝望"是克尔凯郭尔哲学思想的一个重要命题。"对尘世的绝望或对尘世事物的绝望,其实也是对永恒和对自己的绝望,因为这是所有绝望的统一公式。"[2]绝望在人世间以多种形态出现,有无意识的,也有有意识的。无意识的绝望仅仅距离救赎和真理更远

---

[1] 克尔凯郭尔:《克尔凯郭尔文集·6》,京不特译,中国社会科学出版社,2013年,第20页。
[2] Søren Kierkegaard, *Fear and Trembling: A Dialectical Lyric and The Sickness Unto Death*, Walter Lowrie, trans., Princeton: Princeton University Press, 2013, p. 349.

一步,当理查三世决定要做一个"表里如一"的畸形怪物时,他并没有意识到绝望。因为他的不自知,以为王权和皇冠这样的雄图伟业是他的寄托,实际上他走上了自我毁灭之路;然而,真正的绝望在某一刻显现:"我只有绝望了。天下无人爱怜我了;我即便死去,也没有一个人会来同情我;当然,我自己都找不出一点值得我自己怜惜的东西,何况旁人呢?"(第五幕第五场)"Either Caesar or nothing",自古以来,成王败寇。理查此时绝望了,也因此无法忍受自己。绝望是最坏的不幸和痛苦,同时,绝望是一种无限的优势。因为绝望意味着人有自我。人越自知,绝望就越强烈;越自知,越是能够断绝绝望。看似矛盾的悖论使查理三世成为一个有内在性的自我。

五、理查三世的美学内涵和社会伦理价值

由于莎士比亚和克里斯托弗·马洛的努力,历史剧作为一种独立的戏剧体裁在16世纪90年代开始腾飞,并且成为伊丽莎白时代最重要的戏剧形式。乔纳森·贝特说:"公共剧院在莎士比亚时代仍然是新鲜事物,它对文化生活带来的重要变革之一就是出现了讲述英国历史的戏剧。这个时期大概从1588年击败西班牙无敌舰队开始。这是普通人第一次有机会了解自己国家的历史。如果他们想获得这方面的知识,最合适的地方就是剧院。"[1]由此可见,在16、17世纪之交的英格兰,历史剧成为剧院招揽看客的宠儿,是剧作家们竞相搬上舞台的对象。

在《理查三世》中有这样一段描写:女人们组成了希腊式的歌队,她们分别是亨利六世的遗孀玛格莱特王后、爱德华王的遗孀伊丽莎白王后、约克公爵夫人(理查、爱德华及克莱伦斯的母亲);安夫人有时也包括在内,她是被杀的华列克的女儿,爱德华亲王的遗孀,理查的现任妻子。在莎士比亚的任何一部剧中,没有哪个角色像理查三世这样,被这么多女人深恶痛绝地诅咒过这么多次。女人的诅咒和辱骂,必定使舞台的观众相信历史上的理查三世不仅相貌极其丑恶,道德上也是罪大恶极。

弗·史雷格尔(Friedrich von Schlegel,1772—1829)说:"有人觉得这个被强烈渲染的性格有时写得太过分夸张和不大可能。但只是那些不知道人心莫测,或是觉得暴露心底隐事是不适合的人,才会下这种评语。观察过大局面的世情动态,愿意对历史进行思

---

[1] 转引自麦克格雷格:《莎士比亚的动荡世界》,范浩译,河南大学出版社,2016年,第93-94页。

考的人,会觉得他的描述太真实了,太可能了"①。不仅是现实与历史的真实,更是逻辑与心理的真实,就是因为真实才具有更加震撼人心的艺术力量。那么,到底什么是历史真实呢?观众难道就没有想过,也许理查三世是都铎王朝历史编纂的最大受害者呢?②

作为一部剧作,《理查三世》无疑是莎士比亚最成功的典范之一。理查三世作为一个君王的形象,自诞生之日起就是深入人心的。那么,这个形象是如何一步步建立起来的呢?

我们知道,莎士比亚的历史剧部分参考霍林谢德(Raphael Holinshed)的《英格兰、苏格兰及爱尔兰编年史》(*The Chronicles of England, Scotland and Ireland*, 1587)的第二版。但就《理查三世》而言,霍林谢德的史料却又来自爱德华·霍尔(Edward Hall)写的《兰开斯特和约克两大名门贵族的联合》(*Union of the Noble and Illustre Famelies of Lancastre and York*, 1548)。书分为八章,各章的题目很值得寻味:第一章"纷扰不安的亨利四世时代";第二章"亨利五世的丰功伟绩";第三章"多事之秋的亨利六世王朝";第四章"爱德华四世王朝的繁荣";第五章"爱德华五世的悲惨命运";第六章"理查三世的悲惨事迹";第七章"亨利七世时代的政治局面";第八章"亨利八世王朝的盛况"。③

而霍尔此书有关理查三世的部分却主要取材于托马斯·莫尔的《理查三世史》。此书原用拉丁文写作,后来又出版了英文本。莫尔书中的理查(葛罗斯特公爵)"在智力和勇气上与两位兄长不相上下,在身体和才能上却比他们差得很远。他身材矮小,四肢难看,弯腰曲背,左肩比右肩高出很多,面目可憎,放在贵族身上称之为尚武,在其他人身上会有别的说法。他恶毒,爱发火,爱妒忌,在娘胎里就倔强。据说真相是他母亲公爵夫人分娩时难产,不动剪刀就不能把他生出来,双脚先来到世上,就像人死后往坟墓里抬时那样,而且(据说)也不是没有牙齿。或是恨他的人说这是真的,或是大自然从他一出生就改变了进程,在他整个一生中,很多事情都做得不合常理"④。莫尔将理查三世描绘成一位未完全发育成熟就倒着出生的畸形怪物,这一描述对后世产生了巨大影响。进一步追溯发现,《理查三世史》的资料来源于伊利主教约翰·莫顿。然而,莫顿却是本剧中里士满(战败理查三世夺取政权后成为亨利七世)的亲信和顾问,在过去曾遭到理查三世的迫害并长期流亡法国。因此,基于心理和政治原因,莫顿可能对理查三世进行

---

① 转引自杨周翰:《莎士比亚评论汇编》(上),中国社会科学出版社,1979年,第318页。
② 徐嘉:《伦敦塔、录事与恺撒:〈理查三世〉的历史书写》,《外国文学评论》2017年第3期。
③ 方重:《关于莎士比亚的〈理查三世〉》,《外国语文》1982年第5期。
④ 培根:《英王亨利七世本纪》,第6—7页。

了贬低。[1]由此可见,莎剧中理查三世的形象是在前人之上的继承和发挥。

然而,脱去君主的外衣,是否可以隐去偏见,接近一个相对真实的理查三世呢?

根据考证,1484年5月,波西米亚骑士尼古拉斯·范·波佩罗与理查会面。他对理查的外貌描述如下:"理查比他要高三个手指的高度,身材修长,手和脚也很精致。"从尼古拉斯·范·波佩罗的陈述中可以看出,他未提及理查畸形的身体和外貌问题,并且理查给予他舒适印象。苏格兰代表阿奇博尔德·怀特洛在1484年对于理查三世的描写如下:"您是我见过的所有的君主中最为宁静的王子和国王,您拥有最为高贵的名望,且美誉已传到世界上的每一个角落。而且,您拥有最高的正义和伟大的心灵。您还有着难以置信的智慧,这不仅仅是人类的,而是神圣。"从怀特洛的陈述来看,并未涉及理查三世的身体状况,主要称赞其崇高心灵和美德,并将其声誉提升至神圣层次。[2]后世史学家考证,理查三世虽然在位仅两年,但他展现出了非凡的政治才华,而且在推动司法领域无罪推定原则、保释制度等方面发挥过积极作用。

因此,我们不妨认为,莫尔作为学者、圣人和殉道者的声誉,帮助这本传记在接下来的两个世纪里形成了对理查的普遍看法。莫尔在他心目中对反秩序的暴君形象进行了单一化处理,然而实际上,理查三世的真实形象可能并非如此简单。迪安曾指出,在莫尔所写的《理查三世史》中,对于理查三世的描绘始终保持一致,但其实际个性是极其复杂多样的。[3]都铎时期成书的《伦敦大编年史》(*The Great Chronicle of London*)表达了人们对于理查三世遗憾之情:如果他能够以护国公身份忠诚正直地辅佐爱德华四世之子享有荣耀和权势,那么他将会比任何人更加受到尊重和赞扬。然而现在,他却被公开谴责,并失去了人们对他的尊敬(Dockray, 1997)[4]。历史学家也就理查三世登基后的表现给予客观评价。例如,丘吉尔肯定了理查三世政绩:节俭生活、限制奢华场面、宽恕败在手下者、关怀贫困民众。

像许多人文主义学者一样,莫尔坚信历史和文学在教育中的中心地位,并坚持认为,文科的学习对学者的精神和智力发展有直接的影响。莫尔在给牛津大学的信中

---

[1] 孙法理:《从吴宓三境说看莎士比亚〈理查三世〉的创作》,《中国比较文学》1995年第2期。

[2] Kenneth Muir, *The Sources of Shakespeare's Plays*, London: Methuen & Co.Ltd, 1977.转引自周良睿:《〈理查三世〉的史料溯源——以托马斯·莫尔的〈国王理查三世史〉为例》,《作家天地》2020年第15期。

[3] Leonard F. Dean, "Literary Problems in More's 'Richard Ⅲ'," in R.S. Sylvester and Mare'hadour, eds., *Essential Articles for the Study of Thomas More*, Connecticut: Shoestring Press, 1977, p. 318.

[4] Keith Dockray, *Richard Ⅲ: A Source Book*, Bridgend: Sutton Publishing Limited, 1997, p. 12.

(1518)写道:"文科课程'为未来做灵魂的准备。'"[1]理查与这种理解的关联是深刻的,因为他在莫尔的叙事框架内使读者面对自己对暴政本质的评估,并进一步将暴政视为政治文化的产物。通过识别确实经历了社会和心理转变过程的人物,莫尔邀请他的观众与演员形成认同,这些演员被感动去尝试道德行为,从而弥合政治文化与更广泛的道德和伦理责任之间的固有差距。

莎士比亚的《理查三世》影响着人们对历史上金雀花王朝的看法,以及当代人们对理查三世如何在历史和文学写作传统中被视为人物的理解。当然,部分原因是莎士比亚在文化上的无处不在,以及他作为早期现代英国文学代表人物的地位。此外,莎士比亚笔下的理查身上还有很多特质,这些特质使他产生了一种个人魅力,从而成为评论界的磁石。

许多学者认为莎剧《理查三世》(*The Tragedy of King Richard the Third*)写成于《亨利六世》三联剧之后,或许作于1592年6月剧院因瘟疫而关闭之前不久。该剧是莎士比亚为宫内大臣剧团所创作的首部剧作。宫内大臣剧团创办于1594年夏天瘟疫过后剧院重新开张之时。四开本出版于1597年,其标题就彰显出该剧的内容:《理查三世的悲剧。包含他以奸诈的阴谋谋害他的兄长克拉伦斯;对他无辜侄子的残忍谋杀;他残暴的篡位;他可耻的一生,以及罪有应得的死亡。近来由陛下之仆从宫内大臣剧团献演》(*The Tragedy of King Richard the third. Containing, His treacherous Plots against his brother Clarence: the pittiefull murther of his innocent nephewes: his tyrannicall vsurpation: with the whole course of his detested life, and most deserued death. As it hath beene lately Acted by the Right honourable the Lord Chamberlaine his seruants*)。1598年重印时,标题页上出现了莎士比亚的名字(是首批以这种方式署名的印刷版戏剧之一),后又于1602年、1605年、1612年、1622年、1629年和1634年多次再版,证明了该剧受欢迎的程度。[2]

《理查三世》当时的流行离不开社会物质媒介的支撑。印刷书籍的传播渐趋增强。

---

[1] Thomas More, "Thomas More's 1518 Letter to the University of Oxford," in *CW* 15,139 (editor's translation). This understanding of the significance of the arts is not unique to More; cf. Erasmus, "Oration on the Pursuit of Virtue",Brad Inwood, trans., in Elaine Fantham and Erika Rummel with the assistance of Jozef IJsewijn, eds., *Collected Works of Erasmus*, vol. 29, Toronto: University of Toronto Press, 1989, pp. 3-13, esp. 5-9.

[2] 莎士比亚:《理查三世》,孟凡君译,外语教学与研究出版社,2016年,第7-8页。

这一新型媒介与16世纪英格兰文化、政治、经济变革间存在着频繁互动关系。英语印刷品进入政权运作体系。印刷商们都看出这个题材有市场:莎士比亚历史剧的印数相当于其他所有戏剧的总和。此外,还有一些因素对它们的普及起到了推动作用:这些剧本被认为有用,以史实为依据——有人甚而提出——有教化公民的功能。这种说法为剧院经营者提供了很好的武器,对抗批评舞台败坏世风的清教人士。1612年,剧作家托马斯·海伍德在《为演员一辩》中就机智地运用了这一论点:

  戏剧使愚盲之人明锐;使无识者知晓吾国之胜绩:即目不识丁,无由读大事纪年者亦得教诲。试问今日贩夫走卒之中,凡稍有头绪者,尚有谁人于史事不能赞一言耶?盖征服王威廉以降,甚而早至罗马人临岛,至今之诸般大事,剧中皆有言及。此即戏剧之意旨,亦其法度也:使民忠于其君;使知犯上作乱者必不得善终;使知顺从圣意则天恩浩荡,教其忠诚良实,不得作奸犯科也。①

  也就是说,站在剧院里观看历史剧的人们是在学习如何成为奉公守法的好公民,更重要的是学习如何成为女王的忠实臣属。②

  事实上,由于莫尔和莎剧等对理查三世的刻板印象日趋深入人心,直到都铎王朝末期,肩膀不平整的人已约定俗成地被称为"驼背理查",隐喻身体、灵魂都是怪异弯曲的。《牛津英语大词典》中引证《理查三世》作为词条"驼背"的来源。③然而,根据2013年的考古发现和头骨复原,理查三世的五官并没有异于常人,跛脚和手臂萎缩也是子虚乌有,剧中人人喊他驼背丑八怪实在是污名化的表现。而且他虽身材偏瘦,身高却也有五英尺九英寸(约1.75米),也算不上十分矮小。最重要的是,这项发现只能证明理查脊柱

---

① 麦克格雷格:《莎士比亚的动荡世界》,第96-97页。
② 同上书,第97-98页。
③ See Maev Kennedy and Lin Foxhall, *The Bone of a King: Richard Ⅲ Rediscovered*, Boston: Wiley Blackwell, 2015, p. 132.

侧弯①，却丝毫不能表明他驼背。由此可见，理查作为"驼背"一词的源头，本身并不驼背。

六、结语

艾略特在《莎士比亚和塞内加的斯多葛主义》一文中写道："谈到像莎士比亚这样一位伟大的人物，也许我们永远也谈不出真相来……我个人的浅薄意见是，莎士比亚在私生活中所持的意见，跟我们从他那极端富于变化的、发表了的作品中摘录下来的一段两段，有极大的出入。我以为，在他的作品中并没留下什么线索。"②因此我们看到在不同时代，莎士比亚是说不尽的，人们对莎剧也产生了迥异甚至矛盾的理解。诚然如此。"莎士比亚从不明确表明立场……他同情怀疑主义者，对极度绝望的人有着深刻的理解，唯有对厌世主义者敬而远之"③。从这个层面讲，理查三世在生存性选择问题上即使体验着无可言说的忧惧、绝望，在无数人的咒骂中死去，但他绝不是一个厌世主义者。也许正是基于这个原因，莎剧《理查三世》的魅力在悠久的历史沉淀中经久不衰，积累了丰厚的艺术遗产。

参考文献

Erasmus, "Oration on the Pursuit of Virtue", Brad Inwood, trans., in Elaine Fantham and Erika Rummel with the assistance of Jozef IJsewijn, eds., *Collected Works of Erasmus*, vol. 29, Toronto: University of Toronto Press, 1989.

H. A. Kelly, *Divine Providence in the England of Shakespeare's Histories*, MA thesis, Cambridge University, 1970.

---

① 笔者在此处联想到李永毅在翻译维吉尔《农事诗》的过程中发现的一个有趣现象，并以此区分好马和劣马：duplex agitur per lumbos spina，直译：（它）双重的脊柱沿着腰部延伸。然而马不可能有两道脊柱，马的骨骼结构图显示脊柱只有一条。Conington 的注疏说，这是一种 hollow 的脊柱，这里英文的 hollow 也不是"空的"，而是"凹陷的"。他还引用瓦罗的话，说不好的马腰椎是 extans（外凸的）。所以，维吉尔的意思可能是，好马腰部肌肉发达，脊柱位于肌肉之间的凹槽里。人也一样，瘦弱的人，脊柱会突出，健壮的人，脊柱的棱会隐藏，看起来凹陷下去。那么，身体作为一种伦理或者政治隐喻，理查三世被塑造为脊柱外突，是否是莎翁有意为之呢？
② T. S. Eliot, "Shakespeare and the Stoicism of Seneca", in *Selected Essays*, New York: Harcourt, Brace &World, Inc,1964, pp. 107−110.
③ 赫勒：《脱节的时代——作为历史哲人的莎士比亚》，第106页。

Keith Dockray, *Richard III: A Source Book*, Bridgend: Sutton Publishing Limited, 1997.

Leonard F. Dean, "Literary Problems in More's 'Richard III'", in R.S. Sylvester and Mare' hadour, eds., *Essential Articles for the Study of Thomas More*, Connecticut: Shoestring Press, 1977.

Louis Dupré, *Passage to Modernity: An Essay in the Hermeneutics of Nature and Culture*, New Haven: Yale University Press, 1993.

Maev Kennedy and Lin Foxhall, *The Bone of a King: Richard III Rediscovered*, Boston: Wiley Blackwell, 2015.

R. Horrox, *The Parliament Rolls of Medieval England, 1275-1504, XV: Richard III, 1484-1485 & Henry VII, 1485-1487*, New York: Woodbridge, 2012.

Søren Kierkegaard, *Fear and Trembling and The Sickness Unto Death*, Walter Lowrie, trans., Princeton: Princeton University Press, 2013.

Søren Kierkegaard, *Kierkegaard's Journals and Notebooks*, vol.1, Princeton: Princeton University Press, 2007.

T. S. Eliot, "Shakespeare and the Stoicism of Seneca", in *Selected Essays*, New York: Harcourt, Brace & World, Inc, 1964.

Thomas More, "Thomas More's 1518 Letter to the University of Oxford", in CW 15,139 (editor's translation).

培根:《英王亨利七世本纪》,北京时代华文书局,2016年。

王晶:《论理查三世畸形身体中的动物他性和国体隐喻》,《外国文学研究》2022年第1期。

莎士比亚:《理查三世》,孟凡君译,外语教学与研究出版社,2016年。

刘小枫:《现代学的问题意识》,《读书》1994年第5期。

加迪纳:《克尔凯郭尔》,刘玉红译,译林出版社,2013年。

阿尔特:《恶的美学》,宁瑛等译,中央编译出版社,2015年。

赫勒:《脱节的时代——作为历史哲人的莎士比亚》,吴亚蓉译,华夏出版社,2020年。

克尔凯郭尔:《克尔凯郭尔文集·6》,京不特译,中国社会科学出版社,2013年。

麦克格雷格:《莎士比亚的动荡世界》,范浩译,河南大学出版社,2016年。

杨周翰:《莎士比亚评论汇编》(上),中国社会科学出版社,1979年。

徐嘉:《伦敦塔、录事与恺撒:〈理查三世〉的历史书写》,《外国文学评论》2017年第3期。

方重:《关于莎士比亚的〈理查三世〉》,《外国语文》1982年第5期。

孙法理:《从吴宓三境说看莎士比亚〈理查三世〉的创作》,《中国比较文学》1995年第2期。

周良睿:《〈理查三世〉的史料溯源——以托马斯·莫尔的〈国王理查三世史〉为例》,《作家天地》2020年第15期。

文本、理论、跨学科研究

莎士比亚十四行诗的迷雾与猜想

罗朗

摘要：莎士比亚的十四行诗是莎士比亚三年友谊和爱情的象征，是一系列充满个性化激情的描述，是莎士比亚三十岁以前最难忘的一段人生经历。这段人生经历了很多坎坷起伏，充满了很多鲜为人知的谜团。但是，透过这些诗行的描述，可以大体还原莎士比亚的情感经历和思想状况，反映他所经历的一段情感隐伤。也许正是这段情感隐伤，这段强烈的感情冲突，激发了他的创作灵感，使他创作出《罗密欧与朱丽叶》这部伟大的爱情悲剧。

关键词：莎士比亚；十四行诗；南安普顿伯爵；《罗密欧与朱丽叶》

作者简介：罗朗，西南大学外国语学院副教授，硕士生导师，主要研究方向为英美诗歌、欧美城市研究、背包客文化、旅行研究。

1600年，一首诗在英国流行——克里斯托弗·马娄的《多情牧童致恋人》(The Passionate Shepherd to His Love)传唱一时，脍炙人口。诗人借牧童之口，抒发对美丽女子的追求，对美好爱情的向往，充满了富有浪漫气息的田园乐趣。诗歌开篇直抒胸臆："来跟我同住，做我的爱侣"[①](Come live with me and be my love)。没有任何拐弯抹角，也没有婉转暗示，而是直奔主题，直抒胸臆。表明目的后，诗人开始耐心做情人的思想工作，细数这样的田园牧歌可以给他们的爱情带来多少乐趣：

我要用玫瑰花做成床铺，

---

① 屠岸：《英国历代诗歌选》，译林出版社，2007年，第42页。

再编制千百个芬芳的花束；

……

一件细羊毛制成的长袍，

……

腰带是香草和藤苞织成，

扣结是珊瑚，琥珀作饰品。①

从玫瑰花床到羊毛长袍，从琥珀香草的腰带到珊瑚琥珀等饰品，一切来自大自然的馈赠，都是他献给恋人的礼物。除此之外，牧羊人还有一套比较珍贵的器具：盛满食物的银盘、纯金的鞋扣，还有象牙桌子。这些尊贵的小器具，足以说明牧羊人并非一贫如洗，取自大自然的馈赠，也足以积累一定的财富。牧羊人通过层层递进的叙述，描绘了一幅充满田园风光的画卷，而他给恋人献上的花床、长袍、腰带、鞋扣等充满温情的礼物，也足以打动一位少女的芳心。

这首诗的艺术魅力非常强大，从各方面讲，都是一首完美的诗。从音律上看，该诗音律和谐，双行押韵，采用四音部抑扬格，读起来非常上口，适合朗读，也适合歌唱，音调婉转，旋律优美。从结构上看，它的篇幅正好，既不太长，也不太短，7个诗节，每节4行，共28行，正好把牧羊人的感情淋漓尽致地抒发出来。全诗层层递进，先从峰峦、林野、小溪等自然环境开始，过渡到玫瑰花床、香桃裙裾、羊毛长袍、香草腰带等自然馈赠，再到银盘珍馐、五月歌舞等快乐活动，描写的场景从自然风光到温柔梦乡，感染力强，很难不会打动一位少女的心扉。

克里斯托弗·马娄不愧是"大学才子"，不仅这首诗非常出色，其他如《浮士德博士的悲剧》《帖木儿大帝》《马耳他的犹太人》等作品，都热情奔放、雄浑有力、气势恢弘，是英国舞台上颇具影响力的作品。如果马娄不是英年早逝(年仅29岁)的话，他很可能成为莎士比亚最有力的竞争者，双方在诗歌艺术和舞台艺术上都可以一较高下。

由于这首诗广泛流行，在当时就出现了许多仿诗，其中最有名的是沃尔特·雷利爵士的仿诗。沃尔特·雷利爵士是伊丽莎白女王的宠臣，探索过新大陆，为英国占领了弗吉尼亚，又因和女王的侍女私自通婚而被关进伦敦塔，是当时众人瞩目的朝臣。他的仿

---

① 屠岸：《英国历代诗歌选》，第42页。另可参考胡家峦：《英美诗歌名篇详注》，中国人民大学出版社，2008年，第27-30页。

诗《林中仙女答牧童》(*The Nymph's Reply to the Shepherd*)以一种玩笑的口吻讥讽了马娄。他以这样的方式开始假设:

如果世界和爱情不变老,
如果牧羊人的话都可靠,①
但是很快他就推翻了这样的假设:
但河(水)会泛滥,山石会变冷,
……
花(儿)枯萎凋谢,葱茏的大地
屈服于寒冬的任意算计;②

美丽的田园风光也会变成一片荒芜,花儿在冬天的肆虐下枯萎凋谢。至于那些温情脉脉的礼物,"你那玫瑰床、花束和长袍,你那绣花的裙子和鞋帽,很快会干枯、破旧、被遗忘——"(Thy gowns, thy shoes, thy beds of roses/ Thy cap, thy kirtle, and thy posies/ Soon break, soon wither, soon forgotten...)。

雷利爵士先从美丽的自然风光开始,转而说明美丽风光也会消逝,寒冬亦会降临大地,然后逐一细数那些温情的自然馈赠,指出这些东西也很容易干枯破损。因此,牧羊人承诺的这些田园乐趣实际上难以实现,他以嬉戏的口吻嘲讽了马娄的天真。

这首仿诗的构思比较精巧,雷利爵士采用了与马娄的诗歌相同的结构,提到了马娄原诗提到的那些田园乐趣:玫瑰花床、长袍、花束、绣花裙、腰带、珊瑚扣、琥珀钉等。但他把全诗的基调改变了,这些田园乐趣在寒风的摧残下,不堪一击。自然美景中既有春天的温暖,亦有冬天的寒冷萧瑟。他写道:"(既)是春的美梦,(亦)是秋的苦辛。"(Is fancy's spring, but sorrow's fall.)

雷利爵士以林中仙女的口吻作答牧羊人,因为林中仙女和田园牧歌正好契合,林中仙女是青春和美丽的象征,也是牧羊人心中完美的爱恋对象。而林中仙女所拥有的青春和美丽,是不会随着岁月的改变而改变的。这正是牧羊人的田园世界所不具有的性

---

① 参考黄杲炘:《恋歌:英美爱情诗萃》,上海译文出版社,2002年,第81页。黄杲炘没有把"nymph"翻译成"林中仙女",而是翻译成"美女",他把标题译成"美女答牧羊人",但是笔者觉得这样翻译欠妥,因为"林中仙女答牧童"更为贴切。
② 黄杲炘:《恋歌:英美爱情诗萃》,第82页。

质和特征,两者形成了强烈反差。

而且,林中仙女还是智慧的象征。这种智慧不仅让她看到了田园风光美丽的一面,也看到了田园牧歌脆弱的另一面。世间万物,不仅有春光明媚,也有寒霜萧瑟。因此,牧羊人的田园乐趣带有欺骗性质,他以一些足以打动人心的小乐趣,以及美丽的承诺,骗取少女的纯真。而林中仙女以智慧的眼光,拆穿了牧羊人的这些小把戏,揭露了牧羊人的不良动机。诗中准确地写道:"(这些)都在痴想中生,理智中亡。"(In folly ripe, in reason rotten.)

因此,雷利爵士的这首仿诗,以同样的结构、精巧的构思,有力地回击了马娄原诗。他以林中仙女的口吻,揭示了事物的另一方面,是对原诗的有力补充。

对于这首诗,玄学派诗人约翰·多恩(也译为约翰·但恩)也觉得意犹未尽,他也写了一首仿诗。在《诱饵》(The Bait)一诗中,他写道:

金色的沙滩,水晶般溪流,
……河水将汩汩流淌,
…… 在那里着迷的鱼儿徘徊,
央求着要把自个儿出卖。①

这首仿诗中,约翰·多恩把抒情场景完全改变了,田园风光变成了河流湿地,青青草原变成了芦苇鱼塘。草地绵羊消失不见了,取而代之的是沙滩芦苇和鱼儿。

约翰·多恩改变了整首诗的氛围。这首诗把牧羊人和仙女的对话,变成了一场渔夫和鱼儿的较量,原本充满诗情画意的浪漫表白,却变成了一场尔虞我诈的钓与被钓的人生游戏。而且这些鱼儿的行为,也显得如此不可思议,竟然"央求着"要把自个儿出卖。欲望的主体变成了客体,客体变成了主体,施动者成了被动者,被动者又成了主动者。正反互换,阴阳倒置,这样的玄学奇喻,已经颠覆了传统的逻辑关系,模糊了"捉"与"被捉"的界限,模糊了"俘"与"被俘"的角色转换,究竟是"庄周梦蝶",抑或"蝶梦庄周",无可名状了。

1609年,伦敦一个出版商托马斯·索普(T.T.)出版了一本包含莎士比亚154首十四行诗的小册子。但是莎士比亚的研究者却发现,这部诗集与众不同。在一些莎士比亚

---

① 但恩:《约翰·但恩诗集》(修订本),傅浩译,译文出版社,2016年,第131页。

研究学者看来,这部诗集迷雾重重。首先,这部诗集的版权似乎不在莎士比亚手中,而是在出版商索普手中。其次,这部诗集出版之后是一片沉默,莎士比亚没有任何评论,这部诗集也没有再版。而与之相对应的是,莎士比亚其他两部长诗却多次再版。因此,1609年版本至今只有13本存世。①

莎士比亚研究学者罗益民教授专门对此书版本展开了研究。他展示了1609年的版本和1640年的伪本,并指出这两个版本中的许多细节问题,探讨了莎士比亚十四行诗的版权、存伪、主题方面的诸多问题。②

如果我们仔细阅读这部诗集,可以发现这部诗集存在多组相关诗群,并形成不同组诗。这些组诗表达了不同的主题和思想感情,需要读者联系起来阅读。从第1首到第17首,反复规劝一位男子早点儿结婚,好让自己的美貌后继有人;从第18首到第126首,反复表达对这位青年男子的爱慕之情。这位男子有着惊人的美貌、极高的门第,诗人好像是被社会遗弃之人,对这位青年的友谊使他获得了很大安慰。

如果仔细阅读十四行诗第18首至第126首,可以发现诗人跌宕起伏的情感,复杂细腻的情绪,特殊的情感体验。在第20首中,他提到这位男士有一个非常显著的特征:"你有女性的脸儿""你有女性的好心肠""你的眼睛比女儿眼明亮,诚实""你风姿特具,掌握了一切风姿/迷住了男儿眼,同时震撼了女儿魂"。③

这首诗准确地描写了这位男子的气质,不是英俊挺拔的男子气概,而是散发出一种女性柔美的气质。这种独特气质,不仅吸引了女士们,也吸引了男士们的目光,莎士比亚遇到的不是一个普通之人。我们要知道,南安普顿伯爵是英国贵族中爵位很高的贵族,往往跟王室有姻亲关系,一般会在伊丽莎白女王的御前侍奉。所以,莎士比亚能够结识这样的人物,对他的事业发展至关重要。

1591年,27岁的莎士比亚结识了18岁的南安普顿伯爵。这位伯爵8岁丧父,继承爵位,受财政大臣伯利勋爵监护,入学剑桥大学,研修法律。他长相英俊,年轻貌美,正值青春年华,风流倜傥。哈佛大学莎学家斯蒂芬·格林布拉特(Stephen Greenblatt)曾提

---

① Robert Giroux, *The Book Known as Q: A Consideration of Shakespeare's Sonnets*, New York: Vintage Books, 1982, pp. 3–12.
② 参阅罗益民:《莎士比亚十四行诗版本批评史》,科学出版社,2016年。
③ 莎士比亚:《莎士比亚十四行诗》,屠岸译,外语教学与研究出版社,2012年,第41页。另外,本文其他引用莎士比亚十四行诗的地方,皆参考此书译文,引用的译文不再重复书名信息,只标注译者姓名和页码。

道:"最近发现了南安普顿伯爵的一幅肖像画,非常生动地刻画了这位年轻伯爵的形象。他确实如莎士比亚十四行所刻画的那样,几乎被人们认为是一幅女子的肖像画。过去的读者曾认为这是莎士比亚夸张的笔法,而这幅肖像画有力地证明了莎翁并非言过其实,而是的确如此。"①

莎士比亚是如何结识这位年轻伯爵的,历史资料没有说明。根据格林布拉特的猜测,这位伯爵是一位戏剧爱好者,常常前往剧院看戏。因为欣赏莎士比亚的演出,可能亲自前往后台主动结识了莎士比亚,两人结为好友。②还有一件事情也说明了这些情况:1591年,伯利勋爵想把孙女嫁给这位伯爵,伯爵母亲也想攀附权臣,促其成婚,但是南安普顿伯爵本人却推脱不允。

因此,我们看到从第1首到第17首,十四行诗的主题非常明确,极力规劝这位伯爵结婚生子,不要耽误青春时光。伯利勋爵的美意,伯爵母亲的劝说,都没有让这位伯爵转变心意。无奈之下,伯爵母亲只有求助于莎士比亚。此时,莎士比亚刚刚结识南安普顿。南安普顿伯爵不仅风流倜傥,还喜爱文学艺术。此时的莎士比亚在戏剧舞台上崭露头角。他和南安普顿年纪相仿,爱好一致,两人相谈甚欢,非常投缘。③也许伯爵母亲意识到了这一点儿,才托莎士比亚充当说客,撮合这门婚事。在第3首十四行诗中,莎士比亚确实提到了他的母亲:

你是你母亲的镜子,她在你身上
唤回了自己可爱的青春四月天。

(屠岸,第7页)

作为文艺保护人,莎士比亚选择十四行诗作为劝婚手段,既新潮又时髦,还体现了门客价值,确是一种独特的手段。南安普顿伯爵的这门婚事是门当户对的。伯利勋爵的爵位也不低,而且还是女王的财政大臣,他把孙女许配给伯爵,自然是好上加好的婚事。但南安普顿本人却不乐意,这让大家都很尴尬。因此,在其母亲的恳求下,莎士比亚写下了第一批十四行诗,劝他莫负青春,早日成婚。莎士比亚在诗中哀叹:

---

① See Stephen Greenblatt, *Will in the World: How Shakespeare Became Shakespeare*, New York: W. W. Norton & Company, 2004, p. 231.
② Ibid, pp. 226-232.
③ Ibid, pp. 234-255.

这就在丰收的地方造成了饥馑,
你是跟自己作对,教自己受害。

(屠岸,第3页)

莎士比亚以诗歌的语言,埋怨了这位不婚之人。能够和权臣的孙女结婚,这是人人向往的姻缘,却被年轻的伯爵推却。因此,莎士比亚在诗中责备:"温柔的自私者,用吝啬浪费了全部。"(And tender churl, mak'st waste in niggarding.)众人的劝说,勋爵的压力,母亲的催促,还有莎士比亚的十四行诗,都没能挽回南安普顿伯爵的心意。莎士比亚就以这样的方式,卷入了一位高门贵族的家事之中。

有一点儿应该注意,在第17首和第18首之间,出现了一个大大的停顿。17首以前都是非常强烈的劝婚诗,18首之后劝婚的声音消失了。如何解释这个细节?我们只能推测,也许伯爵和莎士比亚有过一番深入交流,伯爵详述了他不能选择这门婚事的理由,因此从18首之后,莎士比亚再没有进行劝婚。

虽然莎士比亚劝婚的热心遇冷,但是两个年轻人之间的交流却日渐频繁。读者可以感觉到,南安普顿伯爵钦佩莎士比亚的艺术才能,而莎士比亚钦慕伯爵的风流倜傥,两人惺惺相惜,俨然已是对方知己。在第22首中,我们读到这样的诗行:

我俩的心儿都交换在对方的胸膛里;
那么,我怎么还能够比你年长?
……
我将小心在胸中守着你的心,
像乳娘情深,守护着婴儿无恙。

(屠岸,第45页)

关于南安普顿拒婚的原因,可能是多方面的。也许伯爵本人并没有看上勋爵的孙女,也许他并不急于建立家庭,他宣称的理由是想追随埃塞克斯伯爵,建立军功,追求荣誉。

埃塞克斯伯爵是女王宠臣,是伊丽莎白朝堂上的一个重要人物,也是南安普顿伯爵崇拜的对象。1588年,西班牙的"无敌舰队"被英国海军击溃,女王非常高兴,特意在威斯敏斯特举办了"持矛骑马比赛",以庆祝这个历史性的胜利,23岁的埃塞克斯伯爵主持了这场盛大的祝捷仪式。1596年6月，埃塞克斯参与英国海军行动，袭击西班牙加的斯港，占领该城，建立了军功。1597年8月，埃塞克斯率领英国舰队远征西班牙亚速尔群岛，南安普顿跟随前往，任花环号舰长。1598年8月，爱尔兰发生叛乱，埃塞克斯被任命为爱尔兰总督，率军征讨，南安普顿随行前往。此时的两位伯爵不仅是密友，也是女王倚重的宠臣，地位和名誉达到了顶峰。[1]

因此，莎士比亚能够攀上这样的权贵，对他来说是莫大的荣幸。他明白文艺赞助者和庇护人的重要性，专门写长诗《维纳斯与阿多尼斯》《鲁克丽丝受辱记》公开献给这位伯爵。不仅如此，他还提笔写下126首十四行诗献给这位年轻贵族。其中，在第37首中，他写道：

> 因为不论美、出身、财富，或智力，
> 或其中之一，或全部，或还不止，
> 都已经在你的身上登峰造极，
> ……
> 既然我从你的丰盈获得了满足，
> 又凭着你全部光荣的一份而生活，
> ……
> 我就不残废也不穷，再没人小看我。
>
> （屠岸，第75页）

这首诗充分说明了这位伯爵朋友的身份地位，所拥有的财富，当然还有俊美的外貌和过人的心智。诗人从他的友谊中，获得了巨大的满足和光荣，当然可能还有不少额外的资助，这是问题的关键。

据考证，这些十四行诗大概写于1592年到1594年，莎士比亚28岁到30岁之间。评论家提到，1592年至1594年正是伦敦腺鼠疫大流行的时期，伦敦剧院全部关闭。那个时期，谁也无法确定这些剧院在何时可以重新开张。公共聚会被禁止，演出场所被关闭。在这种情况下，莎士比亚不仅担心自己的收入来源，同时也担心作为一个戏剧家的发展前途。因此，他转而开始创作诗歌，并以当时流行的方式公开献诗。这方面的证据

---

[1] 参阅《莎士比亚全集·第8卷》，孙法理、辜正坤译，译林出版社，1998年，第433—449页。

是非常确凿的,《维纳斯与阿多尼斯》在1593年出版,《鲁克丽丝受辱记》在1594年出版。从这两首长诗的出版情况和长诗之前的献诗题记来看,确是莎士比亚的手笔,也确是献给南安普顿伯爵的。也就是说,莎士比亚创作这两首长诗的时期,也正是他写下一百多首十四行诗的时期。这两个时期的创作是重叠的、交织的、交互进行的。而且实际情况也证明,《维纳斯与阿多尼斯》和《鲁克丽丝受辱记》非常成功。前者在莎士比亚在世之时至少出了九版,后者出了六版,非常畅销。

《维纳斯与阿多尼斯》取材于古罗马诗人奥维德《变形记》的第十卷,全诗共1194行,由199个六行体小诗节组成。该诗描写了爱神维纳斯向美少年阿多尼斯求爱,可是阿多尼斯却一心一意要去打猎的故事。结果故事的结尾是,阿多尼斯被狂奔的豪猪戳死,化作一朵银莲花。这个故事的寓意本身和他写的第一组十四行诗的劝婚之意是相同的,只是十四行诗非常直接,而这首神话诗则比较委婉。阿多尼斯象征着年轻英俊的南安普顿伯爵,维纳斯象征着爱情,阿多尼斯的打猎象征着伯爵一心想要追求军功,追求荣誉。可是战争的风险极大,不确定因素很多。莎士比亚借用这个神话故事提醒年轻的伯爵,不要意气用事,要珍惜生命,珍惜爱情。

十四行诗和两首长诗都写于1592年到1594年,此时正是莎士比亚和南安普顿伯爵关系最好的一个时期。但是十四行诗不同于两首长诗,两首长诗是文艺作品,公开出版,公开献诗,是诗人向文艺庇护者表达敬意的一种方式;十四行诗则是私下传阅,个体阅读,类似于私人信件之类的一种表达方式。实际上,莎士比亚本人未曾料想这些私人化的十四行诗会被人出版。除第一组劝婚诗之外,莎士比亚在其后的诗中更加强烈地表达了他的情绪。

第29首中,他写道:

我偶尔想到了你呵,——我的心怀
顿时像破晓的云雀从阴郁的大地
冲上了天门,歌唱起赞美诗来;

(屠岸,第59页)

第40首中,他写道:

把我对别人的爱全拿去吧,爱人;

你拿了,能比你原先多点儿什么?
你拿不到你唤做真爱的爱的,爱人;
你就不拿,我的也全都是你的。

(屠岸,第81页)

第43首中,他写道:

不见你,个个白天是漆黑的黑夜,
梦里见到你,夜夜放白天的光烨!

(屠岸,第87页)

对于这种强烈的感情表达,后世批评家,特别是20世纪的评论家,常常将其解读为同性恋倾向。

可是,这种看法可能并不正确。在《鲁克丽丝受辱记》的开篇献词中,莎士比亚也曾使用"love"一词。他写道:"我献给伯爵您的爱是绵绵不绝的。"(The love I dedicate to your Lordship is without end.)[①]

这里的"love"可能具有比较宽泛的概念,并不特指恋人间的爱情。不同历史时期,这个词的词义范围可能会发生变化。比如,我们这个时代的网络热词"亲爱的"(简称为"亲"),其最初的意义是指热恋的对象,可是现在为了表达亲近的含义,对朋友同事也可以这样称呼。可见,这个词的词义范围已经被大大扩展了。因此,莎士比亚公开献诗中的"love"和十四行诗中的"love"一样,也许只是表达对伯爵的敬意,表达亲近的感情,而非现在有些读者所认为的同性恋之情。

莎士比亚和南安普顿伯爵的亲密之情,持续了大约三年多的时间,之后两人关系渐渐疏远。莎士比亚的十四行诗大致写于这个时期,之后基本转入戏剧创作,没有再写十四行诗了。当然,这也许和南安普顿伯爵的政治命运紧密相关。1598年,25岁的南安普顿伯爵和女王的贵嫔伊丽莎白·弗农私通,致该女怀孕,不得不结婚,此事引起女王很大的不满。作为爱尔兰总督的埃塞克斯伯爵,拟任命随军的南安普顿伯爵为参谋长,遭女王拒绝。

[①] Stephen Orgel, *The Complete Pelican Shakespeare*, London: Penguin Books, 2002, p. 25.

更为糟糕的是,在1599年的征讨途中,埃塞克斯和女王发生了争执,对战争部署产生不同意见。埃塞克斯的军事行动损失了12000人,花费了30万英镑,却没有取得任何突破。1599年9月28日,埃塞克斯在没有通报的情况下,突然回英觐见女王,次日即被捕监禁,剥夺一切权利。1600年6月15日,埃塞克斯被指控违抗女王命令,跪地受审达11个小时,指控者包括弗朗西斯·培根爵士。埃塞克斯被囚禁了一段时间后于当年8月26日获释,但被禁止参加任何宫廷活动。凡此种种都暴露出埃塞克斯的轻率和不成熟。①

可是,埃塞克斯伯爵并不甘心这样的命运,他并没有领会女王给他的惩戒和警示。1601年2月8日,埃塞克斯伯爵率其党羽上街,煽动伦敦市民逼迫女王改变政府。结果叛乱失败,埃塞克斯伯爵和南安普顿伯爵被捕,两人均被判处死刑。2月25日,埃塞克斯伯爵被砍头,南安普顿伯爵免去一死,但仍被囚禁在伦敦塔。2月7日,宫内大臣剧团在寰球剧院上演了多年未曾演出的莎剧《理查二世》,埃塞克斯党羽用40先令的酬金买通剧团经理奥古斯丁·菲利普斯等人,安排用弑君篡位的戏来制造舆论。2月18日,剧团经理奥古斯丁·菲利普受审,并写下供词。但是女王并未因为上演《理查二世》之事迁怒剧团或莎士比亚,宫内大臣剧团继续在白厅为宫廷演出。②

这起事件的发生时间正是莎士比亚最危险的时刻,因为宫内大臣剧团是他担任股东的剧团,《理查二世》是他写的剧本,前几年他公开献诗的南安普顿伯爵身陷囹圄,此人正是他的文艺保护人。如果按图索骥,莎士比亚很可能被视为埃塞克斯的党羽而被缉拿归案。可是非常奇怪的是,没有人打扰莎士比亚,宫内大臣剧团照常在白厅上演剧目。

伊丽莎白女王一世时代是个风云激荡的时代。英格兰对外面临西班牙帝国的威胁,西班牙和英国为争夺殖民地,展开了激烈的争夺战。国内的天主教势力也蠢蠢欲动,妄图颠覆英国新教,恢复罗马教皇的权力。北边的苏格兰女王玛丽也是英国王位的顺位继承人之一,有可能取代伊丽莎白,改变英格兰的政治格局。此外,英国国内的清教势力也很强大,其要求宗教改革,革除弊政。这些都是伊丽莎白女王必须面对的困难。

伊丽莎白女王一世精明强干,任用了一批贤德人士,以治乱的手腕开创了一个黄金时代。她积极鼓励海外探险。弗朗西斯·德雷克以海盗起家,是著名的环球航行探险家,伊丽莎白女王亲自登船授予他"海军中将"的称号,并封他为普利茅斯市市长。1588

---

① See Elizabeth Jenkins, *Elizabeth The Great*, New York: Time Inc. Books, 1964, pp. 338–350.
② 参阅《莎士比亚全集·第8卷》,第460–462页。

年7月到8月,弗朗西斯·德雷克联合英国海军上将查尔斯·霍华德,在英吉利海峡彻底击溃西班牙无敌舰队,战斗以西班牙的惨败告终。这场海战改变了世界历史,促使西班牙走向衰落,丧失了原来的霸主地位,而英国的海外贸易和殖民扩张得到了很大发展。1600年12月31日,女王批准"东印度公司"成立,获得印度贸易特权,为英国大规模殖民时代的到来铺平了道路。伊丽莎白女王很重视新大陆的探索,她的宫殿大厅里悬挂着一幅新大陆的地图。她大力资助沃尔特·雷利爵士的美洲探险,尝试建立弗吉尼亚殖民地,并带去了117个定居者。雷利爵士的船队还探索过特立尼达和多巴哥,到达了南美洲的委内瑞拉和苏里南等地。

女王除了有政治才干之外,也非常喜爱文学艺术。她从小受过拉丁文和古希腊文的训练,能说一口流利的意大利语。她非常喜爱诗歌、音乐和戏剧,有才华的廷臣常常写诗献给她。女王也很喜欢华丽的服饰、璀璨的珠宝和宫廷宴会,这些都足以说明她是一位喜欢享乐宴饮的人士,一位陶醉于世俗乐趣,而不追求天国理想的文艺复兴的典型女性。因此,当清教徒纷纷要求禁止戏剧、拆除戏院的时候,女王却暗中支持。

埃塞克斯伯爵和南安普顿伯爵是伊丽莎白朝堂后期崛起的两颗政坛明星,他们想要建立军功,寻求德雷克和霍华德爵士那样的历史功绩,扩大英国的海上霸权。这也是一个巨大的历史机遇,英国正在时代中崛起。如果能把握住这样的历史机遇,两位年轻人也可能创造出历史辉煌,从而名垂千古。因此,当莎士比亚写诗劝诫南安普顿伯爵早日成婚之际,我们的剧作家并不明白伯爵面对的历史机遇。

两位伯爵也确实赢得了军功。1596年7月,英国海军袭击并攻占了西班牙加的斯港,埃塞克斯伯爵参与指挥立功。1597年8月,埃塞克斯伯爵率领英国舰队远征西班牙亚速尔群岛,南安普顿伯爵随行并任花环号舰长。年终,埃塞克斯又被任命为英军统帅,名誉和地位达到了最高峰。

正当两位伯爵达到人生的顶峰之际,1599年却突然出现了命运的巨大翻转,两人从顶峰跌落。1601年2月8日,两人被捕,皆判死刑;2月25日,埃塞克斯被砍头,南安普顿免于一死,但仍然被囚禁在伦敦塔。此时距离莎士比亚公开献诗,只过去了7年时间。正如莎士比亚在长诗《维纳斯和阿多尼斯》中感叹的那样:

刚才迈开步子又急忙转过了身,
时而过分匆忙,时而迟疑犹豫,
仿佛是酒醉办事头脑昏昏沉沉。

文本、理论、跨学科研究

一切都考虑到了,一切都没有看清,
一切都需要去做,一切都难于完成。①

1603年3月24日,伊丽莎白女王去世,终年70岁。4月10日,奉新国王的命令,南安普顿伯爵被释放。5月17日,詹姆斯一世国王指示把原来的"宫内大臣剧团"改组为"国王供奉剧团",莎士比亚被任命为宫廷内侍,同时颁布新王诰令,通知所有的治安官、市长、警察、镇长等,特许他的剧团"自由地"演出,并给予一切便利。这个危机宣告结束了,一切尘埃落定。

可是在1609年6月,伦敦的一位书商在未征询莎士比亚意见的情况下,出版了《莎士比亚十四行诗》。他在献词中感谢了这部诗集的提供者W. H. 先生,以及一位抱有良好愿望的"冒险家"。按照多数莎学家的理解,W. H. 先生是威廉·哈维爵士,南安普顿伯爵母亲的第三个丈夫;那位"冒险家"指的是南安普顿伯爵。此时的伯爵已经36岁,忙于美洲弗吉尼亚殖民地的开拓事业。而此时的莎士比亚已经45岁,是国王供奉剧团首屈一指的剧作家和演员,声名远播,受到国王的恩宠和戏迷的宠爱。莎士比亚十四行诗所写的已是陈年旧事,而且南安普顿的政治沉浮,也让大家不想旧事重提。因此这部诗集出版之后,几乎没有任何评论的声音,迎接诗集的是一片沉默。莎翁当年受人所托而作,而今功成名就,也不想和埃塞克斯的党羽有太多牵连。莎士比亚保持沉默,其他剧作家为了攀附他的盛名,也心照不宣,都保持沉默。从那以后,几乎没人提及这些诗,这些十四行诗沉默了将近三百年。

最后说一下黑肤女郎,因为从第127首到第152首,都是写给这位女郎的。这位女郎有几个特点:一是非常黑,从第127首可知:"我情人的头发像乌鸦般黑/她的眼睛也穿上了黑衣"(屠岸,第255页)。二是她是一个弹奏维琴的乐师,从第128首可知:"我的音乐呵,你把钢丝的和声/轻轻地奏出"(屠岸,第257页)。

莎士比亚认识这位黑肤女郎的时间大概是在1592年年末的时候②。从这些十四行诗可知,莎士比亚最开始的时候,并不为这位黑肤女郎所动,可能是由于音乐的缘故,跟这位女子开始交往。随着认识的加深,两人关系越来越好,逐渐产生感情。情人眼里出西施,在陷入感情的莎士比亚看来,黑色显得那么可爱。在第131首中,"都说你的黑在

---

① 莎士比亚:《莎士比亚全集·第8卷》,第46页。
② Alfred Leslie Rowse, *Shakespeare the Man*, New York: Harper & Row Publishers, 1973, p. 87.

我看来是绝色。/你一点也不黑"(屠岸,第263页)。

第132首中更夸张,"对了,美的本身就是黑,我赌咒,/而你的脸色以外的一切,都是丑"(屠岸,第265页)。

莎士比亚逐渐陷入感情旋涡,在诗中写下了真情实感,第129首:

疯狂于追求,进而疯狂于占有;
占有了,占有着,还要,绝不放松;
品尝甜头,尝过了,原来是苦头;
事前,图个欢喜;过后,一场梦:

(屠岸,第259页)

这样的感情体验是非常深刻的。莎士比亚体会到了"疯狂地追求""疯狂地占有"的滋味。就像他所认识的那样,爱情是一种极致的体验(extreme),是一种甜蜜的忧伤,是一种极乐的痛苦,是一场欢喜的梦,可以让人沉醉,让人疯狂,让人痛苦不已。

莎士比亚在这场恋爱关系中,似乎处于被动地位。黑肤女郎不止一个情人,他处于某种紧张的三角关系之中,而且他还不占优势,另一方的社会地位比他还要高。这种情况给莎士比亚带来了很大的痛苦和忧伤。第135首描述了这样的情况:

你富于意欲,要扩大你的意欲,
你得把我的意图也给添加上。
别让那无情的"不"字把请求人杀死,

(屠岸,第271页)

莎士比亚在这里用了多个"Will",这个词一词多义,既指这位女士的意愿,又指她的另一个情人,还指莎士比亚的昵称,因为William的缩写形式就是Will。通过一语双关,莎士比亚把自己的无奈尴尬、缠绵悱恻的感情,充分表达出来。这也反映出早期的莎士比亚不太自信,在情感和友谊中处于被动尴尬的地位。但是,这些诗句感情热烈,表达真挚,充分体现出莎士比亚的性格:他是一个有话就说、直抒胸臆、感情强烈的人,对待朋友和情人都非常坦诚和直率,可是却遭到了欺骗和背叛。

此外还有一点儿非常重要,《罗密欧与朱丽叶》的写作时间是1595年,正是莎士比亚创作这些十四行诗后不久。此时的莎士比亚刚好30岁,正处于与黑肤女郎三角恋爱的痛苦彷徨期。这段痛苦的经历无疑给了他巨大的情感创伤。爱情的深刻体验,给予了他源源不断的灵感,激发他创作出了世界文学史上最伟大的爱情悲剧。

如果对照罗密欧的台词,那些关于爱情的种种哀伤的表达,和第127首之后的十四行诗,有很多相似的地方。可以说,让莎士比亚陷入情网的那位黑肤女郎给了他足够的伤害,还有南安普顿伯爵对他们美好友谊的最终背叛,等等,这些让他的情感遭受了很大的创伤,也让他饱尝爱情和友谊的折磨,饱尝感情的酸甜苦辣,在29时他就已经饱受这些强烈情感的痛苦折磨。这些经历没有毁灭他,而是重新塑造了他,激发了他。一年之后,他就创作出了伟大的悲剧《罗密欧与朱丽叶》。罗密欧在剧中哀叹:

啊,沉重的轻浮,严肃的狂妄,
整齐的混乱,铅铸的羽毛,
光明的烟雾,寒冷的火焰,
憔悴的健康,永远觉醒的睡眠,否定的存在!
我感觉到的爱情正是这么一种东西,可是我并不喜爱这一种爱情。[①]

所以,莎士比亚的十四行诗,是对他将近三年沉浮经历的友谊和爱情的反映。他从最初认识和攀附南安普顿伯爵,后又被这位伯爵欺骗和背叛;他从最初认识和喜欢黑肤女郎,后又遭这位女郎戏弄和欺骗。这些都给他带来了巨大的情感创伤。但是,年轻的莎士比亚并未沉沦,而是从这些感情旋涡中提取了夺目生辉的诗句,把他郁积的情感注入到这些有力的诗句中,创作出了一部伟大的悲剧。

参考文献

David M. Bergeron, *Shakespeare: A Study and Research Guide*, Lawrence: University Press of Kansas, 1995.

Marchette Chute, *Shakespeare of London*, New York: E. P. Dutton & Co., Inc., 1996.

Jonathan Dollimore and Alan Sinfield, *Political Shakespeare: New Essays in Cultural Materialism*, New York: Cornell University Press, 1985.

[①] 莎士比亚:《莎士比亚全集·第5卷》,第98页。

Robert Giroux, *The Book Known as Q: A Consideration of Shakespeare's Sonnets*, New York: Vintage Books, 1983.

Stephen Greenblatt, Walter Cohen, Jean E. Howard, et al., *The Norton Shakespeare: Based on the Oxford Edition*, New York: W. W. Norton & Company, 1997.

Stephen Greenblatt, *Shakespearean Negotiations: The Circulation of Social Energy in Renaissance England*, California: University of California Press, 1988.

Stephen Greenblatt, *Will in the World: How Shakespeare Became Shakespeare*, New York: W. W. Norton & Company, 2004.

Elizabeth Jenkins, *Elizabeth the Great*, New York: Time Inc. Book, 1964.

Ralph J. Kaufmann, *Elizabethan Drama: Modern Essays in Criticism*, Oxford: Oxford University Press, 1961.

Stephen Orgel and A. R. Braunmuller, *The Complete Pelican Shakespeare*, London: Penguin Books, 2002.

Alfred Leslie Rowse, *Shakespeare the Man*, New York: Harper & Row Publishers, 1973.

Robert Sandler, *Northrop Frye on Shakespeare*, Connecticut: Yale University Press, 1986.

Meredith Anne Skura, *Shakespeare the Actor and the Purpose of Playing*, Chicago: The University of Chicago Press, 1993.

E. M. W. Tillyard, *The Elizabethan World Picture*, New York: Vintage Books, 1959.

Stanley W. Wells, *The Cambridge Companion to Shakespeare Studies*, Cambridge: Cambridge University Press, 1986.

莎士比亚:《莎士比亚十四行诗》,屠岸译,外语教学与研究出版社,2012年。
莎士比亚:《莎士比亚全集》,朱生豪等译,译林出版社,1998年。
钱兆明:《长短诗集》,商务印书馆,2008年。
裘克安:《莎士比亚年谱》,商务印书馆,1988年。
黄杲忻:《恋歌:英美爱情诗萃》,上海译文出版社,2002年。
罗益民:《天鹅最美一支歌:莎士比亚其人其剧其诗》,科学出版社,2016年。
罗益民:《莎士比亚十四行诗版本批评史》,科学出版社,2016年。
罗益民:《莎士比亚评论》(第1辑),河南人民出版社,2023年。

文本、理论、跨学科研究

莎士比亚戏剧中的复仇与司法危机

黄艳丽

摘要：莎士比亚时期是英国现代法律制度的重要调整阶段，诉讼案件呈爆炸式增长态势，人们对法律实践给予了极大热情，因为法律无处不在。复仇剧成为此时最流行的戏剧种类之一。在提倡宽容的基督教社会中，这自然有其深邃的意义。公共复仇是国家司法制度建设的必然要求，然而有缺陷的司法系统本身，往往从一开始就成为复仇的诱因。此时的法律体系并不完善，法律实践也存在诸多问题，如管辖权的争夺、法官的腐败、律师的颠倒黑白等，使得源自日耳曼部落传统的血亲复仇观念仍然有一定的影响力和合理性，因为复仇被认为是一种"原有的正义"，是一种清除社会疾病、保障社会秩序的有效方式。复仇剧的正义危机反映了早期现代英格兰法律体系中的司法危机。

关键词：莎士比亚；复仇；法律；司法危机

作者简介：黄艳丽，贵州工程应用技术学院副教授，主要研究方向为莎士比亚研究。

文艺复兴时期是英国戏剧蓬勃发展的时代，涌现了大批的剧作家和海量的戏剧作品，而复仇剧[1]也在此时获得一定的中心位置。甚至有批评家认为，"从根本上来说，伊丽莎白时期的所有悲剧都必须呈现为关于复仇的悲剧，如果复仇观的全部来龙去脉已然被理清了的话"[2]。的确，除了公认的复仇剧之外，在这一时期的多部悲剧作品难以摆脱复仇元素。不能断言没有复仇元素的戏剧是苍白的，但它无疑给戏剧，尤其是悲剧增

---

[1] "复仇剧"一词于1900年由A.H. Thorndike提出并成为一种戏剧类型。详见John Kerrigan, *Revenge Tragedy: Aeschylus to Armageddon*, Oxford: Oxford University Press, 1996。

[2] Lily B. Campbell, "Theories of Revenge in Renaissance England", *Modern Philology*, 28.3(1931): 290.

添了独特的魅力,呈现出别具一格的视觉盛宴。莎士比亚更是将复仇元素摆弄得炉火纯青,在他的38部戏剧中(包括《两个高贵的亲戚》),只有两部未涉及复仇情节。[1]复仇剧是伊丽莎白时期最流行的戏剧种类之一,在戏院的频繁演出表明观众对此情有独钟。但英格兰不像苏格兰或意大利的弗留里那样,是一种"世仇文化"[2],为什么一个基督教国家屡屡上演复仇剧?在提倡宽容的基督教社会中,复仇剧的普遍流行必然有着深邃的意义。一个封建等级的君主制社会中,舞台复仇者颇为专注暗杀国王或贵族,其中缘由值得思考。

  复仇剧中复仇者选择私人报复无疑是对提供公平与正义的官方机构的不信任。复仇是人与生俱来的天性,也是影响社会秩序的主要元素,更是国家法律的关注重点。在长期的社会动荡中,政治和宗教斗争带来的不仅是精神上的极度忧郁和无法解脱的悲观,而且是肉体的残害与杀戮。结果,死亡成为那个时代文化的中心论题和意象。诉讼案件大量增加,给整个司法机构造成了前所未有的压力。法律逐渐变得"中央集权化"和"专业化",引发巨大的变革。[3]个人复仇的正义与否充满了"不确定性",公众复仇成为社会发展的趋势和秩序社会的条件,因为公众复仇独属于监管得当的(well-policed)社会,我们将其称为司法系统[4]。"有缺陷的司法系统本身,往往从一开始就成为复仇的诱因。"[5]当公众复仇无法实现时,人们倾向诉诸私人复仇。源自塞内加异教传统和基督教传统的两种复仇观是强烈的,也是矛盾的,从来不能被调和;它们因各自的正当性被接受,同样也因各自的不合理性而受到怀疑或谴责。私人复仇和公众复仇的矛盾正是英国现代法律建设进程中的焦虑反映。舞台复仇者经常遇到腐败的法律体系:"上帝的正义可能会缓慢,他的世俗代表腐败了,国家机器失去秩序,因此导致公然的错误不受惩罚。"[6]许多评论家认为,复仇悲剧的流行象征一种更广泛的复仇文化。安塞尔姆·哈

---

[1] 这两部作品是《错误的戏剧》和《爱的徒劳》。
[2] Edward Muir, *Mad Blood Stirring, Vendetta and Factions in Friuli during the Renaissance*, Baltimore: Johns Hopkins University Press, 1993, p. 275.
[3] See Derek Dunne, *Shakespeare, Revenge Tragedy and Early Modern Law*, New York: Palgrave Macmillan, 2016, p. 2.
[4] René Girard, *Violence and the Sacred*, Patrick Gregory, trans., London: Athlone Press, 1988, p. 15.
[5] See Derek Dunne, *Shakespeare, Revenge Tragedy and Early Modern Law*, New York: Palgrave Macmillan, 2016, p. 3.
[6] Anne Pippin Burnett, *Revenge in Attic and Later Tragedy*, Berkeley: University of California Press, 1998, p. 21.

弗坎普声称,复仇像忧郁一样也是伊丽莎白时代的慢性疾病。[①]罗伯特·沃森认为,复仇是警力有限年代对官方司法的重要补充。[②]戏剧中的复仇行为模仿了都铎式的法律,施予被复仇者与其"罪行"相适应的惩罚——小偷的手被砍掉,责骂人的舌头被拴住。[③]当奥赛罗要报复"背叛"自己的妻子时,他采取了对应的报复,使苔丝狄蒙娜窒息在"她玷污的床上"。当泰特斯·安德洛尼克斯的儿子为他报仇时,莎士比亚强调这种对等性:"做儿子的忍心看着他的父亲流血吗?/冤冤相报,有命抵命"(Can the son's eye behold his father bleed? / There's meed for meed, death for a deadly deed)(5.3.64-65)。哈姆雷特放弃了一次复仇的好机会,因为当时"杀父仇人"正在忏悔他的罪行,对其复仇会让他进入天堂,这会让复仇失去对等性,因为被杀害的父亲已不能进入天堂。在许多伊丽莎白时代和詹姆士一世时期的复仇剧中,暴力和复仇者过于浓烈的情感是如此怪诞,任何社会或伦理观察都被淹没在情节中。

《泰特斯·安德洛尼克斯》充满了塞内加式的血腥场景,这部戏剧是莎士比亚少有的复仇悲剧之一。复仇在戏剧开始前就已拉开序幕,罗马将军泰特斯·安德洛尼克斯凯旋并俘虏了哥特女王塔摩拉和她的儿子们,多年与哥特的征战,让泰特斯失去了多个儿子。丧子的悲痛和复仇的欲望,让他杀死了塔摩拉的长子,以祭奠他在战争中死去的亲人,由此推倒了第一张多米诺骨牌。塔摩拉后来成为罗马的皇后,双方的角色互换。塔摩拉和她剩下的儿子展开了疯狂的报复,设计杀死了泰特斯的小儿子,她的两个儿子侮辱了泰特斯的女儿拉维尼娅,并砍去她的双手,割掉她的舌头。遭受厄运的拉维尼娅既无法说出是谁犯下的罪行,又让年迈的父亲为她所受的伤害日日伤心。后来,当泰特斯得知这一切时,他采取了血腥的私人复仇行动,将塔摩拉的两个儿子剁成肉酱,烹调之后骗塔摩拉吃下,自己也被罗马皇帝杀害。最终,他剩下的唯一的儿子又杀死皇帝为父亲和兄弟们报仇。沿袭自日耳曼部落传统的血亲复仇作为主线贯穿全剧。一些批评家对这部戏剧的评价不高,关注点落在剧中的种种暴行上。德国的威廉·希雷格尔认为,这部戏剧是按照错误的悲剧观念创作的,堆积了大量的残忍暴行,使作品除了恐惧之

---

① Harry Keyishian, *The Shapes of Revenge: Victimization, Vengeance, and Vindictiveness in Shakespeare*, Atlantic Highlands, NJ: Humanities Press, 1995, p. 180.
② Robert N. Watson, "Tragedies of Revenge and Ambition", in Claire McEachern, ed., *The Cambridge Companion to Shakespearean Tragedy*, Cambridge: Cambridge University Press, 2002, p. 160.
③ Paul A. Jorgensen, *Our Naked Frailties: Sensational Art and Meaning in "Macbeth"*, Berkeley: University of California Press, 1971, pp. 32-39.

外,再不能给人以任何深刻的印象。①1948年,约翰·多佛尔·威尔逊写道:"这部戏剧就像颠簸、摇晃的破马车,装载着从伊丽莎白时期的绞刑架上解下的血淋淋的尸体,驾驭他的车夫是从疯人院跑出来的刽子手,戴着一顶帽子,穿着喇叭裤。"并且,威尔逊直言不讳地断言这部戏剧没什么价值,如果它的作者不是莎士比亚,那么这部戏剧可能早就被人们淡忘。②然而也有评论家对这部戏剧给予高度评价,认为泰特斯的复仇是对暴君的反抗,将罗马从暴君统治的悲惨境遇中拯救出来。③波斯纳认为,《哈姆雷特》就像《泰特斯·安德洛尼克斯》一样,反映出了对复仇的矛盾态度。这种态度是莎士比亚时期人们对复仇的普遍态度。④

培根将复仇描述为一种"狂野的正义"(wild justice)。曾经担任过大法官的培根,对复仇的态度立场坚定,"人之天性越是爱讨这种公道,法律就越是应该将其铲除。因为犯罪者只是触犯了法律,而对该罪犯以牙还牙则使法律失去了效用"⑤。这段话似乎支持英格兰国家法律的权威性,并否定个人的复仇行为,但也承认了私人复仇的"正义性"。根据《牛津大辞典》的释义,"wild"一词既可表示缺乏管教的,也可表示天生的;"wild justice"表明正义是自然赋予的,从侧面揭露出当时的法律特性——法律与正义并不必然是联系在一起的,有时甚至是矛盾的。亨特发表了类似的观点,将伊丽莎白时代舞台上的报复视为一种腐败的正义形式(perverted form of justice)⑥。同样,他的观点从侧面表明复仇具有一定的正义性质。从二者的定义上看,复仇演变为法律的黑暗孪生兄弟,虽不是全然的正义,但有其存在的合理性。

法律也不能不存在于真空中,它是它所属社会的产物。文学同样也可以作为社会关注的晴雨表。法律和文学的交织在本质上有着悠久而多样的历史,如埃斯库罗斯(Aeschylus)的《俄瑞斯忒亚》(Oresteia)中从复仇到法律的历史旅程,弗朗茨·卡夫卡(Franz Kafka)在《审判》(The Trial)中对司法程序的讽刺。卡夫卡讲述了一个老人被拒

---

① A. W. Schlegel, *Lectures on Dramatic Art and Literature*, London: George Bell and Sons, 1879, p. 442.
② John Dover Wilson, ed., *Titus Andronicus*, Cambridge: Cambridge University Press, 2008, p.xii.
③ Linda Woodbridge, *English Revenge Drama*, New York: Cambridge University Press, 2010, pp. 173-174.
④ Richard A. Posner, *Law and Literature*, 3rd edition, Massachusetts: Harvard University Press, 2009, p. 108.
⑤ Francis Bacon, "Of Revenge", in John Pitcher, ed., *The Essays*, Harmondsworth: Penguin, 1985, pp. 72-73.
⑥ G. K. Hunter, *Dramatic Identities and Cultural Tradition: Studies in Shakespeare and his contemporaries*, New York: Barnes and Noble Books, 1978.

绝进入法律的内殿,并最终死在门外的故事。他为这座可怕的法律大厦描绘了一幅不讨人喜欢的肖像。戏剧作为一种重要的西方文学形式,一直对相应的法律进行深刻的探讨。不管是古希腊,还是现代社会,作为社会产物,文学履行它的社会功能,对有缺陷的法律进行批评。从这个意义上说,文学是社会问题的治病良药。文艺复兴时期戏剧的功能之一就是借助"戏中戏"来隐喻和指涉相似的事件,从而通过符号意象再现真理或政治想象。复仇与社会秩序密切关联。在文艺复兴时期的身体政治和古典医学语境下,复仇被认为是一种医疗手段,能祛除悲剧人物因遭受不道德的伤害而产生的病症。联系当时盛行的大宇宙和小宇宙的类比,复仇也是祛除国家政体疾病的有效路径,能净化日益被污染的民族共同体,整治衰败道德和腐败政治,建立法理一体性。

乔纳森·吉尔·哈里斯发现,人们认为复仇对复仇者造成了生理伤害,这是产生忧郁的主要原因。[1]格雷厄姆·霍尔德内斯提出,对生理学家来说,复仇导致心理和身体上的损害,它是一种"强迫性(obsessive)的浓烈情感,会引起不健康的症状和神经障碍"[2]。普罗塞也表明,复仇的破坏性包括"精神恶化"[3]。很明显,复仇是一种会引起患者心理与身体疾病的事物,因此泰特斯和哈姆雷特将疯癫和忧郁联系在一起。不仅复仇者身患疾病,被复仇者也同样恶疾缠身。根据文艺复兴时期的体液说,人体内的四种体液于健康至关重要。四种体液对应宇宙中的四种元素,四种元素的分布影响宇宙的秩序,四种体液在人体的混合决定了人体的气质、性格和健康状况,人的肉身乃至人的品德与灵魂,都与体液的混合有关。血液多的人情欲过剩,黄胆汁多的人易怒、暴躁,黑胆汁多的人多思、忧郁,黏液多的人胆小、迟钝。罗马皇帝由于"血液过剩"导致"情欲过度",丧失理智将罗马的敌人塔摩拉变成了罗马的皇后,二人的结合意味着坏血与好血交融在一起,健康的罗马政体被感染。同时,少女的纯洁与家族的荣耀息息相关,拉维尼娅的被辱代表着罗马将军家族的纯净血液被异族的败血玷污,最终感染引发社会危机,杀戮和强暴充斥全剧,和谐的秩序荡然无存,整个国家和政体都陷入疾病状态。莎士比亚运用体液修辞书写罗马政体的"患病"始末。在戏剧一开场,泰特斯要求用最"娇贵"的俘虏——塔摩拉的长子——祭奠战争中死去的子嗣。塔摩拉苦苦哀求:泰特斯·安德洛尼

---

[1] Jonathan Gil Harris, *Sick Economies: Drama, Mercantilism, and Disease in Shakespeare's England*, Philadelphia: University of Pennsylvania Press, 2004, p. 101.
[2] Graham Holderness, *Hamlet*, Milton Keynes and Philadelphia: Open University Press, 1987, p. 51.
[3] Eleanor Prosser, *Hamlet and Revenge*, 2nd edition, Stanford: Stanford University Press, 1971, p. 8.

克斯,别用血液玷污了您家的墓地。①这表明异族之血是肮脏的败血。塔摩拉又说:"让我血液(黄胆汁)过剩的儿子们毁掉这朵败柳残花"(Ⅱ.iii.191)。在双手被砍、舌头被割的情况下,拉维尼娅用嘴写出凶手的名字,叔父马科斯惊呼:"什么!皇后被性欲驱使的两个儿子/是这可恨的、血色行为的施暴者"(Ⅳ.i.79-80)。医学术语修辞揭示出施暴者的"情欲"是体液过剩的结果。在马科斯口中,情欲与血色直接相关联。乔特鲁德与克劳狄斯的结合,同样也是坏血污染健康血液的标志。哈姆雷特哀号人世"是一个荒芜不治的花园,长满了恶毒的莠草"。莎士比亚所在时代常用花园隐喻国家,满是莠草的花园无疑是在隐喻社会秩序紊乱,危机四伏。母亲"迫不及待地钻进了乱伦的衾被",这样的行为不比"没有理性的畜生"更高贵,因为其"悲伤得长久一些"。②

  托勒密的宇宙论和体液说是文艺复兴时期最流行的学说和概念,渗透在整个国家的政治思想理念和诗歌、戏剧等文学创作中。以大宇宙、小宇宙的类比为核心的宇宙对应体系,在天体、政体和人体三者之间建立关联性,人体的和谐隐喻国家和宇宙的和谐,人体的疾病隐喻国家的失序和宇宙的混乱,反之亦是如此。黑尔发现,社会和人体之间的相似性类比使用超过了其他任何构建"'伊丽莎白世界图景'的对应关系"③。在这种类比关联网络下,疾病、混乱、腐败、死亡等阴暗词汇连接在一起,成为书写国家政体、社会秩序和人体健康状态的主要修辞话语。英格兰人普遍相信疾病是"身体内部的不平衡状态,由体液紊乱或不足引发",同时外部因素也可能引起疾病,因为身体是开放的,容易遭受"外界病毒的侵入而引起身体内部的体液紊乱"。④每个人都是社会中的个体,社会秩序存在于无数个体的集合中;同样,秩序的破坏是内力与外力共同作用的结果。罗马皇帝引狼入室,让邪恶的塔摩拉一家成为皇室成员,国家的保护者没有履行自己的职责与义务,亲手迎来"外界的病毒",让其进入原本健康的罗马政体;身为将军之女的拉维尼娅被玷污,她纯净的血液沾染了塔摩拉之子的败血,"病毒"将会通过她的身体传染整个家族和罗马帝国。从大宇宙和小宇宙的类比来看,身体的疾病状态、社会秩序的好坏与天体的变化三者建立起联系。当泰特斯发现拉维尼娅的惨状后,又被欺骗

---

① 莎士比亚:《莎士比亚全集(四)》,朱生豪等译,人民文学出版社,1994年,第514页。
② 莎士比亚:《莎士比亚全集(五)》,朱生豪等译,人民文学出版社,1994年,第292-293页。
③ David George Hale, *The Body Politic: A Political Metaphor in Renaissance English Literature*, The Hague: Mouton & Co., 1971, p. 11.
④ Jonathan Gil Harris, *Sick Economies: Drama Mercantilism, and Disease in Shakespeare's England*, Philadelphia: University of Pennsylvania Press, 2004, p. 13.

斩下自己曾挥舞刀剑保卫罗马的手臂,却换来两个儿子被砍下的头颅时,他的悲痛难以克制,叫闹道:"当上天哭泣的时候,地上不是要泛滥着大水吗?当狂风怒吼的时候,大海不是要发起疯来,鼓起了它的面颊向天空恫吓吗?"[1]人体的疾病、社会的失序会带来天气环境的变化。同样,哈姆雷特的抑郁让大地变成"不毛的荒岬",苍穹与屋宇也不过是"一大堆污浊的瘴气的集合"[2]。

既然人体的疾病事关社会秩序和国家政体,那么如何治疗疾病,将混乱的社会秩序导回正轨,恢复国家和谐,便成为戏剧情节的核心任务。复仇成为治愈疾病和拨乱反正的有效方式。在国家机器不能通过发挥司法制度的功能让受害人得到正义时,公共复仇失败了。在这两部复仇剧中,受害人需要向封建等级制度的最高阶级复仇。此时的法律不是正义的体现,而是暴力的行使。不公正的司法制度促使受害人采取私人复仇。诉诸私人复仇表明对保障公平,展现法律和正义的官方机构的不信任,或者说这是在公共复仇不作为下的无奈选择。格雷戈里·塞门扎认为,伊丽莎白时期的复仇表明自治(self-government)的冲动比今天更强烈,因为法律体系不那么有效……也因为旧的家庭义务和权利并不像今天这么遥远。[3]一方面,源自日耳曼部落传统的血亲复仇观念,在伊丽莎白时期的社会上仍然有一定的影响力。此时的法律体系并不完善,法律实践也存在诸多问题,如管辖权的争夺、法官的腐败、律师的颠倒黑白等。另一方面,法律的专业化和中央集权化日益加强。面对此种情形,英格兰人在英国早期法律建设的进程中处于焦虑状态。提倡宽容的基督教义禁止受害者采取私人复仇的行为,但不那么有效的法律机制又不能实现公共复仇,人们陷入了道德困境。"相比同时代的其他戏剧,莎士比亚的戏剧对复仇道德困境的本质渗透得更深……"[4]普洛塞指出,复仇对伊丽莎白时期的人是一种应受谴责的亵渎。她以《哈姆雷特》中的鬼魂为例,认为它是恶魔的标签,因为它命令他人复仇,这违背了基督教教义。[5]但细读这个时期的戏剧文本会发现,复仇是治疗性的。许多复仇者是被剥夺权利的人,被不公正地对待,他们被迫站起来控制局面。这些人物遭受着恶意、不公、背叛、悲伤,以及权利或地位被剥夺。通过复仇,他

---

[1] 莎士比亚:《莎士比亚全集(四)》,第554页。
[2] 莎士比亚:《莎士比亚全集(五)》,第327页。
[3] Gregory M. Colón Semenza, "The Spanish Tragedy and Revenge", in Garrett A. Sullivan Jr., Patrick Cheney and Andrew Hadfield, eds., *Early Modern English Drama: A Critical Companion*, Oxford: Oxford University Press, 2006, pp. 50—60.
[4] Eleanor Prosser, *Hamlet and Revenge*, 2nd edition, Stanford: Stanford University Press, 1971, p. 94.
[5] Ibid, p. 6.

们试图恢复自己的精神完整性。[1] 玛格丽特决定用复仇赶走悲伤,"悲伤使人心软,使人胆怯而丧气,因此,我必须停止哭泣,决心报仇"[2]。泰特斯用复仇减轻内心的哀痛,"上天将要垂听我们的祷告,否则我们要用叹息嘘成浓雾,把天空遮得一片昏沉,使太阳失去它的光辉"[3]。马尔康向麦克德夫提议,"让我们用壮烈的复仇做药饵,治疗这一段惨酷的悲痛"[4]。复仇可以充作药剂,治疗疾病,在某种心理意义上消除最初的伤害。塞内加悲剧中,复仇渴望的受阻"让一个人变得不完整,好像他残缺了",复仇带来了"塞内加的美狄亚所说的一种深深的快乐(voluptas)"。[5]

不仅如此,复仇也被转喻为古典医学中的放血治疗术,体液过剩或体液混合是身体产生疾病乃至社会失序的根源。通过器具割开皮肤放血,是一种快速见效的治疗手段。施暴者"体液过剩",暴行引发复仇者剧烈的悲伤、愤怒、忧郁等情感波动,并致使复仇者体液紊乱。复仇经由外科手术放血,清洗敌人和复仇者自己,二者的疾病得以治疗,体液的和谐状态被重新建立。根据大宇宙和小宇宙的对应关系,身体的疾病治愈也代表了社会秩序的回归正途。伯奈特经研究发现,希腊的神话故事和传说表达了一个观点:所有的秩序都是建立在复仇之上。在一个有序的(regulated)团体中,复仇并不是人们必须废除的犯罪,它并不是像人们认为的那样是秩序的对立面,而是"秩序最原始的形式"。公共复仇的惩罚权力不过是每个人根深蒂固的(ingrained)复仇权力的借用版本。[6]泰特斯复仇的第一步是将契伦和坡勃律斯割喉放血,用他们的污血冲刷他们的罪恶。为了复仇的对等性,泰特斯制订了一套富有仪式感的步骤,要以同样残酷的方式完成对他们的复仇。泰特斯将他们的骨头磨成细粉,头颅捣成肉泥,做成馅饼给塔摩拉吃,整个流程模仿希腊神话中 Philomel 和 Progne 的故事,考虑到文艺复兴时期人文主义者对古希腊文化的推崇,也许莎士比亚这样安排就是为了再现希腊神话故事所传递的复仇重建秩序理念。

拉维尼娅被塔摩拉的儿子侮辱,败血借由精气污染纯净的血液,其父泰特斯模仿罗

---

[1] Harry Keyishian, *The Shapes of Revenge: Victimization, Vengeance, and Vindictiveness in Shakespeare*, Atlantic Highlands and NJ: Humanities Press, 1995, p. 2.
[2] 莎士比亚:《莎士比亚全集(三)》,朱生豪等译,人民文学出版社,1994年,第655页。
[3] 莎士比亚:《莎士比亚全集(五)》,第554页。
[4] 同上书,第262页。
[5] Anne Pippin Burnett, *Revenge in Attic and Later Tragedy*, Berkeley: University of California Press, 1998, pp. 1–2.
[6] Ibid, p. 64.

马共和时期的维琪涅斯将女儿亲手杀死。泰特斯将维琪涅斯作为自己理应效仿的榜样,因为他们的境遇相同。维琪涅斯也曾为罗马浴血奋战,后来却不得不忍受劳迪厄斯的苛待,女儿维琪妮娅被劳迪厄斯侮辱,劳迪厄斯利用伪造的法律手段将她变为逃跑的奴隶而占为己有,腐败的法官助纣为虐,维琪涅斯只能将女儿亲手杀死。泰特斯同样面临着道德堕落、社会腐败的现实语境。拉维尼娅的在场一再勾起他的悲痛,为了平息悲痛,他只能杀死女儿,让自己的悲痛与拉维尼娅一起逝去。体液混合之后,从医学实践来讲,放血手术无法保留好的血液在身体中,只能将败血排出身体之外。而现实语境里,伊丽莎白时期由两性关系引起的疾病是具有传染性的,且几乎无法治愈。既然无法只留下好血,为了不让败血继续传染他人,破坏家族的名誉和健康、社会的稳定与和谐,只能让"患者"流血致死。塔摩拉对罗马政体和社会的危害更大。在她成为皇后之初,莎士比亚借艾伦之口指明她的本性在于旺盛的情欲和迷惑,"这位塞米勒米斯/这位宁芙/这位海妖/她要迷惑罗马的萨特尼纳斯/看他的船只失事,国家遇难"(2.1.21-3)。三人都是希腊神话中的人物,塞米勒米斯是传说中淫荡的亚述女王,宁芙是美丽的山水精灵,塞壬是利用美妙歌喉迷惑海上过往船只的海妖。艾伦对塔摩拉的描述揭露出她的邪恶本性和对罗马的道德腐蚀、社会危害。为了清除塔摩拉带来的毒害,泰特斯也将她放血致死。被恶血感染的罗马帝国"疾病缠身",原本引以为傲的对抗性司法制度在剧中饱受质疑,控辩双方的对抗性修辞话语失去作用场所,陪审团制沦落为徒具其形的法律形式,"隐喻性失聪"揭露出司法腐败的社会现实。

剧院和法庭的基本相似之处是:两者都依赖于以修辞话语的方式向观众或陪审团提供证据和"事实"。法律话语力图以科学方式寻求真相,但其阐释过程是一种语言艺术实践。法律对客观事实的关注,因其依赖既有说服力又矛盾的语言而具有不稳定性。依托法律修辞构建"客观事实"以取信法官和陪审团,是对抗性法律制度的核心。"听"成为彰显正义的必要环节。罗马皇帝萨特尼纳斯本应履行君主的义务,作为国家秩序的最高守护者,倾听国民的诉求,承担公平和正义的维护之责,但他的耳朵从他与塔摩拉的结合开始就埋下了丧失"听力"的隐忧,"这位塞米勒米斯/这位宁芙/这位海妖/她要迷惑罗马的萨特尼纳斯/看他的船只失事,国家遇难"(2.1.21-3)。精灵与海妖的化身将会通过迷惑他,致国家于危难中,稳定的社会秩序受到了毫无防守的耳朵带来的威胁。不久之后,这种隐忧转变为现实。作为"法官"的萨特尼纳斯一再拒绝倾听别人的请求,这事实上是对自己职责的亵渎。都铎王朝时期相关法案中对法官的描述如下:法官的表征应该是"竖起大耳朵而没有眼睛,这表示他应该完全耐心地倾听整个事件的缘由

(cause),而不是亲切地尊重任何一方"①。与此要求相反,萨特尼纳斯在逮捕泰特斯的两个儿子时,立即接受了视觉证据,"如果这事被证明?/你看这已经很明显了"(2.2.292)。但正如泰特斯所说,人的眼睛"是非不明"(5.2.65-66),"法官"要依靠耳朵获取证据与事实,以此平衡正义,而不是依靠凡人"黑白不分"的眼睛。接着萨特尼纳斯剥夺了两兄弟说话的权利,让他们无法为自己辩护,拒绝倾听整个事件的来龙去脉后再做出判断,"让他们一个字也不准说/罪行很清楚"。为泰特斯送信的小丑也被他不问情由就下令处死,"去,马上把他带走,绞死他"(4.4.44)。萨特尼纳斯一直站在"张大耳朵"的英格兰法官对面,他所代表的司法体系难以保障公平、正义,社会秩序陷入危机。

不仅萨特尼纳斯陷入"隐喻性耳聋",罗马的护民官也身染此疾病。泰特斯沿着罗马街道祈求护民官与民众倾听他的诉求,撤除死刑的判决,但没有人听他的哭诉。当路歇斯告诉他这一事实时,泰特斯回答:"即使他们听见/他们也不会关注我"(3.1.33-34)。不管物理的耳朵有没有听见,心灵的耳朵拒绝参与司法公平和正义的实践。萨特尼纳斯用败血污染了整个罗马,尽管他坚信"正义活在/萨特尼纳斯的健康里"(4.4.23-4)。但事实是萨特尼纳斯中毒已深,病毒扩散到整个国家,他无法进行自我排毒。为了恢复国家的道德伦理和社会秩序,只能将萨特尼纳斯的病体毁灭,用罗马将军健康的身体为罗马注入新的血液,治愈久病沉疴的罗马政治。相比之下,哈姆雷特是更合格的"法官"和秩序维护者。在倾听了老国王鬼魂的复仇诉求后,他决定肩负重整乾坤的重任,但他并没有鲁莽行事,而是决定寻找"更确实的证据"(2.2.607-8),唯恐鬼魂是魔鬼化身,要欺骗柔弱的自己。直到借由戏中戏观察到克劳迪斯的反应,并亲耳"听到"他对自己罪行的供认不讳和忏悔,才确定他犯下滔天的大罪。

泰特斯和哈姆雷特没有通过采取法律行动达成复仇的目的。泰特斯首先向法律求助,但法律的执行者拒绝了他,迫使他采取私人复仇的方式获得"对等的复仇"。哈姆雷特看似未考虑公共复仇的可能性,因为在一开始他就知道复仇的对象是法律的执行者,但他严格遵循法庭审判步骤,公正听取双方的陈词,得出事实真相。复仇是治愈性的,它抚平了复仇者的哀伤、悲痛与愤怒;它让"体液紊乱的政治之体"恢复健康,将混乱的社会秩序带回正轨;它是法律的黑暗双胞胎,是狂野的正义。亚里士多德认为,法律的特性是一种秩序,良好的法律就是良好的秩序。法律的本质是政治权威颁布的命令。

---

① Derek Dunne, *Shakespeare, Revenge Tragedy and Early Modern Law*, London: Palgrave Macmillan, 2016, p. 58.

需要注意的是，法律天生带有一定的偏向性，正如柏拉图所观察到的：每一种政体颁布的法律都是有利于自己的；谁不遵守，他就既担违法之罪，又负不义之名。法律应该是赋予秩序与正义的，但法律的本质决定了法律的不确定性，它游走于秩序与混乱、正义与暴力之间，统治者的性质决定了法律的性质。法律实践依赖相关法律专业人士的执行，法律从而被置于被人操纵、引发潜在危机的状态。从都铎王朝开始，英格兰的中央集权化依托王室法庭体系削弱地方领主的权力，争夺的核心是审判权。审判权不仅会带来法庭的组建和相应的权力实践与权威，也会带来大笔的审判费和罚款。崇尚君主绝对权力的詹姆斯一世即位之后，滥用刑室法庭实行个人专制，引发衡平法院和普通法法院的司法权之争。为此，詹姆斯一世和大法官科克(Coke)进行争论。詹姆斯一世认为，法律以理性为基础，国王和法官皆具备理性，法官由国王指任，是国王的代表，国王的理性高于法官的理性。针对国王的观点，科克提出了"自然理性"(natural reason)和"人为理性"(artificial reason)的区别，前者是与生俱来的，后者是法律专业人员的特殊领域，因为法律是一门在人认识它之前需要长期学习和经验的艺术。科克认为，国王个人不应参与到具体的法庭审判中。他承认詹姆斯一世被上帝赋予丰富的科学知识和非凡的天赋，但这不能否认詹姆斯一世没有学习过英格兰国家的法律。不仅如此，科克强调普通法的运行需要正当的程序作为基础，君主的自由干预将对此形成威胁。因为鉴于国王的身份，一旦他做出任何裁定，无人可进行补救。萨特莱勒斯主持的审判，体现了他对担任"法官"所要求的法律专业知识的缺乏。艾伦在拉维尼娅和巴西安纳斯受害的地方，安排了一封"揭露"马歇斯兄弟罪行的信件。他没有按照法律程序检验信件的真实性，当即将信件作为证据；也没有公正倾听双方的陈词，就做出裁定。由此，依靠国家权力和法律的公众复仇失去了正义的必然性。身为统治者的皇帝萨特莱勒斯的放任与偏袒，决定了国家法律复仇的缺席。但人们对秩序和正义的渴望不会停止，私人复仇与公众复仇的错位则成必然之势。

亨德尔观察到，伊丽莎白末期和斯图亚特王朝早期是英国现代法律制度的重要调整阶段[①]，法律的不确定性、程序性和专业性是英格兰人民在法律变革进程中的焦虑所在。英格兰实行的令状制度非常复杂，而令状选择失当即为败诉。他们必须依靠专业的法律人士处理生活中的各种法律事件，与他们的法律生活息息相关的律师，在莎士比

---

① Steve Hindle, "The Keeping of the Public Peace", in Paul Griffiths, Adam Fox and Steve Hindle, eds., *The Experience of Authority in Early Modern England*, Basingstoke: Macmillan, 1996, p. 231.

亚的戏剧中往往备受批判。莎士比亚将律师的负面形象刻画得入木三分。剧中人物一谈到律师，辛辣讽刺之味难以掩饰。在《罗密欧与朱丽叶》第1幕第4场中，茂丘西奥这样描述"春梦婆"："经过律师们的手指，他们就会在梦里伸手讨讼费"(1.4.77–78)。《驯悍记》中的特拉尼奥则说："我们应该像法庭上打官司的律师，在竞争的时候是冤家对头，在吃吃喝喝的时候还是像好朋友一样"(1.2.272–275)。在《李尔王》中，弄人与肯特也对律师嘲弄了一番："肯特：傻瓜，这些话一点意思也没有。／弄人：那么正像拿不到讼费的律师一样，我的话都白说了"(1.4.112)。《哈姆雷特》对律师的颠倒黑白、卖弄言辞也不乏讥讽："谁知道那不会是一个律师的骷髅？他的玩弄刀笔的手段，颠倒黑白的雄辩，现在都跑到哪儿去了？为什么他让这个放肆的家伙用龌龊的铁铲敲他的脑壳，不去控告他一个殴打罪？"(5.1.90–94)。《亨利六世》中更是借由(屠户)狄克之口发愿："第一件该做的事，是把所有的律师全都杀光"(4.2.68)。对律师的这种憎恶，源于律师利用专业知识颠倒黑白，玩弄正义。西方的修辞学传统和对抗性法律体制，使得律师能够在法庭审判中，各自代表控辩双方就共同的"叙事"材料，依据自己对烦琐法律知识的掌握，将故事以法律认可的叙事方式一一讲述，通过操纵陪审团与审判官的方式，达到操纵法律的目的。

　　莎士比亚时期的英国法律体系日益膨胀，伊丽莎白时期的英国人民对法律实践给予了极大热情，因为法律无处不在。据统计，伊丽莎白女王统治末年，英国人口大约有400万，每年要卷入100万诉讼行动中。[①]也就是说，大约每三个人中就有一个卷入诉讼。这种热情当然并不是源于英国人天性好斗，而是社会现实所造就的。随着宗教改革和普通法进入政体，英国法成为产生和维持社会关系的主导机构。[②]诉讼率在此阶段呈爆炸式增长态势，法律事件笼罩了生活的方方面面，法律条文更加专业复杂。哈姆雷特讥讽律师："开口闭口用那些条文、具结、罚款、双重保证、赔偿一类的名词吓人；现在他的脑壳里塞满了泥土，这就算是他所取得的罚款和最后的赔偿了吗？"(5.1.90—98)专业化的法律术语将平常百姓隔离在领域之外，律师与其他法律人员是国王借助司法体制收拢权力的有力助手，司法腐败是法律生活中的常态。但国民的生活可以脱离法律吗？法律不一定是正义的体现和秩序的维护者，但没有法律，国家则必然陷入混乱。国

---

① See B. J. Sokol and Mary Sokol, eds., *Shakespeare, Law and Marriage*, New York: Cambridge University Press, 2003, p. 3.
② 科马克、努斯鲍姆、斯特瑞尔:《莎士比亚与法：学科与职业的对话》，王光林等译，黑龙江教育出版社，2015年，第4页。

家的建立来源于自然状态的不安全性。人们为了追求安全,出于个体意愿放弃自身权利,将权利转移给君主。人们寄望法律带来秩序和自由,没有了法律体系,人们又回归到自然状态,安全性无法得到保障。所以,即使律师的形象被一贬再贬,但法律的必要性却并未受到质疑。《威尼斯商人》中,鲍西亚凭借渊博的专业法律知识,不仅成功达到解救安东尼奥的目的,还对夏洛特进行了严厉的惩戒。面对戏剧性转变的审判结果,原本胜券在握的夏洛特茫然不知所措,只剩一句"法律上是这样说的吗?"(4.1.309),但遭受毁灭性打击的夏洛特并没有诅咒法律或法律的存在。

莎士比亚邀请观众和读者审视的不是法律的存在,而是法律在这个关键性的转变阶段遭遇的法律实践与司法正义实现问题,有缺陷的法律制度与司法腐败无法完成实现正义的本质任务,社会不公平现象大量存在于社会现实中,引发尖锐的社会矛盾,对整个司法机构构成前所未有的威胁,私人复仇自然成为另类的正义获取方式。当然,私人复仇仍然是饱受争议的。对许多人来说,复仇者的死证明了剧作家发现复仇不是基督徒的,他们的死是因为复仇者永远不可能真的是正确的,因为谋杀违反了更高的法律。[1]古希腊神话中,复仇者在复仇后或飘然而去,或得到民众的理解。这种结局有一定的合理性,却完全没有考虑伊丽莎白末期和斯图亚特早期英国的法律语境。都铎时期的法官判决严厉,法律体系建立在相应的惩罚制度上,新教的信仰与恩典破坏了以往以功绩为基础的奖赏。事实上,基督教本身关于复仇的教义就是矛盾的。《旧约》提倡"以牙还牙,以血还血",而《新约》认为只有上帝有复仇的权力。舞台复仇者经常遇到腐败的法律体系:"上帝的正义可能会缓慢,他的世俗代表腐败了,国家机器失去秩序,因此导致公然的错误不受惩罚。"[2]剧场内,泰特斯呐喊正义女神艾斯特莱雅(Astraea)已离开罗马,罗马陷入了黑暗和混乱;而剧场外,伊丽莎白女王被当作艾斯特莱雅女神的化身。鉴于莎士比亚常用戏剧世界影射现实社会,正义女神的离开揭露了伊丽莎白女王晚年时期英国司法系统的腐败和正义的缺失。即便是在提倡宽容的基督教社会,一个封建等级严明的国家,稳定和谐的社会秩序是国家安定的必要条件,如果统治者无法运行国家机器保障社会秩序,基于对提供公平与正义的官方机构的不信任,复仇者不会一直等待上帝缓慢的正义,而是进行私人复仇,因为"有缺陷的司法系统本身,往往从一

---

[1] Linda Woodbridge, *English Revenge Drama*, Cambridge: Cambridge University Press, 2010, p. 25.
[2] Anne Pippin Burnett, *Revenge in Attic and Later Tragedy*, Berkeley: University of California Press, 1998, p. 21.

开始就成为复仇的诱因"[①]。复仇者哈姆雷特虽因此失去性命,但"天使们将唱歌让他安息"(5.2.303)。莎士比亚复仇剧的核心之正义危机,在非常真实的意义上反映了早期现代英格兰法律体系发生的危机。

参考文献

A. W. Schlegel, *Lectures on Dramatic Art and Literature*, London: George Bell and Sons, 1879.

Anne Pippin Burnett, *Revenge in Attic and Later Tragedy*, Berkeley: University of California Press, 1998.

B. J. Sokol and Mary Sokol, eds., *Shakespeare, Law and Marriage*, New York: Cambridge University Press, 2003.

David George Hale, *The Body Politic: A Political Metaphor in Renaissance English Literature*, The Hague: Mouton & Co., 1971.

Derek Dunne, *Shakespeare, Revenge Tragedy and Early Modern Law*, London: Palgrave Macmillan, 2016.

Edward Muir, *Mad Blood Stirring, Vendetta and Factions in Friuli during the Renaissance*, Baltimore: Johns Hopkins University Press, 1993.

Eleanor Prosser, *Hamlet and Revenge*, 2nd edition, Stanford: Stanford University Press, 1971.

Francis Bacon, "Of Revenge", in John Pitcher, ed., *The Essays*, Harmondsworth: Penguin, 1985.

G. K. Hunter, *Dramatic Identities and Cultural Tradition: Studies in Shakespeare and His Contemporaries*, New York: Barnes and Noble Books, 1978.

Graham Holderness, *Hamlet*, Milton Keynes and Philadelphia: Open University Press, 1987.

Gregory M. Colón Semenza, "The Spanish Tragedy and Revenge", in Garrett A. Sullivan Jr., Patrick Cheney and Andrew Hadfield, eds., *Early Modern English Drama: A Critical Companion*, Oxford: Oxford University Press, 2006.

Harry Keyishian, *The Shapes of Revenge: Victimization, Vengeance, and Vindictiveness in Shakespeare*, Atlantic Highlands, NJ: Humanities Press, 1995.

John Dover Wilson, ed., *Titus Andronicus*, Cambridge: Cambridge University Press, 2008.

John Kerrigan, *Revenge Tragedy: Aeschylus to Armageddon*, Oxford: Oxford University Press, 1996.

[①] See Derek Dunne, *Shakespeare, Revenge Tragedy and Early Modern Law*, New York: Palgrave Macmillan, 2016, p. 3.

Jonathan Gil Harris, *Sick Economies: Drama Mercantilism, and Disease in Shakespeare's England*, Philadelphia: University of Pennsylvania Press, 2004.

Lily B. Campbell, "Theories of Revenge in Renaissance England", *Modern Philology*, 28.3 (1931): 290.

Linda Woodbridge, *English Revenge Drama*, Cambridge: Cambridge University Press, 2010.

Paul A. Jorgensen, *Our Naked Frailties: Sensational Art and Meaning in "Macbeth"*, Berkeley: University of California Press, 1971.

René Girard, *Violence and the Sacred*, Patrick Gregory, trans., London: Athlone Press, 1988.

Richard A. Posner, *Law and Literature*, 3rd edition, Massachusetts: Harvard University Press, 2009.

Robert N. Watson, "Tragedies of Revenge and Ambition", in Claire McEachern, ed., *The Cambridge Companion to Shakespearean Tragedy*, Cambridge: Cambridge University Press, 2002.

Steve Hindle, "The Keeping of the Public Peace", in Paul Griffiths, Adam Fox and Steve Hindle, eds., *The Experience of Authority in Early Modern England*, Basingstoke: Macmillan, 1996.

莎士比亚:《莎士比亚全集(三)》,朱生豪等译,人民文学出版社,1994年。

莎士比亚:《莎士比亚全集(四)》,朱生豪等译,人民文学出版社,1994年。

莎士比亚:《莎士比亚全集(五)》,朱生豪等译,人民文学出版社,1994年。

科马克、努斯鲍姆、斯特瑞尔:《莎士比亚与法:学科与职业的对话》,王光林等译,黑龙江教育出版社,2015年。

饥饿、寓言与天气
——《科利奥兰纳》中吃的意图

胡鹏

摘要：莎士比亚的罗马悲剧向来以其深刻而广泛的政治寓意受到研究者的重视，但是研究者的目光多集中在剧本如何反映罗马政治生活、如何塑造政治英雄人物等方面。作为莎士比亚罗马剧的最后一部，《科利奥兰纳》以主人公的起伏经历讲出了一个不可一世的英雄人物自取灭亡的悲剧。本文拟从剧中开场导致罗马市民暴动的饥荒出发，从人们的"饥饿"、米尼涅斯"肚子寓言"及同时代暴动、天气因素等方面分析剧中吃的逻辑，指出莎士比亚在改编罗马历史叙事以拷问政治制度的同时，暗含的"脱责"意图，以更好理解此剧内涵。

关键词：《科利奥兰纳》；吃；饥饿；寓言；天气

基金项目：本文系国家社科后期资助项目"莎士比亚与早期现代英国物质文化研究"（项目编号：19FWWB017）的阶段性研究成果。

作者简介：胡鹏，四川外国语大学莎士比亚研究所教授，主要研究方向为莎士比亚研究。

一、导论

莎士比亚最后一部罗马悲剧《科利奥兰纳》（以下简称《科》）讲述了公元前5世纪古罗马城邦的阶级斗争状况，其中主人公与护民官、民众、元老院贵族等之间的政治博弈尤为激烈。该剧向来备受研究者关注，但研究多从政治角度出发，如研究政府组织功能、统治者品质、贵族与民众关系,甚至同时代政治状况等。[1]莎士比亚主要依据古希腊史学家普鲁塔克《名人传》中的科里奥兰纳传记构思这一罗马悲剧,使用的是诺斯的英译本(1579),但其主要的改编是将两次国内的动乱合二为一。在普鲁塔克的文本中,贫穷的民众恼怒于高利贷而非谷物价格及饥荒,在元老院无法做出处理决定时,他们抛弃并离开了城市。米尼涅斯通过肚子和四肢的寓言安抚平民,保民官是指定而非民选的。传记中只有在攻取科瑞欧利的战役之后,才提及了食物短缺带来的饥馑(耕地荒废、战时缺乏运输工具及时间、不许进口外国粮食)。[2]显然,莎士比亚则认为戏剧中民众的暴动一次就能达到戏剧效果,从而将本剧重点放在平民的饥荒及他们认为贵族囤积大量的粮食之上。本文则试图将此剧放置在饥荒、暴动和小冰期的背景之下,从"吃"这一细节出发,剖析剧中政治博弈背后莎士比亚的隐含意图。

二、饥饿

《科》很可能是在1608年创作初演的。[3]那时,英格兰全国都陷入了食物短缺的困境,因此批评家们都注意到此剧的时事性。[4]我们毫不奇怪地看到戏剧甫一开场,饥饿的罗马市民手持棍棒及其他武器准备暴动,他们下定决心"宁可死不愿挨饿"(320):

> 我们不过是穷百姓,贵族才是'好'市民。那些掌权的吃饱喝足了。剩下的才救济我们。要是他们趁着那些过剩的食品还没有发霉变质就施舍给我们,我们还以为他们的救济是出于人道之心;但他们太抬举我们了。我们那副骨瘦如柴的苦相,我们那副受苦受难的模样,是一张用来衬托他们财富的清单;他们的收获来自我们的苦难。让我们

---

[1] Stephen Orgel and Sean Keilen, eds., *Political Shakespeare*, London and New York: Routledge, 1999.; John A. and Sean D. Dutton, *Perspectives on Politics in Shakespeare*, Lanham: Lexington Books, 2006.; Robin H. Wells, *Shakespeare's Politics: a Contextual Introduction*, London and New York: Continuum, 2009.

[2] 普鲁塔克:《希腊罗马名人传·上》,席代岳译,吉林出版集团,2009年,第404-405页、第410页。

[3] Stanley Wells, Gary Taylor, John Jowett and William Montgomery, eds., *William Shakespeare: A Textual Companion.*, Oxford: Clarendon Press, 1987, pp. 124-125, p. 131.

[4] E.C. Pettett, "*Coriolanus* and the Midlands Insurrection of 1607", *Shakespeare Survey*, 3(1950): 34-42.; Annabel M. Patterson, *Shakespeare and the Popular Voice*, Oxford: Basil Blackwell, 1989, pp. 127-146.; W.G. Zeeveld, "*Coriolanus* and Jacobean Politics", *Modern Language Review*, 57.3(1962):321-324.; Richard Wilson, *Will Power: Essays on Shakespearean Authority*, New York: Harvester Wheatsheaf, 1993, pp. 88-117.

举起钉耙来报仇雪恨,趁我们还没有瘦成骨架。天上的神祇知道我说这话是出于饥饿,而不是渴于复仇(320-1)。①

剧中的市民们抱怨统治他们的罗马贵族,同时也对比了饱受饥饿之苦的市民和脑满肠肥的贵族,更是鲜明地指出了暴动的原因——饥饿,而并非我们在《凯撒》等剧中看到的出于政治目的的暴动。暴动的根本原因似乎是贵族与平民之间源于粮食问题的尖锐矛盾,就如同平民所控诉的那样:"让我们忍饥挨饿,他们的谷仓却堆满粮食;颁布了庇护高利贷的法令;针对有钱人的法令取消了,替代的是苛刻的束缚穷人的条文。"(《科》:323)他们的怒火指向了一个个体,即凯厄斯·马修斯(即科利奥兰纳)这个"老百姓的头号敌人"(《科》:320),认为只要杀死他,粮食问题便可迎刃而解。而科利奥兰纳之所以成为民众的第一个对付对象,"全体人民的众矢之的"(《科》:321),是因为他是最典型、最激进的贵族代表,他认为不应该满足民众的请愿,平白分配给他们粮食,瞧不起这些只会空口白话、毫无贡献的愚民。但是正如盖尔·克恩·帕斯特(Gail Kern Paster)指出的那样,此剧根本不允许我们查明平民控告囤积粮食的贵族是否正确。②

由此,我们可以进一步梳理剧中其他人物及群体有关"吃""饥饿"的细节,特别是连接科利奥兰纳和其母亲的食物及喂养意象上。我们看到剧中伏伦妮娅有两次都提到了母乳喂养,第一次是在第一幕第三景中,她让儿媳维吉莉娅劝诫丈夫英勇杀敌时说道:"当赫卡柏哺乳赫克托时,她的乳房还不及赫克托流血的额头姣美,这额头把血轻蔑地溅向希腊人的利剑。"(《科》:338)第二次是在第三幕第二景中,她鼓励儿子时又讲道:"你只管干吧,你的勇敢是吮吸了我奶汁才获得的,你的骄傲却属于你自己。"(《科》:421)这两处指涉无疑会让读者和观众认为科利奥兰纳所有的才能和力量都源于母乳喂养。珍妮特·阿德尔曼(Janet Adelman)从精神分析角度详细梳理了此剧的食物及喂养主题,她将伏伦妮娅第一段关于乳汁的话这样解读:

血液比乳汁、伤口比乳房、战争比和平的喂养都更美……赫克托将婴幼儿的母乳喂养转移到流血的伤口,而乳房和伤口之间无言的中介者则是婴儿的嘴唇:在这一想象性

---

① 莎士比亚:《科利奥兰纳》,《新莎士比亚全集·第6卷》,汪义群译,河北教育出版社,2000年。本文出自该著作的引文,将随文在括号内标出该名称首字和引文出处页码,不另作注。
② Gail Kern Paster, "To Starve with Feeding: The City in *Coriolanus*", *Shakespeare Studies*, 11(1978): 123-144, p. 126.

转移中,喂养即受伤,嘴成为伤口而乳房成为刀剑……但同时正如伏伦妮娅的想象指出了哺乳中固有的脆弱性,同样也指出了避开脆弱性的一种方法。在她的想象中,哺乳/消化吸收转化成为倾吐,一种具有进攻性的驱逐排出行为;伤口再次变成了能吐的嘴……伤口流血没有由此变成脆弱性的符号而是进攻的手段。①

在斯坦利·卡维尔(Stanley Cavell)看来,一方面,赫克托既蔑视希腊人的刀剑,但同时自己也使用刀剑战斗,因此"嘴似乎变成了一把切割武器;哺乳的母亲似乎变成了被英雄儿子劈砍的对象,被她所喂养的对象吞噬"。另一方面,将母乳与男子鲜血相提并论,意味着"男人在战场上流血战斗并不是简单的攻击,同样也是以男性的方式在提供食物"。②科利奥兰纳母子俩一直都处于持续性的"饥饿"状态且贯穿全剧始终,"母子俩以人类的名义或定义展示了这种饥饿状态,展示出一种贪得无厌、不知足(insatiability)的状态(由喂养带来的饥饿,喂养即贫困/剥夺)。有时,这种状态也被描述为强加在有限身体上欲望的无限性。但他们母子俩的饥饿体现出这种无限性不是人类不知足的原因,而是结果"③。此外,母子俩的饥饿对象实际上从食物转向了荣誉。科利奥兰纳反复告诫我们要提防吃的欲望,在荣誉面前克制身体欲望。他忍受着内心的厌恶出现在市民面前,公开展示自己作战的伤口,但却在市民走后吐露心声:"我们宁可死去,宁可挨饿,也不愿向别人乞求我们应得的工价。我为何披着这身粗羊皮的外衣,站在这儿向每一个路过的人乞讨那不必要的担保?习俗逼着我这样做。"(《科》:387)甚至于他后来被放逐时也谈道:"让他们宣判将我从峻峭的大帕岩上推下,将我放逐、鞭打、囚禁起来,每天只给吃一粒谷子;我也不愿用一句好话做代价买通他们的慈悲,更不愿为了乞求他们的恩赐而短了自己的志气,去向他们道声早安。"(《科》:428)而在科利奥兰纳被放逐之后,米尼涅斯询问伏伦妮娅是否愿意一起用膳时,她如此回应:"愤怒是我的食物;光是咽下这么多的愤怒便要把我撑死。"(《科》:438)这句话正好与早前科利奥兰纳"宁可死去宁可挨饿"的话一致。可见,科利奥兰纳乃至她的母亲伏伦妮娅都是饥饿的,他们想

---

① Janet Adelman, "'Anger's my meat': feeding, dependency and aggression in *Coriolanus*", in Murray Schwartz and Coppélia Kahn, eds., *Representing Shakespeare*. Baltimore: The Johns Hopkins University Press, 1980, p. 131.
② Stanley Cavell, "'Who Does the Wolf Love?': *Coriolanus* and Interpretations of Politics", in Patricia Parker and Geoffrey Hartman, eds., *Shakespeare and the Question of Theory*, New York: Methuen, 1985, p. 253.
③ Ibid, p. 249.

"吃"的"食物"不是普通的粮食,而是所谓的"血气"还有荣耀。[1]

进一步而言,食人与同类相食贯穿整部戏剧。首先,民众是贵族的食物。我们不能忽视的是,市民在控诉贵族时所讲的话,"咱们要是不死在战场上,也会死在他们的手里!(if the war eat us not up ,they will),这就是他们对我们的爱护"(《科》:323)。这意味着贵族就像捕食者,而平民则成为猎物。因为这是一个饥荒的时代,同时也是面临战争和被入侵的实际威胁而充满危机的年代。其次,贵族也可能是他人的食物。我们需要注意的是,米尼涅斯问护民官西西涅斯和勃鲁托斯:"请问,狼喜欢什么?"西西涅斯回答:"羔羊。"而米尼涅斯则回应:"正是,为的是把它一口吞掉,正像饥饿的平民恨不得把尊贵的马修斯吞下肚里一样。"而勃鲁托斯则说:"他实在是一头羔羊,叫起来却像头熊"。(《科》:363)显然这里反转地说明了那些如科利奥兰纳这样的"羔羊"也是贵族"狼"的食物。再次,米尼涅斯也谈到了可能发生的食人现象:"善良明智的天神不会允许我们名扬四海的罗马蚕食自己的儿女,像一头灭绝天性的母兽一样!"(《科》:412)最后,我们还可以看到食人的循环往复,即进食者被他们所吃的食物所吞没,贵族与平民可以将角色置换颠倒,乃至互相吞没毁灭。如同科利奥兰纳对市民所言:"攻击尊贵的元老院,是怎么回事?若不是他们在诸神的帮助下使你们慑手畏惧,你们早就彼此相食了。"(《科》:328)而科利奥兰纳后来被放逐,从贵族沦为平民,被各方利用也说明了这一点。因此我们可以这样认为,剧中的所有人都处于一种"饥饿"状态,而由此带来的有关"吃"与"食人"的逻辑则贯穿了整部戏剧,实际上《科》就是一部"吃"的戏剧。

三、寓言

戏剧一开场的暴动让我们看到了罗马城的分裂状态,当市民准备冲向议会时,米尼涅斯登场试图劝说、安抚民众,在最初的辩护无果的状态下,他决定讲一个"有趣"的故事——肚子的寓言,这实际上也就是一个关于"吃"的故事。米尼涅斯从人的生理学概念出发,向饥饿的暴民解释元老院在罗马政治生活里的中心地位。他将元老院比作身体中的胃,想象着肚子与身体其他器官争辩,它们指责它:"像只无底洞占据身体中央的

---

[1] 参见陈雷:《对罗马共和国的柏拉图式批评——谈〈科利奥兰纳斯〉并兼及"荣誉至上的政体"》,《外国文学评论》2012年第4期;彭磊:《荣誉与权谋——〈科利奥兰纳斯〉中的伏伦妮娅》,《国外文学》2016年第3期。

部位,终日无所事事,无所作为,只顾着把食物往里面装,却从不分担别人的劳苦。"(《科》:324)面对这种潜在的叛乱,肚子则这样回应。尽管它接收了食物,但把精华都输送给了其他器官,他告诉那些不满的器官:"是我通过你们血液之河把这食物输送到心脏的宫殿和头脑的宝座;并流经曲折的管道和各个脏器,最强健的筋肉和最微小的血管得以生存,都因从我这儿获得精力的滋养。"(《科》:325-6)

米尼涅斯的故事源于古老的寓言和人们已有的认知,因为他自己就承认这个寓言很可能听众都听过,"你们或许已经听过,但我还得老生常谈一遍"(《科》:323),以此来抚慰市民们对元老院统治日益增长的不满。①虽然他的故事似乎没有提到医学知识,但却说出了一个当时的流行观点,即有形的个体身体的运作可以用来解释无形的政治身体的运转。当时的流行医学理论认为,所有身体器官都在这一过程中扮演了至关重要的作用。迈克尔·费尔特(Michael Schoenfeldt)就指出,这一时期的解剖学家和医生认为,消化是发生在整个身体内部的,这一过程一直持续到各个器官吸收并获取需要的营养后才会完成。②其结果就是消化并不是由胃分配的过程,也不是身体其他部分被动接受的过程,而是构成身体的所有器官平等、相互依赖、通力合作的系统性过程。因此,我们看到的米尼涅斯有关肚子的寓言,正回应了古代医学家盖伦所描述的胃,即不是被动接受而是主动提供营养的仓库,仿佛主动把麦子和糠分开:"就像工人熟练地制备麦子一样,将混在里面对人体有害的泥土、石头或外国种子清除,胃的功能就在于将那些(无用的、有害的)东西往下推排,而把那些剩下的、有营养的物质分配到胃肠延伸的血管中。"③盖伦认为,消化道在维持身体体液平衡方面十分重要,如果肠胃受到损害,那么身体其他官能也将受损。"很多文艺复兴时期的作家将身体分为政治之体和由大脑、心脏、肚子组成的三位一体等级秩序之体,而大脑往往指上层阶级、肚子则是下层阶级。"④从这点来看,这些描述是与盖伦有关或与工人类比一致的。但市民们曾在米尼涅斯的故

---

① 有关此寓言故事来龙去脉,参见 David G. Hale, "Intestine Sedition: The Fable of the Belly", *Comparative Literature Studies*, 5.4(1968):377-388。
② Michael Schoenfeldt, "Fables of the Belly in Early Modern England", in David Hillman and Carla Mazzio, eds., *The Body in Parts: Fantasies of Corporeality in Early Modern Europe*, New York: Routledge, 1997, p. 245.
③ Galen, *On the Usefulness of the Parts of the Body*, vol.1, Margaret Tallmadge May, trans., *Cornell Publications in the History of Science*, Ithaca: Cornell University Press, 1968, p. 204.
④ Joan Fitzpatrick, *Food in Shakespeare: Early Modern Dietaries and the Plays*, Burlington: Ashgate, 2007, p. 95.

事中途插话,讲出了另一个表述:"那戴着王冠的头,那警惕的眼睛,那运筹帷幄的心,那打仗的手臂,那作为坐骑的腿,那作为号手的舌,联合起来我们这个组织里各尽其职的防御部门……要是他们受制于贪婪的肚子,那个身上的下水道。"(《科》:324–5)安德鲁·哈德菲尔德(Andrew Hadfield)就指出,市民有关不同身体部分相互依赖共同作用造就一个健康整体的身体政治观念的表述,实际上"更加符合早期现代政治话语中对身体隐喻的用法"。[1]但也正如费尔特指出的那样,《科》中肚子的寓言故事是对身体政治秩序典型阐释的违背,因为"基于上层和下层区分的等级秩序"被"基于中心和边缘区分的等级秩序"所取代,后者"强调了消化、分配食物以维持身体各个部分的极度重要性"。费尔特将米尼涅斯的寓言看作一个"有关社会资源自然而然从少数特权阶级流向大众"的幻想,"(利用)有关胃部生理上的中心位置将社会的不平等神秘化,并掩盖了作为生产和分配食物的一部分实际劳动"。[2]我们看到米尼涅斯的解释却并未得到市民的认可,市民甲就反问:"你引用这话用意何在?""我是大趾头!为什么是那个大的?"(《科》:326)米尼涅斯试图让饥民们理解贵族的视角,实际上也就是他自己的视角。他的话激起市民的愤怒,提出、展示了问题却并未给出解决方案,因此并未成功安抚愤怒的市民。正如帕斯特指出的那样,米尼涅斯的寓言"最深刻的意义是作为城市稳定的喜剧可能性,剧中无情的主要行动留下了孤立和悬而未决的痕迹,标志着理想与现实之间的分裂,标志着可能的想象,甚至有时会导致喜剧与无法避免的悲剧之间的分裂"。[3]也正如卡维尔将莎士比亚笔下的米尼涅斯与西德尼在《为诗辩护》中的米尼涅斯对比时指出的那样,莎士比亚的米尼涅斯是"党徒,有限的……作为故事的讲述人"。[4]而情况在马修斯进场之后变得更加恶化,因为他坚持认为市民们是"暴乱的无赖"和"疥癣"(《科》:327),恨不得"将那成千个砍成碎段的奴才堆成尸山"(《科》:329)。

进一步而言,我们必须注意到科利奥兰纳采用了食人的想象来指责当时罗马的民主。在他看来,恰恰是贵族的独裁专制震慑了平民,得以避免他们"彼此相食"(《科》:

---

[1] Andrew Hadfield, *Shakespeare and Renaissance Politics*, London: Thomason Learning, 2004, p. 174.

[2] Michael Schoenfeldt, *Bodies and Selves in Early Modern England: Physiology and Inwardness in Spenser, Shakespeare, Herbert, and Milton*, Cambridge: Cambridge University Press, 1999, p. 29.

[3] Gail Kern Paster, "To Starve with Feeding: The City in *Coriolanus*", *Shakespeare Studies*, 11(1978): 123–144, p. 126.

[4] Stanley Cavell, "'Who Does the Wolf Love?': *Coriolanus* and the Interpretations of Politics", in Patricia Parker and Geoffrey Hartman, eds., *Shakespeare and the Question of Theory*, New York: Methuen, 1985, pp. 245–272.

328)。这实际上又再次提醒着我们,肚子的寓言是一个有关人的生理乃至人"吃"东西(食物与人)的故事。从这一角度讲,莎士比亚特意透过米尼涅斯将罗马的"头和心脏"——元老院沉降到了"腹部",显然是与口腹之欲相关。诚然,剧中米尼涅斯是出于谈话效果而特意选择器官,同时也契合罗马社会财富增长过程中贵族所起的作用,即财富是由贵族对外掠夺获得,而非由平民劳动获得。但若从戏剧效果上看,这则寓言实际上也将贵族、元老院与下层阶级等同,说明了所有人实际上都处于一种"吃"与"被吃"的状态之下。

四、暴动与天气

那么为何莎士比亚会将饥饿与吃放置于如此重要的地位呢？实际上,此剧写成时,英国先后发生过1597年的粮荒、牛津郡民起事和1607年至1608年英格兰中部各郡的骚乱。1607年6月28日,英国王室曾发表公告称:"国内最低微的民众近来多诱人啸聚作乱。"[①]1586—1587年制定的相关法令《王国救济及粮食饥荒……法令》(*Orders...for the reliefe and stay of the present dearth of Graine within the Realme*)在1594年、1595年、1608年及后反复颁布。其中规定法官有权检查囤积粮食的商人,让他们将囤货上市、抑制粮价、雇佣失业者,同样也鼓励富农以"慈善的价格"卖粮食给穷人。[②]诚然有很多富人出于慈善施舍穷人钱用于买食物或直接提供食物,但有时却是在当局的压力下不得已而为之。例如1597年在布里斯托尔"所有城市中有能力的人均被责成给每八个穷人一顿肉"。同年,伍斯特最富有的市民"收留了200多名穷人和老人并供养他们"。[③]某些城镇也自建粮仓以备粮备荒,这种行为就同剧中马修斯所说那样,敌人"伏尔斯人有的是谷子,把这些耗子带去,去啃啮他们的谷仓"(《科》:331-2)。城镇当局就利用这些谷仓在饥荒之年购入粮食,以补贴价售卖给穷人。比如1596年,在布里斯托尔,当局购买了3000夸脱的波罗的海黑麦,以低于市场价的价格出售,"并向城市的穷人分发了许

---

① Alexander Leggart, *Shakespeare's Political Drama: the History Plays and Roman Plays*, London: Routledge, 1982, p. 208.
② R.B. Outhwaite, *Dearth, Public Policy and Social Disturbance in England, 1550-1800*, Basingstoke: Palgrave Macmillan, 1991, p. 40.
③ John Walter, *Crowds and Popular Politics in Early Modern England*, Manchester: Manchester University Press, 2006, p. 153.

多食物"。①如果补贴销售的数量足够大,那么以这种方式使用粮食库存也可以降低市场价格。但是在1590年代中期后,英国其他地区收成逐渐恢复的时候,米德兰兹地区依然谷物缺乏且价格上涨。其中一个重要原因就是都铎时代盛行的圈地运动,将原来公有的开放耕作土地变成了富农养羊的牧场。这一"羊吃人"运动的快速发展导致农民群体被迫变得更穷更饿,甚至谷物价格没有在收获前的夏季达到峰值,反而略有下降——这表明需求的下降足以抵消日益严重的短缺,因为"穷人已经用完了他们的现金储备,转而购买燕麦等劣等谷物"。②实际上,农村的动荡在1607年并非新出现的现象。他们"既没有宗教也没有广义上的政治要求,起义者所抗议的是圈地和食物短缺,并将前者视为后者的主要原因"③。不愿失地的农民能抵抗圈地的唯一方式就是暴力,而且失地农民也易于被纳入叛乱者队伍,威胁社会稳定。虽然都铎时期政府也曾颁布一系列反圈地法令,但由于经济发展潮流的不可违逆而收效甚微。正如约翰·马丁(John Martin)所指出那样,这是"在像中部这样的地区,农业资本主义者与农民阶级在为商业放牧而圈地和改地为牧场的问题上发生了正面冲突"④。但实际上,圈地只是导致农业减产和粮食价格上升的原因之一。

另一个关键原因其实是气候,因为古代农业本来就是靠天吃饭。根据气候史家的观点,从14世纪初开始,人类气候进入了长达近5个半世纪的小冰期。这一时期的气候变得不可预测,更加寒冷,时常出现暴风雨和极端气候。而全球范围内同期出现的极寒期(1590—1610),恰好与莎士比亚的写作年代(1590—1613)吻合。⑤小冰期带来的不仅仅是气温下降,还使得植物生长季节变短,粮食减产,谷物价格上升,造成全球各地饥馑与瘟疫频发。因此,小冰期也是暴乱、死亡及王朝更迭的高发期。文艺复兴时期,英国文学所谓的"黄金时代"大概指1575—1625年间,与之相应的就是我们熟知的小冰期,

---

① Quoted in John Walter, *Crowds and Popular Politics in Early Modern England*, Manchester: Manchester University Press, 2006, p. 156.
② John E. Martin, *Feudalism to Capitalism: Peasant and Landlord in English Agrarian Development*, London: Macmillan Press, 1983, p. 162.
③ Peter Holland, ed., *Coriolanus*, London and New York: Bloomsbury, 2017, p. 57.
④ John E. Martin, *Feudalism to Capitalism: Peasant and Landlord in English Agrarian Development*, London: Macmillan Press, 1983, p. 132.
⑤ See Brian Fagan, *The Little Ice Age: How Climate Made History 1300-1850*, New York: Basic Books, 2000, pp. 48-50.

中世纪温暖的时期被寒冷所替代。①杰弗瑞·帕克(Geoffery Parker)专注于17世纪中期欧洲的"普遍危机(General Crisis)"。他将气候科学与历史研究相结合,指出"主要气候类型的改变,特别是冬季更长更冷、夏季更加潮湿……带来了饥荒、营养不良及疾病;物质条件恶化,战争、暴动、革命频发"。②而且正如沃尔夫刚·贝林格(Wolfgang Behringer)与布莱恩·费根(Brian Fagan)指出的那样,气候的改变是文化反应及创新的巨大推动力。③1575—1625年间,英格兰、苏格兰、威尔士及欧陆大部分地区都经历了气候的干扰,潮湿夏季之后急剧变化的冬季导致了一连串的歉收。16世纪90年代,严寒笼罩着伊丽莎白一世统治下的英格兰,坚冰紧锁横贯伦敦的泰晤士河。贝林格就指出:当冰层能够承载足够的重量时,首都伦敦的生活就会转移到泰晤士河上,其中包括货摊交易和冬季运动。④16世纪90年代为16世纪最冷的十年,1591—1597年作物歉收,举国抱怨食物匮乏,甚至很多郡县都发生了食物暴动,市民生活举步维艰。一篇1596年的日志记录了当年的饥荒情况:"市场上谷物供应有限,市民也没有钱买得起粮食。供应萎缩导致市场上时常发生哄抢,哀鸿遍野,这在以前是闻所未闻的。"⑤到了17世纪初,严寒依旧,在反常的极端天气影响下,饥民们往往被迫揭竿而起。⑥而1607年英国爆发了史称"米德兰兹起义(The Midlands Revolt)"的民众起义运动,短短一个月的时间就席卷了北安普敦郡、莱斯特郡及沃里克郡。部分原因在于长期以来,特别是1590年代中期以来的粮食歉收所造成的饥荒人数激增,死亡率上升,社会动荡。⑦布莱特·斯特林(Brents Stirling)认为米德兰兹地区叛乱对戏剧是有影响

---

① "小冰期"最初由马修斯于1939所使用。F. E. Matthes, "Report of Committee on Glaciers, April 1939", *Transactions, American Geophysical Union*, 20.4(1939): 518−523.

② G. Parker, *Global Crisis: War, Climate and Catastrophe in the Seventeenth Century*, New Haven and CT: Yale University Press, 2013.

③ Wolfgang Behringer, *A Cultural History of Climate*, London: Polity, 2011.; Brian Fagan, *The Little Ice Age: How Climate Made History, 1300−1850*, New York: Basic Books, 2000.

④ 贝林格:《气候的文明史:从冰川时代到全球变暖》,史జ译,社会科学文献出版社,2012年,第107页。See also H. H. Lamb, *Climate, History, and the Modern World*, New York: Routledge, 1995, pp. 230−231.

⑤ Brian Fagan, *The Little Ice Age: How Climate Made History 1300−1850*, New York: Basic Books, 2000, p. 90.

⑥ See Brian Parker, ed., *The Oxford Shakespeare: The Tragedy of Coriolanus*, Oxford: Oxford University Press, 2008, p. 6.

⑦ R.B. Outhwaite, *Dearth, Public Policy and Social Disturbance in England, 1550−1800*, Basingstoke: Palgrave Macmillan, 1991, pp. 46−47.

的。①而皮特特也指出,"1607年叛乱在《科》中的反映有着非常好的基础"。②他们的研究为我们理解同时代文本及戏剧的可能创作年份提供了基础,因为悲剧《科利奥兰纳》恰好写作于这一时期,剧中穷人们的诉求是古罗马社会矛盾尖锐的体现,同时也是小冰期伊丽莎白一世统治下粮食危机的写照。③剧中诸如"冰上的炭火""阳光中的雹点"之类的修辞,也具有现实基础。马修斯将平民的无信比作"冰上的炭火",实际上指涉的是1607—1608年冬季的"大严寒"(Great Frost)。据埃德蒙·豪斯(Edmund Howes)记载:"12月8日开始的严寒持续了7天……同月20日严寒再次袭来,仅仅4天之内人们即可行走于泰晤士河中间的冰面上……乃至横穿河面……很多人在冰上摆摊设点售卖商品……"而在1607/8年1月8日的一封信中,约翰·张伯伦(John Chamberlain)写道:"确信的是有年轻人在冰上加热一加仑的红酒,让所有的路人都参与其中。"1608年,作家托马斯·德克(Thomas Dekker)写了一本小册子《大严寒》(The Great Frost),描绘了"数锅的炭火"怎样被放置在冰面上供路人取暖的。④因此,我们对莎士比亚通过米尼涅斯劝告民众的话感到毫不奇怪,他实际上是在为政府与贵族乃至粮食商人"脱罪",把饥荒的罪责归咎于天:

至于因为贫困和饥荒,你们便要举起棍棒来反抗罗马政府,那我奉劝你们倒不如去打那老天,因为罗马政府始终如一地替你们解除种种困难,那困难比你们的反抗所造成的危害要严重得多。因为这次灾荒是上天而不是贵族造成……

(《科》:322-3)

实际上,莎士比亚透过米尼涅斯与马修斯的对白,明确表达出对平民这群乌合之众的蔑视。因为在马修斯看来,平民的要求是无理的、空想的、不切实际的:

---

① Brents Stirling, *The Populace of Shakespeare*, New York: AMS Press, 1949, p. 225.
② E.C. Pettett, "*Coriolanus* and the Midlands Insurrection of 1607", *Shakespeare Survey*, 3(1950):34−42, p. 35.
③ 在普鲁塔克原文中,饥馑是由平民脱离运动导致的废耕及战时交通运输不便造成的,与天气无关。See Arthur Hugh Clough, et al., eds., *Plutarch: The Lives of the Noble Grecians and Romans*, John Dryden, trans., New York: Modern Library, 1932, p. 270.而莎士比亚在剧中添加了某些寒冷的词汇表达,显然是与同时代的天气相关的。
④ Quoted in Brian Parker, ed., *The Oxford Shakespeare: The Tragedy of Coriolanus*, Oxford: Oxford University Press, 2008, p. 5.

米尼涅斯:要按他们的要求分配谷物,他们说城里储藏着好多粮食。

马修斯:绞死他们! 他们说! 他们只会坐在火炉旁边,假装知道议会里发生的事情。

(《科》:328)

剧中的平民是只管肚子饿不饿,而不会理会政府、贵族等是否真的有罪。他们性格暴躁、易冲动、极其易变、容易被煽动,根本没有理性思维,每一个作为个体的罗马平民在人口众多的罗马城中微不足道,倘若政局发生重大变化,他们就能够汇聚成一股不容忽视的政治力量登上舞台,表现出让人难以想象的力量。正如古斯塔夫·勒庞所言:孤立的个人很清楚,在孤身一人时,他不能焚烧宫殿或洗劫商店,即使受到诱惑,他也很容易抵制这种诱惑。但是在成为群体的一员时,他就会意识到人数赋予他的力量,这足以让他生出杀人劫掠的念头,并且会立刻屈从于这种诱惑。[1]因此,正如乔纳森·贝特(Jonathan Bate)所言:"小冰期时代的饥馑与粮食短缺,可以为理解莎士比亚作品提供新的思路。"[2]正是在缺粮和饥荒的状态下,罗马市民会让整个社会陷入失序和动荡。

五、结语

杰妮·阿彻(Jayne Archer)和她的两个同事通过仔细梳理历史文献,发现来自斯特拉特福镇的这名剧作家作为粮食商人以及房产主的不为人知的细节,而他的一些行径有时候也会和法律发生冲突。"在15年间,他不断地购买和储藏谷物,然后以高价卖给邻居和当地商人。"她还说莎士比亚"喜欢找那些无法(或者说不会)全额支付购买其谷物的人,然后用这些收益进一步扩大其放贷活动"。甚至在1598年,他还因为在粮食短缺时期囤积谷物而被起诉过。因此,对于当时粮食危机的了解可以帮助我们更好地了解莎士比亚的作品,其中就包括《科》:"记住把莎士比亚当作一个肚子会饿的人,这么一想的话,我们就觉得他更加有人性,更加可以理解,也更加复杂。"[3]而且在阿彻看来,莎士比亚不单单以写作来为其粮食买卖的投资提供资金支持,同时也呈现及再定义对都铎王朝后期和斯图亚特王朝前期政治中的核心观点——可持续性(sustainability)的争

---

[1] 勒庞:《乌合之众:大众心理研究》,冯克利译,中央编译出版社,2000年,第27页。
[2] William Shakespeare was a Ruthless Profiteer: Study. *CNBC*. 1 April, 2013. 3 April, 2013.
[3] Ibid.

论,包括琼·菲茨帕特里克(Joan Fitzpatrick)及罗伯特·阿佩尔鲍姆(Robert Appelbaum)等学者都注意到了莎士比亚戏剧中食物及食物相关意象的重要性。[1]"由身体政治与自然政治所支撑的营养与食物的政治,已经写入了社会结构、粮食,乃至莎士比亚自己笔下的角色、语言与情节之中。"[2]阿彻提醒我们,要注意莎士比亚粮食商人及地主的角色,因此我们有必要将莎士比亚与粮食联系起来解读。[3]值得注意的是,莎士比亚写作《科利奥兰纳》剧作时的1607—1608年,正是米德兰兹起义的时段。此时,莎士比亚自己的财产也受到了威胁,《科》剧展示出外族入侵是罗马城的命运,以及如何最好地应对"饥荒",是否应该囤积粮食。剧中的俚语"饥饿能毁墙""狗也要吃食""肉是为果腹""天神降五谷不仅为富人"(《科》:329)等无疑佐证了这一点。莎士比亚学者乔纳森·贝特对媒体说,阿彻和她的同事们做了非常有价值的工作,说他们的研究"给在《科》悲剧中因为粮食囤积而发生的抗议与真实的抗议活动发生在同一时代的观点注入了新的证据"。[4]

因此,我们可以说莎士比亚通过《科》剧透露出其商人的思维逻辑。首先,他透过第一幕让平民发泄自己的饥饿怨气,实际上疏导了同时代观众的怨气。其次,他也为政府、贵族乃至自己这样的囤粮商人脱罪,引导观众把导致饥荒的罪责归咎于气候。最后且最重要的是,剧作家也由此探讨了政治的本质问题,那就是——"吃",在这一点上,粮食等谷物与人实际上是一样的。

参考文献

Alexander Leggart, *Shakespeare's Political Drama: The History Plays and Roman Plays*, London: Routledge, 1982.

Andrew Hadfield, *Shakespeare and Renaissance Politics*, London: Thomason Learning, 2004.

---

[1] 相关研究著作有 Joan Fitzpatrick, *Food in Shakespeare: Early Modern Dietaries and the Plays*, Burlington: Ashgate, 2007.; Joan Fitzpatrick, *Renaissance Food from Rabelais to Shakespeare: Culinary Readings and Culinary Histories*, Aldershot: Ashgate, 2010.; Robert Appelbaum, *Aguecheek's Beef, Belch's Hiccup and Other Gastronomic Interjections: Literature, Culture and Food among the Early Moderns*, Chicago and IL: University of Chicago Press, 2006。

[2] Jayne Elisabeth Archer, Howard Thomas and Richard Marggraf Turley, "Reading Shakespeare with the grain: sustainability and the hunger business", *Green Letters: Studies in Ecocriticism*, 19.1(2015), pp. 13−14.

[3] Quoted in Jayne Elisabeth Archer, Howard Thomas and Richard Marggraf Turley, "Reading Shakespeare with the grain: sustainability and the hunger business", *Green Letters: Studies in Ecocriticism*, 19.1(2015): 16.

[4] William Shakespeare was a Ruthless Profiteer: Study. *CNBC*. 1 April, 2013. 3 April, 2013.

Annabel M. Patterson, *Shakespeare and the Popular Voice*, Oxford: Basil Blackwell, 1989.

Brents Stirling, *The Populace of Shakespeare*, New York: AMS Press, 1949.

Brian Fagan, *The Little Ice Age: How Climate Made History 1300−1850*, New York: Basic Books, 2000.

Brian Parker, ed., *The Oxford Shakespeare: The Tragedy of Coriolanus*, Oxford: Oxford University Press, 2008.

David G. Hale, "Intestine Sedition: The Fable of the Belly", *Comparative Literature Studies*, 5.4 (1968): 377−388.

E. C. Pettett, "Coriolanus and the Midlands Insurrection of 1607", *Shakespeare Survey*, 3(1950): 34−42.

F. E. Matthes, "Report of Committee on Glaciers, April 1939", *Transactions, American Geophysical Union*, 20.4(1939): 518−523.

G. Parker, *Global Crisis: War, Climate and Catastrophe in the Seventeenth Century*, New Haven and CT: Yale University Press, 2013.

Gail Kern Paster, "To Starve with Feeding: The City in Coriolanus", *Shakespeare Studies*, 11 (1978):123−144.

Galen, *On the Usefulness of the Parts of the Body*, vol.1, Margaret Tallmadge May, trans., Cornell Publications in the History of Science, Ithaca: Cornell University Press, 1968.

H. H. Lamb, *Climate, History, and the Modern World*, New York: Routledge, 1995.

Janet Adelman, "'Anger's my meat': Feeding, Dependency and Aggression in Coriolanus", in Murray Schwartz and Coppélia Kahn, eds., *Representing Shakespeare*, Baltimore: The Johns Hopkins University Press, 1980.

Jayne Elisabeth Archer, Howard Thomas and Richard Marggraf Turley, "Reading Shakespeare with the grain: sustainability and the hunger business", *Green Letters: Studies in Ecocriticism*, 19.1 (2015):8−20.

Joan Fitzpatrick, *Food in Shakespeare: Early Modern Dietaries and the Plays*, Burlington: Ashgate, 2007.

Joan Fitzpatrick, *Renaissance Food from Rabelais to Shakespeare: Culinary Readings and Culinary Histories*, Aldershot: Ashgate, 2010.

John A. and Sean D. Dutton, *Perspectives on Politics in Shakespeare*, Lanham: Lexington Books, 2006.

John E. Martin, *Feudalism to Capitalism: Peasant and Landlord in English Agrarian Development*, London: Macmillan Press, 1983.

John Walter, *Crowds and Popular Politics in Early Modern England*, Manchester: Manchester University Press, 2006.

Michael Schoenfeldt, "Fables of the Belly in Early Modern England", in David Hillman and Carla Mazzio, eds., *The Body in Parts: Fantasies of Corporeality in Early Modern Europe*, New York: Routledge, 1997.

Michael Schoenfeldt, *Bodies and Selves in Early Modern England: Physiology and Inwardness in Spenser, Shakespeare, Herbert, and Milton*, Cambridge: Cambridge University Press, 1999.

Peter Holland, ed., *Coriolanus*, London and New York: Bloomsbury, 2017.

R. B. Outhwaite, *Dearth, Public Policy and Social Disturbance in England, 1550–1800*, Basingstoke: Palgrave Macmillan, 1991.

Richard Wilson, *Will Power: Essays on Shakespearean Authority*, New York: Harvester Wheatsheaf, 1993.

Robert Appelbaum, *Aguecheek's Beef, Belch's Hiccup and Other Gastronomic Interjections: Literature, Culture and Food among the Early Moderns*, Chicago and IL: University of Chicago Press, 2008.

Robin H. Wells, *Shakespeare's Politics: A Contextual Introduction*, London and New York: Continuum, 2009.

Stanley Cavell, "'Who Does the Wolf Love?': Coriolanus and Interpretations of Politics", in Patricia Parker and Geoffrey Hartman, eds., *Shakespeare and the Question of Theory*, New York: Methuen, 1985.

Stanley Wells, Gary Taylor, John Jowett and William Montgomery, eds., *William Shakespeare: A Textual Companion*, Oxford: Clarendon Press, 1987.

Stephen Orgel and Sean Keilen, eds., *Political Shakespeare*, London and New York: Routledge, 1999.

W. G. Zeeveld, "Coriolanus and Jacobean Politics", *Modern Language Review*, 57.3(1962): 321–324.

William Shakespeare was a Ruthless Profiteer: Study. *CNBC*. 1 April, 2013. 3 April, 2013.

Wolfgang Behringer, *A Cultural History of Climate*, London: Polity, 2011.

普鲁塔克:《希腊罗马名人传·上》,席代岳译,吉林出版集团,2009年。

莎士比亚:《新莎士比亚全集·第6卷》,汪义群译,河北教育出版社,2000年。

陈雷:《对罗马共和国的柏拉图式批评——谈〈科利奥兰纳斯〉并兼及"荣誉至上的政体"》,《外国文学评论》2012年第4期。

彭磊:《荣誉与权谋——〈科利奥兰纳斯〉中的伏伦妮娅》,《国外文学》2016年第3期。

贝林格:《气候的文明史:从冰川时代到全球变暖》,史军译,社会科学文献出版社,2012年。

勒庞:《乌合之众:大众心理研究》,冯克利译,中央编译出版社,2000年。

《鲁克丽丝受辱记》中的"艺格符换"与性别政治

许庆红　李玉婷

摘要：莎士比亚的长篇叙事诗《鲁克丽丝受辱记》是一首跨艺术诗歌，具有隐含性别政治的艺格符换式书写——男性凝视下的女性身体刻画、鲁克丽丝对"特洛伊"画作的解读以及鲁克丽丝尸首的视觉呈现。这些揭示了作为视觉艺术的绘画与作为语言艺术的诗歌之间的互动关系。通过"观看"这一动作，该诗揭示了语言与图像背后暗含的性别政治，以及女性作为"艺格符换"主体所蕴含的言说潜力。女性尸首的视觉呈现使得整首诗从个人的微观空间转向公众的宏观政治空间，即罗马共和的建立。莎士比亚在该诗中赋予语言以视觉性和抒情性，使语言不仅能够召唤读者的图像感知，还能穿透他们的情感联想。同时，绘画作为视觉艺术并非处于静默状态，它参与了诗歌文本意义的建构，在诗歌阐释的过程中产生了巨大的言说潜力和政治意图，实现了诗歌中的审美与政治的联姻，也使诗歌具有了史诗般的维度。

关键词：《鲁克丽丝受辱记》；艺格符换；性别政治

作者简介：许庆红，安徽大学外语学院教授，博士生导师，主要研究方向为英美诗歌中的跨艺术与跨媒介；李玉婷，安徽大学外语学院硕士研究生，主要研究方向为英语语言文学。

一、引言

　　诗歌从诞生之日起，就与音乐、舞蹈、绘画等艺术门类之间有着密不可分的关系。跨艺术诗学指的是诗歌批评的跨艺术研究，关注诗歌与绘画、音乐等非语言艺术的相互影响以及诗歌文本与绘画、音乐等非诗歌文本之间的转换或改写，又称"艺格符换诗学"（Poetics of Ekphrasis），它"关注不同艺术媒介之间的互动和不同艺术文本之间的互文性"[1]。其中,"艺格符换"(Ekphrasis)是跨艺术诗学中的核心概念。"Ekphrasis"来自希腊语"ekphrasizein",其中"ek"指"说出来","phrasizein"指"详尽讲述"。[2]"艺格符换"作为古希腊罗马时期的修辞文化传统,是一种演讲术中的修辞手段。首部《修辞学初阶训练》(*Progymnasmata*)中就包含十几项修辞训练,"艺格符换"就是其中之一。《修辞学初阶训练》对该词的定义是对任何事物、人物、场景、艺术品等进行细致而生动的描述,"把主题生动地呈现在人们眼前"[3]。美国学者克里格(Murray Krieger)在《艺格符换:自然符号的幻觉》(*Ekphrasis: The Illusion of the Natural Sign*)中指出,艺格符换早期的含义"在古希腊修辞中是不受限制的:它指对生活或艺术中的事物,几乎是任何事物的语言描述"[4]。为了达到呈现在眼前的效果,修辞学家大多追求语言描述的生动性,即"生动描述"(Enargeia),它是艺格符换的核心。Enargeia不仅归于修辞学范畴中对演讲的要求,它还经常被用来形容诗歌的生动性,听众或读者可以通过语言这一媒介做出想象性反应,将自己置身于所描述的情景中。

随着20世纪后期比较文学的兴起,西方学者对"艺格符换"重新界定,沿着西方一直以来的"诗如画"(Ut Pictura Poesis)传统,将之运用于诗歌批评。美国学者赫佛南(James Heffernan)的界定被广为接受,"艺格符换"指诗歌中"视觉再现的语言再现"[5]。因此,我们可以看到"艺格符换"在古代指对任何事物的描述,而到了现代则局限于对艺术品(绘画、雕塑)的真实再现。其中,再现的媒介为文字性的语言或口头描述,而要使语言能在读者或听众心中产生情感,听众也必须参与其中,调动自身的感官、认知、情感等,努力使自己"沉浸"在作者所呈现的场景中。

《鲁克丽丝受辱记》(*The Rape of Lucrece*)是莎士比亚的一首长篇叙事诗,讲述的是鲁克丽丝被罗马王子塔昆强奸,并通过对卧室内一幅"特洛伊画"进行观看和思考,选择了自杀,从而引发古罗马向"共和"转变的故事。该诗中有大量艺格符换式描述,均由语

---

[1] 欧荣等:《语词博物馆:欧美跨艺术诗学研究》,北京大学出版社,2022年,第11页。

[2] James A. W. Heffernan, *Museum of Words: The Poetics of Ekphrasis from Homer to Ashbery*, Chicago: University of Chicago Press, 1993, p. 191.

[3] Ruth Webb, *Ekphrasis, Imagination and Persuasion in Ancient Rhetorical Theory and Practice*, Burlington: Ashgate Publishing Company, 2009, p. 14.

[4] Murray Krieger, *Ekphrasis: The Illusion of the Natural Sign*, Baltimore: Johns Hopkins University Press, 1992, p. 7.

[5] James A. W. Heffernan, *Museum of Words: The Poetics of Ekphrasis from Homer to Ashbery*, Chicago: University of Chicago Press, 1993, p. 3.

言(口语)这一媒介实现:第一,男性凝视下对女性所做的图像式的描述,其隐喻性和侵略性的语言暗含着性别政治思想。第二,鲁克丽丝对"特洛伊"画的解读,实现了从绘画到诗歌的"艺格符换"。受辱后的鲁克丽丝羞于指控,因此莎士比亚聚焦于对鲁克丽丝肉体和尸身的视觉展示。[1]在这一场景中,鲁克丽丝同样像一幅画一样被当众展示,像艺术品一般被政治利用,乃至其身体激怒了民众对该行径的反抗。通过"观看"这一动作,该诗揭示了语言与图像背后暗含的性别政治,以及女性作为"艺格符换"主体所隐含的言说潜力。女性尸首的视觉呈现使得整首诗从个人的微观抒情空间转向公众的政治空间[2],即罗马共和的建立。莎士比亚在该诗中赋予语言以视觉性和抒情性,使语言不仅能够召唤读者的图像感知,还能穿透他们的情感联想。同时,绘画作为视觉艺术并非处于静默状态,它参与了诗歌文本意义的建构,在诗歌阐释的过程中产生巨大的言说潜力和政治意图,实现了诗歌中审美与政治的联姻,也使诗歌具有了史诗般的维度。

二、从语言到绘画:男性"看"画背后的女性物化

韦伯(Ruth Webb)在其论著《艺格符换,古典修辞理论与实践中的想象与劝导》(*Ekphrasis, Imagination and Persuasion in Ancient Rhetorical Theory and Practice*)中指出了古代与现代关于"艺格符换"定义之间的联系与差异:

> 古代和现代的定义之间存在谱系联系,这种联系反映在视觉性在两者中的重要地位。但是,视觉的不同作用是二者定义背后的概念之间深刻差异的关键。对于现代定义,视觉性是所指物的品质,是对现实的再现。对于古代修辞学家来说,"艺格符换"的影响是视觉上的;它是对观察结果感知后的转换,使听众仿佛看见。……它是一种心理作用,并且它模仿的不是现实,而是对现实的感知。它不寻求再现物,而是要在观众的脑海中产生模仿观看行为的效果。[3]

---

[1] 梁庆标:《从"特洛伊画"到"罗马共和"——〈鲁克丽丝受辱记〉中的艺术与政治》,《外国文学评论》2018年第4期。

[2] Marion A. Wells, "'To Find a Face Where All Distress is Stell'd: 'Enargeia', 'Ekphrasis', and Mourning in 'The Rape of Lucrece' and the 'Aeneid'", *Comparative Literature*, 52.4 (2002): 98.

[3] Ruth Webb, *Ekphrasis, Imagination and Persuasion in Ancient Rhetorical Theory and Practice*, Burlington: Ashgate Publishing Company, 2009, pp. 37-38.

莎士比亚对语言生动性的讲究有其时代的修辞文化传统。文艺复兴时期注重对古典文化的推崇和复兴，其中，作为古典修辞学中的一门训练，"艺格符换"无疑是诗人创作时所运用的一门技巧。鲍德温（T. W. Baldwin）认为，莎士比亚可能熟知古罗马修辞学家西塞罗和昆提利安，对语言生动性的强调可能出现在莎士比亚在文法学校遇到的修辞教科书中[1]。莎士比亚诗中的"艺格符换"就是古代时期的定义，是主体感知后的一种心理再现，所追求的是一种心理效果，即在读者或听众心中产生图像，视觉性是其重要特征。

鲁克丽丝在丈夫柯拉廷对其美貌与贞洁的夸赞和吹嘘中进入王子塔昆和读者的视野："是何种无与伦比的、艳丽的嫣红与白嫩，/在她迷人的面容——……，/那儿，人间的星辰，亮似天国的银星。"[2]叙述者称"美色"自有其言说的权威，用不着如簧之舌，就能把众人说服，而邪念的出现往往是因为"我们的耳朵，会败坏我们的心灵"[3]。正是柯拉廷对鲁克丽丝的形象做的视觉化呈现，使塔昆萌生了邪念和情欲。鲁克丽丝是男权社会中附庸于丈夫的一个客体。在柯拉廷看来，妻子是上天赐予他的无比珍贵的财富，是无双的宝物、稀世之珍和独占的财富。这里的鲁克丽丝已经被柯拉廷所物化和客体化。米利特（Kate Millet）在《性政治》（*Sexual Politics*）中指出，男权制允许父亲对妻子和孩子拥有几乎绝对的所有权，在将亲属关系视为财产的制度下，作为一家之长的父亲是所有者，拥有至高无上的权力。[4]因此，在男权制下，两性的关系是支配与从属的关系，鲁克丽丝在根本上处于依附地位，是柯拉廷的私有财产。但是，鲁克丽丝的"美"只是激起塔昆炽热情欲的一部分原因。塔昆认为，地位低下的臣子柯拉廷竟然享用了作为尊长"也不曾享用的佳运"，因此，是男性对"奇珍异宝"的羡慕刺痛了塔昆那高傲的自尊。对未得之物的渴望和情欲加速了塔昆前进的步伐，他来到柯拉廷的城堡，一睹鲁克丽丝美丽的容颜："觑见她的面颊间，美与德相互竞赛，/……/德的莹洁的白色，美的浓艳的红装，/在鲁克丽丝的脸上，显示出瑰丽的纹章"[5]。塔昆使用了一系列的军事隐喻——他奸邪的眼睛看见百合与玫瑰两支队伍在鲁克丽丝的脸上正展开着无声的战争。在这里，叙述者一开始就强调了眼睛的重要作用。正如拉康（Jacques Lacan）所言："在可视领域，

---

[1] T.W. Baldwin, *William Shakespeare's Small Latine and Less Greeke*, vol.1, Urbana: University of Illinois Press, 1944, p. 197.
[2] 莎士比亚：《莎士比亚全集·11》，朱生豪、绿原等译，人民文学出版社，1988年，第65页。
[3] 同上书，第67页。
[4] 米利特：《性的政治》，钟良明译，社会科学文献出版社，1999年，第50-51页。
[5] 莎士比亚：《莎士比亚全集·11》，第67-68页。

凝视在外面,我被注视,也就是说,我是一幅图画。"[1]其中,塔昆作为观看主体,鲁克丽丝则被看作一幅美丽的画一般被邪恶地欣赏、凝视。从"奸邪的眼睛"到"惊奇的两眼",莎士比亚借塔昆之眼揭示了语言无法完全再现所见之物,目之所及比言说更优越、更有说服力。因而,塔昆觉得柯拉廷对鲁克丽丝的盛赞简直是一种"污蔑",认为他的口才如此"贫乏",根本不足以对鲁克丽丝的美貌进行颂扬。

在艺格符换中,对某一艺术品或某事物(无论真实或虚构)详尽地描述所达到的效果,叫作"生动描述"(Enargeia),它的特点是"生动性"。"生动描述"可以追溯到柏拉图和亚里士多德,它同时也与斯多葛派关于"心象"(Phantasia)的讨论密切相关。古罗马修辞家昆提利安将"心象"定义为"将不存在的事物的图像呈现在头脑中,从而使我们似乎能用眼睛看到它们,并使它们呈现在我们面前"[2]。亚里士多德说明了"心象"的作用:"通过我们的'心象',我们可以将各种事物视觉化或形象化,就像人们为了适应自己,在记忆系统中安排图像的顺序一样。因为在某种方式上,'心象'必须属于意识,必须有某种现实与之对应,因为语言是现实的指示。"[3]因此,生动的语言具有可视化的能力,它能在听众的脑海激起相应的图像和情感联想,这便是古典时期艺格符换的视觉性。不过,"生动描述"中涉及的"心象",即语言描述的方式能创造出一种类似于存在的感觉,但实际上却不存在。它的能力或作用在于,演讲者或作家可以将听众或读者的想象力带回或推进到所谈论的事件当中。因此,"生动描述"的重点不是修辞,而是它激活了艺术创作者和接受者想象的能力。此外,它还可以在听众内心发挥作用,并产生强烈的情感效果。正如昆提利安所说,生动的语言可以"穿透情感"[4]。有效的艺格符换应该使听众或读者亲历所描述的事物,即去想象而非用眼睛去看。莎士比亚在诗中就实现了"生动描述"这一语言的品质。塔昆的欲望和行动便是艺格符换的有效结果,正是"生动描述"使得鲁克丽丝被辱的故事开始了,柯拉廷对妻子容貌的描述成功地让塔昆着了迷。塔昆在脑海中用时间性的词语建构了空间性的、虚假的视觉想象,也就是鲁克丽丝的形象,从而达到"心灵之眼"的美学效果。柯拉廷利用"生动描述"这一手法,用文字"画"出鲁

---

[1] Jacques Lacan, *The Four Fundamental Concepts of Psychoanalysis*, Alan Sheridan. trans., Harmondsworth: Penguin, 1977, p. 106.
[2] Alexandros Kampakoglou and Anna Novokhatko, *Gaze, Vision, and Visuality in Ancient Greek Literature*, Boston: Walter de Gruyter GmbH & Co KG, 2018, p. 375.
[3] Gerard Waston, *Phantasia in Classical Thought*, Galway: University of Galway Press, 1988, p. 22.
[4] Ruth Webb, *Ekphrasis, Imagination and Persuasion in Ancient Rhetorical Theory and Practice*, Burlington: Ashgate Publishing Company, 2009, p. 98.

克丽丝的容颜,其情感效果在于它刺激了塔昆想要占有那幅用语言生动描绘出的原画的欲望。当塔昆也像一位画家一样用颜料在画上填充时,他也试图用语言还原鲁克丽丝的美貌,却发现语言无法再现鲁克丽丝的容貌,只能用"沉思遐想来补偿",并且"噤默无言地凝望"。[1]塔昆对鲁克丽丝着迷般地凝视,揭示出口头描述已经让位于更完整的视觉想象。这种对一个形象的心灵"填充"就是亚里士多德所说的心象,或形象的视觉化,表明鲁克丽丝的形象早已在塔昆脑海中内化。

米切尔(W.J.T.Mitchell)在《图像理论》(*Picture Theory: Essays on Verbal and Visual Representation*)中谈到,在西方文化中,一直以来,"文本中的图像被视为女性,言说或观看主体被视为男性"[2]。他指出,艺格符换中隐含着性别政治,其中词语是男性的,而图像是女性的。在《鲁克丽丝受辱记》中,柯拉廷和塔昆都试图用词语观看和定义女性,并将女性图像化。这形成了词语与图像之间的对立,而词语与图像之间的竞争,已然暗含了男性话语对女性意象的暴力入侵。它在凝视中将意象变为他者,以实现词语对意象的控制和权力欲望。观看是男性对女性意象施加暴力的方式,在观看过程中,男性的语言建构了意象女性他者的身份。[3]因此,文字对图像的再现,既展示了男性对美丽女性的窥阴式的占有欲望与想象,又展现了男性因担心美丽女性剥夺他们的话语权,而试图将她们置于被控制的地位。[4]"观看"或者视觉在男性"看"画中扮演重要角色。该诗通过男性凝视下的"生动描述",向我们展示了一幅美丽、诱人、被动的女性"他者"图像。

"生动描述"的风格原则是通过许多具体化的细节来实现的。这些细节创造了现实的效果,使得抽象的、不存在的事情在接受者的当下变得具体和显而易见[5]。首先,鲁克丽丝第一次被"辱"是通过塔昆的眼睛实现的。塔昆如同捕捉猎物一般,在鲁克丽丝的床榻转动着贪婪的眼珠,而鲁克丽丝则像一尊贞洁的石像,让他那淫亵的目光尽情赞美艳羡。这里鲁克丽丝被描述成一尊"石像",一个被他人注视的、沉默的艺术品。其次,通过他"眈眈的目光""焦灼的眼睛",塔昆对鲁克丽丝进行了大量隐喻性的、具体的艺格符换描述:百合般纤手、玫瑰色腮颊、金丝秀发、玉石般肌肤、淡青色筋络、红似珊瑚的唇

---

[1] 莎士比亚:《莎士比亚全集·11》,第69页。
[2] Mitchell, W. J. T. *Picture Theory: Essays on Verbal and Visual Representation*, Chicago: University of Chicago Press, 1994, p. 181.
[3] 王安、罗怿、程锡麟:《语象叙事研究》,科学出版社,2019年,第122页。
[4] 王安:《美杜莎式语象叙事、性别政治与再现的困境》,《符号与传媒》2020年第1期。
[5] Heinrich F. Plett, *Enargeia in Classical Antiquity and the Early Modern Age: The Aesthetics of Evidence*, London and Boston: Brill Academic Publishers, 2012, p. 4.

吻、雪白而含涡的下颔、娇红嫩白的姿容等。[1]这些细致的肢体容貌刻画,使看的动作产生了更多其他不同形式的、用于满足感官的欲望,而男性对一个美丽女人图像的主动凝视,激发了其占有和侵犯该身体的欲望。面对这"沉睡的贞女",看着她胸前的"象牙墙",他的情欲愈益昂扬,他"悍然打开了突破口,进入这迷人的城郭"[2]。这里,塔昆的语言充满了浓厚的侵略性——鲁克丽丝的胸脯是"圆塔",是"她全部领土的中心",不仅她被当成男性淫欲、窥视的对象,其身体还被隐喻成一座"未经征服"、即将被攻下的城堡,等待着敌人的"入侵"。在叙述者看来,"眼睛已享有一切,仍未能满足心意/……贪欲永远无底"[3],作为征服者和篡夺者,塔昆瞪着毒龙一般的致人死命的眼珠,像盗贼一般掠夺了鲁克丽丝"纯洁的贞德的宝库"[4]。

男性不仅主动观看,还使语言为其服务。法国女性主义者、语言学家伊瑞格蕾(Luce Irigaray)认为,西方文化对视觉的推崇与单一男性主体性的延续有关[5]。在西方罗格斯中心主义中,男性在语言符号体系和视觉方面都占据主导地位。可以看出,在《鲁克丽丝受辱记》中,柯拉廷和塔昆代表了语言,鲁克丽丝代表静止的图像。因而,鲁克丽丝的形象、身份以及地位都是由语言建构的。行暴之后,塔昆为自己的恶行进行开脱——"若是你想斥责我,我已经先发制人:/是你那诱人的美貌,陷你到今宵的困境"[6],他之所以要进攻她的"堡垒",是鲁克丽丝"那双媚眼,煽惑了我这双眼睛"。他声称,过错并不在他,是因为鲁克丽丝的美貌和眼睛如此诱人,"你未经征服的堡垒;责任应由你担承"[7]。悲伤的鲁克丽丝在塔昆行暴前,用语言进行劝说,她边挥洒眼泪,边祈求他的怜悯和宽恕,指出他的淫邪和暴行对于君王来说是何等的罪过,但是,这不仅遭到了塔昆的拒绝,还使其奔涌的欲望越涨越高:"别说下去了""住口吧""我发誓,决不再听你一言;/依顺我的爱情吧"。[8]受辱后的鲁克丽丝进行了大量的独白,此时叙述者把鲁克丽丝比作"伤心的菲罗墨拉"。奥维德《变形记》(Metamorphoses)中的菲罗墨拉因年轻貌

---

[1] 莎士比亚:《莎士比亚全集·11》,第85页。
[2] 同上书,第88页。
[3] 同上书,第69页。
[4] 同上书,第99页。
[5] Teresa Brennan and Martin Jay, *Vision in Context: Historical and Contemporary Perspectives on Sight*, New York and London: Routledge, 1996, p. 129.
[6] 莎士比亚:《莎士比亚全集·11》,第89页。
[7] 同上书,第88页。
[8] 同上书,第96—97页。

美而被姐夫忒柔斯强奸,后被割舌并关进小屋里囚禁。割舌意味着丧失了话语权。在两性对立的情况下,男性对女性的控诉充耳不闻,不平等的地位决定了女性的语言是无效的,因而处于失语、失声状态的鲁克丽丝真正地失去了贞洁,无法掌控自我的形象与命运。父权社会中,贞洁对女性来说至关重要,失贞如同失去生命,鲁克丽丝只好选择用自杀来证明自己的清誉。可见,《鲁克丽丝受辱记》中的女性是男性语言和视觉的客体,既丧失主体性,也没有话语权,其身体也被物化、"色情化"为静止美丽的图像。

三、从绘画到语言:女性"看"画背后的困境共情与主体重塑

在西方文艺批评史上,贺拉斯的"诗如画"(Ut Pictura Poesis)理论一直被奉为文艺复兴时期对待文学与视觉艺术关系的圭臬。在这一时期,"诗如画"可以用来说明修辞性的描述应达到图像般的生动效果;而莎士比亚式的艺格符换,即语言能让读者"看见"的能力,可以进一步说明这一时期文学与视觉艺术有着亲密关系。作为古典时期修辞学中的一项训练,当时艺格符换的目的主要是作为史诗中的一个插叙,用来阐释古典文学中的史诗情节,如《伊利亚特》(Iliad)中荷马对"阿基里斯之盾"的精彩描述,或是像在《画记》(Imagines)中大菲洛斯特拉托斯对艺术品进行如实、逼真的呈现,这些使得古罗马时期的艺格符换更具有文学性。文艺复兴时期的人文主义者在研读古典著作时发掘了修辞学和演讲术,对艺格符换的训练和使用,让人文主义者得以再现古典时期的语词习惯。[①]这一时期的画家,如波提切利(Sandro Botticelli)、拉斐尔(Raffaello Santi)、提香(Titian)等根据前人作品中对绘画、艺术品的描述进行再创作,也有瓦萨里(Giorgio Vasari)在其《名人传》(Lives of the Artists)中对不同时期名人的绘画进行细致的文字描述。莎士比亚延续了古典时期的修辞学传统,在《鲁克丽丝受辱记》中插入了艺格符换这一修辞手法。不同学者曾指出,莎士比亚在该诗中对视觉艺术品(特洛伊画)的文学转换和再现有着不同的灵感来源。比如,在《埃涅阿斯纪》(Aeneid)第二卷中,维吉尔(Virgil)描述了埃涅阿斯在狄多神庙的墙上观察并描述特洛伊城陷落的情节。米克(Richard Meek)指出,《鲁克丽丝受辱记》是这一时期诗人对艺格符换和"诗如画"观念迷恋的产物。诗中,鲁克丽丝偶遇了特洛伊陷落的绘画再现,这也许是莎士比亚式艺格符换最清晰、最明确的例子。这个艺格符换为莎士比亚进一步探索诗歌与绘画之间的

---

① 李骁:《西方艺术史中的描述与阐释传统》,上海大学,2018年,第101页。

竞争提供了一次机会。[1]

在《鲁克丽丝受辱记》中,女性的"观看"不是一个被动的现象,即通过眼睛接受外部世界,而是主体对世界进行选择和解释的过程。在对这幅画进行描述的同时,鲁克丽丝不再是被观看的客体,而是从受害者转变成一个动态的、不断变化的主体。她有选择性地看画,为画中人物发声的同时也揭示了自己所处的困境,通过对受苦人物的认同来表达悲痛的情感。厌倦了眼泪和叹息的鲁克丽丝不再哭泣,"后来,她终于想起了:房里挂着一幅画,/精妙绝伦地画着普里阿摩斯的特洛亚"[2]。在观画过程中,女性的"怨诉"起着关键作用。"'怨诉'为莎士比亚提供了一种诗歌模式,使莎士比亚能够塑造那些通过讲述而非行动来创造自我形象的人物。"[3]通过将"怨诉"作为深思熟虑后采取行动的手段,鲁克丽丝在"怨诉"中重写了自己。也就是说,通过读画或艺格符换这一方式,鲁克丽丝不仅通过个人倾诉为自己申冤,揭示画中的历史情节,还向读者揭示了男性的暴行。

首先,作为史诗的观看者,鲁克丽丝在视觉与想象中与画中人物共情——面对来势汹汹的希腊军队,特洛伊成百上千的形象"都画得悲苦动人,/艺术凌驾造物主,造出无生命的生命",画家的笔巧夺天工,使得"这幅奇妙的作品,竟这样精巧传神:/从那些远处的眼睛里,能看出悲痛的表情"[4]。鲁克丽丝看着画中特洛伊王后赫卡柏的脸上有着"时序的摧残、忧患的折磨、姿容的凋谢"[5];她的脸上"汇聚着一切苦难的面孔",包容着所有的哀愁和不幸。纽曼(Jane Newman)认为,莎士比亚有选择地阅读了菲罗墨拉和赫卡柏等女性受害者的经典故事,这些故事消除了女性暴力的可能性,创造了一个适合父权制意识形态的鲁克丽丝。[6]莎士比亚在诗中塑造了一个借用一幅画重构过去,从而为自己创造新选择的女性角色——鲁克丽丝。莎士比亚在诗中插入艺格符换,使得读画成为鲁克丽丝反抗男权压迫、救赎自我的一种方式。悲伤的鲁克丽丝在赫卡柏脸上找到了情感认同,她的目光停留在画上,"以她的悲戚来迎合这位老妪的哀痛"[7]。面对

---

[1] Richard Meek, *Narrating the Visual in Shakespeare*, Routledge: Taylor & Francis Group, 2009, p. 56.
[2] 莎士比亚:《莎士比亚全集·11》,第131页。
[3] Mary Jo Kietzman, "'What Is Hecuba to Him or [S]he to Hecuba?': Lucrece's Complaint and Shakespearean Poetic Agency", *Modern Philosophy*, 97.1(1999): 22.
[4] 莎士比亚:《莎士比亚全集·11》,第132页。
[5] 同上书,第135页。
[6] Jane O. Newman, "'And Let Mild Women to Him Lose Their Mildness': Philomela, Female Violence, and Shakespeare's *The Rape of Lucrece*", *Shakespeare Quarterly*, 45.3 (1994): 304–326.
[7] 莎士比亚:《莎士比亚全集·11》,第136页。

着受伤的丈夫、即将灭亡的特洛伊城,绝望的赫卡柏已经变了模样——一具僵死的躯壳,脸上布满皱纹和皲裂,脉管渐渐枯竭,由蓝血变成了黑血。鲁克丽丝显然把赫卡柏当成了受害的自己,她抱怨画家不能赋予她声音,"给了她这许多苦难,不给她舌头一根"①。于是鲁克丽丝用悲怆的曲调去咏唱她的哀愁,用指责的言语去咒骂希腊人、引起这场战争的海伦,以及罪魁祸首特洛伊王子帕里斯,这罪责是由他的欲念和好色所引起,"你看:在这儿——特洛亚,由于你眼睛的罪过,/父亲和儿子双亡;夫人和女儿俱殁"②。当鲁克丽丝为赫卡柏发声时,她为女性创造了一种在经典来源中不存在的能动性选择,即一种在重建自我的同时也改变了他人的言语,一种在为画中人发声的同时也为自己创造了机会的言说。

其次,作为诗中"艺格符换"的女性聚焦者,鲁克丽丝强调的是个人的悲伤和损失,而不是特洛伊的陷落对罗马随后崛起的政治和历史影响③。但是,她在强调个人悲伤的同时也做出了相应的选择,即复仇。这一抉择使得整首诗从个人的微观抒情空间转变为公众的宏观政治空间,即罗马共和的建立,而这一空间的转换也是由鲁克丽丝的身体展示实现的。给丈夫写信时,鲁克丽丝不愿再诉诸絮烦的言语,因为她发现没有任何言语能形容这种罪恶,也没有什么说辞能摆脱她的厄运。于是她通过自己的容貌、服饰和行动为自己代言,使他人"看见"自己所经历的苦难,从而证明自身的清白和纯洁,因为"看到悲惨的景象,比听人讲它更难过;/因为我们的眼睛,瞧见了苦难的始末,/等到尔后眼睛把它传达给耳朵,/于是,各个感官,都承当了一部分灾厄;/我们耳朵听到的,只能是一部分惨祸"④。归来的丈夫、父亲以及朋友看到了鲁克丽丝披着黑色的丧服,以及她悲伤的脸庞,这脸庞犹如一幅画,画满了人间惨苦。在说出塔昆名字之后,她用刀子刺进自己的身体,这身体流出了热血,一部分血液依旧鲜红纯洁,一部分变黑了,而那污秽来自塔昆。这里的匕首隐喻男性的阴茎,而黑色的鲜血隐喻了屈辱和失贞。

希腊文学研究者戈德希尔(Goldhill)指出,西方视觉文化是从荷马的诗歌以及对英雄的身体公开展示开始的,而英雄的身体和社会价值是在他人的注视中构建的。⑤鲁克

---

① 莎士比亚:《莎士比亚全集·11》,第136页。
② 同上。
③ Marion A. Wells, "'To Find a Face Where All Distress Is Stell'd: 'Enargeia', 'Ekphrasis', and Mourning in 'The Rape of Lucrece' and the 'Aeneid'", *Comparative Literature*, 52.4 (2002): 117.
④ 莎士比亚:《莎士比亚全集·11》,第129页。
⑤ Teresa Brennan and Martin Jay, *Vision in Context: Historical and Contemporary Perspectives on Sight*, New York and London: Routledge, 1996, p. 17.

丽丝虽不是史诗中的英雄,但在该诗结尾,勃鲁托斯看到了鲁克丽丝身体的政治价值,他断定鲁克丽丝的尸身一定能激起罗马民众的反抗。于是,他们将鲁克丽丝的遗体抬去游行,"游遍罗马全城,展览这流血的尸身,/这样向市民披露塔昆万恶的罪行"[1]。这一身体的公开展示给罗马民众带来了视觉上的冲击,罗马人民一致同意将塔昆家族驱逐出境。这样,鲁克丽丝的身体最终被当成了一件深富寓意的"艺术品"或"寓意画"和一个"政治文本"[2]。在诗歌的开始,鲁克丽丝的容貌就被丈夫"广为传布";在结尾,她的尸体同样被"展示"。从作为个人的私人物品、财富,到作为公众的政治武器,鲁克丽丝的身体完成了诗歌从个人到公众的政治空间转向。

四、结语

"艺格符换"及图像理论为文学批评提供了新的跨艺术诗学研究视角,拓宽了诗歌的阐释边界。《鲁克丽丝受辱记》这首跨艺术诗歌包含了由语言到绘画,再由绘画到语言的"艺格符换"双向动态过程。前者揭示了作为语言的男性与作为图像的女性之间的性别政治思想,即男性试图用语言与视觉物化女性,从而达到占有和控制的目的;后者则使女性转变成诗中的言说者,通过观画再现女性个体的困境及其苦难共情,以反抗男性的压迫并实现自我救赎和主体重塑。女性的身体被图像化并被政治地利用,使得该诗完成了从个人到公众的政治空间转向,也完成了诗歌中审美与政治的联姻,从而使得整篇叙事诗具有了史诗般的维度。

参考文献

Alexandros Kampakoglou and Anna Novokhatko, *Gaze, Vision, and Visuality in Ancient Greek Literature*, Boston: Walter de Gruyter GmbH & Co KG, 2018.

Gerard Waston, *Phantasia in Classical Thought*, Galway: University of Galway Press, 1988.

Heinrich F. Plett, *Enargeia in Classical Antiquity and the Early Modern Age: The Aesthetics of Evidence*, London and Boston: Brill Academic Publishers, 2012.

---

[1] 莎士比亚:《莎士比亚全集·11》,第155页。
[2] 梁庆标:《从"特洛伊画"到"罗马共和"——〈鲁克丽丝受辱记〉中的艺术与政治》,《外国文学评论》2018年第4期。

Jacques Lacan, *The Four Fundamental Concepts of Psychoanalysis*, Alan Sheridan, trans., Harmondsworth: Penguin, 1977.

James A. W. Heffernan, *Museum of Words: The Poetics of Ekphrasis from Homer to Ashbery*, Chicago: University of Chicago Press, 1993.

Jane O. Newman, "'And Let Mild Women to Him Lose Their Mildness': Philomela, Female Violence, and Shakespeare's The Rape of Lucrece", *Shakespeare Quarterly*, 45.3 (1994): 304–326.

Marion A. Wells, "'To Find a Face Where All Distress is Stell'd: 'Enargeia', 'Ekphrasis', and Mourning in 'The Rape of Lucrece' and the 'Aeneid'", *Comparative Literature*, 52.4 (2002): 97–126.

Mary Jo Kietzman, "'What Is Hecuba to Him or [S]he to Hecuba?': Lucrece's Complaint and Shakespearean Poetic Agency", *Modern Philosophy*, 97.1(1999): 22.

W. J. T. Mitchell, *Picture Theory: Essays on Verbal and Visual Representation*, Chicago: University of Chicago Press, 1994.

Murray Krieger, *Ekphrasis: The Illusion of the Natural Sign*, Baltimore: Johns Hopkins University Press, 1992.

Richard Meek, *Narrating the Visual in Shakespeare*, Routledge: Taylor & Francis Group, 2009.

Ruth Webb, *Ekphrasis, Imagination and Persuasion in Ancient Rhetorical Theory and Practice*, Burlington: Ashgate Publishing Company, 2009.

T. W. Baldwin, *William Shakespeare's Small Latine and Less Greeke*, vol.1, Urbana: University of Illinois Press, 1944.

Teresa Brennan and Martin Jay, *Vision in Context: Historical and Contemporary Perspectives on Sight*, New York and London: Routledge, 1996.

莎士比亚:《莎士比亚全集·11》,朱生豪、绿原等译,人民文学出版社,1988年。

米利特:《性的政治》,钟良明译,社会科学文献出版社,1999年。

王安、罗怿、程锡麟:《语象叙事研究》,科学出版社,2019年。

王安:《美杜莎式语象叙事、性别政治与再现的困境》,《符号与传媒》2020年第1期。

李骁:《西方艺术史中的描述与阐释传统》,上海大学,2018年。

欧荣等:《语词博物馆:欧美跨艺术诗学研究》,北京大学出版社,2022年。

梁庆标:《从"特洛伊画"到"罗马共和"——〈鲁克丽丝受辱记〉中的艺术与政治》,《外国文学评论》2018年第4期。

跨国语境中的莎士比亚

17至18世纪德国对莎士比亚的接受

唐雪

摘要:17世纪初期,莎士比亚戏剧开始在德国上演,经由启蒙运动时期的戏剧改革,成为德语文学的重要榜样,更是广泛影响了狂飙突进运动时期以歌德为代表的年轻一代。本文以17至18世纪德国对莎士比亚的接受情况为研究对象,结合时代背景,历时性梳理了德国文学界对莎士比亚的译介、研究与评判,动态化展示了莎士比亚对德语文学的影响,并初步探究了莎士比亚接受状态变化的原因。

关键词:17至18世纪;德国;莎士比亚;接受

基金项目:本文系国家社科基金一般项目"中国古代文论在德语世界的传播研究"(项目编号:23BWW008)的阶段性研究成果。

作者简介:唐雪,西南大学外国语学院教师,主要研究方向为比较文学。

莎士比亚戏剧在英国首演几年后,就在德国[①]的舞台上上演了。[②]英国流浪剧团从15世纪90年代到16世纪60年代在欧洲大陆的第一次巡演,推动了莎士比亚戏剧在德国的传播。该剧团带着几部莎士比亚及其同时代的戏剧,走遍了从荷兰到拉脱维亚的广大地区,并在不同场所演出,从美因河畔法兰克福的集市到俄罗斯加里宁格勒的公爵城堡,向来自不同社会和文化背景的观众展示了莎士比亚戏剧。然而,直到一个半世纪之后,莎士比亚才真正成为德国家喻户晓的剧作家,其戏剧作品才成为剧院长盛不衰的

[①] 本文中的"德国"指17至18世纪的德意志地区,主要包括德意志神圣罗马帝国及其邦国、普鲁士王国。
[②] Ernst Leopold Stahl, *Shakespeare und das deutsche Theater. Wanderung und Wandelung seines Werkes in dreiundhalb Jahrhunderten*, Stuttgart: W. Kohlhammer Verlag, 1947, p. 10.

经典之作。而在这一百多年的历程中,德语文学界对莎士比亚的接受经历了忽视、批判、盛赞和反思四个阶段,德语文学也经由启蒙运动和狂飙突进运动得到迅速发展。莎士比亚对这一时期的德语文学无疑产生了深远影响。本文从比较文学接受研究的角度出发,以时间为线,梳理了德国在肇始期、启蒙运动时期和狂飙突进运动时期对莎士比亚的译介与接受,并对该时期最重要的作家歌德对莎士比亚的接受进行个案分析,以期初步探究莎士比亚对17至18世纪德语文学的影响。

一、接受肇始期

1626年6月24日,英国流浪剧团在德累斯顿上演了《哈姆雷特》。这也是该戏剧第一次在德国演出。剧团在德累斯顿驻足数月之久,除了《哈姆雷特》之外,还上演了《罗密欧与朱丽叶》(1626年6月2日)、《裘力斯·凯撒》(1626年6月8日)和《李尔王》(1626年9月26日)。学界对于英国流浪剧团的演出对促进莎士比亚在欧洲大陆兴起的反映不一,如有学者认为,17世纪流浪剧团的戏剧与18世纪后半叶莎士比亚的批评和戏剧兴起之间的连续性证据不足。[1]在20世纪,英国流浪剧团很少被视为欧洲国家接受莎士比亚的一个组成部分。这种忽视不无历史原因:在巡演初期,大多未受过专业教育的剧团演员需要克服绝大多数观众听不懂英语的障碍,加之演出条件有限,因此他们不得不在演出时对剧本进行大刀阔斧的改动,如简化台词和情节,忽视原文的格律,创作即兴对话,加入音乐及舞蹈等,并将精力放在夸张的肢体表演上以吸引观众。这导致了对莎翁剧的严重改编。除了语言与条件的双重限制外,剧团多驻足于市民集市,竭力为受教育程度普遍较低的平民百姓营造欢乐的喜剧氛围,因此剧团带去的莎翁剧多活跃在底层民众之间。然而,不可否认的是,这次时间跨度长、地点范围广的巡演,开创了英国与欧洲大陆的莎士比亚交流传统,随着对莎士比亚和戏剧表演研究的深入,剧团的演出进一步证实了舞台实践的重要性。因此,进入21世纪以来,学者们更愿意承认英国流浪剧团为莎士比亚戏剧的传播和实践发挥了重要作用。

虽然英国流浪剧团的演出推动了莎士比亚戏剧的普及,但并未真正引起当时掌握文化话语权的上层的关注,最明显的表现是德国学界对剧作家莎士比亚的忽视。直到

---

[1] Simon Williams, *Shakespeare on the German Stage: Volume 1, 1586–1914*, Cambridge: Cambridge University Press, 1990, p. 27.

1682年,在文学通史研究奠基人摩尔霍夫(Daniel Georg Morhof)的《德语语言和诗歌教程》(*Unterricht von der Teutschen Sprache und Poesie*)书中,莎士比亚的名字才出现在欧洲大陆的印刷品上。[1]但摩尔霍夫对莎士比亚的评论是相当负面的:"约翰·德莱顿最擅长描写戏剧诗歌。他在这里提到的英国人莎士比亚、弗莱彻、博蒙特,在这些人中我还没有发现有价值的东西。"[2]

二、启蒙运动时期的戏剧改革与莎士比亚接受

直到启蒙运动时期,莎士比亚才真正成为德国文坛的焦点之一。德国的启蒙运动者们围绕着莎士比亚,展开了一系列关于英国和法国文学的争论。首先,1741年,普鲁士驻伦敦外交官冯·博尔克(C.W. von Borcke)以《将裘力斯·凯撒之死的悲剧翻译成合订本的尝试》(*Versuch einer gebundenen Uebersetzung des Trauerspiels von dem Tode des Julius Casar*)为名翻译了《裘力斯·凯撒》。这是第一部莎翁剧德译本。该译作并非全译本,且译者并未采用经典的抑扬格五音步,而是采用了当时流行的法语亚历山大体诗行进行翻译,所以对原作进行了大量改编。除了开启莎士比亚戏剧德译的序幕之外,该译本引起了一位重要人物的关注——当时德语文坛的核心人物和德国戏剧的公认立法者戈特舍德(Johann Christoph Gottsched)。他对冯·博尔克译本的批评不是出于译者的不准确,而是莎士比亚在戏剧创作中对规则的完全无视,他尖锐地提出:"即使是我们庸俗喜剧演员最拙劣的历史剧,也很难像莎士比亚的这部作品一样,充满了违反舞台规则和常识的失误和错误。"[3]另一位大名鼎鼎的莎士比亚反对者则是普鲁士国王腓特烈二世(Friedrich Ⅱ),他针对当时莎翁剧在德国的演出提出:"在这里,你会看到莎士比亚可憎的作品被翻译成我们的语言,当听到这些可笑的闹剧时,所有的观众都会轻松地沉醉其中,这些闹剧不愧是加拿大野蛮人的作品。"[4]

德国启蒙运动早期盛行模仿法国古典主义文学的风气。上述两位莎士比亚的反对者是这一风气的促使者和推动者。推行"开明君主专制"的腓特烈二世极度推崇法国文

---

[1] J. G. Robertson, "The Knowledge of Shakespeare on the Continent at the Beginning of the Eighteenth Century", *The Modern Language Review*, 100.5(2005): 105.
[2] Roy Pascal, *Shakespeare in Germany: 1740-1815*, Cambridge: Cambridge University Press, 1937, p. 37.
[3] Ibid, p. 39.
[4] George Henry Lewes, *The Life of Goethe*, London: Smith, Elder, &Co., 1890, pp. 249-250.

化,深受法国启蒙思想影响,甚至因为羞于说德语而只说法语,并用法语撰写过一篇批评讥他嗤之以鼻的德国文学的文章《德意志文学》("De la littérature allemande")。上述对莎士比亚的批评就是出自这篇贬低德语文学的文章。

戈特舍德认为,亚里士多德的《诗学》以近乎教条的严谨态度影响着法国的古典戏剧。①他以法国古典主义戏剧家高乃依和拉辛为创作榜样,宣扬照搬法国文学模式。因此,法国新古典主义秉承的"三一律"和亚历山大体诗行一度成为德国戏剧创作的原则。冯·博尔克译本使用亚历山大体诗行,自然是基于这一文化语境。为肃清当时盛行政治嬉闹剧(Haupt-und Staatsaktion)的风气,戈特舍德进行了一系列大刀阔斧的改革,如确立了模仿法国古典主义戏剧的基本纲领,在剧本创作、舞台表演、舞台布景和观众要求等方面制订了一系列规则,整顿戏剧创作和剧团表演,并推行标准德语,从而使戏剧明确地具有了教育功能。他的理论被称为"规则诗学"(Regelpoetik)。

戈特舍德的弟子约翰·埃里阿斯·施莱格尔(Johann Elias Schlegel)是德国第一位莎士比亚评论家,他无意破坏其师的"规则诗学",同样认为冯·博尔克的译本是非常糟糕的,而莎士比亚却可以媲美德国戏剧家格吕菲乌斯(Andreas Gryphius)。在对比两位剧作家时,施莱格尔对莎士比亚的全面评价显示了与当时文学风气相左的客观性。他虽然批评了莎士比亚作品中的不规范、场景的杂乱无章、滑稽与崇高的混杂,但承认莎士比亚在表现人物性格和情感方面比格里菲斯更胜一筹。因此,他提出了另一种戏剧创作的可能性,即与亚里士多德式的、为教化而创作的表现具有道德意义的行为悲剧相对的英国式悲剧。这种悲剧没有特定的目的,仅是为了揭示人性,因此结构并不是绝对重要的因素。尽管文章发表后的20年里,德语文坛对莎士比亚的兴趣似乎有所减退,但施莱格尔作为德语区第一位全面评论莎士比亚的学者,为莎士比亚的接受奠定了重要的理论基础。

然而,对法国文学近乎全面接受导致了德语文学的停滞不前,教条的模仿并没有让德语文学孕育出响亮的名字,因此学者们开始反对倡导这一文坛风气的戈特舍德等人。在启蒙运动中后期,德语文学批评在对德国戏剧的未来走向问题上分成了两个阵营:一方坚持以法国古典主义为榜样,另一方则提倡向英国戏剧学习。在此背景下,莎士比亚成为这场持续数十年的德语文学界争论的焦点。瑞士知名学者博德默(Johann Jakob Bodmer)和布莱丁格(Johann Jakob Breitinger)与戈特舍德的激烈论战,成为1730年至

---

① Christian Schacherreiter, *Man muss nur Aug und Ohren dafür haben*, Linz: Verlag Grosser, 1997, p. 38.

1745年德国文坛最为热闹的事情。他们在批评戈特舍德忽视本国传统的同时,指责他对英国文学视而不见。① 1753年的一篇匿名文章为莎士比亚无视统一性及其双关语辩解,指出为莎士比亚的错误开脱是愚蠢的,但对他的突出优点漠不关心也是同样荒谬的。莎士比亚远离了研究式的艺术,追随自然,他经常使用双关语是时代错误造就的缺陷。因此,以此来批评他是不公平的。1758年,由瑞士巴塞尔的人文主义者西蒙·格里诺伊斯(Simon Grynaeus)翻译的《罗密欧与朱丽叶》问世。他是第一个尝试用抑扬格五音步翻译莎士比亚作品的德译者。这一时期最著名的评论则来自德国启蒙运动最重要的代表之一莱辛(Gotthold Ephraim Lessing)。他在1760年写道:"一个法国化的剧院,却不去研究这个法国化的剧院是否适应德国人的思维方式……如果将莎士比亚的代表作稍加改动就翻译给我们的德国人,我可以肯定地说,效果一定会比让他们如此熟悉柯奈(Corneille)和拉辛(Racine)的作品更好……除了索福克勒斯的《俄狄浦斯》之外,世界上没有一部戏剧比《奥赛罗》《李尔王》等更能激发我们的激情。"② 对莱辛而言,观众是否被舞台上的情节所吸引才是关键,而时间和地点的单一性是次要的。但是,莱辛也并不希望德国作家们盲目模仿莎士比亚。他认为,莎翁作品中人物的复杂性,人物塑造的现实意义,以及让观众产生强烈的情感共鸣,应该是作家们的学习榜样。但他也对莎士比亚作品中过多的次要情节,悲喜剧元素的混合以及一些不自然、不可能的对话,持批评态度。因此,他提出:"莎士比亚需要被研究,而不是被掠夺。"③

莎士比亚在德国的普及要归功于维兰德(Christoph Martin Wieland)。他在1762年到1766年翻译了21部莎士比亚戏剧,其译作使所有受过教育的德国人都了解了莎士比亚。他的译作一经问世就深受欢迎,成为赫尔德、席勒和歌德等年轻一代了解莎士比亚的重要途径,也印证了前述的文学论战对关注文学的公众产生的巨大影响。自此,启蒙运动时期文学界关于莎士比亚的争论才在真正意义上与舞台演出产生了相关性。然而,尽管公众对维兰德的成就普遍持积极态度,但因维兰德的英语知识不足,导致了许多翻译错误,并且他的脚注过于遵循新古典主义。④ 这也招致了一些批评。此外,当时

---

① 吴涵志:《德国文学简史》,外语教学与研究出版社,2008年,第43页。
② Karl Lachmann, ed., *Lessings sämtliehe Schriften Bd. 8*, Stuttgart: G. J. Göschen'sche Verlagsbuchhandlung, 1892, pp. 41–44.
③ Renata Häublein, *Die Entdeckung Shakespeares auf der deutschen Bühne des 18. Jahrhunderts*, Tübingen: Max Niemeyer Verlag, 2010, p. 21.
④ Ibid, p. 23.

文学翻译范式正处于转换时期,一些读者希望译者能尽可能精确地再现包括错误在内的原文,而另一些读者则期望译者为当代读者构建一个参考框架。因此,针对维兰德的批评,既有译本过于贴近原文,也有译者为符合时代和国家背景而将莎士比亚同化。[1]

三、狂飙突进运动时期的接受状况

在德国启蒙运动后期,即18世纪60年代晚期到80年代早期,一群青年作家反对启蒙运动的单一性,反对唯理主义、唯进步论和唯规则论,以及样板化的人物形象和不正常的社会规则,在德国发起了一场追求个性解放和表达个人情感的运动,被称为"狂飙突进运动"。他们批判戈特舍德的"规则诗学",认为成功的创作应体现出创造力与激情,而不是那些学来的规则。因此,他们在文学创作时不再遵循条条框框,而强调创作的感性、情感和想象。狂飙突进运动的拥护者们推崇"天才(Genie)不需规律"的思想,他们提倡文学中的自然,莎士比亚被认为是作家中最具有这种特质的人。因此,这一时期的青年作家们对莎士比亚有着极高的崇拜之情。在此背景下,莎士比亚成为狂飙突进运动的"守护神",最重要标志莫过于三位狂飙突进运动重要代表关于莎士比亚的论著:赫尔德(Johann Gottfried Herder)的《莎士比亚》、歌德(Johann Wolfgang von Goethe)的《致莎士比亚日》以及伦茨(Jakob Michael Reinhold Lenz)的《论戏剧》。赫尔德从探究古希腊戏剧的起源出发,来解释为什么亚里士多德的戏剧理论在他的时代是合理的,但并不适用于现在的英国和德国。他提出,"索福克勒斯的戏剧和莎士比亚的戏剧是两回事,它们在特定的方面也鲜有共同的名字",并且"北方它(戏剧)不是也不可能是它在希腊所是的那种东西"。他认为,亚里士多德"也是根据他的时代的大势来从事理论化的工作的",然而"随着世上一切的变化,作为希腊戏剧的真正创造者的自然注定也要变化",因此莎士比亚戏剧的"新鲜、创新和不同"同样是时代所造就的。他辛辣讽刺了法国古典主义对希腊戏剧的模仿,认为法国戏剧"缺乏精神、生命、自然(本质)、真理","它(法国戏剧)与希腊戏剧的相似性"如同雕像与真人的相似性。[2]伦茨在《论戏剧》中比较了莎士比亚和伏尔泰对凯撒大帝之死的改编,指出莎士比亚在各方面都优于伏尔泰,并

---

[1] Renata Häublein, *Die Entdeckung Shakespeares auf der deutschen Bühne des 18. Jahrhunderts*, Tübingen: Max Niemeyer Verlag, 2010, p. 25.

[2] Gunter E. Grimm, ed., *Johann Gottfried Herder: Schriften zur Ästhetik und Literatur 1767-1781*, Frankfurt am Main: Deutscher Klassiker Verlag, 1993, p. 500.

得出了最终结论:"……同样的技巧,同样强大的各方面能力,他(莎士比亚)为全人类创造了一个剧场,每个人都可以在这里站立、惊叹、欢欣,并找到自己,从最高层到最低层。"[1]

狂飙突进运动时期对莎士比亚的第一批评论也开始为莎士比亚正名,海因里希·威廉·冯·格尔斯滕贝格(Heinrich Wilhelm von Gerstenberg)是这一群体中的优秀代表。他的《论文学特性书简》(*Briefe über Merkwürdigkeiten der Litteratur*)于1776年出版,其中包含了自施莱格尔时代以来对莎士比亚的首次全面评价。格尔斯滕贝格首先恢复了施莱格尔关于两种悲剧类型的理论,即亚里士多德式的悲剧和英国式的悲剧;其次提出戏剧的本质会随着历史的变迁而改变,因此没有必要听从亚里士多德的法则,因为它们只严格适用于希腊悲剧。此外,他还指出,莎士比亚的兴趣主要在于表现人物性格,但这并不意味着其无法唤起观众的激情,莎士比亚将自己与他笔下的人物融为一体,他的作品是完整的,观众需要发挥想象力。

四、歌德对莎士比亚的接受研究

歌德在1771年为法兰克福市的莎士比亚纪念日发表的讲话《致莎士比亚日》,是狂飙突进运动时期最著名和最重要的莎士比亚评论。这篇仅有约1220个单词的讲话稿集中体现了歌德在狂飙突进运动时期的文艺思想。首先,歌德激情昂扬地表达了对莎士比亚的崇敬,"读完他的第一个剧本,我仿佛像一个天生的盲人,瞬息间,有一只神奇的手给我送来了光明",并且盛赞莎士比亚的天赋,他将自己比作以"最快的速度疾速奔走"的漫游者,而莎士比亚"则穿着七里靴","走两步就等于前者一天的行程"。其次,歌德在文中毫不留情地批判了法国古典主义戏剧的僵化规则,坚定地反对"三一律"。他认为,地点的统一犹如监牢一般可怕,情节和时间的统一是我们想象力难以忍受的枷锁。他也讽刺了法国古典主义的模仿,所有的法国悲剧也都是对自己的嘲弄。最后,他推崇艺术的自然,对莎士比亚作品中的这一本质给予极高的评价:没有什么比莎士比亚的人物更为自然了。歌德强调艺术需要有机统一,并反驳了莎士比亚缺乏统一性的批判:他的布局,按照通常的看法,不是什么布局,但他所有的剧本都围绕着一个秘密点运

---

[1] Carl Conrad Hense, *Shakespeare: untersuchungen und studien*, Halle: Buchhandlung des Waisenhauses, 1884, p. 229.

转(这个点还没有一位哲学家看到和确定过);在这个点上,我们的自我所特有的东西,我们的意愿所要求的自由与整体的必然进程相冲突。[1]

莎士比亚对歌德戏剧创作的影响则体现在其成名作《铁手骑士葛兹·封·贝利欣根》中。该剧由散文体写作,无视"三一律",忽略情节编排,将所有戏剧事件加在主人公一人身上,并以其死亡结束,完全不关心主人公是否实现其奋斗目标。[2]腓特烈二世在批判莎士比亚的《德意志文学》(De la litterature Allemande)中也严厉指责了歌德的这部成名之作:"葛兹·封·贝利欣根出现在舞台上,这是对那些糟糕的英国作品的可恶模仿,令人憎恶,全场报以热烈的掌声,因此坚决反对重复这些令人厌恶的陈词滥调!"[3]

歌德从狂飙突进运动开始创作,直到魏玛古典主义时期才最终完成的《威廉·迈斯特的学习时代》,是莎士比亚贯穿歌德创作生涯的集中体现。歌德在书中将《哈姆雷特》作为素材,以主人翁威廉·迈斯特所在剧团排练该剧作为重要情节。《威廉·迈斯特的学习时代》共计7本,第一本书于1778年完成,最终在1795年出版。其中,《哈姆雷特》的情节大多写于1785—1786年。1785年年底,他基本完成了小说的前六部,意大利之行(1786—1788)打断了他的创作。意大利之行开启了歌德创作的新阶段,这几乎等同于一次彻底转变。他的新艺术哲学让他开始反思自己早期的作品,他认为这些作品充满了奢华的生活气息,但缺乏形式感。正是在意大利逗留期间,歌德完成了《艾格蒙特》,这是他最后一部承认受到莎士比亚影响的戏剧。

回国后,直至1794年,他都迟迟未能完成《威廉·迈斯特的学习时代》。他在绝望中将版权卖给了书商,并承诺完成它。重新提笔之后,歌德研究了之前的手稿,并决定对其进行修改。在修订版中,剧院的戏份被大大缩减,但威廉·迈斯特讨论《哈姆雷特》的情节完全未变。最终,在好友席勒的鼓励下,他在1794年至1796年完成了该作品,并以《威廉·迈斯特的学习时代》(Wilhelm Meisters Lehrjahre)为名出版。其中,莎士比亚主题在第五本之后被完全删除。但毫无疑问,《威廉·迈斯特的学习时代》中的"哈姆雷特"主题是该作品的重要组成部分,尤其是歌德在创作初期仍然深受莎士比亚的影响——研究《哈姆雷特》并被其形象所吸引。从成长小说(Bildungsroman)的角度而言,歌德将自己的经历客观化,威廉·迈斯特被赋予了诗人自身所有的奋斗和理想,以及自身创作

---

[1] 参见歌德:《歌德文集:论文学艺术》,范大灿、安书祉、黄燎宇等译,人民文学出版社,1999年,第1-5页。
[2] 孙芳颐:《莎士比亚在德国的经典化历程》,《青年文学家》2021年第15期。
[3] George Henry Lewes, The Life & Works of Goethe, London: Smith, Elder,&Co., 1890, p. 250.

能力的一部分。他把莎士比亚对自己的影响作为一种象征,从而将莎士比亚的戏剧编织进自己的小说中,因此书中关于哈姆雷特的情节大多写于1785—1786年。

1790年,被烧毁的魏玛宫廷剧院重新开放,歌德被任命为负责人并享有政策上的绝对自由。他利用魏玛剧院来实践其戏剧理念,邀请了汉堡市民剧院的经理,也是当时最著名的戏剧导演和演员施罗德(Freidrich Ludwig Schröder)来魏玛。施罗德自1776年开始改编莎士比亚戏剧,总共改编了包括《哈姆雷特》等七部莎翁剧。他的改编版本已成为德国舞台上莎士比亚的标准版本。施罗德认为,剧院必须赚钱,因此需要尊重观众的品位,最理想的模式就是经济上的成功能与好的戏剧相协调。为此他主张改编莎士比亚戏剧,以适应当时的舞台。但歌德最初对迎合公众口味的想法兴趣甚微,这一点可以在新剧院于1791年上演的第一部莎士比亚戏剧《李尔王》是未改编版得到证明。1792年,剧院上演了由文学理论家和文学史学家埃申堡(Johann Joachim Eschenburg)用散文翻译的《亨利四世》(第一、二部分)。同年,上演了施罗德改编的第二版《哈姆雷特》。三年后,施罗德改编的第二版《哈姆雷特》再次制作上演,歌德也进行了一些修改。这也表明,歌德转变了初期的态度,已经接受了改编莎士比亚作品的必要性。这部作品在魏玛剧院收获了较大成果,曾连续几晚上演。1796年上演了施罗德改编的《李尔王》,但反应平平。此后,歌德一度回避了莎士比亚的作品。歌德和席勒之间的通信表明,后者试图再次使歌德和莎士比亚和解。席勒反对歌德对法国古典主义者日益增长的偏爱,并尽最大努力向他保证,莎士比亚在某些方面比法国人更接近亚里士多德。1800年,席勒给歌德带去了他翻译和改编的《麦克白》。这个版本的《麦克白》成为魏玛宫廷剧院最成功的作品,在接下来的十年中多次上演,至今仍是德译《麦克白》的标准版本。歌德在这部剧中首次运用了他对舞台技巧的新思考。该剧的成功使他在1803年写出了《剧作家准则》("Regeln für Schauspieler")。该文章提倡一种风格化、正式的表演模式,特别注重语言的节奏感和清晰的发音。他认为,莎士比亚因为遵循时代被迫将许多不和谐的东西集中在一起,以迎合当时的观众口味。而他的改编原则是集中所有最有趣的东西,并使其和谐一致。歌德对1803年上演的由德国浪漫派理论家奥古斯特·威廉·施莱格尔(August Wilhelm von Schlegel)翻译的《裘力斯·凯撒》,进行了一些他认为必要的修改。1811年上演的《罗密欧与朱丽叶》是歌德制作的最后一部莎翁戏剧。他重写了这部莎翁戏剧。从上述歌德参与的莎士比亚戏剧项目可以看出其戏剧思想的转变,他最终认可了施罗德的观点,接受了改编莎士比亚以适应当时德国戏剧舞台的必要性。

《说不尽的莎士比亚》("Shakespeare und kein Ende")是歌德对莎士比亚成熟和最终

的评价。第一部分写于1813年,发表于1815年;第三部分写于1816年,发表于1826年。在第一部分"莎士比亚作为一般意义上的作家"中,歌德首先强调了莎士比亚作品中想象的重要性:他让一些容易想象的事,甚至一些最好通过想象而不是通过视觉来把握的事,发生在他的剧本中。但同时也批判到,一些过多需要依靠想象的细节,会在表演时显得累赘碍事。因此,莎士比亚是通过有生命力的词句发生影响的,而诵读是最好的阅读方式。通过诵读让听众"闭目倾听",较之演员朗诵的效果更好。此外,他还强调了时代的重要性,将莎士比亚的成就归功于当时的英国:莎士比亚跟他生活的时代融为一体,展示了当时英国社会的方方面面。在第二部分"莎士比亚与古代和今人之比较"中,歌德用哲学术语区分了古代戏剧和现代戏剧,并阐述了戏剧艺术的基本原理,提出莎士比亚将古今衔接。在莎士比亚的剧作中,他将本该由内部迸发的愿望,通过外在的机缘激发出来,从而让愿望变成了某种应当;将古代戏剧中"应当与现实"的矛盾,与现代戏剧中"愿望与现实"的矛盾结合在一起。在第三部分"莎士比亚作为剧作家"中,歌德通过定义和区分"史诗"、"对话"、"戏剧"和"舞台剧"这四种文学种类,重塑了对莎士比亚的评价,即莎士比亚并不是一位真正的戏剧家。歌德认为,戏剧是在行动中进行的对话,即使这种对话只是靠想象力进行的。在这一点上,莎士比亚的作品是富有戏剧性的,而符合歌德戏剧表演的文学种类却是"史诗"、"对话"和"戏剧"相结合的"舞台剧",因为它使视觉也参与工作。在此意义上,莎士比亚的戏剧并不符合舞台表演的要求。歌德认为,舞台的要求在他(莎士比亚)看来是无足轻重的,因此莎士比亚的整个创作方法与真正的舞台是有抵触的。歌德由此肯定了施罗德对莎翁剧的改编,提出改编后的戏剧更符合当时的舞台。[①]

五、结语

自17世纪初期以来,历经近两百年历程,从不知姓名的英国剧作家到成为德国众人皆知的文学巨匠,莎士比亚在德国文坛遭受过最猛烈的抨击,也接受过最激昂的盛赞。德国学者对莎士比亚的不同态度是基于时代背景及其思想理论所产生的结果,并反映了这一时期德国文学的发展脉络。启蒙运动前期,以戈特舍德为代表的理论家,为了捍卫其"规则诗学"对莎士比亚全盘否定。从客观角度而言这是极端的,且有失偏颇的;但从

---

① 歌德:《歌德文集:论文学艺术》,第234-248页。

另一方面而言，戈特舍德的戏剧改革无疑极大程度规范了德国戏剧和德语语言，为后继的文学发展奠定了重要基础。而启蒙运动后期，莱辛等人为反对戈特舍德派的僵化模仿，转而将莎士比亚代表的英国戏剧作为榜样，同样是为了给予停滞的德国文学以创新之风气。狂飙突进运动时期，德国对莎士比亚的接受高潮更是继承和发展了莱辛等人的观点，加入了德国青年作家们的激情、个性和自然。在莎士比亚的影响和启发下，以歌德为代表的德国青年一代终于成长为德语文学乃至世界文学的大师。因此，通过对莎士比亚在德国17至18世纪的接受梳理可以发现，他作为德语文学界的"社会集体想象物"，是德国学者们的思想投射，始终反映了接受者的不同情感、精神生活和时代环境。对德国对莎士比亚的接受进行探究，可以为我国德语文学研究提供一个新的"他者"视角。

参考文献

Carl Conrad Hense, *Shakespeare: untersuchungen und studien*, Halle: Buchhandlung des Waisenhauses, 1884.

Christian Schacherreiter, *Man muss nur Aug und Ohren dafür haben*, Linz: Verlag Grosser, 1997.

Ernst Leopold Stahl, *Shakespeare und das deutsche Theater. Wanderung und Wandelung seines Werkes in dreiundhalb Jahrhunderten*, Stuttgart: W. Kohlhammer Verlag, 1947.

George Henry Lewes, *The Life & Works of Goethe*, London: Smith, Elder,&Co., 1890.

Gunter E. Grimm, ed., *Johann Gottfried Herder: Schriften zur Ästhetik und Literatur 1767–1781*, Frankfurt am Main: Deutscher Klassiker Verlag, 1993.

J. G. Robertson, "The Knowledge of Shakespeare on the Continent at the Beginning of the Eighteenth Century", *The Modern Language Review*, 100.5(2005): 105.

Karl Lachmann, ed., *Lessings sämtliehe Schriften Bd. 8*, Stuttgart: G. J. Göschen'sche Verlagsbuchhandlung, 1892.

Renata Häublein, *Die Entdeckung Shakespeares auf der deutschen Bühne des 18. Jahrhunderts*, Tübingen: Max Niemeyer Verlag, 2010.

Roy Pascal, *Shakespeare in Germany: 1740-1815*, Cambridge: Cambridge University Press, 1937.

Simon Williams, *Shakespeare on the German Stage: Volume 1, 1586-1914*, Cambridge: Cambridge University Press, 1990.

歌德：《歌德文集：论文学艺术》，范大灿、安书祉、黄燎宇等译，人民文学出版社，1999年。

孙芳颐：《莎士比亚在德国的经典化历程》，《青年文学家》2021年第15期。

吴涵志：《德国文学简史》，外语教学与研究出版社，2008年，第43页。

莎士比亚与萧伯纳作家人格的形成

陈鑫

摘要：莎士比亚是英国文学的丰碑之一，同时在世界文学史上也享有崇高地位。很少有作者公开批判莎士比亚，而乔治·萧伯纳算是"倒莎"少数派的代表人物。生于爱尔兰的萧伯纳被公认是英国戏剧的第二人。而他对第一人则充满竞争意识，多番攻讦莎士比亚。但回顾萧伯纳的作家生涯，我们会发现莎士比亚是萧伯纳作家人格形成的重要媒介。作为爱尔兰人，萧伯纳想征服英国的语言与文学。他就像是一个叛逆的儿子，不仅叛逆性地继承了莎士比亚的文学遗产，更是希望重新创造一个作为"父亲"的莎士比亚。本文将从其爱尔兰性、社会表演性以及时代性出发，考察萧-莎关系。

关键词：莎士比亚；萧伯纳；爱尔兰性；社会表演；时代性

基金项目：本文系中央高校基本科研项目"乔治·萧伯纳的表演性跨媒介书写研究"（项目编号：XJ2023003901）的阶段性研究成果。

作者简介：陈鑫，西南大学外国语学院讲师，主要研究方向为萧伯纳戏剧及维多利亚晚期戏剧。

在莎士比亚批评史上，给莎士比亚投反对票的人并不算多，其中列夫·托尔斯泰与萧伯纳或许是作家圈中名声最著的两位。"除了荷马这个例外（因为荷马不是单个的作家），当我和莎士比亚互较头脑时，我对任何知名作家，包括沃尔特·斯科特爵士，都没有讨厌到如我讨厌莎士比亚的地步。"[1]这段话出自1896年萧伯纳在《周日评论》(*Sunday Review*)上发表的一篇题为《斥责诗人》("Blaming the Bard")的文章。这或许是评论家

---

[1] Bernard Shaw, "Blaming the Bard", *The Saturday Review*, 1896.

们最常引用的萧伯纳对莎士比亚的恶评。哈罗德·布鲁姆(Harold Bloom)在其编辑的《乔治·萧伯纳》一书引言的开头便印上了这段话[1]。对于布鲁姆而言,莎士比亚是西方文学经典的中心,其后来者都或多或少辗转于他的阴影之下,而萧伯纳正是因为意识到"他在机智上无法与福斯塔夫相比",不能轻松地赞美自己的心志,从而"鄙薄莎士比亚"。[2]从某种角度而言,萧伯纳胸臆中对莎士比亚确实有一种布鲁姆所言的"自相对立"的意识,这是一种作家间,尤其是戏剧家同行间的影响焦虑。

但是萧伯纳对莎士比亚的态度,比单纯的"作家影响"更为复杂。批评家们在引用这段恶评时,似乎经常忽略下面一段中萧伯纳提到的"我不得不加一句,我可怜那些无法欣赏莎士比亚的人"。萧伯纳对于莎士比亚的评价难以一言蔽之,而在试图和莎士比亚对抗的过程中,他的野心也远比布鲁姆设想的更大。萧伯纳不仅仅试图超越福斯塔夫和莎氏喜剧,更是将莎剧中最好的悲剧剧本当作自己的范本和假想敌。在其戏剧生涯的最后一部剧《莎 vs 萧》(Shakes versus Shav)中,代表莎士比亚的木偶问道:"你的哈姆雷特在哪里,你能写出《李尔王》吗?"萧伯纳说道:"如果让女儿们都活着,你能写出《伤心之家》吗?看看我的李尔王吧。"[3]萧伯纳的回复重点不只在于他认为《伤心之家》的主角萧特非船长(Captain Shotover)比得上李尔王,更在于他自认为在"让女儿们都活着"的情况下走出了新的戏剧道路。一方面,他认为"无人能写出比李尔王更好的悲剧"[4],李尔王有一种"亵渎的绝望"(blasphemous despair)[5],并在《伤心之家》的序言中引用拜伦的话"死去并不困难,活着反而困难得多"[6],来试图为莎士比亚的"悲观主义"找到另外的解决方案。另一方面,他认为无人能在技巧和技艺上超越莎士比亚,但同时又对莎士比亚的思想与理念嗤之以鼻。

有一个细节可以体现他与莎士比亚的"较劲"技巧——他不会侵入莎士比亚的全部战场,但总会在与莎士比亚的比对中为自己留出足够的地盘和退路。萧伯纳的第三本

---

[1] Bloom Harold and Chelsea House Publishers, *George Bernard Shaw*, New York: Chelsea House, 1987, p. 1.
[2] 布鲁姆:《西方正典》,江宁康译,译林出版社,2005年,第36页。
[3] Bernard Shaw, *Buoyant Billions, Farfetched Fables, & Shakes Versus Shav*, London: Constable, 1950, p. 141.
[4] Bernard Shaw, *Shaw on Shakespeare: An Anthology of Bernard Shaw's Writings on the Plays and Production of Shakespeare*, Milwaukee: Hal Leonard Corporation, 1961, p. 111.
[5] Ibid.
[6] Bernard Shaw, *Heartbreak House, Great Catherine, and Playlets of the War*, London: Constable, 1920, p. xxxiii.

戏剧集《清教徒戏剧三种》(*Three Plays for Puritans*)序言题为"比莎士比亚更好？"(Better than Shakespeare?)，其取巧之处在于留了个问号。在晚年回忆中，他揭露了自己留下的这个小伏笔，让观众注意这个问号，并指出某些人说他"轻率地声称我的戏或者其他人的戏比莎士比亚写得更好"这种说法是很荒谬的[1]。这种看似极端，其实圆融的批评手段，散见于其他莎剧评论意见中。

同样地，在戏剧实践上，他也从未把"打倒莎士比亚"作为最终信条，相反不得不承认他在莎士比亚那里获得了不少方便和启发。萧剧中遍布对莎剧情节与人物的改写、翻案、重构，乃至倒转。从萧伯纳眼中的莎士比亚形象，可以管窥萧伯纳的文艺观和世界观。更重要的是，莎士比亚就像一面镜子，萧伯纳鉴照于它，其反射镜像成为萧伯纳解释世界与开展文学事业的蓝图。甚至可以说，萧伯纳"创造"了一个自己的莎士比亚，这从他将莎士比亚名字拼作"Shakespear"就能看出，这个自创的莎士比亚，成为其作家人格不可缺少的一部分。本文试图从三个方面勾勒出莎士比亚在萧伯纳作家人格形成过程中起到的重要作用。

一、莎士比亚与爱尔兰——"反征服"的流散人格

莎士比亚戏剧中提及爱尔兰的地方不多，基本都出现在其历史剧中，唯一的爱尔兰角色便是《亨利五世》中的麦克摩里斯（Macmorris）上尉，而在《理查二世》中，理查二世也入侵过爱尔兰。但从某种程度上来讲，莎士比亚对爱尔兰的看法带有某种殖民主义视角，而他作为大英帝国文化殖民力量的中心，其作品也深刻影响了爱尔兰文化圈。在寻求国族解放与独立的过程中，莎士比亚成为许多爱尔兰作家的"靶子"，尤其是那些爱尔兰文艺复兴中的旗帜性人物，比如乔伊斯、叶芝、辛格、贝克特，乃至于作为流散作家的王尔德与萧伯纳都在其列。和萧伯纳类似，很多爱尔兰作家一方面"写反对莎士比亚的篇什"，另一方面又在"重新征用莎士比亚"。[2]乔伊斯对莎士比亚的崇敬与有意识借用广为人知，而叶芝则通过重新解读莎士比亚笔下那位阴晴不定、刚愎自用的理查二

---

[1] Bernard Shaw, *Sixteen Self Sketches*, London: Constable, 1949, p. 142.
[2] Robin E. Bates, *Shakespeare and the Cultural Colonization of Ireland*, New York: Routledge, 2008, p. 1.

世,将某种爱尔兰性格投射在它身上。①在所有抵抗莎士比亚文化影响的爱尔兰人中,"最为强劲的反抗,来自萧伯纳"②。

和叶芝等人试图调和莎士比亚与爱尔兰相比,萧伯纳对于莎士比亚的敌意更为明显。叶芝认为,莎士比亚更加共情理查二世这类角色,相反对亨利四世更多是笑着去看,"就像人们看见了一匹很英俊的烈马一样"③。这是一种疏离于角色,并带着一丝反讽(irony)的笑。但萧伯纳却认为,莎士比亚对他的大部分角色都抱持这种反讽。他认为,莎士比亚的悲观主义背后并非一种绝望,而是一种"不可压抑的天才之快感",它是一种反讽,"是在悲观主义中获得快感的玩闹"。④在萧伯纳看来,莎士比亚是沉湎于自己的文字天才中,而缺乏对其笔下角色之苦难的共情。

这个评价表面上有失公允,但是从深层次反映出萧伯纳对莎士比亚的批评术语与对照物并不仅仅是文学作品,还有以德国音乐为主的歌剧传统。萧伯纳不止一次提及莎士比亚作品的最大艺术特点是一种"音乐性"。作为萧伯纳文学事业的起始,其音乐批评对其艺术观的塑成起着重要作用。"莎士比亚的力量在于他深谙于如何掌控言辞-音乐(word-music)"⑤。言辞-音乐(word-music)这个术语应是受了瓦格纳式的"总体艺术"(Gesamtkunstwerk)的启发。这种总体艺术强调言辞(诗歌)、音乐以及舞蹈之间的无缝融合。在《完美的瓦格纳主义者》(*The Perfect Wagnerite*)中,萧伯纳改造了瓦格纳的框架,"音乐—情感—理念"的三位一体成为其解释音乐史发展(以及瓦格纳地位)的

---

① 叶芝的解读出自"At Stratford of Avon"。这篇文章将理查二世和亨利五世进行对比。他认为,现实且稳重的亨利五世不仅是"典型的盎格鲁—撒克逊人",更是"莎士比亚为英国树立的榜样"(157)。而作为其对立面的理查二世,更像是一位"未成熟的哈姆雷特"(162)。在叶芝看来,理查二世反而是"瓷器"(vessel of porcelain),而亨利五世是"陶器"(vessel of clay)(163)。(参见:William Butler Yeats, *Ideas of Good and Evil*, London: AH Bullen, 1914。)罗宾·贝茨认为,叶芝之所以要将这种"美"赋予理查二世,是因为对他来说"美和政治密切相关",重新强调爱尔兰的美,"是重新强调爱尔兰自治的政治过程一部分"(Robin Bates, *Shakespeare and the Cultural Colonization of Ireland*, New York: Routledge, 2008, p. 72.)。

② Philip Edwards, "Shakespeare and the Politics of the Irish Revival", in Joseph McMinn, ed., *The Internationalism of Irish Literature and Drama*, Maryland: Barnes & Noble Books, 1992, p. 47.

③ William Butler Yeats, *Ideas of Good and Evil*, London: AH Bullen, 1914, p. 164.

④ Bernard Shaw, *Misalliance: The Dark Lady of the Sonnets, and Fanny's First Play—With a Treatise on Parents and Children*, London: Constable, 1914, pp. 219-220.

⑤ Bernard Shaw, *Shaw on Shakespeare: An Anthology of Bernard Shaw's Writings on the Plays and Production of Shakespeare*, Milwaukee: Hal Leonard Corporation, 1961, p. 2. 在其他很多地方萧伯纳也提过类似的观点,比如对《皆大欢喜》《安东尼与克里奥帕特拉》《辛白林》和《终成眷属》等剧的批评中,常常见到类似的术语。其中其最明显的展现是在《十四行诗的黑夫人》这部剧及其序言中。

重要参照。他评价贝多芬的交响乐"表达了高贵的情感(feeling),但是没有思想",而瓦格纳的重要性就在于"加上了思想并创造了音乐戏剧(music drama)"①。但从其莎剧批评来看,音乐—情感—思想显然溢出了单纯的音乐批评。"莎士比亚的弱点在于他在最高的思想领域完全是乏力的。"②所以在萧伯纳眼里,莎士比亚的作品至少短了一只脚——莎士比亚只擅长用言辞-音乐传递情感,甚至因为本身的思想限制,他与他所传达的情感(或者角色)之间,形成了一道屏障。莎士比亚便站在屏障外,陶醉于其文字天才,而对他施加于角色身上的"折磨"却视而不见。

这种音乐性和情感的分离,被萧伯纳用作《十四行诗的黑夫人》这部剧的主题。"黑夫人"(The Dark Lady)指的是莎士比亚十四行诗第127首到第152首中出现的倾慕对象,阶段性地表达了莎士比亚对"黑夫人"从爱慕到厌弃的过程。萧伯纳认为,莎士比亚并非因为黑夫人不曾回应他的爱而伤心,而是在用自己的诗对黑夫人施加某种"言语暴力"。非常典型的一段情节就是当剧中的黑夫人觉得莎士比亚的爱慕有些过分时,提醒他"你有些越界了,请节制一下你的爱慕",莎士比亚重复吟咏了一遍黑夫人的"请节制一下你的爱慕",并喃喃自语道:"这是音乐啊,你听不到吗?"③莎士比亚对于自身情感力量的表达,在萧伯纳看来,似乎都耽溺于字面的"word-music"上。萧剧中的莎士比亚自比为"言辞之王"(king of the words),强调"诗歌的永恒力量",却否认自己对黑夫人的爱是"残忍的"。他以朱庇特和塞勒莫的神话④自比,承认"无法控制自己的雷电(言辞的力量)去伤害她"⑤。因此,表面上萧伯纳似乎是在批判莎士比亚的剧本"悲观主义"和"缺乏思想",但深层次上是在指责莎士比亚无法控制自己的天才,无法从word-music的表面深潜进去,从而使得他笔下的角色(尤其是女角色)都在无言地接受其言语暴力。

萧伯纳的这种批评思路反映出两个问题。第一个是他的理论或艺术参照物并非来自英国传统,而是来自欧洲大陆(尤其是德国),这是其批评中反殖民性的一端。第二个

---

① Bernard Shaw, *The Perfect Wagnerite: A Commentary on the Niblung's Ring*, London: Constable, 1913, p. 139.
② Bernard Shaw, *Shaw on Shakespeare: An Anthology of Bernard Shaw's Writings on the Plays and Production of Shakespeare*, Milwaukee: Hal Leonard Corporation, 1961, p. 3.
③ Bernard Shaw, *Misalliance: The Dark Lady of the Sonnets, and Fanny's First Play—With a Treatise on Parents and Children*, London: Constable, 1914, p. 235.
④ 神话中,凡人之女塞勒莫(Seleme)爱上了众神之王朱庇特,她求朱庇特在她面前显出神容,但凡人无法直视神的力量,最后被朱庇特的雷电劈死。
⑤ Bernard Shaw, *Misalliance: The Dark Lady of the Sonnets, and Fanny's First Play— With a Treatise on Parents and Children*, London: Constable, 1914, p. 241.

或许更为重要,即他所描绘的莎士比亚-黑夫人关系,某种程度上也能成为"英国-爱尔兰"关系的隐喻。在萧伯纳的剧本中,许多成熟或寻求独立的女性,似乎都有过遭受男方语言暴力的经历。最为典型的可能是其最流行的剧本《皮格马利翁》,希金斯对于卖花女艾丽莎多有言语上的轻蔑和打击,但最后艾丽莎没有选择和希金斯在一起,而是打算和"次一等"的弗莱迪结婚。这种女性独立的情节毫无疑问深受易卜生《玩偶之家》的影响。但需要注意的是,对于爱尔兰文学而言,易卜生《玩偶之家》中的娜拉出走,在某些场合会被政治性解释为爱尔兰从英国的独立。在萧伯纳、辛格和奥凯西等人的作品中都出现过娜拉(Nora)的同名角色,而他们对娜拉男女关系的相异设定,某种程度上也反映了作者们对爱尔兰问题的不同倾向。在萧伯纳唯一一部以爱尔兰为背景的长篇剧《英国佬的另一个岛》中,娜拉就是一位典型的爱尔兰女性,她爱着剧中的爱尔兰人拉里·多伊尔,但最后仍然选择跟代表英国对爱尔兰进行经济与政治殖民的汤姆·博饶本结婚。在这部剧中,博饶本对于爱尔兰的想象是一种典型的异国想象,他对爱尔兰的喜欢如同十四行诗的黑夫人中莎士比亚的爱慕那般,并非对对象实质的喜爱,而是对他们构建的想象客体之美的喜爱。尽管在萧伯纳的剧中,娜拉最后选择与博饶本结婚,但是这个选择是由她自己做出来的。"女性的选择权"是贯穿萧伯纳戏剧的一个重要主题。从某种角度上讲,这种"选择权"背后也带着一定的爱尔兰情结。

萧伯纳对于莎士比亚的反抗,带有一定的社会表演性,某种程度上也是其作为爱尔兰流散作家对于故乡身份的确证。在萧伯纳小的时候,莎士比亚在某种程度上是其重要的精神食粮。"在阅读莎士比亚的过程中,他找到了生活的全部,除了他实际在场的身体……"[1]但是在其成长的过程中,他对莎士比亚的看法和立场也变得越来越复杂。萧伯纳尽管也说英语,但他认为他的母语是"斯威夫特的英语",而非"19世纪中期伦敦报纸的黑话"。[2]由于斯威夫特也是爱尔兰作家,因此对萧伯纳而言,大不列颠的英语及其代表莎士比亚无法构成其真正的语言认同,而是构成其反面。

萧伯纳没有成形的宗教崇拜观念,但是他很自豪于自己的爱尔兰新教背景。他将这种新教传统理解为一种反抗精神:"新教主义对我来说是一项伟大的历史运动,是关

---

[1] Michael Holroyd, *Bernard Shaw, Volume 1: The Search for Love, 1856-1898*, London: Random House, 1988, p.41.

[2] Bernard Shaw, et al., *The Matter with Ireland*, 2nd edition, Gainesville: University Press of Florida, 2001, p.38.

于改革、抱负与反对精神暴君的自我肯定的历史运动。"①临近他去世之前,萧伯纳仍然向外界坚持自身的爱尔兰身份,"我是个外乡人——是个爱尔兰人——所有外乡人中最外乡人的……"②。萧伯纳对于爱尔兰英语和爱尔兰新教传统的自豪,反映出大卫·克莱尔所言的两种心态。一种是爱尔兰国教徒(Irish Anglican)对于英国本土的"更加稳定而被低估的敌意"③。这种敌意并未因为它与英格兰在宗教上的同源性而弥合,相反,他们对爱尔兰本地事物(包括爱尔兰天主教)更抱有同情的态度。一种则是作为某种"有文化的奴隶(cultured slave)",爱尔兰人所带有的对于英国文化的优越感④。就像著名的爱尔兰后殖民主义批评家戴克兰·基博德(Declan Kiberd)所说的,萧伯纳"把英国当作一个实验室,来定义什么叫作爱尔兰"⑤。这其实代表着一种反向殖民或者反向征服,也就是基博德引用的萧伯纳那句著名的话:"英国已经征服了爱尔兰,那么要做的事情就只有反过来征服英国。"⑥这种反向征服更多是一种文化上的征服以及语言上的征服。因此萧伯纳和莎士比亚的争端,以及爱尔兰作家和莎士比亚的争端,在某种程度上也是爱尔兰文化以及英国文化之间冲突的缩影。

在这种英爱冲突中,萧伯纳和莎士比亚有过一些侧面交锋。其中最主要的例子应该是萧伯纳在英爱战争期间完成的《圣女贞德》。莎士比亚在《亨利六世》中塑造的贞德诡计多端,浪荡放肆,如同《麦克白》中那些阴险的女巫一般。萧伯纳的贞德则非常"新教徒",她不相信任何世俗机构,只相信自己所听到的"声音"。这位意志坚定、领导力强,甚至有些性别不明的贞德,某种程度上是当时反抗英国的爱尔兰起义者们的形象。尽管萧伯纳在他20岁离开都柏林后,主要活动场所都在伦敦,但是他一直都在侧面介入现代爱尔兰事务当中。1916年,当时复活节起义领袖之一罗杰·凯斯曼(Roger Casement)被英军逮捕,萧伯纳试着为他写一出独白剧,让他在法庭上演出并为自己(以及爱尔兰起义)辩护,来帮助他逃脱死刑。尽管最后没有成功,但起义领导人们的审判,

---

① Bernard Shaw, et al., *The Religious Speeches*, University Park: Pennsylvania State University Press, 1963, p. 50.
② Bernard Shaw, *Sixteen Self Sketches*, London: Constable, 1949, p. 70.
③ David Clare, *Bernard Shaw's Irish Outlook*, London: Palgrave Macmillan, 2016, p. 41.
④ Ibid, p. 17.
⑤ Declan Kiberd, *Inventing Ireland*, Cambridge: Harvard University Press, 1996, p. 51.
⑥ Ibid, p. 62.

"也部分启发了贞德最后的虚构自辩场面"①。从立场上来说,爱尔兰民族主义和以爱尔兰天主教为主的起义运动,都不太符合萧伯纳心中关于爱尔兰问题的解决办法。和莎士比亚的反派化处理不同,萧伯纳并不愿意因为某个"阵营"而去为民族主义战争划定正与反,是与非。正如他在《圣女贞德》序言中所说:"这部剧中没有任何反面人物(villain)。"在他看来,简单地将英国树立为敌人,并不能从根本上解决爱尔兰问题。这或许也可以说明他对莎士比亚乃至整个英国文化的矛盾态度。他并非完全反战,只是他认为一切问题的解决前提是爱尔兰自治。因此,萧伯纳尽管不算一位爱尔兰民族主义者,但是他对爱尔兰文化身份的渴求,仍然使得他走上了想要反向征服英国,乃至征服莎士比亚的路上(尽管萧伯纳对莎士比亚的态度比他看上去的要谦卑许多)。

二、跨媒介社会表演——作为戏剧家/批评家的人格

相比于莎士比亚,萧伯纳更像是一个"半路出家"的戏剧从业者。他是在将近不惑之年,也就是莎士比亚写出《哈姆雷特》《麦克白》的年纪,才出版了自己的第一部戏剧《鳏夫之家》。在此之前,他写过五部小说,分发过各种政论小册,发表过大量音乐批评和新闻报道。萧伯纳最初本想利用小说创作来扩大自身的影响力,但可惜并未得到太多反响。从其文学生涯看,戏剧是萧伯纳的"成熟期",而它和莎士比亚的"不成熟"呈现出一种独特的互补性,这反而让萧伯纳为直面莎士比亚另辟蹊径。他认为莎士比亚去世太早,"未熟先殁",而将他和莎士比亚做比较对后者极不公平,因为"他比莎士比亚多活了将近30年"②。他丝毫不怀疑莎士比亚在之后能创作出更伟大的作品。从其批评来看,他隐约将莎剧的"缺点"归因于莎士比亚的不成熟。

萧伯纳的这种批评思路,有一些"以己度人"的感觉,因为他自己就有过这样一个从"不成熟"到"成熟"的转变。他说莎士比亚"没有信仰也没有规划(programme),他的情节就像用旧的衣服那样(reach-me-downs)"③。而他评价其早期小说时,也有着类似的

---

① James Moran, "Meditations in Time of Civil War: Back to Methuselah and Saint Joan in Production, 1919-1924", *SHAW Annual: The Annual of Bernard Shaw Studies*, University Park: Penn State University Press, 2010, p. 155.
② Hesketh Pearson, *Bernard Shaw: His Life and Personality*, Chicago: House of Stratus, 2015, pp. 230-231.
③ Ibid, p. 230.

评语,"它们太幼稚且劣质了,我不会再写它们了"①。在萧伯纳那里,不成熟与"粗制滥造""杂乱无章"等特点相关,它反映的是一种思想的散漫和经验的缺乏。某种程度上,"成熟"是萧伯纳戏剧最重要的主题之一,其刻画的"超人"形象,多是稳重、睿智且富有领导力的。从不成熟到成熟,既可以说是一种性格转变,也可以说是一种"角色"转变。

有不少学者讨论过萧伯纳从小说到戏剧的过渡,包括其主题、风格、角色以及心理的嬗变。其中,某种"政治性"因素是萧伯纳放弃小说,转向戏剧创作的直接原因。"萧伯纳对小说渐渐不再感兴趣,是因为他逐渐贯注于社会主义,以及他作为社会改革者的角色(role)"②。但在某些学者看来,尽管他停止了小说写作,但"萧伯纳从未考虑完全放弃扮演自己作为小说家的角色(role)"③。这两句评论中的"角色",其实暗合了萧伯纳文学事业的一个突出特性,即社会表演性。这种社会表演涉及公众(名人)形象的塑造、相应的社会表演规则等。

和他著名的矛盾修辞法一样,萧伯纳对小说创作抱着既决裂又延续的态度。这和他对莎士比亚的态度似乎又不谋而合,言语上摈弃又从未置于脑后。萧伯纳对其小说的看法,从几部小说的标题或许就能看出来,尤其是《无理之节》(*The Irrational Knots*)、《不成熟》(*Immaturity*)以及《不社会的社会主义者》(*An Unsocial Socialist*)等。在这几本多少带些半自传性质的小说中,不理性、不成熟以及社会性的分离等性质,既是萧伯纳站在第三人称视角不断去剖析的,也或多或少是他站在第一人称视角不断自我感知的。这些小说是萧伯纳"内在作者(Interior Author)的初步创成"④。只是作为小说家的社会表演,或许有些过于孤单和独白化。因此对于萧伯纳而言,小说并非其作家身份的理想媒介。由于他本人强烈的论辩性和对话性,戏剧或许确实是更符合他特点的"表演媒介"。印刷媒介并不适合传播他的各种观念及讨论,因此他试图"融合纸媒以及戏剧媒介来创造一个新的政治—文学论场"⑤。这种融合使得他的戏剧文本具有丰富的副文

---

① Bernard Shaw and Dan H. Laurence, *Collected letters, 1874-1897*, New York: Dodd, Mead & Company, 1965, p. 550.
② Dietrich Richard F., *Portrait of the Artist As a Young Superman: A Study of Shaw's Novels*, Gainesville: University of Florida Press, 1969, p. 67.
③ Stanley Weintraub, *Bernard Shaw, Novelist*, University Park: The Pennsylvania State University, 1956, p. 269.
④ Lagretta Tallent Lenker, "Bernard Shaw's Interior Authors: The Novels", *Shaw*, 41.1(2021): 96.
⑤ Elizabeth Carolyn Miller, *Slow Print: Literary Radicalism and Late Victorian Print Culture*, Redwood City: Stanford University Press, 2020, p. 132.

本,尤其是和其戏剧一样出名的戏剧前言(preface)。其小说及其他纸媒创作,可以看作这种萧式前言的"前言"。有些时候,前言本身比戏剧都长,甚至在戏剧中会出现某种元戏剧散文文本(比如《人与超人》中的《革命者手册》)。

这种跨媒介、跨文本的作家身份,既包括作为戏剧作家的萧伯纳,也包括作为散文作家和批评家的萧伯纳。因此,从"不成熟"到"成熟"的转变,更是一种从单媒介到多媒介的社会性角色的转变。这是萧伯纳真正觉得自己可以和莎士比亚并肩的地方。萧伯纳需要一个从不成熟到成熟的剧本,莎士比亚则暂时成为其早期的"反面人物"。但成熟的萧伯纳和不成熟的莎士比亚之间,反而形成了一种特殊的时间关系。它不仅仅关乎生物时间,同时还牵扯萧伯纳世界观的时间特性,以及文学文本的不朽性与当代性。

萧伯纳初登剧坛是在19世纪的最后十年,同时这几年也是他早期对莎士比亚开火最猛烈的时候。萧伯纳早期戏剧目标是围绕易卜生建立一种新的现代戏剧规范,而莎士比亚便是要被易卜生主义打破的头号偶像之一。1889年,萧伯纳最重要的批评著作之一《易卜生主义的精髓》(*The Quintessence of Ibsenism*)(以下简称《精髓》)初次发表。早期版本的《精髓》中,莎士比亚虽然被提得不多,但是后续"批判"莎士比亚的标准已经被定下。据弗兰克·哈里斯(Frank Harris)回忆,萧伯纳在那时,对台前台后各类事务都用《精髓》的标准去衡量,而莎士比亚成了"最显眼的受害者"[1]。1894年,萧伯纳在结束为《世界》杂志撰写音乐评论后,便在哈里斯主编的《周六评论》(*Saturday Review*)上发表戏剧评论,其中相当一部分都是对莎士比亚演出及戏剧的批评。而批评标准就是他在《精髓》里提出的"腓利士人—唯心主义—现实主义"三分法,其中最重要的就是唯心主义和现实主义的对立。这种现实主义者虽和现实主义文学传统有渊源,但更融合了萧伯纳的超人精神、生机论以及左翼激进思想等,更强调其颠覆性与否定性。在他看来,唯心主义者(idealist)"在理想中寻得庇护",是因为"他恨自己并以自己为耻",而现实主义者则"深深地尊敬自己,相信自身意志的有效性"。[2]现实主义力求揭破面纱,寻求未来可能性的实现。

莎士比亚并没有被划在这一类"现实主义者"之中,但是萧伯纳将其排除的理由并非莎士比亚是"唯心主义者",而是莎士比亚"过时"了。在《精髓》的后续增补中,他提到

---

[1] Bernard Shaw, *Sixteen Self Sketches*, London: Constable, 1949, p. 185.

[2] Bernard Shaw, *The Quintessence of Ibsenism: Now completed to the Death of Ibsen*, London: Constable, 1913, p. 27.

托尔斯泰以及易卜生并非比莎士比亚与莫里哀更有天赋,他们之所以能够在当下开创格局,是因为某种"理念进化的一般规律"①。拉马克式进化论以及叔本华和尼采的意志论是这种进化规律的主要外观。新的时代需要新的理念,而创造新理念的人本身也预兆了新时代的到来。在这个意义上,莎士比亚是被"淘汰"而非"否定"。而前述的成熟与未成熟,反映的并非生理时间或个体时间的差异,而是一种整体的时代差异。

但这种时代差异并非一种简单的线性差异。首先就是尼采和萧伯纳的"超人观",都带着某种"不合时宜性"。尼采在《不合时宜的沉思》中指出,历史只能"由强有力的人格来催生",而"弱小的人格则会完全被其灭绝"。②这种不合时宜被阿甘本解读为某种"同时代性"(contemporariness)——与时代同步的人,在某种程度上一定是悖谬于时代的,真正属于那个时代的人"是那些从未完美地和时代同步或者没有适应时代需求的人……但正是通过这种切断与时代错误,他们相比其他人更能感知和把握他们的时代"③。自称是英国尼采的萧伯纳,其笔下角色也具有某种"时代错乱"(anachronism)的特征,而这种"时代错乱",是一种和过去时间的断裂。因此对萧伯纳来说,"成熟"是一种超越时代的进化隐喻,它不是连续的,相反是断裂的。事实上,以生命力量为主导的创造性进化永远不会结束,除非人类失去自己的肉体,达到凭思想永生的地步。这使得萧伯纳的时间观呈现出一种奇怪的悖论:一方面,人类还未达到真正的成熟,故而所有的未成熟都是"同时代的";另一方面,"成熟"并非时间的线性演进,相反每一次"成熟",都代表和过去"未成熟"状态的决裂。这种矛盾也体现在他对莎士比亚的评论上。

和早期剑拔弩张的态度不同,萧伯纳后期对莎士比亚的态度显得更加复杂,但其实也更加敢于直面莎士比亚。如前所述,萧伯纳在对莎士比亚的批评中,其实都留下了一些退路。如在早期的互文性作品《凯撒与克里奥帕特拉》中,萧伯纳看似与莎士比亚"对立",但其实更像是与莎士比亚"互补"。他说:"莎士比亚虽然如此了解人类的弱点,但却从不知道凯撒这类人的强力。"④他将自己的超人角色看作莎士比亚没有写过的角色,

---

① Bernard Shaw, *The Quintessence of Ibsenism: Now completed to the Death of Ibsen*, London: Constable, 1913, p. 174.
② Friedrich Nietzsche,. *Nietzsche: Untimely Meditations*, Cambridge: Cambridge University Press, 1997, p. 86.
③ Giorgio Agamben, *"What Is an Apparatus?" and Other Essays*, Redwood City: Stanford University Press, 2009, p. 40.
④ Bernard Shaw, *Three Plays for Puritans: The Devil's Disciple, Cæsar and Cleopatra, and Captain Brassbound's Conversion*, London: Constable, 1929, p.xxix.

同时也是在划定自己所扮演的这个戏剧家角色的"演出范围"。但是在后期,他更多的是想要"改造"莎士比亚(详见下一小节)。他曾经改写过《辛白林》的最后一幕,并认为重写这一幕的标准要参照"如果莎士比亚是在后易卜生(Post-Ibsen)、后萧伯纳(Post-Shaw)而非后马娄的情况下会怎么写"①。这种希望把莎士比亚"移植到"当代的想法,其实暗合了萧伯纳时间观的同时性特征。莎士比亚被易卜生取代,是因为他"过时"了,这种过时不是因为他生在前而易卜生(萧伯纳)生在后,相反是因为易卜生(萧伯纳)开创了一个和过去的"不成熟"相迥异的新理念与新时代;但是这种"过时"并不影响莎士比亚可以在某种程度上成为萧伯纳的"同时代人",他存在某种变得"成熟"或者说变成"后易卜生""后萧伯纳"的可能性。或许更准确点说,并非莎士比亚变成萧伯纳的同时代人,而是萧伯纳变成莎士比亚在这个时代的延续。某种程度上,萧伯纳是一个"叛逆"的莎士比亚继承者。他的特殊性在于,一方面他以一种对立姿态继承莎士比亚的戏剧遗产;但另一方面,就是这个"叛逆的儿子",打算创造另一个版本的莎士比亚"父亲"。

在萧伯纳的作品中,"互补"和"改造"的并置并不绝对。相反,这两种策略贯穿了萧伯纳对莎士比亚的反思、接受、批评与再创作。回到其戏剧生涯的早期,萧伯纳其实就已经在尝试着改造一个自己的莎士比亚。一个非常典型的例子是他对著名的莎剧演员亨利·欧文(Henry Irving)的批判。他认为欧文对莎士比亚的表演只是在演他自己,"除了他自己,他这一生中没有理解和阐释过任何一个作家的角色"②。萧伯纳对欧文的敌意,一方面来自其"情节剧"(melodrama)式的表演方式,也包括两人的戏剧分歧(比如欧文对易卜生的排斥);另一方面来自两者作为戏剧从业者的不同。欧文是当时有名的演员-经理(actor-manager),代表着19世纪后期以著名演员为中心的莎士比亚演出系统。而世纪之交既是欧陆新戏剧传入英国并产生重要作用的时期,也是莎士比亚戏剧进入斯提安(J. L. Styan)所谓的"莎士比亚革命"中。③这场革命最重要的趋向就是演员中心变成了导演中心,同时戏剧批评的影响力迅速擢升,很多演员开始转向"学者型"演员。世纪之交就是一个重新发明莎士比亚戏剧演出的过程,而这个过程中萧伯纳也处于中心圈层的附近。他的莎剧批评,以及他对威廉·珀尔(William Poel)、哈利·格兰威尔-巴克等重要莎剧表演改革者的影响与亲近关系,使得他成为这场莎士比亚革命的隐秘推

---

① Bernard Shaw, *Geneva; Cymbeline Refinished; &, Good King Charles*, London: Constable, 1946, p. 136.
② Bernard Shaw, *Shaw on Shakespeare: An Anthology of Bernard Shaw's Writings on the Plays and Production of Shakespeare*, Milwaukee: Hal Leonard Corporation, 1961, p. 53.
③ John Louis Styan, *The Shakespeare Revolution*, Cambridge: Cambridge University Press, 1983.

动者。他对莎剧批评的贡献,不仅仅体现在他本人的观点上,他对于英国独立剧场以及先锋戏剧的影响(公众讨论场的形成,对相关从业人员的支持和影响,提高批评家的话语权,等等),也是这场"莎士比亚革命"的重要推力之一。

但反过来,因为莎士比亚,新的戏剧表演模式、理念乃至新的从业者的角色变换(演员—导演,演员—批评家,批评家—导演,等等),使得萧伯纳作为戏剧家和批评家的社会表演有了足够的舞台和剧目。这也为他在后期回应乃至"改写"莎士比亚,并与莎士比亚之间形成更为复杂的"同时代"关系打下了基础。

三、重写与改写——双向成就的"不朽"人格

萧伯纳说在他小的时候,莎士比亚是他"下意识决定要从襁褓中重新转世(reincarnate)成为的人"[①]。这种莎士比亚"情结"可谓贯穿了萧伯纳一生。所谓"转世",并非萧伯纳想要成为莎士比亚,而是想要成为"另一个"莎士比亚(The Other Shakespeare),同时也是一个完全不是莎士比亚的人(Other than Shakespeare)。而这种矛盾的特性,最后交织成为《莎vs萧》的两名木偶角色。在此剧的一开场,代表莎士比亚的木偶指责某个毁坏他名声的人:

【莎】:我,威廉·莎(William Shakes),生于斯特拉特福,
此地经年,常设盛典,来祝我的名,
非一代之名,乃万世之名,
故我愠怒,
有无耻狡徒前来诟辱,
他自命不凡到失心,
竟将我的名缩成"萧",还敢
装作是我转生(reincarnate)到这里

从某个角度来说,在萧伯纳的绝笔中,两个互相比斗文德的角色,与其说是萧伯纳和莎士比亚,不如说是两个版本的莎士比亚,或者两个版本的萧伯纳。他们彼此成为对

---

① Bernard Shaw, *Immaturity*, London: Constable, 1931, p.x.

方的"转世",这一点成为萧伯纳戏剧/作家人格中最奇特的一面。和莎士比亚在晚期戏剧(比如《暴风雨》等)中呈现的和解倾向不同,萧伯纳到最后都没有寻求一个完美的解决。或许是受到瓦格纳"无尽旋律"(Unending Melody)的影响,也可能是因为内化了进化论、意志论等永久斗争的模型,萧伯纳的戏剧结尾充满了妥协、压抑而非冲突的解决与张力的释放。这种"非卡塔西斯"型的戏剧结尾,既是萧伯纳政治宣传的一部分,目的是"刺痛"无忧无虑、沉醉于情节剧的中产阶级,但另一方面可能也是其思想、观念乃至作家人格本身的形式性表征。这种非释放性结局在《莎vs萧》也很明显。剧中莎士比亚和萧伯纳斗拳,先是萧伯纳被打倒在地,然后数到九时,萧伯纳站起来回击了一拳,最后莎士比亚被击倒十秒判负。看起来似乎是萧伯纳赢了,但之后莎士比亚马上用自己的"不朽性"找补回来。两人进行了一系列作品角色的比拼,最后萧伯纳大量引用《暴风雨》和《哈姆雷特》的台词,指出无论是自己还是莎士比亚,都是世界的过客,无法永恒。为了清晰展现这种互文关系,允许我引用一长段最后的结尾。

【萧】:你并非首个唱诵伤心之人,

而在我之前,无人教你

那无信的泰门疗愈那伤痕

【莎】:你教的是你不知的,能的话就唱吧

我高入云霄的楼台,辉煌的宫殿,

宏伟的庙宇,以至整个儿地球

地面上的一切,都将烟消云散——[①]

【萧】:我们这短小的憨戏,

留不下半点影痕。[②]

我说过,这世界远比我们留得更久

明日明日复明日,

我们这些木偶,还得重演此幕,

同时,不朽的威廉,身后化成了泥土,

[①] 化用自《暴风雨》(The Tempest)第四幕第一场,第148—154行,此处译文参考方平译本。参见:莎士比亚:《莎士比亚全集》,方平等译,上海译文出版社,2010年。

[②] 此处代表"萧伯纳"的木偶接续着化用了《暴风雨》引文的下面两行:And, like this insubstantial pageant faded, Leave not a rack behind.(IV.i.155—156)。

只配去堵塞漏风的门户
别看这泥土,生前称霸称雄,
只落得挡风防雨,填补墙洞①。
【莎】:这是我的词,不是你的!
【萧】:安静,小气(jealous)的诗人,
我俩都是凡人,在世匆匆受苦,
我微明的火烛,照过来了。

  这里萧伯纳用莎士比亚的台词来说明其不朽性的虚妄。但很有意思的是,当莎士比亚指责他挪用自己的句子时,萧伯纳竟然用"小气"(jealous)来形容莎士比亚。在英语中,jealous既可以表示嫉妒,也可以表示对自身所有物的强烈占有欲。在这里,萧伯纳可能表面上是在批评莎士比亚太过在意自己台词的所属权。但从深层次讲,他说莎士比亚不是第一个"唱诵伤心的人",但他是第一个教会那位没有信仰的泰门如何治疗自己伤痕的人。这里萧伯纳引用莎士比亚的句子,或许也是在讽刺莎士比亚这些描述世界变化、无物居留的句子,也不是"第一次"出现的。因此在萧伯纳眼中,莎士比亚或许是在"嫉妒"自己的"第一次"。

  需要阐明的是,萧伯纳所谓的"第一次"并非指某种"原创性"。相反萧伯纳并不把"原创性"看作"不朽性"的必要前提。"动辄称誉某些东西有无与伦比的原创性(original),就像一些轻率地崇拜我的人做的那样,是一件很危险的事情:这个世界所称的原创性只是一种让人不习惯的挠痒痒(tickling)罢了。"②萧伯纳丝毫不讳认自己受过的影响,甚至现在批评家们研究萧伯纳时,都是顺着他给出了这一长串名字来挖掘其思想线索:马克思、尼采、瓦格纳、叔本华、拉马克、柏格森等。在他看来,"原创性"只是一种时兴,或者说它更多是以一种"新瓶装旧酒"的方式体现出来,正如在某种程度上他对于莎士比亚的描述那样。对萧伯纳而言,真的新戏剧需要"新理念",(当时的)人们需要的不是更好的戏剧,而是更新的戏剧。他引用斯图尔特·格伦尼的话"没有新哲学,就没有新戏剧"③,并补充道:"莎士比亚和歌德缺了对方都无法存在,而一个哲学时代中也不

---

① 这四行化用自《哈姆雷特》第五幕第一场,第220-223行,只是主语从凯撒大帝换成了威廉·莎士比亚。
② Bernard Shaw, *Shaw on Shakespeare: An Anthology of Bernard Shaw's Writings on the Plays and Production of Shakespeare*, Milwaukee: Hal Leonard Corporation, 1961, p. 212.
③ Ibid, p. 208.

可能有两个莎士比亚。"①萧伯纳的补充说明在这里显得很有意思,一方面他认为一个时代只会有一个巨人,这个巨人可谓赢家通吃,会分走后来者的大部分荣光。另一方面,一个巨人想要成为巨人,就必须有另一位巨人的借鉴,没有歌德对于莎士比亚的推崇,莎士比亚的声名不会如此闻达;但如果没有莎士比亚,那么歌德也无法将自己树立为一个新时代的神像。

只有从这两点入手,我们才能解释清楚,为什么萧伯纳并不会将"改写"或者"挪用"莎士比亚当作羞耻,反而当成是一份需要严肃对待与准备的事业。因为在萧伯纳看来,改写是用思想改装旧剧,但这种改装本身却成就了双方,如同歌德和莎士比亚互相成就那样。萧伯纳对于莎士比亚的改写,不仅是塑造自身的"先锋"身份,同时也让莎士比亚"再活一次"。对于一位信奉进化论以及坚持新教徒打破偶像传统的作者而言,萧伯纳的哲学世界中并不能存在某种"永恒的雕像"。相反,真正的永恒来源于某种进化过程中的观念嬗变、试错与成熟。另外,萧伯纳对于"原创性"的否定,以及对于某种"不朽性"称呼的鄙夷,一方面可能是一种逆反心理,另一方面也符合其"讨论剧"的形式设定。萧伯纳尽管经常被看作"说教作家",但是他的戏剧中却从来不止一个声音,他声称会给予正面以及反面人物同样的比重。换句话说,他的戏剧体现出一种多声部特征。这种多声部特征部分接近巴赫金所说的"复调"。但巴赫金认为"复调"一般只能出现在社会化的长篇小说中,而诗歌和戏剧当中则很少出现。这从某个角度上也说明了萧伯纳的戏剧文本更带有小说的特征(尤其是将其和各类副文本,例如序言和后记等结合起来看的时候)。从某种角度来说,《莎 vs 萧》与《暴风雨》最后的戏中戏结构是类似的,作者和角色都面临一种不同的身份。而这部剧也是萧伯纳对于自己"表演者"、"批评者"与"创作者"身份相结合的作家人格的一次反思。这是一种"作者完全操控权的不可能性","戏剧家发现他和角色们处在同等的位置上"。②

因此,改写对于萧伯纳而言,其实是一种更加复杂乃至高级的文学活动。一方面,它糅合了萧伯纳戏剧家、批评家和社会表演者的角色;另一方面,这些角色的融合并非和谐而稳定的。相反,萧伯纳在不同的"角色"中间,不断地打着各种游击战。在这场怪异的战争中,莎士比亚既是他的敌人,又是他的盟友。以他对《辛白林》结尾的改写

---

① Bernard Shaw, *Shaw on Shakespeare: An Anthology of Bernard Shaw's Writings on the Plays and Production of Shakespeare*, Milwaukee: Hal Leonard Corporation, 1961, p. 208.

② Christopher Wixson, "Authorship and Shaw's Shakes Versus Shav", *Shaw*, 33.1(2013): 88.

(Cymbeline Refinished)为例,相比原著强调宽容的结局,萧伯纳版的终幕以"争辩"为主题。伊摩琴(Imogen)并不原谅波赛摩斯(Posthumus),他将这一幕改写成和《玩偶之家》类似的场景,伊摩琴质问波赛摩斯她到底何处不忠,并痛诉"笑容融解了太多憎厌,宽宥了太多罪恶"[1]。而两位失踪的王子也不再欲求团圆,相反他们怀念起了在山洞的生活。尽管这些人物思维非常的"萧伯纳",但是萧伯纳在改写文本中所做的,不仅仅是粗暴地加入自己的角色和思想。相反,他是力图重新"演化"莎士比亚的剧本。在改版的第五幕最后,萧伯纳保留了莎士比亚的台词:"战争从未因为这和平而停止,直到沾血的双手洗净。"(《辛白林》第五幕第五场,第590—591行)这句本来指代罗马、英国以及诸角色间的和解之语,反而成了萧伯纳暗中"批评"莎士比亚的地方。在他看来,莎士比亚没有弥补波赛摩斯曾经对伊摩琴的伤害,同时也为了大团圆结局"扭曲"了两位山洞中长大的王子的性情。在萧伯纳的解读中,"沾血的双手洗净"毋宁算是一种清算而非妥协,而这种从未因和平停下的战争,也可以解读为一种"不断处在战争状态中的和平"。在萧伯纳这里,和平仅仅意味着非暴力,但并非"无冲突",相反,它意味着不同理念的彼此对抗和更新。他认为莎士比亚没有给自己笔下的角色足够的理念(idea),也没有产生足够有力的对话。因此,他不仅改写了《辛白林》的角色与主题,更是改写了其形式。在试图保留莎士比亚角色与情节框架的情况下,正面扭转结局的"仓促"和"刻意"。

在萧伯纳对莎士比亚的改写文本中,我们都至少可以听到萧伯纳和莎士比亚两个声音。但这两个声音并不完全是本人的。萧伯纳的不同角色,反映的是他和文本之间的距离(在文本外,在文本内,在文本间)。文本外的萧伯纳是一个掌控文本全局的作家,文本内的萧伯纳是一位抒发己见的第一人称批评家,而在文本间的萧伯纳,则是试图勾连起两个时代、两种理念,乃至两种作家身份。萧伯纳的作家身份与其说是"大写的一",不如说是"大写的二"。他代表着萧伯纳的作家人格本身的双元性,也就是必须有一个人同他一样站在时代的两端,才能够形成他自身的作家人格。而伴随着这个作家人格诞生的,也是一个被他全面改造过的,另一个版本的对应作家。从萧伯纳职业生涯来看,莎士比亚或许便是这个"大写的二"的另一端的核心。

参考文献

Bernard Shaw and Dan H. Laurence, *Collected letters, 1874–1897*, New York: Dodd, Mead &

---

[1] Bernard Shaw, *Geneva; Cymbeline Refinished; &, Good King Charles*, London: Constable, 1946, p. 149.

Company, 1965.

Bernard Shaw, "Blaming the Bard", *The Saturday Review*, 1896.

Bernard Shaw, *Buoyant Billions, Farfetched Fables, & Shakes Versus Shav*, London: Constable, 1950.

Bernard Shaw, et al., *The Matter with Ireland*, 2nd edition, Gainesville: University Press of Florida, 2001.

Bernard Shaw, et al., *The Religious Speeches*, University Park: Pennsylvania State University Press, 1963.

Bernard Shaw, *Geneva; Cymbeline Refinished; &, Good King Charles*, London: Constable, 1946.

Bernard Shaw, *Heartbreak House, Great Catherine, and Playlets of the War*, London: Constable, 1920.

Bernard Shaw, *Immaturity*, London: Constable, 1931.

Bernard Shaw, *Shaw on Shakespeare: An Anthology of Bernard Shaw's Writings on the Plays and Production of Shakespeare*, Milwaukee: Hal Leonard Corporation, 1961.

Bernard Shaw, *Sixteen Self Sketches*, London: Constable, 1949.

Bernard Shaw, *Misalliance: The Dark Lady of the Sonnets, and Fanny's First Play—With a Treatise on Parents and Children*, London: Constable, 1914.

Bernard Shaw, *Shaw on Shakespeare: An Anthology of Bernard Shaw's Writings on the Plays and Production of Shakespeare*, Milwaukee: Hal Leonard Corporation, 1961.

Bernard Shaw, *The Perfect Wagnerite: A Commentary on the Niblung's Ring*, London: Constable, 1913.

Bernard Shaw, *The Quintessence of Ibsenism: Now completed to the Death of Ibsen*, London: Constable, 1913.

Bernard Shaw, *Three Plays for Puritans: The Devil's Disciple, Cæsar and Cleopatra, and Captain Brassbound's Conversion*, London: Constable, 1929.

Bloom Harold and Chelsea House Publishers, *George Bernard Shaw*, New York: Chelsea House, 1987.

Christopher Wixson, "Authorship and Shaw's Shakes Versus Shav", *Shaw*, 33.1(2013): 79-94.

David Clare, *Bernard Shaw's Irish Outlook*, London: Palgrave Macmillan, 2016.

Declan Kiberd, *Inventing Ireland*, Cambridge: Harvard University Press, 1996.

Dietrich Richard F., *Portrait of the Artist as a Young Superman: A Study of Shaw's Novels*,

Gainesville: University of Florida Press, 1969.

Elizabeth Carolyn Miller, *Slow Print: Literary Radicalism and Late Victorian Print Culture*, Redwood City: Stanford University Press, 2020.

Friedrich Nietzsche, *Nietzsche: Untimely Meditations*, Cambridge: Cambridge University Press, 1997.

Giorgio Agamben, *"What Is an Apparatus?" and Other Essays*, Redwood City: Stanford University Press, 2009.

Hesketh Pearson, *Bernard Shaw: His Life and Personality*, Chicago: House of Stratus, 2015.

James Moran, "Meditations in Time of Civil War: Back to Methuselah and Saint Joan in Production, 1919-1924", *SHAW Annual: The Annual of Bernard Shaw Studies*, University Park: Penn State University Press, 2010.

John Louis Styan, *The Shakespeare Revolution*, Cambridge: Cambridge University Press.

Lagretta Tallent Lenker, "Bernard Shaw's Interior Authors: The Novels", *Shaw*, 41.1(2021): 87-118.

Michael Holroyd, *Bernard Shaw, Volume 1: The Search for Love, 1856-1898*, London: Random House, 1988.

Philip Edwards, "Shakespeare and the Politics of the Irish Revival", in Joseph McMinn, ed., *The Internationalism of Irish Literature and Drama*, Maryland: Barnes & Noble Books, 1992.

Robin Bates, *Shakespeare and the Cultural Colonization of Ireland*, New York: Routledge, 2008.

Stanley Weintraub, *Bernard Shaw, Novelist*, University Park: The Pennsylvania State University, 1956.

William Butler Yeats, *Ideas of Good and Evil*, London: AH Bullen, 1914.

莎士比亚:《莎士比亚全集》,方平等译,上海译文出版社,2010年。

布鲁姆:《西方正典》,江宁康译,译林出版社,2005年。

莎士比亚东瀛"行脚"论
——"美"的传播与接受历程

卢昱安

摘要：作为西方戏剧艺术典范的莎士比亚自19世纪中叶传入日本以来，在戏剧、文学等方面激励着近代日本社会的发展。明治维新后在西方启蒙思想的影响下，日本积极吸收西方文化，莎士比亚戏剧被搬上了日本的剧院舞台。莎士比亚戏剧有着日本传统戏剧无法表现的西方魅力与审美治愈性，如何处理好东西方文化的差异成为日本近代知识分子思考的难题。本文按时间顺序梳理莎士比亚戏剧之美在日本的传播与接受历程，继而考察东西方文化在交流与碰撞中所折射出的日本近代知识分子的思想转变问题。

关键词：莎士比亚戏剧；日本近代知识分子；审美治愈性；跨文化传播

基金项目：本文系中央高校基本科研业务费专项资金资助项目"中国当下'治愈'文化趋势对日本'治愈系'文化的语境迁移研究"（项目编号：SWU2309712）的阶段性研究成果。

作者简介：卢昱安，西南大学外国语学院日语系教师，主要研究方向为日本近现代文学、比较文学与比较文化研究。

一、引言

"行脚"（あんぎゃ）在《日本国语大辞典》中有两种含义。一是作佛教用语，指的是佛教的僧侣或为自我修行，或为教化他人而广游四方。游方之僧人，又可称为"行脚僧"。二是佛教用语以外的用法,有行走、游历于各国之意。①追根溯源,这个词是由中国传到日本去的,杜牧在《大梦上人自庐峰回》中写道:"行脚寻常到寺稀,一枝藜杖一禅衣。"该"行脚"对应佛教用语的含义。另外,南宋文学家杨万里在《和文远叔行春》中写道:"行脚宜晴翠,看云恐夕黄。"其中"行脚"指的就是佛教用语以外的"行走"之意。笔者为何以莎士比亚东瀛"行脚"论为题,在此想要做出一些解释。首先,笔者所用的"行脚"也指的是"行走、游历"之意。提及莎士比亚与日本的关系,人们往往想到的是莎士比亚在日本的接受史、日本的莎士比亚研究与在日本的莎剧演出等,抑或是从比较文学的角度探讨莎翁剧对日本戏剧发展的影响,这些都是从日本如何接受莎士比亚的角度出发的。笔者在这里用"行脚"一词,是将莎士比亚戏剧在日本的传播拟人化,从莎士比亚戏剧"探访"东瀛并且"游走"于日本的各个时代这一角度出发,梳理和论证莎士比亚戏剧之美在东瀛传播与接受的过程。

二、莎翁踏入东瀛——从"莎士比亚"姓名的日语表记谈起

要想了解莎士比亚是如何传入日本的,首先要了解日英文化交流的起源。第一位来到日本的英国人是和莎士比亚同年出生的航海家威廉·亚当斯(日本名:三浦按针)。1600年4月29日,经过了19个月的航海,威廉乘坐的利夫得号船漂流到日本的丰后地带(今大分县)。②后来德川家康将这位踏入日本的英国人威廉聘为外交贸易顾问,封他为日本的武士,赐予佩刀,并赐名"三浦按针",使得威廉成为日本的第一位白人武士。威廉为德川家康翻译过英国国王詹姆士一世的国书,这也逐渐拉开了日本和英国文化交流的序幕。

最早将"莎士比亚"这个名字介绍到日本的是江户幕府末期的《英文鉴》一书。值得一提的是,该书出版于1841年,是由涩川敬直将美国文法家Lindley Murray(1745—1826)的 *English Grammar* 翻译成荷兰语的版本。"莎士比亚"的名字在日本最早就是在这本荷兰语的《英文鉴》中,按照荷兰语的发音,以「シャーケスピール」的日语表记出现的。日本的"莎士比亚"居然是由荷兰语引进的,虽说有些奇怪,但是考虑到当时日本的国情,这又是情理之中的。1639年幕府正式颁布了"锁国令",除了中国和荷兰,日本断

---

① 日本大辞典刊行会『日本国語大辞典〔縮刷版〕』第一卷、小学館、1979年、546。
② 甘茵:《19世纪的日本英语教育及启示》,《新西部》2016年第6期。

绝了同其他国家的外交往来。江户中后期的日本主要借助荷兰语翻译介绍西方近代科技知识。[1]江户时期的日本学者借助荷兰语接触西方文化，兴起了一场名为"兰学"的学术运动。日本的洋学可以说是在"兰学"的基础上发展而来的。因此，"莎士比亚"踏入东瀛是由荷兰语引进的也就不足为奇了。除了《英文鉴》以外，江户时期莎士比亚的名字还出现在《暎咭唎纪略》《英国志》两本书中。《暎咭唎纪略》是清朝江苏江都人陈逢衡（1778—1885）所著，荒木謇对其施以日语训读，并于1853年在日本再版刊出，属于和刻本汉籍。这本书中提到，英国有书画，有地图、户籍，有医学、法学，还有善于写诗文的四人，其中一人就是"沙士比阿"，这也是"莎士比亚"第一次以汉字的表记出现在日本。[2]另外一本《英国志》是由长期居住在上海的英国宣教士慕维廉（1822—1900），依据英国托马斯·米纳尔原著编译成汉语，于1856年由墨海书馆印刻而成。该书中提到的"舌克斯毕"，指的就是莎士比亚。[3]该书后来传入日本，于1861年在长州藩（现山口县）再版刊出，以同样的汉字表记"舌克斯毕"指代莎士比亚。就这样，从江户时期开始，莎士比亚的名字正式踏入东瀛。

不难发现，《英文鉴》《暎咭唎纪略》《英国志》这几本书都不是直接从英语翻译成日语的书籍，而是通过对荷兰语、中文进行翻译或加以日语训读得以出版。这和前面提到的日本"锁国令"相关。日本对于莎士比亚的了解，最开始是从英文语法书，或介绍英国国情的书籍中获取的，大众仅仅是知道英国有善于写诗作文的莎士比亚这个人。后来在日本，莎士比亚的日语表记多为片假名。尤其是明治时期，莎士比亚的日语表记更是有很多种，包括「セークスピヤ」「シャクスピール」「セクスピア」「シェークスピア」「シェイクスピア」等。莎士比亚在日本以"沙翁"的表记出现也是在明治时期。现今日本的莎士比亚主要以「シェイクスピア」表记为主，比如作为日本莎学研究阵地的日本莎士比亚协会（日本シェイクスピア協会）也是用的该表记。[4]

---

[1] 徐克伟：《汉译西书之于日本江户兰学的借鉴意义》，《国际汉学》2021年第1期。
[2] 陈逢衡：《暎咭唎纪略》，荒木謇训读，和泉屋善兵卫出版，1853年，第7页。汉语为笔者译。
[3] 邹振环：《〈大英国志〉与晚清国人对英国历史的认识》，《复旦学报》（社会科学版）2004年第1期。
[4] 此部分内容主要参照荒井良雄、大場建治、川崎淳之助『シェイクスピア大事典』、日本図書センター、2000年、669。

三、行走明治、大正

根据现存文献资料的记载,虽然"莎士比亚"的名字在1841年才正式被介绍到了日本,但早于这个时间,有着"日本莎士比亚"美誉的剧作家近松门左卫门(本名:杉森信盛)的《释迦如来诞生会》(1695年)、《妹背山妇女庭训》(1771年)、《心谜解色丝》(1810年)这三部作品中都有和莎士比亚戏剧类似的情节,比如《释迦如来诞生会》中"割肉"的情节和《威尼斯商人》相似,《妹背山妇女庭训》《心谜解色丝》中也有一些和《罗密欧与朱丽叶》相似的情节,但至今日本的学术界还没弄清这究竟是巧合还是有着一定的必然性。

1. 谁是莎士比亚戏剧的日本"引路人"?

有研究认为,日本第一部莎士比亚戏剧的翻译作品是出版于1884年的坪内逍遥的《该撒奇谈——自由太刀余波锐锋》。这是一部将莎士比亚的《凯撒大帝》按照人形净琉璃剧本风格进行翻译的作品。[①]还有研究提到,1883年2月27日—4月11日,河岛敬藏以《欧洲戏剧凯撒大帝》为题,将莎士比亚戏剧的翻译连载刊登在名为《日本立宪政党新闻》的报纸上,这是最早的按照莎士比亚戏剧英文原文进行的翻译。[②]此外,还有研究认为,日本莎士比亚的翻译始于1875年连载于《平假名绘入新闻》上假名垣鲁文的《西洋歌舞伎叶武列士》。[③]以上研究中,都提到了"最早"翻译莎士比亚戏剧的相关内容,但为什么会出现不同的作家和作品呢?笔者认为,谁是莎士比亚的"引路人",并将莎剧传入日本,即莎士比亚戏剧的日本翻译起源的这个问题需要重新梳理。

据考证,1871年,日本明治时期著名学者中村正直所的《西国立志编》中就提到过莎士比亚的《哈姆雷特》这部作品。和江户时期的闭关锁国政策不同,明治维新之后的日本加速了"西化"的进程,大量引进西方启蒙书籍、科学技术书籍,并翻译了当时西方流

---

① 安西徹雄「四つの時代区分—序論に代えて」、『日本シェイクスピア一〇〇年』、荒竹出版株式会社、1998年、3。
② 同上书、632。
③ 道行千枝「日中シェイクスピア受容—導入期についての一考察—」、『福岡女学院大学短期大学部紀要』、2005年、103。在这里笔者想补充说明的是,假名垣鲁文本名野崎文藏,1829—1894年,是日本文明开化时期著名的小说家。《平假名绘入新闻》是《东京绘入新闻》的前身,报纸主要刊登日语平假名的文章,并配插画。『西洋歌舞伎葉武列土』题目中和式汉字的发音就是ハムレット(哈姆雷特)。这部作品也是假名垣鲁文根据日本歌舞伎剧本的风格所改编的《哈姆雷特》。

行的概念。就是在这样的社会背景下,启蒙思想家中村正直翻译了英国斯迈尔斯(Samuel Smiles)的《自助论》,取名为《西国立志编》。①这本宣扬西方价值观的畅销书,多次提到莎士比亚和莎剧的台词片段。②先于莎士比亚的原作剧本,日本一开始是对由英国浪漫主义作家查尔斯·兰姆和玛丽·兰姆改编的《莎士比亚戏剧故事集》(Tales from Shakespeare,1807)进行的翻译。假名垣鲁文在1875年的《平假名绘入新闻》上连载三期的作品《西洋歌舞伎叶武列士》,就是根据兰姆姐妹的底本进行的翻译。值得一提的是,当时发表在报纸上介绍这部戏剧的原作者是以《英国的狂言作者莎士比亚》为题的,从故事概要中也可以发现这部作品是假名垣对原作进行改编的"翻案"剧。③明治初期的日本虽然积极引进西方的文化,但由于对异国文化认知缺乏常识,所以一开始也会有些"消化不良"。看惯了江户时期传统戏剧的日本人,面对新兴的外来戏剧文化,比如陌生的西洋的人名、奇特的异国风俗等都不便于理解。因此,当时最流行的翻译方式就是"翻案",即把一个外国故事嫁接到本国的某个历史时期的背景中,风俗、地名等都改成本土的内容。④比如,1877年由藤田茂吉翻译的《胸肉的奇诉》,1883年由井上勤翻译的《人肉质入裁判》,都是依据兰姆姐弟的《莎士比亚戏剧故事集》中的《威尼斯商人》改编的"翻案"小说。以上的"翻案"都是对兰姆姐弟的底本进行的翻译,而日本最早对莎士比亚的原作进行翻译的是1883年河岛敬藏的《欧洲戏剧凯撒大帝》。1884年5月,同样是对《凯撒大帝》原作进行翻译的坪内逍遥的《该撒奇谈自由太刀余波锐锋》问世。⑤从时间上来看,河岛敬藏的翻译稍稍早于坪内逍遥的,但是坪内逍遥却是日本翻译莎士比亚戏剧全集的第一人。据明治时期的文学家、翻译家柳田泉的记载,坪内逍遥在翻译《该撒奇谈自由太刀余波锐锋》时也曾参考了河岛之前的译本,"日本最初"这个名号非《欧洲戏剧凯撒大帝》的译者河岛莫属。⑥

明治时期以来,莎士比亚的戏剧随着"开国""西化"的浪潮涌进日本,中村正直通过翻译西方的思想启蒙书,介绍了一些莎士比亚戏剧中的名言名句。假名垣鲁文、藤田茂吉等人对由兰姆姐弟改编的《莎士比亚戏剧故事集》进行"翻案"创作,后来,河岛敬藏、

---

① 夏晓虹:《晚清女报中的西方女杰——明治"妇人立志"读物的中国之旅》,《文史哲》2012年第4期。
② 郝田虎:《莎士比亚在晚清中国新探》,《福建师范大学学报》(哲学社会科学版)2021年第2期。
③ 吉田弥生「葉武列土倭錦絵」,『文京学院大学外国語学部文京学院短期大学紀要』、2005年、268-269。
④ 胡纹馨:《如何并置东方与西方:莎剧歌舞伎的三个案例》,《戏剧艺术》2023年第2期。
⑤ 同上。
⑥ 柳田泉「西洋文学の移入」,『明治文学研究』第七卷、春秋社、1974年、122。

坪内逍遥等则直接对莎士比亚原著进行翻译。莎士比亚在这些"引路人"的引领下,将西方的戏剧逐渐渗透进东瀛的世界。

2."他乡"遇"故知"——莎士比亚戏剧与日本传统戏剧

1885年5月6日,由宇田川文海编排的《何樱彼樱钱世中》登上大阪的"戎座"。这是莎士比亚戏剧在日本的第一次演出。该剧将时代背景设置在了江户幕府末期,是将《威尼斯商人》根据日本的歌舞伎剧本风格改编的"翻案"剧。明治时期,日本对外国剧本翻译改编有两种并行的方式:一个是大体忠实于原著的面貌进行剧本的翻译;还有一个是将国外的剧本翻译并改编移植为日本故事,即本土化的"翻案"。对于对外来新兴事物和文化还缺乏认知的日本人来讲,依据"翻案"改编本土化的戏剧更易于接受,其演出的影响也更大。选择以歌舞伎演出第一部莎士比亚戏剧,是置于东方的世界之中的日本人在面对西方戏剧文化冲击的一次大胆尝试。

在谈及日本的莎士比亚戏剧翻译之时,不能不提到坪内逍遥(1859—1935),他是英国文学专家、小说家和戏剧导演。逍遥作为日本翻译莎士比亚戏剧全集的第一人,对莎士比亚文学在日本的传播有着丰功伟绩。和以往的"翻案"不同,逍遥将莎士比亚戏剧由"翻案"转为忠实于原著的翻译。1884年5月,他将莎士比亚的《朱利叶斯·凯撒》以《该撒奇谈自由太刀余波锐锋》为题译出刊行;1901年7月,又将这部剧搬上了"明治座"的剧院舞台,这也是莎士比亚戏剧在日本的第二次演出。虽然是致力于原著的翻译,但逍遥还是以模仿日本的古典舞台艺术形式之一人形净琉璃(文乐)剧本的风格进行翻译。作为西方戏剧代表的莎士比亚文学来到了东瀛,为什么始终摆脱不掉日本传统戏剧的影响呢?坪内逍遥曾在《该撒奇谈》的附言中谈到,莎士比亚戏剧并不是当时日本人所理解的"戏剧"。[①]由歌唱、舞蹈、乐曲等来演绎的歌舞伎、能、狂言都是日本传统"戏剧",而莎士比亚戏剧则是由对白写成,这对日本来说并不是传统意义的"戏剧"。其实,当时的日本人还没有"戏剧"这一概念,对他们来讲,歌舞伎、能、狂言都是"戏曲"。戏曲最早是由中国传入日本的,后经演变成为日本的传统艺能,并且融入了歌唱、舞蹈、乐曲、杂技等表演形式。因此,缺乏了这些表演要素的莎剧对日本人来讲,并不是他们所认知的传统"戏剧"。戏剧文本与舞台演出是不可分割的,因此在戏剧翻译的过程中,译者必须考虑剧本以外的因素,比如对白的节奏、音调、强度等是否符合观众的审美趣味。

---

① 坪内雄蔵「該撒奇談自由太刀餘波鋭鋒」、『明治文化全集』第22卷、日本評論社、1927年、334。

这些因素在孤立的文本阅读时往往不容易被察觉,但对于戏剧翻译的译者来说,首先想到的是文本要具有舞台性。以何种方式来演绎脱离了传统"戏曲"表演形式的莎士比亚戏剧,对日本人来说成了难题。日本传统戏剧侧重于"曲",而莎士比亚戏剧的精彩之处在于台词的演绎。为了调和东西文化的差异,坪内逍遥想出了"和洋折衷"的办法,将日本传统戏剧剧本的风格套入莎士比亚戏剧的翻译文本之中。1934年10月10日,在逝世前约4个月,坪内逍遥完成了《麦克白》的最后一次修订和翻译工作,在病后卧床静养休息中,他写了下面这段话:

我对莎士比亚戏剧产生浓厚兴趣的契机是想将其作为改进我们国家戏剧的参考资料。我的目的不是把他的作品当作英国文学的经典来研究,而是从功利主义的角度出发,把它看作为我国戏剧改革提供经验的璞玉。换句话说,我并没有把莎士比亚当成英国文学家,而是从剧本作家的角度出发来研究。①

坪内逍遥翻译莎士比亚戏剧的创作动机是为了改进日本的传统戏剧。他山之石,可以攻玉。在莎士比亚戏剧这块"沃土"中培育日本传统戏剧,是他的翻译理念和创作动机。逍遥有意识地移植西方戏剧,将翻译和借鉴西方剧作为推进日本传统戏剧改良的手段,为日本传统戏剧的"古木"插上莎士比亚戏剧的"新枝"。这反映出面对东西文化碰撞所产生的差异,以及日本知识分子的心态和对策,可以说这是一个日本对莎士比亚戏剧摸索和实践的时代。

四、迷途昭和

昭和是日本天皇裕仁在位期间使用的年号,时间是1926年12月25日—1989年1月7日。历经62年零13天,也是日本年号中所用时间最长的。20世纪30年代,日本介入第二次世界大战,导致国家全面崩溃和最后投降,各行各业大萧条,日本人称之为"昭和萧条"。后来,日本抓住机会从50年代开始高速发展经济,又创造了"昭和奇迹"。在这样一个动荡变化的时期,莎士比亚戏剧的传播也发生了相应的变化。

---

① 坪内逍遥「跋に代えて」,『新修シェークスピヤ全集』第二九卷、中央公社論、1935年、8。

1. 昭和前期——异乡人的身份彷徨

明治维新以后,日本的戏剧经历了改良运动,主要是对西方戏剧的"翻案"改编。后来,致力于戏剧的改革者意识到仅是对西方戏剧进行翻译,难以实现日本戏剧的近代化,所以在引进、接受翻译西方戏剧的同时,也开始注重新内容和新形式两个方面。由此,日本的传统戏剧迎来了近代改良的新局面,于1909年前后有组织地开展了话剧运动,在日本戏剧史上称为"新剧"。由小山内薰、市川左团次发起建立的自由剧场,由坪内逍遥、岛村抱月创办的"文艺协会",两者成为日本话剧运动的起点。[①]在任何时代,当人们尝试新方法或面对新事物时,就算出发点是好的,也难免会出现一些问题。日本近代戏剧的先驱者小山内薰曾两次出访欧洲,考察过英、法、苏联等国家的戏剧现状,深感戏剧是现代欧洲的象征。他回国后不久便创办了《戏剧与评论》杂志,致力于介绍欧洲新兴的表现主义戏剧。1924年5月1日,小山内薰与友田恭助、和田精等人创办了筑地小剧场。但筑地小剧场刚创办之时,几乎无人为其提供创作剧本,连续两年一直采取上演西方翻译剧的方针。其中,包括易卜生、契诃夫以及莎士比亚的戏剧等,都取得了很大成功。据统计,筑地小剧场五年共演出剧目117部,西方翻译剧就有90部,日本本土原创戏剧的数量少之又少。这样的演出形式受到日本小说家、戏剧家菊池宽等人的批评,直言小山内薰上演方针的问题,以及筑地小剧场需要反省等。进入昭和时代,筑地小剧场仍多次上演过莎士比亚的《麦克白》《仲夏夜之梦》,但本来就饱受争议的剧场,随着小山内薰的去世也变得四分五裂。后来又以土方与志为中心成立了新筑地小剧场,新筑地受当时的马克思主义的影响,其口号是在社会制度允许的范围内呈现进步的意识形态戏剧,并通过戏剧向大众传播马克思主义。1940年8月,政府以"带有浓烈的社会主义色彩不符合本国的国情"为由强制其解散了。

这个时期,日本对莎士比亚戏剧的接受态度也发生了变化,莎翁的戏剧由台前转为幕后。从以演出为目的的莎士比亚戏剧变成了作为文学文本研究的"学院派"的莎剧,日本英国文学评论家中野好夫(1903—1985)称这是莎士比亚的"不遇时代"。莎士比亚戏剧为什么会经历从为传统戏剧提供经验的"璞玉"到遭受"不遇"的变化? 随着维多利亚时代繁荣的衰落,英国开始失去其作为强国的吸引力,不只对英国戏剧感兴趣,从英国戏剧扩展到学习西欧整体是当时日本戏剧界的明显转向。易卜生、高尔基、契诃夫的戏剧被纷纷搬上舞台。福原麟太郎曾指出,英国文学是"成年人的文学"。所谓成年人

---

① 唐月梅:《日本戏剧史》,昆仑出版社,2008年,第443页。

文学是在自我权衡的人生观下看待人生的物语,是写给善于思考人生问题的读者的。但当时的日本人追求的不是莎士比亚说教式的成人的文学,而是"青年的文学"。[①]其实,当初坪内逍遥笔下的莎士比亚戏剧就遭到过夏目漱石的批评,漱石在题为《坪内逍遥与哈姆雷特》的剧评中提到过,坪内逍遥的莎士比亚戏剧一点都不有趣。[②]虽然逍遥尝试"忠实"原著的翻译,但以改良日本传统戏剧为目的,并将传统戏剧的风格融入莎士比亚戏剧翻译之中,可以说是一次"不忠实"的失败。在面对东方传统文化与西方新兴文化的差异时,夏目漱石认为不能以功利主义为目的,只从形式上套用西方戏剧,这样的翻译无法诠释出莎士比亚戏剧真正的精髓。但如何从本质上解决"东方"与"西方"的二元对立,当时的日本人也没有更好的办法,昭和前期就是日本近代知识分子对这一问题进行思考与追问的时代。莎士比亚戏剧由舞台转向幕后,看似停滞不前,但适当驻足是为了更好地出发。不能否认的是,苦恼于"东方"与"西方"二元对立的日本近代知识分子在思考与追问的过程中,也终于将莎士比亚的戏剧从日本传统戏剧的枷锁中解放出来。

2. 昭和后期——疗愈人心的莎剧复兴

大正到昭和前期,莎士比亚戏剧逐渐从戏剧舞台淡出,成为日本学界研究英国文学作品的典范。当时日本莎学家的研究方向主要分为四大类:①莎士比亚传记、作品研究;②比较文学研究;③海外莎士比亚研究的翻译;④莎士比亚戏剧剧场的研究。第二次世界大战结束后,经历军国主义统治后的日本又将莎士比亚戏剧重新拾起。二战结束后的二十年,再次迎来日本莎士比亚戏剧表演的复兴与再生时期。以1946年6月《仲夏夜之梦》在帝国剧院的盛大演出为开端,随着"前进座"剧院的巡回公演、莎士比亚专业剧团、现代剧院的出现等等,莎剧又如雨后春笋般不断被搬上舞台。[③]其中最重要的是1955年"文学座"剧院上演的《哈姆雷特》,由福田恒存翻译并导演。他所执导的莎士比亚带有浓厚的西方风格,已经完全摆脱了歌舞伎的色彩。[④]福田不仅向日本戏剧界提供了现代日语的莎士比亚戏剧翻译,而且还从当时的英国舞台引进了简易的布景和舞

---

① 福原麟太郎「大人の文学」、『愚者の知恵』、新潮社、1957年、77-78。
② 河竹登志夫『近代演劇の展開』、NHK市民大学叢書、1985年、23-24。
③ 同上书、653。
④ 野田学:《蜷川幸雄莎士比亚作品中的镜像和文化错位》,《戏剧》(中央戏剧学院学报)2009年第4期。

台装置,演出给观众留下了难忘的印象,获得了成功和好评。①1954年,福田在伦敦的剧院观看了由理查德·伯顿主演的《哈姆雷特》,在英国看到正宗的莎剧表演令他大受感动,并以此为契机开始了莎士比亚戏剧的翻译和导演工作。在福田的努力下,曾经被当作"成年人的文学"而遭受"不遇"的莎士比亚戏剧终于能够"含冤昭雪"。福田认为,莎士比亚戏剧体现了戏剧的精髓,是能够疗愈近代日本人"自我"意识和孤独感的一剂良药。他希望通过莎士比亚戏剧,日本人能够认识自我,建立自我,最终实现超越自我。②

从70年代初开始,小田岛雄志开始发表他的莎士比亚译本。福田和小田岛的翻译都重视台词的节奏感,更加口语化,富有生气。但是小田岛最大的特点是他的译文融入了年轻人的语言情感,并致力于莎士比亚戏剧的语言游戏和双关语的翻译。小田岛的译本逐渐被搬上舞台。1975年1月,由出口典雄主导的莎士比亚剧院成立;同年5月,该剧院采用小田岛的译本来编排和上演莎士比亚戏剧的所有作品。剧院为了一改往日莎士比亚戏剧晦涩难懂的形象,呈现出更加"亲民"的莎士比亚,演员都穿着便装表演,因此被观众称为"牛仔裤莎士比亚"。二战后,日本知识分子和剧作家开始重新审视"东方"与"西方"这一二元对立问题。不同于坪内逍遥在"东方"与"西方"之间求同、折中的态度,以福田恒存为代表的日本人开始认真思考"东方"与"西方"之间的存异。如何通过以莎士比亚为代表的西方戏剧来确立日本的"近代",完成"近代的超克",是关注的重点。

五、跨越平成、留步令和

莎士比亚的作品被著名导演黑泽明搬上了大荧幕。黑泽明在日本电影界影响力非凡,他推动了日本战后电影的发展,让日本电影走向世界。黑泽明的《蜘蛛巢城》《恶汉甜梦》《乱》分别是《麦克白》《哈姆雷特》《李尔王》的改编电影,其电影中融入了大量的日本传统能乐元素。借助莎士比亚的"品牌效应",黑泽明让世界看到了日本传统艺能文化。二战后,莎士比亚戏剧不光重返戏剧舞台,日本对"莎学"的研究也蒸蒸日上。这里不能不提到日本莎士比亚协会的重建。在迎来莎士比亚诞辰400周年的三年前1961年,日本莎士比亚协会重新建立。日本莎士比亚协会的创办推进了莎士比亚文学在日

---

① 中野里皓史:《日本的莎士比亚研究与莎剧演出》,《复旦学报》(社会科学版)1980年第1期。
② 難波田紀夫「福田恒存とシェイクスピア―せりふ劇を通しての近代の確立と超克」,『日本のシェイクスピア一〇〇年』、荒竹出版株式会社、1998年。

本的研究,为莎学研究家提供了可以发表研究成果的平台。该协会自创办以来,每年都要举办一次研究年会。2023年10月14日—15日,日本立正大学召开了"第61届莎士比亚学会"。除了召开学术会议以外,还发行研究年刊、综合性学术杂志和学会会报。2016年,为纪念莎士比亚逝世400周年和日本莎士比亚协会成立55周年,该协会出版了论文集《莎士比亚重生》。从20世纪70年代开始,英国的皇家莎士比亚剧团陆续来日演出。随着两国戏剧界交流的加深,加速了莎士比亚戏剧在日发展。以蜷川幸雄为代表的新生代戏剧导演脱离以西方为正统的束缚,根据日本人自己的理解演出莎士比亚戏剧。他认为,莎士比亚戏剧不是外国的故事,而应该是日本人自己的故事。[1]蜷川在执导《哈姆雷特》时曾思考,过往的"哈姆雷特"能否成为今天的"哈姆雷特",日式的《哈姆雷特》能否成为世界的《哈姆雷特》。[2]这部于2003年在东京涩谷文化村Cocoon剧场演出的《哈姆雷特》,获得了极大的成功,剧场魅力被发挥得淋漓尽致,从表演到舞台意象形成了"激情万象"的面貌。[3]蜷川导演完成了对上演形式多样化的莎士比亚戏剧的再发现与再定位,外来西方戏剧实现了具有日本特色的本土化转变。蜷川的"日本的莎士比亚",超越了东西之分,实现了东方与西方的会通;超越了古今之辨,实现了传统与现代的融合。

六、结语

日本自明治维新以来,不断吸收西方先进文化,莎士比亚戏剧的引进体现了日本知识分子对"洋气"的追求。莎士比亚的戏剧蕴含着日本传统戏剧所不具备的浪漫主义色彩。莎士比亚舞台剧浪漫主义场景的设置、诗意美学风格的台词、精致的布景装饰等,给日本人带来了审美的新体验。莎士比亚文学有着日本文学无法表现的西方魅力与审美治愈性。东西方戏剧的美学碰撞,拓印传统或复制西方,对"东方"与"西方"二元对立的质疑,通过西方确立和重构近代日本形象,是日本人面对外来文化时的不同心态。在不断地摸索、实践中,莎士比亚戏剧走向了"美"的历程与文化重塑的曲折道路。面对外

---

[1] 濑户宏:《蜷川幸雄的戏剧导演艺术——基于其莎士比亚作品》,《郑州轻工业大学学报》(社会科学版)2021年第4期。
[2] 刘恩平:《"成长"于千眼千刃——管窥蜷川幸雄导演的自我越界》,《上海艺术评论》2018年第2期。
[3] 韩煦:《极简风格与激情万象:从导演视角谈蜷川幸雄〈哈姆雷特〉的舞台美术设计》,《装饰》2021年第2期。

来文化,日本一直坚持建设性态度,在拥抱先进与共性的同时,也时刻秉持对外来文化的批判态度。在不断思考"我"来自何方,又该去向何方之时,"和魂"之"体"不仅没有丧失,反而得到了丰富和发展,坚持了文化认同,树立了文化自信,实现了与先进文明的价值对接。

参考文献

日本シェイクスピア協会編、『シェイクスピア案内』、研究社出版株式会社、1964年。

佐々木隆編、『日本シェイクスピア総覧』、株式会社エルピス、1990年。

ピーター・ミルワード、中山理訳著、『シェイクスピアと日本人』、株式会社講談社、1997年。

荒井良雄、大場建治、川崎淳之助編、『シェイクスピア大事典』、日本図書センター、2000年。

高橋康也、大場建治、喜志哲雄、村上淑郎編、『研究社　シェイクスピア辞典』、研究社印刷株式会社、2000年。

安西徹雄編、『日本のシェイクスピア一〇〇年』、荒竹出版、1989年。

水崎野里子著、『日本近代文学とシェイクスピア』、日本図書センター、2003年。

日本シェイクスピア協会編、『新編シェイクスピア案内』、株式会社研究社、2007年。

河竹登志夫:《戏剧舞台上的日本美学观》,丛林春译,中国戏剧出版社,1999年。

河竹繁俊:《日本演剧史概论》,郭连友、左汉卿、李凡荣等译,文化艺术出版社,2002年。

唐月梅:《日本戏剧史》,昆仑出版社,2008年。

濑户宏:《莎士比亚在中国:中国人的莎士比亚接受史》,陈凌虹译,广东人民出版社,2017年。

马克思主义与莎士比亚

《雅典的泰门》与莎士比亚时期炼金术情感生产及交易制度

史敬轩

摘要：在《雅典的泰门》中，泰门因为破产而失去朋友，债主登门，泰门饱尝了人情凉薄。他在宴会上痛斥众人的势利。泰门隐居洞穴，运用他所发现的黄金驱使阿西比亚德斯攻陷雅典城。《雅典的泰门》是莎剧众多诅咒剧中的一种，但莎士比亚并未完成全剧。泰门的破产是马克思政治经济理论中资本家对土地所有者的胜利。但同时，泰门对雅典的诅咒也是希腊人感性意识中感觉和精神之间的抽象敌对。泰门用黄金实现了他的诅咒，也正是私有财产所表现出的中世纪神明力量的物化，是莎士比亚时代对于货币概念的基本思想。

关键词：货币；情感；生产；私有财产；交换

基金项目：本文系重庆市哲学社会科学规划项目"马克思主义莎士比亚批评研究"（项目编号：2023NDYB157）、2022年度重庆市社会科学规划社会组织项目"莎士比亚四大悲剧朱生豪译本音乐性研究"（项目编号：2022SZ44）的阶段性研究成果。

作者简介：史敬轩，重庆邮电大学外国语学院教授，主要研究方向为莎士比亚与古英语文学。

虽然在钱伯斯看来，莎士比亚并未完成《雅典的泰门》（以下简称《泰门》）全剧，[①]但是福尔杰莎士比亚图书馆的迈克尔·罗摩尼克断定：莎士比亚至少曾在《泰门》一剧中扮

[①] E. K. Chambers, *William Shakespeare: A Study of Facts and Problems*, vol. 1, Oxford: Clarendon Press, 1930, p. 482.

演过诗人这个角色。[1] 这也许能间接说明,莎士比亚自己并不是对这个剧作毫无兴趣,或者像钱伯斯所说的,"因为身心双重压力过大,导致崩溃"[2],才放弃了《泰门》。

因为《泰门》已经是公认的莎士比亚在他人的作品基础上改编的剧作,[3] 而且还是和别的剧作家合作的产物,[4] 所以通过剧情来推断作者的思想,这不太可能说得通。那么,如果看看《泰门》中的诗人到底说了什么,也许对于我们理解莎士比亚的真实想法会有一定帮助。因为这个角色并不出现在前人的《泰门》作品之中。《泰门》中的诗人台词共有113行,分别集中于第一幕第一场和第五幕第一场。诗人和剧中另一个人物埃皮曼特斯在一开始就警告过泰门要警惕那些趋炎附势的朋友。但和埃皮曼特斯不同的是,他既没有那么愤世嫉俗,也没有那么厌世消极,反而表现出的是一种对"拜金主义"默认的态度:"瞧,慷慨的魔力!群灵都被你召唤前来,听候驱使了。"[5]

一

这一点尤为重要,以往的评论家会更关注《泰门》所表现出的社会批判性。最具代表性的无疑是马克思。马克思在他的《资本论》和《政治经济学手稿》中都特意引用了《泰门》第四幕第三场中泰门那段对黄金的评价:"金子!黄黄的,发光的,宝贵的金子!……"[6] 马克思引用泰门的这段话旨在论证货币本质中所具备的特性,但是马克思

---

[1] Michael LoMonico, *The Shakespeare Book of Lists: The Ultimate Guide to the Bard, His Plays, and How They've Been Interpreted (And Misinterpreted) Through the Ages*, New Jersey: The Career Press, 2001, p. 165. 罗摩尼克引用了纽约瓦萨学院的唐纳德·韦恩·福斯特的莎士比亚文本数字分析技术,得出了20部莎士比亚戏剧中,莎士比亚可能扮演的角色。

[2] E. K. Chambers. *William Shakespeare: A Study of Facts and Problems*, Vol. 1, Oxford: Clarendon Press, 1930, p. 483.

[3] 1567年,威廉·潘特的意大利故事集《逍遥宫》(*Palace of Pleasure*)中就有《雅典的泰门》。更早一些的有2世纪希腊化时代的卢西恩的《对话录》(*Dialogues*),其中也有名为《泰门,或慈善家》("Timon, or the Misanthrope")的短故事。

[4] 除了钱伯斯认为《泰门》是莎士比亚与人合著的作品(E. K. Chambers, *William Shakespeare: A Study of Facts and Problems*, Vol. 1, Oxford: Clarendon Press, 1930, p. 482.),还有查理斯·耐特(Charles Knight, *The Comedies, Histories, Tragedies, and Poems of William Shakspere: King Lear, Timon of Athens, Troilus and Cressida*, Vol. 9, London: Charles Knight and Co., 1843, p. 171.)、尼克劳斯·德利乌斯、古廉·沃普兰克等人。(参见 Harold James Oliver, ed., *The Arden Edition of the Works of William Shakespeare: Timon of Athens*, London: Methuen, 1986, p.xxii。)

[5] 莎士比亚:《莎士比亚全集·第8卷》,朱生豪、苏福忠、马爱农译,新星出版社,2014年,第164页。

[6] 同上书,第225页。

并没有对货币(黄金)的特性进行更多的道德批判。虽然在后文中,格奥尔格·韦伯激烈地认为"这种构成货币本质的抽象,是一切祸害的起因"①,并且引用摩莱里的话"在没有任何财产的地方,也就不能产生财产造成的恶果"②,但这显然不是马克思的本意或者真正的态度。马克思从没有说过类似取消或者没收财产的话。格奥尔格·韦伯的认识本身就颠倒了唯物主义有关物质决定意识的先后次序。马克思只是强调了货币在私有化阶段才会表现出人的异化中所体现的"一种非人的力量统治一切"③。此处,马克思所说的"非人的力量"很难说他指的是某种抽象的力量,或者是某种自然的力量。因为他在书中对自然的力量有明确的定义,即人对于自然界,如土地肥力、人的直接生活资料的加工改造。

马克思反而用了一个非常具有通灵术色彩的词:神力。在他看来,莎士比亚在《泰门》中对黄金的论述揭示的正是货币成为有形的神明,"这种神力包含在它的本质中,即包含在人的异化的、外化的和外在化的类本质中。它是人类的外化的能力"④。也就是说,马克思并不把金钱的恶看作是金钱与生俱来的,反而是把金钱看作是人的能力的外化。

而更值得我们注意的是,这并不是马克思首次或者偶尔才使用类似的词汇,马克思反而在他的书中频繁地用到类似的词。那么,在严肃的哲学著作中,用类似的词,马克思是在运用文学比喻吗?还是说他的确将其视作严肃的问题在讨论?如果是前者,那么诗意化的语言就会妨碍马克思主义的科学性和严肃性;如果是后者,就有必要进一步探讨马克思的意图何在了。

马克思曾把包括文艺复兴之前的欧洲称为"精神化的世界"(welt vergeistigt),那个时代是以各种各样的"怪影"(Gespenst)呈现在读者的面前的。⑤也就是说,历史上的欧洲呈现出的是一种纯粹唯心化的形态,欧洲的古代人是世界的精神化者,他们在这种精神化的过程中,解释了世界的奥秘,将诸多现象形成文本,并将之归诸灵异。这也就能

---

① 《马克思恩格斯全集·第3卷》,人民出版社,2002年,第642页。
② 同上书,第644页。
③ 同上书,第349页。
④ 同上书,第363页。此处的"神力",马克思德文做"die göttliche Kraft",即英文的the divine power。希腊文作 δὲ δύναμις。参见 Karl Marx, Ökonomisch-philosophische Manuskripte aus dem Jahre 1844, Hamburg: Felix Meiner Verlag, 2005, p. 123。
⑤ 参见《马克思恩格斯全集·第3卷》,第167–169页。德文版参见 Karl Marx and Friedrich Engels, Die Deutsche Ideologie, Berlin: Dietz Verlag, 1960, pp. 151–154。

理解为什么在《泰门》开篇,诗人就说:"瞧,慷慨的魔力!群灵都被你召唤前来,听候驱使了。"① 这句话一方面是指泰门手中的金钱所表现出的力量;另一方面,它并不是诗人的文学修辞式的语言,而是文艺复兴时代所反映的真实思想。人们笃信黄金所具有的魔力,并不仅仅是因为它的货币价值,更是因为相信"它是有形的神明,它使一切人的和自然的特性变成它们的对立物"②。 所以,人是必死的,但黄金却可以使人永生(elixir)。③ 这也是泰门那段对黄金的论述所表述的意义。货币的力量可以使得事物以它非自然的状态呈现出来。死亡本是自然的,但黄金却可以使得时光永驻,生命不朽。

这是今天的我们所难以理解的。因为在欧洲"精神化的世界",世界的构成不是具体的人,而是马克思所说的十种"怪影":"最高本质,神、本质、世界的空虚、善和恶的本质、本质和它的王国、'诸本质'、圣子,基督、人、民族的精神,和把'一切'变为幽灵。"④ 所以,泰门所痛恨的并不是世态炎凉、人情淡薄,而是在神的本质下,那层温情脉脉的面纱被揭掉以后,作为财富所有者的泰门在失去自己的"神力"后所看到的善和恶的神圣圭臬。无论是雅典的元老们,还是趋炎附势的卢修斯这样的贵族,他们本身并没有任何变化。因为他们对于黄金的追逐,对于财富的渴望是自然的、正常的,是人之常情。神圣道德上的指责并不能改变这个客观现象,正如马克思语:"神学家……用原罪来说明恶的起源,就是说,他把他应当加以说明的东西假定为一种具有历史形式的事实。"⑤ 那么,既然是历史的,也就说明恶的存在是暂时的,并不是永恒的。这为道德家们谴责当下人类的堕落,期望未来的乌托邦、人类的恶会消失,提供了非常好的安慰和"救命稻草"。

然而,事实是善恶的本质只不过是"怪影"世界中精神上神意的体现。因为,假如对于黄金的追求是恶的,那么这和中世纪人通过炼金术来追求永恒显然是相矛盾的:人怎么可能一方面追求黄金,但同时又痛恨自己呢?或者说,人怎么可能在相信黄金等同于善的同时,又像格奥尔格·韦伯一样认为它是一切祸害的起因?

所以,也许最好的理解就是,这种明显的双重标准依赖于针对什么样的人来解释。

---

① 莎士比亚:《莎士比亚全集·第8卷》,第164页。
② 《马克思恩格斯全集·第3卷》,第362页。
③ 参见 Michela Pereira, "Alchemy", in Edward Craig, ed., *Routledge Encyclopedia of Philosophy*, New York: Routledge, 1998, p. 157.
④ "Gespenst"即英文中的"Spectre",也可以译为幽灵、神灵,或者鬼魅。德文版参见 Karl Marx and Friedrich Engels, *Die Deutsche Ideologie*, Berlin: Dietz Verlag, 1960, pp. 151-154。
⑤ 《马克思恩格斯全集·第3卷》,第267页。

正如马克思所说:"土地所有者炫耀他的财产的贵族渊源、封建往昔的纪念(怀旧)、他的回忆的诗意、他的耽于幻想的气质、他的政治上的重要性等等……同时,他把自己的对手描绘为狡黠诡诈的,兜售叫卖的,吹毛求疵的,坑蒙拐骗的,贪婪成性的,见钱眼开的,图谋不轨的,没有心肝和丧尽天良的,背离社会和出卖社会利益的,放高利贷的,牵线撮合的,奴颜婢膝的,阿谀奉承的,圆滑世故的,招摇撞骗的,冷漠生硬的,制造、助长和纵容竞争、赤贫和犯罪的,破坏一切社会纽带的,没有廉耻、没有原则、没有诗意、没有实体、心灵空虚的贪财恶棍。"①

在马克思看来,贵族对对手的咒骂正表明了土地所有者败给了资本所有者。马克思引用堂吉诃德来说明类似泰门这样的雅典农奴主:不理解工业动产本质(而这是完全对的)。② 从这里可以看出来,马克思并不认为工业资本主义是邪恶的或者不道德的,反而,相对于农奴制来说,它是完全对的。那么,泰门的破落是否就是现代资本的凯旋呢?

二

第二幕第二场,在管家和泰门的对话中,管家说:"伟大的泰门,光荣高贵的泰门,唉!花费了无数的钱财,买到人家一声赞美……"③这也就是说,泰门与那些从他手中获得金钱的贵族和艺人们构成了某种事实上的交易关系。交易的产品是实物或赞美,艺人和贵族们向泰门出售画作、诗篇、戏剧及礼物来换取金钱,而泰门则出钱购买这些有形或者无形的商品。他们已经构成了事实上的商人或生产者和消费者的货币关系。正如格奥尔格·韦伯语:"货币的本质表现为不折不扣的价值,表现为抽象的价值,这种抽象是货币为自己的神明本质提供的外观。"④马克思也使用了相同的词来形容事物的交换价值:"金钱是以色列人的妒忌之神;在他面前,一切神都要退位。金钱贬低了人所崇奉的一切神,并把一切神都变成商品。金钱是一切事物的普遍的、独立自在的价值。因此它剥夺了整个世界——人的世界和自然界——固有的价值。"⑤也就是说,一幅画或者

---

① 《马克思恩格斯全集·第3卷》,第285—286页。
② 同上书,第286页。
③ 莎士比亚:《莎士比亚全集·第8卷》,第193页。
④ 《马克思恩格斯全集·第3卷》,第641页。
⑤ 同上书,第194页。

一首诗到底值多少金币,只有金钱的神明才知道。对别人来说也许不如一块面包值钱,但对泰门来说,它或许就值一大笔钱。那么,我们是不是该把泰门的慷慨和高雅嘲笑为犯傻呢?

胡鹏教授认为,泰门的慷慨是有问题的,其关键在于他对如何、怎样赠与礼物,缺乏恰当的判断。[①]或者说,他唯一的问题就是管家所说的"傻头傻脑地乐善好施"[②]。但事实是,即便在工业资产社会,资本家一掷千金来购买名画或者艺术品,或者慷慨赠与赞美他的诗人或者艺术家,都是很常见的,而且并不一定要求回赠礼物。我们会看到泰门与他人的关系都是相互的,几乎没有单方面的礼物赠与。

在《艺术的培养》(1874)中,作者认为,富裕阶层纯粹为了作秀而在奢侈品上花费,这是愚蠢而该受谴责的,"但是,若经济状况良好,用钱合理,甚至收支允许,那么满足单纯自然的品味,让美的情感引领他们进入伟大艺术丰碑的富丽堂皇之中,那就是另一回事了"[③]。泰门并非如马克思所说的是庸俗的拜金的犹太人,或者说"仿佛他的无节制的挥霍浪费和放纵无度的非生产性消费决定着别人的劳动"[④]。泰门把那些贵族、元老和艺人们幻想成是依附于他的奴隶或者需要帮助的可怜人,如他帮助被捕入狱的文蒂狄斯脱困一样。从给别人的帮助中(通过金钱)获得虚荣心的满足,是类似于高高在上的神明对别人命运的主宰感。也就是说,他购买的商品是具有生产情感这一功能的,他花钱交易的方式也是以物易情的。因为这种交易从实物价值上来说等价性很差,所以管家才觉得不公平。

因此,即便如泰门自己所说,他的土地一直通到斯巴达,但由于地产并不能像资本那样具有流动性,也就没有了除地租外的商品利润。那么,当土地被分割和出售给他人的时候,泰门也就破产了,而之前与艺人和贵族的交易也就终止了。也只有在这个时候,他才会从幻想中醒来,从浪漫主义的灵光中跌入尘埃。不过,泰门不会意识到问题出在地产在动产面前势必会商品化,从而使像他这样的贵族破产。他反而把这一切归咎于世人在道德上的伪善。

他没有意识到,他的慷慨大方"无非是给奴隶以较多工资,而且既不会使工人也不

[①] 胡鹏:《友谊、金钱与政治:〈雅典人泰门〉的礼物经济》,《英美文学研究论丛》2019年第1期。
[②] 莎士比亚:《莎士比亚全集·第8卷》,第187页。
[③] A. R. Cooper, *The Cultivation of Art, and Its Relations to Religious Puritanism and Money-Getting*, New York: A. K. Butts & Co., 1874, p. 23.
[④] 《马克思恩格斯全集·第3卷》,第349页。

会使劳动获得人的身份和尊严"①。也即，工人付出劳动，制造产品，并将产品交于资本家来获得工资，而泰门的艺人和贵族同样将自己的产品交给泰门，来获得工资。如果泰门意识到了这个问题，那么他在情感上就不会有这么激烈的变化了。

三

所以，货币本是无罪的，黄金也不过是金属。但是，在《泰门》中，金钱却承担起了另一个重要的功能，那就是泰门情感的外化。正如前文所说，货币包含的神力是人类外化的能力。所以有人认为，《泰门》中人物性格反差太大，前后极不自然，②并得出这不是莎士比亚的作品，但这个观点的说服力是不够强的。《泰门》和《李尔王》具备的共同特征就是剧中主人公在梦幻破灭以后的大段诅咒。

在第四幕第一场开篇和第三场开篇，泰门使用了两段长篇诅咒来攻击雅典和它的市民。诅咒是通灵文学艺术手法诅术（malediction）中最常用的语言形式。此外，常见的诅术还有盟誓、告祝、诅牌、谶语、诟詈诗（curse poetry，或又称为诅咒诗）等。③按照通灵文学的理论，这些诅咒并不仅仅是人物情感的宣泄，还要真正发挥作用。如柏林大学教授比戎·奎林（Björn Quiring）所说：诅咒属于运用一套工具来发挥力量，通过将主体客观化来进行瓦解和统治。④无论是诅咒朋友们中毒而死，还是元老们手脚瘫痪，都是泰门渴望能重新驾驭这些人，或者恢复和左右原先交易关系的表现。如奎林所说："在威权的基础上，诅咒主张与至高无上的力量进行关联，表明对公正的运作施加重构的影响力。"⑤这也就是为什么泰门在两段诅咒中召唤了包括太阳在内的天上的一切神明。从这个角度来说，作为古代雅典贵族的泰门不可能是个无神论者。这也就意味着，他确实相信他的诅咒会被神灵听到，并且真的能降灾于雅典。因此，泰门诅咒的力量就不单单是power，而是"the divine power"（法力）。这样一来，我们就不能把《泰门》单纯地看作

---

① 《马克思恩格斯全集·第3卷》，第278页。
② See E. K. Chambers, *William Shakespeare: A Study of Facts and Problems,* Vol. 1, Oxford: Clarendon Press, 1930, p. 86.
③ 参见罗益民：《莎士比亚评论·第1辑》，河南人民出版社，2023年，第189-203页。
④ Björn Quiring, *Shakespeare's Curse,* London: Routledge, 2020, p. 7. 又参见 Michel Foucault, "The Subject and Power", in Hubert L. Dreyfus and Paul Rabinow, eds., *Michel Foucault: Beyond Structuralism and Hermeneutics,* Chicago: University of Chicago Press, 1983, p. 208.
⑤ Björn Quiring, *Shakespeare's Curse,* London: Routledge, 2020, p. 3.

一部社会讽刺剧了,它和莎士比亚的其他作品一样,法术、魔力、灾异充斥其中。

文艺复兴戏剧的独特之处也恰在于此。与后世的戏剧不同,文艺复兴戏剧并不是单纯的演出或者娱乐,而是承担着从古希腊戏剧就开始的移情、医疗、诅咒、祝福、预言、煽动等实际的功能。① 这对于当时的人来说,并不是什么荒唐的迷信。我们不能以今天的视角来看待当年的文学作品。泰门也对着诗人说:"你们这两个奴才!你们替我做了工了,这是你们的工钱;去!你有炼金的本领,去把这些泥块去炼成黄金吧。"② 一方面,我们可以看到,泰门也承认他和诗人、画师之间构成的劳动雇佣关系,虽然与此前的态度不同,他表现出了极端的愤恨,但事实就是这样。另一方面,文学诗歌在泰门看来就是炼金的技艺。③ 文学等同于炼金术,或许并不在于它能化腐朽为神奇,反而是因为它像黄金一样可以使人永生。正如莎士比亚所言:

死神夸不着你在他影子里踯躅,
你将在不朽的诗中与时间同长;
只要人类在呼吸,眼睛看得见,
我这诗就活着,使你的生命绵延。④

文学属于魔法,能够点石成金,这一观念自从古埃及时代就已经存在。从通灵文学理论的角度来讲,人们都希望美好的愿望能成真、华丽的祝福能实现,或者会担心不小心一语成谶,或者希望对痛恨的人的诅咒能够应验……这些想法可以说从文学产生的时候就有了,并且也和文学一样延续至今。诗歌承担着祝福、许愿、诅咒,还包括求神问

---

① 法兰西斯·柯克曼所著的《神机妙算,又名步步高》(*The Wits or Sport upon Sport*)在1662年版开篇的一段话中就凸显了这个问题。在"致读者"部分中,出版商有一段简短的致辞:"它能行医术、健身体,它能平定众多痼疾久痛,它还能缓酒瘟、退高烧发热,它是包治百病万灵药,它是快乐逍遥长生丹。现在,列位晓得整个故事,先生们,这些散剧(Rump Drolls),为了上述缘由,请铭记在心。"这部出版于王政复辟时期的不到一百页的小册子,包含了27部谐剧和闹剧,这些谐剧大多是当年很多名剧中的经典桥段,例如《哈姆雷特》中掘墓人的对话、《温莎的风流娘们》中福斯塔夫被整蛊的情节等。(See Francis Kirkman, *The Wits, or, Sport upon Sport. Part I in Select Pieces of Drollery*, London: Henry Marsh, 1662, A3v–A4v. 该版本现藏于美国密歇根大学图书馆。)
② 莎士比亚:《莎士比亚全集·第8卷》,第247页。
③ 彼得拉克在致朋友的信中称:因为他喜欢荷马、维吉尔,因为他是诗人,所以就被人称为了通灵师(necromanticus)。(See Francisci Petrarcæ, *Epistolæ De Rebus Familiaribus Et Variæ*, Florentie: Felicis Le Monnier, 1862, p. 234, p. 240.)
④ 莎士比亚:《莎士比亚十四行诗》,屠岸译,重庆出版社,2008年,第36页。

卜、寻医问药的实际功能。诗人们既是巫师,也是音乐家和史学家。他们所创作的作品,例如史诗、预言诗、咒语、招魂词,或者挽歌、战歌、赞美诗等,都被认为有着超自然的神秘功效。

那么,假如泰门确信文学具有超自然的功能,从今天科学实证的角度来看,真实性似乎不攻自破。但是实际上,正如奎林所说:"在早期现代话语语境中,戏剧诅咒非常理想地适用于展示疑难、解谜式的戏剧结构,诸如基督教式的王权合法问题和神学所支持的法律权力问题。"① 泰门所面对的就是原本由金钱所支撑的合法权利的丧失:他无法消费,他无法借债,他失去了生活能力,他失去了驾驭他人的能力。他把这一切归咎于朋友的背信弃义,但不如说是"货币作为激进的平均主义者把一切差别都消灭了"②。而这对于早已习惯了既慷慨大方又高高在上,既傲慢自负又随心所欲,喜好幻想的贵族泰门来说,显然是难以接受的。

所以,泰门固然值得同情,但也是咎由自取。他既没有经商头脑,也不懂得投资再生产,他并不力求从自己的领地取得最大可能的收益。相反,他消费那里的东西,并且心安理得地让农奴和租地农场主去操心新财源的开辟。他的管家弗莱维厄斯反复警告他财务出现了赤字,他却置之不理。他只是旧时代的代表。从他失去金钱的那一刻起,金钱的法力就离他而去了,直到他重新发现黄金的那一刻。也就是在这个时候,他的诅咒才得以发挥作用,有了效验(virtutem et opera)③。

无论是他把黄金送给两个窃贼让他们去雅典盗窃杀人,还是他出钱资助阿西比亚德斯进攻雅典,"奉行天罚"④,他都是在借助黄金的法力(如前文所述,黄金作为一种有形的神明存在)来实施他的诅咒。最明显的证据就是每当他给上述人等黄金的时候,都会伴随着三四百字的对雅典的诅咒。⑤ 金钱在这里为他的负面情感提供了外化的真实力量。

---

① Björn Quiring, *Shakespeare's Curse*, New York: Routledge, 2020, p. 16.
② 中共中央马克思恩格斯列宁斯大宁著作编译局:《资本论·第1卷》,人民出版社,2004年,第155页。
③ 语出:Petri Garsie, *Petri Garsie episcopi vsselen. ad sanctissimum patrem et dominum innocentium Papam VIII in determinationes magistrales contra conclusiones apologiales Ioannis Pici Mirandulani concordie comitis proemium*. Rome: Eucharium Silber alias Franck, 1489, n. p。原文为:Tertio quia nó est probabile quo deus conferat verbis quibus conque virtutem ad effectus ptrarios virtuti:vel qui ver guit in muriá creatoris: quéadmodii cótingit in operibus magos。
④ 莎士比亚:《莎士比亚全集·第8卷》,第229页。
⑤ 例如,泰门在给盗贼黄金的时候,亲口说道:"快快运用你的法力,让他们互相砍杀,留下这个世界来给兽类统治吧。"(莎士比亚:《莎士比亚全集·第8卷》,第237页。)

如果说,之前泰门运用金钱的力量是为了满足自己虚荣的情感,那么他慷慨大方的与人交往方式也正是旧时代的情感交易制度。而之后他用黄金来驱使他人杀人屠城,同样满足的是自己的复仇情感,他的诅咒下谶同样是一种情感交易制度。此前的交易制度,如泰门在诅咒中所尝试破坏的,是古代的封建伦理道德,是君臣、主奴、父子、夫妻等交易的前提原则。而此后的交易制度,泰门则着力破坏上述交易关系,力图颠覆已有的社会交易构成原则。

显而易见,泰门的诅咒并没有完全实现,剧终的时候,阿西比亚德斯赦免了雅典人。这个情节并没出现在潘特(William Painter)的《逍遥宫》(*Palace of Pleasure*)中,以及卢西恩(Lucian)的《对话录》(*Dialogues*)里面,很可能是莎士比亚自己为戏剧加的结尾。这样一个结尾也说明莎士比亚并不希望给出一个类似《哈姆雷特》那样同归于尽、玉石俱焚的结局。这使得原故事的戾气得以缓和,历史上的阿西比亚德斯也确实没有毁灭雅典。这或许并不是因为莎士比亚打算忠于历史——莎士比亚的不少历史剧都曾篡改历史。这或许更多是因为他"不像某个无名的诗人着墨于泰门的毁灭,莎士比亚的诗歌能够缓和而不是激化政治原则"①。这无疑表现出了莎士比亚对于现有制度保守的而不是激进的态度。

或者说,作为《泰门》的作者,莎士比亚并不憎恨泰门之前那种忠仆义主的交易关系,那种高朋满座的情感交易制度。莎士比亚的态度绝不是愤世嫉俗的,反而是"随波逐流"的。他并不痛恨金钱贸易。也许,只需要使得地产"降到牟利价值的水平"②,原有的情感交易制度就可以得以维护,而不是彻底摧毁它。③

四

那么,这样的结局是否也会被当时的观众所接受呢?遗憾的是,在莎士比亚生前,

---

① Jerome C. Foss, "Revisiting Shakespeare's *Timon of Athens* with Leo Paul S. de Alvarez", *Ramify Symposium*, (2019): p. 7.
② 《马克思恩格斯全集·第3卷》,第262页。
③ 胡鹏论证:莎士比亚自己就是个高利贷放贷人,他很可能也曾经借钱给贵族们。(参见胡鹏:《洛佩慈、宗教与高利贷》〈威尼斯商人〉的地点与归宿》,《四川戏剧》2014年第3期。)而且,他还用他在伦敦的收入在家乡购买了房产"新房子"(New Place)。

并没有《泰门》的演出记录。《泰门》最早的演出也在莎士比亚死后将近一百年了。①剑桥大学布拉德布鲁克教授(Muriel Clara Bradbrook)认为:"在任何正常的戏剧中,主人公的死都不该被略去;伊丽莎白时代的观众或者演员都不会允许这样的事情。"②这或许能间接说明为什么《泰门》是一部未完的戏剧。也许莎士比亚就没打算把它搬上戏台。

诅咒诟詈的场面在莎士比亚的其他戏剧中并不缺乏。如果不是因为这个原因,那就只可能是该剧所涉及的某些东西并不是当时的人所认可的。观众可以接受台上哈姆雷特中剑而死,也可以接受罗密欧殉情,甚至国王理查三世当场被诛。这都没什么问题,但为什么一个雅典贵族的死反而很不寻常?芝加哥大学的贝文顿(David Martin Bevington)就暗示,豪奢慷慨的泰门却下场悲惨,就算是牵强附会,也可能会使得当时的观众想到是对詹姆士一世的批评。③胡鹏也提到,詹姆士一世沉溺于慷慨的赏赐乃至负债累累。④这种现象是伊丽莎白-詹姆士王朝贵族生活的实际表现:一方面生活奢靡,大量馈赠;另一方面又四处借贷,债台高筑。

在这一背景下,如果《泰门》真的会被贵族们看到,那么它的谏诤用意是不言而喻的。但莎士比亚并没有给出解决之道。如前所述,他并不反对贵族们的情感交易——诗人最后不也用诗歌去向泰门换取黄金了吗?文学也许就是莎士比亚最好的炼金术。胡鹏也认为,戏剧家和演员们都是由贵族庇护和赞助的,因此戏剧就成为现成的工具。⑤这意味着,戏剧也许是莎士比亚最重要的收入来源,是他和贵族交易的有力产品。根据古尔(Andrew Gurr)的记载,当时看戏的价格在10个便士到4个先令不等。贵族可能还会额外付随从仆佣几个钱,或者换取在戏台边上搭个凳子就近观看的"嘉宾座"。⑥环球剧院能容纳3000多人,以此推算,一场戏的收入不会少于125镑。这个金额差不多相当于今天的两万英镑,约为20万元人民币。也就是说,莎士比亚的一场戏,毛收入不会低于20万元。一些热门的剧目还会频繁上演,收入是非常可观的。

---

① 1761年的时候,《雅典的泰门》才首次在都柏林,而不是伦敦的斯莫克·艾里剧院(Smock Alley Theatre)上演。(参见John Jowett , ed., *Timon of Athens*, Oxford: Oxford University Press, 2004, p. 93。)
② Muriel Clara Bradbrook, *The Tragic Pageant of "Timon of Athens"*, London: Cambridge University Press, p. 24.
③ David Martin Bevington, "James I and *Timon of Athens*", *Comparative Drama*, 33.1(1999): 67.
④ 参见胡鹏:《友谊、金钱与政治:〈雅典人泰门〉的礼物经济》,《英美文学研究论丛》2019年第1期。
⑤ 胡鹏:《洛佩慈、宗教与高利贷:〈威尼斯商人〉的地点与归宿》,《四川戏剧》2014年第3期。
⑥ See Andrew Gurr, *Playgoing in Shakespeare's London*, Cambridge: Cambridge University Press, 2002, p. 265.

因此,还有什么比戏剧更赚钱呢？这或许才是莎士比亚的炼金术:莎士比亚的戏剧能够激发情感,人们付钱来获得情感上的满足。这和泰门的情感交易并无二致。在这一点上,莎士比亚是相信他的语言可以产生一种力量的,他在他的戏剧世界里,运用包括诅咒在内的各种通灵技巧所生发出的力量,创造了一个超自然的世界,一个他相信而且观众也相信的可以用语言来影响真实世界的戏剧场域。[1]这也许才是文艺复兴时期人们理解戏剧的方式:钱能通神。

参考文献

A. R. Cooper, *The Cultivation of Art, and Its Relations to Religious Puritanism and Money-Getting*, New York: A. K. Butts & Co., 1874.

Andrew Gurr, *Playgoing in Shakespeare's London*, Cambridge: Cambridge University Press, 2002.

Björn Quiring, *Shakespeare's Curse*, London: Routledge, 2020.

Charles Knight, *The Comedies, Histories, Tragedies, and Poems of William Shakespeare: King Lear, Timon of Athens, Troilus and Cressida*, vol. 9, London: Charles Knight and Co., 1843.

David Martin Bevington, "James I and Timon of Athens", *Comparative Drama*, 33.1(1999): 67.

E. K. Chambers, *William Shakespeare: A Study of Facts and Problems*, vol. 1, Oxford: Clarendon Press, 1930.

Francis Kirkman, *The Wits, or, Sport upon Sport. Part I in Select Pieces of Drollery*, London: Henry Marsh, 1662.

Francisci Petrarcæ, *Epistolæ De Rebus Familiaribus Et Variæ*, Florentie: Felicis Le Monnier, 1862.

Harold James Oliver, ed., *The Arden Edition of the Works of William Shakespeare: Timon of Athens*, London: Methuen, 1986.

Jerome C. Foss, "Revisiting Shakespeare's Timon of Athens with Leo Paul S. de Alvarez", *Ramify Symposium*, (2019): p. 67–77.

John Jowett, ed., *Timon of Athens*, Oxford: Oxford University Press, 2004.

Karl Marx and Friedrich Engels, *Die Deutsche Ideologie*, Berlin: Dietz Verlag, 1960.

Karl Marx, *Ökonomisch-philosophische Manuskripte aus dem Jahre 1844*, Hamburg: Felix Meiner Verlag, 2005.

Michael LoMonico, *The Shakespeare Book of Lists: The Ultimate Guide to the Bard, His Plays, and

---

[1] 罗益民:《莎士比亚评论·第1辑》,第203页。

How They've Been Interpreted (And Misinterpreted) Through the Ages, New Jersey: The Career Press, 2001.

Michel Foucault, "The Subject and Power", in Hubert L. Dreyfus and Paul Rabinow, eds., *Michel Foucault: Beyond Structuralism and Hermeneutics*, Chicago: University of Chicago Press, 1983.

Michela Pereira, "Alchemy", in Edward Craig, ed., *Routledge Encyclopedia of Philosophy*, New York: Routledge, 1998.

Muriel Clara Bradbrook, *The Tragic Pageant of "Timon of Athens"*, London: Cambridge University Press.

胡鹏:《友谊、金钱与政治:〈雅典人泰门〉的礼物经济》,《英美文学研究论丛》2019年第1期。

莎士比亚:《莎士比亚全集·第8卷》,朱生豪、苏福忠、马爱农译,新星出版社,2014年。

《马克思恩格斯全集·第3卷》,人民出版社,2002年。

罗益民:《莎士比亚评论·第1辑》,河南人民出版社,2023年。

莎士比亚:《莎士比亚十四行诗》,屠岸译,重庆出版社,2008年。

中共中央马克思恩格斯列宁斯大宁著作编译局:《资本论·第1卷》,人民出版社,2004年。

胡鹏:《洛佩慈、宗教与高利贷:〈威尼斯商人〉的地点与归宿》,《四川戏剧》2014年第3期。

唯物主义与莎士比亚：女权主义及以后

陈小凤

摘要：唯物主义成为马克思主义莎士比亚批评独树一帜的理论症候，在不同时期、不同地域、不同民族、不同文化中表现出异质同构的理论共性。经典马克思主义创始人以"莎士比亚化"和"福斯泰夫式的背景"来阐述辩证唯物主义、历史唯物主义的文艺批评原理。苏联马克思主义莎评经历了从以阶级性和人民性为纲的片面批评立场到历史唯物主义的转变。西方马克思主义莎评着重关注资本主义生产关系对人的异化。中国马克思主义莎评先后受苏联马克思主义莎评和西方马克思主义莎评的影响。

关键词：唯物主义；莎士比亚；女权主义

基金项目：本文系重庆市社会科学规划项目"马克思主义莎士比亚批评研究"（项目编号：2023NDYB157）的阶段性研究成果。

作者简介：陈小凤，西南大学博士研究生，主要研究方向为莎士比亚研究。

作为对新批评的回应，20世纪60年代以来，文学批评出现了外部转向，开始重视文学与世界的关联，包括新历史主义、文化唯物主义、女性主义和马克思主义。这几个流派的共同点在于对物的关注，物成为历史与现实之间的文学观照，其理论基础可以溯源至经典马克思主义唯物史观。马克思主义论题的提出和佐证常常离不开文学辅助，"文学成了他有力的战斗武器"，成了他"精神上的支持、游戏的材料、论战的弹药"。[①]从"莎

---

① 柏拉威尔：《马克思和世界文学》，梅绍武、苏绍亨、傅惟慈等译，生活·读书·新知三联书店，1980年，第537页。

士比亚化"[①]批评原则到"福斯泰夫式的背景"[②]描写,马克思、恩格斯借用莎士比亚戏剧人物和文学隐喻来建构唯物史观,这反过来发展了世界范围内马克思主义莎士比亚批评。

一、经典马克思主义莎士比亚批评与唯物史观

在《莱茵报》工作期间,马克思便"第一次遇到要对所谓物质利益发表意见的难事"[③]。他在《政治经济学批判·第一分册》序言中写道:"我们决定共同阐明我们的见解与德国哲学的意识形态的见解的对立,实际上是把我们从前的哲学信仰清算一下。"[④]从前的哲学信仰主要指席勒、康德、黑格尔等发轫于德国的唯心主义思潮,马克思则不自觉地流露出了唯物主义倾向。在梳理了家庭关系与国家关系后,他盖棺定论地总结道:"法的关系正像国家的形式一样,既不能从它们本身来理解,也不能从所谓人类精神的一般发展来理解,相反,它们根源于物质的生活关系。"[⑤]在政治、经济社会活动中,物的生产、流通与再生产组建起家庭到社会再到国家层面的社会运作模式。社会存在的第一性正是马克思、恩格斯唯物主义不同于以青年黑格尔为代表的德国唯心主义基本立场,马克思、恩格斯明确指出:"思想、观念、意识的生产最初是直接与人们的物质活动,与人们的物质交往,与现实生活的语言交织在一起的。人们的想象、思维、精神交往在这里还是人们物质行动的直接产物。"[⑥]二人反复在《德意志意识形态》中表达了唯物主义基本原理,即物质先于意识,物质决定意识。

马克思批评"青年黑格尔派的意识形态家们尽管满口讲的都是所谓'震撼世界的'词句,却是最大的保守派"[⑦]。马克思和恩格斯不仅通晓莎士比亚戏剧涉及的人物、语言、主题等,还熟知相关的评论,"震撼世界"的说法显然借鉴了罗伯特·格林(Robert

---

[①] 1859年4月19日,马克思在给拉萨尔的信中告诫后者文艺创作要"更加莎士比亚化",不要"席勒式"。参见《马克思恩格斯全集·第29卷》,人民出版社,1972年,第574页。
[②] 《马克思恩格斯全集·第29卷》,第585页。Falstaff多译为福斯塔夫。本文采用中共中央马克思恩格斯列宁斯大宁编译局编译的《马克思恩格斯全集》的译名福斯泰夫。
[③] 《马克思恩格斯全集·第31卷》,人民出版社,1998年,第411页。
[④] 同上书,第414页。
[⑤] 同上书,第412页。
[⑥] 马克思、恩格斯:《德意志意识形态》(节选本),人民出版社,2018年,第16页。
[⑦] 同上书,第10页。

Greene)评价莎士比亚的典故。更加意味深长的是,莎士比亚的确震撼了舞台,而唯心主义过于片面的理论立场却不可能震撼世界,这种隐晦的对比反映了唯物论与唯心论之间的对立。为了更加明晰地阐释物质与精神之间的关系,马克思深刻地阐释了骨相原理。他认为精神蕴含在头盖骨中,"在最后一点生命的火花熄灭之后,这具残骸的各个组成部分就分解了,它们重新化合,构成新的物质"[1]。也就是说,精神只有参与了生命形态的物理再生产,才能抵御随生命消亡而被迫肢解的结局。这样,精神也便实体化、物质化了。马克思、恩格斯的头盖骨隐喻,不难从莎士比亚的《哈姆莱特[2]》中发现文本关联,不过前者侧重物质再生产体系,后者试图表达循环时空的生命哲学。

莎士比亚对马克思、恩格斯的影响是显性的。马克思、恩格斯也毫不避讳地谈及自己对莎士比亚的喜爱,[3]多次在著作和书信中引用莎士比亚诗文,[4]将莎士比亚视为唯物主义先驱。马克思晚年在家里组建了莎士比亚戏剧读书会,称为"道格培里俱乐部"(Dogberry Club)[5]。马克思以"莎士比亚化"与"席勒化"两种文艺批评范式来区别唯物主义与唯心主义、现实主义与浪漫主义。尽管浪漫主义盛行于英国,却发轫于德国,席勒便是其中的杰出代表。据诗人对待自然的不同态度,席勒认为古希腊诗人"与自然融为一体,本身就是自然"[6],因此不会像现代人那样对自然产生多愁善感的情愫,便产生了朴素的诗。在工业化的人类文明进程中,自然逐渐脱离了人类生活,诗歌中对自然的讴歌表达了人类对理想生活的美好愿景。因此,感伤的诗能够表现诗人大胆突破感性与理性的对立局面,寻求人与自然和谐相处的主观能动性。他说:"我们知道,一切现实都落后于理想,存在的一切总是有限的,但思想却是无限的。因此,朴素诗人遭受到一切感性事物所遭受的限制,反之,观念力量的绝对自由则有利于感伤诗人。"[7] 观念的自由,即诗歌的想象力,随后在华兹华斯、科勒律治等英国浪漫主义诗人的文学演绎中达

---

[1] 马克思、恩格斯:《德意志意识形态》(节选本),第7页。
[2] 现多译为哈姆雷特。本文根据人民文学出版社2016年朱生豪译本译为哈姆莱特。本文中的莎士比亚戏剧引文都出自此版本。
[3] 马克思在《〈政治经济学批判〉导言》及《自白》中盛赞并推崇莎士比亚,称后者是自己最喜爱的三位作家之一。
[4] 据统计,马克思、恩格斯直接或间接地谈及莎士比亚共计两百多处。参见孟宪强:《马克思恩格斯与莎士比亚》,陕西人民出版社,1984年,第220—222页。
[5] 道格培里是莎士比亚《无事生非》里的狱警。See P. N. Fedoseyev, et al., *Karl Marx: A Biography*, Yuri Sdobnikov, trans., Moscow: Progress Publishers, 1973, p. 518.
[6] 杨冬:《西方文学批评史》,吉林教育出版社,1998年,第187页。
[7] 章安祺:《缪灵珠美学译文集·第2卷》,中国人民大学出版社,1998年,第267页。

到极致。莎士比亚在戏剧中表现的冷漠无情让席勒有些恼怒,他无法理解莎士比亚何以在悲痛的情绪中玩弄戏谑,让丑角扰乱情绪,消解了悲剧的严肃氛围。他略感无奈地说:"这位诗人[笔者注,莎士比亚]总不让我捉住,总不想同我谈心,这使我十分难堪。"[1] 从浪漫主义兴起的时代背景来看,席勒采取了一种回避式的文艺策略,他似乎可以避开工业革命产生的一系列社会矛盾,将解困之道转向远离尘世的大自然,而这种避世的哲学观被马克思批评为"席勒式地把个人变成时代精神的单纯的传声筒"[2]。席勒的好友歌德也基于唯物论立场对主观创作方法提出疑问,他说:"我主张诗应采取从客观世界出发的原则,认为只有这种创作方法才可取。但是席勒却用完全主观的方法去写作,认为只有他那种创作方法才是正确的。"[3] 与席勒不同,莎士比亚因其客观性、普遍性、跨时代性而备受马克思推崇,"莎士比亚化"成为马克思主义文艺理论的基石。

恩格斯说,不要"为了席勒而忘掉莎士比亚",也就是"不应该为了观念的东西而忘掉现实主义的东西"[4]。恩格斯用观念与现实的殊异来类比席勒与莎士比亚的不同,将席勒等同于观念,将莎士比亚视为现实主义的代表。他在1888年4月初写给英国女作家玛格丽特·哈克奈斯的信中定义了现实主义:"据我看来,现实主义的意思是,除细节的真实外,还要真实地再现典型环境中的典型人物。"[5] 在规约现实主义文艺思潮时,人物塑造和环境因素得以凸显,二者相互影响,相得益彰,实现了人与环境协作式推进。恩格斯笔下那个"五光十色的平民社会"[6] 成为唯物主义理论的一个重要症候,它能够真实地还原社会生活图景,将社会活动中的生产、交换、流通活动视为马克思主义唯物论的文学源流。

马克思将唯物主义视为唯心主义的对立面,主张物质第一性。恩格斯将马克思的唯物论置于社会化生产生活活动中,将福斯泰夫式的背景视为16世纪末17世纪初英国转型时期历史语境的文本映射和现实观照。这样,唯物主义摆脱了牛顿力学中机械唯物主义倾向,增加了历史唯物主义维度,将文本视为生产关系和意识形态的文学表征。据《文学理论核心术语》对马克思主义词条的释义,唯物论者主张社会思潮和历史事件

---

[1] 章安祺:《缪灵珠美学译文集·第2卷》,第237页。
[2] 《马克思恩格斯全集·第29卷》,人民出版社,1972年,第574页。
[3] 爱克曼:《歌德谈话录》,朱光潜译,人民文学出版社,1982年,第221页。
[4] 《马克思恩格斯全集·第29卷》,人民出版社,1972年,第585页。
[5] 《马克思恩格斯全集·第37卷》,人民出版社,1971年,第41页。
[6] 《马克思恩格斯全集·第29卷》,人民出版社,1972年,第585页。

的物质第一性,表现为"人类可感知的物理世界,人们的劳动工具及工作本身。辩证唯物主义也是一种历史的思维模式,因为历史能解释物质实践对事件和文化的作用机制,观念会随物质变化而改变"①。在马克思主义哲学体系中,物质性蕴藏于生产关系中,生产关系成为一切社会活动的中枢,它衍生的社会分工和分配方式产生阶级及阶级对立。马克思主义旗舰学者特里·伊格尔顿(Terry Eagleton)阐释了唯物论的学理基础:"物质是宇宙的本源形态……从蚂蚁到小行星,世界是一个相互关联的动态复合体,万物皆呈运动之势,量变转换为质变。"②马克思主义社会学的物质演进学说无异于自然界中猿到人的进化过程,进化使人类逐渐学会使用工具、改造工具。生产方式、劳动工具和收入差异最终发展为阶级对立及代表各自阶级利益的意识形态,"意识形态使阶级的社会地位和物质利益合理化"③。其中,文学也参与了这种合理化过程。

二、苏联与东欧时期莎士比亚批评与人的能动性

马克思主义莎评林立于世界莎学批评史离不开苏联学者的推动。20世纪上半叶,在深刻的阶级斗争和时代矛盾中,以普希金、别林斯基、赫尔岑、车尔尼雪夫斯基为代表的人文学者洞悉了莎士比亚戏剧包含的反抗性和斗争性,将莎士比亚戏剧视为阶级斗争的文学锐器。因此,这一时期的莎评,从思想内容上强调莎士比亚的时代性、阶级性和人民性;着重挖掘他的人文主义、乐观主义和推动社会进步的积极意义。从艺术上则强调他的现实主义和创新精神。④除人民性、乐观主义、现实主义以外,杨周翰强调苏联马克思主义莎评"力图贯彻唯物主义"⑤的特点。然而,当唯物主义观点被放到历史发展和阶级斗争中去考察时,不免印上评论家的主观倾向,夸大了哈姆莱特等人的斗争性和反抗性,以至于失去了唯物主义应有的客观、审慎的批评立场。

20世纪80年代,苏联马克思主义莎学逐渐摆脱了教条主义倾向,从历史角度构建文本与时代的关联,逐渐凸显出莎士比亚戏剧的深刻性和艺术性,代表学者包括卢卡

---

① Mary Klages, *Key Terms in Literary Theory*, London and New York: Continuum, 2012, p. 51.
② Terry Eagleton, *Materialism*, New Haven and London: Yale University Press, 2016, p. 7.
③ Paul N. Siegel, *Shakespeare's English and Roman History Plays: A Marxist Approach*, Cranbury and NJ: Association University presses, Inc., 1986, p. 16.
④ 张泗洋、徐斌、张晓阳:《莎士比亚引论》(下),中国戏剧出版社,1989年,第449页。
⑤ 杨周翰:《二十世纪莎评》,《外国文学研究》1980年第4期。

契、卢那察尔斯基、莫洛佐夫和阿尼克斯特。卢那察尔斯基强调了人的主体能动性,表现出人对蒂利亚德呈现的文艺复兴等级秩序的颠覆和反叛,这与莎士比亚戏剧诞生的时代背景有关:

  以前,你生为农民、仆人、手工业者、农村地主或名门望族,——那么,你的一生就像签了约似的再也不会变了,任何人都知道此人今后该过什么日子。一代代人的生活和他们父辈过的日子如出一辙,没有人会越出以前的生活轨道。然而,这里一切都超出了常轨,一切都混淆起来,新的生活开始了,革命开始了,紧接着便是人民暴动和名副其实的国内战争,阴谋、逮捕、处决接连不断。在这样的社会风暴中,完成了封建农业英国向资本主义英国的过渡。①

  在那个动乱的年代,社会充斥着各种不确定性。一方面,海外殖民带来的巨额财富刺激了工业和贸易,市场呈现奢靡的繁荣盛况。另一方面,社会上涌现出大量被剥夺了土地的农民、机器大生产中的工人和其他无产者,贫富差距引发了尖锐的社会冲突,处于中间的小资产者面临着哈姆莱特式"生存还是毁灭"②的抉择,他们可能通过努力实现阶层跃升,亦可能不幸堕落为社会的群氓。在这样的社会语境下,中世纪延续的神学观被解构,人的主体意识开始觉醒,动乱、冲突、战争被赋予了人类主体自由的时代内涵。卢那察尔斯基在"莎士比亚人物陪衬下的培根"小节中将理查三世、伊阿古、埃德蒙和哈姆莱特视为培根的文学隐喻。实际上,卢那察尔斯基借用英国唯物主义先驱、现代实验科学鼻祖培根来暗示莎士比亚戏剧的唯物主义倾向,以此实现人物、作者、历史的互文。在莎士比亚戏剧中,人物的反叛精神具有现实指涉性,是对亨利七世至詹姆斯一世为代表的英国王室的不满。卢那察尔斯基还大胆推测了莎士比亚本人的政治企图,即通过埃塞克斯的密谋行为传达戏剧家超越文本的写作意图。③卢那察尔斯基试图借用莎士比亚的时代背景和人物形象来映射苏联国内的矛盾,显性地呈现了历史唯物主义批评视角。

  阿尼克斯特是苏联马克思主义莎士比亚批评的集大成者,代表成果包括《英国文学史纲》《莎士比亚》《莎士比亚时代的戏剧》《莎士比亚的创作》。《莎士比亚的创作》对莎士比亚生平、时代背景、艺术技巧等方面做出了系统梳理和全面介绍,许多观点今天依然

---

① 卢那察尔斯基:《论欧洲文学》,蒋路、郭家申译,百花文艺出版社,2011年,第355页。
② 莎士比亚:《莎士比亚全集·Ⅸ》,朱生豪译,人民文学出版社,2016年,第150页。
③ 参见卢那察尔斯基:《论欧洲文学》,第402页。

值得关注。18世纪英国批评家约翰逊(Samuel Johnson)在肯定莎士比亚普遍性的前提下,对莎士比亚的道德性提出疑问,这种论点及至20世纪的萧伯纳和伏尔泰。[1]然而,学院派莎士比亚评论家对此持否定观点。爱尔兰剧作家伊丽莎白·格里菲斯(Elizabeth Griffith)最早为莎士比亚的道德观辩解,她逐一阐释了莎士比亚戏剧的伦理属性,将伦理视为莎士比亚戏剧的重要因素。[2]此外,弗兰克·夏普(Frank Chapman Sharp)、威尔逊·奈特(G. Wilson Knight)、阿尔弗雷德·哈贝奇(Alfred Harbage)、哈罗德·福特(Harrold Ford)[3]等不同程度地肯定了莎士比亚戏剧的道德属性和教化作用。两派学者吵吵嚷嚷,争论不休,以至于20世纪英国评论家斯图厄特(J. I. M. Stewart)在评述莎士比亚道德观时表现出一种"不可知论"[4]。

那么,莎士比亚为何让坏人在明知为恶的情况下作恶呢?阿尼克斯特从艺术手法和社会背景两方面给予观照。就人物塑造而言,他认为,莎剧中最崇高的英雄同样具有平凡人的种种弱点,也会犯错误;反之,莎士比亚笔下的恶人,尽管行事极端灭绝人性,却也不乏这样的品质:能叫人相信,他们依旧是人。[5]这便是善恶同体人性论的普遍反映,表现了莎士比亚人物的真实性和客观性。现实中,鲜少人至纯至善,也没有毫无悔意的恶魔。阿尼克斯特关于莎士比亚戏剧人物善恶论的阐释,成为马克思关于英国悲剧混合了"崇高和卑贱、恐怖和滑稽、豪迈和诙谐"[6]论述的跨时代回响。更令人信服的是,阿尼克斯结合早期英国社会转型时期的历史背景给予恶行发生学阐释,因为"他们[恶人]把精力全用在争夺权力与财富上……这种凶恶性在文艺复兴时代的特别表现

---

[1] See Samuel Johnson, "The Preface to *The Plays of William Shakespeare*", in Robert Demaria Jr., Stephen Fix, and Howard D. Weinbrot, eds., *Samuel Johnson: Selected Works*, New Haven: Yale University Press, 2021, p. 433.; Bernard Shaw, *Shaw on Shakespeare: an anthology of Bernard Shaw's writings on the plays and production of Shakespeare*, Edwin Wilson, ed., New York: Dutton, 1961, p. 236.; Voltaire, *Philosophical Letters, Or Letters Regarding the English Nation*, Prudence L. Steiner, trans., John Leigh, ed., Indianapolis and Cambridge: Hackett Publishing Company, Inc., 2007, p. 69.

[2] See Elizabeth Griffith, *The Morality of Shakespeare's Drama Illustrated*, London: Frank Cass & Co. Ltd., 1971, p. 3.

[3] See Frank Chapman Sharp, *Shakespeare's Portrayal of the Moral Life*, New York: Charles Scribner's Sons, 1902, p. 14.; G. Wilson Knight, *The Wheel of Fire: Interpretations of Shakespearian Tragedy*, London and New York: Routledge, 2001, p. 284.; Alfred Harbage, *As They Liked It: A Study of Shakespeare's Moral Artistry*, Harper & Brothers, 1947, p. 14.; Harold Ford, *Shakespeare: His Ethical Teaching*, London: Smiths' Printing Co. Ltd., 1922, p. 28.

[4] 杨周翰:《二十世纪莎评》,《外国文学研究》1980年第4期。

[5] 阿尼克斯特:《莎士比亚的创作》,徐克勤译,山东教育出版社,1985年,第61页。

[6] 《马克思恩格斯全集·第13卷》,人民出版社,1998年,第215页。

形式是：征服者和商人冒险家不仅看重实际的财富，而且珍惜财富的美感价值，他们想过美好的生活，让艺术家和诗人前后趋奉，在豪华阔绰中消度光阴"①。当戏剧被置于更加广阔的时代背景时，恶行被理解为资本主义制度下达尔文式的竞争法则，恶行由此获得了现实的文本指涉，恶人随即得到观众的原谅，观众似乎会忍不住同情夏洛克的悲惨命运，愿意为理查三世准备一匹解困的战马。

从普希金的引荐到阿尼克斯特的推动，苏联学者成功确定了马克思主义莎评独树一帜的批评范式，对西方马克思主义莎评和中国马克思主义莎评产生了积极影响。

三、西方马克思主义莎士比亚批评与物化论

20世纪80年代，西方马克思主义随着英国文化唯物主义和美国新历史主义进入莎士比亚批评领域②，蔚然成风，成为莎士比亚研究的中坚力量，代表学者包括特里·伊格尔顿（Terry Eagleton）、雷蒙·威廉斯（Ramond Williams）、理查德·哈尔本（Richard Halpern）、伊沃·坎普斯（Ivo Kamps）、珍·霍华德（Jean E. Howard）等。他们自觉地将马克思主义原理和方法运用于莎士比亚研究，使西方马克思主义莎士比亚批评久盛不衰。

（一）幽灵的物化

《共产党宣言》以幽灵开头："一个幽灵，共产主义的幽灵，在欧洲游荡。"③幽灵来自英文spectre④，该词条的拉丁语词源为spectrum，意为可视的幽灵、幻影、鬼怪，与specere（看）同源。灵魂不灭的观念可以追溯至柏拉图的《斐多》篇，苏格拉底信誓旦旦地阐释了转世说。莎士比亚持相似观点，他借哈姆莱特之口道："至于我的灵论，那是跟他自己同样永生不灭的。"（第一幕第四场），鬼魂被莎士比亚物质化、实体化，哈姆莱特不仅能够凭肉眼看见鬼魂，注意到鬼魂的着装变化，还能与鬼魂自由对话，鬼魂俨然一个鲜活的个体。马克思在《共产党宣言》中借鉴了鬼魂的可视化意象，用幽灵来指代马克思主

---

① 阿尼克斯特：《莎士比亚的创作》，第63页。
② Gabriel Egan, *Shakespeare and Marx*, Oxford: Oxford University Press, 2004, p. 2.
③ 《马克思恩格斯选集·第1卷》，人民出版社，2012年，第399页。
④ 原文："A SPECTRE is haunting Europe—the spectre of Communism." See Karl Marx and Frederick Engels, *Manifesto of the Communist Party*, Frederick Engels, trans. & ed., Chicago: Charles H. Kerr & Company, 1946, p. 11.

义学说。西方马克思主义学者柏拉威尔论述道:"它(笔者注,《共产党宣言》)从一开头就充满了可以正当地称之为'文学上的'形象化的比喻的东西:从口头和书写的文学,从出版物,从舞台演出中取得的比喻和形象。"① 比喻使抽象的观点具体化、形象化,幽灵去掉共产主义的神秘色彩,它不是令人恐惧的鬼魅,而是如老哈姆莱特鬼魂般清晰、可视,更重要的是,共产主义对欧洲革命的感召力将如同老王对哈姆莱特的影响力般振聋发聩。

理查德·哈尔本(Richard Halpern)在《不纯粹的幽灵史:德里达、马克思、莎士比亚》中刻意关联了哈姆莱特与德里达、马克思与幽灵。"德里达有意识地充当了哈姆莱特这一角色,被父亲的鬼魂缠住,这个父亲的鬼魂就是马克思主义的幽灵。"② 通过鬼魂与幽灵的拓扑学空间形变,德里达与哈姆莱特,老王与马克思实现了不同文本空间的等价连通,即文本间性。此时,幽灵不仅被去魅,还被擢升为理论家。如果鬼魂与马克思主义的类比仍然停留在抽象的理论层面,那么当代美国学者皮特·斯达里布拉斯(Peter Stallybrass)关于"老田鼠"(old mole)的唯物论阐释更加具体。他在文章中探讨了如下两个问题:"唯物论者马克思何以通过老哈姆莱特的幽灵来戏仿革命?国王的幽灵为何被降格为田鼠?"③ 答案可以从哈姆莱特对老王的称呼及老王的着装变化中洞悉幽微。

戏剧中,哈姆莱特前后三次提到自己的父亲老哈姆莱特。在露台看见鬼魂的时候,哈姆莱特内心的不安伴随着兴奋,他以鬼魂来证实猜测,以此坚定复仇决心。哈姆莱特呼喊着:"我要叫你哈姆莱特,君王,父亲。"(第一幕第四场)君王和父亲的双重身份在哈姆莱特心中发酵,升格为太阳神和战神。他有"太阳神的卷发,天神的前额,像战神一样威风凛凛的眼睛,像降落在高耸苍穹的山巅的神使一样矫健的姿态"(第三幕第四场),这不仅符合英国资产阶级革命前君权神授的君王塑像,还暗示了鬼魂话语的权威性。当鬼魂强迫哈姆莱特立誓报仇时,哈姆莱特的称呼发生了变化:"啊哈!孩儿!你也这样说吗?你在那儿吗,好家伙?来;你们不听见这个地下的人怎么说吗?"(第一幕第五场)斯达里布拉斯从语义层面分析了"孩儿""好家伙""地下的人"的语篇意义,表现出说

---

① 柏拉威尔:《马克思和世界文学》,第184页。
② Richard Halpern, "An Impure History of Ghosts: Derrida, Marx, Shakespeare", in Jean Howard and Scott Cutler Shershow, eds., *Marxist Shakespeares*, London: Routledge, 2001, p. 32.
③ Peter Stallybrass, "Well grubbed, old mole", in Jean Howard and Scott Cutler Shershow, eds., *Marxist Shakespeares*, London: Routledge, 2001, p. 23.

话者贬低和不信任的情感态度。①最后,哈姆莱特索性将老国王贬斥为一只鼹鼠:"说得好,老鼹鼠!你能够在地底钻得这么快吗?好一个开路的先锋。"(第一幕第五场)老国王从天神到地底的空间移位反衬了哈姆莱特对鬼魂的情感变化。此外,老国王的着装差异也颇具异曲同工之妙。从露台上身着甲胄的战士到王后寝宫里的睡袍懒汉,鬼魂形象逐渐世俗化,马克思对此持褒扬态度。他故意将哈姆莱特的"说得好,老鼹鼠!"改为"掘得好,老田鼠!"②,用田鼠隐喻暗流涌动的无产阶级革命势力,"掘"字暗示资产阶级掘墓人——无产阶级的革命声势。马克思《在〈人民报〉创刊纪念会上的演说》中提道:"在那些使资产阶级、贵族和可怜的倒退预言家惊慌失措的现象当中,我们认出了我们的勇敢的朋友好人儿罗宾,这个会迅速刨土的老田鼠、光荣的工兵——革命。"③据《辞海》解释,田鼠能消灭害虫,对农业有益。正如工人阶级在经济建设中的重要作用。从居高临下的天神到兢兢业业的鼹鼠,从具有指令特征的"说"到具有行动特征的"掘",幽灵在斯达里布拉斯的阐释中实现了物的客体实在性和劳动生产的创造性,这种自上而下的空间转移契合了马克思主义无产阶级唯物论的阶级立场。

(二)货币的异化

马克思在《1844年经济学哲学手稿》中整段引用了泰门关于金钱万能的论述④,借此表现货币与人的异化关系,即货币作为外部力量颠覆了人的主体性和能动性,造成人与货币主客体关系的错位和倒置,使仅具交换价值的客体变成了具有导向作用的主体。马克思将货币视为"个性的普遍颠倒:它把个性变成它们的对立物,赋予个性以与它们的特性相矛盾的特性"⑤,异化成为货币的本质属性。马克思注意到,莎士比亚特别强调了货币的两个特性:(1)它是有形的神明,它使一切人的和自然的特性变成它们的对立物,使事物普遍混淆和颠倒;它能使冰炭化为胶漆。(2)它是人尽可夫的娼妇,是人们和各民族的普遍牵线人。⑥在莎士比亚戏剧中,《雅典的泰门》和《威尼斯商人》最能表现金钱的异化。

---

① Peter Stallybrass, "Well grubbed, old mole", pp. 24–25.
② 《马克思恩格斯选集·第1卷》,第760页。
③ 同上书,第776页。
④ 除《1844年经济学哲学手稿》以外,《资本论》《德意志意识形态》《英国的金融舞弊》《政治经济学批判》等文章中反复出现泰门的形象,以此阐明金钱的本质。
⑤ 《马克思恩格斯全集·第3卷》,人民出版社,2002年,第364页。
⑥ 同上书,第362–363页。

《威尼斯商人》是一出以兑换为题材的城市剧。在以威尼斯为代表的早期资本主义兴起的城市,经济关系超越城邦制度和伦理法规,成为立法的主要依据。① 戏剧冲突的焦点在于加倍还款还是割肉赔偿。法庭辩护环节,鲍西亚应允了夏洛克的一磅肉诉求,"不准流一滴血,也不准割得超过或是不足一磅的重量"②。关于些微差别的评价标准,鲍西亚用"一根头发(a hair)"③来度量。当得知安东尼奥的商船失事时,鲍西亚承诺赔付双倍的欠款,而不希望好朋友"损伤一根头发"④。鲍西亚避开肉的生物学属性,而将话题转向头发,将头发视为与肉一样重要的身体之物。加布里埃尔·伊根(Gabriel Egan)认为头发不仅是身体的一部分,也代表着身体的完整性,失去一根头发意味着身体的完整性遭受侵害。⑤ 据《牛津英语词典》释义,头发(hair)常不进行单复数的区分,它表示整体概念,谓语使用三人称单数形式,复数hairs表达该词的引申义,指过度细节的划分。夏洛克拒绝了"比他的欠款多二十倍"⑥的总量,而是将整体做了量上的切割,使"六千块钱中间的每一块钱都可以分作六份"⑦。夏洛克的局部观与鲍西亚代表的白人基督权贵的主流价值观迥异,后者既强调了一根头发的单数性,又暗示了头发的无限性和不可分割性。在伊根看来,鲍西亚口中的头发象征着财富,头发的不可分意味着财富的整一性,财富积累成为早期资本主义发展的必经途径,鲍西亚本人即受益人之一。

得知安东尼奥的商船失事时,鲍西亚允诺拿出六千块还债,大约相当于今天的五百四十万英镑⑧。鲍西亚的经济地位决定了她在司法体系中的话语权,以至于她几乎主导了整个法庭审理环节。最后,夏洛克因为"异邦人企图用直接或间接手段,谋害任何公民"(第四幕第一场)的罪行被没收了全部财产。"然而,这种财产处罚形式意味着某种不公平,因为种

---

① Gabriel Egan, *Shakespeare and Marx*, Oxford: Oxford University Press, 2004, p. 105.
② 莎士比亚:《莎士比亚全集·Ⅱ》,第308页。
③ 原文: If thou tak'st more/ Or less than a just pound, be it but so much /As makes it light or heavy in the substance / Or the division of the twentieth part / Of one poor scruple – nay, if the scale do turn / But in the estimation of a hair, / Thou diest, and all thy goods are conficate." See William Shakespeare, *The Merchant of Venice*, M. M. Mahood, ed., Cambridge: Cambridge University Press, 2003, Act 4, Scene 1, Line 322-328.
④ 莎士比亚:《莎士比亚全集·Ⅱ》,第290页。
⑤ Gabriel Egan, *Shakespeare and Marx*, Oxford: Oxford University Press, 2004, p. 104.
⑥ 莎士比亚:《莎士比亚全集·Ⅱ》,第290页。
⑦ 同上书,第300页。
⑧ Peter Holland, "The Merchant of Venice and the Value of Money", *Cahiers Élisabéthaisn*, 60.1(2001), p. 16.

族属性早已先天地融进了夏洛克的血液。"① 这便体现了金钱与人物赤裸裸的异化关系,正如马克思所说:"货币是受尊敬的,因此,它的占有者也受尊敬。货币是最高的善,因此,它的占有者也是善的。"② 夏洛克的财富实际上正面临缩水。在资本主义迅速发展的上升期,财富常常因为工人和机器生产的总量而扩大,这导致单位数量的货币购买力贬值。因此,在通货膨胀期间,囤积钱财必然是会贬值的。③ 夏洛克的放贷做法实际上使用了货币流通原则,是有效的货币增值手段。然而,夏洛克拒绝利息,用一磅肉还债的做法使他的财富总量受到损失。由于宗教信仰和种族歧视,犹太人夏洛克甚至还需要定期或不定期向威尼斯政府交纳赋税。这一点可以在马洛的《马耳他的犹太人》中发现端倪。显然,大量的赋税和罚金不利于夏洛克的财富积累,使他在经济上处于法庭判决的劣势。据伊根考证,以利率为目的的借贷关系符合当时资本主义经济发展初期的契约精神,夏洛克的一磅肉诉求显然是对借贷伦理的悖反,为他可悲可叹的落魄结局埋下伏笔。

借贷关系同样出现在《雅典的泰门》中。泰门仗义疏财,试图用货币来置换名声,实际上破坏了财富增值的经济运行规则,最终演绎了一场人与人之间的信任危机。"在资产阶级财富关系中,只有当物品具有交换价值时,它的价值才得以体现。"④ 也就是说,物品的价值存在于明码实价的等价交换,货币的功用和地位得以凸显。然而,"事实上,那些真正属于自身且能表征个体身份的财富不能置换,比如一件破烂的外套,它保存了我们关于时间和场所的珍贵记忆"⑤。关于可置换的商品和不可置换的情谊,泰门显然弄不清二者在经济学意义上的差别,在财物散尽后,他选择离群索居。非消费空间的意义在于否定了货币的一切属性,也在客观上瓦解了泰门与外界的情感关联,意味着他同时解构了物质性的货币和非物质性的人际情感。泰门的愤世嫉俗是由于"异化的、外在的"货币"使一切人的和自然的性质颠倒和混淆"⑥,他痛苦地意识到:这东西,只这一点点儿,就可以使黑的变成白的,丑的变成美的,错的变成对的,卑贱变成尊贵,老人变成少年,懦夫变成勇士。这无异于《麦克白》中女巫"美即丑恶丑即美"的呓语,这种颠覆违背了人伦纲常,表现了人的异化。

---

① Gabriel Egan, *Shakespeare and Marx*, Oxford: Oxford University Press, 2004, p. 104.
② 《马克思恩格斯全集·第3卷》,第362页。
③ Scott Cutler Shershow, "Shakespeare Beyond Shakespeare", *Marxist Shakespeares*, (2013): 245-264, p. 259.
④ Gabriel Egan, *Shakespeare and Marx*, Oxford: Oxford University Press, 2004, p. 111.
⑤ Ibid.
⑥ 《马克思恩格斯全集·第3卷》,第363页。

(三)织物生产与女性的物化

人的异化亦渗透于机器大生产中。其中,女性作为主要的劳动生产者,异化程度最甚。马克思在《1844年经济学哲学手稿》中引用了舒尔茨《生产运动》的一组数据,表明从事纺织业的男女工人比例:

在英国的纺纱厂中就业的只有158818个男工和196818个女工。兰开斯特郡的棉纺织厂每有100个男工就有103个女工,而在苏格兰甚至达到209个。在英国利兹的麻纺厂中每有100个男工就有147个女工;在邓迪和苏格兰东海岸甚至高达280个。在英国的丝织厂中有很多女工;在需要较强劳力的毛纺织厂中男工较多。1833年在北美的棉纺织厂中就业的,除了18593个男工以外,至少有38927个女工。①

这一组数据表明女性从业者数量增加,这同时也意味着女性"生产得越多","能够消费的越少","创造价值越多","自己越没有价值、越低贱",女性似乎被她们自己生产的产品控制了,这种无力感刚好暴露了劳动本质的异化。②在资本主义发展的历史阶段,机器生产首先进军纺织业。"圈地运动"不仅提供了生产原料,也提供了大量失去土地的廉价劳动力,由此衍生出马克思学说中的二元立场。二元论不仅反映了生产关系,也呈现于性别伦理,文学成了疏解这种对立关系的试金石。正如朱丽叶·狄森伯莉(Juliet Dusinberre)所言:"意识形态、文学、社会变革及自我意识等社会主流话语都进入了莎士比亚和他同时代作家的剧本里。"③其中,经济问题在英国文艺复兴时期的戏剧中尤为突出,因为"经济开始渗入人际交往:钱成了价值评估的唯一手段,利润成了人类行动的唯一动力"④。

邓普钠·卡拉汉(Dympna Callaghan)《留心照看你的织物:〈奥瑟罗〉和莎士比亚时代的英国女性和文化生产》一文以19世纪英国女作家玛丽·兰姆(Mary Lamb)因针线活引发暴怒情绪后残忍弑母的骇人故事切入,展开探讨了性别的差异化社会分工。写作主要被视为男性活动,而女性大多从事缝纫、刺绣、纺纱或织布等工作。缝纫不仅隶属

---

① 《马克思恩格斯全集·第3卷》,第234页。
② 同上书,第269页。
③ Juliet Dusinberre, *Shakespeare and the Nature of Women*, London and Basingstoke: The Macmillan Press Ltd., 1975, p. 1.
④ David Hawkes, *Shakespeare and Economic Theory*, London: Bloomsbury, 2015, p. 74.

于经济生产活动,也是"女性美德的装饰品"①,成为文化生产的性别表征。然而"17世纪,这类活动不再被界定为一项工作,仅仅是因为从业者均为女性"②。《奥瑟罗》中,手帕、床单等织品受到男性权威的过度凝视,成为女性贞洁的监视者,以此形成了物与人本末倒置的社会关系。正如爱米莉亚所说:"男人是一张胃,我们是一块肉;他们贪婪地把我们吞下去,吃饱了,就把我们呕出来。"③胃与食物的比喻生动地阐释了主体和他者之间支配与被支配、生产与消费的二元关系。女性生产织物,同时赋予了织物经济属性和文化属性;男性消费织物,同时消费女性的性别属性。卡拉汉认为,苔丝德梦娜的手绢等同于婚床床单,手绢上的红色草莓象征着床单上留下的处女血迹。④对奥瑟罗来说,手帕成为女性贞洁的象征,失去手帕则意味着失去贞洁。

学者曾经质疑奥瑟罗的轻信,苔丝狄蒙娜和凯西奥不可能在短时间内认识便私通,这似乎有违常识和逻辑。⑤这种莫名的嫉妒和疑虑实际上受到当时女性地位和社会风气的影响。在经济生产中失语的女性不得不以出卖身体来维持生计。伊阿古责骂爱米莉亚道:"叫你们管家,你们只会一味胡闹,一上床却又十足像个忙碌的主妇。"(第二幕第一场)上床忙碌具有明显的性暗示。奥瑟罗甚至联想起"全营的将士,从最低微的公兵起,都曾领略过她的肉体的美趣"(第三幕第三场),这无异于妓女的现实写照。莎士比亚戏剧中不乏对妓女这个特殊群体的描述,包括凯西欧的情妇比恩卡、《亨利四世》中的桃儿·贴席等。快嘴桂嫂甚至明确地把妓女与针织结合起来,她自己打算结婚,就不再"招留房客啦",而是请了"十三四个娘儿们——尽管人家都是好女人,规规矩矩,靠做针线过日子"。女人们表面上靠做针线过日子,实际上是"开了一个窑子啦"⑥。多数没有收入的寡妇、被遗弃的女人等低收入群体以卖淫为生,她们在结束纺织厂白天的工作

---

① Susan J. Wolfson, "Explaining to her Sisters: Mary Lamb's *Tales from Shakespear*," in Marianne Novy, ed., *Women's Re-Visions of Shakespeare: On the Responses of Dickinson, Woolf, Rich, H. D., George Eliot, and Others*, Urbana and Chicago: University of Illinois Press, 1990, p. 16.
② Dympna Callaghan, "Looking well to linens: women and cultural production in *Othello* and Shakespeare's England", in *Marxist Shakespeares*, New York: Routledge, p. 55.
③ 莎士比亚:《莎士比亚全集·X》,第159页。
④ Dympna Callaghan, "Looking Well to Linens: Women and Cultural Production in *Othello* and Shakespeare's England", p. 57.
⑤ 聂珍钊、杜娟:《莎士比亚与外国文学研究》,商务印书馆,2020年,第198页。
⑥ 莎士比亚:《莎士比亚全集·Ⅳ》,朱生豪译,人民文学出版社,2016年,第124页。

以后,或许还不得不"求助于商业性行为"①。这成为妇女在陷入经济困境时勉力维生的手段。马克思引用了查·劳顿在《人口等问题的解决办法》(1842年巴黎版)中的统计数据,称"估计英国卖淫者的数目有6—7万人。贞操可疑的妇女也有那么大的数目"②。在差异化的社会分工中,男性占据经济活动的有利地位,从事针织活动的妇女逐渐异化为被消费的商品。为此,卡拉汉不无同情。

四、中国马克思主义莎士比亚批评与物的文化表征

中国马克思主义莎评先后受到苏联马克思主义莎评、西方马克思主义莎评影响。20世纪80年代以前,中国马克思主义莎评强调莎士比亚戏剧的革命性和战斗性。1944年,杨晦在译文《雅典人台满》(今译《雅典的泰门》)的序言中提到,黄金对人的异化解释了莎士比亚对英国社会的疯狂鞭打,这个故事"虽然出自雅典,实际上,却对当时的英国社会,很像把衣裳给剥光,用鞭子在疯狂地鞭打一样,而且这鞭打的不是社会的某些疮疤,而是这个社会的本身"③。杨晦转向本文外部因素,将莎士比亚戏剧视为社会批判的利器,泰门俨然成了英国广大劳动人民的代言人,"可以说这是中国人第一次试用马克思主义观点来分析莎士比亚的作品"④。此外,卞之琳的《莎士比亚的悲剧〈哈姆雷特〉》、吴兴华的《亨利四世》、方重的《理查三世》、方平的《捕风捉影》《亨利五世》等都从阶级性、人民性、时代性的角度,对莎士比亚戏剧做了符合意识形态论点的评价和阐释。不难看出,这一时期中国莎士比亚研究曾受到苏联和东欧马克思主义莎评的影响。

20世纪80年代以后,中国马克思主义莎士比亚批评受到西方马克思主义的影响,逐渐淡化莎士比亚戏剧的意识形态属性,开始由外及内地进行文本转向,将马克思主义辩证唯物主义和历史唯物主义的批评立场应用于莎士比亚研究,阐释文本语言、人物特征、主题思想及历史语境特征,实现了文学、历史、文化视角的跨时空互文。孙家琇的《马克思恩格斯和莎士比亚戏剧》和孟宪强辑注的《马克思恩格斯与莎士比亚》,总结和梳理了《马克思恩格斯全集》中马克思、恩格斯借鉴和引用莎士比亚人物和台词的情况,

---

① Olwen Hufton: *The Prospect Before Her: A History of Women in Western Europe 1500-1800*, New York: Vintage, 1995, p. 332.
② 《马克思恩格斯全集·第3卷》,第235页。
③ 孟宪强:《中国莎士比亚评论》,东北师范大学出版社,2014年,第72页。
④ 张泗洋、徐斌、张晓阳:《莎士比亚引论》(下),第521页。

通过文本和数据来证实马克思、恩格斯对莎士比亚的喜爱程度及后者对前者产生的重要影响,具有综述性和介绍性,是马克思主义莎士比亚研究的入门书籍。张泗洋等著的《莎士比亚引论》,从生平、批评简史、美学思想、文学创作艺术、文本批评、舞台创作与演出等维度做了百科全书式的评价,包括莎士比亚的艺术性和思想性,与杨周翰主编的《莎士比亚评论汇编》遥相呼应,对世界范围内莎士比亚的批评与实践做出了系统梳理和深入阐释,成为新时期国内莎士比亚研究的力作。其中,《莎士比亚引论》(下篇)专章介绍了马克思与莎士比亚,将泰门、夏洛克和福斯塔夫视为马克思政治经济学原理的生动诠释者。"他(笔者注,泰门)揭示的不仅是金钱本身,而是资本主义制度的罪恶。夏洛克体现了资本家的贪婪和资产阶级的剥削本性,'一磅肉'几乎成了马克思用在这方面的代词,替他省了许多需要说明、解释的语言。福斯塔夫则是被资本异化了的代表,失去了人类应有的一切美好的品德,成了毫无廉耻的赤裸裸的四脚兽。"[1]无论是作为主体的资本家还是被异化的他者,人类俨然失去了理性、情感和道德判断,成为被金钱网罗和收买的商品,这便解释了资本主义制度的冷酷和血腥。尽管作者试图表现莎士比亚戏剧人物的现实生命力,却难免镌刻马克思、恩格斯创作时期的历史语境,使文艺批评陷入阶级矛盾和政治话语的窠臼。

21世纪以来,中国马克思主义莎士比亚研究学者表现出敏锐的世界立场,开始不满足于笼统的马克思主义批评方法,重视传统马克思主义莎士比亚批评与英国文化唯物主义、美国新历史主义批评之间的细微差异,建构起唯物主义与性别、权力的关联,代表学者包括杨林贵、李伟民、张薇等。杨林贵说:"由于持有文学'相对自主'的观点,新马克思主义者从经典马克思主义中脱离出来。唯物主义者把人的主体置于非人类结构——一种由经济力量所决定的社会关系网之中。"[2]与传统马克思主义不同,新马克思主义兼收文化唯物主义与新历史主义视角,结合历史背景,挖掘与主流价值体系相悖的文学符号和文化表征。[3]莎士比亚戏剧的深刻性在于还原文本与历史的姻亲关系,在文本中挖掘隐藏线索,以期揭露历史事件背后隐藏的意识形态。正如文化唯物主义领军人物艾伦·辛菲尔德(Alan Sinfield)所言:"传统评论家以连贯作为阅读的旨趣,文化

---

[1] 张泗洋、徐斌、张晓阳:《莎士比亚引论》(下),第466页。
[2] 杨林贵:《莎士比亚与权力》,《外国语文》2009年第4期。
[3] 参见赵国新、袁方:《文化唯物主义》,外语教学与研究出版社,2019年,第51页。

唯物主义者强调阅读的不连贯性。"[1]文本的不连贯性恰好解释了意识形态"试图掩盖的真相和重塑的幻影"[2],这种改变和颠覆往往表现在文学的沉默之处,包括被物化的劳动关系及社会再生产所必需的劳动工具。这样,马克思唯物主义解构了自浪漫主义延续至心理分析的人物中心论,物成为经济生产和权力关系的切入点。《威尼斯商人》中,伪装成法官的鲍西亚要求巴萨尼奥赠送象征忠诚和稳固的戒指,后者原初的一丝顾虑被安东尼奥的劝说瓦解,最终巴萨尼奥背弃对鲍西亚的承诺,送出戒指,以此来挽救安东尼奥。袁方认为,戒指的取舍问题暗示了巴萨尼奥的性取向,与鲍西亚的异性婚姻既是为了权衡经济收益,也是为了延续子嗣,符合早期现代英国社会规约。[3]

经历近百年的栉风沐雨,中国马克思主义莎士比亚批评不断壮大,成为中国莎士比亚批评的重要组成部分。美中不足的是,国内研究仍然表现出苏联和西方马克思主义批评的痕迹,尚未完全建立独立的批评范式和话语体系,尚待进一步发展与完善。就应用层面而言,马克思主义莎士比亚批评要坚持唯物史观,在课堂教学、戏剧改编等文化活动中增加中国元素,有利于在全球化语境中弘扬中国文化、展现中国形象,壮大中国学者在世界莎士比亚批评舞台上的学术声音。

五、结语

经典马克思主义莎评、苏联马克思主义莎评、西方马克思主义莎评和中国马克思主义莎评既呈现了历时的渐进式发展脉络,又表现了马克思主义在不同地域、不同文化、不同民族之间的共时性融合。唯物主义提供了一个阐释文化特殊性、连接理论共性的学术视角,体现了人类对生产生活方式及性别差异等社会属性的共同思考。莎士比亚的戏剧成为切入口,他提供了大量"关于他所生活时代的有价值的线索"[4]。从马克思主义唯物史观来看,莎士比亚的作家身份被消解,文本成为社会的直接产物,这在一定程度上呼应了罗兰·巴特关于"作者已死"的文学主张。唯物主义批评家"先擦除了笼罩在

---

[1] Alan Sinfield, *Cultural Politics-Queer Reading*, Philadelphia: University of Pennsylvania Press, 1994, p. 38.

[2] Nicos Poulantzas, *Political Power and Social Class*, Timothy O'Hagan, trans., London: New Left Books, 1973, p. 207.

[3] 袁方:《文化唯物论视阈下莎士比亚戏剧中的性别政治》,《外国文学动态研究》2017年第1期。

[4] Paul N. Siegel, *Shakespeare's English and Roman History Plays: A Marxist Approach*, 1986, p. 19.

莎士比亚身上超验主义式的神秘光环,将他视为一个历史主体,后肢解对剧本的盲目崇拜,使文本自身成为政治场所,一个包容冲突意识形态的场所"①。在物与意识形态的神秘关系中,物成为文本表征,意识形态则是主导因素,尽管这种主次关系是隐性的。早期社会生产方式和权力关系反映了商品社会化大生产的起源,关于社会结构的历史追溯可以预测和探索未来世界体系的发展格局。②这样,文学实现了历史与未来的桥接。

参考文献

Alan Sinfield, *Cultural Politics-Queer Reading*, Philadelphia: University of Pennsylvania Press, 1994.

Alfred Harbage, *As They Liked It: A Study of Shakespeare's Moral Artistry*, Harper & Brothers, 1947.

Bernard Shaw, *Shaw on Shakespeare: An Anthology of Bernard Shaw's Writings on the Plays and Production of Shakespeare*, Edwin Wilson, ed., New York: Dutton, 1961.

David Hawkes, *Shakespeare and Economic Theory*, London: Bloomsbury, 2015.

Dympna Callaghan, "Looking Well to Linens: Women and Cultural Production in Othello and Shakespeare's England", in *Marxist Shakespeares*, (2013): 53-81.

Elizabeth Griffith, *The Morality of Shakespeare's Drama Illustrated*, London: Frank Cass & Co. Ltd., 1971.

Frank Chapman Sharp, *Shakespeare's Portrayal of the Moral Life*, New York: Charles Scribner's Sons, 1902.

Fredric Jameson, "Radicalizing Radical Shakespeare: The Permanent Revolution in Shakespeare Studies", in lvo kamps, ed., *Materialist Shakespeares: A History*, London: New York: Verso, 1995.

G. Wilson Knight, *The Wheel of Fire: Interpretations of Shakespearian Tragedy*, London and New York: Routledge, 2001.

Gabriel Egan, *Shakespeare and Marx*, Oxford: Oxford University Press, 2004

---

① Yang Lingui, "Materialist Criticism and Shakespeare", *Foreign Literature Studies*, 1 (2012): 40.
② See Fredric Jameson, "Radicalizing Radical Shakespeare: The Permanent Revolution in Shakespeare Studies", in lvo kamps, ed., *Materialist Shakespeares: A History*, London: New York: Verso, 1995, p. 328.

Harold Ford, *Shakespeare: His Ethical Teaching*, London: Smiths' Printing Co. Ltd., 1922.

Juliet Dusinberre, *Shakespeare and the Nature of Women*, London and Basingstoke: The Macmillan Press Ltd., 1975.

Karl Marx and Frederick Engels, *Manifesto of the Communist Party*, Frederick Engels, trans. & ed., Chicago: Charles H. Kerr & Company, 1946.

Mary Klages, *Key Terms in Literary Theory*, London and New York: Continuum, 2012.

Nicos Poulantzas, *Political Power and Social Class*, Timothy O'Hagan, trans., London: New Left Books, 1973.

Olwen Hufton, *The Prospect Before Her: A History of Women in Western Europe 1500–1800*, New York: Vintage, 1995.

P. N. Fedoseyev, et al., *Karl Marx: A Biography*, Yuri Sdobnikov, trans., Moscow: Progress Publishers, 1973.

Paul N. Siegel, *Shakespeare's English and Roman History Plays: A Marxist Approach*, Cranbury and NJ: Association University presses, Inc., 1986.

Peter Holland, "The Merchant of Venice and the Value of Money", *Cahiers Élisabéthaisn*, 60.1 (2001): 13–31.

Peter Stallybrass, "Well Grubbed, Old Mole", in Jean Howard and Scott Cutler Shershow eds., *Marxist Shakespeares*, London: Routledge, 2001.

Richard Halpern, "An Impure History of Ghosts: Derrida, Marx, Shakespeare", in Jean Howard and Scott Cutler Shershow, eds., *Marxist Shakespeares*, London: Routledge, 2001.

Samuel Johnson, "The Preface to The Plays of William Shakespeare", in Robert Demaria Jr., Stephen Fix, and Howard D. Weinbrot, eds., *Samuel Johnson: Selected Works*, New Haven: Yale University Press, 2021.

Scott Cutler Shershow, "Shakespeare Beyond Shakespeare", *Marxist Shakespeares*, (2013): 245–264.

Susan J. Wolfson, "Explaining to her Sisters: Mary Lamb's Tales from Shakespear," in Marianne Novy, ed., *Women's Re-Visions of Shakespeare: On the Responses of Dickinson, Woolf, Rich, H. D., George Eliot, and Others*, Urbana and Chicago: University of Illinois Press, 1990.

Terry Eagleton, *Materialism*, New Haven and London: Yale University Press, 2016.

Voltaire, *Philosophical Letters, Or Letters Regarding the English Nation*, Prudence L. Steiner, trans., John Leigh, ed., Indianapolis and Cambridge: Hackett Publishing Company, Inc., 2007.

William Shakespeare, *The Merchant of Venice*, M. M. Mahood, ed., Cambridge: Cambridge University Press, 2003.

Yang Lingui, "Materialist Criticism and Shakespeare", *Foreign Literature Studies*, 1 (2012): 32-43.

杨周翰:《二十世纪莎评》,《外国文学研究》1980年第4期。

阿尼克斯特:《莎士比亚的创作》,徐克勤译,山东教育出版社,1985年。

《马克思恩格斯全集·第13卷》,人民出版社,1998年。

《马克思恩格斯选集·第1卷》,人民出版社,2012年。

《马克思恩格斯全集·第3卷》,人民出版社,2002年。

聂珍钊、杜娟:《莎士比亚与外国文学研究》,商务印书馆,2020年。

莎士比亚:《莎士比亚全集·Ⅳ》,朱生豪译,人民文学出版社,2016年。

孟宪强:《中国莎士比亚评论》,东北师范大学出版社,2014年。

杨林贵:《莎士比亚与权力》,《外国语文》2009年第4期。

赵国新、袁方:《文化唯物主义》,外语教学与研究出版社,2019年。

袁方:《文化唯物论视阈下莎士比亚戏剧中的性别政治》,《外国文学动态研究》2017年第1期。

柏拉威尔:《马克思和世界文学》,梅绍武、苏绍亨、傅惟慈等译,生活·读书·新知三联书店,1980年。

《马克思恩格斯全集·第29卷》,人民出版社,1972年。

《马克思恩格斯全集·第31卷》,人民出版社,1998年。

马克思、恩格斯:《德意志意识形态》(节选本),人民出版社,2018年,第16页。

孟宪强:《马克思恩格斯与莎士比亚》,陕西人民出版社,1984年。

杨冬:《西方文学批评史》,吉林教育出版社,1998年。

章安祺:《缪灵珠美学译文集·第2卷》,中国人民大学出版社,1998年。

爱克曼:《歌德谈话录》,朱光潜译,人民文学出版社,1982年。

《马克思恩格斯全集·第37卷》,人民出版社,1971年,第41页。

张泗洋、徐斌、张晓阳:《莎士比亚引论》(下),中国戏剧出版社,1989年。

卢那察尔斯基:《论欧洲文学》,蒋路、郭家申译,百花文艺出版社,2011年。

莎士比亚:《莎士比亚全集·Ⅸ》,朱生豪译,人民文学出版社,2016年。

莎士比亚在中国

莎士比亚戏剧在中国戏曲中的重生
——以越剧改编为中心

刘昉

摘要：本文在梳理戏曲莎剧百年史的基础上，以越剧《第十二夜》和《王子复仇记》为例分析"越莎"[①]在"异化重生"与"归化重生"中的利弊得失，进而辐射归纳莎剧在中国戏曲中重生的路径与方式。经笔者研究发现：在极具兼容性、向心力的中华文化中孕育而生的戏曲莎剧，跨越并融合了中西方戏剧文化；"创造性叛逆"让混血的戏曲莎剧焕发出了蓬勃的生命力；其勃兴之路应在有效把握莎剧精髓的同时，充分发挥中国戏曲文化特色，在化融中实现内容与形式的双重审美叠加，在借船出海中促进中西文明的交流互鉴。

关键词：戏曲莎剧；"越莎"；归化重生；创造性叛逆；化融

基金项目：本文系浙江省哲社规划项目"经典莎剧的中国戏曲阐释研究——以越剧为例"（项目编号：14NDJC079YB）、教育部人文社科项目"莎剧在当代中国的跨文化戏曲改编研究"（项目编号：18YJC752020）的阶段性研究成果。

作者简介：刘昉，绍兴文理学院元培学院副教授，主要研究方向为跨文化戏剧。

一、引言

中国戏曲历史悠久、分布广泛、种类繁多。除了享有"国粹"之称的京剧之外，地方戏曲的种类也曾达300种以上。但中国戏曲自诞生之初便被放逐于民间，一直被主流

---

① "越莎"，文中对越剧改编的莎剧的简称，"京莎"、"昆莎"等不同戏曲剧种改编的莎剧以此类推。

价值鄙弃；自晚清戏曲改良开始，又因其内容陈旧，与现实脱节而饱受诟病，成为与"现代化"背道而驰的存在。新中国成立后的戏改虽在一定程度上改善了这一状况，但戏曲的文化意蕴与其他文艺形式相比还相对匮乏。随着改革开放的深入，在国际化、市场化背景下，加强戏曲文本的创作，促使其意识内涵层面的现代化显得尤为重要。同时，面对日新月异、丰富多彩的视觉艺术，戏曲观众同样需要新的审美对象、新的感知方式，以更新他们的审美体验。他们需要在舞台上寻找一种"陌生感"。而在大部分戏曲观众的心理定势中，戏曲是历史的、写意的，这本身就是一种"陌生化"。也正是这种"陌生化"的审美需求，让戏曲工作者把眼光投向了异域经典。两种异质文化、艺术的碰撞，异域经典与戏曲的"嫁接"，现代观念与古典艺术的融合，成为关注的焦点。京剧《圣母院》《王者俄狄》《悲惨世界》，昆剧《血手记》（《麦克白》改编），川剧《欲海狂潮》（《榆树下的欲望》改编）的成功，不约而同地掀起了异域经典改编的热潮。越剧也借此契机大放异彩。浙江越剧院的《茶花女》女主角穿着欧式大蓬裙唱起了傅派唱腔；杭州越剧院在2006年至2008年间连续推出了《心比天高》（《海达·高布尔》改编）、《海上夫人》和《简·爱》；上海越剧院上演了《第十二夜》、《王子复仇记》（《哈姆雷特》改编）；浙江小百花越剧团上演了《春琴传》、《马龙将军》（《麦克白》改编）；等等。异域经典的改编俨然成了越剧舞台上一道亮丽的风景。其中，莎剧堪称经典中的经典，亦是被改编最多的异域经典。

二、戏曲莎剧百年史中的"越莎"

中国戏曲改编莎剧已有百年历史。早在1914年，四川雅安川剧团的王国仁就曾把莎剧《哈姆雷特》改成川剧《杀兄夺嫂》演出，开创了中国地方戏曲编演莎剧的历史。20世纪40、50年代，上海掀起以袁雪芬、傅全香为代表的越剧名角莎剧演出热潮。焦菊隐根据话剧《罗密欧与朱丽叶》改编的京剧《铸情记》，在北京公演后也大获好评。早期戏曲莎剧演出所使用的剧本多是根据已有的莎剧译本或话剧剧本改编。地方戏曲改编原版莎剧文本的实践集中开始于1986年的首届莎士比亚戏剧节。其间，上演了5部由莎剧原著改编的戏曲（京剧《奥赛罗》、越剧《第十二夜》、越剧《冬天的故事》、昆剧《血手记》和黄梅戏《无事生非》）。若在此之前的戏曲莎剧尚处于尝试、探索阶段，那在此之后的戏曲莎剧便迈入了成熟期。1994年第二届国际莎剧节上，越剧《王子复仇记》的成功再次掀起了戏曲演绎莎剧的热潮；丝弦剧《李尔王》和京剧《岐王梦》（《李尔王》改编）在之后的世界莎士比亚大会、莎士比亚国际研讨会上也备受国际莎学界的关注。与此同时,港台地区也纷纷涌现此类经典之作,如吴兴国版的京剧《欲望城国》(1986/2016)(《麦克白》改编)、罗家英版的粤剧《英雄叛国》(1996)(《麦克白》改编)等等。进入新世纪后,更多地方剧种加入到莎剧改编的浪潮中,戏曲莎剧在色彩纷呈的演出中呈现出了更多的实验色彩。截至2016年第三届国际莎士比亚戏剧节,全国共有约20个戏曲剧种编演过莎剧。其中,越剧上演8个莎剧剧目,位列各剧种之首。

越剧虽与浙江有着天然的血肉联系,但其成熟发展却依托在以上海为代表的市民文化中,肇基于整个江南吴语区的文化底蕴。在不断丰富发展中,越剧还向京剧和昆剧学习音乐、身段、调度和舞台排场等,其古典与时尚并存的艺术气质,正契合背负着数千年文明迈入现代化的中国社会。因此,在广大的江南农村,越剧的传统剧目紧密地嵌入代代传承的民俗生活中;而在日新月异的城市文化中,越剧的才子佳人故事吸引着都市青年的浪漫潮流。越剧以不断拓展的艺术形式、极具包容的演出方式,逐渐成为中国现代戏曲的代表、莎剧编演的翘楚。

经笔者调研发现:"越莎"演出的专业剧团从雪声越剧团、全香越剧团到上海越剧院、浙江小百花越剧团,都是越剧各个发展时期的代表剧团;且聚集了袁雪芬、傅全香、茅威涛、赵志刚等越剧名角;再加上于伶、刘厚生、胡伟民、苏乐慈等著名导演的加盟和大量创作经费的投入,高质量的作品产出实属情理之中。但究其深层原因,还是越剧与莎剧内在的相通性。其一,题材内容的一致性。作为江南地方剧种的越剧,大多取材于民间故事和历史传记,多反映百姓生活,歌颂美好爱情。莎剧故事也都源于先前的剧本、小说、编年史。周恩来总理就曾向外国友人介绍越剧经典《梁祝》是中国的《罗密欧与朱丽叶》。纵观"越莎"剧目,《罗密欧与朱丽叶》是被改编最多,也是契合度最高的。其二,越剧一直在寻找能代表现代人思想的作品,也一直在作品中挖掘现代意识。莎剧便是很好的参考。莎士比亚对于人性的深刻洞察让他的剧本跨越时代,焕发着无限的生命力。越剧对莎剧的改编大大促进了其内涵意蕴层面的现代化。其三,美学上的共性。传统的越剧大多是关于女性的戏,既有《红楼梦》《梁祝》这类悲剧,也有《西厢记》《孟丽君》这类喜剧。缠绵悱恻的剧情、清丽婉转的唱腔,再加上女班时期开始的女演员独领风骚的局面,让越剧获得了"女子戏曲"的美名。莎士比亚在其喜剧作品中也刻画了很多个性鲜明的女性形象,诸如《第十二夜》这类剧目,就特别适合越剧改编。但上海越剧院在改编《哈姆雷特》这出似乎和越剧不太契合的莎剧时却另辟蹊径,利用男女合演的优势,在赵志刚柔美的唱腔中增添了阳刚的旋律,又借鉴了其他剧种的武打、身段,让"沙漠王子"成功变身成了莎士比亚笔下的"忧郁王子"。

"越莎"的成功在于重质量、重投入,与时俱进、敢于创新、兼收并蓄,从改编到演出的一丝不苟、精益求精。这也是百年越剧在传统与现代并存的道路上阔步向前的底气。

三、"越莎"《第十二夜》的异化重生

《第十二夜》是莎士比亚喜剧艺术的巅峰之作,融汇了古典喜剧、浪漫喜剧、讽刺喜剧、音乐喜剧等多种喜剧风格,营造出了复杂有趣的喜剧氛围,体现出了丰富多彩的喜剧效果。它运用多种喜剧语言,有高雅喜剧绮丽含蓄的对白,有欢快喜剧活泼开朗、幽默风趣的对话,也有通俗喜剧的插科打诨,粗俗滑稽却又不失机智风趣。特别是剧中两个中心人物薇奥拉和马伏里奥,均被置于喜剧与闹剧的场景之中,形成了鲜明的对比。马伏里奥假冒的失败增添了他的痛苦,薇奥拉乔装的成功带来了她的幸福。莎士比亚用散文体加强了闹剧的"阳刚之气",又用韵文描述了浪漫场景的"阴柔之美"。

"越莎"《第十二夜》由上海越剧院第三团于1985年2月首演,之后参加1986年首届莎士比亚戏剧节,是胡伟民导演的代表作之一。与西方传统戏剧注重戏剧语言表达不同,"越莎"《第十二夜》既以中国戏曲程式刻画人物性格,展现人物心理,又不拘泥于此。它采用"洋装洋扮"的方式,在融合大量西方文化元素的基础上,以形式美服从于人物性格的塑造、剧情的发展,建构青春与欢乐、幽默与诙谐。在充分尊重原作的前提下,编剧用异化的改编方式在对西方经典致敬的同时,努力挖掘作品的现代意义。除了将莎士比亚原剧中公爵、薇奥拉、奥利维亚的三角恋作为主线外,还保留了马伏里奥对女主人荒谬的"白日梦"等副线,尽可能保留原作对婚恋主题探讨的丰富性。

虽然越剧的唱腔极富特色,但为了更好地塑造莎剧人物,演员在继承传统唱法的基础上又广泛吸收了其他剧种流派的唱法。比如,女主角薇奥拉由吕派孙智君扮演,除了从《红娘》《金枝》《三看御妹》等经典剧目中吸收吕派旦角唱腔的精华外,还结合西洋音乐元素来更好地表达人物情感。这种新唱腔唱出了女主角女扮男装时的洒脱和力度。她和公爵的对唱"陈陈细乐柔如柳,牵动心底层层愁,只道是,爱情犹如花芬芳,却不料,伊甸园中苦寻求。情海深邃容九州,方寸之心,拒不留。她一双秋水冷如冰,我满腔热情独向隅,几次求婚遭严拒,伊人柔肠铁铸就,心绪如麻理还休,纵然是,天堂仙乐也难解忧"[①],通过痴情的唱、舞,生动刻画了薇奥拉的真挚多情、勇敢英气。

---

① 越剧《第十二夜》剧本,上海越剧院提供。

该剧最出彩的马伏里奥由史济华扮演。他的精彩表演也堪称该剧表演史上的一座里程碑。范派唱腔的史济华吸收了徐派、绍兴大班、京剧、河北梆子等音乐唱腔。比如，在花园求爱这场刚开场的四句唱词"戴上假头发，脸上涂粉搽，穿上黄袜子，袜带子扎进我血脉"[①]中，"穿上黄袜子"用高腔，结合京剧嘎调和徐派唱腔特色；"袜带子扎进我血脉"又用范派特色甩腔。史济华还借鉴西洋歌剧唱法，真假声结合，表现马伏里奥得意忘形的丑态。之前在花园拾信读信这场中，他不仅表演了传统戏曲的起霸、搓步、顿步，还跳起了芭蕾、华尔兹的舞步，以表现马伏里奥的得意洋洋、轻佻可笑。但当他向伯爵小姐展示自己的黄袜子时，又用了川剧勾袍、踢袍的程式化动作。这种中西互补的全新诠释形式实现了从话剧到戏曲的转换，使莎剧与越剧的融合达到了更高的层次。

　　"越莎"《第十二夜》的编导、演员和舞美都没有因循守旧，创造性地运用富有个性的艺术语言表达具有时代精神的主题，在创作实践中不断丰富和拓展戏曲表现形式，这是它最大的成功。此外，该剧的成功还在于具有通达现代观众心灵的力量，引发他们对人性的思考，产生对美的共鸣。从该剧的改编实践以及审美效果看，这种重构是建立在以越剧独特的表现方式来演绎莎剧故事的基础上，突出原作的人文主义思想，讴歌真挚的爱情和纯洁的友谊。该剧的"洋装洋扮"无论是在演出形式上还是在艺术感染力上，都是在"真"与"美"之间寻求和谐与平衡，努力在内涵与写意之间达到双重审美叠加。但批评界对此剧褒贬不一。李如茹认为这次过于"忠实"的改编"是一次失败的尝试"[②]。也有不少观众对"越味"太少感到遗憾。

四、"越莎"《王子复仇记》的归化重生

　　上海越剧三团充分吸取了《第十二夜》的经验与反馈，之后的《王子复仇记》另辟蹊径走上了本土化适应的道路，以越剧为主，莎味辅之，用中国戏曲的写意表达莎剧精神，用中国人的面孔呈现莎剧人物。该剧于1994年8月6日由上海越剧院明月剧团首演于人民大舞台，之后参加1994年上海国际莎士比亚戏剧节演出，受到了广大观众的热情关注。在保留莎剧原著的基本情节、人物关系的基础上，该剧将时空定位在中国古代，服化道都

[①] 越剧《第十二夜》剧本，上海越剧院提供。
[②] Li Ruru, *Shashibiya: Staging Shakespeare in China*, Hong Kong: Hong Kong University Press, 2003, p. 175.

采用"中国古装",人名、地名也做了"中国化"处理。导演苏乐慈概括了执导"越莎"《王子复仇记》的总体原则:"思想内涵上保存精华,表达内涵实质;故事情节上大胆去枝蔓,明晰条理;角色人物上运用中国戏曲的音乐、舞蹈等艺术手段,精心塑造主要人物;关键场次增加篇幅,着力渲染;风格样式上将莎剧的恢宏、凝重、深刻与越剧的柔美、抒情、细致结合起来;表现形式上充分发挥越剧艺术本体特点,同时汲取兄弟剧种的表现手法。"①

《哈姆雷特》历来被公认为莎士比亚戏剧艺术的巅峰。虽然从表面看,它归属于当时颇受欢迎的"复仇悲剧",但莎士比亚特别注重通过悲剧主人公哈姆雷特的内心独白来表现其性格和思想,人物形象丰富,语言极具个性化。无论是舞台版还是银幕版,《哈姆雷特》的改编不计其数,许多演员也因扮演哈姆雷特而闻名于世。深受观众喜爱的赵志刚扮演的王子,既有哈姆雷特的复杂性格,又有中国古代王子的风采。原剧中的独白、对白都改用越剧念白和唱段展现。编剧薛允璜指出,"唱"是戏曲抒情的主要手段,也正是因为这一点,他们决定改编厚实、深刻的《哈姆雷特》,挑战其哲理性与越剧抒情性的矛盾;他们认为主人公复杂的内心,可以展现越剧"唱"的魅力,将人物刻画得淋漓尽致。这些抒情唱段中,自然带出了美丑、善恶、是非、生死等哲理思考……抓住特殊的人物关系,以情说理,情理交融。②

莎剧原作是五幕二十场,越剧改编成"遇魂""劝宴""试探""演戏""祈祷""责母""阴谋""祭吊""饮毒"九场。编导没有把该剧处理成情节曲折的复仇悲剧,而是着重展现王子为重整乾坤与篡位者展开的一系列斗争,注重人物心理刻画,再现该剧的"莎味"。

当然,该剧在改编过程中也存在一些瑕疵。比如删减太多,导致情节铺垫不足,人物表现稍显单薄。例如王子与雷莉亚的爱情副线分量太轻,雷莉亚发疯的心路历程没有很好展现,导致悲剧效果有所削减。此外,中西方文化的差异让归化的改编带有"夹生感"。例如该剧开场,新国王大张旗鼓地迎娶新丧夫的寡嫂;而在中国古代,这样的行为似乎与传统的伦理纲常背道而驰。

但从总体上看,观众普遍认为该剧拓宽了越剧题材,"越剧王子"赵志刚的表演有所突破,成功塑造了一个刚柔相济、内在冲突激烈的"忧郁王子"形象。演出过程中热烈的掌声、喝彩声不断。剧场门口观众送来的花篮林林总总,不少观众散场后还等在剧场出

---

① 陈君:《浅谈〈哈姆雷特〉在越剧〈王子复仇记〉中的异化与归化》,《淮海工学院学报》(人文社会科学版)2015年第2期。
② 孙福良:《94'上海国际莎士比亚戏剧节论文集》,上海文艺出版社,1996年,第46页。

口处向扮演哈姆雷特的演员赵志刚表示祝贺。[①]

五、莎剧在中国戏曲中重生的路径与方式

中国是一个始终具有开放性的实体存在。[②]在强大的向心力漩涡效应下凝成的中国文化本身,就是多种文化互化与融合而成的混成体。

在这内含天下、极具兼容性的中华文化中孕育而生的戏曲莎剧,跨越并融合东西方文化,是跨文化戏剧的集大成者。中国戏曲以开放包容的姿态接受、互化、融合莎剧经典,以本土文化模式展现莎剧情节、人物,又从异质文化中获得了当代影响,推动了戏曲的现代化。"它提倡对于文化差异性的包容和文化多样性的尊重,代表了一种面向未来的价值观。"[③]

随着霍米·巴巴的"第三空间"和"杂糅"理论的提出,西方的文化霸权逐渐消解,国际化视角下的多元文化观念逐步确立。"杂糅性原则上指一种动态的混杂文化的创建。"[④]戏曲莎剧通过中西两种文化的杂糅,营造出异质文化间的张力和空间,创造出文化重塑的多元拓展性。这一杂糅了中西方戏剧风格的中西合璧,呈现出一副混血的面孔。戏曲在阐释莎剧主题与内容的同时,既改编了文本,又改变了形式。这种创造性叛逆并不为文学翻译所特有,它实际上是文学传播与接受的一个基本规律。[⑤]

(一)戏曲莎剧的重生路径

纵观中国戏曲改编莎剧的历史,从最初的尝试走向成熟,一路都充满了实验与创新。我们看到戏曲莎剧的从业者既关注莎剧精神的表达,又注重戏曲艺术的表现,让莎剧在色彩纷呈的中国戏曲中获得了重生。其中,既有"越莎"《第十二夜》、"京莎"《奥赛罗》等的异化重生,也有"越莎"《王子复仇记》、"昆莎"《血手记》等的归化重生,还有英文版京剧《奥赛罗》唱响海内外。

[①] 曹树钧:《莎士比亚的春天在中国》,天马图书有限公司,2002年,第196页。
[②] 赵汀阳:《中国作为一个政治神学概念》,《江海学刊》2015年第5期。
[③] 何成洲:《作为行动的表演——跨文化戏剧研究的新趋势》,《中国比较文学》2020年第4期。
[④] 陈靓:《美国本土文学研究中的杂糅特征理论探源——从生物杂糅到文化杂糅的概念流变》,《西安外国语大学学报》2009年第3期。
[⑤] 谢天振:《译介学(增订本)》,译林出版社,2013年,第109页。

1986年首届莎士比亚戏剧节上,上海越剧院第三团、北京实验京剧团在演出"越莎"《第十二夜》、"京莎"《奥赛罗》时都尽可能地保留了莎士比亚原作的人物、时间、地点、风俗等。演员们身着欧式服装,在舞台上结合戏曲的表现程式和话剧的表演形式,再现了欧洲中世纪的精神风貌。这种"异化重生"最大的优点在于接近原著,"混血感"强。但若对西方文化与中国戏曲程式间的相通性把握不好,矛盾就会更多一些。此届戏剧节上还有与之形成鲜明对比的另一种改编模式:身着昆剧戏服,遵循传统戏曲表演程式的"昆莎"《血手记》同样赢得了观众的阵阵掌声。该剧和"越莎"《王子复仇记》一样,将莎剧中的人物、时间、地点、风俗都嫁接到了中国古代。作为我国最古老的剧种,昆剧善于将人物内心与外部表现高度结合,具有强烈的艺术审美。比如《闺疯》一场,编导增加了"喷火"这一传统表演形式。四个被害者的鬼魂上场时彩火开路,"怒火中烧"的鬼魂们一起向铁氏(麦克白夫人)喷火。面对步步逼近的鬼魂,铁氏的身心几近崩溃,终于在凄厉的狂笑和惨烈的悲歌中走向了死亡。观众身临其境地追随着铁氏的心路历程,恐惧与怜悯随之而生。在对莎剧不太熟悉的前提下,这种"归化重生"经过本土化适应更能通达观众心灵,也更能发挥戏曲的艺术特色。故之后的戏曲莎剧基本都采用这种路径。但是,归化也会丢形而同时失神,把握中庸状态是艺术,是妥协,是调和。[①]

除上述两种路径之外,还有一种更具挑战性和实验性的路径——用戏曲演绎英语莎剧。20世纪80年代,有"第一女花脸"之称的齐啸云改编创作了英文版京剧《奥赛罗》。2015年3月29日,沈阳师范大学的苗瑞珉、王嘉嘉将再次创新的《奥赛罗》带到了第10届萨姆·沃纳梅克戏剧节,同样收获了巨大的成功。但这种路径对演员的语言和艺术素养要求极高,所以鲜有尝试。此外,还有一些话剧表演中穿插了一些戏曲表演形式。比如,1981年上海戏剧学院用藏语编演的《罗密欧与朱丽叶》,被"重新阐释、彻底颠覆、完全重构"[②]的后现代小剧场"昆莎"《我,哈姆雷特》。

从总体上说,莎剧在中国戏曲中的"归化"移植与改编是其重生的主要路径。戏曲莎剧对中西两种不同戏剧文化的互化与融合,不必固守传统的程式和手段,应在充分遵循艺术法则的前提下,协调好"莎味"与"戏曲味",创造性地实现"化融"。

[①] 罗益民:《等效天平上的"内在语法"结构——接受美学理论与诗歌翻译的归化问题兼评汉译莎士比亚十四行诗》,《中国翻译》2004年第3期。
[②] 杨林贵、乔雪瑛:《莎剧改编与接受中的传统与现代问题——以莎士比亚的亚洲化为例》,《四川戏剧》2014年第1期。

(二)戏曲莎剧的内容

谢天振在《译介学》一书中指出:改编的叛逆仅在于文学作品的样式和体裁的变化上,对原作内容的传达应是比较忠实的。[1]这是戏曲莎剧"忠实"阐释莎剧精神的方向性命题。虽然周氏兄弟曾对本土化处理后的"不忠的美人"颇多微词,但李健吾认为,"改编越具备再创造的情况,价值也就越大"[2]。笔者更偏向于柯灵的观点:"创作也好,翻译也好,改编也好,一切决定于质量。"[3]

莎剧原作的演出多在三小时以上,但中国戏曲"唱念做打"的程式化表演节奏缓慢,需时更长。若要在有限的时间内演绎完整部作品,须对原著做大量删减,尽可能地保留原作精华,突出主要人物和事件。比如,"京莎"《欲望城国》与"昆莎"《血手记》均改编自莎剧《麦克白》。莎剧原作展现的是野心和欲望如何一步步吞噬人心的过程,改编后的京剧和昆剧却对原作的理解产生了偏颇,把主人公的悲剧归咎于女巫的诱导。但在莎剧中,女巫只是导火线,人性的贪婪才是此剧的中心。小百花越剧团演出的同样改编自《麦克白》的"越莎"《马龙将军》,就牢牢地抓住了这一中心,发挥越剧长于抒情的特点,用抒情化的唱段淋漓尽致地刻画了人物心理转变的过程,凸显了戏曲"以歌舞演故事"[4]的特色。

西方的悲剧,从亚里士多德起就被普遍认为会激起观众的怜悯和同情。莎士比亚在剧本开头先把麦克白的英勇无畏、能征善战展示给读者。之后,这些优秀品质逐渐被欲望侵蚀。莎士比亚非常注重刻画他在这一过程中的矛盾与挣扎。麦克白并不缺乏自省,这种自省时刻折磨着他。对于观众,他的悲剧同样发人深省,警示人们在善恶的斗争中清醒地认识人性,做出正确的抉择。这也正是此剧的深刻之处。"越莎"《马龙将军》将莎士比亚原剧移植到春秋时代,英姿飒爽的马龙将军一登场即营造出心怀天下、功勋卓著的英雄形象。同时,马龙对妻子的情深义重也被大肆渲染,不仅为之后剧情的发展埋下了伏笔,也为"有情有义"的马龙将军结下了不错的观众缘。随着剧情发展,马龙在欲望驱使下一步步走向深渊,观众"尽管深感恐怖,却禁不住要赞美麦克白,同情他的痛苦,怜悯他"[5]。吴凤花饰演的马龙将军发挥了越剧长于抒情的特点,人性拿捏到位。但

---

[1] 谢天振:《译介学(增订本)》,第123-124页。
[2] 李健吾:《李健吾戏剧评论选》,中国戏剧出版社,1982年,第200页。
[3] 柯灵:《剧场偶记》,百花文艺出版社,1983年,第74页。
[4] 王国维:《王国维戏曲论文集》,中国戏剧出版社,1984年,第163页。
[5] 朱光潜:《悲剧心理学》,江苏文艺出版社,2009年,第110页。

因大幅度删减,越剧人物谱系又比较单一扁平,人物形象的丰富性与原著相比存在一定的差距。虽然该剧对中国戏曲人物"善恶分明"的类型化特点有所改进,但大量"减法"让改编显得被动与无力,人物塑造略显苍白与不真实。同样改编自莎剧《麦克白》的"昆莎"《血手记》,为迎合中国观众的审美做了一些"加法"。改编者把铁氏(麦克白夫人)的死从幕后推到了台前,在此之前又增加了一个鹦鹉泄密被夫人当场掐死的情节。这一情节展现了铁氏的残忍与恐惧,也反衬出马佩(麦克白)四面楚歌的危急境遇,大大渲染了该剧的戏剧效果。

除了上述删减情节线的做法,还有一些改编在基本保留原作情节线的基础上对内容进行了适当压缩。如"越莎"《第十二夜》保留了原作的四条爱情线,通过越剧常用的过场戏、重场戏,将主线、副线处理得脉络分明;与此同时,该戏也对次要线索和次要人物做了较大删减,但总体不影响剧本的完整性。在时间允许的情况下,这种尝试更能突破传统戏曲一人一事的模式,更好地展现莎士比亚原著的丰富性。总之,"剧本,只有在深入理解它,用心去钻进它以后,你才能进行谨慎而大胆的艺术构思……首先是谨慎,然后才谈得上大胆。"[1]

(三)戏曲莎剧的形式

中国戏曲具有独特的表现形式,如程式化的表演、空灵的舞台时空等。特别是程式化的表演,不仅仅是唱念做打、四功五法,还包括特殊的表演模式与舞台形式之间的相互依存与补充。这种戏曲文化模式不仅根植于戏曲艺术本身,也深深印刻于国人心中。当下的戏曲观众大致分为两类:一类是比较成熟的戏迷,出于爱好经常看戏,不仅了解戏曲的基本知识,对此还有一定的研究;另一类是好奇的"伪戏迷",本身的戏曲知识相当有限,更追求一种猎奇的"陌生化"体验。对于后一类观众,实验性、先锋性更容易吸引他们,但真正能留住他们的是戏曲的独特性。俗话说"内行看门道,外行看热闹",只有真正的戏曲门道和名角绝活才能吸引稳定的戏曲观众群。所以,中国戏曲改编莎剧除了对莎剧原著有深入的理解之外,还须结合中国戏曲的特点,将莎剧"变形",套进戏曲这个"模子"里面。

改编是"阐释性和创造性的行动"[2],行当的突破创新和综合运用十分重要。在"越

---

[1] 黄佐临:《我的写意戏剧观》,中国戏剧出版社,1990年,第536页。
[2] 哈琴、奥弗林:《改编理论》,任传霞译,清华大学出版社,2019年,第76页。

莎《第十二夜》中,史济华的表演并没有简单套用传统戏曲的程式,而是创造性地综合了老生、花脸、小生、小丑等多种行当形式,成功塑造了马伏里奥这一滑稽可笑的人物形象,让观众在阵阵欢笑声中回味无穷。当马伏里奥在下人面前颐指气使时,史济华以老生、花脸的行当表演;当他独自一人读假情书时,史济华以小生的行当表演;当他来到伯爵小姐面前求爱时,史济华又以小丑的行当表演。这种非此非彼、亦此亦彼的境界,正是戏曲莎剧追求的艺术境界。

同时,各戏曲剧种必须扬长避短、兼收并蓄,才能彰显出各自特有的艺术魅力。"越莎"《王子复仇记》中王子的扮演者赵志刚,是越剧舞台上的男小生"名角"。但一向以"女子戏曲"著称的越剧擅长抒情,武戏并不多见,阳刚之气略显不足。赵志刚在其柔美的唱腔中融合了阳刚的旋律,并借鉴了京剧的武打动作,与西洋剑法糅合在一起。这种文武戏搭配的创意,既创造了戏剧张力,又突破了剧种局限,不失为一次成功的尝试。但该剧对王后这一角色的处理,因删减过多而稍显无力。改编导致原著信息的损失是必不可免的,然而有所失也有所得,而这个"得"往往来自戏曲程式的魅力。[①]改编并不是一味地做减法,中国传统戏曲中的艺术精华是可以被不断挖掘吸收的加法。

在不同文化符码重重编码下的"京莎"《王子复仇记》和"越莎"《王子复仇记》,是形似而神不似的"枳"与"橘"[②]。该剧将故事背景从丹麦搬到中国古代的"赤诚国",将"生存还是毁灭"等精彩独白改编成了颇具哲理风格的经典唱段。在人物塑造上,王子子丹以不戴髯口的文武老生形象出场,表演中融合了武小生的特点,凸显其英武阳刚之气。开场子丹夜遇父亲鬼魂时,便运用趟马、甩发、翎子、僵尸、朝天蹬等程式化技巧,展示了人物心理,也很好地吸引了观众的注意。该剧在保持莎剧总体框架原貌的基础上,为唱、念、做、打腾出足够的空间,既在京剧传统乐队的配置下充分展示各个行当的声腔特点,以程式化的表演成功塑造西方经典人物,又深入挖掘京剧和话剧的表演手法,创造性地融合写意表现和写实再现的中西戏剧审美范式,呈现出京剧化、多样化和国际化的"京莎"特色。编剧冯钢认为,戏曲对莎剧的归化移植与改编,更能体现中国戏曲的亮点,比如舞台形式、表演技艺等更能体现中国文化的底蕴。[③]该剧从2005年诞生至今,先后赴丹麦、荷兰、德国、法国、西班牙、英国、墨西哥、秘鲁、智利、厄瓜多尔、哥伦比亚、

---

① 费春放、孙惠柱:《戏曲程式的表意和文化信息——以几个取材于西方剧作的戏曲演出为例》,《艺术百家》2015年第5期。
② 宫宝荣:《从〈哈姆雷特〉到〈王子复仇记〉——一则跨文化戏剧的案例》,《戏剧艺术》2012年第2期。
③ 刘昉:《经典莎剧的中国戏曲阐释研究》,浙江大学出版社,2019年,第135页。

美国、加拿大等十几个国家巡演,所到之处掀起阵阵京剧旋风,还曾获得2011年爱丁堡国际艺术节"先驱天使奖"。民族色彩浓郁、地域特征鲜明的中国戏曲通过莎剧的"地域化"重构,获得了全球化的阐释空间。①戏曲莎剧的跨文化圆形之旅是具有创新性、能动性的动态开放的演出、文化"事件","是一个由众多不同性质的因素构成的复杂网络,包含艺术的、社会的、经济的等等因素"②。

六、结语:从重生走向勃兴

《孟子·尽心上》曰:"所过者化,所存者神。"中国具有"以变而在"的无限性,是以中国能够像一个"世界"那样存在,具有"世界性"容纳能力,能以"不是之是"的方式生长。③在全球化时代,中国文化身份建构不只是自身传统的承继,还有他者文化的参照,是一种你中有我、我中有你的交融互化、多元并存。回顾戏曲莎剧的百年历程,中国戏曲以开放包容的姿态接受、互化、融合莎剧经典,以本土文化模式展现莎剧情节、人物,又从异质文化中获得了当代影响,推动了戏曲的现代化,也促进了中西文化的交流。恰如布洛克所言:"莎士比亚的春天在中国。"④莎剧在中国戏曲中获得了重生并焕发出了蓬勃的生命力。在文明互鉴的时代潮流下,戏曲莎剧更应秉承文化自信的原则,充分挖掘中国文化特色,在"化融"中创造性地实现内容与形式的双重审美叠加。同时,其勃兴之路也应充分借鉴其他国家对莎剧经典"民族化"演绎的经验,探索具有中国特色的"民族化"演绎与全球化传播战略。

参考文献

Li Ruru, Shashibiya, *Staging Shakespeare in China*, Hong Kong: Hong Kong University Press, 2003.

陈君:《浅谈〈哈姆雷特〉在越剧〈王子复仇记〉中的异化与归化》,《淮海工学院学报》(人文社会科学版)2015年第2期。

孙福良:《94'上海国际莎士比亚戏剧节论文集》,上海文艺出版社,1996年。

---

① 李伟民:《莎士比亚戏剧在中国语境中的接受与流变》,中国社会科学出版社,2019年,第698页。
② 何成洲:《作为行动的表演——跨文化戏剧研究的新趋势》,《中国比较文学》2020年第4期。
③ 赵汀阳:《中国作为一个政治神学概念》,《江海学刊》2015年第5期。
④ 李宣海:《上海市科技教育党委系统改革开放30年实录》,上海人民出版社,2008年,第133页。

曹树钧：《莎士比亚的春天在中国》，天马图书有限公司，2002年。

赵汀阳：《中国作为一个政治神学概念》，《江海学刊》2015年第5期。

何成洲：《作为行动的表演——跨文化戏剧研究的新趋势》，《中国比较文学》2020年第4期。

陈靓：《美国本土文学研究中的杂糅特征理论探源——从生物杂糅到文化杂糅的概念流变》，《西安外国语大学学报》2009年第3期。

谢天振：《译介学（增订本）》，译林出版社，2013年。

罗益民：《等效天平上的"内在语法"结构——接受美学理论与诗歌翻译的归化问题兼评汉译莎士比亚十四行诗》，《中国翻译》2004年第3期。

杨林贵、乔雪瑛：《莎剧改编与接受中的传统与现代问题——以莎士比亚的亚洲化为例》，《四川戏剧》2014年第1期。

李健吾：《李健吾戏剧评论选》，中国戏剧出版社，1982年。

柯灵：《剧场偶记》，百花文艺出版社，1983年。

王国维：《王国维戏曲论文集》，中国戏剧出版社，1984年。

朱光潜：《悲剧心理学》，江苏文艺出版社，2009年。

黄佐临：《我的写意戏剧观》，中国戏剧出版社，1990年。

哈琴、奥弗林：《改编理论》，任传霞译，清华大学出版社，2019年。

费春放、孙惠柱：《戏曲程式的表意和文化信息——以几个取材于西方剧作的戏曲演出为例》，《艺术百家》2015年第5期。

宫宝荣：《从〈哈姆雷特〉到〈王子复仇记〉——一则跨文化戏剧的案例》，《戏剧艺术》2012年第2期。

刘昉：《经典莎剧的中国戏曲阐释研究》，浙江大学出版社，2019年。

李伟民：《莎士比亚戏剧在中国语境中的接受与流变》，中国社会科学出版社，2019年。

李宣海：《上海市科技教育党委系统改革开放30年实录》，上海人民出版社，2008年。

莎士比亚戏剧汉译批评百年回顾与展望

孙媛

摘要：莎士比亚戏剧翻译在中国历经120年，取得了辉煌的成就，所以对莎剧翻译研究进行适时的历史性回顾与技术性展望，对于指导莎剧翻译教学、确定莎剧翻译研究切入点而言具有重要意义。本文结合文本细读和可视化文献计量软件Citespace5.8.R3，钩沉、梳理了1917年以来的莎剧翻译研究成果，从共时和历史角度绘制了该领域的知识图谱，探测了研究热点、前沿及不足。研究发现，早期莎剧翻译思想成果卓著，但对后人的学术滋养有限。当代莎剧翻译研究视野宏阔，但主题高度集中，学科发展不均衡。目前，该领域在早期莎译批评、历史剧翻译研究，以及朱生豪、梁实秋以外的其他译者/译本探查等方面尚欠缺，这也给当下的莎译研究提供了巨大的腾挪空间。另外，傅光明莎剧翻译研究有望成为最具前沿性的话题，语料库技术在该领域仍大有可为。

关键词：莎剧汉译批评；可视化；前沿热点；语料库

基金项目：本文系国家社科重大项目"莎士比亚戏剧本源系统整理与传承比较研究"（项目编号：19ZDA294）的阶段性研究成果。

作者简介：孙媛，河南大学博士研究生，主要研究方向为莎士比亚研究、语料库翻译学。

一、引言

自1903年我国第一部莎剧汉译本《澥外奇谭》问世，到2018年以来傅光明新译《莎士比亚全集》陆续出版，莎士比亚戏剧翻译在中国取得了辉煌的成就。有翻译就有翻译批评，莎士比亚作品的翻译批评是莎士比亚在中国的传播达到一定程度的表现。[1]随着

---

[1] 李伟民：《中国莎士比亚翻译研究五十年》，《中国翻译》2004年第5期。

莎剧的传播,我国译学界对莎剧的翻译批评虽已历经百年,但仍方兴未艾,尤其是20世纪80年代以来,莎剧翻译研究成果日渐增多,主题不断深化,已经构成了中国莎士比亚学的一个重要方面[①]。

李伟民[②]、李涛、徐芳[③]、朱安博[④]等曾分别就莎剧翻译的批评述题、译者研究和批评范式做了综述,整合了此前莎译批评的主要信息,为后人的研究提供了参考。但三人的考察时段从10年到50年不等,均没有覆盖莎译批评的全部进程。纵观莎译批评的百年历程,整个学科发展到底呈现了怎样的学术样貌、具有哪些特征、如何演变,仍缺乏一种全域性的俯瞰。而这种俯瞰不仅可以加深我国译学界对莎剧如何进入中国的理解,还可促进莎剧翻译教学,精准定位研究切入点,甚至对中国文学作品"走出去"都具有重要的参照意义。

因此,本文综合运用数字人文技术下的远读和近读优势互补研究模式,采用文献钩沉、文本细读、可视化呈现等手段,对莎剧译评文献进行宏观与微观、历史与当代相结合的梳理,力争以科学、客观的视角,对莎剧翻译批评的学术动态、学科特点和发展轨迹进行回顾,对其未来的发展趋势进行技术性预判,并揭示莎剧翻译120年研究的特征与规律,为后来者的莎剧译学研究提供借鉴。

二、百年莎剧汉译批评文献总趋势

需要指出的是,早期莎剧翻译批评文献由于数量较少,可以通过文本细读来分析,但当代文献数量巨大,必须借助数字人文技术来完成。大数据透视已成为人文研究的大趋势,被认为是与科学实验、理论分析、计算模拟并列的科学研究"第四范式",对社会科学的变革具有重大意义。据此,本文借助科学计量工具CiteSpace5.8.R3软件来完成对当代莎剧翻译批评的透视。该软件能够通过共引分析(cocitation analysis)和多种网络算法(network scaling)等特定功能对大批量文献进行科学计量莎剧翻译研究领域的文献集合,并以可视化图谱形式呈现出学科领域演化的关键路径、知识转折点、学科演

---

① 李伟民:《中国莎士比亚翻译研究五十年》,《中国翻译》2004年第5期。
② 同上。
③ 李涛、徐芳:《莎士比亚戏剧汉译研究新进展》,《当代外语研究》2015年第1期。
④ 朱安博:《中国莎剧汉译批评范式之嬗变》,《外语研究》2019年第6期。

化的动力机制、学科发展的前沿[1],是本研究的有效助力。

本文研究数据取自全国报刊索引、大公报、CNKI三个中文数据库。前两个数据库收录了新中国成立前莎剧翻译批评的早期文献,后一个数据库收录的是当代文献,三者之间是很好的互补。以"莎士比亚"和"翻译"为检索主题、关键词,且排除"十四行诗",共检索到相关论文836篇,其中全国报刊索引数据库19篇,大公报数据库1篇,CNKI数据库816篇。这些文献基本覆盖了莎剧翻译研究各个时期的主要成果,剔除与莎剧翻译研究主题不相关的文献后,剩下793篇论文,构成本文的研究对象。

三、结果与分析

根据取得的数据分析发文量总趋势、早期文献特征、当代文献研究热点对莎剧翻译批评的研究前沿做了预估。这些分析能够清晰显示莎剧翻译批评的宏观样态,有助于研究者对该领域形成一定的认识,助力其研究方向和切入点的选择。

(一)文献发表总趋势

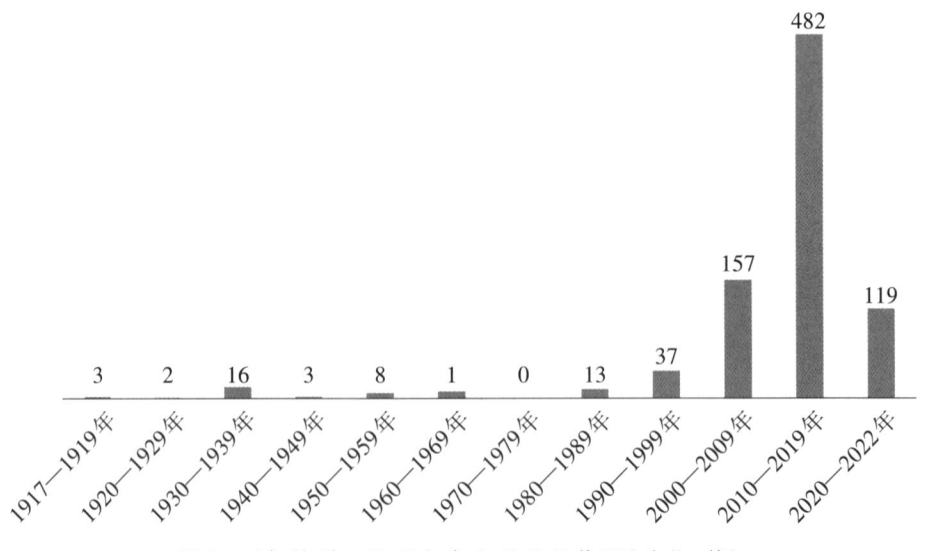

年份	篇数
1917—1919年	3
1920—1929年	2
1930—1939年	16
1940—1949年	3
1950—1959年	8
1960—1969年	1
1970—1979年	0
1980—1989年	13
1990—1999年	37
2000—2009年	157
2010—2019年	482
2020—2022年	119

图1 百年莎剧翻译研究发文量总趋势图(单位:篇)

---

[1] 陈悦、陈超美、胡志刚等:《引文空间分析原理与应用:CiteSpace实用指南》,科学出版社,2014年,第12页。

为了清晰地显示百年来莎士比亚翻译批评的整体趋势,研究者将相关主题的文章发文量以每10年作为一个切片,绘制了自1917年到2022年间的发文趋势图(见图1),直观显示了莎译研究成果的历时动态。

据目前史料来看,钱玄同于1917年发表在《新青年》的《通信:独秀先生鉴胡适之君之"文学改良刍议"》揭开了莎剧翻译批评的帷幕。之后随着莎剧翻译的日渐繁荣,莎剧翻译研究也逐渐增多,并在1930年代达到了第一个小高峰。1940年代,莎剧的文学研究大增,但其翻译批评数量大降。1950年代,莎译研究有所起色,却在此后的20年间近乎陷入沉寂。

20世纪80年代初,随着我国人文社会科学研究的整体恢复,莎剧翻译研究也开始复苏,成果数量开始缓慢增长,基本维持在每年5篇左右,整个10年发表量只达到半个世纪前的水平。1990年代,莎剧翻译研究开始发力,仅这10年的研究成果基本达到了之前研究量的总和。

进入21世纪之后,莎士比亚翻译研究才算是进入真正的繁荣。21世纪第一个10年,研究总量急速攀升到157篇,第二个10年更是进入爆发式生长期,达到482篇。2016年,是在莎士比亚逝世400周年,莎剧翻译研究发文量达到年发文量的峰值,48篇。2020年以来,仅过了两年,119篇的发文量就直追21世纪前10年的总和。这些数据表明,莎剧翻译研究的相关学术力量在不断增强,成为中国莎学研究的一个有力增长点。

如图1所示,莎剧翻译批评集中出现在1980年以后,这也是本文研究的重点。CNKI收录的第一篇莎士比亚翻译研究论文是戈宝权发表于1964年的《莎士比亚的作品在中国——翻译文学史话》。为了便于表述,笔者以此为界,将该文之前(含该文)的莎剧翻译批评文献统称为早期文献。这些文献由于年代较早且数量较少,一直被莎译研究忽略,但它们却是该领域的奠基之作,对学科溯源意义重大,是莎译研究不可分割的一部分,有必要对其进行适当回顾。

(二)早期莎剧翻译批评概览

早期莎剧翻译批评可分为两个阶段来考察,民国时期和新中国成立后。民国时期的莎剧翻译批评者主要有刘半农[1]、郑振铎[2]、焦尹孚[3]、罗皑岚[4]、纪乘之、水天同[5]、邢光祖[6]、孙大雨[7]等。他们多以林纾、田汉、梁实秋译本为批评对象,最常见的批评视角为文体、文本和风格批评。文体批评主要涉及两方面内容,一是刘半农对林纾使用文言文翻译莎剧的批评,二是多位译评者对梁实秋采用散文形式翻译莎剧的诟病。文本批评主要是语义勘误,如罗皑岚、纪乘之分别就田汉译的《哈孟雷特》和戴望舒译的《麦克倍斯》,找出误译分别达31处、40处之多,凸显了早期莎译批评者勇于纠错、善于纠错的担当。这一阶段,最大的批评热点是针对梁实秋译本的风格批判,如失了神韵[8]、风格以简陋窘乏见长[9]等负面评价。

新中国成立后的莎译研究是对前一阶段的延续,朱生豪和曹未风译本出版发行后,影响渐增,开始进入译评者眼中。顾绶昌[10]比较了朱、曹、梁三译本,认为梁译本枯燥乏味、曹译本文字生硬、朱译本过于铺张渲染,其评价可谓抓住了三个译本的典型特征,在一定程度上锚定了后人的研究结论。日趋稳定的国内生活和学术环境,也使考察莎士比亚如何进入中国、如何翻译、如何得到广泛传播成为可能。林子朴[11]则明确指出朱生豪译文"质量较好"。戈宝权于1964年第一次全面介绍了我国莎士比亚翻译和传播情况,尽管文内个别信息有误,但鉴于戈宝权对待莎士比亚来源的谨慎[12],仍不失为一篇莎剧译介研究的"元典性文献"[13]。此时的卞之琳翻译了《哈姆雷特》,他的"以顿代步"思想也日臻成熟。此阶段较前一阶段的批评量更少,话题更为分散,没有突出的研究热点。

早期莎剧翻译研究最大的特点是,只有极个别文献被后人关注、阅读、引鉴,其学术

---

[1] 刘半农:《老实说了:刘半农随笔》,北京大学出版社,2010年,第98-115页。
[2] 郑振铎:《林琴南先生》,《小说月报》1924年第11期。
[3] 焦尹孚:《评田汉君的莎译:"罗蜜欧和朱丽叶"》,《洪水》1926年第9期。
[4] 罗皑岚(化名"山风大郎"):《卓宾鞋和田汉的翻译》,《幻洲》1927年第12期。
[5] 水天同:《书评:略谈梁译莎士比亚》,《国闻周报》1937年第1期。
[6] 邢光祖(化名"不平"):《论翻译莎士比亚:与梁实秋先生讨论莎士比亚的翻译》,《光华附中半月刊》1937年第3-4期。
[7] 孙大雨:《译莎剧"黎琊王"序》,《民族文学》1943年第1期。
[8] 邢光祖(化名"不平"):《论翻译莎士比亚:与梁实秋先生讨论莎士比亚的翻译》,《光华附中半月刊》1937年第3-4期。
[9] 孙大雨:《译莎剧"黎琊王"序》,《民族文学》1943年第1期。
[10] 顾绶昌:《评莎剧〈哈姆雷特〉的三种译本》,《翻译通报》1951年第3期。
[11] 林子朴:《一个比较》,《读书月报》1957年第3期。
[12] 郝田虎:《弥尔顿在中国:1837—1888,兼及莎士比亚》,《外国文学》2010年第4期。
[13] 孙媛:《"重复建设"还是"多重建设"——文献计量学视野下的中国哈姆雷特研究40年》,《四川戏剧》2018年第11期。

养分远未能被后世汲取,与当代研究基本呈断裂状态。然而就翻译思想而言,这一时期成果卓著,最为瞩目的是孙大雨提出的"音组"论。该思想不仅指导了孙大雨本人的莎剧翻译,还启发了卞之琳的"以顿代步",使之成为中国诗歌翻译的重要形式原则之一,可谓影响深远。除了孙大雨的"音组"论,早期文献中还衍生出一些其他批评思想,如焦尹孚[①]的"文体补偿"论、邢光祖[②]的"莎剧翻译五原则"、李辰冬[③]的"意象忠实"论等,这些思想有力地促进了当时的莎剧翻译实践,它们的意义和内涵亟待进一步挖掘,由于篇幅所限,笔者将另文探讨。

(三)当代莎剧翻译热点分析

研究热点可以反映一个学科发展健康与否,是研究者切入一个学科之前对于该学科的必要认识。通过CiteSpace5.8.R3的核心功能共现分析(Co-occurence Analysis),可以得到1978年后绝大多数莎剧翻译研究的关键词共现(Keyword Co-occurence)、聚类(Keyword Cluster)等知识图谱。通过阐释知识图谱中所体现出来的当代莎译研究热点,可以从共时和历时角度描绘莎剧翻译研究的演变历程和学科特点。

1.关键词共现情况

节点关键词的共现频次和中介中心性可以揭示其在莎剧翻译知识网络中的重要性。共现频次反映了关键词在知识网络结构中出现的次数,中介中心性反映了关键词在整个网络结构中占据的位置,二者共同衡量了节点关键词在整个知识网络中作为媒介者的能力。节点越大,中心性越高,说明该关键词在学科网络中的共现频次越高,其地位就越重要,研究热度也就越高。节点之间的连线表示两个节点之间的共现关系,连线越粗表示共现关系越强。运行CiteSpace5.8.R3,得到莎剧翻译研究的568个关键词,将最低出现频次设置为8,得到共现频次在8以上的关键词共现网络图(图2)。

[①] 焦尹孚:《评田汉君的莎译:"罗蜜欧和朱丽叶"》,《洪水》1926年第9期。
[②] 邢光祖(化名"不平"):《论翻译莎士比亚:与梁实秋先生讨论莎士比亚的翻译》,《光华附中半月刊》1937年第3—4期。
[③] 李辰冬:《柔密欧与幽丽叶》,《文化先峰》1944年第24期。

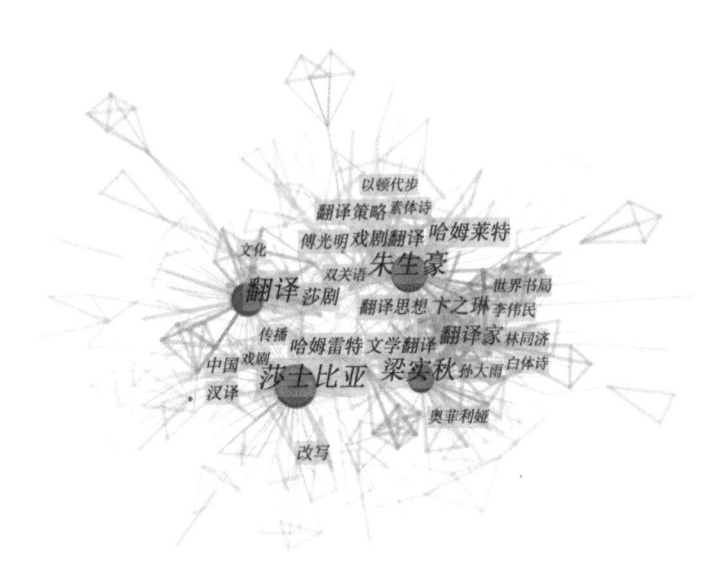

图2 高频关键词共现网络图

从图2中,可以清晰看到四个硕大的节点,"莎士比亚""朱生豪""翻译""梁实秋",说明它们在莎剧翻译研究中有着极高的出现频次,占据着研究的中心位置。其他小节点分别围绕在"朱生豪""梁实秋""莎士比亚""翻译"周边,前一组节点密度显然远高于后一组节点密度。这说明莎剧翻译研究主题大致分为两大类,一类是关于"翻译家""卞之琳""哈姆莱特""翻译策略"等的微观研究,另一类是关于"文化""传播""改写"等的宏观研究,整体研究以微观研究为主。图2最大的特点是节点集中出现在共现网络图的中心位置,外围很少有出现频数在8次以上的关键词,说明莎剧翻译研究的关键词分布非常不均衡。

为了更清晰地显示莎剧翻译研究的主题分布特点,将出现频率排前10的高频关键词的频次及其中介中心性数据整理如下(见表1):

表1 高频关键词频次及中介中心性

关键词	莎士比亚	朱生豪	翻译	梁实秋	翻译家	哈姆莱/雷特	莎剧	文学翻译	翻译策略	戏剧翻译
频次	181	175	131	108	47	28	24	20	19	19
中介中心性	0.48	0.36	0.41	0.26	0.37	0.12	0.05	0.04	0.05	0.05

如表1所示,前四个关键词的出现频次都在100次以上,而第五个关键词"翻译家"的频次骤降到47。同时,节点的中介中心性也从"翻译家"的0.37猛跌至"哈姆莱/雷特"

的0.12。这两个数值的下降意味着莎剧翻译研究存在主题分布的断崖现象。当一个节点的中介中心性高于0.1时,该节点可被看作关键节点[①],然而当一个节点的中心性大幅低于0.1时,难言其还具有关键性。可以说,"哈姆莱/雷特"及之后的关键词在共现网络中的重要性很低,基本不曾得到充分的研究涵养。

结合图2和表1可以得出,莎剧翻译研究主题过于集中,呈现出高密度、高集中性的结构特征。结合CNKI数据,这个特征更为明显。CNKI显示,莎剧翻译研究中主题为"朱生豪"和"梁实秋"的文章分别为270篇和192篇,对二人的研究占据了整个莎译研究总量793篇的58.3%,更是占据了译者研究量的65.5%(见表2)。

表2 莎剧译者研究量

译者	篇数	译者	篇数	译者	篇数	译者	篇数	译者	篇数
朱生豪	270	梁实秋	192	方平	67	卞之琳	54	林纾	36
孙大雨	33	傅光明	20	田汉	16	曹未风	7	徐志摩	6
吴兴华	3	辜正坤	2	杨德豫	1	彭镜禧	1	戴望舒	1

此外,剧本翻译研究的重心依次为《哈姆雷特》、《罗密欧与朱丽叶》、《李尔王》、《威尼斯商人》及《仲夏夜之梦》,其他剧本非常少见。在图2中,只能看到哈姆雷特和奥菲利亚两个剧中人物,其他绝大多数人物形象在莎剧翻译研究中缺位。以上种种,均说明整个莎剧翻译研究的学科生态呈现出一种拥挤的聚集态。

2.关键词聚类情况

莎剧翻译研究关键词的共现情况展示了其学科热点的共时结构特征,其历时聚类呈现的则是该领域的历时演进过程。同一聚类的节点按照时间顺序被分布在同一水平线上,每个聚类的文献就像串在一条时间线上,展示出该聚类的历时成果。[②]莎剧翻译研究关键词形成了"莎士比亚""翻译""朱生豪""梁实秋""莎剧""汉译""戏剧翻译""文学翻译""戏剧家""意识形态""傅光明""文化转向""哈姆雷特""改写""基督教"等15个时间线关键词聚类[③],涵盖了译者研究、译本研究、文学翻译、戏剧翻译、意识形态与宗

[①] Chaomei Chen, "CiteSpace Ⅱ: Detecting and visualizing emerging trends and transient patterns in scientific literature", *Journal of the American Society for Information Science and Technology*, 57.3 (2006): 362.

[②] 陈悦、陈超美、胡志刚等:《引文空间分析原理与应用:CiteSpace实用指南》,科学出版社,2014年,第76页。

[③] 由于时线图占幅较大,且图中聚类节点关键词字形过小,导致印刷效果不佳,故此处省略该图。读者如有需要可联系本文作者:15516173676@163.com。

教、文化转向与改写等六大研究方向。

莎剧翻译研究热点的生成大致可分为三个时间阶段。第一阶段从1945年到1980年,只有一个聚类"朱生豪",说明"朱生豪"研究的热度从诞生开始一直延续到现在。1980年到1998年间,"哈姆雷特""梁实秋""戏剧家""翻译""莎士比亚"等聚类次第成为热点,其他聚类基本诞生于2004年以后。就这些聚类的发展趋势来看,"文化转向""改写""基督教"自2018年以来就不再有文献发表,说明与这几个话题相关的研究量已减少,同时"莎剧""文学翻译""哈姆雷特"三个聚类也有变冷趋势。

15个聚类中,只有"翻译""朱生豪""梁实秋""汉译"的热度不减,尤其是"朱生豪",堪称莎剧翻译研究中的永恒主题。结合每个聚类的各个节点,可以对上述四个聚类的发展进程、研究视角、阶段性热点等有更清楚的认知。

聚类"翻译"最初的研究热点为"简洁优美""冗词赘语""独白"等文本性批评话语,后逐渐成为包含"赞助人""文学史""会话含义""概念整合"等关键词的意识形态、认知语言学视角的翻译批评,近期的批评更是体现了"拼搏""奉献""敬业"的爱国主义思想。不难看出,这是一个经历了从文本到理论,又上升到爱国主义翻译思想的批评历程,整个聚类侧重宏观研究。

聚类"朱生豪"的研究热点从时间轴上可大致分为三个发展阶段。第一阶段为1983—1998年间,以秀洲中学、宋清如、世界书局、日译本等节点为热点的关于朱生豪生平和译莎动力的考证。秀洲中学、宋清如、世界书局分别代表了朱生豪的少年、青年、成年阶段。节点词"日译本"的出现彰显了朱生豪翻译莎剧的最大动力,乃以自己独特之方式对抗日本对中国的军事侵略和文化诋毁。第二阶段为2004—2007年间,批评界开始关注杨德豫、吴兴华等被忽略的莎剧译者,以及他们在莎剧翻译研究中的贡献;同时,哈姆雷特、雷欧提斯等剧中形象也得以体现。第三阶段为2010年之后,学界开始关注诗词创作、审美特征等莎剧翻译批评中的文本特性。可见,聚类"朱生豪"包括了历史、译者、政治、剧中形象、作品审美等元素,从对译者的历史考证到对译本的文学性、美学性的阐释,呈现出一种从宏观到微观、从历史到文本的收缩性趋势。

聚类"梁实秋"的节点类型比较复杂,从共时角度大致可分为三类。第一类是由卞之琳、闻一多、徐志摩、王佐良、邢光祖、傅东华、鲁迅等构成的莎剧译评群体,他们贯穿了梁译莎剧批评的始终。第二类是以白体诗、以诗译诗、求真、悖论、审美、诗人、转喻、隐喻等为主的文体、文学、修辞类的翻译批评话语。第三类包括阐释学、历史观、人性论、人文精神、文化精英、古典主义、文学创作等主题,体现的是翻译伦理、翻译阶级性及"文化转向"

的宏大叙事。从该聚类的历时发展角度来看,其研究热点从莎剧的早期译介转变为文学性批评,近期又迁移到对莎剧早期批评的关注,呈现出一种螺旋上升的动态历程。

值得一提的是,邢光祖、傅东华和鲁迅等节点人物与梁实秋曾展开过旷日持久的翻译笔战,鲁迅和梁实秋之间发生了"信、顺"之争。梁实秋[1]批评傅东华译的《失乐园》像大鼓,像莲花落,就是不像弥尔顿;而邢光祖[2]又尖锐批判了梁译莎剧的风格问题。这些笔仗看似混乱,实则产生了很多译学思想闪光点,其内涵即使在今日也未能全部挖掘出来,需要进一步诠释。

聚类"汉译",涵盖了剧本、显化、人际功能、情感语义、语料库、决策过程等节点。显然,这是一个基于系统功能语言学和语料库等当代视角的研究聚类。自从卡特福特[3]首次自觉将级阶和范畴语法理论运用到翻译研究中,经贝克[4]、贝尔[5]、胡壮麟[6]、张美芳[7]等的继续发展,系统功能语言学已成为翻译研究中最为普遍和有效的手段之一。系统功能语言学视角下的莎译批评主要是对"sir""how now""can""lord"等具有人际意义的词汇的功能进行考证。语料库莎剧翻译研究在2009年后得到长足发展,其中最为瞩目的成果是胡开宝及其团队建立的基于朱生豪、梁实秋、方平译本的莎士比亚戏剧语料库。在此基础上,胡开宝团队完成了一系列莎剧汉译研究成果,后付梓为《基于语料库的莎士比亚戏剧汉译研究》一书,堪称语料库视角莎剧翻译研究的集大成之作。

综上,不同聚类有着各自的显著特征。聚类"翻译"和"汉译"侧重从语言学视角观照莎剧翻译,在语言理论、语料库等数字人文手段加持下,长于宏观研究。聚类"朱生豪""梁实秋"更侧重历史、审美、修辞研究,更关注微观探求。整体来说,高频关键词的共现和聚类情况分别展示了莎剧翻译研究中两种截然不同的样态,前者反映了莎剧翻译研究主题分布高度集中,而后者反映了莎剧翻译批评路径异常多元。这意味着,人们对莎剧的理解局限在为数不多的特定主题上,但在方法论意义上,各种翻译理论、语言学理论被广泛应用在莎剧汉译研究领域中。

---

[1] 梁实秋:《傅东华译的〈失乐园〉》,《图书评论》1933年第2期。
[2] 邢光祖(化名"不平"):《论翻译莎士比亚:与梁实秋先生讨论莎士比亚的翻译》,《光华附中半月刊》1937年第3-4期。
[3] J. C. Catford, *A Linguistic Theory of Translation*, London: Oxford University Press, 1965, p. 20.
[4] Mona Baker, *In Other Words: A Course on Translation*, London: Routledge, 2018.
[5] R. T. Bell, *Translation and Translating: Theory and Practice*, London: Longman,1991.
[6] 胡壮麟、朱永生、张德禄等:《系统功能语言学概论》,北京大学出版社,2017年。
[7] 张美芳、黄国文:《语篇语言翻译学与翻译研究》,《中国翻译》2002年第3期。

四、前沿预估

研究前沿是学科未来的发展方向,也是研究者确定研究方向的重要参数之一。准确预估前沿热点对于研究者有重大意义。可以通过CiteSpace5.8.R3软件探查关键词的引用突变强度(Burstness)来确定莎剧翻译研究的学科前沿。引用突变强度是度量关键词前沿性的重要参数,如果某关键词的被引频次在某个年份突然变大变强,就意味着该关键词成为本学科领域的前沿热点。

首先,笔者共抽取到11个最强引用突变关键词,生成莎剧翻译研究的最强引用突变关键词(Burst Terms)时序图(图3)。这11个关键词代表着不同年份莎译研究的前沿热点和变化趋势。从突转强度上来看,关键词"朱生豪"的强度指数最高,达6.9,说明相关研究在1986年以后突然变得密集起来,这种密集状态一直持续到1995年。在此期间,"朱生豪"一直都是莎剧翻译研究的前沿热点。从持续时长来看,关键词"翻译家"的前沿地位从1984年开始形成,到2003年结束,持续了约20年。它不仅是该领域生成时间最早,也是迄今为止持续时间最长、译学者探讨最为积极的主题。

值得注意的是,关键词"语料库"的前沿热点地位持续时间最短,始于2013年,终于2015年,仅持续了2年时间。主要原因有两点:第一,语料库方法对研究者的数字人文技术要求较高,长期浸润在莎剧研究领域的大多数学者不使用语料库技术。第二,胡开宝团队的研究方向在2015年之后发生了巨大的转变,从莎剧翻译研究转向了政治翻译研究,这就使关键词"语料库"的热点状态后继乏力。

关键词	检索起始年	强度	出现年	结束年
翻译家	1964	4.75	1984	2003
朱生豪	1964	6.9	1986	1995
宋清如	1964	3.51	1986	2003
哈姆莱特	1964	4.09	1994	2001
戏剧翻译	1964	3.05	2008	2013
语料库	1964	3.08	2013	2015
汉译	1964	5.42	2015	2019
傅光明	1964	4.47	2018	2022
莎剧汉译	1964	4.22	2020	2022
方平	1964	3.01	2020	2022
副文本	1964	2.92	2020	2022

图3 最强引用突变关键词时序图(前11位)(1964—2022年)

其次,判定具体关键词是否有可能成为当下的前沿热点,还要结合三个变量,即出现时间、是否延续、强度指数进行综合考量。如果某关键词目前一直保持热点地位,其出现时间越晚,强度指数越高,则其成为前沿热点的可能性就越大。从图3中可以看出,出现时间最晚并仍在持续发展的突变关键词依次为"傅光明""莎剧汉译""方平""副文本",距今都不到5年时间。其中,"傅光明"和"莎剧汉译"的突变强度指数分别为4.47和4.22,均超过中位数4.09,强度较强。这说明,傅光明译本有极大概率会成为莎剧翻译研究的前沿热点。傅光明从2012年开始重译莎剧全集,目前已出版了多部译本,受到学界关注,其莎学研究甚至被称为"傅莎学"[1]。"方平"和"副文本"两个关键词的前沿性也初显头角。方平主持翻译了我国第一套诗体莎剧,本应受到关注,但以往研究通常聚焦于朱、梁二人的译本,方平译本多少受到了冷遇。"副文本"可以显示译本形成过程中的参与因素、再现其重要历史事件[2],尤其在勘察译者的心路历程、决策选择等方面起着不可替代的作用。

"傅光明""方平""副文本"作为引用突变关键词同时出现,显露出莎剧翻译研究的两个新趋势。一方面,莎剧译学界除了把目光集中投向朱生豪和梁实秋之外,译者研究的多样性结构初露良好端倪。另一方面,莎剧翻译研究从文本导向逐渐转向文化导向,将译本引入历史语境,有助于探究译者、译本、社会语境之间的关系,观察译者及赞助人对特定译本的情感态度、历史评价,甚至复杂的意识形态争夺,使得莎剧翻译研究视野更为宏阔。这两个趋势有利于莎剧翻译研究长期、健康地向广博及纵深发展。

五、莎剧翻译研究不足与展望

通过以上分析可以发现,目前我国莎剧汉译研究取得了丰硕的成果,尤其是研究视野丰富宏阔,宏观、微观、语言学、哲学、文化学、译介学等理论应用多角度并举,保证了该领域的蓬勃发展。但其最大特点是高度集中,研究资源向为数不多的对象倾斜,这种学科样态的优势有利于对特定对象进行持续深入的观察、理解和阐释。其不足之处也很明显,集中度高意味着主题单一,研究面狭窄即学科发育不均衡。

这些不均衡主要体现在以下几个方面。第一,译者方面,除了朱生豪和梁实秋,我国大部分莎剧译者,如早期的顾仲彝、曹未风,新中国成立后的章益、杨德豫,近期的陈才宇、覃学岚等都被忽视,甚至被湮没。第二,译本方面,研究对象过于集中在前文所提

---

[1] 陈淑芬:《台湾莎学视角论傅新译"莎士比亚戏剧"与新"傅莎学"》,《名作欣赏》2018年第28期。
[2] 刘泽权:《数字人文视域下名著重译多维评价模型构建》,《中国翻译》2021年第5期。

到的五部常规悲喜剧中,而作为莎剧的一个重要组成类别的历史剧,长期遭受译学界的漠视,个别历史剧的翻译研究甚至为空白。第三,研究内容方面,当代莎剧汉译研究热衷于翻译策略、翻译思想等宏观主题,修辞、意象、称谓、情态、情感、双关语、隐喻、风格等微观话题相对欠缺。随着数字技术的质的飞跃,李伟民在20年前指出的研判整部莎剧或莎作全集翻译特点、风格相对较难、莎剧译文风格阐释缺乏令人信服的深入的定量研究等困境[1],已得到了相当程度的解决。但一些基本性问题,如读者为什么会对不同译文产生不同的喜好,仍缺乏精确而有说服力的解释,对译本特点及风格的分析,仍未能彻底解决。第四,历史方面,当下的译学界对早期莎剧翻译少有涉足,早期莎译研究与当代莎译研究之间呈断裂状态。这种断裂现象不利于莎译研究整个学科的继承和发展,亟待改观。早期莎剧翻译的研究文献、译学思想也需及时整理、辑录,并进一步挖掘。除了梁实秋的"求真"、孙大雨的"音组"论,刘半农的"汉语西就"、焦尹孚的"文体补偿"、邢光祖的"神韵忠实"等思想都值得探究。至于莎剧在我国的译介,许多学者都做过介绍,但这些信息散落在不同文献中,缺乏一种纵横捭阖的总体历史观书写。第五,研究手段方面,莎译研究中数字人文要素不足。此前的莎译研究大都是花絮漫谈式的印象评价,缺乏有力的证据。2009年后,语料库的应用大幅提升了莎剧译者、译本风格分析的大数据处理能力,研究过程更为客观。胡开宝团队建设的莎剧英汉平行语料库,为其研究提供了充分的数据支撑。由此可见,大型语料库堪称翻译研究的基础工程,其重要性随着文本数据量的增大而愈来愈显著。但随着该团队主要研究兴趣的转移,语料库方法在莎译研究中再次缺失。

以上种种导致了一个现象,即对莎剧译本的研究结论往往大同小异,如顾绶昌[2]评价梁译本枯燥乏味、朱译本铺张渲染;刘炳善[3]认为梁译本旨在"求真",以"信""达"见长,朱译本意在"神韵",以"达""雅"取胜。多年后,这些说法仍在译本/译者研究中通行。这一方面固然是译本本身的特质使然,另一方面又何尝不是莎剧翻译研究开拓性不足的缘故。因此,莎剧翻译研究必须拓展新的研究栖息地,避免研究扎堆、结论同质的倾向。

根据以上分析可以得出,莎剧译学目前有三个广阔的施为空间:早期莎译研究、历史剧翻译研究、"朱梁"之外的其他译者。早期莎译研究已有了风向标,莎士比亚主要研

---

[1] 李伟民:《中国莎士比亚翻译研究五十年》,《中国翻译》2004年第5期。
[2] 顾绶昌:《评莎剧〈哈姆雷特〉的三种译本》,《翻译通报》1951年第3期。
[3] 刘炳善:《莎剧的两种中译本:从一出戏看全集》,《中国翻译》1992年第4期。

究者之一李伟民已开始关注民国时期莎剧经典化问题,这很可能会在一定程度上引发早期莎译研究热。历史剧翻译研究也逐渐起步,CNKI中可查的《亨利六世》翻译研究文献为3篇,《理查三世》7篇,《亨利五世》11篇。至于其他译者,如林纾、曹未风、章益、辜正坤、覃学岚等同样也在莎剧的翻译文学经典化历程中付出了巨大的努力和贡献,皆值得译学界的关注和尊重。这三个研究方向,有助于缓解当前莎译研究主题的拥挤程度,助力其均衡、多元化发展。

六、结语

本文回顾了1918年以来的莎剧翻译研究历程,总结了研究现状,指出了研究中存在的问题,预测了新兴热点和学科前沿,并发现早期莎译研究含括丰厚的翻译思想,却和当代莎译研究之间基本断裂,二者之间亟待学术贯通,相互滋养。当代莎剧翻译研究涉及词汇学、语义学、语用学、功能语言学、认知语言学等多种语言学科分支,但研究主题主要集中在"朱生豪""梁实秋"等热点话题,关于傅光明、方平的莎剧翻译研究有望成为最新的学科前沿。总的来说,我国的莎剧翻译研究取得了巨大的成就,理论自觉、研究视角、挖掘深度等方面都在向好发展,但在译者/译本的选取、研究内容和方法等方面还有待改进,尤其是研究结构需要优化,以保证莎译研究的行稳致远。

另有一点毋庸置疑,语料库可以有效整合定量和定性两种分析模式,从根本上改善李伟民提出的风格研究困境。虽然语料库方法本身存在一定的不足,对剧中具体情节、人物、冲突等戏剧基本要素的再现解释力可能会力有不逮,但刘泽权《红楼梦》系列研究在一定程度上克服了上述缺陷,尤其是对王熙凤、刘姥姥等人物形象在各译本中的再现分析,合理地解释了语境化建构对人物重塑的作用,为莎剧翻译研究的数据解读和人物阐释之间的深度结合提供了极具参考价值的范本。因此,作为一种方法论,语料库在莎剧翻译研究中仍然大有可为。

参考文献

Chaomei Chen, "CiteSpace Ⅱ: Detecting and visualizing emerging trends and transient patterns in scientific literature", *Journal of the American Society for Information Science and Technology*, 57.3 (2006): 359-377.

J. C. Catford, *A Linguistic Theory of Translation*, London: Oxford University Press, 1965.

Mona Baker, *In Other Words: A Course on Translation*, London: Routledge, 2018.

R. T. Bell, *Translation and Translating: Theory and Practice*, London: Longman, 1991.

李伟民:《中国莎士比亚翻译研究五十年》,《中国翻译》2004年第5期。

李涛、徐芳:《莎士比亚戏剧汉译研究新进展》,《当代外语研究》2015年第1期。

朱安博:《中国莎剧汉译批评范式之嬗变》,《外语研究》2019年第6期。

陈悦、陈超美、胡志刚等:《引文空间分析原理与应用:CiteSpace实用指南》,科学出版社,2014年。

刘半农:《老实说了:刘半农随笔》,北京大学出版社,2010年。

郑振铎:《林琴南先生》,《小说月报》1924年第11期。

焦尹孚:《评田汉君的莎译:"罗蜜欧和朱丽叶"》,《洪水》1926年第9期。

罗皑岚(化名"山风大郎"):《卓宾鞋和田汉的翻译》,《幻洲》1927年第12期。

水天同:《书评:略谈梁译莎士比亚》,《国闻周报》1937年第1期。

邢光祖:《论翻译莎士比亚:与梁实秋先生讨论莎士比亚的翻译》,《光华附中半月刊》1937年第3-4期。

孙大雨:《译莎剧"黎琊王"序》,《民族文学》1943年第1期。

顾绶昌:《评莎剧〈哈姆雷特〉的三种译本》,《翻译通报》1951年第3期。

林子朴:《一个比较》,《读书月报》1957年第3期。

郝田虎:《弥尔顿在中国:1837—1888,兼及莎士比亚》,《外国文学》2010年第4期。

孙媛:《"重复建设"还是"多重建设"——文献计量学视野下的中国哈姆雷特研究40年》,《四川戏剧》2018年第11期。

李辰冬:《柔密欧与幽丽叶》,《文化先锋》1944年第24期。

梁实秋:《傅东华译的〈失乐园〉》,《图书评论》1933年第2期。

胡壮麟、朱永生、张德禄等:《系统功能语言学概论》,北京大学出版社,2017年。

张美芳、黄国文:《语篇语言翻译学与翻译研究》,《中国翻译》2002年第3期。

陈淑芬:《台湾莎学视角论傅新译"莎士比亚戏剧"与新"傅莎学"》,《名作欣赏》2018年第28期。

刘泽权:《数字人文视域下名著重译多维评价模型构建》,《中国翻译》2021年第5期。

刘炳善:《莎剧的两种中译本:从一出戏看全集》,《中国翻译》1992年第4期。

译坛论莎

译坛论莎

《无事生非》双关语的语内和语际翻译[①]

袁帅亚

摘要：莎士比亚喜剧《无事生非》包含大量的双关语。因为时代和语言文化的差异，原作双关语在现代英语和汉语译本中表现出不同的形式。现代英语译本与原作有同一语言文化基础，部分双关语得到自然保留，但因为表达明确的追求，多数情况下译文取消了原作的双关语。汉语译者在翻译双关语时，往往依据汉语自身的条件，要么亦步亦趋，要么另辟蹊径。用双关译双关，往往更能达到与原作一致的、绝妙的修辞效果。

关键词：《无事生非》；双关语；语内翻译；语际翻译

作者简介：袁帅亚，郑州航空工业管理学院副教授，主要研究方向为翻译和比较文学。

双关语（pun）是运用一个词语来暗示两层或两层以上意思或不同的联想，或者运用两个或两个以上同音异义或音近异义词的修辞手段。双关语通常有语义双关（ambiguity）和谐音双关（paronomasia）两种表现。语义双关是利用词语的多义性，构成表里两层意思。谐音双关是利用同音或近音的条件构成双关。运用双关语可以使语言新鲜活泼，诙谐有趣，收到滑稽幽默、冷嘲热讽，甚至悲剧性的效果。[②]莎士比亚喜剧《无事生非》中包含大量的双关语。因为时代和语言文化上的差异，理解和翻译这些双关语都有一定难度。本文通过剖析《无事生非》双关语的巧妙之处，展示这些双关语在该剧

[①] 本文所引莎士比亚戏剧原文出自新剑桥版莎士比亚 *Much Ado About Nothing*，F. H. Mares 编；现代英语译文出自"巴伦教育系列" *Much Ado About Nothing* 译本，Christina Lacie 译；汉语译文出自人民文学出版社《无事生非》朱生豪译本。引文中所有粗体均为笔者所加。

[②] 徐鹏：《莎士比亚的修辞手段》，苏州大学出版社，2001年，第251页。

本的语内翻译和语际翻译译本中的不同表现,以加深对莎士比亚双关语的理解和翻译的认识,更好地欣赏莎士比亚剧作。

一、双关语的翻译

多义性是文学文本的重要特点,双关语更是把这一特点外化,成为文学性的一个重要体现。因此,双关语的翻译是文学翻译研究中一个重要而有趣的热点。中国古典名著《红楼梦》的英译者霍克思在翻译这部小说时说:"凡是书里存在的,都有它的意图,所以总要设法表达出来。"霍克思恪守的一条翻译原则就是:"要把一切都译出来,甚至包括双关语在内。"[①]双关语的成功翻译,也是霍克思这部伟大的文学翻译文本有卓越造诣的一个重要成因。《红楼梦》第二十回中有一个非常有意思的情境,就是回目"林黛玉俏谑娇音"概括的故事。心直口快的史湘云看到贾宝玉和林黛玉天天在一处玩,自己备受冷落,心中很是不平。见到贾和林二人又在一起玩,史湘云就走过来责备他们两个:

二人正说着,只见湘云走来,笑道:"爱哥哥,林姐姐,你们天天一处玩,我好容易来了,也不理我理儿。"黛玉笑道:"偏是咬舌子爱说话,连个'二'哥哥也叫不上来,只是'爱'哥哥'爱'哥哥的。回来赶围棋儿,又该你闹么'爱'三了。"[②]

发音不清楚的"咬舌子"是史湘云真实可爱形象的一个生动表现。林黛玉抓住史湘云这个缺点,戏谑地模仿她"二"和"爱"发音不清,取笑她现在"二哥哥""爱哥哥"叫不上来,将来下围棋又该说"么'爱'三了"。"二"和"爱"在汉语中发音相近,如何在英语中传达这一谐音双关,是一个难度极大的翻译挑战。霍克思自然不会轻易放过这个对人物形象塑造起到关键作用的双关修辞。他的解决方案是在另外一种语言中再造一个"咬舌子"说话的情境,让小说人物在英语里"咬舌"——借助英语中/s/和/ð/发音相近:

Just then Xiang-yun burst in on them and reproved them smilingly for abandoning her:

[①] 曹雪芹:《红楼梦·第1卷》,大卫·霍克思译,上海外语教育出版社,2014年,第56页。
[②] 同上书,第486页。

'**Couthin** Bao, **Couthin** Lin: you can **thee** each other every day. It'th not often I get a **chanthe** to come here; yet now I have come, you both ignore me!'

Dai-yu burst out laughing:

'Lisping doesn't seem to make you any less talkative! Listen to you: "**Couthin!**" "**Couthin!**" Presently, when you're playing Racing Go, you'll be all "**thicktheth**" and "**theventh**"!'

语言大师莎士比亚更是运用双关语的妙手。18世纪,莎士比亚评论家约翰逊有一句名言:"双关语对他来说,就如同他爱上了给人带来致命灾难的埃及艳后克娄巴特拉。为了它,即便是失去一切,他也甘心情愿。"①意思是说,莎士比亚一见有运用双关语的机会,就不顾一切,非用不可。尽管他的一些早期喜剧中出现了不顾思想表达、单纯追求双关语的现象,但莎士比亚剧本中那些大量的双关语主要还是为戏剧效果服务,有其戏剧作用的。为了说明在中国出版莎士比亚注释本的必要性,裘克安先生曾分析过莎士比亚剧本中一个典型双关语例子。他举的例子是《哈姆雷特》剧中男主角出场后最初讲的几句话:

King	But now, my cousin Hamlet, and my son—
Hamlet[Aside]	A little more than **kin**, and less than **kind**!
King	How is it that the clouds still hang on you?
Hamlet	Not so, my lord. I am too much i' the **sun**.

莎士比亚让哈姆雷特使用了 kin 和 kind 以及 son 和 sun 两组双关语,kind 一词又有双重意义。哈姆雷特在旁白里说:比亲戚多一点——本来我是你的侄子,现在又成了你的儿子,确实不是一般的亲戚关系啊;然而却比 kind 少一点——kind 有两层意思,一是"同类相求"的亲近感,一是"与人为善"的善意感,我同你没有共同语言,我也不知道你是安的什么心。这话只能对自己说,在舞台上假定对方听不到。哈姆雷特的第二句话是公开的俏皮话:哪里有什么阴云呀,我在太阳里晒得不行呢。sun 是跟 clouds 相对,太阳意味着国王的恩宠,"你对我太好了,我怎么会阴郁呢";sun 又跟 son 谐音,"做你的儿

---

① 徐鹏:《莎士比亚的修辞手段》,第251页。

子,我领教得够了"。原文含义太复杂,有隐藏的深层感情,无论如何也只能译出一个侧面。这里仅以莎士比亚剧本最出色的译者朱生豪的译文为例:

王　　　　可是来,我的侄儿哈姆莱特,我的孩子——
哈[旁白]　超乎寻常的亲族,漠不相干的路人。
王　　　　为什么愁云依旧笼罩在你的身上?
哈　　　　不,陛下;我已经在太阳里晒得太久了。

双关语是翻译的难点,甚至有人还认为双关语根本无从翻译。因为,不管技艺如何高超,即使是霍克思也不可能在英语里一语双关"二"和"爱",即使是朱生豪也不可能在汉语里一语双关 sun 和 son。鲁迅先生在谈文学翻译的困难时说:"譬如一个名词或动词,写不出,创作时候可以回避,翻译上却不成,也还得想,一直弄到头昏眼花,好像在脑子里面摸一个急于要开箱子的钥匙,却没有。"①双关语更是如此,译者不可能对其存在视而不见,文学翻译家更是迫切需要一把打开双关语翻译的箱子的钥匙。

二、《无事生非》及其现代英语译本

《无事生非》是莎士比亚喜剧艺术达到成熟的一部作品,大致创作于1598年之后,在莎士比亚全部作品里的地位相当重要。主要故事是阿拉贡亲王唐·彼得罗(Don Petro)庶弟唐·约翰(Don John),企图破坏佛罗伦萨少年贵族克劳狄奥(Claudio)和梅西那总督里奥那托(Leonato)的女儿希罗(Hero)的婚事,对他们进行诬陷,最后以失败告终。而实际上,最吸引人的乃是另一对个性很强且嘴不饶人的青年男女里奥那托的侄女贝特丽丝(Beatrice)和帕度亚少年贵族培尼狄克(Benedick)。他们出身高贵,有灵活的头脑与敏捷的口才,只是都太高傲了,不肯向人低头,尤其是不肯在异性面前服输。一个因此不肯嫁,一个因此不愿娶。舌锋似剑的两个年轻人遇在一起便互相讥诮,直到都被捉弄,并认为对方强烈地暗恋自己,最终回心转意且互诉爱慕。女主角贝特丽丝直爽、活泼、乐观、谈锋犀利,才华过人。她和培尼狄克互不相让、唇枪舌剑的交锋,仿佛是一场展示机智才华的盛宴。特别是她那心直口快、妙语连珠的风趣谈吐,令人喜爱倾

---

① 鲁迅:《且介亭杂文二集》,人民文学出版社,2006年,第143页。

倒,玩味无穷,最是本剧精彩之处。

《无事生非》是一部所谓的"高尚的喜剧"(High Comedy)。剧中重要人物都是受过教育的上层人士,他们惯于玩弄智力游戏和进行机智的反驳,谈话充满风趣,十分幽默俏皮。尤其是一对青年男女的口舌之争,有时很精彩,有时也很庸俗。这种舌战是莎士比亚时代观众所欣赏的。莎士比亚善于运用修辞手段,语言丰富多彩,用词生动有力。修辞的运用可以追溯到古希腊和罗马。在从古希腊、罗马开始约两千年中,演讲被视为教育本身的最高层次,修辞学作为一门学科或作为教学的一个原则,被置于教育过程的中心位置。文艺复兴时期,英国的教育也把修辞学作为一门重要的必修课。莎士比亚曾进入家乡的文法学校就读,在那里,他打下了坚实的古典文学基础,掌握了丰富的修辞学知识。就双关辞格而言,据统计,仅在《罗密欧与朱丽叶》一剧中就至少运用了175处[①];《无事生非》一剧,梁实秋译本"例言"特别指出原文多"双关语",以及各种典故,无法逐译时则加注说明,而在全剧136条译者注中明确出现"双关语"字眼的就有11条之多。

莎士比亚剧本研读是现代英美人文教育的一项重要内容。莎士比亚剧本是四百多年前的作品,今天的英美读者如果没有一定的古典作品阅读训练,读其原作会很感困难。造成原作阅读困难的因素除社会文化背景之外,还包括伊丽莎白时代的语言在句法和词汇上与现代英语的差异,以及莎士比亚丰富的修辞手段,尤其是大量的双关语等。为了方便阅读,甚至为了应付考试,英美的教育和出版机构也在莎士比亚的剧本上大做文章,各种校注本、评析本、演出本、图像本层出不穷。有的出版机构还出版了莎士比亚剧作的现代英语翻译本。语言学家雅各布森从符号学的观点出发,把翻译分为三类:语内翻译、语际翻译、符际翻译。语内翻译是一种在同一语言内部的翻译,也就是把一种语言符号译成同一语言中的其他符号。[②]用现代英语翻译莎士比亚的剧本,自然也属于一种形式的语内翻译。

美国巴伦教育系列(*Barron's Educational Series*)于21世纪初推出了莎士比亚剧本的现代英语译本丛书,首度发行13个剧本,是莎士比亚剧本语内翻译的一项重要成果。该丛书总题目即为"莎士比亚不再难读系列"(*SHAKESPEARES MADE EASY SERIES*),正文前附有介绍剧作家和剧本概况的导读文章。剧作家介绍包括他的生平和创作成就

---

① 徐鹏:《莎士比亚的修辞手段》,第251页。
② 方梦之:《中国译学大辞典》,上海外语教育出版社,2011年,第133页。

等,剧本介绍包括该剧的创作时期、题材来源、演出和批评的历史等。正文包括莎士比亚的剧本原作及现代英语翻译两部分,剧本原文的对面页是现代英语的逐句翻译。正文之后是为理解和进一步研习该剧本而设计的研习问题。"终于,莎士比亚有了人人都能读懂的语言""是的,当代语言翻译让莎士比亚不再难读,让你轻松考高分,还能享受大师卓越作品的永恒之美"。①我们能从这些广告语中看出该丛书的读者对象和出版目的。仅以《无事生非》译本开场为例,里奥那托总督得到信使(Messenger)报告培尼狄克一行即将到来:

Enter **Leonato**, governor of Messina, **Hero** his daughter, and **Beatrice** his niece, with a Messenger.

Leonato　　I learn in this letter, that Don Pedro of Arragon comes this night to Messina.
Messenger　　He is very near by this, he was not three leagues off when I left him.
Leonato　　How many gentlemen have you lost in this action?
Messenger　　But few of any sort, and none of name.

Standing in front of his home, **Leonato**, *with his daughter* **Hero** *and niece* **Beatrice**, *receives a letter delivered by a messenger of* Don Petro of Arragon.

Leonato　　The letter states that Don Petro of Arragon will be arriving in Messina this morning.
Messenger　　Yes, he is very close; when I left he was only about nine miles away.
Leonato　　How many gentlemen were killed in this most recent battle?
Messenger　　Very few were lost and none of any importance or ranking.

在现代英语译本中,舞台提示更清楚;人物台词是现代英语,更便于理解剧情。然而,莎士比亚剧本是语言艺术的杰作,在绝大多数情况下以诗体形式呈现,所谓的抑扬格五音步素体诗。翻译,无论是语际翻译还是语内翻译,都会破坏原作固有的形式,尤

---

① William Shakespeare, *Much Ado About Nothing*, Christina Lacie, trans., New York: Barron's Educational Series, Inc., 2009.

其是原作的诗体特征和修辞技巧。语内翻译在同一语言的不同历史阶段,或在其不同变体之间进行,有一致的语言文化基础。语际翻译在不同语言之间进行,要跨越语言文化的鸿沟,难度更大。然而,文学翻译是一种补偿和平衡的艺术,原作的内容和形式在译本中得到全新呈现,同一原作的语内和语际译本所能达到的文学高度不可以想当然地判定。考察莎士比亚剧本双关语在现代英语和汉译本里的不同表现,不失为语内和语际翻译比较研究的一种有效途径。

三、《无事生非》双关语的翻译

莎士比亚剧作的汉译始于20世纪初期。20世纪20年代,田汉最先翻译了《哈姆雷特》和《罗密欧和朱丽叶》。此后,朱生豪、梁实秋、曹未风、卞之琳、方平等都翻译过。朱生豪的译文优美畅达,一直是最受读者喜爱的译本。梁实秋是中国迄今为止唯一一个独立完成莎士比亚全部作品汉译的翻译家。梁译本有详尽的注释,学术含量较高。卞之琳采取"以顿代步、韵式依原诗、等行翻译"的方法,其诗体译本成就卓著。方平也是莎士比亚剧作重要的诗体译家。《无事生非》就是朱生豪的译名,梁译本作《无事自扰》,方译本作《捕风捉影》。本文中双关语的语际翻译译本采自朱生豪译本,语内翻译译本采自Christina Lacie的现代英语译本。依据剧中双关语在汉译本中的再现方式,笔者将代表性译例分为四类:(1)亦步亦趋,基本对应;(2)丢卒保车,存其大体;(3)另辟蹊径,改头换面;(4)无能为力,完全放弃。并比较这四类双关语在语内和语际翻译中的不同表现。

1.亦步亦趋,基本对应

在语义双关中,双关语利用词语的多义性,构成表里两层意思。一词多义现象在任何语言中都很常见,但一个词语在一种语言中的若干义项很少能在另一种语言中完全对应。然而,在两种语言之间,仍有一部分基本意义相同的词汇的引申意义也大致相同或相近。遇到此类词语构成的双关,译文可以亦步亦趋地紧跟原文形式而得到基本对应的效果。以本剧第二幕第三场中pains两个不同义项构成的双关为例:

Beatrice   Against my will I am sent to bid you come in to dinner.

Benedick   Fair Beatrice, I thank you for your **pains**.

Beatrice   I took no more **pains** for those thanks, than you took **pains** to thank me, if it had been **painful** I would not have come.

Beatrice　　Against my wishes, I have been sent here to ask you to come in to dinner.

Benedick　　Beautiful Beatrice, thank you for your **efforts**.

Beatrice　　Actually, I have no more **effort** for those thanks than you make effort to thank me. If it had been too **much effort**, I wouldn't have come.

贝特丽丝　他们叫我来请您进去吃饭,可是这是违反我自己的意志的。
培尼狄克　好贝特丽丝,有劳枉驾,**辛苦**您啦,真是多谢。
贝特丽丝　我并没什么**辛苦**可以领受您的谢意,就像您这一声多谢并没有**辛苦**了您。要是这是一件**辛苦**的事,我也不会来啦。

彼得罗与克劳狄奥和里奥那托一起设下圈套捉弄培尼狄克,他们故意让他偷听他们在一起谈论贝特丽丝如何疯狂地爱着他,却又不敢向他表露内心的激情。他们故意表示担心培尼狄克一旦知道贝特丽丝对他的热恋,会对她大加嘲讽。培尼狄克因此确信贝特丽丝爱自己,决定回报她的这份情。当贝特丽丝极不情愿地出现在他面前请他赴宴时,培尼狄克答谢她的邀请:thank you for your pains。英文用法中pains有两层意思:一层是客套语中的"麻烦";一层是基本义"痛苦"。培尼狄克的意思显然是"多有麻烦"。贝特丽丝则一贯地对其冷嘲热讽:I took no pains for those thanks, than you took pains to thank me。这里pains的意思是"痛苦":我来请您去赴宴并不痛苦,您向我道谢倒是很痛苦啊。贝特丽丝接下来说的一句话中的painful一词更是确认了这种解释。pains一词表示"麻烦"的用法在现代英语中已经不常用,所以这段对白的现代英语译本用efforts一词,在汉译本中用"辛苦"一词,表演和阅读时可以通过夸张或重读,基本上能保留原文的一语双关。

2.丢卒保车,存其大体

还有一类双关语是借眼前的事物来讲述所说的意思,双关语所用的音形义三方面都能关涉两种事物,双关语不必只是一个词,而可以是一个或几个句子。[①]本剧第二幕第一场中就有这样的一例:God sends curst cow short horns。更为复杂的是,这个双关句

[①]　陈望道:《修辞学发凡》,复旦大学出版社,2008年,第84页。

子中的horn一词还同时还是个多重双关语。汉译本在翻译这个双关句的时候，只能丢卒保车，存其大体，原文讲述的主要意思得到保留，双关句中又嵌入的双关词则付之阙如：

Antonio　　In faith, she's too curst.

Beatrice　　Too curst is more than curst, **I shall lessen God's sending that way: for it is said, God sends a curst cow short horns, but to a cow too curst, she sends none.**

Leonato　　So, by being too curst, God will send you no **horns**.

Antonio　　I swear that she is too quarrelsome.

Beatrice　　Too quarrelsome is more than just quarrelsome. **If that is true I will decrease God's punishment according to the proverb that says, "God sends short horns to a quarrelsome cow, but sends none to a too quarrelsome cow."**

Leonato　　Then, God will not send you **horns** because you are so quarrelsome.

安东尼奥　　可不是，她这张嘴尖利得过了分。

贝特丽丝　　尖利过了分就算不得尖利，那嚒"**尖嘴姑娘嫁一个矮脚郎**"这句话可落不到我头上来啦。

里奥那托　　那是说，上帝干脆连一个"**矮脚郎**"都不送给你啦。

贝特丽丝在描述她心中的白马王子时，说唐·约翰和培尼狄克离她的标准差得如何远。里奥那托提醒她，说话太刻薄会让她找不到丈夫。列里奥那托的弟弟安东尼奥插话说她这张嘴太尖利（curst）。贝特丽丝顺着curst一词说下去，引用一句谚语God sends a curst cow short horns。这句谚语中curst的意思"坏脾气的"，"上帝让脾气坏的牛只生短角"，意思是说上帝让本性凶恶的事物没有了伤人的利器。既然让脾气坏的牛只生短脚，那么脾气过分坏的牛，干脆就不让它生角了。因此，当安东尼奥说到too curst时，贝特丽丝接下去说，她这样就减少了上帝的赠与（I shall lessen God's sending that way）。因为角亦是上帝的赠与，不使牛生角就是减少了上帝的赠与。贝特丽丝表面上是在说上帝让凶恶的事物没有伤人的利器，实际上是说自己乐得独身，这是整句话的双关语。汉译本抓住了这个关键意思，将这个谚语译为"尖嘴姑娘嫁一个矮脚郎"，并在这

317

个谚语的基础上进一步说,过分尖利了上帝干脆连一个"矮脚郎"都不送了。谚语原文中 horn 一词则是进一步的语义双关。horn 除了有"动物头上的角"这项基本义外,还有"妻子与人私通者头上所生的(假想的)角",即"绿帽子"的比喻义。[①]贝特丽丝所说的"减少上帝的赠与",则可理解为上帝既不令她嫁得丈夫,当然就不可能令人有头上生角之虞。horn 还是男性生殖器(penis)的隐语,a short horn/penis 隐指"一个无能的丈夫"。列奥那托说的 God will send you no horns 自然也是指上帝不令她嫁得丈夫了。这样的性隐喻用法在莎士比亚剧作中是很常见的。原文中 horn 这么多的义项显然不能完全翻译出来,译者只能丢卒保车。然而,在语内翻译的译文中 horn 一词没有翻译,双关得到自然保留,只是当代读者对这个词的基本义项之外的意义已经很陌生了,没有足够的注解很难理解其中复杂的含义。

3. 另辟蹊径,改头换面

短语或成语不能从字面上理解其含义。巧妙利用短语或成语的字面义也可以构成一种双关语。这种双关语进行语际翻译的难度更大,而在语内翻译中则可以保持原状。本剧第五幕第一场中的一段对白,就是利用 side 和短语 beside one's wit(发疯)中 beside 的谐音构成双关。此类双关语在语际翻译中不可能被复制出来,译者只能发挥创造性,再造新的双关语表达形式。

Claudio　　We have been up and down to seek thee, for we are high proof melancholy, and would fain have it beaten away, wilt thou use thy wit?

Benedick　　It is in my scabbard, shall I **draw** it?

Don Pedro　　Dost thou **wear thy wit by thy side**?

Claudio　　Never any did so, though very many have been **beside their wit**: I will bid thee **draw**, as we do the minstrels, **draw** to pleasure us.

Claudio　　We have been up and down looking for you because we are downhearted and would gladly have itchased way. Will you use your wit to help?

Benedick　　It in my scabbard. Shall I **pull it out**?

Don Pedro　　Are you **wearing your humor on your side**?

Claudio　　No one **carries their wit on their side**, although some have been **beside**

[①] 刘炳善:《英汉双解莎士比亚大词典》,河南人民出版社,2002年,第537页。

their wit. Please, **draw** your wit as the musicians **draw** their bows. Make us happy.

克劳狄奥　　我们到处找着你，因为我们一肚子都是烦恼，想设法把它排遣排遣。你给我们讲个笑话吧。

培尼狄克　　我的笑话就在我的剑鞘里，要不要拔出来给你们瞧瞧？

彼得罗　　你是把笑话随身佩戴的吗？

克劳狄奥　　只听见把人笑破"肚皮"，可还没听说把笑话插在"腰"里。请你把他"拔"来，就像乐师从他的琴囊里拿出他的乐器来一样，给我们弹奏弹奏解解闷吧。

培尼狄克和贝特丽丝互诉爱慕之后，培尼狄克发誓会为贝特丽丝做任何事情以证明爱她。贝特丽丝因为不能替密友希罗报受克劳狄奥诬陷之仇而绝望，她的信念让培尼迪克相信希罗的清白。于是培尼狄克向昔日好友挑战。彼得罗和克劳狄奥不知道培尼狄克到来是为了挑战，仍像以往一样希望他能带来轻松愉快。克劳狄奥让培尼狄克讲个笑话排解愁闷，培尼狄克说他的笑话就在剑鞘里，要不要拔出来给他们瞧瞧(It is in my scabbard, shall I draw it?)。他的意思是要拔剑挑战。没有意识到问题的严重性，彼得罗取笑培尼狄克"把笑话随身佩戴"(Dost thou wear thy wit by thy side?)，克劳狄奥更是利用彼得罗这句话中的 side 和短语 beside one's wit 中的 beside 谐音，打趣培尼狄克。汉译者在这里另辟蹊径，模仿原文中双关语形成的机制，再造了一个类似的汉语双关语——只听见人笑破"肚皮"，可还没听说把笑话插在"腰"里——再现了原作这一重要情节。将固定短语"笑破肚皮"拆开来解读，造成和原文将 beside one's wit 拆开来解读类似的幽默风趣，可谓翻译得非常成功。此外，原文中还有 draw 这个单词也是一语双关（"拿出"和"弹奏"）。汉译本没能用对应的双关语译出来，现代英语译本先是将其翻译为 pull it out，待到该词再次出现而一语双关的时候就保持原样，不再翻译了。

4. 无能为力，完全放弃

当双关语的一词多义方式在另一种语言中完全找不到合适的方式对应的时候，译者实在无能为力，对这类双关语只好完全放弃。本剧第二幕第三场就有一处这样的双关语：

Balthazar　　**Note** this before my **notes**,
There's not a **note** of mine that's worth the **noting**.

Don Pedro　Why these are very crotchets that he speaks, **Note notes** forsooth, and **nothing**.

Balthazar　But what you **need to know** before I sing my **notes** is that there's not a **note** of mine that is worth **noting**.

Don Pedro　What strange ideas he is speaking of; **note, notes**, in truth he is speaking of **nothing**.

鲍尔萨泽　在我未唱以前,先要声明一句:我唱的歌儿是一句也不值得你们注意的。
彼得罗　他在那儿净说些不值得注意的废话。

彼得罗、克劳狄奥和里奥那托三人故意在花园里引诱培尼狄克前来偷听他们的议论。彼得罗的仆人鲍尔萨泽和一群乐工也在这个时候来到花园。彼得罗建议大家欣赏音乐,并让鲍尔萨泽唱歌。絮絮叨叨的鲍尔萨泽开唱前说的一句话中note出现了四次。在note this和worth the noting短语中,note的意思是"注意";在my notes短语中,note的意思是"曲调"或"乐谱";在not a note of mine短语中,note的意思是"音符"。汉译本尽管翻译出了整句的意思,但note的双关付之阙如。现代英语译本为了尽可能表达明确,将note this中的note译为need to know,其余三个原封不动,双关得到部分保留。彼得罗对鲍尔萨泽的絮叨很不耐烦,说他的话全是奇怪的字谜(crotchet又有两解:"四分音符"和"怪念头"),然而却不忘在note的一语双关上再叠加一层:note与nothing也关联了起来(nothing当时可以读作noting,th通常情况下发字母t的音)。以上诸多复杂的含义,实在让任何语际翻译的译者都感束手无策,现代英语译本为了表意明确也大大降低了原作的双关负载。

四、结语

双关语在《无事生非》剧作中的大量存在,对刻画人物性格和表现剧作主题有着极其重要的作用。尤其需要指出的是,本剧的剧目 *Much Ado About Nothing* 本身就有两重双关,而这两重双关又关涉对本剧主题的解读。首先,nothing和noting在那个时代发音相同,构成谐音双关,因此关涉剧中反复出现的"偷听"和"欺骗"主题。其次,在莎士比亚的词法中，nothing 因其"空无一物"的含义，还暗指"女性器官"，因此关涉该剧的"性"、"两性关系"和"厌恶女性"主题。这些都是该剧的现代主题批评所发掘的主要内容。因此，双关语可以说是该剧鉴赏和翻译的锁钥。

本文通过分析《无事生非》中双关语的理解和翻译，尤其是考察其在汉译本中的再现方式，对比其在语内和语际翻译译本中的得失，展示出译者在翻译双关语时的苦心，以及在语言自身的客观条件差异限制下，翻译所能为和所不能为的极限，对理解和欣赏莎士比亚剧作，对理解和认识翻译本身，都有一定的启示意义。

参考文献

William Shakespeare, *Much Ado About Nothing*, Christina Lacie, trans., New York: Barron's Educational Series, Inc., 2009.

徐鹏:《莎士比亚的修辞手段》，苏州大学出版社，2001年。

曹雪芹:《红楼梦·第1卷》，大卫·霍克思译，上海外语教育出版社，2014年。

鲁迅:《且介亭杂文二集》，人民文学出版社，2006年。

方梦之:《中国译学大辞典》，上海外语教育出版社，2011年。

陈望道:《修辞学发凡》，复旦大学出版社，2008年。

刘炳善:《英汉双解莎士比亚大词典》，河南人民出版社，2002年。

莎律朱韵 高山流水
——基于语料库的莎士比亚四大悲剧朱生豪译本音乐性研究

刘佯

摘要：本文以莎士比亚四大悲剧朱生豪译本为研究对象，运用语料库的研究方法，从用韵、节奏和语调三方面对译本音乐性开展定量考察和定性分析。研究结果表明，朱译采用了头韵、行内韵、隔行韵、尾韵及其他修辞手段来再现莎剧原文的韵式，意组节奏表现形式丰富，意顿律、声韵律突出，但平仄律使用相对有限。朱生豪从对文本音乐性的深刻认知出发，凭借深厚的古典诗词功底，对莎剧原文韵律和节奏进行改造和创新，贴切地再现了莎士比亚诗剧的语体原貌，把新文与旧辞巧妙地融合成义明音泽的诗化语言，为莎士比亚作品在中国的传播作出了独特的贡献。

关键词：语料库；莎士比亚四大悲剧；朱生豪译本；音乐性

基金项目：本文系重庆市社会科学规划社会组织项目"莎士比亚四大悲剧朱生豪译本音乐性研究"（项目编号：2022SZ44）的阶段性研究成果。

作者简介：刘佯，西南大学外国语学院博士研究生，主要研究方向为文学翻译、莎士比亚研究。

一、引言

莎士比亚是英国文艺复兴时期的伟大剧作家，"他的剧作是全人类所共有的宝贵精神财富"[1]。中国学者孟宪强认为，"莎士比亚的悲剧不仅是他个人创作的最高成就，同

---

[1] 曹树钧：《朱生豪论莎士比亚：纪念朱生豪诞生100周年》，《上海戏剧》2012年第12期。

时也代表了文艺复兴时期英国戏剧乃至整个欧洲戏剧的最高水平"[1]。国际著名莎学家、美国耶鲁大学戴维·斯科特·卡斯顿教授指出,四大悲剧是莎士比亚艺术宝库的四大支柱,它们既是莎士比亚伟大与崇高的明证,也是莎士比亚不朽文坛声誉的源泉。[2]四百多年来,莎士比亚创作的四大悲剧——《哈姆雷特》《奥赛罗》《李尔王》《麦克白》——被翻译成多种文字,在世界各国的舞台上盛演不衰,受到人们的普遍喜爱,引起了评论家的高度关注,相关的研究著作浩如烟海。

自1903年上海达文书社出版了我国最早的莎剧故事译本《海外奇谭》至今,莎士比亚戏剧在中国的译介已逾一百二十年。据不完全统计,除开单行本、选集等,仅以《莎士比亚全集》之名出版的中文译本就超过十种[3],以朱译本为基础的莎士比亚全集经过多次校订[4],重印和再版逾七十次,总印数超过一百万册。出版行业对朱译莎剧的长期青睐,在中国翻译史上是一种罕见的现象。而事实上,翻译过莎士比亚戏剧的中国译者除朱生豪外,还有梁实秋、曹未风、方平、卞之琳等,他们有的是诗人,有的是学者,有的是文学评论家,有的甚至身兼多重身份,但他们几乎都在自己的莎剧译作序言中承认参考了朱生豪的译本。朱生豪译本之所以得到同行们的肯定,成为他们学习和借鉴的对象,不仅仅在于译文语言的优美、典雅和晓畅,更在于它含有目前尚未完全揭示的内在特质:音乐性。

---

[1] 孟宪强:《莎士比亚创作分期新探》,《社会科学战线》1994年第6期。

[2] See David Scott Kastan, "'A rarity most beloved': Shakespeare and the Idea of Tragedy", in Richard Dutton and Jane E. Howard, eds., *A Companion to Shakespeare's Works, Volume I: The Tragedies,* Oxford: Blackwell Publishing Ltd., 2003, p. 4.

[3] 比较知名的《莎士比亚全集》包括1957年台北世界书局版,朱生豪和虞而昌合译;1967年台北远东图书公司版,梁实秋译;1978年人民文学出版社版,朱生豪等译,吴兴华等校;1996年长春时代文艺出版社版,朱生豪等译,苏福忠等校;1997年长沙新世纪版,肖运初校;1998年南京译林版,朱生豪等译,裘克安等校;2000年河北教育出版社版,方平等译;2016年外研社版,辜正坤等译;2021年新星出版社版,朱生豪、苏福忠译。

[4] 以朱生豪译本为基础的莎士比亚全集历经的主要校订包括1957年台北世界书局邀请虞尔昌做的修订补译,1978年人民文学出版社组织杨周翰、方重、张谷若等对朱生豪所译的三十一个剧本进行的校订和补译,1998年南京译林出版社组织辜正坤、裘克安、何其莘等进行的校订,以及21世纪以来翻译家苏福忠先生参与的多次校订与补译。

二、双语平行语料库的创建

(一) 语料的选取与输入

在世界书局首版《莎士比亚戏剧全集》的"译者自序"中,朱生豪直言自己是以一册牛津版莎士比亚全集为英语原文。[①]另据朱生豪的妻子宋清如回忆,"他(朱生豪)采用的是一九二八年出版的牛津版莎士比亚全集一卷本"。[②]无独有偶,1905年牛津大学出版社出版了克雷格(W. J. Craig)编写的牛津标准作者版《莎士比亚全集》(*The Oxford Standard Authors edition of Shakespeare's Works*),全书仅一册,于1928年第12次重印[③]。从时间以及译者身处的历史和社会实际情况推测,朱生豪翻译莎士比亚戏剧时,使用该版作为源文本的可能性最大。因此,本研究选择了1905年牛津标准作者版《莎士比亚全集》中的四大悲剧作为英语源文本,便于精准地考察源文本与译本的对应关系。

朱生豪历经10年握管不辍,翻译出31部半莎士比亚戏剧。1947年,世界书局出版了朱生豪翻译的《莎士比亚戏剧全集》3辑共27种,其中四大悲剧悉数出现在该版第2辑中[④]。此后,朱译莎剧历经多次校改,反复重印再版,于原译难免失真陨形。为最大程度地存留朱译莎剧原貌,本研究选取了1947年世界书局首版《莎士比亚戏剧全集》(第2辑)中的四大悲剧作为中文语料。

确定源语料后,笔者从权威网站下载了克雷格(W. J. Craig)编写的牛津标准作者版《莎士比亚全集》,又通过文献传递找到了1947年世界书局版朱生豪译《莎士比亚戏剧全集》(第二辑),从中提取出莎士比亚四大悲剧的英语原文本和朱译本,并转化为纯文本格式。为保证语料质量及研究的可靠性,笔者对输入的语料做了人工校对,以避免拼

[①] 原文为:"越年(即1936年)战事发生,……仓卒中惟携出牛津版全集一册,及译稿数本而已。"见莎士比亚:《莎士比亚戏剧全集》(第一辑),世界书局,1947年,译者自序第2页。

[②] 宋清如:《朱生豪与莎士比亚戏剧》,《新文学史料》1989年第1期。

[③] 该书封面为《莎士比亚全集》(*Shakespeare: Complete Works*),版权页注明是牛津标准作者版《莎士比亚全集》(*The Oxford Standard Authors edition of Shakespeare's Works*),并说明该书于1905年首版发行后,多次重印。See William Shakespeare, *Shakespeare: Complete Works*, W. J. Craig, ed., London: Oxford University Press, 1905.

[④] 据朱生豪译《莎士比亚戏剧全集》(第一辑)目次显示,《漢姆莱脱》(今译《哈姆雷特》)为该辑第2个剧目,《奥瑟罗》(今译《奥赛罗》)为第3个剧目,《李尔王》(今译《李尔王》)为第4个剧目,《麦克佩斯》(今译《麦克白》)为第5个剧目。为避免莎剧指称混淆,本文采用今译。见莎士比亚:《莎士比亚戏剧全集》(第一辑),朱生豪译,世界书局,1947年。

写错误及其他语码问题。

(二)语料的分词和标注

笔者采用中科院计算机技术研究所开发的NLPIR/ICTCLAS分词系统对朱生豪译莎士比亚四大悲剧和牛津版英语原文分别进行了英汉语词语切分和词形标注。以《李尔王》(King Lear)第1幕第1场第38—47行为例,完成分词标注处理的中英文语料示例图,如图1、2所示:

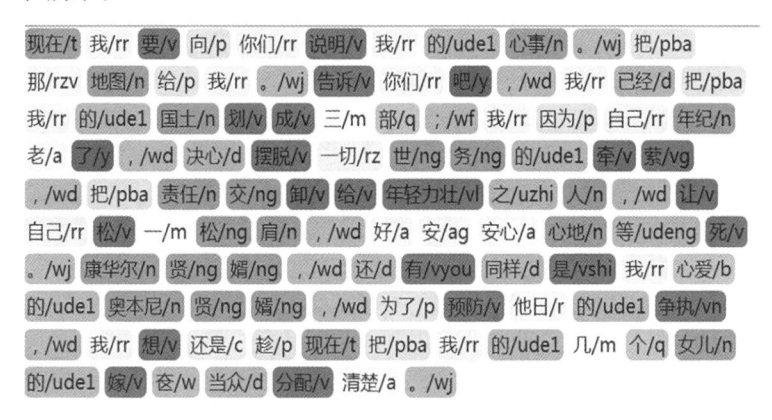

现在/t 我/rr 要/v 向/p 你们/rr 说明/v 我/rr 的/ude1 心事/n 。/wj 把/pba 那/rzv 地图/n 给/p 我/rr 。/wj 告诉/v 你们/rr 吧/y ,/wd 我/rr 已经/d 把/pba 我/rr 的/ude1 国土/n 划/v 成/v 三/m 部/q ,/wf 我/rr 因为/p 自己/rr 年纪/n 老/a 了/y ,/wd 决心/n 摆脱/v 一切/rz 世/ng 务/ng 的/ude1 牵/v 萦/vg ,/wd 把/pba 责任/n 交/ng 卸/v 给/v 年轻力壮/vl 之/uzhi 人/n ,/wd 让/v 自己/rr 松/v 一/m 松/ng 肩/n ,/wd 好/a 安/ag 安心/a 心地/n 等/udeng 死/v 。/wj 康华尔/n 贤/ng 婿/ng ,/wd 还/d 有/vyou 同样/d 是/vshi 我/rr 心爱/b 的/ude1 奥本尼/n 贤/ng 婿/ng ,/wd 为了/p 预防/v 他日/r 的/ude1 争执/vn ,/wd 我/rr 想/v 还是/c 趁/p 现在/t 把/pba 我/rr 的/ude1 几/m 个/q 女儿/n 的/ude1 嫁/v 奁/w 当众/d 分配/v 清楚/a 。/wj

图1 朱译莎士比亚四大悲剧分词标注示例图

Meantime/v we/rzt shall/vyou express/v our/rr darker/v purpose/n ./wj Give/v me/rzv the/rzt map/n there/rzs ./wj Know/v that/c we/rzt have/vyou divided/vd In/p three/m our/rr kingdom/n ;/n and/c tis/n our/rr fast/a intent/n To/pba shake/v all/a cares/v and/c business/n from/p our/rr stage/n ,/wd Conferring/v them/rzt on/p younger/a strengths/vi ,/wd while/c we/rzt Unburden/a ^/n d/o crawl/v toward/p death/n ./wj Our/rr son/n of/p Cornwall/a ,/wd And/c you/rzt ,/wd our/rr no/rzt less/rzs loving/a son/n of/p Albany/nz ,/wd We/rzt have/vyou this/r hour/n a/rzv constant/a will/vyou to/pba publish/vd Our/rr daughters/n ^/n several/rzs dowers/n ,/wd that/c future/n strife/n May/vyou be/vshi prevented/vd now/d ./wj

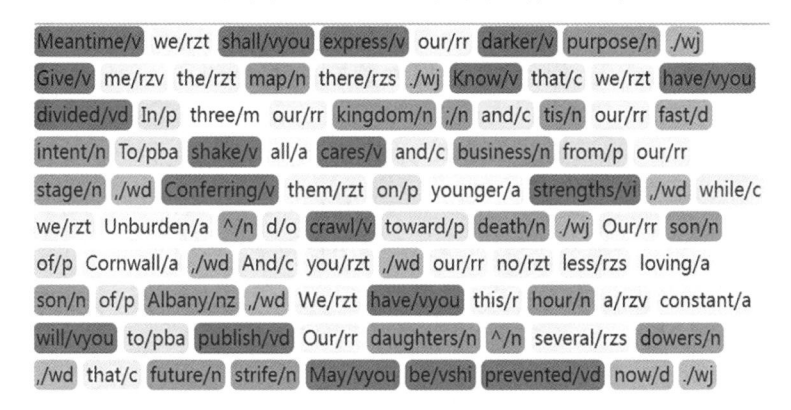

图2 牛津版英语原文分词标注示例图

为考察文本音乐性,笔者又做了汉语自动注音,并按照严韵、宽韵、通韵(常通和偶通)对四部朱译莎剧台词进行句内和句间押韵标注,对朱译莎士比亚四大悲剧的押韵形式进行分类,以统计译本的韵律、节奏和修辞情况。由于朱译本在语言方面有文白交融的特点,为避免舛误,需要依靠工具书人工校对。

（三）语料的平行对齐

为保持源文本与译本语言层面的一一对应关系，笔者使用了软件ParaConc来实现英语原文与朱译本的平行对齐。首先以戏剧中的人物对话为单位，做到段落层面的对齐，再依靠人工标记实现句子层面的对齐。语料平行对齐浏览窗口如图3所示：

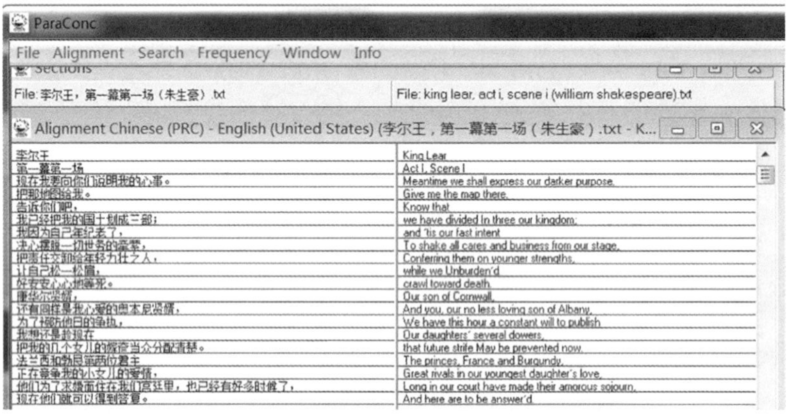

图3 语料平行对齐浏览窗口示例图

至此，莎士比亚四大悲剧汉英双语平行语料库建成，其中包含牛津版英语源文本137564字符，世界书局版朱译本430254字符，共计56万余字符。

三、莎士比亚四大悲剧的音乐性

莎士比亚戏剧主要由两种语体构成：诗体和散文体。早在1964年，我国著名翻译家王佐良就注意到，莎士比亚善于运用素体无韵诗（blank verse，以下简称无韵诗），而这种诗体"更善于捕捉戏剧性和发扬音乐性"[1]，因为它有着严谨的音律，十个音节依照声音的强弱组成五个音步，通过音势（即声音强弱）产生强烈的诗歌节奏。

（一）诗体与散文体：量的观察

莎士比亚戏剧在英美国家舞台和银幕上演出时，演员们朗诵的台词字句铿锵，节奏井然，自有一种协和声调之美，所以莎剧又被称为诗剧，因为莎剧的台词里具有诗歌的显著特点。四大悲剧作为莎士比亚成熟期的作品，在语体方面更加纯熟，诗体和散文体

---

[1] 王佐良：《英国诗剧与莎士比亚》，《文学评论》1964年第2期。

的篇幅差异十分明显。

1968年,英国莎学家布莱恩·威克斯曾大致统计过莎剧中诗体和散文体台词的比例,数据显示,四大悲剧文本中,诗体所占比例都在75%以上:《麦克白》高达95%;《奥赛罗》次之,占80%;《哈姆雷特》和《李尔王》诗体所占比例都是75%。[1]2008年,休梅克(Shewmaker)也指出,莎士比亚的戏剧语言中,大约有3/4是诗体(verse)。[2]由此观之,诗体在莎士比亚戏剧中的使用十分普遍。

(二)诗体与散文体:质的考量

1. 诗体与文本音乐性

在莎士比亚四大悲剧中,诗体大致有三类:韵诗、歌谣和无韵诗台词。以《哈姆雷特》为例,第3幕第2场中戏部分共有149行诗,且全部都是双行押韵,即abab韵式,这是该剧韵文最为集中的地方。除此之外,第2幕第2场哈姆雷特在波洛涅斯面前装疯时,说出的4行民谣也是韵文,含头韵和尾韵;第5幕第1场掘坟的小丑甲唱了3段共12行abab韵式的歌谣;第4幕第5场中奥菲利娅所唱的歌谣虽然是断断续续,但8处44行中仍能感受到音乐的韵律。在幕、场结尾的地方,押韵的诗行更是比比皆是。刘勰《文心雕龙·声律篇》有云:"异音相从谓之和,同声相应谓之韵。"莎士比亚四大悲剧,从韵式来看,既有"异声相合",又有"同声相应",韵诗与歌谣使文字的意义借助声音形象得以对应、强化和贯穿起来,从而营造出无与伦比的文字音乐美。

无韵诗早在13世纪便盛行于意大利,16世纪初由萨里伯爵(Henry Howard, Earl of Surrey)引进英国。1587年,马洛(Christopher Marlowe)的《帖木儿大帝》(Tamburlaine)问世后,无韵诗便在英国盛行起来,同时也成为当时戏剧创作的标准体式。[3]莎士比亚在无韵诗的使用方面虽比马洛晚,但却是这方面的集大成者:戏剧情节中不论是插科打诨,还是抒情叙事,他都能恰如其分地用这种无韵诗体表达;舞台上的人物不论是欣喜若狂,还是暴跳如雷,五音步抑扬格的节奏也能把情绪烘托得惟妙惟肖,哈姆雷特著名

---

[1] Brian Vickers, *The Artistry of Shakespeare's Prose*, London and New York: Routledge, 2005, p. 433.
[2] Eugene F. Shewmaker, "An Introduction to Shakespeare and His Language", in *Shakespeare's Language: A Glossary of Unfamiliar Words in His Plays and Poems*, 2nd Edition, New York: Facts On File, Inc., 2008, p.xv.
[3] Charles Boyce, *Shakespeare A to Z: The Essential Reference to His Plays, His Poems, His Life and Times, and More*, New York: Dell Publishing Group, Inc., 1990, p. 65.

的独白"to be or not to be"就是其中最具有代表性的实例。

美国莎学家赖特认为,抑扬格五音步包含可量化的音节和独特的重音形式。[①]作为一种诗歌语言,乍一看它似乎形式简单,但却拥有令人印象深刻的力量。莎剧无韵诗每行由轻重交替的音节组成,"因为它不受押韵和韵式的束缚而获得跨行的自由,既保持了诗行节奏鲜明的诗歌特点,又最接近于富于伸缩、自由表达的散文优势"[②]。跨行有助于意义的延续,即行断意续。在节奏的驱动下,文本音乐性得以实现,同时又推动戏剧的情节向前发展,使观众从听觉和视觉等方面获得多重审美体验。

2. 散文体与文本音乐性

到目前为止,评论家们对于莎剧中使用散文体的部分有以下两点共识:第一,莎士比亚会根据人物的身份来量身定制言语风格,如王公贵族台词多用无韵诗,小丑、傻子、伶人、侍从或其他受教育程度不高的戏剧人物则用散文体。第二,场合不同,人物的语体也随之各异,如哈姆雷特装疯时在公共场合用散文体,独白却是大段的无韵诗。在《麦克白》和《奥赛罗》两部剧中,信件的内容用散文体来暗示它们在戏剧情节发展中的"他者"身份。

莎士比亚四大悲剧中,诗体和散文体彼此结合、相互协调,共同演绎莎士比亚笔下的人间百态,这就好比一首乐曲中两条独立的旋律线,以不同的声部演奏出一唱三叹的复调音乐——如果说诗体是莎剧文本中的主旋律,那么散文体就是其中不可或缺的衬腔。

四、莎士比亚四大悲剧朱译本中的音乐性

1944年4月,朱生豪记述了他十年埋头伏案翻译莎剧的经历:翻译前,朱生豪收集了各种版本的莎士比亚戏剧集,研究诵读十余遍,自认为对莎士比亚戏剧"颇有会心",他还购买了数量高达"一二百册"之巨的莎剧注释、考证和批评著作,以作参考、研究之用。[③] 1935年春,时任上海世界书局英文编辑的朱生豪在前辈同事詹文浒先生的鼓励下,着手尝试翻译莎士比亚戏剧,及至1942年翻译四大悲剧时,他已历经七年的探索阶

---

① George T. Wright, *Shakespeare's Metrical Art,* Berkeley and Los Angeles: University of California Press, Ltd., 1988, p. 289.
② 蓝仁哲:《莎剧的翻译:从散文体到诗体译本——兼评方平主编〈新莎士比亚全集〉》,《中国翻译》2003年第3期。
③ 莎士比亚:《莎士比亚戏剧全集》(第一辑),译者自序第2页。

段,对莎士比亚的语言特点深有体悟,对剧本的音乐性心领神会。"译者的文笔益进于熟练、流利,所谓炉火纯青的境地。"[①]

朱译莎剧自问世以来便蜚声译坛,赞美之声不绝。台湾大学虞尔昌教授说:"一九四七年秋,我国首次出版的《莎士比亚戏剧全集》译作三辑传到海外,欧美文坛为之震惊,许多莎士比亚研究者简直不敢相信中国人会写出这样高质量的译文。"[②]桂扬清评价朱生豪的译文"既忠实于原文,又流畅自然,也颇典雅"[③]。四大悲剧作为朱译中最令人称道的作品,特别能体现朱生豪的翻译风格和审美取向。

(一)合辙押韵:形散神聚

朱生豪在《译者自序》中说:"每译一段竟,必先自拟为读者,察阅译文中有无暧昧不明之处。又必自拟为舞台上之演员,审辨语调之是否顺口,音节之是否调和。一字一句之未惬,往往苦思累日。"[④]可见他不但追求译文的流畅度,也注重语调和音节的搭配,即韵律的和谐。

1.宏观押韵特征

综合考察朱译莎士比亚四大悲剧的押韵情况,我们发现四个译本中都普遍使用了押韵手段,如图4所示:

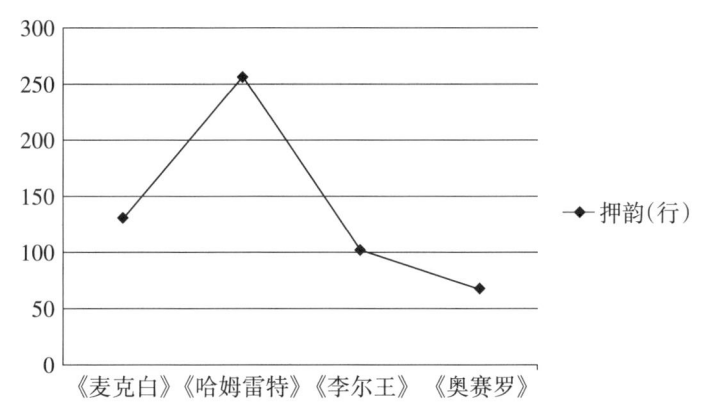

图4 朱译莎士比亚四大悲剧押韵诗行数量统计图

---

① 朱尚刚:《诗侣莎魂:我的父母朱生豪、宋清如》,华东师范大学出版社,1999年,第249页。
② 吴洁敏、朱宏达:《朱生豪传》,上海外语教育出版社,1990年,第129-130页。
③ 桂扬清:《莎剧译文探讨》,《外国语》1986年第4期。
④ 莎士比亚:《莎士比亚戏剧全集》(第一辑),译者自序第2页。

从押韵诗行的数量来看,《奥赛罗》最少,只有68行;《哈姆雷特》最多,高达256行;《麦克白》和《李尔王》的韵诗数量居中。

《奥瑟罗》英语源文本中双行同韵的地方,朱译本不但严格遵循原文的韵式,甚至连音步都亦步亦趋,可谓神形兼备。比如第1幕第3场公爵与勃拉班修时的对话共计18行韵诗,译文保留了原文aa bb cc dd (ee)的韵式,且每行10个音节,与源文本的五音步节奏完全相同。第2幕第3场中,伊阿古的歌谣隔行押韵,5行中第1、3、5行是一个韵,第2、4行是另一个韵,译文也保持了这种隔行押韵的形式。

《哈姆雷特》英语源文本中,戏中戏是韵文,所以译文中押韵的诗行最多不足为奇,这也从一个侧面反映出朱生豪译文在文本音乐性方面的忠实;戏中戏的英语原文是隔行同韵(即abab韵式),译文也保留了这种韵式。第4幕第5场王后的台词中有4行诗,为aabb韵式,朱译不但保留了双行同韵这种韵式,且每行10个字,读起来工整雅训,朗朗上口。奥菲利娅疯癫之后唱了8段歌谣,共计42行,诗行长短各不相同,朱生豪同样以长短不一的歌谣形式译出,唱词还统一使用了abab韵式,这在无形中增添了译文的韵律感和音乐美。

统计数据显示,朱译《李尔王》和《麦克白》的押韵也主要集中在原文为诗体台词的部分,可见诗体台词押韵具有普遍性。除此之外,朱生豪还充分发挥了译者主体性,把英语源文本中一些原本不押韵的无韵诗和散文台词也做了押韵处理。总的来说,朱译莎士比亚四大悲剧中的押韵诗行主要有戏中戏、十四行诗、歌谣、唱词、戏剧人物的对话,以及收场诗,朱生豪在这些诗体译文中展现出对译文韵律的重视,尤其是对音步的苛求;除传统的四言、五言、七言律诗外,朱生豪还尝试了每行八字、九字、十字,甚至十二个字的诗行,力求押韵的诗行之间字数相等,音节相同,节奏近似于英语源文本。

2.微观押韵模式

朱译莎士比亚四大悲剧的押韵类别主要有严韵、宽韵和通韵(偶通和常通)三种,分类统计数据如图5所示:

从图5可以看出,朱译莎士比亚四大悲剧以严韵为主,通韵次之,宽韵最少。以《哈姆雷特》第1幕第2场第87行至第117行为例,31行台词中共有3处押韵:第一处"行"和"动"押宽韵,"心"和"性"是常通,韵式为aabb;第二处句内"起"和"止"押严韵,韵式为aa;第三处"里"和"子"、"臣"和"欣"为严韵,韵式为abab。

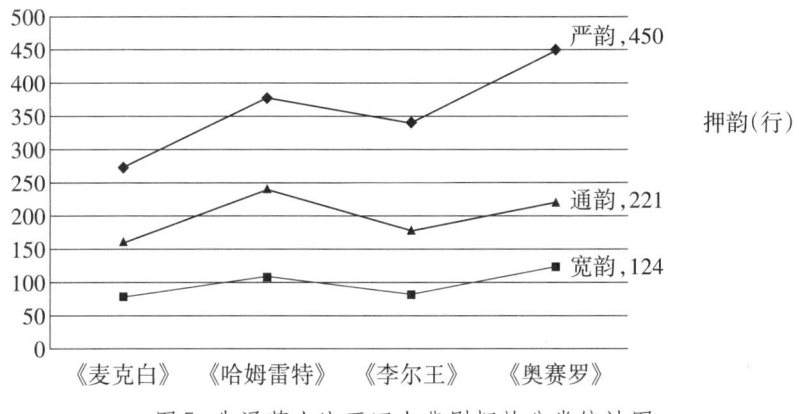

图 5 朱译莎士比亚四大悲剧押韵分类统计图

从分布的位置来看,朱译莎士比亚四大悲剧的押韵主要有句内押韵和句间押韵两种。《李尔王》第3幕第4场的译文"我的良心不允许我全然服从您的女儿的无情的命令"①属于句内押韵,"心"和"您"押的是人辰辙,"情"和"令"押的是中东辙。《麦克白》第1幕第6场译文"我们的犬马微劳,即使加倍报效,比起陛下赐给我们的深恩广泽来,也还是不足挂齿的;我们只有燃起一瓣心香,为陛下祷祝上苍,报答陛下过去和新近加于我们的荣宠"②是句间押韵,"劳"和"效"是遥条辙,"香"和"苍"是江阳辙。这段译文共两个层次,以分号隔开;每个层次3个小句,头两个小句连续押韵,第3个小句不再押韵,从而产生一定的间离效果。随着两个层次的韵脚开口度逐渐加大,声音的洪亮度渐次增加,两个层次叠加形成一种递进关系,麦克白夫人刻意对邓肯国王呈现出来的感激之情显得格外堂皇。这种句尾的开音反复具有强调意味,有助于增强表达的效果,节奏与音色的结合与剧情的发展达到了高度的一致。

音韵是诗歌的基本美学特征之一。以上统计数据和译本实例清楚地表明,押韵是朱译莎士比亚四大悲剧最为突出也最为普遍的语言特点。朱生豪凭借深厚的古典文学功底,灵活运用了头韵、句内韵、句间韵、尾韵等来增强译本的音乐性。这些反复出现的音韵能更好地营造出声音循环往复的音乐感,既有利于内容的表达,也有助于感情的抒发。三种音韵类别中,严韵的声音协调度最高,在朱译莎士比亚四大悲剧中数量也最多,这在一定程度上能够弥补莎士比亚戏剧中素体诗音韵上的缺失。在保留原有韵式的基础上,朱生豪还刻意增译了原文散文语体的音韵,这有助于形成规律性的声韵叠加

---

① 莎士比亚:《莎士比亚戏剧全集》(第一辑),第66页。
② 同上书,第15页。

效果,能有效增强译文的节奏感和音乐性,也更符合汉语译文读者的审美期待。

(二)意顿严密:节奏昭彰

朱光潜把"节奏"定义为"声音大致相等的时间段落里所生的起伏"①。这"大致相等的时间段落"就是声音的单位,比如英语诗歌中的音步与行,汉语诗歌中的句读;"起伏"主要指声音的长短、高低和轻重。英语中凡是两个音节以上的单词都有明确的重音,轻重音节相间排列构成音步(foot),这是英语节奏的基本单位。汉语是以单音节语素为主的语言,每个音节由声母、韵母和声调三部分组成。在汉语的七种节奏形式中,音顿律、声韵律和平仄律是主旋律。②

1.音顿律

音顿律是指由等音节或等音步语句排列组合形成的汉语语音链上的节奏。③音顿律主要利用词、句的艺术安排,通过句序的灵活变动,形成整齐的对仗、排比及偶句等,它最突出的特点便是音节数目或音步数量相同或近似。如《奥赛罗》第1幕第3场公爵的台词"没有更确实显明的证据,单单凭着这些表面上的猜测和莫须有的武断,是不能使人信服的"④中,"表面上的猜测"和"莫须有的武断"就是音节和音步完全相同的音顿律。朱译莎士比亚四大悲剧中,这种对偶句式不胜枚举,四部译本的音顿律总数量如图6所示:

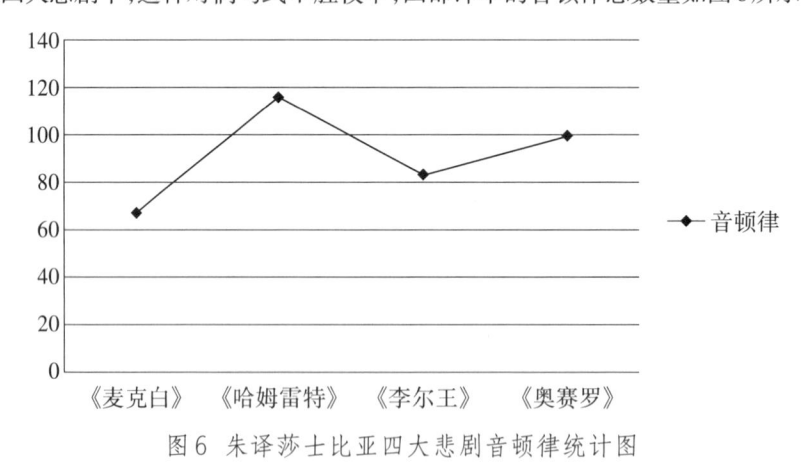

图6 朱译莎士比亚四大悲剧音顿律统计图

---

① 朱光潜:《诗论》,安徽教育出版社,1997年,第139页。
② 倪宝元:《语言学与语文教育》,上海教育出版社,1995年,第114-115页。
③ 秦凌燕、梁华:《和谐的节律:现代散文语音形式美构建模式》,《广西社会科学》2009年第8期。
④ 莎士比亚:《莎士比亚戏剧全集》(第一辑),第15页。

显而易见,《哈姆雷特》音顿律数量最多,这与朱生豪在《莎士比亚戏剧故事》提要中述及的四大悲剧特点有关:《哈姆雷特》侧重人物内心的观照,音顿律能通过相同的句式叠加烘托人物思想活动和心理变化,递进式渲染舞台气氛。

2. 声韵律

在汉语构词中,双声、叠韵、叠音是最常见的语音修辞手段。音色相同或相异的汉字组合有规律地交替出现会产生循环往复的声韵美,这也是汉语节奏的一大特色。朱译莎士比亚四大悲剧中,声韵律的使用比较显著,尤其是借助汉语助词"的"字和"了"字构成的句式出现非常高。译本语料检索的结果显示,"的"字是词频最高的,共8694次;"了"字在词频排列中位居第三,共2019次。数据显示,"的"字主要出现在句末或句中,前者(即"的"字在句末)的频次为762次,后者7932次。根据汉语句法常识,"的"字在句末属于语气助词,往往表达肯定的语气,而"的"字出现在句中就是结构助词,起调节句子节奏的作用。显然,在朱译莎士比亚四大悲剧中,"的"字在绝大多数情况下都是结构助词,它的连续出现形成声韵律。再进一步限定"的"字前后搭配的汉字数量及词类,笔者发现,"的"字前后字数相同的类型相对较少,"的"字后面是双音节词,前面字数并不相等的类型数量较多,具有普遍性。

在《哈姆雷特》第3幕第4场哈姆雷特痛斥母亲时,他说:"一个杀人犯,一个恶徒,一个不及你前夫二百分之一的庸奴,一个戴王冠的丑角,一个盗国窃位的扒儿手!"①这段台词中有两种形式的声韵律和两种音顿律。声韵律包括五组由"一个"领衔的偏正短语和三组"X+的+双音节词"结构(X代表音节不等的汉字组合),音顿律指的是"徒"和"奴"押严韵,"角"和"手"是偶通。朱生豪在这段译文中将声韵律和音顿律结合起来,语音的重复与语义的递进珠联璧合,产生了比单一节奏更有力的情绪推进,将哈姆雷特内心的愤慨与失望表达得淋漓尽致。

3. 平仄律

"汉语是方块字,声调语言,一个字只有一个音节,并无明显确切的重音,因此主要以平仄音调组成诗句,使音节和谐。"②"音乐旋律一般也由两个层次构成:底层是节拍节奏,音的长短、强弱及其相互关系是旋律的基础;上层是调式音阶,由处在一定高低关系

---

① 莎士比亚:《莎士比亚戏剧全集》(第一辑),第82页。
② 黄新渠:《中英诗歌格律的比较与翻译》,《外国语》1992年第4期。

中的固定的几个音构成,通过有规律的重复变化制约音乐中的音高关系。"[①]音乐的声音特征与语言的韵律具有一定的象似性和互拟性,所以在考察文本音乐性时,可将平仄律与乐律贯通起来。

平仄交替的语音模式往往会取得跌宕起伏、错落有致的音乐效果,在莎士比亚四大悲剧英语源文本中,歌谣和韵诗主要通过抑扬格来体现音调的起伏,朱生豪译本中则采用了相对比较松散的平仄律来之对应,如《麦克白》里女巫的唱词:"绕釜环行火融融,毒肝腐脏置其中。"两行唱词前四个字是工整的平仄对称,后三字是完全相同的平仄相叠,平仄律与意顿律交融,读起来对称、均衡、和谐,富有诗意。

语言的音韵和节奏特色同语音密切相关,与词句的搭配安排和句子结构也不无关联。从语料库统计的数据来看,朱译莎士比亚四大悲剧的平仄律使用相对于意顿律和声韵律而言比较有限,平仄相间的现象也并不突出,这从一个侧面反映出朱生豪利用平仄律加强译本音乐性的主观动机并不明显。一方面,这可能是因为文本类型使然,戏剧终究要围绕故事情节展开,因此叙述居于首位,抒情退居其次。另一方面,朱生豪生活的时代正值白话文的文学地位不断上升,这也促使译者在翻译过程中尽可能遵循当时的翻译规范,即更倾向于口语体散文和白话诗体。

五、结语

中国古代文学的诸种样式中,诗歌与音乐的关系最为密切。我国最早的诗歌总集《诗经》里就有颂歌、弦诗、歌诗等,诗歌与音乐的深度融合造就了诗乐一体的文学传统,一直延续至今。在西方的文艺传统中,诗歌与音乐最初也是一体的,它们共同起源于酒神祭典:主祭官与祭祀者披戴着植物枝叶,伴随着竖琴以及其他乐器的演奏对唱,后来演变为朗诵颂神诗,再后来是悲剧表演,这一点在欧里庇得斯《酒神的伴侣》、亚里士多德《诗学》、尼采《悲剧的诞生》中都记述。

然而,每一种语言都有自己独特的语音特点和构成文本音乐美的独特手段。汉语和英语分属不同的语系,在翻译活动中完全移植几乎是不可能的。本文通过实证研究的方法,检测出朱生豪在翻译莎士比亚四大悲剧时在文本音乐性方面做出的不懈努力:

[①] 转引自李飞跃:《中国古典诗歌平仄律的本质与功能》,《北京大学学报》(哲学社会科学版)2016年第3期。

从音韵的悦耳和谐到节奏的抑扬顿挫,从丰富的用韵到音顿律和声韵律的精彩呈现,从韵式的亦步亦趋到格律的开拓创新。在语言的音乐性方面,朱生豪是莎士比亚的知音:朱译莎士比亚四大悲剧不仅贴切地再现了莎士比亚诗剧的语体原貌,也把新文与旧辞巧妙地融合成义明音泽的诗化语言,既为译文增色,也为原文添彩。从这个意义上说,朱译莎剧为莎士比亚作品在中国的传播作出了独特的贡献。

参考文献

Brian Vickers, *The Artistry of Shakespeare's Prose*, London and New York: Routledge, 2005.

Charles Boyce, *Shakespeare A to Z: The Essential Reference to His Plays, His Poems, His Life and Times, and More*, New York: Dell Publishing Group, Inc., 1990.

David Scott Kastan, "'A rarity most beloved': Shakespeare and the Idea of Tragedy", in Richard Dutton and Jane E. Howard, eds., *A Companion to Shakespeare's Works, Volume I: The Tragedies*, Oxford: Blackwell Publishing Ltd., 2003.

Eugene F. Shewmaker, "An Introduction to Shakespeare and His Language", in *Shakespeare's Language: A Glossary of Unfamiliar Words in His Plays and Poems*, 2nd Edition, New York: Facts On File, Inc., 2008.

George T. Wright, *Shakespeare's Metrical Art*, Berkeley and Los Angeles: University of California Press, Ltd., 1988.

曹树钧:《朱生豪论莎士比亚:纪念朱生豪诞生100周年》,《上海戏剧》2012年第12期。

孟宪强:《莎士比亚创作分期新探》,《社会科学战线》1994年第6期。

宋清如:《朱生豪与莎士比亚戏剧》,《新文学史料》1989年第1期。

莎士比亚:《莎士比亚戏剧全集》(第一辑),朱生豪译,世界书局,1947年。

王佐良:《英国诗剧与莎士比亚》,《文学评论》1964年第2期。

蓝仁哲:《莎剧的翻译:从散文体到诗体译本——兼评方平主编〈新莎士比亚全集〉》,《中国翻译》2003年第3期。

朱尚刚:《诗侣莎魂:我的父母朱生豪、宋清如》,华东师范大学出版社,1999年。

吴洁敏、朱宏达:《朱生豪传》,上海外语教育出版社,1990年。

桂扬清:《莎剧译文探讨》,《外国语》1986年第4期。

朱光潜:《诗论》,安徽教育出版社,1997年。

倪宝元:《语言学与语文教育》,上海教育出版社,1995年。

秦凌燕、梁华:《和谐的节律:现代散文语音形式美构建模式》,《广西社会科学》2009年第8期。

黄新渠:《中英诗歌格律的比较与翻译》,《外国语》1992年第4期。

李飞跃:《中国古典诗歌平仄律的本质与功能》,《北京大学学报》(哲学社会科学版)2016年第3期。

译坛论莎

近二十年国内莎士比亚汉译研究博士学位论文调查述评

杨斐然

摘要：近二十年来，莎士比亚汉译研究的博士学位论文已初具规模。作为国内莎士比亚研究的重要组成部分，莎士比亚汉译研究的博士学位论文包含新颖原创的学术思路，多维创新的研究方法，具有重要的学术意义。本文拟对这一时期国内莎士比亚翻译研究博士学位论文进行调查，依据艾布拉姆斯艺术四要素理论，即从文本、译者、读者和世界四个视角出发，总结各角度之下莎士比亚汉译研究的特征与重点。透过这一时期的博士学位论文，厘清近二十年来中国莎士比亚汉译研究的现状，阐述各侧重的特征，发现其中存在的问题，进行学术史的梳理，以期促进未来中国莎士比亚汉译的研究。

关键词：莎士比亚；翻译研究；博士学位论文；艾布拉姆斯

作者简介：杨斐然，西南大学外国语学院博士研究生，主要研究方向为文学翻译、莎士比亚研究。

一、引言

莎士比亚的名字进入中国以来，至今一百多年的时间里，掀起了一段"说不完且译不完"的"莎学"浪潮。1949年以后，中国的莎士比亚翻译及研究虽然兴盛，但是各类学术期刊与报纸上发表的对后世有影响的文章只有150篇左右[1]。20世纪末，中国莎士比亚学会的成立使这种状况有了很大改观。特别是进入21世纪以来，中国莎学的研究无

---

[1] 陆谷孙：《莎士比亚研究十讲》，复旦大学出版社，2005年，第153页。

疑进入了鼎盛时期：中国学者开始有规模、有组织地参加国际莎学盛会；各地成立莎士比亚学会、研究会，举办一系列活动、论坛、戏剧节等等；莎士比亚翻译、评论、教学、演出、文化交流与互鉴等领域百花齐放。

莎士比亚作品的翻译、评论与研究、戏剧的演出，形成了中国莎士比亚传播史上三足鼎立的局面。前者是后两者的基础，占据重要地位。但是我们在以往的莎学研究中，却忽视了对莎士比亚翻译研究特点的了解以及理论上的归纳。[1]我国翻译研究已进入独立学科阶段，21世纪以来的头二十年是我国译学发展史上最富成果的时期。[2]在此背景下，总结回顾近二十年国内莎士比亚作品翻译研究成果，无疑是必要的。

21世纪以来，莎士比亚作品汉译研究在我国已取得丰硕成果，期刊论文、学术著作、学位论文等层出不穷。其中，博士学位论文是高等学校或研究机构的学生完成学业的最终成果，论文的选题往往涉及本学科的热点和难点，展示了该领域的前沿成果，反映了学科的潜在发展趋势，有相当高的学术参考价值，以及独特的科研价值。莎士比亚作品翻译研究博士学位论文是莎士比亚翻译研究的重要组成部分，目前学界尚未对这部分的博士学位论文进行系统性研究。本文以近二十年国内莎士比亚作品翻译研究博士学位论文为研究对象[3]，以艾布拉姆斯艺术批评四要素为视角，对博士学位论文进行综观整合研究，探索21世纪以来莎士比亚汉译研究的特色、动向甚至不足，从博士学位论文视角勾勒出一段21世纪以来中国莎士比亚汉译研究的学术史。

二、艾布拉姆斯艺术四要素理论与翻译研究

艾布拉姆斯在他的著作《镜与灯：浪漫主义文论及批评传统》(*The Mirror and the Lamp: Romantic Theory and the Critical Tradition*)(1958)中提出了艺术批评的坐标系，由四个要素构成，即作品(work)、艺术家(artist)、世界(universe)和受众(audience)[4]。该理论指出，任何艺术作品都包含四个分析层面，即作品本身、作品的创作者、与作品相关

---

[1] 李伟民：《中国莎士比亚批评史》，中国戏剧出版社，2006年，第273页。
[2] 方梦之：《中国译学的主体性和原创性——新范畴、新概念、新表述探源》，《中国翻译》2023年第3期。
[3] 本文的研究对象为2000—2022年期间，国内关于莎士比亚作品汉译研究相关的博士学位论文。资料主要来源于中国知网、万方数据、中国国家图书馆等数据库，以及北京大学、清华大学、北京外国语大学等高校图书馆学位论文数据库。
[4] 艾布拉姆斯：《镜与灯：浪漫主义文论及批评传统》，郦稚牛、张照进、童庆生译，北京大学出版社，2004年，第4页。

的历史社会环境,以及作品的欣赏者。作品处于中心位置,关联着文学活动四个要素,整个活动是围绕着作品展开的。文学批评的进行需建立在以作品为核心的基点上,四个要素在文学活动中相互渗透、相互依存、相互作用。作品的艺术形态凝聚着现实与艺术家的联系,是创作活动的成果,也是连接艺术家与受众的桥梁。受众通过作品去理解与感受生活,扩大生活的视野。文学研究必须从整体性出发,避免孤立地分析各个要素。这一理论与系统论的原则不谋而合,也为人们进行艺术分类、构建理论体系、探索不同的文艺思潮和流派,以及比较不同的理论及其演变提供了依据和方法。[1]艾布拉姆斯提倡批评的多元化、视角的多样性,而且多重视角的整合能够得到"深度视角"。[2]

文学作品的翻译不单是语言的转换,或是语言外形的变化,还是语言学、文学、美学等学科知识的综合性运用。一方面,从文学的视角来看,文学的语言具有丰富的内涵,文学的形式存在文学性,这是文学区别于其他艺术门类的根本特性。[3]从语言学的视角来看,翻译应该首先从文本出发,关注文学作品本身的语言形式、风格特征等。另一方面,人们总以为作品不是由作品本身来解释的,而是由作者的人格或者由决定这种人格的环境来解释的[4]。作者是文本的生产者,产出的文本汇聚了审美经验与情感意义,读者赋予了文本意义,延长了文本存在的生命。所以,艾布拉姆斯的艺术批评四要素可以用于框定翻译研究的对象。

20世纪下半叶以来,当代西方翻译研究实现了三大根本性的突破:翻译研究从语言间的对等研究深入到对翻译行为本身的深层探究,翻译研究不再局限于文本本身,重点关注译作的生产和消费过程,并且翻译被放在一个宏大的文化语境中去审视。[5]学界逐渐认识到翻译研究作为一门独立学科的性质,看到了翻译研究的多学科特征,与语言学、文学,还有社会学、心理学等学科密不可分。可见,西方翻译研究的关注点从译本、译者逐渐转向社会文化,即宏大的世界。在近三十多年的时间里,中国学界通过翻译或影印原书,出版了"国外翻译研究丛书""外研社翻译研究文库""当代西方翻译研究译丛"等系列丛书。这些引进著作为中国的翻译研究者提供了一手文献,开阔了他们的学

---

[1] 周宪:《艺术四要素理论与西方文论的演变——艾布拉姆斯〈镜与灯〉评述》,《南京师大学报》(社会科学版)1986年第4期。
[2] 高继海:《艾布拉姆斯诗学观简论》,《英美文学研究论丛》2012年第2期。
[3] 朱立元:《当代西方文艺理论》,华东师范大学出版社,2014年,第2页。
[4] 杜夫海纳:《美学与哲学》,孙非译,中国社会科学出版社,1985年,第156页。
[5] 谢天振:《当代西方翻译研究的三大突破和两大转向》,《四川外语学院学报》2003年第5期。

术视野,中国的翻译理论逐渐与国际译论高度融合。[①]于是,受国际翻译研究的影响,中国的翻译研究也出现文化转向,译者逐渐"登场",语言学派翻译理论一统天下的格局被打破,而后翻译研究的路径出现了多元化趋势。

因此,翻译活动不是孤立的,而是一项具有复杂性、整体性和多维性的活动。作品即原文与译文,占据翻译活动的核心地位,与其余几个要素相互角力。若仅仅局限在一个领域进行研究,则无法揭示翻译的性质及活动规律。艾布拉姆斯提出的艺术批评四要素正好契合翻译研究的各角度。

三、作品文本视角:语言、文化及文体之争

艾布拉姆斯的艺术批评四要素是一个完整的艺术系统,作品是中心,将其他三要素关联起来。翻译研究的角度里,作品即是原文本与译文本。近二十年国内莎士比亚翻译研究博士学位论文中,大部分是从文本角度进行探究。其中,对文本中的语言、意象、文体、文化及译本质量等进行的研究占据大多数。

作为语言大师的莎士比亚,在其作品中展示了独特的语言创造能力以及善于操纵和发展语言词汇意义的能力,使其语言成为讨论的热门话题。如在笔者收集的博士学位论文中,多有涉及莎剧中的称谓、双关语、话语标记词、人称代词、情态谓词、语序变异、指令表达等语言现象的讨论。

从近二十年相关博士学位论文来看,研究莎士比亚戏剧译本中语言现象的论文主要出自北京外国语大学。王瑞的《莎剧中称谓的翻译》[②]主要研究莎剧全集中的人名以及《温莎的快活娘子》[③]、《亨利四世·上》、《亨利四世·下》和《亨利五世》中的第二人称代词you和thou以及名词性称谓的翻译,采用社会—语用分析视角,对现有几个主要的莎剧翻译版本相关内容进行比较,对三类称谓进一步分类,针对具体类别尝试提出相应的原则和方法。这篇博士论文不仅呈现了莎剧中的"称谓"翻译,还展示了莎剧原文本以及汉译本的爬梳,以及"称谓"的系统比较和背后的文化因素等。段素萍的《莎士比亚戏剧中语序变异的汉译——以〈哈姆雷特〉译本为例》[④]以功能语言学为理论框架,调查《哈姆雷特》

[①] 王克非:《关于翻译理论及其发展史研究》,《上海翻译》2021年第6期。
[②] 王瑞:《莎剧中称谓的翻译》,北京外国语大学,2007年。
[③] 即《温莎的风流娘儿们》(朱生豪译名)。
[④] 段素萍:《莎士比亚戏剧中语序变异的汉译——以〈哈姆雷特〉译本为例》,北京外国语大学,2013年。

中不改变命题意义的非常规语序句,分析原文中语序变异的理据,讨论现有5个译本的处理,寻求实现译文与原文在语序形式与功能上最大程度契合的途径。除了段素萍的研究是句法层面的讨论,其余都是对特定词汇的研究。谢世坚的《莎士比亚剧本中话语标记语的汉译》以韩礼德(Halliday)和哈桑(Hassan)关于语言三大元功能的理论为基础,探讨《罗密欧与茱莉叶之悲剧》[①]、《一报还一报》和《温莎的风流娘儿们》三部戏剧中9个话语标记语的用法、意义、功能及其翻译。管兴忠的《莎士比亚〈温莎的风流娘儿们〉剧中的指令及其汉译》[②]对《温莎的风流娘儿们》一剧中一种重要而常见的言语举动"指令"汉译进行分类,比较朱生豪、梁实秋及方平的译本,从句法、词汇和篇章手段探讨剧中指令的表达及其语力传译。吴边的《莎士比亚〈一报还一报〉里情态谓词的汉译研究》[③]和庞密香的《莎剧 Measure for Measure 和 Romeo and Juliet 中人称代词汉译的语用学和语义学研究》[④]将莎剧中的特定词汇、情态谓词(can, may, must, will 和 shall)及人称代词(we 和第三人称代词)作为研究对象,把译文分为"形式和意义都对应""形式不对应,意义对应""形式对应,意义不对应""形式和意义都不对应"四种情况,分别从翻译对等角度及语用学和语义学的角度进行探讨。以上6篇博士论文均是对莎剧中某一语言现象的汉译进行深入挖掘,除此以外,上海交通大学刘慧丹的博士论文《基于语料库的莎士比亚戏剧汉译本中情感意义的再现与重构研究》[⑤]以15部莎剧中的典型情感词及其表达的情感意义为研究对象,考察梁实秋和朱生豪译本中对原文情感意义的传达。

值得一提的是,大多数莎译研究者忽略了原文的版本问题。莎士比亚著作的版本,不仅是一个学术问题,也是一个理论问题。[⑥]莎剧的版本之多,再现原作的精神风貌必然涉及原作的版本问题。[⑦]以上博士论文大多指出了原剧本、版本及译本的选择,所以必须考虑各译本所依据的差异。这样的研究基础可靠,得出的结论铿锵有力。

从语言学视角对莎作译本进行考察是一大趋势,对剧文本中意象、概念隐喻等文化维度翻译的探究又是另一大研究热点。仇蓓玲的《美的变迁——论莎士比亚戏剧文本

---

① 即《罗密欧与朱丽叶》(朱生豪译名)。
② 管兴忠:《莎士比亚〈温莎的风流娘儿们〉剧中的指令及其汉译》,北京外国语大学,2013年。
③ 吴边:《莎士比亚〈一报还一报〉里情态谓词的汉译研究》,北京外国语大学,2017年。
④ 庞密香:《莎剧 Measure for Measure 和 Romeo and Juliet 中人称代词汉译的语用学和语义学研究》,北京外国语大学,2019年。
⑤ 刘慧丹:《基于语料库的莎士比亚戏剧汉译本中情感意义的再现与重构研究》,上海交通大学,2015年。
⑥ 罗益民:《莎士比亚十四行诗版本批评史》,科学出版社,2016年。
⑦ 陈国华:《论莎剧重译(下)》,《外语教学与研究》1997年第3期。

中意象的汉译》①通过分析莎剧译本中的意象在朱生豪、梁实秋、方平译本中的传递,审视经典文学作品复译这一既定的历史现象,由此解读翻译主体审美心理和文化心态的变迁。刘翼斌的《概念隐喻翻译的认知分析——基于〈哈姆雷特〉对比语料库研究》②对梁实秋和朱生豪《哈姆雷特》译本中的概念隐喻进行了穷尽而系统的识别,对剧中的"悲"主题、"仇""玄""喜"次主题下的隐喻意象进行认知解读,重构悲剧意义方面的特色和得失,管窥译者的认知理据和心理机制。莎剧中的隐喻及意象等丰富多彩,两位作者都对某一主题下的意象进行了分类,举例阐述其特点和作用,将最新莎学成果融入了莎译研究中,具有重要的理论及实践意义。

除了对莎士比亚作品译本中某一语言现象进行深究,对莎剧译本进行综合性研究也有一定占比。龚芬的《论戏剧语言的翻译——莎剧多译本比较》③通过对戏剧语言特征的分析,戏剧翻译理论的论述,个案研究如《罗密欧与朱丽叶》的可演性翻译以及《哈姆雷特》的多译本比较,对戏剧语言的翻译进行了多角度的讨论。李春江的《莎士比亚戏剧汉译研究》④对莎剧译本中的典故、习俗、意象、宗教等文化维度的因素进行了调查。他认为,译者在处理文化因素的过程中,社会意识形态与文化语境对译者的选择产生了重要的影响。莎士比亚戏剧翻译实践的发展,与莎士比亚戏剧原文本和译文本的文体之争是动态发展的。综观莎士比亚戏剧汉译史,一直存在"散文体译本"和"诗体译本"的讨论。李春江在文中探讨了莎士比亚诗剧的美学特征,译者对原文文体的处理方法及效果,素体诗与散文体对戏剧美学的贡献。该博士论文涉及了莎士比亚戏剧译本的文化、文体等各方面内容,具有重要的实践指导意义。张威的《莎士比亚戏剧汉译定量分析研究》⑤采用实证研究方法对梁实秋和朱生豪四部莎剧译本进行定量分析,分别从译本的基本特征、"音乐化"、"欧化"、"译语化"等视角进行考察,并对译者和译作风格进行阐释。此类研究多数集中在朱生豪、梁实秋及方平的译本,剧本倾向于众人熟知的四大悲剧和四大喜剧,运用了翻译研究中的数字人文方法,避免了传统经验性的分析,具有一定的理论与实践意义。萧文乾的《历久弥新:〈哈姆雷特〉汉译研究:1867—2013》⑥

---

① 仇蓓玲:《美的变迁——论莎士比亚戏剧文本中意象的汉译》,南京大学,2005年。
② 刘翼斌:《概念隐喻翻译的认知分析——基于〈哈姆雷特〉对比语料库研究》,上海外国语大学,2010年。
③ 龚芬:《论戏剧语言的翻译——莎剧多译本对比》,上海外国语大学,2004年。
④ 李春江:《莎士比亚戏剧汉译研究》,四川大学,2009年。
⑤ 张威:《莎士比亚戏剧汉译定量分析研究》,上海外国语大学,2014年。
⑥ 萧文乾:《历久弥新:〈哈姆雷特〉汉译研究:1867—2013》,清华大学,2015年。

则聚焦《哈姆雷特》的百年汉译史,对该剧的汉译历程进行了提炼浓缩,对17个汉译译本进行个评,最后将"格律"作为观察点进行深入研究。该研究获取第一首《哈姆雷特》汉译入华的第一手史料,译史资料翔实,译评规范,为学界的《哈姆雷特》汉译研究提供了崭新一瞥。张汩的《朱生豪莎士比亚戏剧翻译手稿及刊印本版本对比研究》[①]则另辟蹊径,以朱生豪莎士比亚戏剧翻译手稿以及不同时期的刊印本为语料,采用"描写——解释"的研究方式对语料进行研究,找出手稿修改处和书稿与刊印本之间的差异后进行深度描写与分析,并对这些翻译行为进行解释。此研究关注文本生成的动态过程,并且通过研究手稿,也揭示了译者的动态决策过程。

莎士比亚是一名伟大的戏剧家,也是一名技艺精湛的诗人。他创作的十四行诗被认为是英国诗歌,甚至世界文学领域的巅峰之作。近二十年国内莎士比亚作品汉译研究博士学位论文中,对莎士比亚十四行诗的研究也不少。万江松的《翻译中的诗学:莎士比亚十四行诗汉译研究》[②]以翻译诗学为理论框架,对莎士比亚十四行诗的汉译进行翻译诗学的构成性研究和功能性研究,细考译本形态,探索翻译与诗学的相互影响,同时对屠岸、曹明伦、辜正坤译本进行了全译本分析研究。陈庆的《诗歌意象翻译情感研究:基于情感计算的认知分析》[③]创新地采用人工智能与人类智能结合的方式,结合认知语言学和人文研究质性方法,计算《莎士比亚十四行诗》译作的各种情感值,研究译作的情感表现和背后的根源,将情感研究从纯思辨型推向量化和定性结合的范式。这些研究既采用了传统翻译研究范式,又大胆尝试了人工智能研究方法,体现了学者们勇于创新的学术思维和精神。

四、译者视角:从隐形到显形的转变

作为原作与译作对接的桥梁,译者在翻译活动中扮演着重要角色。在早期的翻译研究中,译者处于边缘地位,常被看作原作者的仆人、舌人、搬运工等。溯源中西方翻译史,可发现原作与译作、原作者与译者的关系常是二元对立的。道格拉斯·鲁宾逊(Douglas Robinson)在著作《译者登场》(*The Translator's Turn*)中提出了一种新的翻译

[①] 张汩:《朱生豪莎士比亚戏剧翻译手稿及刊印本版本对比研究》,北京航空航天大学,2017年。
[②] 万江松:《翻译中的诗学:莎士比亚十四行诗汉译研究》,四川大学,2015年。
[③] 陈庆:《诗歌意象翻译情感研究:基于情感计算的认知分析》,广东外语外贸大学,2017年。

研究范式,解构西方主流翻译理论中的二元论,提出"翻译身体学"(the somatics of translation),将翻译研究的重点聚焦在"人"上,关注译者在翻译过程中的个人身体感受和主观能动性。[1]劳伦斯·韦努蒂(Lawrence Venuti)在代表作《译者的隐身:一部翻译史》(*The Translator's Invisibility: A History of Translation*)中提出,应该改变译者的隐身状态,提高译者的身份,译者与原文作者享有同等地位。[2]由此,近年来翻译研究的文化转向促使译者从"隐形"向"显性"转变[3],译者逐渐从边缘走向中心。近二十年来关于莎士比亚翻译研究的博士学位论文中,不缺少对莎士比亚作品译者的研究,研究角度各异,对译者的翻译观、翻译风格、翻译策略等有详细的讨论。

对于莎剧译者的研究主要以朱生豪和梁实秋为中心,旁及方平、卞之琳、英若诚诸人;对于莎士比亚十四行诗译者的研究则围绕屠岸、梁宗岱、辜正坤、曹明伦等人进行讨论。严晓江的《梁实秋中庸翻译观研究》[4]从分析梁实秋翻译的《莎士比亚全集》入手,从宏观和微观上构建梁实秋的翻译观,指出梁译莎作具有明显的"中庸"特点。《梁实秋与西方文学》[5]是吉林大学文学院赵慧的博士论文。该文对梁实秋的文艺思想和西方文学翻译进行了全面客观的评价。梁实秋的翻译作品众多,但是成就最高,最能体现他的翻译观和翻译风格的就是对莎士比亚全集的翻译。作者指出,梁实秋的莎译忠信可靠却文采不足,瑕瑜互见,文采不足是忠信可靠的代价,是"学者的译本",具有不可取代的地位。山东大学文学院吕丽丽的《梁实秋文学翻译研究》[6]梳理了梁实秋的文学翻译史,考察了梁实秋对中国文学和翻译学的历史影响和当代价值。梁实秋凭一己之力完成四十册《莎士比亚全集》的翻译,历经五四运动、抗战以及新中国三个时期。梁实秋的莎译研究是该文的一部分,作者回归文学历史语境,结合文学活动、文艺思想、文化立场等多维度视角,对梁实秋的莎译活动进行了拓展研究。

对朱生豪译莎活动专门进行研究的博士学位论文有两篇。刘云雁的《朱生豪莎剧翻译——影响与比较》[7]是第一部关于朱生豪翻译研究的博士论文。该论文从影响和比较的角度,探讨了朱生豪译文产生的文学传统背景以及对中国的长期影响。段自力的

---

[1] Douglas Robinson, *The Translator's Turn*, Baltimore: The Johns Hopkins University Press,1991.
[2] Lawrence Venuti, *The Translator's Invisibility: A History of Translation*, New York: Routledge,1995.
[3] 王亚、文军:《国内译者研究30年:现状与展望》,《外国语文》2023年第4期。
[4] 严晓江:《梁实秋中庸翻译观研究》,南京大学,2007年。
[5] 赵慧:《梁实秋与西方文学》,吉林大学,2015年。
[6] 吕丽丽:《梁实秋文学翻译研究》,山东大学,2021年。
[7] 刘云雁:《朱生豪莎剧翻译——影响与比较》,浙江大学,2011年。

《朱生豪莎剧翻译经典化研究》①以文学经典化理论为依据,从定量和定性的视角,探索了朱译莎剧经典化的内外因素及其在经典中形成的作用。朱生豪在战火纷飞、条件极端艰苦的情况下,翻译卷帙浩繁的《莎士比亚全集》,积劳成疾,英年早逝。两篇博士论文从不同角度均谈到朱译的影响以及对当代的启示,提供了两个全面立体的研究成果。

除了对莎译两大巨头——朱生豪和梁实秋的研究,近二十年国内博士学位论文中还有触及其他译者的。田汉翻译的《哈孟雷特》是中国第一部用白话文完成的莎士比亚剧作。在王林的《论田汉的戏剧译介与艺术实践》②一文中,虽没对其翻译的《哈姆雷特》和《罗密欧与朱丽叶》进行细节性研究,但是对田汉进行莎作翻译的历史背景做了注解。任晓霏的《"译者登场"——英若诚戏剧翻译研究》③在系统整体范式的指导下,对英若诚的翻译实践进行全景式研究,其中涉及英若诚翻译的莎剧《请君入瓮》(*Measure for Measure*)。作者研究发现,英若诚的戏剧翻译实践注重"舞台性",时刻以戏剧舞台表演为参照,对《请君入瓮》译本中意象、话轮转换、声韵、节奏等进行分析,发现此译本保留了优美诗篇和叫座好戏的双重艺术生命力。莎作翻译的另一大家是卞之琳。肖曼琼的《翻译家卞之琳研究》④在对卞之琳的译介活动做了全景扫描的基础上,探索其翻译思想以及翻译研究的思想和价值。卞之琳对莎士比亚四大悲剧的诗体翻译在翻译界产生了巨大影响。人们对莎剧译本重译的争论,主要是批评它们没有做到以诗译诗⑤。该文作者研究发现,卞之琳通过对英汉诗歌音律的深入研究,坚持用五音顿不押韵诗行翻译四大悲剧中五音步一行的素体诗。卞之琳的译本也不是纯诗体译本,而是莎剧丰富多彩形式的忠实呈现。

近年来,认知科学与翻译学的深度融合,促使了认知翻译学的迅速发展,越来越多的学者致力于通过"认知翻译学"来探索译者行为等译者认知活动和心理行为的研究⑥。由此,现已有将认知翻译学引入莎士比亚汉译译者研究的博士学位论文。董典的《文学翻译中的认知识解操作——以〈麦克白〉的五个汉译本为例》⑦研究了莎士比亚戏剧中心理描写的佳作《麦克白》,通过对比辜正坤、戴望舒、朱生豪、梁实秋、卞之琳五名译者的

---

① 段自力:《朱生豪莎剧翻译经典化研究》,四川大学,2013年。
② 王林:《论田汉的戏剧译介与艺术实践》,复旦大学,2003年。
③ 任晓霏:《"译者登场"——英若诚戏剧翻译研究》,上海外国语大学,2008年。
④ 肖曼琼:《翻译家卞之琳研究》,湖南师范大学,2010年。
⑤ 陈国华:《论莎剧重译(上)》,《外语教学与研究》1997年第2期。
⑥ 文旭、张钰奇:《认知翻译学研究新进展》,《上海翻译》2023年第1期。
⑦ 董典:《文学翻译中的认知识解操作——以〈麦克白〉的五个汉译本为例》,西南大学,2021年。

译本,探索译者在文学翻译过程中的认知识解操作。作者在文中说,该研究采用的是将传统的描写与解释结合的方法用于探索翻译的认知活动,存在一定的局限性。文章虽是以现有文本作为出发点,但作者在其中发现,翻译是译者"认知"的结果,译者认知的核心要素便是认知识解。由此来看,该文探讨了认知识解分析对于文学翻译研究和评价的意义,具有一定的参考价值。

对于莎士比亚作品译者的研究,近二十年国内博士学位论文大多集中在以上的翻译家,但是莎士比亚作品汉译译者是一个数量不少的群体,还有部分莎作译者亟待深入式研究。

五、译本读者视角:接受主体与审美距离

受众(audience)是艾布拉姆斯提出的艺术批评坐标系下的要素之一,既是翻译研究中的读者,也是一个完整翻译活动中的一环。从接受美学的角度来看,译文本身不能产生独立的意义,读者的阅读才是文学审美观照活动的开始。译文的再现过程也是读者的接受过程,如此才能达到文本的彻底完成。莎士比亚进入中国以来的一百多年时间里,翻译主体和译本接受群体也在不断发生变化。在近二十年国内莎士比亚翻译研究博士学位论文中,研究者们使用了多元化的手段来观察读者对译文的接受度。

仇蓓玲的《美的变迁——论莎士比亚戏剧文本中意象的汉译》通过剖析20世纪30年代至今中国读者的接受特征发展演变,了解了莎剧朱生豪、梁实秋、方平三种译本的目的语读者期待视野的变化。刘云雁的《朱生豪莎剧翻译——影响与比较》关注的是,相比其他译者的译文,受众对朱生豪译本的好感度。于是在最后一个章节中,作者使用了问卷调查的方式对此进行考察。段自力的《朱生豪莎剧翻译经典化研究》将朱生豪译莎剧的传播和接受看作其经典化的外因。由此,在文学经典的建构中,读者分为两类,知识精英和普通读者。对于朱译莎剧的接受研究,作者区分为专家学者的接受以及大众读者的接受,读者群体覆盖专家、教育界、翻译家、出版社、普通读者、话剧及戏剧观众。作者别具匠心地将朱生豪莎剧原译的"补译和校译"看作其接受的一个特殊层面,这是不少研究者忽略的一部分。

近二十年国内莎士比亚作品翻译研究博士学位论文中,除了对莎士比亚戏剧译本读者进行考察以外,对莎士比亚十四行诗的读者接受也有涉及。申玉革的《多视角下的莎士比亚十四行诗经典化研究》中提到翻译作为文学系统中的一个要素,参与了莎士比

亚十四行诗经典的塑造。对于莎士比亚十四行诗在中国的读者接受,作者通过梳理它在中国的翻译史及研究史发现,异彩纷呈的莎士比亚十四行诗翻译推动了它在中国的传播和影响,使其不局限于专家学者学院式的考证,也被普通读者所接受。反之,从精英化到通俗化,受众的增加也促使了莎士比亚十四行诗的经典化。

六、世界视角:社会、文化及思想

艾布拉姆斯提出的universe,一般译为宇宙或者世界,在翻译研究中,可以理解为除了译者和译本读者以外的其他外部环境因素。正如安德烈·勒菲弗尔(Andre Lefevere)所说,"翻译不是在真空中发生的"[1]。由于现实原因,译者受意识形态、赞助人、诗学等的影响进行翻译活动。反过来看,莎士比亚作品的汉译在中国又影响着目的语的社会、文化和思想,也融入到其发展之中。

叶庄新的《跨越文化的戏剧旅程:莎士比亚于中国现代戏剧》[2]探讨了20世纪上半叶50年间莎士比亚在中国的译介、演出、评论的演进,论述了莎士比亚对中国现代戏剧的历史作用。作者研究指出,莎士比亚的作品没有在中国话剧史上引起轰动效应,但是却处处留痕,在中国现代剧坛留下了若隐若现的足迹。

侯靖靖的《婆娑一世界,扮演两扇门——1949—1966年间英美戏剧在中国的译介研究》[3]和温年芳的《系统中的戏剧翻译——以1977—2010年英美戏剧汉译为例》,尽管研究理论基础和研究方法不一样,但是前者是后者的研究起点,两者贯通了1949年至2010年的英美戏剧译介史,其中涉及莎士比亚戏剧在中国的译介研究。侯靖靖谈到了1949—1966年诗学理论对莎士比亚的选择。经过分析得出,莎士比亚戏剧在此期间以译介34部之多高居榜首,主要原因是当时的赞助体系、诗学理念、特殊的国际关系历史语境、莎剧自身的艺术魅力及其所蕴含的现实主义精神。温年芳将1977—2010年的英美戏剧汉译看作翻译文学的子系统,分为三个时期进行历时性考察。通过剖析三个时期中的意识形态、戏剧诗学、赞助体系、翻译选材变化以及文化建构作用,探索这一时期英美戏剧翻译的全貌。其中,莎士比亚戏剧的翻译贯穿三个时期,在各时期现实影响下

---

[1] Andre Lefevere, *Translation History Culture: A Sourcebook*, New York: Routledge, 1992, p. 14.
[2] 叶庄新:《跨越文化的戏剧旅程:莎士比亚于中国现代戏剧》,福建师范大学,2007年。
[3] 侯靖靖:《婆娑一世界,扮演两扇门——1949—1966年间英美戏剧在中国的译介研究》,上海外国语大学,2008年。

呈现出不同特点。

五四时期戏剧的翻译以狂奔突进之势介入新文化运动,莎士比亚戏剧的译介是这一时期不可不提及的话题。卢贝贝的《五四时期戏剧翻译研究》[①]从五四语境、翻译戏剧的文本特征、副文本与翻译戏剧的接受、戏剧翻译中的误译与改写以及对中国话剧创作的影响出发,探究了五四时期中国的翻译戏剧。文中虽未对莎士比亚戏剧翻译进行专题研究,但是通过分析,作者指出,莎士比亚戏剧虽被主流话语边缘化,但仍有不少译介。魏策策的《思想视域下的莎士比亚符码》[②]则另辟蹊径,从符号学和传播学角度对现代中国思想视域下的莎士比亚译介、演出及经典化进行深度挖掘。文中专设章节对早期莎剧译介与现代中国民族国家的建构进行细微洞察,深入论证莎剧对中国社会的思想、政治、文化等领域的影响。

七、未结束的结语

近二十年国内莎士比亚汉译的博士学位论文研究涉及翻译学、外国语言学及应用语言学、英语语言文学、比较文学与世界文学、中国现当代文学等学科,由此可见莎士比亚汉译研究的跨学科性和多学科性。不同学科下的研究范式不尽相同,显示出翻译研究范式的多元化特征。

莎作翻译文本视角下的研究,自然离不开从作品的语言现象入手。一方面,从近二十年此领域的博士学位论文可看出,以语言学为主,如系统功能语言学、认知语言学、语料库语言学等,对莎作译本的研究仍是研究者的首选出发点之一,且都倾向对多个译本中的语言现象、文化意象、典故等进行比较研究。另一方面,随着现代科学的发展,除了传统质的观察外,研究者愈加热衷于采用数字人文技术,使其研究更具科学性与说服力。对于莎剧文类的选择,大多集中在悲喜剧和十四行诗,对长诗、历史剧、传奇剧等译本的研究占比较少。莎士比亚作品译者的研究主要从译者主体性、译者风格、译者翻译思想、译者经典化等视角进行剖析,但是研究重合度较高,大多偏重21世纪以前的莎作译者。由于《莎士比亚全集》的翻译活动一直持续到21世纪的今天,朱生豪、梁实秋、方平等译者的译本不断再版的同时,也有其他译者加入其中。新世纪以来,莎士比亚研究

---

① 卢贝贝:《五四时期戏剧翻译研究》,西南大学,2021年。
② 魏策策:《思想视域下的莎士比亚符码》,华东师范大学,2013年。

有了新成果,翻译研究有了新发展,莎士比亚作品翻译也有了新版本,对于这部分的莎作译者,研究相对零散,未来也可增加对这部分译者群像的研究;研究的方法也可从"译者行为批评"等创新性理论视角进行系统性探索。

读者接受是衡量作品译介效果的重要标尺,莎士比亚作品汉译的读者接受研究在近二十年来的博士学位论文中并不丰硕,而是载于其余视角的研究中,主要从读者期待视野、接受美学及视域融合等角度进行考察。研究者通过收集学者的评论与批评、网络书评、图书馆记录、读者问卷、访谈等材料进行调查,兼顾专家型与大众型读者的接受,给莎作译本的读者研究带来了新的可能。如今,随着莎士比亚的普及度越来越高,针对不同年龄段的读者有不同翻译改写版的莎士比亚作品,如罗益民针对青少年读者翻译的《莎士比亚漫画版》(2023)、针对儿童读者翻译改编的《给孩子讲莎士比亚》系列等。对这一部分读者接受进行考察,可以补缺莎士比亚作品翻译改编在中国低龄人群中的接受传播研究。

世界视角下的莎士比亚汉译研究主要集中在各特定历史时期的意识形态、诗学理念、赞助人等视角,剖析各时期莎士比亚的译介与社会、文化、思想的相互影响。莎作译本中承载的各类政治、经济、社会、文化、博物学等知识,尚待学界深入挖掘,以继续探寻这一人类文学奥林匹克上的宙斯的奥秘。

四百年来,莎士比亚成了一个万人迷,各行各业的饭碗、文化的衣食父母[①]。更甚的是,莎士比亚的作品包罗万象,是那个时代的精神产品[②]。莎士比亚作品的汉译则是无数中国人的精神食粮,上至龙钟老叟,下至满面红光的孩童,纷纷转动这一绚丽万花筒,打开美丽新世界。近二十年来,国内莎士比亚翻译研究已攀高峰,特别是这一领域的博士学位论文,每一篇都凝聚着研究者对莎士比亚以及翻译研究学术上的热情与智慧,值得每一位读者认真品味。二十年是一时段,足以见思想之演变、范式之兴替、问题之浮现。本文是莎士比亚汉译研究学术史沧海中的一粟,以期能为我国莎士比亚研究学术推进贡献一份薄力。

---

① 罗益民、康方:《四百年莎士比亚的身份与形象》,《外国文学研究》2016年第6期。
② 苏福忠:《瞄准莎士比亚》,人民文学出版社,2017年,第327页。

参考文献

Andre Lefevere, *Translation History Culture: A Sourcebook*, New York: Routledge, 1992.

Douglas Robinson, *The Translator's Turn*, Baltimore: The Johns Hopkins University Press, 1991.

Lawrence Venuti, *The Translator's Invisibility: A History of Translation*, New York: Routledge, 1995.

陆谷孙：《莎士比亚研究十讲》，复旦大学出版社，2005年。

李伟民：《中国莎士比亚批评史》，中国戏剧出版社，2006年。

方梦之：《中国译学的主体性和原创性——新范畴、新概念、新表述探源》，《中国翻译》2023年第3期。

艾布拉姆斯：《镜与灯：浪漫主义文论及批评传统》，郦稚牛、张照进、童庆生译，北京大学出版社，2004年。

周宪：《艺术四要素理论与西方文论的演变——艾布拉姆斯〈镜与灯〉评述》，《南京师大学报》（社会科学版）1986年第4期。

高继海：《艾布拉姆斯诗学观简论》，《英美文学研究论丛》2012年第2期。

朱立元：《当代西方文艺理论》，华东师范大学出版社，2014年。

杜夫海纳：《美学与哲学》，孙非译，中国社会科学出版社，1985年。

谢天振：《当代西方翻译研究的三大突破和两大转向》，《四川外语学院学报》2003年第5期。

王克非：《关于翻译理论及其发展史研究》，《上海翻译》2021年第6期。

王瑞：《莎剧中称谓的翻译》，北京外国语大学，2007年。

段素萍：《莎士比亚戏剧中语序变异的汉译——以〈哈姆雷特〉译本为例》，北京外国语大学，2013年。

管兴忠：《莎士比亚〈温莎的风流娘们儿〉剧中的指令及其汉译》，北京外国语大学，2013年。

吴边：《莎士比亚〈一报还一报〉里情态谓词的汉译研究》，北京外国语大学，2017年。

庞密香：《莎剧 Measure for Measure 和 Romeo and Juliet 中人称代词汉译的语用学和语义学研究》，北京外国语大学，2019年。

刘慧丹：《基于语料库的莎士比亚戏剧汉译本中情感意义的再现与重构研究》，上海交通大学，2015年。

罗益民：《莎士比亚十四行诗版本批评史》，科学出版社，2016年。

陈国华:《论莎剧重译(下)》,《外语教学与研究》1997年第3期。

仇蓓玲:《美的变迁——论莎士比亚戏剧文本中意象的汉译》,南京大学,2005年。

刘翼斌:《概念隐喻翻译的认知分析——基于〈哈姆雷特〉对比语料库研究》,上海外国语大学,2010年。

龚芬:《论戏剧语言的翻译——莎剧多译本对比》,上海外国语大学,2004年。

李春江:《莎士比亚戏剧汉译研究》,四川大学,2009年。

张威:《莎士比亚戏剧汉译定量分析研究》,上海外国语大学,2014年。

萧文乾:《历久弥新:〈哈姆雷特〉汉译研究:1867—2013》,清华大学,2015年。

张汨:《朱生豪莎士比亚戏剧翻译手稿及刊印本版本对比研究》,北京航空航天大学,2017年。

万江松:《翻译中的诗学:莎士比亚十四行诗汉译研究》,四川大学,2015年。

陈庆:《诗歌意象翻译情感研究:基于情感计算的认知分析》,广东外语外贸大学,2017年。

王亚、文军:《国内译者研究30年:现状与展望》,《外国语文》2023年第4期。

严晓江:《梁实秋中庸翻译观研究》,南京大学,2007年。

赵慧:《梁实秋与西方文学》,吉林大学,2015年。

吕丽丽:《梁实秋文学翻译研究》,山东大学,2021年。

刘云雁:《朱生豪莎剧翻译——影响与比较》,浙江大学,2011年。

段自力:《朱生豪莎剧翻译经典化研究》,四川大学,2013年。

王林:《论田汉的戏剧译介与艺术实践》,复旦大学,2003年。

任晓霏:《"译者登场"——英若诚戏剧翻译研究》,上海外国语大学,2008年。

肖曼琼:《翻译家卞之琳研究》,湖南师范大学,2010年。

陈国华:《论莎剧重译(上)》,《外语教学与研究》1997年第2期。

文旭、张钺奇:《认知翻译学研究新进展》,《上海翻译》2023年第1期。

董典:《文学翻译中的认知识解操作——以〈麦克白〉的五个汉译本为例》,西南大学,2021年。

叶庄新:《跨越文化的戏剧旅程:莎士比亚于中国现代戏剧》,福建师范大学,2007年。

侯靖靖:《婆娑一世界,扮演两扇门——1949—1966年间英美戏剧在中国的译介研究》,上海外国语大学,2008年。

卢贝贝:《五四时期戏剧翻译研究》,西南大学,2021年。

魏策策:《思想视域下的莎士比亚符码》,华东师范大学,2013年。

罗益民、康方:《四百年莎士比亚的身份与形象》,《外国文学研究》2016年第6期。

苏福忠:《瞄准莎士比亚》,人民文学出版社,2017年。

人物专访

人物专访

林纾：莎士比亚戏剧汉译的先声

柳杨

众所周知，莎士比亚戏剧在中国的前经典化，在很大程度上得益于兰姆姐弟根据莎士比亚戏剧改写的儿童读物《莎士比亚戏剧故事集》(Tales from Shakespeare)。1903年，上海达文社出版的《澥外奇谭》[1]是该书的第一个汉译本，但遗憾的是，这个译本只选取了《莎士比亚戏剧故事集》中的十个故事，且译者不详。1904年7月，商务印书馆出版的《吟边燕语》是《莎士比亚戏剧故事集》的第一个汉语全译本。

首版《吟边燕语》扉页注明原著作者为"英国莎士比"，翻译者是闽县林纾与仁和魏易[2]。译者林纾在《序》中特意提到了魏易，以及二人合作翻译的过程：

挚友仁和魏君春叔，年少英博，淹通西文。长沙张尚书既领译事于京师，余与魏君适厕译席，魏君口述，余则叙致为文章。计二年以来，予二人所分译者，得三四种，拿破仑本纪为最巨本，秋初可以毕业矣。夜中余闲，魏君偶举莎士比笔记一二则，余就灯起草，积二十日书成，其文均莎诗之记事也。[3]

如林纾所述，魏易是他的"挚友"。二人共事时，魏易口述，林纾聆听、领会后，叙述成文。

---

[1] 根据中国国家图书馆藏本，该书封面的书名为"澥外奇谭"，但叙例、目次及内页书耳位置印的书名都是"海外奇谭"，本文采用了封面书名。
[2] 据史料记载，林纾为福建闽县（今福州市）人，魏易为浙江省杭州市仁和县人。
[3] 此处原文为繁体字，为方便读者阅读，笔者改用现代汉语录入。参见莎士比：《吟边燕语》，林纾、魏易译，商务印书馆，1904年，第2页。

夜晚休息时，魏易偶尔会讲一两个莎士比亚戏剧故事，林纾便就着灯光奋笔疾书，二十天后，《吟边燕语》译成。

林纾尤其重视莎士比亚的诗人身份，他在《序》中称莎士比亚为"诗家"，并认为"莎氏之诗，直抗吾国之杜甫……"[1]。对于莎剧的产生过程，他解释为"彼中名辈，耽莎氏之诗者，家弦户诵，而又不已；则付之梨园，用为院本"[2]。可见他清楚地知道，莎士比亚是像杜甫一样伟大的诗人，莎剧是诗体，因广泛传颂而为剧院所用。除此之外，林纾认为莎士比亚的艺术特色在于"立义遣词，往往托象于神怪"[3]，所以他将译本定名为《吟边燕语》，颇类似于蒲松龄的《聊斋志异》。翻译莎剧标题时，林纾一律采用两个字的传奇式标题，如《肉券》《训悍》《李误》等；有些标题刻意突出了神怪主题，如《神和》《蛊征》《鬼诏》《仙狯》等。

《吟边燕语》全文采用汉语文言翻译，行文简练，叙述生动，寥寥数语便勾勒出主要人物间的关系。以《女变》（今译《李尔王》）为例，开篇译者便介绍了李尔王三个女儿的婚姻状况，与标题呼应，并为下文情节的展开做好铺垫：

> 英王李亚有三女，长曰贡吕儿，嫁阿本内公爵；次曰李甘，嫁康华而公爵；季曰高地丽，待字也。时法王及卑根豆公爵咸欲得之。二氏以欲得高地丽故，咸集英伦。顾李亚年逾八秩，在倦勤之时，思以国政属之季女，得颐养残年。[4]

林译简洁明了，不但大大缩减了篇幅，在情节的凸显方面更是功不可没。正因如此，《吟边燕语》发行时虽是袖珍的口袋书，却引起时人的强烈反响，汪笑侬于1905年发表的《题英国诗人吟边燕语二十首》便是其中代表。

《吟边燕语》收录的二十个莎士比亚戏剧故事中，有喜剧、悲剧和传奇剧，但没有历史剧。林纾为弥补这一遗憾，又与陈家麟合作，用文言译出了五个莎士比亚历史剧故事，即《雷查得记》《亨利第四纪》《亨利第六遗事》《凯彻遗事》《亨利第五纪》。其中，《亨利第六遗事》被列为商务印书馆的"说部丛书"之一，印成单行本出版。

---

[1] 莎士比：《吟边燕语》，林纾、魏易译，商务印书馆，1904年，第1页。
[2] 同上。
[3] 同上。
[4] 兰姆：《吟边燕语》，林纾、魏易译，商务印书馆，1981年，第61页。

林纾"不审西文",做翻译时需依靠合作者的口译,故自称"勉强厕身于译界者"[1],然而林译小说数量之巨,时人无可比肩者;风靡程度,亦无出其右者——莎士比亚戏剧故事的翻译便是其中最为典型的代表。作为译者,林纾善于领会原作的主旨与风格,并以生动传神的译笔再现莎剧故事梗概,这种移花接木式的翻译与当时人们的阅读习惯契合,因而在出版方面取得了空前的成功。除此之外,林译莎剧故事还引起了当时电影行业的关注,《铸情》不久便登上了中国荧幕。尤其值得一提的是,林纾翻译的莎士比亚戏剧故事在内容方面涉及莎翁创作的喜剧、悲剧和历史剧,这为国人较为全面地认识和了解莎士比亚戏剧提供了契机,促进了近代中国文明戏演出的兴盛,堪称莎士比亚戏剧汉译的先声。

---

[1] 却而司迭更司:《孝女耐儿传》,林纾、魏易译述,商务印书馆,1915年,第1页。

我的父亲朱达与朱氏一族的译莎、研莎之旅

朱小琳

又一个曈昽冬日，飞云如卷，我怀念应邀为伯公朱生豪先生撰文纪念的旧岁，而今又增新的怀念——怀念我的父亲朱达教授。他已经离开我们三百天，而我终于能够按捺住翻卷的情愫去呈上一份深沉的思念。在2023年农历冬月来临的今日，我思念他温润的笑容、爽朗幽默的妙语和他对莎士比亚翻译与研究的执着。他给予我对莎士比亚这位文坛巨擘的启蒙，带着朱氏家族先贤未竟的心愿，点燃了我的文学求索之心，也将这份对莎士比亚的热爱播撒于他的学生之中。

父亲出生于1942年，自幼沉浸在祖父翻译和研究莎学的氛围里。中学毕业于百年名校成都七中，这里培养了蒲富恪等多名中科院、工程院院士，并具有浓郁的人文学风。"审是迁善，模范群伦"是校训，也是父亲一生的写照。若从伯公朱生豪先生算起，父亲是朱氏一门中承继莎士比亚译研的第三人。他自1962年到四川师院任教，一直致力于外国文学研究与教学，后在国家的战略需求下又从俄文转攻英语文学，成为该校第一个俄语背景下获得正高级职称的英语教授。他是该校第一个与获得诺贝尔文学奖作家建立书信联系的学者。他还担任系主任，为系部发展鞠躬尽瘁，成果卓越。我至今仍记得，从幼年起便存目的父亲深夜伏案的背影，是家中无声而最为醒目的标志。无论何时，他总是以乐观的态度面对人生的挑战，用最阳光的一面感染他人，同事们也都乐于与之亲近。

在莎士比亚研究方面，他笔耕不辍，常念伯公朱生豪先生年仅23岁便以报国为信念着手莎士比亚戏剧翻译，在战乱年代心血耗尽溘然长逝。伯公译出莎剧31部半，遗愿谓其兄弟，即祖父朱文振先生继而完成所有戏剧翻译。祖父于四川大学以戏曲体译

出余下莎剧,但终因时局动荡遗失了完整手稿,只存有部分译稿片段。后无意中得知手稿曾在旧书古玩市场昙花一现,终究寻找无门。每念及此,父亲扼腕叹息。伯公及祖父均为人温和,但他们对莎士比亚翻译与传播的热忱刻入了父亲的文学追求。

父亲在20世纪80年代访学美国之际,曾探访美国福吉莎士比亚图书馆。他介绍了中国的莎学翻译研究情况,并捐赠了莎学研究成果作品,在世界莎学研究中增添了中国学者的贡献。多年后,在我去往纽约访问福吉莎士比亚图书馆之际,馆长热情相待,还取出了父亲当年留赠与我共情。回想起来,年幼的我便是端坐在父亲书房的地板上,从书柜中取出一本本伯公翻译的《莎士比亚全集》,由此完成了我对莎士比亚文学的启蒙。午后斜阳,父亲的书房总是一个美妙所在。我总会在此找到我心仪的文学名著。在大学里,父亲的藏书是数一数二的,除了莎学研究作品与译本等,他也嗜好收集其他中外文史书籍。我的诗词启蒙来自他所收藏的龙榆生的《唐宋名家词选》。我被密集的竖行排版惊呆,也沉迷于繁体字表述诗意的视觉感性。他的中文修养是很好的,这也影响了我对文学研究的基本态度:对文学的研究首先建立于文本的艺术属性及美学特征,乃至于文学文本研究的文字表意也应具有一定的文学性。

父亲早年尤爱诗歌,以及与诗歌有关的音乐艺术。他吹笛鸣箫,探究音律。他还是演奏小提琴的一把好手。我记得他拉琴时的专注。对于他,琴韵与诗律同样美妙。因此,他秉承祖父对莎剧的诗剧翻译观,致力于研究莎士比亚戏剧的传统诗体汉译,撰文发表,还留下了大量笔记,手稿累累,至身体危殆,竟成未竟之遗作,令人扼腕。在祖国各地及海外的学生纷纷表达对恩师的怀念与哀悼,追忆当年进校面试时父亲的音貌与学养风度,感同入学第一课。学生周保和作诗悼挽:"谦谦乃君子,暖暖胜温玉。潇洒蕴真知,谆教如春雨,未及报恩泽,仙骨还太虚。得道邀苍宇,天宫种桃李。"在这寂静的深夜,抬眼看去,天穹星光,望之欲止。突然想起那句民谚,只要我们还记得,他就永远活着。是为之记。

屠岸与莎士比亚

章燕

1950年,上海文化工作社出版了《莎士比亚十四行诗集》,这是中国第一部莎士比亚十四行诗的全译本,译者为屠岸。屠岸年轻时对英诗产生了极大兴趣,并在1941年发表了他的第一首汉译英诗,此后他又陆续发表了多首外国诗歌汉译作品。1943年底,他在上海"古今书店"找到了他非常喜爱的莎士比亚十四行诗集的英文原版书。该书制作小巧精美,由伦敦德拉莫尔出版社于1904年出版,夏洛蒂·斯托普斯(Charlotte Stopes)编注。屠岸获得此书,如获至宝,在20世纪40年代中期便着手翻译。当时,屠岸的同窗好友张志镳患肺结核去世,为了寄托对这位挚友的怀念,屠岸发愤将莎士比亚十四行诗全部译出,并在扉页上题写了献词:"献给已故的金鹿火同志。""金鹿火"是"镳"字拆分开来的三个字。屠岸在翻译之初就被这些十四行诗的艺术所征服,但在翻译过程中也遇到不少困难。他找来其他注释本进行查阅比对,如克雷格(W.J. Craig)编的牛津《莎士比亚全集》一卷本(1926)。他还曾经写信求教当时的复旦大学教授葛传椝,并得到他的指点。1948年,这部诗集的翻译临近尾声,但因当时的政治形势,翻译工作停了下来。1950年3月,屠岸在登门向胡风约稿时,受到胡风的鼓励,立即着手完成了最后的译稿。当年11月,中国第一部《莎士比亚十四行诗集》出版。书中在每首十四行诗之后附有较详尽的"译解",受到冯至的称赞。该译本在"文革"前多次再版。1964年,该译本经全面修订之后交给上海文艺出版社(上海译文出版社前身),但未及出版"文革"开始。"文革"期间,该译本以手抄本的形式在民间流传,很多人能够将其中的诗篇背诵出来。改革开放之后,上海译文出版社找到了这本莎翁十四行诗翻译稿的修订稿原稿,经屠岸再一次修订之后于1981年出版。此后,屠译《莎士比亚十四行诗》不断再版,形式更加多样,有英汉对照版、插图版、线装版、手迹版等，累计印数达50余万册，成为名副其实的经典常销书，在读者中产生了广泛影响。

20世纪90年代中期，上海译文出版社方平筹备出版《新莎士比亚全集》，约屠岸翻译莎士比亚的历史剧《约翰王》和莎士比亚除《维纳斯与阿董尼》（当时已有方平的译本）之外的其他长篇诗作。屠岸欣然应允，反复研读《约翰王》这部历史剧，并以诗体形式，即抑扬格五音步无韵体诗歌形式，翻译了这部剧作。在翻译莎士比亚长诗时，屠岸让女儿章燕参与了翻译。由章燕翻译初稿，屠岸进行修改、审定。他们共同翻译了《卢克丽丝失贞记》《热情的朝圣者》《恋人的怨诉》等诗作。这些作品一并收入了由方平主编，河北教育出版社1999年出版的《新莎士比亚全集》中。屠岸晚年有一个强烈的心愿，要出一本莎士比亚诗歌全集汉译本。2015年，屠岸与章燕再度合作翻译，完成了莎士比亚的另一首长诗《维纳斯与阿多尼》的翻译。2016年，《莎士比亚诗歌全编》分上下册由北方文艺出版社出版，上册为屠岸翻译的《莎士比亚十四行诗》，下册为《莎士比亚长篇叙事诗》。至此，屠岸翻译了莎士比亚诗歌的全部作品和莎剧《约翰王》。

除翻译之外，屠岸还结合他的翻译撰写了有关莎士比亚十四行诗的学术研究论文和翻译研究论文。屠岸的莎士比亚诗歌和戏剧翻译，尤其是他翻译的《莎士比亚十四行诗集》，为中国莎士比亚诗歌的翻译和研究做出了突出贡献。

刘炳善雕龙莎士比亚
——写在《刘炳善文集》出版之际

彭弱水

老来何事习雕龙?只缘痴情耽莎翁。
敢以苦学追少壮,窃把勤耕比劳农。
一字未稳几片纸,三思始得半日功。
心血倘能平险阻,好与来者攀高峰。

这是于2010年仙逝作古的《莎士比亚大词典》编纂者,我国改革开放以来英国文学的奠基者、开创性学者,蜚声四海的莎士比亚研究者,河南大学博士生导师刘炳善,于1997年6月9日,为他的皇皇巨著英汉双解《莎士比亚大词典》正编(因后有续编,故如此指称)竣工写自序作结的即兴赋诗。

其时,刘炳善先生已届古稀之年,仍笔耕不辍。他编纂的这部《莎士比亚大词典》,真可谓是"褴褛筚路"。可以想象的类似情形包括:18世纪的巨人萨缪尔·约翰逊(Samuel Johnson, 1709—1784)于1755年出版的第一部英语词典,20世纪末至21世纪初引领众人编纂中国最大的英汉大词典的陆谷孙先生。然而,还有一个惊人的相似之处在于,这三位都同时以词典编纂、莎学研究左右开弓而流传于世且名垂千古。这些事情联系在一起,不可不算是一段佳话。刘炳善、约翰逊、陆谷孙,他们的名字,在莎士比亚与语言发展漫长历史长河中具有里程碑意义。

在刘炳善先生的正编《莎士比亚大词典》出版之际,李赋宁与前一年仙逝的戴镏龄为该词典作序。这也与莎士比亚戏剧集第一对开本(*First Folio*)的情形如出一辙:有他人撰序,也有本人自序。李赋宁与戴镏龄先生的算是一种题序,曾在《外语与外语教学》上分期发表。刘炳善先生的《莎士比亚大词典》还附上了他1996年4月在美国洛杉矶第六届世界莎士比亚大会上的英文发言稿。

可以看出,刘炳善先生写这首诗不仅仅说明了他汲汲做莎士比亚事业的决心、坚持、勤劳和智慧,他足足凑集了43箱方便面箱子的卡片,更让人想起了钱锺书近十大麻袋的读书笔记,吴宓的多卷本自废纸卡片与纸烟盒上留下的日记,美国女诗人艾米莉·狄金森写在废纸片和火柴盒上的近1800首诗歌!所以,用"褴褛筚路"来形容,可以说是恰如其分!

刘炳善先生的雕龙之功,从由河南人民出版社(之前还在上海外语教育出版社出版过,后改为河南人民出版社出版)出版的《英国文学简史》印数达100万册以上就可以看出,他经年累月,锱铢积累,用色带和机械打字机做出的莎士比亚文字大全,与之前美国艺术、科学院院士约翰·巴特利特(John Bartlett)于1896年做出的《莎士比亚词汇语句大典》(*A New and Complete Concordance or Verbal Index to Shakespeare*),德国人亚历山大·施密特(Alexander Schmidt)1902年所编的《莎士比亚词典》(*Shakespeare-Lexicon*),堪称"三座高峰"。后来的数字技术语料库,恐怕都来自三者的"贪天之功"的产品之一。刘炳善先生的双解,不仅多了汉语译文,而且加入了其他莎士比亚学习与研究者所需要的莎士比亚生平略传、创作年表、戏剧故事梗概,还附有莎士比亚专有名词读音表、莎士比亚用语特点、莎士比亚诗歌格律、历史剧阅读参考材料、莎士比亚在中国(简况)等。刘炳善先生逝世后整理出版了续编《莎士比亚大词典》。这两本皇皇巨著,对中国学生与学者来说,是极好的入门莎学的工具大全。刘炳善先生把他人生的后20年全部都投入其中,心无旁骛。更为传奇的是,他的妻子储国蕾女士,也成为他的助手,配合他的工作,这真像Gladys Yang配合杨宪益译《红楼梦》,大粉丝詹姆斯·鲍斯韦尔(James Boswell, 1740—1795)之于约翰逊,历史天赐般地授予先生一个助手,玉成了这一项伟大的工程。主编了中国最好最大的英汉词典的陆谷孙先生曾经在与本人的交流中慨叹,纸版本词典成了一种大而无当的累赘(white elephant),有了电子词典之后,纸版本词典开始走向它的历史终点。笔者教"文学翻译"课程时,要求学子每人购买一本《莎士比亚大词典》。一是其具有标志性,二是可以作为财产继承。他们究竟怎么看,谁知道呢?电子时代开始,如当年天主教会说:爱迪生发明了电灯,魔鬼就来到了人间。因为,有些人再也不肯在晚上休息了。因此,电子时代开始,有些人再也不读纸版本的叫作书的东西了。尽管如此,笔者仍然认为,人类文明最方便的记录方式,也许就是书和辅助读书的工具书了。莎士比亚在他的收笔之作《暴风雨》中,借普洛斯佩罗的口说:"我呢,一个可怜的人,书斋便是我广大的公国。"(朱生豪译)书于人类,正如高尔基所说,是"人类进步的阶梯"。在今天,书是否产生了拓扑学的等价形变?它还是人类进步的阶梯吗?

刘炳善先生在打字机上一下一下弹指按下去打出来的卡片,被河南大学博物馆收藏,河南人民出版社准备出版,意义何在?是乔治·吉辛(George Gissing, 1857—1903)《草堂笔记》里写的寒食街穷酸,还是伦敦充满陋室的德里巷繁华的落寞?多少文人,多少诗歌,不都是在穷酸中成长起来的吗?有说"愤怒出诗人",有说"诗可以怨",穷酸、落寞、愤怒、怨就是诗吗?果真如此,那就再来一次?

在《刘炳善文集》出版之际想想这些问题,或许是有益处的。

人物专访

苏福忠及其对莎士比亚研究的贡献

洛州牧

苏福忠先生早年毕业于南开大学，就职于人民文学出版社，进入20世纪90年代，他接手了《莎士比亚全集》的重版工作，因此把十一卷改为六卷，每一卷前面放了一张目录，为读者查阅全集篇目提供了方便。不过，六本书也是不小的体量，他希望参照国外流行版本出一个单本全集。巧合的是，时代文艺出版社的邢爱光先生赴京出差，表示非常有兴趣出版一个全新的莎士比亚全集版本。在双方共同努力下，1996年两卷本《莎士比亚全集》出版，首印26000套，据说加印到了50000册。尽管距离单卷本还多一本，但终归前进了一大步。在编辑过程中，苏福忠先生遇到精彩的句子时便随手写了下来，后来在东方出版社著名出版人刘丽华的积极推动下，出版了《莎士比亚语言精髓录》。

书是有力量的，它的存在是人类积累积极元素的结果。苏福忠先生的老师黄雨石，也是他的老同事，不幸患了帕金森病。他对黄先生说："你有什么特别想说的话，如果写出来困难的话，试着搞个录音吧。"想不到他在他老师的录音里听到了这样的叙述：

关于朱生豪旧译莎士比亚的问题，我也简单说几句。我到文学出版社的时候，出版社已经印出一本洋洋大观的五年出书计划，差不多把英文作品所有有名气的都列在上面。莎士比亚当然是一个重点。当时编辑部已经决定抛弃朱生豪的译本，另外组织人翻译莎士比亚。我把朱生豪的本子仔细看看，觉得译得很不错，现在要赶上他可不是一件容易的事。

苏先生听到后刹那间感到"如获至宝"。这促成他一有空闲就研读朱生豪译文的习惯。退休后，他把朱译三十一个剧本逐一校订。不期这是个越做越上瘾的活儿，朱生豪一个又一个出彩的翻译例子让这看似枯燥的活儿充满了乐趣。他常说他享受了朱生豪的福气,比如他因此写出了《朱莎合璧》一书,该书出版后颇受读者和专家学者的青睐。他也经常说沾了莎士比亚的仙气,比如他在阅读和编辑 E. M. 福斯特、安东尼·特罗洛普、乔治·吉辛、奥斯卡·王尔德、弗吉尼亚·伍尔夫、乔治·奥威尔、威廉·萨默塞特·毛姆、纳撒尼尔·霍桑、亨利·戴维·梭罗、杰克·伦敦、马克·吐温、斯科特·菲茨杰拉德、约翰·厄普代克、塞巴斯蒂安·巴里等等这些大名鼎鼎的莎士比亚的超级粉丝的过程中,能翻译就翻译他们的作品,能够做他们的文集和单本就尽力推进出版。经过多年努力和经营,出版了《伍尔夫文集》《福斯特文集》和众多单本,如《巴塞特的最后纪事》《索恩医生》《霍华德庄园》《最漫长的旅程》《道连·格雷的画像》《一九八四》《动物农场》;《杰克·伦敦短篇小说选》《海狼》《马丁·伊登》《汤姆·索亚历险记》《赫克贝利·芬恩历险记》《兔子富了》《夫妇》和《漫漫长路》。又在积累经验和实践的基础上,出版了《译事余墨》《席德这个小人儿》《编译曲直》《瞄准莎士比亚》《朱莎合璧》等专著。并两度与新星出版社合作,推出了十二卷《莎士比亚全集》插图本,其中包括莎翁遗作《一错再错》,合作剧本《法弗沙姆的阿登》,以及一些遗佚的散诗,使得该全集成为国内最完整的版本。

苏先生以人民文学出版社的传统为基础,创立了独树一帜的翻译原则性理论,倡导翻译中的4M(即 Meaning, Message, Information 和 Image)说,并提出了"展、转、腾、挪"的翻译策略,其理论与策略切实可行,对翻译实践具有实际的指导意义。除此之外,苏先生还两度组编英汉对照的名著名译,为英语语种的学习与汉译提供了可资借鉴的范本,对翻译教学做出了卓越的贡献。

从英语这个专业角度看,他就业的环境也是有福的,碰上了几个专业素质很高的老同事。他们尽职尽责,不显山不露水,却建立起一种相对稳定的审稿标准,为出版社推出好译本做出了贡献。这让他个人受益无穷。因此借此机会,向他这几位默默无闻的老同事,如吴钧燮、石永礼以及施咸荣诸位老前辈致敬,以表达对他们的感激和纪念。

前沿快递

《莎士比亚作品选读》的教学文化启示

今至

早在20世纪上半叶,莎士比亚已是众多高校外语系的必开课程。目前,莎士比亚相关课程继续在大学人文教育中占据重要地位。然而,莎士比亚戏剧应该如何走进大学课堂、相关教材应该如何编写,这些依然是中国学者们热烈讨论的问题。罗益民认为,鉴于莎士比亚这门课程的特殊性,适当的教师主体是必要的,进而提出了五种结合的教学建议,即文本与表演结合、讲解与讨论结合、细读与研讨结合、课堂与作业结合、教研与教学结合,最终达到"传授最好或是最有代表性的人文精神"的教学目标。人文精神乃莎士比亚作品的核心,在这一点上,《莎士比亚作品选读》(2022年由高等教育出版社出版,下简称《选读》)的编著者之一的黎志敏与罗益民的看法是一致的。黎志敏提出,文学的核心是人,"是人的心灵和人与人之间关系的揭示,是人与自然、与社会的冲突和调和"。在《选读》中,黎志敏着力凸显莎士比亚人文精神,并在此基础上对教材每一章的内容做了大幅度调整,如将导读部分拆分为导读与赏析,另外还添加了思考题与延伸阅读,在教材的编排中透显出莎士比亚课程的设计理念。这种理念提倡多元式引导、沉浸式课堂以及发散式讨论,正好与罗益民提出的"五种结合"教学思路形成呼应。

首先,莎士比亚课程的教授者以及相关教材的编著者需以多元引导的方式带领学生认识到莎士比亚剧作兼容并包的时代性与现代性。一方面,莎士比亚创作生涯的开端正值伊丽莎白一世统治的全盛时期。这位教养良好的女王开创了一种热衷于学习与探究的文化。莎士比亚分享着这个时代的激情,凭借敏锐的洞察力精确地捕捉住该时代的风俗百态及社会基调,又以人道的温情创作出一个个独具魅力的人物角色。对于莎士比亚时代的探讨以及对莎剧人物与时代的互动性分析是引领学生走近莎士比亚作品极为重要的一步。另一方面,教师应启发学生看到莎士比亚超越时代的一面。莎士比亚作品的力量虽来源于他诞生的时代,但并未拘泥于时代;相反,英国文艺复兴时期赋予莎士比亚的探索精神使他勇于向该时期的某些价值观念发起挑战。例如,在《选读》中,黎志敏就讨论了莎士比亚在《终成眷属》中对荣誉问题的重新诠释,而《特洛伊罗斯和克瑞西达》中的反英雄性以及对于战争与人生意义的质疑则很容易与现代读者及观众产生连接,揭示出莎士比亚戏剧的批判性与现代性。

其次,如果多元式引导只是让学生"走近"莎士比亚,那么文本细读以及沉浸式的课堂体验则让学生真正"走进"莎士比亚的戏剧世界。"沉浸式"一词来自"沉浸式戏剧",是对观与演关系的一种新探索,而沉浸式课堂则是对教与学关系的一种新的尝试。沉浸式课堂的开展离不开学生在教师指导下对原文剧本进行文本细读,再根据自己理解演绎出来。诚然,对于刚接触莎士比亚作品的学生而言,阅读整部原文剧本存在一定难度。因此,黎志敏从莎士比亚的每部剧中挑选出最能彰显人文精神的片段,并辅以详尽的注释与自由诗式的翻译,帮助学生在跨越语言障碍的同时,在细读的过程中能够充分沉浸于莎士比亚绚丽多姿的语言世界中,领略到阿伽门农气势恢弘的史诗式铺排,哈姆莱特充满哲学思辨性的学者式语言,辨识到麦克白的语言就如同他内心世界一般幽暗曲折,罗密欧诗意流动的语言与福斯塔夫市井气息浓重的言语之间形成了鲜明差异……此外,在《选读》中,黎志敏鼓励学生将选段作为朗读以及小规模演出的素材。表演其实是一种再创作的过程,在剧本中舞台指导有限的情况下,学生需补充剧本以外的元素,如在念出某句台词时角色的内心活动,与台词相匹配的表情、声调以及身体动作等,在实现从文本到舞台的过渡过程中,也实现了从教学与接受客体到创作与表演主体的身份转换,这不仅有利于学生加深对莎士比亚戏剧人文精神内核的理解,而且有助于学生发挥想象力,提高学生的自信心。

最后,发散式的讨论与延伸阅读为学生进一步深入学习、探究莎士比亚戏剧提供了思路。莎士比亚在作品中留下的关于人性、人类生存的普适性问题叩击着一代又一代读者的心灵,在四百多年以后的今天依然能够引起共鸣。人何以为人,如何为人,是什么决定了人的行为,人在多大程度上享有自由选择的权利,又在多大程度上受制于他人与时代环境……莎士比亚将这些问题抛给读者,邀请读者与其笔下的角色共同去了解人性的复杂,在失序的世界中寻找意义。但无论是对人性复杂面的把握,还是对人生意义的探寻,都不是一件容易的事情。教师需在此过程中肩负起引路人的责任。黎志敏所编著的《莎士比亚作品选读》充分体现了这份责任感。他通过发散式的问题启发学生的思考,并以一步步深入的学术论文作为延伸阅读的材料,为学生打开研究莎士比亚戏剧之门。

时代共鸣：与莎士比亚的永恒对话，写在《芳华》之后

朱鑫宇

莎士比亚戏剧是人类文明的一大宝库，除了阅读和观赏之外，更重要的是通过参与戏剧表演，切身感受莎剧的魅力。戴丹妮教授主编的《青春舞台 莎园芳华——首届"友邻杯"莎士比亚（中国）学生戏剧节实录暨莎剧教学与实践论文集》（以下简称《芳华》）独树一帜，围绕莎士比亚戏剧的改编与表演展开，将莎士比亚从书本搬到舞台，赋予新的生命。这也印证了莎士比亚写作的本来目的：首先是为了呈现在舞台上给人看的，而能作为文本阅读是后来的事情。

《芳华》既是首届"友邻杯"莎士比亚（中国）学生戏剧节（以下简称戏剧节）实录，又是莎剧教学与实践学术论文集。戏剧节的宗旨是通过莎士比亚经典戏剧的中英文表演和基于莎剧的戏剧创作，提高中国青年学生的文学艺术修养，跨文化交流及中英文表达能力，发挥莎士比亚人文主义资源在我国社会文化发展中的现实作用，并以此加强校园文化与美育建设。负责人南京大学的从丛老师和武汉大学的戴丹妮老师分别撰写此书的"序"和"前言"道出此次戏剧节薪火相传的历史，两校联袂的渊源。由于病毒肆虐，戏剧节采用"线上＋线下"模式开展，通过互联网搭建了一个跨越空间的学术交流和戏剧表演平台。

学习和研究莎士比亚戏剧，都可以归结于一个问题，那就是培养一个怎样的人。莎士比亚之所以能够跨越时空，具有历久弥新的经典力量，其中一个重要环节就是教学。此书收录论文的作者，都来自莎学界，他们不仅是莎士比亚的研究者，更是戏剧教育的

践行者。武汉大学的戴丹妮教授分享了疫情期间的线上结课式,呈现了一场学术研讨和表演艺术的盛宴;浙江传媒学院的顾颖婕老师从剧场运营管理角度出发,探讨了如何上好戏剧课,让学生通过参与剧场运营管理,学会"做"好一部剧;深圳大学的迈克尔·加雷斯·福斯特作为一名在中国教授莎士比亚戏剧的外籍教师,从第二外语的角度探讨了莎士比亚戏剧教学中的问题。

当今,大学校园是莎士比亚戏剧教育的主要阵地,大学生是莎剧表演的重要群体,因而除了大学生以外的莎士比亚学习者常被忽略。此书的另一个亮点就是将中学生纳入莎剧教学实践环节,鼓励中学生走进戏剧,激发中学生的英语学习兴趣,使得莎剧以一种更加"稚嫩"的方式被诠释。这里的"稚嫩"并非贬义,而是指中学生可以更加具有想象力、创造力地对莎士比亚进行解读。这恰恰反映了每个人心中都应该有一个自己的莎士比亚。同时,莎剧教育与实践从大学到中学的"下沉",将打破人们对莎剧晦涩难懂、严肃高雅的刻板印象,有利于让我们走近莎士比亚,让莎士比亚走进我们的生活。

除此之外,《芳华》还体现了中国莎学研究的跨文化视角,将莎士比亚与中国传统文化联系起来,中西方思想在此碰撞。厦门理工学院的刘芭教授大胆地将中国少数民族的元素融入莎剧,让我们看到了莎剧与中国戏曲结合的可能。艺术无国界,莎翁作品也因不同文化的演绎而更显深刻。

莎士比亚的作品不像那些已经画上句号的东西,更像一个包容的容器[①]。通过剖析莎士比亚的作品在当代语境中的新生,《芳华》显现出文学在文化交流中的力量,展现了经典在当代的鲜活适应力,证明了文学作为时代反映与文化桥梁的双重身份,能够促进不同文化的价值共振,实现创新与融合。

---

① 陆谷孙:《莎士比亚研究十讲》,复旦大学出版社,2005年,第46页。

画中有戏：从文字到绘画的舞台
——"莎士比亚漫画版"的特色和魅力

木子李

近年来，儿童绘本盛行，让儿童在画与文字的交叉互动中走进莎士比亚的艺术世界。这可以解释为什么作为作家的兰姆姐弟改写了莎士比亚的戏剧故事。这种改写本身，也已成为一种经典。兰姆姐弟的莎士比亚故事被一再继续改写、续写和翻译，并加入了插图。这说明，绘画的直观感，对理解莎士比亚戏剧，是有明显的帮助的。这一点又可以让人想到，在舞台的直观感与文字的想象魅力之间，需要沟通的桥梁。于是，我们可以想象，从插图到绘本是一种过渡，也是一种超越。当今的绘本还被附上了扫码即听的音乐和朗读，由此，文字、绘画与声音阅读，就融合贯通，成为一体了。

孩子的认知和感受，更高地基于想象和直观。因此，从插图到绘本的跨越，表明了直观的必要性。早在电子信息尚未充分发展的时代，就有一种由简易的绘画和少量的文字构成的图书，在当时被称为"连环画"。这些连环画培养了孩子的读书兴趣。如今的漫画绘本，也许可以说是连环画的延伸。连环画对经典文学作品的宣传，可以说功不可没，其效果与影响难以估量。这或许也可以解释，为什么漫画绘本会再次繁荣起来。

英国作家史蒂夫·巴洛与史蒂夫·斯基德莫尔对莎士比亚戏剧进行创意改编。就整个情节来说，他们忠实地领悟和再现了莎剧的原意。以《仲夏夜之梦》为例，其漫画绘本中，人神共舞，神仙和凡人纠缠不清，现实与戏剧排演交相辉映，神仙的喜怒哀乐影响人间阴晴圆缺，梦境与现实若隐若现，尽力在文字和漫画的表达与互相配合方面做得天衣无缝，文笔奇巧，绘画生动，既画出了龙的骨架，又点化了龙的传神的眼睛。让孩子们以图画与文字为双重媒介,进行想象,走入莎士比亚的世界。

"莎士比亚漫画版"还有一大特色是一般绘本童书没有的,那就是该丛书的书前与书末信息。一般说来,孩子需要的故事,内容要精彩,以满足孩子的新奇愿望;情节要有起伏,能够让孩子想象前后的联系,拓展想象的空间;人物要有特色,或悲怆引起怜悯,或幽默导致捧腹,或发人深思,或教化善恶好坏;知识拓展并不是文学类绘本的主要目的。

可能编创者感觉到了必要性,在每个故事前加上了作家传记、故事梗概、名言精粹、人物列表,使得小读者可以了解作家和故事主要内容,并品读文中吸引人的精粹之处,还能对即将上场的人物进行简要勾画。在小读者做好这些准备以后,进入故事时就能有豁然开朗之感。在每个故事后加上了故事点评,故事探源,主题浏览,语言、格律分析,版本状况,演出历史概要,戏院结构,票价行情,莎士比亚年表。如此一来,小读者不仅仅是在读故事,还能建立起一个知识结构,知道了什么是莎士比亚,莎士比亚是什么样子。莎士比亚虽是今人并不陌生的大作家,但莎士比亚的世界如此丰富广大,值得孩子们了解。所以,这些材料不仅能让孩子增长知识,在某些方面甚至可以触及高层次教学、阅读,引发研究灵感。举个例,关于《麦克白》故事的历史来源和莎士比亚妙手回春的改编,可以让读者体会到莎士比亚创作这出著名的四大悲剧之一的伟大之处。

真实的麦克白治国十七年,戏中却只为王几个月;历史上的邓肯并非因为谋杀致命,而是因为吃了败仗,自取灭亡。莎士比亚的神笔妙转,只是为了暗示,詹姆斯一世王位未稳,为顾全大局,犯上弑君是不可取的,因而才让谋杀者麦克白不得好死,酿成了人间的最大悲剧。为了达到这个目的,莎士比亚还创造了女巫连环计、森林移步计、凡人非妈生等一些离奇的故事。由此可见,这些知识,看起来旁敲侧击,事实上可以加深读者的理解和增强读者的好奇心,把读者和莎士比亚的关系再拉近一步,以达到绘本阅读的真正目的。

笔者注:

"莎士比亚漫画版"指由贵州人民出版社于2023年出版的以漫画形式演绎的五部莎士比亚经典戏剧,包括《哈姆雷特》《罗密欧与朱丽叶》《暴风雨》《麦克白》《仲夏夜之梦》,文字内容均由笔者翻译而成。

英文摘要

Zhu Shenghao's Sinicization of Shakespeare's Plays with a Note on Shakespeare Studies in China / YANG Lingui

Abstract: Upon the Bard's introduction into China, Shakespeare studies run through the shaping process of modern Chinese culture. The sinicization of Shakespeare's works consequently not only involves the strategies and methods of translating his canon, but also has profound cultural and political implications. Zhu Shenghao's sinicization of Shakespeare's plays, as informed with the essence of Chinese aesthetic and, in a crystallization of the creativity of Zhu and Shakespeare, appeals to tastes of both highbrow and lowbrow, thus having influenced generations of Chinese readers, adaptors, and researchers. For one thing, Zhu Shenghao's rendering of Shakespeare's plays has enriched the Chinese lexicon with an amazing vocabulary, which is a great contribution to the development of modern Chinese language; for another, his flexible use of ancient Chinese allusions has preserved the charm and essence of Chinese culture in the vernacular transformation of the language. Therefore, his contributions to world Shakespeare lie not only in facilitating the reception of Shakespeare's classics in the Chinese context, but more importantly, in his sinicizing exploration of foriegn literature that offers great inspiration and reference for the practice of international dissemination of Chinese culture as in a current catchphrase. His translation, furthermore, has provided us with valuable experience in handling the relationship between form and content as often addressed in translation theory and practice. That is to say that with or without the cliched terms of domestication and foreignization with the latter often being privileged, both transplanting and literal rendering of foreign texts may be viable approaches; or to be more specific, westernizing of Chinese works and the sinicizating of foreign ones can both be effective ways to spread Chinese culture and wisdom.

Key words: Zhu Shenghao; sinicization; Shakespeare's plays; Shakespeare Studies in China

The Little Ice Age and Shakespearean Ecological Criticism / ZHANG Jun

Abstract: Literature, like all things in human society, is a product of specific temporal and spatial contexts. Examining the ecological space attributes of texts helps to more fully understand the nature of literary expression. This article first emphasizes the important bridging role of the Little Ice Age between literary classics and modern science, then traces the climate issues in Western literary criticism from a historical perspective, and finally explores the current application and future prospects of the Little Ice Age in Shakespearean ecological criticism.

Key words: The Little Ice Age; ecological criticism; Shakespeare

Man under the Spell and Beasts out of the Cage: King, Daughters and Animals in William Shakespeare's Family-Nation Tragedy *King Lear* / CHEN Guicai

Abstract: The deformation of the characters into animals is a distinctive feature of William Shakespeare's family-nation tragedy *King Lear*. Through the strategy of animalization by self-identification and identification by others, Shakespeare deforms ancient British King Lear spellbound with patriarchal and monarchical power into a series of animals in accordance with the changes of his status and Lear's daughters Goneril and Reagan temporarily free of the bondage of patriarchal and monarchical power and unscrupulously fighting for power and wealth into a variety of fierce birds and beasts and even evil snakes and transforms the small world of the family and the big world of the family and nation seeking viciously for power and wealth into a crisis-ridden animal world and successfully weaves the family-nation tragedy that the family undergoes heavy destruction and severe deaths and the nation irrevocable collapse in the artful links among the king, daughters and animals. The reason for the family-nation tragedy is the cumulating result of the lack of legitimate heir to the throne, the reckless strategy of division and rule without distinguishing right from wrong, the disorderly competition for power, the crazy deconstruction of the center of patriarchy and monarchy, the deformation of acting subjects into animals and the severe condition of domestic troubles and foreign aggression.

Key words: Shakespeare's family-nation tragedy; *King Lear*; king; daughters; animals

Angst, Despair and Death: The Choice of Being in *Richard III* / LIU Huimin

Abstract: Shakespeare's historical play *Richard III* is a renowned masterpiece that delves into the existential quest for self-identity and self-fashioning during the early modern era. Within this play, Richard III, portrayed as a morally corrupt antagonist, emerges as a despised outcast in society. However, through an analysis of character scenes and dialogue distribution, and combining with the relevant dimensions of Kierkegaard's philosophical thoughts, this paper argues that Richard III's anxiety, despair, and contemplation of death actually serve to evoke readers' own existential angst while reflecting Shakespeare's exploration of the spirit of individualism prevalent in the early modern period.

Key words: *Richard III*; being; angst; despair; death

The Mysteries and Conjectures of Shakespeare's *Sonnets* / LUO Lang

Abstract: Shakespeare's Sonnets are symbols of Shakespeare's three-year friendship and love, a series of descriptions full of personalized passion, and the most memorable experiences of Shakespeare's life that had gone through lots of ups and downs and filled with many little-known mysteries before the age of thirty. However, through Sonnets, Shakespeare's emotional experiences and thoughts can be generally restored, reflecting the hidden emotional wounds he experienced. Perhaps the emotional wounds and the strong emotional conflicts inspired him to create the great love tragedy, *Romeo and Juliet*.

Key words: Shakespeare; *Sonnets*; Earl of Southampton; *Romeo and Juliet*.

The Revenge and Judicial Crisis in Shakespeare's Plays / HUANG Yanli

Abstract: Shakespeare's England was at an important adjustment stage of modern legal system, which was expanding day by day, and lawsuits were increasing explosively. People had been crazy about legal practice because law was everywhere. Revenge play became one of the most popular genres of drama at that time, which was specially significant in a Christian society advocating mercy. Public revenge is the necessity and requirement of national legal construction. However, the flawed justice system often functions as a spur to vengeance at the very beginning. The flawed legal system caused many problems in legal practice, such as jurisdictional disputes, corrupt judges, and lawyers reversing right and wrong. This made the traditional concept of blood revenge originating from the Germanic tribes still have a certain influence and rationality, because revenge was considered to be an "wild justice" to eliminate social diseases, and an effective way to ensure social order. The crisis of justice in revenge play reflects the judicial crisis of the early modern English legal system.

Key words: Shakespeare; revenge; law; judicial crisis

Famine, Fable and Weather: The Allusion of Eating in *Coriolanus* / HU Peng

Abstract: Shakespeare's *Coriolanus* has long been a favorite topic for political studies, with focuses ranging from Roman political system to political allusions to the Elizabethan England. While most studies consider *Coriolanus* versus citizens as the core of the tragedy, this paper argues for critical attention toward the role and function of eating in this play. Through close reading, the author analyzes the famine, the illusions of Mininuas' "Fable of Belly", and contemporary riots and weather condition. The paper also emphasizes on the significance of Shakespeare's adaptation of Roman history in order to inquiry and his logic of hunger business.

Key words: *Coriolanus*; eating; famine; fable; weather

The Ekphrasis and Sexual Politics in Shakespeare's *The Rape of Lucrece* / XU Qinghong, LI Yuting

Abstract: Shakespeare's long narrative poem *The Rape of Lucrece* is an interart poem, with ekphrastic features that imply gender politics, such as the depiction of the female body under the male gaze, Lucrece's interpretation of the painting of the Trojan War, and the visual representation of Lucrece's corpse. These manifest the interactive relationship between painting as a visual art and poetry as a language art. Through the act of "gazing", the poem connotes the gender politics behind the language and images, as well as the speaking potential of women as the subject of "ekphrasis". The visuality of the female corpse shifts the poem from the personal micro space to the public macro political space, i.e. the establishment of the Roman Republic. In this poem, Shakespeare endows language with much visuality and lyricism, arousing the reader's perception of image and penetrating their emotional associations. At the same time, as a visual art, painting is no longer in a silent state but participating in the construction of the poetic meaning. It produces a powerful potential of speech and political intention in poetry interpretation, hence establishing the connection of aesthetics and politics in poetry and adding this poem an epic dimension.

Key words: *The Rape of Lucrece*; ekphrasis; sexual politics

A Preliminary Study of the Reception of Shakespeare from 17th to 18th Centuries in Germany / TANG Xue

Abstract: Since the early 17th century, Shakespeare's dramas have been performed in Germany. After the drama reform during the Enlightenment in Germany, they have become an important role model for German literature, and they have widely influenced the younger generation represented by Johann Wolfgang von Goethe during the period of Sturm und Drang. Taking the reception of Shakespeare in Germany from the 17th to the 18th centuries as the research object, this paper takes a chronological overview of Shakespeare's translation, research and judgment in the German literature in the context of time background, dynamically demonstrates Shakespeare's influence on German literature, and preliminarily explores the reasons for the changes in the state of Shakespeare's reception.

Key words: 17th to 18th centuries; Germany; Shakespeare; reception

Shakespeare and the Making of Bernard Shaw's Writing Personality / CHEN Xin

Abstract: Shakespeare is one of the monuments of English literature, and enjoys a high position in the history of world literature. Few authors have openly criticized Shakespeare, and George Bernard Shaw is a representative of the "anti-Shakespeare" minority. Born in Ireland, George Bernard Shaw is recognized as the second man in English drama. While he was competitive with the first man and repeatedly attacked Shakespeare, if we look back at his career as a writer, Shakespeare was an important medium for the formation of his personality as a writer. Being Irish, he wanted to conquer the English language and literature. He was like a rebellious son who not only inherited Shakespeare's literary heritage rebelliously, but also wanted to recreate Shakespeare as a "father". This study will examine the Shaw-Shakespeare relationship from the perspective of its Irishness, social performativity, and contemporaneity.

Key words: Shakespeare; George Bernard Shaw; Irishness; social performativity; contemporariness

Shakespeare's "Traveling" in Japan: The Course of the Transmission and Reception of "Beauty" / LU Yu'an

Abstract: As a model of Western dramatic art, Shakespeare has inspired the development of modern Japanese society in drama and literature since it was introduced to Japan in the mid-19th century. After the Meiji Restoration, under the influence of Western enlightenment ideas, Japan actively absorbed Western culture, and Shakespeare's plays were put on the Japanese theater stage. Shakespeare's plays have Western charm and aesthetic healing that traditional Japanese plays cannot express. How to deal with the differences between Eastern and Western cultures has become a difficult problem for modern Japanese intellectuals. This paper chronologically analyzes the dissemination and acceptance of the beauty of Shakespeare's plays in Japan, and then examines the ideological transformation of modern Japanese intellectuals reflected in the exchange and collision of Eastern and Western cultures.

Key words: Shakespeare's plays; Japanese modern intellectuals; aesthetic healing; cross-cultural communication

Shakespearean Alchemy: The Production and the Exchange of Feelings in *Timon of Athens* / SHI Jingxuan

Abstract: Timon, an Athenian nobleman lost his friends when he broke. When his creditors came calling, Timon had no resources to pay them and felt the coldness of human nature. Timon hosted a second party. He made a speech denouncing them, and also harangued them with a bitter tirade against mankind generally. The disillusioned Timon went to live as a recluse outside Athens and also involved himself with Alcibiades' plot to wreck Athens in revenge. *Timon of Athens* is one of the Shakespeare's curse plays. But Shakespeare did not finish the whole play. Timon's bankruptcy is the capitalist's victory over the land owner according to Marx's political economic theory. Meanwhile, Timon's curse upon

Athens is a sort of abstract opposition between the sense and the spirit in the Athenian sensible conscious. Timon's curse got its virtue through the gold, which is the materialized divinity reflected through the private property in the middle age. That is the original ideology about the currency at Shakespeare's age.

Key words: currency feeling; production; private property; exchange

Materialism and Shakespeare: Feminism and Beyond / CHEN Xiaofeng

Abstract: As a cornerstone of Marxism, materialism has exemplified heterogeneity in different ages, regions, ethnicities and cultures. Marx and Engles take "Shakespeare-like" and "Falstaffian background" as theoretical illustrations for dialectical materialism and historical materialism. In Soviet Union, Marxist Shakespeare criticism has transferred from class differentiation and people orientation towards historical materialism. Western Marxist Shakespeare criticism has laid stress on human's alienation in terms of economical production relationships. Chinese Marxist Shakespeare criticism has been chronologically influenced by Soviet Union and the western school, striving to new theoretical vitality in modern Chinese context.

Key words: materialism; Shakespeare; feminism

Adapting Shakespearean Dramas in Traditional Chinese Theatre: A Case Study in Yue Opera / LIU Fang

Abstracts: On the basis of sorting out the centennial history of Xiqu Shakespeare, this paper analyzes the alien adaptation of *Twelfth Night* and the domestic adaptation of *Hamlet*, and summarizes various methods in adaptation. The author found that the compatible and centripetal Chinese culture gave birth to the combination of Shakespeare and traditional Chinese theatre, and "creative treason" makes the mixed-blood Xiqu Shakespeare glow with vitality. The road to its prosperity should retain the essence of Shakespeare while giving the traditional Chinese theatre full play. This transfigurative Xiqu Shakespeare with dual aesthetic superposition of content and form promotes exchange and mutual learning between civilizations.

Key words: Xiqu Shakespeare; "Yue Sha"; domestic adaptation; creative treason; transfiguration

Retrospect and Prospect: Criticism of Chinese Translations of Shakespeare's Plays for 100 Years / SUN Yuan

Abstract: The translation of Shakespeare's plays has made a brilliant achievement in China over the last 120 years. Therefore, a historical retrospect and a technical prospect of the study of Shakespeare plays translation is of great significance for both Shakespeare's translation pedagogy and the academic pointcut in the field. This paper is set to comb the Shakespeare translation criticism since 1917 combining a close reading with the visualized bibliometric software Citespace5.8.R3. By mapping the knowledge of the field and detecting the research hotspots and frontiers from synchronic and diachronic perspectives, we find that the early Shakespeare translation studies entail remarkable translation thoughts, but few of them could nourish the studies. And contemporary Shakespeare translation studies are conducted on a wide horizon, yet with over-concentrated themes and an unequilibrated disciplinary development. So far, there are still deficiencies regarding early Shakespeare translation critics, historical plays translation studies, translators other than Zhu Shenghao and Liang Shiqiu, but the positive side is that deficiencies provide a huge academic maneuver space for the current Shakespeare translation studies. It is also found that Fu Guangming's translation could be the next hotspot in Shakespeare translation studies, and corpus is expected to have great potential in this academic field.

Key words: Shakespeare's plays; Chinese translation; visualization; hotspots; corpus

Inter-and Intra-lingual Translations of Puns in Shakespeare's *Much Ado About Nothing* / YUAN Shuaiya

Abstract: Shakespeare's *Much Ado About Nothing* contains a large number of puns. Because of the differences in time and language and culture, the puns in the play take different forms in modern English and Chinese translation. The modern English translation shares the same linguistic and cultural basis with the original, and some of the puns in the original are naturally retained, but in most cases the translation has canceled the punning rhetoric of the original because of the pursuit of expressive clarity. When translating puns, Chinese translators often rely on their own linguistic conditions, either following the same path or taking a different one, using puns to translate puns, which often achieves a consistent and marvelous rhetorical effect with the original work.

Key words: *Much Ado About Nothing*; puns; intra-lingual translation; inter-lingual translation

"The true concord of well-tuned sounds": A Corpus-Based Study of Musicality in Zhu Shenghao's Translations of Shakespeare's Four Tragedies / LIU Yang

Abstract: This paper takes Zhu Shenghao's translations of Shakespeare's four tragedies as the research focus, using the corpus as research method to carry out quantitative investigation, hereby studies their musicality. The results show that Zhu's translations apply alliteration, in-line rhyme, interline rhyme, end rhyme and other rhetorical means to reproduce the rhyme patterns of Shakespeare's four tragedies. In addition, Shakespeare's rhythm is represented by Zhu Shenghao in rich forms, of which the parallel rhythms along with repetitive ones are prominent, while the use of level and non-level rhyme is relatively limited. In this sense, Zhu Shenghao's translations are "the true concord of well-tuned sounds" to Shakespeare's four tragedies: They remained the original style of Shakespeare's metrical arts, as well as made full use of Chinese language and played up its unique beauty in rhyme and rhythm, thus making unique contribution to the dissemination of Shakespeare's plays in China.

Key words: corpus-based; Shakespeare's four tragedies; Zhu Shenghao's translations; musicality

A Critical Survey of Doctoral Dissertations on Shakespeare's Chinese Translation Studies in China, 2000–2022 / YANG Feiran

Abstract: Since the 21st century, the doctoral dissertations on Shakespeare translations have been developed into a scale. As an integral part of Shakespeare studies in China, the doctoral dissertations on the study of Shakespeare translations in Chinese are characterized by their original and creative research contents and multi-dimensional innovative methods. They are of great academic significance. This study investigates the tendency of these dissertations from the perspective of Abrams' four elements: work, artist, universe and audience. Based on the analysis, the paper summarizes the characteristics and shortcomings of the existing research and clarifies the academic history of this field in order to promote future study of Shakespeare translations in Chinese.

Key words: Shakespeare; translation studies; doctoral dissertations; Abrams' four elements